TWIN

A
NOVEL

STUDIES

KEITH MAILLARD

Published with the generous assistance of the Canada Council for the Arts and the Alberta Media Fund.

 Canada Council for the Arts   Conseil des Arts du Canada   Alberta Government

Freehand Books
515 – 815 1st Street sw   Calgary, Alberta   T2P 1N3
www.freehand-books.com

Book orders: LitDistCo
8300 Lawson Road   Milton, Ontario   L9T 0A4
Telephone: 1-800-591-6250   Fax: 1-800-591-6251
orders@litdistco.ca   www.litdistco.ca

Library and Archives Canada Cataloguing in Publication
Maillard, Keith, 1942–, author
Twin studies : a novel / Keith Maillard.
Issued in print and electronic formats.
ISBN 978-1-988298-31-3 (softcover).   ISBN 978-1-988298-32-0 (epub).
ISBN 978-1-988298-33-7 (pdf)
I. Title.
PS8576.A49T85 2018   C813'.54   C2018-902941-2   C2018-902942-0

Edited by Lee Shedden
Book design by Natalie Olsen, Kisscut Design
Author photo by Mary Maillard
Printed on FSC® recycled paper and bound in Canada by Friesens

Twin and twinlike relationships are valued
and admired by nearly everyone, most of all
by those lucky enough to have them.

NANCY L. SEGAL

Entwined Lives:
Twins and What They Tell Us about Human Behavior

I think many adults (and I am among them)
are trying, in our work, to keep faith with
vividly remembered promises made to
ourselves in childhood.

EVE KOSOFSKY SEDGWICK

Tendencies

NE

1.

Bauer

From:	Jamiedevon Oxley-Clark [geminiforever@pacificnet.com]
Sent:	Wednesday, August 26, 2009 11:18 PM
To:	Dr. Erica Bauer
Subject:	Website Email Form Submission

This message has been automatically generated from the contacts section of the Interdisciplinary Twin Studies Program website.

Name & Email:

NAME:	Jamiedevon Oxley-Clark
EMAIL:	geminiforever@pacificnet.com

COMMENTS: Dear Interdisciplinary Twin Studies Program,

We are identical twins and we very much want to be in your Twin Study. We read about it on the net. Our name is Jamie and Devon Oxley-Clark, we were born together on December 12, 1996, at St. Paul's Hospital in Vancouver, British Columbia, Canada. Our parents told us we are fraternal but we are identical. We google twins and visit all the websites and we wish we could be in a twin club or go to twin conferences. We think we are a very rare kind of identical, we bet you have never studied identicals like us, we hope you will study us. We are definitely monozygotic, we bet we had the same placenta too. We think something weird happened to our egg when it split, we hope you can tell us what, we bet we are really rare. Please read this letter all the way to the end and let us be in your Twin Study.

We are going into grade 8 at Palmerston, we are in AP. Our best friends are twins, they are identical, nobody ever tells them they are fraternal. We think maybe we should have an operation to make us totally identical, then people would stop telling us we are fraternal but why should we have to do that? If people let us alone to be identical we would be happy. We hope you can help us, we do not want to be separated.

We live with our mother. Our father lives in California so plus being twins we are double citizens. We are afraid he will split us up again. They bisected us when we were little. Our Mom got to keep Jamie and our little sister and the house and our Dad got to keep Devon, so Devon went down to California and lived with our Dad. It was not like in The Parent Trap, we always knew about each other, we always knew we were twins, we always talked to each other on our birthday, it was not a big deal. Last summer our Dad let Devon come to West Vancouver to visit, it was amazing, we were identical. Our parentals were like no no you are not identical you are fraternal. We were like who are you, are you on crack, we are identical, we were distraught. Devon went back to California, we talked online every night, our Dad found out and we were cut. We had to send letters in the mail, it really sucked. We can not tell you how cruel it was, it was depressing, but we talked on the phone in the dark of the night and decided if they were going to split us up forever we would have to commit suicide. Do you know other twins who got split up? Can you tell us about them and what happened to them? Did any of them commit suicide?

Here is how we were going to do it, we were going to Home Hardware and get long rubber hoses and connect them to the exhaust pipes of the cars and run the hoses in the windows and seal them up with duck tape, like sit in the car, we know how to start a car, and talk on the phone and just go to sleep and our souls would fuse. Our Mom intercepted Devon's snail mail about this, family drama to the max. Our Dad was like OK Devon can go back up to Canada for the rest of grade 7 and we will see how it works out, Devon is on loan. Mom is like we never should have split you up, no one is going to split you up ever again unless you do it yourselves but she can not say this to Dad because he has custody of Devon. We were so happy to be reunited, we can not tell you. We went to Palmerston, we did not have issues, we were not inappropriate, we got good grades, every body was amazed. We hope Dad notices this and does not split us up. We do not want to have to commit suicide, that would be really depressing.

Now we are trying to be as identical as we can. There are lots of ways to be identical you would not think of at first, you have to think all the time. Mom is like you have an obsessive compulsive disorder and should be in therapy but it has got so bad these days the minute you walk in the office all they know how to do is reach for their prescription pads, she does not believe in kids being on medication like this drug that makes kids commit suicide, have you heard about it, so she gives up. Do you know any other twins who try to be identical? If you do, could you tell us what happened to them? We do not want to be in therapy or take some weird drug that makes you commit suicide when you do not want to.

We do not know what else you want to know about us, please write back and tell us and we will tell you everything you want to know. Please let us be in your Twin Study. We do not want to be split up. We want to meet other twins and talk to them and find out what happened to them, we hope we can find out what happened to our egg, we bet we are really rare, so you can see why we want to be in your Twin Study. Please write back soon.

We are most sincerely yours,
Jamie Oxley-Clark
Devon Oxley-Clark
5837 Skyview Drive
West Vancouver
British Columbia

Interdisciplinary Twin Studies Program   August 27, 2009

Dear Jamie Oxley-Clark and Devon Oxley-Clark:
Let me introduce myself. My name is Erica Bauer, and I am a researcher in the Interdisciplinary Twin Studies Program here at the University. I have sent to your mother, under separate cover, detailed information about the particular Twin Study I am conducting as well as a Parental Consent Form. I cannot interview you unless your mother signs the Consent Form. I am emailing you now, however, because your letter raised some concerns that I believe should be addressed quickly.

It is important for you to know what twin type you are, but making the correct assessment is sometimes surprisingly difficult. If each of you had your own placenta, that, in itself, does not mean that you are fraternal twins. Doctors are often misinformed about this fact.

Even though they have the same genes, identical twins are not exactly alike. From the moment that the egg separates, co-twins are subjected to different environmental events, some of which can impact them profoundly, making them less like each other. On the extreme end of the scale, it is possible for identical twins to be discordant in significant ways. Sometimes, for example, one twin will inherit a disease and the other one will not. What all this boils down to is that sometimes identicals can be strikingly different from each other.

As you probably know, fraternal twins share approximately fifty percent of their genes. What happens with the other fifty percent is the luck of the draw, so, by chance, it might turn out that fraternal twins resemble each other very strongly just as singleton siblings can sometimes resemble each other very strongly. There have been studies of fraternal twins who were so much alike that even trained observers thought that they were identical twins.

Parents are not usually good judges of twin type. The only way for you to know your twin type with absolute certainty is to have a blood test. If you enroll in my Twin Study, one of the first things we will do is have you tested at the University Hospital. This is a simple procedure which involves nothing more than giving a blood sample.

Because you so clearly wish to be reared together, I am glad to hear that you have been reunited, but I am deeply concerned about your mention of suicide. If you ever again have thoughts of suicide, you must immediately talk to someone you trust. If you don't want to talk to one or both of your parents, then consider talking to the counselor at your school, or, if you belong to a church, synagogue, or temple, please consider talking to someone there. If all else fails, you can always go into the nearest Family Services Unit and ask to speak to a counselor. But the important thing to remember is that if you ever have thoughts of suicide, you should talk to someone. Thoughts of suicide are not something that the two of you should try to deal with on your own, nor should you have to. There are trained professionals who can help you cope with the "dark" moments in your lives. If your mother consents to participation in my study, I look forward to meeting you. If, for whatever reasons, she withholds her consent, I wish you the very best. You should always remember that being a twin is a special blessing.

Sincerely yours,
Dr. Erica Bauer

Dear Doctor Bauer,

Thank you so much for writing back to us. We liked your letter a lot. We made sure our mother signed the Parental Consent Form, we watched her sign it, we took it and mailed it ourselves, you should have it by now, do you have it? We want to meet you and tell you everything you want to know. We are so excited to be in your Twin Study.

We do not know if we had the same placenta. Our Mom does not remember. You would think your Mom would remember something like this but she does not, she is like I was off in lala land, give me a break. The doctor said we are fraternal, she is like it is obvious you are fraternal, we know we are identical. We are discordant identical, we are glad you told us this, we googled it. The kind of discordant identical we are is really rare, you will have lots of fun studying us and learn lots too. Thank you for telling us about dark moments. We have lots of dark moments. We do not go to a church except for Christmas and Easter, we do not think people at the church would talk to us, they do not know us, plus our school counselor hates us. Where is Family Services, we do not know about it, we googled it. Our Mom is like if you so much as set foot in Family Services I will never talk to either one of you ever again or drive you anywhere or give you a single cent even if you live to be a hundred and ten.

We know that being a twin is a special blessing, we are so lucky, we feel sorry for kids who are not twins. We do not want our Dad to have custody of Devon, he could take Devon back any time he wants. We want to stay with Mom but it would be OK to go to live with Dad for a while, we just want to be together. Our Dad does not want both of us, he does not want Jamie. We have many dark moments about this. How could you want one of us and not the other one? Every body we talk to on the net says twins should stay together, we are glad you think we should stay together. We are so excited to be in your Twin Study, please write back and tell us when we can meet you, we hope it is soon!!!!

Sincerely yours,
Jamie and Devon

Interdisciplinary Twin Studies Program   September 7, 2009

Dear Jamie and Devon:

Thank you for your letter. Yes, I did receive the signed Parental Consent Form from your mother. I am looking forward to meeting you. I will make arrangements to interview you and I may also want to interview other members of your family who will consent to talk to me.

Your mother did not fill out the Preliminary Questionnaire. Perhaps she found the questions confusing or intrusive. I don't need the Preliminary Questionnaire filled out before I can proceed, although it would help, but I do need for her to return my calls. I have called your house several times, and I always get the answering machine. I have left a detailed message each time I called. If you would still like me to interview you, perhaps you might suggest to your mother that she return my calls.

I am sorry if I was not clear enough in my last letter. I did not say that you are "discordant identicals." I was only trying to tell you that sometimes identical twins can be very different from each other. I don't want you to think that there is a twin type called "discordant identical." "Discordant" is only a fancy word we use when we mean "different." To find out exactly what twin type you are, we need to do a blood test, as I said before. I will arrange for this as soon as possible.

If you are participating in my Twin Study, I could also arrange for you to see a counselor here at the university. No trained professional would automatically put you on medication, and you might find it very helpful to have someone outside your family with whom to discuss your problems.

Sincerely yours,
Erica Bauer

Dear Erica,

Boy, are we mad!!! We are so sorry Mom did not call you back. We thought she did, we bugged her and bugged her but she is like my life is nuts, it is out of control, what else is new. She did not fill out the Preliminary Questionnaire because she does not ever fill out anything like if she has to fill out anything she just throws it away, plus she is like if you want to talk to some crazy doctor this is fine, I give up, but one thing for sure I am not going to encourage any more of this crazy twin crap, this sucks for us. You can see us any time you want, do you want her to call you and tell you this? Do you want her to write this to you and sign it? It would be easy for her to send you an email, is it OK for her to send you an email?

We do not know about the rest of our family talking to you. We know for sure Dad will not talk to you, he is deep unlisted. We will tell you about our Dad. He is like I am not Bill Gates but I am doing OK, people pay him a million bucks just to put his name on their letter heads. When he and mom split up he went back to California, he has a new wife, she is the youngest wife yet. We have a little sister in California, her name is Avery, she is our half sib. Mom is sorry she ever let Dad have custody of Devon, she is like I must have been out of my bloody mind. Our Dad is supposed to talk to us on the phone but lots of times he is too busy, he does not want us to be identical, we do not tell him about being identical, he is like Devon you are coming back here for high school and don't you forget it, you can see why we are glad he is in California and we are in Vancouver.

For sure Mom will talk to you like no no I do not want to talk to any body but once she gets going she will not be able to help herself. We have a little sister, she is our full sib, she looks a little bit like us, her name is Paige, she is ten, do you want to talk to some body who is ten? She is a major drama queen, she goes to theatre camp, she is annoying, she takes ballet, she thinks she is so cool, she is inappropriate, she wants to be a hottie and have a boy friend, we do not know if she will tell you this. We have a brother five years older than us, his name is Cameron, he is our half sib, we only have a few genes in common with him, he does not look like us, he is very tall. Our Mom and Cameron's Dad have joint custody but Cam lives with us because his Dad hates him. Cam is blowing off high school, he has issues, he is failing every thing, he is doing cocaine, Mom is like the flu my ass, how stupid do you think I am, do you think I can not see the blood running out of your nose. Cam is so random, we do not think Cam will talk to you.

This is all of our family except for Mom's boy friend, his name is Drew. Mom says Drew is part of our family but he is not our real family, you do not have to talk to him, he tries to act like he is our father, this sucks for us, he is always in your face, it is awkward. Mom is like you kids do not want me to have a sex life, this is not true we do not care if Mom has a sex life, we wish she would find a new boy friend to have a sex life, Drew is like if you keep on going with this crazy twin crap you will make yourselves into freaks of nature and no body will want to marry you and all you will be able to do is work in a circus, he thinks this is funny, we hate him.

We want to have a blood test. We want every body to know we are identical. We are sick of people saying we are fraternal. We liked what you said about discordant identical, we know it means different, we bet we are discordant identical but we do not know for sure, can you tell us? Can you fix discordant identicals with an operation? We googled it but it is not on google. We are scared to have an operation. Our Mom will not talk about it, she is like shut up do not talk to me about operations, you can see why we have issues. We do not want to make trouble, we do not want to be inappropriate, it really sucks. Mom is like do you think you are living in a manga? No we do not think we are living in a manga, we are not retards. We want to be identical. What is wrong with that? We do not know what else to tell you, we are so excited to meet you and be in your Twin Study.

Your friends, Jamie and Devon

From: Karen Oxley [karenoxley@pacificnet.com]
Sent: Sunday, September 13, 2009 2:07 AM
To: Dr. Erica Bauer
Subject: Website Email Form Submission

This message has been automatically generated from the contacts section of the Interdisciplinary Twin Studies Program website.

Name & Email:

NAME: Karen Oxley
EMAIL: karenoxley@pacificnet.com

COMMENTS: Dear Dr. Bauer,

My name is Karen Oxley. I am the mother of the twins Jamie Oxley-Clark and Devon Oxley-Clark. It is alright with me if you come to interview them. We live at 5837 Skyview Drive, West Vancouver, British Columbia. Can you come this Thursday September 17 2009 at 4 oclock? This would be a good time for you to come.

                    Thank you for your kind attention.
                                        Karen Oxley

2.

A BLACK CAR was shooting down the driveway straight at her, coming way too fast. Before her mind could register what was happening, Erica had already kicked the brakes. Her seat belt grabbed her, jerked her back so hard it hurt—and fuck, the other car kept right on coming. All she could do was watch—oh my god, watch it *stop*? No, she was going to get hit and there was not a thing she could do about it. A rolling jolt, a dull smack—metal on metal. Was it over? Hey, she thought, that's not too bad. I can live with that.

The blonde woman in the black car was staring at her through their two windshields. It wasn't just any old black car but an SUV, a small one, and not just black but a gleaming spaceship black—inside, not just a blonde woman but a blonde child, both of them shocked and staring. The woman threw up her hands in helpless despair—then put her car into reverse and made a *come on* gesture. Erica clicked into low and inched upward after her.

The driveway led to a turn-around big enough to park half-a-dozen cars. Erica pulled over and turned off her engine. I have just been in an accident, she thought—a pissy-ass stupid pointless little accident. She was in *full burn*—that's what her mind called it. She usually chased the burn but now it was chasing her. She'd told nobody about the burn and she would tell nobody about it. The burn was private, the burn was hers, the burn was this—sweating, sucking air, her heart trying to hammer its way out of her chest. She couldn't see right. Her thoughts were scrambled.

The blonde woman was getting out of her car, so Erica thought that she should get out of hers too. The module of Erica's mind that recognized humans and processed them as being human must have turned itself off because she saw the woman walking toward her as virtual, as a YouTube video titled "tall hot blonde." The omega on the woman's jacket didn't mean The End, it meant lululemon. "Are you all right?"

"Oh, I'm fine," Erica said, although she wasn't. She was surprised that she could talk at all. Adrenaline was fouling her mouth like hot pennies.

The blonde woman bent down to look at Erica's car, emitted the word "shit" as a soft puff of sound.

There was nothing for Erica to do but pretend to be normal. She looked too, saw a short deep scoring in her left front quarter-panel. Now the woman was walking away. She was inspecting her own car—a BMW. How absolutely and utterly wonderful—Erica's Golf had just been dinged by fifty-thousand-bucks'-worth of high-end German engineering.

Was this woman the twins' mum? Her eyes were astonishing—huge and golden, true amber, rare in humans. She'd emphasized them with mascara. She was using them now to shoot a blast of anger at Erica—"You don't expect to run into somebody in *your own driveway.*"

"I'm sorry," was what a normal person would say, so Erica said it.

Now the woman seemed to be checking out Erica the same way she'd checked out the damage. "Oh, what a ridiculous— But it *is* my fault. Absolutely. No doubt about it. I was going too fast. Let's leave ICBC out of this, okay?"

The woman's sea-blue workout gear fit her tightly enough to show off a figure to die for—maybe she really did work out, maybe she spent half her life in the gym—and to top it off, she was naturally blonde. At the roots, all the honey did was turn to copper. Just the kind of woman Erica loathed on sight. "I'm Karen Oxley, by the way."

Okay, so Erica had picked the right driveway. Until then she hadn't been absolutely sure—not in this pretentious upscale neighbourhood where people didn't give a shit whether you could read the numbers on their houses or not. And this must be the twins' house—concrete and glass, a classic example of West Coast Architecture ready to be photographed for a glossy coffee-table book. Mile-high hemlocks and cedars and firs blocked it off from its neighbours. Worth a couple of million bucks easy— No, that was nowhere near enough. Three million? More? How could anybody afford a house like this?

Erica was slowing her breathing so her heart rate would drop. If she'd been alone, she would have monitored her pulse. The burn, as it always did, had given her the illusion of meaning, but now she was sinking back into the flat pointless home movie where she usually lived these days. "I'm Erica Bauer," she said.

She reached for a card but couldn't hand it over yet because the mum was still pumping out the words, going blah blah blah, all about the accident. The BMW had suffered nothing more than a five-centimetre stripe of blue paint on its bumper. "I'm not even going to bother with this. Look, Erica . . . Would you mind? . . . I'm sorry—"

A small blonde clone of her mother was leaping out of the BMW. The car was so high off the ground that for a child, it really was a leap. A drawn-out wail: "Mu-um!"

The twins' emails had introduced Erica to the major players, so this must be the little sister, Paige, costumed perfectly for her role—in pink leotard, pink tights, and pink ballet slippers crammed into unlaced pink running shoes, her hair up in a ballet student's bun—a blue-eyed tow-head blonde. She was jumping up and down. "Mu-um! *Mu-um!* We're going to be laaaa-aaate!"

Mum's golden eyes shot a sizzling bolt at her daughter. "I am *so* sorry," she said to Erica. "Would you mind? . . . Just take your car to a body shop and send me the bill."

"Sure. No problem." Fuck you, Erica thought.

The woman's face had fallen into an expression of inquiry—polite but unmistakable—*who the hell are you, and what are you doing in my driveway?*

Explanations—Erica wasn't sure she could do them. Parents, when they first met her, never believed that she was old enough to be who she said she was. She and her sister had always looked younger than their age. In high school, they'd been mistaken for grade eights—in university, for teenagers. "You'll be glad when you're forty," their mum had told them, but Erica was years away from forty and Annalise would never see it. The taste in her mouth was absolutely foul. She needed water. *Focus,* she told herself.

Her card usually did the trick. It had the university's distinctive green-and-gold logo. It said that she was *Doctor* Bauer.

The woman looked down at the card then up at Erica.

"Did I get the day wrong?" Erica asked, keeping her voice neutral. She knew perfectly well that the twins had sent the last email—the one that had invited her—and not their mother.

"How should I know?" The woman held Erica's gaze a moment longer then turned to address the house. "Hey, Gemini Forever, get your asses out here."

The twins must have been watching from just inside the open front door. They came slumping down the steps with the hangdog air of kids who knew they were in deep shit—and oh my god, they were boys.

Erica had been expecting girls—but why? They had gender-neutral names, so maybe it was their verbal fluency or the mention of *The Parent Trap* or something girlish in their emails. It had never crossed her mind that they might be boys. The researcher in her was automatically assessing them for twin type, looking at the big important markers—hair, eyes, height and weight. They got a check on all four—a pair of dark-haired, brown-eyed boys, matched in size. If they'd always been told that they were fraternal, she could see their problem. They could well be identical.

"You want to explain this?" their mother was asking them.

They obviously didn't—staring down at their scuffed black dress shoes. Still in their private-school uniforms—grey pants, white shirts, striped ties, navy blazers with the school crest on the pockets. Wearing the same haircuts—a fly-away style that curled around the sides to cover most of their ears and fell in the front into long ragged bangs.

"Nothing to say? . . . Okay, let me introduce you to *Doctor* Bauer. She's from the Interdisciplinary Twin Studies Program at the university. She's driven all the way out here to see you. If I wasn't running late, I wouldn't even be here . . . Isn't it odd that *Doctor* Bauer would show up at exactly this time?"

"Mum!" one twin said.

"This is like," the other twin said, "awkward."

"Oh, you bet it's awkward . . . Dr. Bauer . . ."

"Erica."

"Erica. Okay, let's get one thing straight here. You are not going to put my kids on antidepressants."

"I can't put your kids on anything. I'm not a medical doctor."

"So you're . . . ?"

"I'm a psychologist. I study twins."

"And now you want to study mine?"

"Yes. With your permission."

The woman looked away—not at her kids but at the sky. She was holding Erica's card in her right hand, snapping it repeatedly into the palm of her left. Then she looked into Erica's eyes. "Well, you've hit the jackpot today, *Doctor* Bauer. If you want twins, you've got twins. You can just study the hell out of them."

HOLY CRAP! The small-town Alberta girl inside Erica was blown away by this house. Glass, floor to ceiling. A whole wall of glass—it went on forever. Past a steel-and-pine dining room, past a steel-and-granite kitchen, all the way to the big French doors that opened onto a balcony set with white patio furniture and a stainless steel barbecue—and there was not a single fingerprint on a single centimetre of any of that glass—and the purpose of all that glass was to reveal a spectacular multi-million-dollar view—the long reach of the sea, coastal mountains etched in the distance, sailboats dotting the postcard water. The low sun was blazing in, striking Erica from the side, bathing her and everything else in spun gold straight from the vaults of heaven. None of this could possibly be real—there was just no way *any of this* could be real. She felt like she'd just stepped into a rerun of *The O.C.*

One of the twins had brought her the glass of water she'd asked for. She'd wanted tap water but hadn't said so. She'd got Perrier and it would do just fine. She liked the bubbles. "Thank you," she said and told herself to smile. Now she had to act like an adult, take charge. If she was studying the twins, they were also studying her.

She'd chosen a chair at an angle to the sun, hoping they would sit together on the couch with the light full on them—and they did. MZ twins—even those separated at birth—often walked, stood, and sat much like each other, but these two didn't. One perched tensely on the edge of a cushion; the other flopped back into the couch as loose-limbed as a cat.

"Are you in trouble with your mum?" Erica said—not a safe way to start; it was like an invitation to the twins to conspire with her against their mother, but she didn't care. She had to pretend to be conducting an interview but she wasn't, so it didn't matter what she said just so long as she got them relaxed and talking.

"She'll get over it," the tense twin said.

They didn't have the startling good looks of their younger sib but they were attractive children. In three months they'd turn thirteen but neither displayed visible signs of puberty. On weight and height distributions for boys their age, they'd fall to the left of the bells—lighter and shorter than the norm. The tense twin was a few centimetres taller than his brother and slightly more muscular—and hey, wait a minute, they had different coloured eyes! It would be hard to see if they weren't sitting side by side with the sun shining on their faces—a subtle difference, but unmistakable. The taller twin's eyes were simply a clear medium brown the colour of milk chocolate. His brother's eyes were slightly lighter and had small flecks of gold mixed into the brown. No matter how much they looked like each other, they were almost certainly DZ.

"Okay," Erica said, "which of you is which?"

"I'm Jamie." The tense one with the darker eyes.

"I'm Devon." The relaxed one with the gold flecks.

Thank god for the sun—it was better than turning a spotlight on them. Their hair was a brown that was nearly black and the colour was just too vibrant and rich to be natural. When they'd got their identical haircuts, they must have had their hair dyed to match—oh, but their *eyebrows* didn't match. Jamie's were just as dark as his hair, Devon's a lighter chestnut brown. A blood test would nail it, but now Erica was absolutely certain they were DZ. "How do you like Palmerston?" she asked them.

"Meh," Jamie said.

"It's okay," Devon said.

"Better than public school?"

They both answered, riding over each other's voices. "School sucks," Devon said, "like . . . Palmerston's better, but . . ." "I had issues at Inglewood," Jamie said, "but like . . ."

A pause as they stopped for each other—then Devon said, "The teachers are always in your face . . . but it's okay."

"Mum's happy. We're in AP."

"AP?"

"Advanced Placement. In Literature. Weird. I have a learning disability."

"You do not," Devon said.

"Yes, I do," Jamie said. "Mum had me *tested*."

"A learning disability?" Erica said.

"Yeah, I have writing issues."

That scratchy exchange seemed to have stopped things dead. Jamie was giving his brother a meaningful stare—saying what? Shut up? Devon rolled his eyes. School and learning disabilities must be loaded topics. Erica wanted to break their awkward silence. She wanted them to trust her. She was looking for the next question, but before she could find it, Jamie said, "Hey, do you want to see our rooms?"

Erica stood and followed them. A high heat was coming off the twins like radiation. It wasn't physical; it was in Erica's mind. It hurt her and she needed it—the crackle of their twinness. It was bitter and she wanted it. Could they be feeling it too? If it had cost her a tremendous amount of time and effort to get here, it had cost them just as much to bring her here. She knew why she was here—*all suicide threats should be taken seriously, especially with children*—but what did they want from her?

"We were each supposed to have our own room," Jamie was telling her, "but we wanted to share all our stuff . . ."

"Like we wanted one room to be the office, and the other the bedroom, but Mom won't let us sleep together . . ."

"Like she won't even let us sleep in the same *room*."

"Lots of twins sleep together."—something Erica should *not* have said. She should be observing, not commenting. She didn't care. "It's absolutely normal for twins," she said. But it wasn't just twins—she thought that humans had been designed to sleep with each other, that it was cruel and unnatural to put babies and children in separate beds. She hated sleeping alone. She and her sister had slept together until Annalise got her Ed degree.

"This is the office," Devon said. "*I* have to sleep in here." A frantic confusion of colourful images, all four walls plastered with pictures, Japanese anime characters with enormous eyes, photos of real kids. Their friends? These boys must be really attracted to girls—nearly all of the pictures were of girls.

One space seemed to be devoted to famous twins. Erica recognized Mary-Kate and Ashley, Tegan and Sara. Both Hayley Mills and Lindsay Lohan were there. "Which version of *The Parent Trap* do you like better?"

"Hayley Mills!" they both said at once.

"They're different. They're both good," Jamie said. "We've got the DVDs."

"But Hayley Mills *is* better," his brother said. "We've watched them both like a gazillion times. We can say all the lines."

Erica and Annalise had watched the Hayley Mills version a gazillion times too—and could say all the lines. Someone must have given them the video when they'd been little—it was an obvious present to give identical twins—and Erica remembered *The Parent Trap* as something that had always been there, an eternal narrative of their childhood, more fundamental than Cinderella. When the Lindsay Lohan version came out, she and Lise had still been in Edmonton—still sleeping in the same bed. When they'd gone to see the movie, it had been just the two of them, no boys invited. It was fun to see the story again from a different angle, and Lindsay Lohan did a good job, but the Hayley Mills version was impossible to match—"It's mythic for us," Annalise said.

I can't do this, Erica thought. I really can't. This happened to her a lot now. She would be walking through the world, knowing exactly where she was going. Everything would be where it was supposed to be—a table was a table and a chair was a chair—but then, with no warning, an enormous black hole would open under her feet, and she would fall right down it, and then a table wasn't a table anymore and a chair wasn't a chair. Nothing was anything anymore.

The twins were talking to her. She was missing what they were saying. *Focus*, she told herself again. *All you have to do is pay attention.*

Erica walked around the room and checked things out. The centerpiece was the computer setup. The twins showed her how the system worked. They sat facing each other, each with his own monitor, mouse and keyboard, but everything was hooked up to a single computer. When they looked slightly to the left of their monitors, they were looking directly into each other's eyes. "What happens when you both type at once?"

"Random shit," Devon said, laughing, "everything's scrambled." That was interesting—technologically enforced cooperation.

They surfed the net, they told her, looking for other twins. They visited blogs and chat rooms. "We talk to lots of twins but we've never met twins like us—"

"Mum's like, if you keep talking to strangers on the net, some weird sick pedophile is going to hit on you," Jamie said, "but we never give out our address or phone number . . . or even our real names—"

"Like the minute somebody starts perving, we just block them—"

"She doesn't understand how easy this is."

"Yeah, Mom thinks we don't have any street smarts," Devon said. "We're not retards!"

She'd got what she wanted—they were relaxed, talking quickly, both talking at once. Erica could hear how different they were. At first she'd thought that Jamie's voice was deeper but that wasn't right. They were in the same register, but Jamie's voice had a muffled blurry quality to it. He swallowed the ends of his sentences or let the pitch drop—leaving his thoughts incomplete. Devon spoke more precisely, in a clear bright voice. It made him sound older, more expressive. Their slang was slightly different too. Devon said "like" more often. But there was something else— oh, it was obvious. Jamie had a Canadian accent, Devon an American one.

The low bookcases were crammed with Japanese comic books, the pocket-sized kind that came in series. "You like Japanese comics, eh?"

"They're *manga*," Jamie corrected her. "We don't read *comics*."

"Oh, right." Erica returned to the pictures on the wall. "Who are these people?"

They were more than happy to tell her. She was amazed that they could remember so many Japanese names. But they didn't have just pictures of anime characters, they had pictures of real kids too. "That's Morgan and Avi . . . our best friends." Two pretty little redheads who looked like mirror images of each other, obviously MZ. "They want to be in your twin study. Can they be in your twin study?"

"Sure."

"Our dad hates twins," Jamie said.

What? Erica thought. That came out of nowhere. It must have jolted Devon too. He'd stopped right in the middle of his sentence, was giving his brother a puzzled look.

"Our dad doesn't want us to be identical," Jamie said in his blurry monotone. "He thinks we should be split up forever. Come on, I'll show you the bedroom."

23

Erica followed Jamie to the room next door. "I sleep in here," he said.

It was just as messy as most kids' spaces, unmade double bed and clothes flung everywhere—and then Erica was stopped, her thoughts fragmenting. A pleated kilt was crumpled up on a chair. That didn't make any sense.

The floor of the closet was the dumping ground for shoes, many of them just what you'd expect for boys, but girls' shoes too—running shoes with pink stripes, flats with bows on the toes. Erica couldn't believe it had taken her so long to get it. She felt like an idiot. There'd been plenty of clues. She'd been right the first time. They were girls.

SO MUCH FOR the detached, highly trained observer—Erica hadn't even been able to read their sex right. It was like a visual illusion from a text-book unit on perception studies. The one she remembered had been made up of black blobs on a white background. Depending on the gestalt your brain created, it looked either like a flying goose or a crouching lion, and once you'd seen it one way, it was next to impossible to see it the other way. When she'd seen the twins as boys, their haircuts looked too long—a bit too pretty. Now that she saw them as girls, the same haircuts looked too short— not pretty enough. What on earth were they doing wearing boys' uniforms?

Jamie picked up her kilt from the balloon-back chair so Erica could sit. "Why are we such a big problem? Everybody think we're such a— We just want to be identical. What's wrong with that?"

"Nothing," Erica said.

The bedroom must have originally been Jamie's. It had none of the manic we-did-it-ourselves look of "the office," instead was a space designed by an adult—pale lavender walls, white drapes, a white dresser and matching chairs, a queen-sized bed with a floral comforter. If Jamie finished picking up the clothes and putting them away—that's what she was doing—it would look spacious, almost bare, nearly formal, very feminine. Erica couldn't imagine any little girl liking a room like this. It had to be the work of their loathsome mother.

"Dad thinks we're sick!" Jamie said.

"No he doesn't." Devon had collapsed onto the floor and was sprawled with her back against the wall.

"Yes, he does. *He's* the freakin' problem."

"He's not so bad," Devon said quietly, but Jamie's voice rode over hers. "I haven't seen him since I was *seven*."

Devon laughed. "I didn't see him that much either. And I was like living with him. He works all the time."

"What's your dad do?"

"I don't know . . . exactly." Devon struggled with it. "He's like . . . He's on boards and shit like that. When that . . . like commercial paper? You know about that? It was a big freakin' deal. He had to go to some heavy meeting and they came and got him *in a helicopter.*"

Jamie was ignoring her sister. "We don't understand why we're a problem. We really don't." She was giving Erica a dark searching look like she expected an explanation right there on the spot. "Maybe someday we'll want to be individuated and independent but right now we don't, okay? What's wrong with that?"

"Nothing," Erica said.

The twins must be getting some kind of counseling to pick up terminology like that—and if some counselor saw them as having a problem, what was it? Maybe it wasn't related to twinship at all. Non-conformity with gender norms? They were tomboys who wore boys' uniforms, but Erica hadn't read them as boys merely because of the uniforms—there *was* something boyish about them. Maybe it was more complicated than just being tomboys. "We think maybe we should have an operation to make us totally identical," they'd written in their first email. Did one of them have a genital birth defect that needed to be fixed? That would be so embarrassing for kids their age they'd have a hard time even talking about it.

There was only one picture in the room, a big poster, matted and framed, that took up most of a wall—yet another colourful anime image, this one with big bold splashy Japanese script running down the left side. It must be special to be separated from the cartoon images in the other room, to be given a place of honour in this one. "Who are those kids?"

In a single surprising leap, Devon was on her feet. "That's Kagami and Makoto!"

Jamie's fingers lovingly traced the Japanese characters. "*Two from One Fire.* It's our favourite manga—"

"We got the poster *from Japan!* Akime got it for us. She's the president of the Anime Club."

"They're identical twins," Jamie said. "They were separated when they were little."

"That's like you," Erica said.

"Yeah, they are like us, and it's—" Devon seemed to be searching for words. "It's like . . . not just our favourite manga. It's like—"

"Like it was written for us," her sister said.

In the picture two teenagers with huge cartoon eyes were staring at each other from opposite sides of a pane of glass. On the right was a girl dressed in black. She was suspended from a rope, climbing down it hand over hand. "That's Kagami," Devon said. "She's a scavenger."

Kagami's leather catsuit fit her so tightly it could be stretch fabric but it had the dull gleam of leather. It was crisscrossed with zippers and hung with clips and various metallic gadgets, a knife worn just above her hip bone. The picture caught her in mid-descent, one hand clutching the rope, the other moving for a new hold, one broad boot kicked out to steady herself against the pane of glass. "She's like, you know, a cat burglar. She's climbing down into Makoto's buildings to steal shit . . . and like that."

On the left was another girl, this one barefoot, dressed in what appeared to be loose white pajamas. She was barefoot, caught in midstride, stepping toward the glass. "That's Makoto," Jamie said. "He's heard her like sliding down the windows and he got out of bed to see what's happening."

"That's *a boy?*"

"Yeah. In manga, lots of the boys look like girls . . . but they're really boys."

The characters were staring at each other with expressions of stunned amazement. Their faces were identical. Their hair styles were identical. "Hey, you've got the same haircuts!" Erica said.

The twins giggled. "Yeah," Jamie said, "we brought the manga to show the stylist. She's like, 'You wanna look like that? That's easy. I can do that.'"

"She did a great job."

"Yeah, she did," Devon said, "and Mom was sooo mad. She wanted to kill Jamie. She was like, 'Oh, your beautiful hair! You broke my heart!' Jamie had hair down to here." Devon drew an imaginary line halfway down her back.

"Meh," Jamie said, "it was too freakin' much work," and then, pointing, she directed Erica's attention back to the picture. "This is like the first time they see each other . . . like after they've been separated for ten years."

"Yeah, they're like, 'What the . . . We're *twins!*' You gotta read it. It's crazy cool."

"It's a work of genius," Jamie said with absolute conviction.

The three of them were standing in front of the framed poster. The twins were looking at her expectantly. Then her mental gestalt rearranged itself again. They weren't *both* girls.

They did have a problem—and if they wanted to be identical, it was a *big* problem. Did they have any idea how ambiguous their gender presentations were? Maybe they did. Maybe they did it intentionally.

"When I first got your emails," she said, "I thought you were both girls. Then when I first saw you, I thought you were both boys. Now I've changed my mind again, but I'm not sure. Could you please just tell me."

They were both startled but had very different reactions. Jamie drew herself into a stubborn defensive stance, arms wrapped around her chest. Devon was giving Erica a look of blameless innocence, hands offering an open-handed peace-making gesture.

"What do you think we are?" Jamie said. It was probably the same tone she would have used if she'd said, "Fuck you, lady." Oh, my goodness, Erica thought, you are a tough little cookie, aren't you?

"I'll tell you what I think . . . but you tell me first."

Jamie said it like a challenge: "I'm a girl."

Devon laughed, shrugged. He seemed to want to drain away anything serious. "I'm a boy."

"That's exactly what I thought," Erica said. "Okay, so if you're not the same sex, you can't be identical. You know that, don't you?"

Devon was still giving her his hapless apologetic charming smile. He was probably getting through life on that smile. "Yeah, but we *are* identical."

Jamie wasn't smiling. "We *know* we're identical."

"We're MZ twins discordant for sex," Devon said with a shining triumphant grin that said he'd nailed it.

"Okay," Erica said evenly. "Why are you wearing a boy's uniform?" she asked Jamie.

"It's a *girl's* uniform."

"Yeah, but you're the only girl who wears it," her brother said, laughing. "It says in the Palmerston dress code that girls can wear pants instead of kilts, so Jamie went to the principal and—"

"I wear a kilt sometimes."

"Yeah, but you're like the only girl who ever wears pants," and then, to Erica, "Sometimes we want to dress alike, and *I* can't wear a kilt."

"Well, you *could*," Jamie said.

THEY WERE BACK where they'd started—on the couch in the living room. Erica felt like she'd been talking with the twins forever. The sun was setting, leaving behind a long purple smudge over the water. The light flowing through the vast expanse of glass was flat and radiant. The burn was long gone, a memory. She felt drained and tired.

Erica was more than familiar with a ninety-two-page document titled "University Guidelines on Research with Human Subjects." Written in a dry repetitive style designed to nail meaning to the desktop, the Guidelines did its best to cover every contingency. The suicide threat in the twins' first email was clear and unmistakable, so what she should have done was forward it to the Chair of ITS but she hadn't done that. With every exchange, she'd gone farther off the Guidelines, and this visit to their home was the last straw. She wasn't tenured yet. If things went sideways on her, she had just destroyed her academic career. "How are you guys doing with the dark moments?" she said.

Jamie shrugged. "Okay."

"Yeah, it's all good."

"That thing with the cars," Erica said, "it won't work, you know. Modern cars have catalytic converters. There wouldn't be enough carbon monoxide. All you'd do is give yourselves headaches."

"Yeah, Mom told us that too," Devon said.

Jamie's tone was matter-of-fact. "If we have to, we'll probably just hang ourselves. Lots of kids hang themselves."

Erica was shocked. "So you're still thinking about it?"

"No," Jamie said, "we're not *thinking* about it. We don't need to think about it. It's just something that's going to happen."

"If we get separated," Devon said.

"Let me get this straight, okay? So you've made a suicide pact—?"

"No, no," Jamie said, "it's not like that. That's what Mum says too . . . *a suicide pact.* But it's—"

"It's *not* a suicide pact," Devon said. "It's just gonna happen, you know, like automatic. If we get separated."

"If you kick the chair out from under yourself, you can't chicken out," Jamie said like that explained everything.

"I wish there was a better way," Devon said. "We googled everything we could think of, and you can screw it up so easy. That'd be horrible. You know, to wake up and— There's like no pill you can just   So, yeah, we'll probably just hang ourselves. But when I think about somebody finding our bodies, it's so sad . . . You know, if it was Mom or Paige."

"We can call 911 first," Jamie told her brother, "like just before it's going to happen."

"I don't know," he said. "Sometimes they can get somewhere real fast." Then, looking directly at Erica—"You've gotta tie the rope someplace that will like support your weight. And then the rope's gotta be thick enough so it won't cut you but not too thick . . . so we're gonna use nylon. It's real strong. And we're gonna stand on kitchen stools, you know, cause they're higher than chairs, so there's no way we can like reach the floor. And then we'll count to three and kick the stools . . . and it'll be like . . . just a couple of minutes. And then our souls will fuse."

Oh fuck, Erica thought.

"Don't tell Mom," he said. "She'll just worry about it. We don't want her to worry about it."

"She knows anyway," Jamie said, "and it's not going to happen unless we get separated. She knows that."

"She doesn't know exactly how it's gonna happen."

29

Jamie gave Erica a nasty smug little smile. "Tell her if you want. We've got another way too. But it's a secret."

You little bitch, Erica thought, I'm sure glad *I'm* not your mum—and where was their mum? Why hadn't she come home yet?

Erica was absolutely required to report this. Well, fuck that. She wasn't a clinical psychologist but she knew pretty much what would happen if she did report it and she didn't think that the "qualified professionals" would do any better with these crazy kids than they had with her. She took out a business card, turned it over and wrote her cell number on it. "Before you do it," she told them, "you owe me a phone call."

They were giving her a look that was almost identical—big grave eyes. "This is my *personal* number," Erica said. "Only my family and my friends have it. If you call me on it just for fun, I'll get really pissed off at you. Like really *really* pissed off. You only call me if things are serious. Do you understand me?"

They nodded.

"If you call me, I'll do everything I possibly can to keep you from being separated. *Everything*. Do you understand me?"

"Can we text you?" Devon said.

"Yeah, you can text me. Just so I get the message. But you've got to promise that you won't do anything to yourselves until you've talked to me. Do you promise?"

They nodded again. Erica offered her hand to Jamie. The girl's hand was cold and moist. "Swear to it," Erica said.

Jamie's dark eyes lit with anger and she tried to pull her hand away. Erica hung on. No, you don't, Erica thought. I'm not going to let you off so easy. "Swear to it."

Blood flowed into Jamie's face. For a moment she was actually fighting to get her hand free—but then she changed tactics, squeezed Erica's hand hard. They were locked together, hurting each other.

"I swear to it!"

"Good."

Erica let go and offered her hand to Devon. He was grinning madly. Instead of taking her hand, he wrapped his arms around her. "I swear to it too."

3.

"I'M NOT SURE I like the girl very much but the boy's a sweetheart."

Erica was glad to have something to talk about other than herself. She'd lost more weight since the last time Stacey had seen her, so she'd worn a loose cardigan to try to hide it. Now she was deliberately eating a slice of warm sourdough and slathering it with butter that she didn't want. "They're very bright," she said, "very articulate once they get going. Spoiled rotten. Oh my god, you should see their house. It's like a movie set. I don't understand those people. It's like they live on a different planet."

"Oh, West Vancouver," Stacey said, laughing. "It *is* a different planet."

Erica laughed too. She'd been listening to herself. I'm doing all right, she thought—I sound normal. "Yeah, all that frigging money," she said. "It's kind of obscene."

Stacey had made the first move—had called her up and invited her out—so Erica was trying to recreate one of their nice carefree dinners the way they used to be back in the day when their friendship had been easy, when the most ordinary of things had created the illusion of meaning. She thought of Stacey as her best friend in Vancouver—or that's the way she *used* to think of her. Even though their offices were directly across the hall from each other, Erica had hardly seen Stacey all summer—and when she had, Stacey had scurried by furtively with a "Got to run, call you," and nobody had called anybody. Stacey must be embarrassed about the long silence. The minute they'd sat down at their table, she'd been sure to let Erica know that she'd been to *three* conferences.

Erica was hurt—no, it was more complicated than that. Her feelings were muddy and conflicted. The long silence was just as much her own fault as it was Stacey's—phone lines run both ways—but she'd burned Stacey out in the spring and had wanted to give her a break. There's a limit to how long somebody can put up with you when you're inconsolable, when you're crying all the time. Stacey hadn't asked yet how Erica was doing, but she was bound to, and when she did, Erica would tell her that she was doing much better, thanks, even though she wasn't. People can only take so much. Nobody wanted to hear that you weren't getting any better.

ERICA THOUGHT OF HERSELF as the unlikeliest of candidates to be Stacey's friend. "Brilliant" was the word most often used to describe Dr. Stacey Chou. Her PhD was from Harvard. As a postdoc at McGill, she'd published several shit-hot papers that everybody and their dog in her field was citing. "She's a fabulous hire for us," Bill had said—that was Dr. William Ingram, the Chair of ITS. If Erica wanted promotion and tenure, he was the main person she'd have to please. "And she's genuinely nice too . . . warm and engaging. You'll love her."

Erica looked at two of Stacey's papers—"Induction of Immunogenic Ciliogenesis Negatively Regulates Tβ-positive CD4 T Cells through IL-4 Production," "Human IL-47-responsive type 2 innate lymphoid cells differentially express ADF1 in monozygotic twins discordant for diabetes mellitus." Holy fuck, she thought.

She emailed Annalise. "I don't have a clue what she's working on. I can't even begin to read her papers—they're in another universe. But we're the new hires and we're supposed to get along. What if she doesn't like me?"

"Of course she's going to like you," Annalise said, "you're the dominant twin with the social skills."

Erica understood her sister's resentment—on top of their genetic connection they had a lifetime of shared experience, so of course she understood it—and Erica resented it too, that she and Annalise had allowed themselves to be channeled too easily into roles the world had created for them, but the joker in the deck was this—in order to be the dominant twin with the social skills, you've got to be functioning as half of a twin unit and they were no longer a twin unit. They were separated. "Thanks a lot, jerk," she wrote back.

"*Of course* she's going to like you, Ricki," Annalise said on the phone later. "Stop worrying so much," and Stacey did like her—or at least she seemed to—and she liked Stacey, was in awe of her actually. The brilliant Dr. Chou turned out to be warm and friendly and chatty—and much to Erica's surprise, a totally down-to-earth girl. The first time they'd met—it had been at an ITS luncheon—she'd caught Stacey staring at her. Their eyes met and Erica saw something on Stacey's face she couldn't read—amusement? Afterwards, when they were walking away from the Faculty Club, Stacey said, "Both of us must have the same final clause in our JDs."

Erica didn't have a clue what she was talking about. With only the faintest suggestion of a smile, Stacey said, "You know, the clause that says, 'The successful candidate will not exceed 162 centimetres in height.'"

Erica laughed so hard she had to stop walking. Stacey had nailed the absurd improbability of it—how the hell could ITS have managed to hire *two* pint-sized PhDs?

After that, everything was easy. Dinner? Sure. "Anywhere but Chinese," Stacey said, so they parked on a quiet block near the university and walked into the first restaurant they saw. It was vaguely French, trying to be upscale but not succeeding, dim and brown and slightly tacky, enough like a small-town restaurant for Erica to feel at home. The entrées, mostly sauce-drenched meat, were too expensive, but neither of them could eat a full meal anyway, so they usually had appetizers and salads. Neither of them drank much—sometimes Erica would have a beer and Stacey a glass of white wine. They took turns picking up the bill. The restaurant had a name, but in their private joke they called it "Anywhere."

They had no problem talking to each other—as different as they were, it was amazing what they had in common. They both looked younger than their age and were frequently mistaken for teenagers. They both came from big families and liked having people around. They both had left boyfriends behind—Erica in Madison, Stacey in Montreal—and both felt uneasy about it, a mixture of sadness and relief. They both hoped to get married someday—to the right boy—but certainly not before they were tenured. Erica admitted that Vancouver scared her, but Stacey had grown up in Richmond so the Lower Mainland was home. "This is one of the great cities of the world. You doing anything tomorrow?"

It was late July, that time when Vancouver creates the illusion of paradise, so they walked the beach at Spanish Banks. They had lattes in Kits and Stacey drove them around Stanley Park, across the Lions Gate and halfway up Cypress to the lookout so Erica could see all of Vancouver laid out below her like a tiny glittering toy city. They could see the mountains on Vancouver Island, the beach where they'd just been, the glassy downtown, and distant Burnaby—even Mt. Baker across the border in the States—and for the first time Erica thought that she might understand the geography of this strange place. Then Stacey took the highway and shot them over to Main Street to poke around in the funky used furniture stores where Erica bought an antique dresser. They headed back toward Erica's apartment in the twilight and Stacey stopped at an amazing little Jamaican restaurant on the Drive where they ate fried plantain, jerk chicken and oxtail. It had been a perfect day and they knew each other quite well by then.

They were the first new hires to be specifically cross-appointed between their home departments and the rapidly expanding Inter-disciplinary Twin Studies Program. They were both wildly enthusiastic about their research. Stacey was a molecular biologist—generally a human geneticist, specifically an immunologist. Her research involved MZ twins discordant for heritable diseases. Erica was a social psych-ologist whose work had been in the area of group socialization. As a postdoc at Wisconsin, she'd been part of a team studying MZ twins in late childhood and early adolescence. "I still can't believe ITS hired me," she told Stacey, "that I'm actually *a professor*. I'm so lucky. It's the perfect job for me."

For Stacey, twins were high-class laboratory rats. If one MZ twin had Type I diabetes and the other didn't, that was *interesting* and Stacey had to find out why. But Erica had always been fascinated by twins because she was one. It was the most fundamental fact about her. She was an MZ twin—half of a twin unit.

Singletons never got it about MZ twins. They said they did, but they didn't. "So tell me," Stacey said.

"Okay. So you know you're separate. You're not connected by mental telepathy. You're stuck inside of your own head just like everyone else. But there's a barrier singletons have between themselves and other people—it's like a bubble—and you and your twin have always been inside the same bubble. The feeling's hard to describe.

"There are moments like . . . I don't know, *transformative insights?* When something goes click, when you really *know* something. I'll tell you one that was really important to me."

In grade five Erica and Annalise got in trouble and were sent to the principal's office. They didn't get in trouble a lot when they were kids, but they hadn't been angels either, not by a long shot. Erica couldn't remember what they'd done. "There've been some studies on this," she told Stacey. "Most children don't remember what they're punished for. They remember *the punishment*."

The principal gave them a good chewing out and then delivered that standard predictable line: "What do you girls have to say for yourselves?"

Erica came up with the standard required answer. She said they were sorry and that they'd never do it again—whatever it was. She was proud of herself. She'd given him far more than the minimum. She'd laid it on fairly thick. She'd been positively eloquent. "Okay," he said, "and how about you, Annalise?"

Erica and Annalise looked at each other. That was unusual. Most of the time they knew each other's thoughts so well that they didn't need to look at each other but this was so horrible that they couldn't even begin to deal with it.

The principal did not understand about twins. What was his problem? Erica was the one who talked to grown-ups and she did it for both of them. They were *twins* and she'd been speaking for Annalise too. She'd said "we," hadn't she? Why didn't he get it?

"Annalise?" he said.

A single tear ran down Annalise's cheek and Erica's heart broke. Annalise could not say a word.

They stood there in silence for what felt like a hundred million years. Then the principal said, "Annalise, one of these days you're going to have to learn to stand up for yourself," and let them go.

"And that's when the click happened," Erica had told Stacey. "Of course we knew we were twins. We'd always known that—it was the most basic thing in the world—but that was the first time I'd felt the full . . . I don't know how to say this . . . just how *massive* it was. I knew that I could never possibly feel about another human being the way I did about Annalise and that somehow . . . that Annalise didn't have to learn how to stand up for herself because she had me to do it for her. But that's still not right. Okay, let me try it this way. We weren't two separate people. When I was standing up for her, she *was* standing up for herself."

35

NOW ERICA HAD achieved exactly what she'd wanted—a perfectly ordinary moment with Stacey. They'd chatted with their waitress last year so she knew that they were professors—despite how ridiculously young they looked—just as they knew that she was an undergrad English major, a perfectly nice, perfectly ordinary girl. "Two spoons?" she was asking with a wicked grin.

"Oh, come on," Erica said to Stacey, "I'll share it with you."

This sisterly conspiracy was about something just as ordinary as it should be—*about chocolate.* "Okay," Stacey said, giving in with a smile.

All Erica had to do was hold it together for another half an hour. Soon they would have triple-chocolate mousse to distract them and she was still getting mileage out of the Oxley-Clark twins. She was trying to make her voice sound more than merely normal—she was trying to make it sound concerned and engaged and alive. "I don't know what's going on with them exactly, but I can sense it . . . something about gender norms."

And the identical thing? Okay, so for whatever reasons, the Oxley-Clark twins needed to feel identical, she said—and to try to act like they were—but their obsession with twins, and with themselves as twins, would probably go away on its own in a year or two. Well, it would just so long as they weren't separated—but there was not a whole hell of a lot she could do about that one.

Listening to herself, Erica realized that this line of conversation was getting dangerous. Making house calls on prospective interviewees was not something she ordinarily did, but she didn't know if Stacey knew that or not. She couldn't really explain herself without talking about the suicide threat—and she couldn't do that—but if she kept on going, she might paint herself into a corner, so it was time to change the subject. "Oh," she said, "driving's getting a lot better."

The last time she and Stacey had talked, driving was still making Erica so anxious that even the familiar route from her apartment to the university was a major ordeal and she hadn't been able to drive on highways at all. Sometimes she'd get full-blown panic attacks and have to stop and pull over. Even *riding* in a car made her anxious. "I've been working on systematic desensitization like right out of the textbook," she said.

She'd written out a hierarchy of anxiety-producing situations. The least fear-producing item was standing next to a car and thinking about getting into it; the most fear-producing was driving highways in poor weather conditions—in particular, making highway entrances. She'd imagined each scene and gradually worked her way up the hierarchy. Once she'd been able to imagine it, she'd been able to do it. "Good for you," Stacey said. "Vancouver's impossible if you can't drive."

Erica had beaten Stacey in the reach for the credit card. Now they were standing on the street outside the restaurant. Either twilight was settling in or the sky was thickening with rain clouds—she couldn't tell which—but the streetlights hadn't come on yet. They always hugged each other goodbye but tonight Stacey seemed reluctant to let go. "Erica," she said, "are you any better?"

Okay, here it is. "Yeah," Erica said, "a little. It just takes time." Bullshit. But Erica *had* accomplished what she'd set out to do—successfully imitated normalcy, and that was, she supposed, a victory. *You see, Stace, we can still be friends. I won't embarrass you or make you sad.*

MZ twins often had trouble with socialization. When they tried to form friendships outside the twin bond, they got too close too fast and wanted too much. *You see, Stace, I won't ask for something you can't give me.*

Erica and Annalise had been born with a sense of smell far more acute than normal. If one of their girlfriends snuck out for a smoke, they could smell it on her for hours afterward—even over Halls or mouthwash. Half a block from the house, they knew what they were having for dinner. "We must be part dog," Lise said.

Stacey was wearing, as she usually did, the faintest mist of perfume—not a floral scent, but something sharp and citrusy. The main note was lime. It suited her. "I burned you out in the spring," Erica said. "I'm sorry."

"Yeah, you did. I'm sorry too."

They'd been hugging each other for so long it was awkward. Erica stepped back. "If you ever want to talk," Stacey said, "if you ever . . . need anything. Call me. Okay?"

Erica said she would, but she wouldn't. She drove away. She was heading east toward the highway. She was terrified of the Port Mann Bridge so that's where she was going.

ERICA HADN'T TOLD STACEY that the systematic desensitization she'd been practicing had gradually morphed into her personal brand of implosion therapy, a variation on the crude but effective "flooding" technique. If you experienced what was frightening often enough, you became habituated to it and lost your fear. It was pretty much the same as taking a kid who's terrified of the water and chucking her into the deep end. Of course the kid must already know how to swim. Erica did know how to drive. She'd been driving since she was sixteen.

She was making it work for her. Flooding herself with the most frightening items near the top of the hierarchy had drained away the fear from the items near the bottom. She could drive in normal city traffic now, no problem, but she was far from habituated to the items near the top. Highways still gave her the burn.

In the voice of her coach from her softball days—"Go for the burn, girls"—the heat at the edge of pain in the weight room, changes she could feel in her body—that was the metaphor. On the highway the burn was a foul taste, a foul smell—acrid and metallic—and the sting of sweat, the tight cap of tension on her head, on her neck, and her heart hammering her ribs like a rig-mounted breaker. It was adrenaline—more than adrenaline, a set of complex chemical interactions—but she didn't want to think about any of that or she would see herself, as she too often did, as nothing more than a sophisticated bio-mechanical device cleverly designed by several billion years of evolution. When she was in the burn, all she wanted to do was feel it. She wanted to believe in it.

She wanted driving to be a mixture of animal fear and alertness. She wanted to be forced to make crucial decisions at lightning speed. It was addictive. Her body liked it—although it left her afterward in an unresolved state, exhausted and jumpy. The burn made her high—created the illusion of meaning. While she was in the burn, she had to believe in the illusion because if she didn't, she could die. There was something unquestionably wrong with her—that it took death to inject meaning, that it was death that canceled meaning.

She was doing a hundred clicks on the highway in the dark and trucks were still passing her in the left-hand lane. She was in full burn but it still hadn't used up all of her mind. She didn't care about much these days but she cared about the Oxley-Clark twins. Oh my god, they had their hanging-themselves scenario down pat. They even knew what kind of rope they were going to use. They'd refused the label "suicide pact," had said, instead, "automatic." How can you kill yourself *automatically?* Did she really think she could save those crazy kids by making them promise to call her? Who the hell was she kidding?

ERICA WAS LOST IN SURREY looking for the King George Highway that would take her home—although it wasn't *home*; it was just where she went when she ran out of anywhere else to go. Her colleagues had tried to talk her out of renting in East Van—"You don't want to be all the way over *there*"—but when she'd first seen her little apartment, it had been June and the sunlight shining in through the small windows had made the converted attic in an old house near Commercial Drive seem quaint, even charming, like a Bohemian artists' den in an old-school romantic story—anyhow that's how she'd *wanted* to see it and that's how she'd described it to Annalise—and the clincher was the low rent. Even with an assistant professor's salary, Erica was still enough of a small-town girl to want to save every penny—but winter transformed her cute garret into a cramped murky little prison where she was sentenced to solitary.

She found the highway and it was taking her back to the Drive so everything was familiar now—routine—and the illusion of meaning was draining away. She was able to park not too far away, climbed the three flights of stairs, unlocked her door and walked in to the sound of the CBC. She kept her radio on all the time whether she was there or not. She needed the sound of the voices; it didn't matter what they were saying. One of the reasons for the cheap rent was the low headroom—not a problem for Erica. Her bedroom was so small that her single bed and antique dresser took up all the space in it. Her IKEA desk took up most of the living room; her bulletin board was behind it—a panel of Donnacona screwed to the wall with Robertson heads just the way their dad had taught her to do it when she'd been twelve. Writing inspirational or instructional notes to themselves and posting them on bulletin boards was something Erica and Annalise had done their entire lives. Shortly after she'd come back to Vancouver in January, Erica had pinned up the current note.

Nothing feels good but some things feel better than others.
Being at school is better than not being at school.
Being busy is better than not being busy.
Being with people is better than being alone.
Maybe you will feel better someday.
Until you feel better do not go back to the Hat.

Erica and Annalise were the first members of their family to go to university. It was a big deal; everybody was so proud of them. "My two little geniuses," their mum called them. They'd both been good students, but Lise had been the more adventurous, the more creative. Erica's primary talent was an ability to learn whatever her teachers wanted her to learn.

Erica had written her PhD thesis to please her supervisor and he had been pleased. As a postdoc, she'd had her name attached to three papers that were being cited by the leading scholars in her field and a fourth was due out any day now. She was an assistant professor at a first-rate institution and SSHRC had given her a reasonably good-sized grant, enough to set up her lab. Her research was going well. If she kept on saying and doing the right things, she would be promoted to associate and granted tenure. She would gradually build an international reputation and be promoted to full professor and become the Chair of the ITS Program. That's how things were supposed to go. The problem was that nothing in that scenario felt good enough to make her want to get out of bed in the morning. Much of what she'd been saying and writing and teaching she no longer believed to be true. Some of it she now believed to be as false as Hippocrates' theory of the four humours.

Erica kept a journal in which she recorded her overall mood score for the day and a record of her weight and how much she'd eaten and slept. Even when she was focusing on it and trying to do better, her eating was sketchy at best; she'd lost twelve and a half pounds since Christmas. Three hours of sleep at a single stretch was the best she could hope for, and the highest mood score she'd given herself had been a five on a scale of ten.

She'd seen four doctors—one in Medicine Hat, one at the University Hospital and one at the walk-in clinic near where she lived. The clinic doctor had admitted to feeling out of her depth and had referred Erica to the fourth doctor, a psychiatrist who'd told Erica that she was suffering from post-traumatic stress disorder and was clinically depressed. It was serious, he'd said—which she should know perfectly well, being a psychologist—and she would not get better on her own. It was essential that she comply with treatment. She'd only seen him once.

She *had* tried to help herself. The doctor at the University Hospital had told her that the four pillars of treatment for depression were Cognitive Behaviour Therapy, regular aerobic exercise, meditation and antidepressants. She hadn't been convinced. The "four pillars" approach sounded too formulaic to her—but what did she have to lose? She'd done the assignments in the CBT workbook until she'd realized that the evidence supporting her worst fear—her "hot thought"—usually turned out to be one hundred percent. She had no problem with grinding herself through a fitness circuit—she'd been a gym rat since her softball days—but with all the shit at school it was hard to get into the gym often enough and she hated being alone there. When she'd tried a meditation class, the instructor—a sweet white-haired lady in sweatpants—had devoted the entire hour to breathing exercises designed to open the Heart Chakra and had told everyone to read Deepak Chopra.

All four doctors had prescribed drugs—Zopiclone for sleep and other psychoactive agents that varied from doctor to doctor. In all, Erica had received prescriptions for Prozac and Zoloft, Trazodone and Desipramine, Clonazepam and Diazepam. Of course Erica was well aware of the meta-analyses that suggested that antidepressants don't work any better than placebo for all but the most severely disturbed patients, and even in those patients, any positive results could be equally explained by regression toward the mean. But okay, she'd thought, maybe I'm one of those few who might actually be helped—*maybe*—so every time Erica received a prescription, she filled it. Then she Googled the drug and read about it. A dozen little plastic pill bottles were lined up on the counter in her bathroom. She had not taken a single pill from a single bottle.

She hadn't been back to the Hat since the accident. Right after it had happened she'd stayed there because she hadn't been able to think of anything else to do. She'd stayed through Christmas and on into the

41

new year—she'd missed her first week of classes—but she didn't remember that time very well and what she did remember was a narrative she'd created later. What Erica had learned from her sister's death was the truth about the world.

Before the accident she wouldn't have been able to imagine crying so much that it was like a physical illness. She'd been taught that the human brain is incapable of remembering pain *as pain* but could only remember narratives *about* pain, so anything she thought about it now was another narrative added onto the previous narratives, including ideas such as this: you could snatch anyone out of the prime of their life—no matter how healthy, optimistic, self-confident, and robust they might be—and if you tortured them methodically, day after day, they would want to die.

"Don't throw anything away," she'd told both their mother and Mark, Annalise's husband, "not *anything*." As a twin, Erica felt that she had the right not merely to ask but to demand. Yes, she wanted the memory box that Mum had been keeping for Annalise. Yes, she wanted all of Annalise's university papers. Yes, she wanted her lesson plans and to-do lists. Yes, she wanted all of her clothes. Yes, she wanted her perfume and her toothbrush and her makeup and her hairbrush with her hair still in it. She'd left much of that stuff in the Hat and had promised to go back for it, but she'd brought the essentials to Vancouver—the memory box, everything that had been in Annalise's car, everything that had been on her vanity table the day she'd died.

It wasn't as bad as it had been right after the accident. She'd had classic PTSD symptoms. Whenever she tried to go to sleep, she would see vivid images of Annalise dead—or she'd be driving frantically to the hospital, sure she could save her. She'd thought constantly about killing herself. She hadn't been able to pick up a kitchen knife without imagining ramming it into her chest, hadn't been able to walk out onto a balcony without imagining throwing herself off of it, hadn't been able to drive a car without imagining swerving into oncoming traffic. The same words kept appearing in her mind so often they turned into an endlessly repeating tape loop—"You want out of this shit? That's easy. Kill yourself." She'd worked through that terrible time by turning

Annalise's death into a research project, and she had to admit that the worst seemed to be over. Those hallucinatory images had stopped recycling through her mind, and now she could sleep in short stretches, but she wished she could just turn everything off. It must be such a relief to be able to stop thinking altogether. Maybe she should try the sleeping pills—but she was afraid of them, afraid of what they might do to her brain chemistry.

Erica was terrified by the loss of consciousness that sleep required. The edge between sleeping and waking was intolerable. If it went on too long, she simply gave up and got out of bed. The best way for sleep to overcome her was suddenly, her body's demand for it having become irresistible. Now, on the edge, as one ugly thing morphed into another, she was still driving the highway—it felt like Alberta. Nothing bad was happening yet, and a part of her knew that she was going to sleep. *My brain waves are changing*, she thought. Her brain waves could be studied and measured, particularly now that there were no other cars on the road. The sky was flat and radiant like tarnished pewter in window light. Did Mum own pewter like that? It felt like a real window and real pewter. Maybe it would snow, or maybe not, and maybe it was real snow. She didn't know if she was driving home or leaving it.

How could she have forgotten those furry little animals? They were like rabbits or mice. Their quiet sad little voices were saying, "But you promised to take care of us." Erica opened the carton and there they were, packed in tight. They had been turned into fur for coats. How could she have forgotten the little animals? How could she have let that happen to them?

She pulled back from her sorrow, first realized that she was in REM sleep and then, immediately afterward, that she was awake. She got up, lit all the lights, noted the time and wrote it into her journal, adding: "First attempt to sleep, made it all of 40 min. I'm afraid I can't stand this much longer."

4.

"YOUR MUM DIDN'T come with you?"

"No," Jamie said, "she was double-booked."

"She's really sorry," Devon said.

I bet she is, Erica thought.

Their elusive mum, however, had filled out the questionnaire. It had been riding around in Devon's knapsack and looked a bit worse for wear, but there it was; he was handing it to her. Maybe the twins had filled it out themselves—they were perfectly capable of that.

"We've got all the stuff for Morgan and Avi too," Devon said, shoving more rumpled paper at her. "Thanks," Erica said, "I'll set up an appointment for them."

Devon's sunshine grin was telling her that he was glad to see her. Well, she was glad to see him too, so glad that she didn't trust it—how personal it was, how immediate. It was like a shudder across a sensitive membrane.

There was nothing gender-ambiguous about the Oxley-Clark twins today. They were in their school uniforms and Jamie was wearing a kilt and girly scuffed flats. When Erica smiled at her, Jamie did a small maneuver, not enough to call it a pirouette, but an awkward look-at-me gesture. Look at what? That I'm really a girl? Erica met her eyes but couldn't read them. Jamie was a closed door that Erica wanted to open—

No, that wasn't right. Erica didn't want to open anything. She was afraid of how this particular set of twins created the illusion of meaning for her. She was afraid of feeling too much, afraid of the illusion. She was afraid of feeling responsible for them. She wanted to be nothing more than a detached observer, an extension of her computer.

Erica offered her hand. It was a non-threatening way to make physical contact and it also gave her a chance to gauge their emotional state. Devon's hand was warm, his sister's cold and moist. Erica could feel the tension coming off the girl like a draft through a crack in a window. "There's nothing to be nervous about," she said. "Are you nervous about being videotaped?"

Big-eyed and silent, both kids shook their heads no. "Just forget about the camera. I haven't turned it on yet. I'll tell you when I do. Nobody's going to see the tapes but me and my grad students. If anybody else saw them, I'd get in big trouble with the university. Okay?"

"Yeah, sure," Devon said. He didn't give a shit about the camera.

Erica was now in the early stages of testing her hypothesis that MZ twins had personality traits that distinguished them from the rest of the human population, including a special bond between a subset of MZ co-twins that was unique to them. There was plenty of anecdotal evidence to support that hypothesis but anecdotal evidence was so much crap—without something to quantify and measure, there was no science. She hoped to develop an inventory accurate enough to identify MZ twins and measure the bond between them. She had her work cut out for her. She would have to interview not only MZ twins but DZ twins, non-twin sibs and pairs of unrelated same-age friends. To get statistically significant results, she needed large sample sizes. It would take years—but in the meantime she'd better start generating some papers or she wouldn't get her grant renewed and then she wouldn't get tenure.

It had taken Erica a while to get things off the ground, but everything was running smoothly now. As the Principal Investigator, she did not ordinarily gather data. Her grad students did that—conducted the interviews and scored them. Her postdoc, Andrew, supervised her grad students and she supervised him. When she'd told him that she was going to conduct this particular interview herself, he'd looked at her like she'd grown an extra head. "Just want to keep my hand in," she'd said airily—which, of course, was ridiculous. Andrew was a steady-as-you-go sort of guy, pretty much unflappable, but he'd gaped at her open-mouthed—obviously shocked, maybe even offended. God knows what he'd thought. Well, he'd get over it.

"Okay, here goes," she said to the twins. "I'm turning on the camera. I'm just going to ask you a series of questions. You can answer any way you want."

Even with the small samples she'd collected so far, Item One was beginning to look significant. "I'm going to start off by interviewing each of you separately," she said. "I would like one of you to stay and one of

45

you to leave. Okay? Now one of you should go out into the waiting room and we'll call you when it's your turn."

"Which one of us do you want?" Jamie said.

"It doesn't matter."

The twins looked at each other. "You want me to go first?" Jamie said.

"I don't care."

"I don't, ah . . . Maybe I should go first."

Devon shrugged. "I'll go first if you want."

"No, maybe I should." Jamie looked away, then at her brother, then at Erica, then back at her brother. "No, you go first."

"Okay."

Jamie stared hard at Erica, her eyes asking for permission. Erica nodded. Jamie was not a happy camper. She slouched out of the room, slamming the door behind her. When Erica's grad students scored the interview, they would record how long it had taken the twins to decide who would go first.

All the tension seemed to have left the room along with Jamie. Devon fell onto one of the chairs and lay there in his catlike sprawl. He looked relaxed, even happy, and he seemed to enjoy being interviewed. The items were designed to test the strength of the twin-bond—how much each twin knew about the other, how cooperative they were, how much they depended on each other. Erica was still in the early stages of developing her instrument and many of the items were pure guesswork. Some of them, she knew, would eventually turn out to be statistical junk and have to be discarded. When Erica got to the questions about friends, Devon said, "That's easy. Morgan and Avi Lynas are our best friends. They're identical like us."

Before Erica could present the next item, he said, "Like in deep time they're our sisters."

What Erica was supposed to do was move right along through the inventory but that's not what she did. "Okay," she said, "what do you mean by deep time?"

"That's the time you could see if you could see the entire world stack."

Science fiction stuff. Where was he getting it? How much did he believe it? If she kept on going off-script, her grad students would think

46

she'd lost her mind. But there was no way she could use this interview—she'd already fucked her data—so it didn't matter what her grad students thought. "World stack?" she said.

"It's like . . . Okay, none of us can see the entire world stack without a major consciousness morph, but if we could, we'd see deep time."

"Where'd you get that idea?"

He shrugged. "Stuff I read. Like from stuff on the net. Like *Two from One Fire*."

"The manga? The one with the picture on your wall?"

"Yeah."

"So what's a world stack?"

"You really want to know? . . . Okay. Worlds are like . . . *replications?* You can like push the top world until it pops and then you get a new world. You can't like, you know, just jump around from world to world, but some people have got their souls linked like across these little bridges. Like Einstein-Rosen bridges. You still can't *see* deep time, but you can like feel it . . . Jamie and I can feel it. Morgan and Avi can too."

WHEN IT WAS Jamie's turn to be interviewed, she got hung up on exactly the same item that her brother had—the question about best friends. She was uncomfortable in a skirt—or just uncomfortable, period. She was sitting with her knees crammed together and her feet splayed out, tapping the toes of one foot on the floor. She sighed, rolled her eyes, her expression saying: "This is *so* a waste of time!" but answered—"Morgan and Avi."

Jamie seemed angry. This is interesting, Erica thought. "But they're not just . . ." Jamie said.

Erica waited until she saw that Jamie had no intention of finishing her sentence. She could push Jamie right along through the inventory or she could go off-script again. "They're not just what?"

"I had a girl crush on Morgan."

Jamie seemed to have surprised herself with what she'd just said. She sent Erica a look like a startled bird taking off.

Okay, Erica thought, my grad students are just going to *love* this one. Instead of moving on to the next item in the inventory, she said, "A girl crush?"

47

"Like . . . you know . . . another girl? Like a *girl* crush?"

"I've heard other kids use that term but I don't know what it means exactly. Do you want to tell me?"

"Like . . . you don't want to *do her*, but she's . . . You want to be with her all the time. You want to be *like* her. I don't know. It's like . . . real intense."

"Okay."

Jamie was picking at loose threads in her kilt.

"Do you want to tell me about it?" Erica asked.

For a moment it looked like the answer was no, but then Jamie said, "A lot of the kids were scared of them . . . the kids at school? But Dev like just walked up and started talking to them."

Morgan and Avalon were in the anime club and Devon was into all that stuff too—like totally into it—and so the three of them were like, oh my god, *The Ghost in the Shell*, oh my god, *Neon Genesis*, and Jamie didn't know what they were talking about.

"So you weren't into anime before?" Erica asked her.

"Not so much. No, I wasn't a fan. Not until *Two from One Fire* . . . but Dev's like . . . Morgan and Avi invited us over after school. They downloaded all this shit like off the net, and they had every freakin' episode of *Utena* and we had to watch every freakin' one of them, like *hours*."

Jamie looked quickly into Erica's eyes then away, and in that brief flash, Erica saw something like panic. What was going on?

Jamie probably didn't understand the point of the interview. Maybe she thought she was in a therapy session where she was supposed to reveal deep dark secrets. Even if she hadn't actually been in therapy before, she would have seen dramatizations on TV. Okay, Erica thought, any idiot could play Carl Rogers. "They invited you to go home with them?"

"Yeah, and I like couldn't talk. I couldn't say a freakin' word, and Devon was like . . . oh my god, he never shut up."

"You didn't feel like part of the group?"

"No. I was like, oh, this is so fucking retarded."

"And you had a girl crush on Morgan?"

"Like I thought I would die."

Jamie's eyes were focused on a spot on the wall. "You ever walked across the Lynn Valley Suspension Bridge?" she said.

"No."

"There's this sign . . . We go there on the weekend, and this sign's like, 'No Running,' so Morgan and Avi just run across the bridge and all the way back. There's people on it. Like, 'Girls! Girls!' Freakin' scary. I'm not afraid of heights, but Dev's afraid of heights . . . We get out in the middle of the bridge and they start . . . and Morgan and Avi start swinging it and . . . I'm not kidding, like really swinging it, and I'm like, whoa . . . It's really scary and Devon's like scared. He's hanging onto the . . . It's high up on . . . sort of like wires? Devon's yelling at them to stop, like 'Come on, come on,' and they're laughing and making the bridge swing harder, and I'm getting like whoa, I'm going to be sick."

Jamie took a deep breath and held it. Then she let it out slowly. "Are you afraid of heights?"

"Yes," Erica said, "a little bit. Not so it's a phobia. About the same as most people."

"You ever get this feeling like . . . You look over and it's like, eeew, I'd hate to fall off but . . . then like, maybe I *want* to fall off. What if I jump?"

It was the first time Erica felt that Jamie was talking *to* her and not just *at* her. "That's common," she said. "A lot of people get that feeling."

"Morgan and Avi are like, 'Hey, let's go for a swim,' and it's way down and the river's fast, like crazy fast . . . and Morgan goes to jump over, she's got her whole leg over the railing and I'm like, 'Stop it, this isn't funny,' and Avi goes to like push Morgan over and I'm like . . . I just start crying, like *crying really hard*, and there's this guy and he's like, 'Kids! Get off this bridge *now!*' and I just run off the bridge and he's like, 'You kids have to leave now. That was insane,' and we start walking back to the bus stop and Morgan and Avi are like, 'Jamie, hey,' and I'm like, 'Don't touch me,' and I won't talk to them. I was just so fucking . . ."

"Humiliated?"

"Yeah."

"Because they made you cry?"

"Yeah. I'm like I hate my life. Dev's walking with them and I'm like *traitor!*"

They took the bus back to West Van. Jamie wouldn't talk to her brother or to the Lynas twins. She walked a half a block behind them. "I'm like this sucks balls. Should I kill myself now or later?"

The other kids bought food at the DQ and then walked down to the beach. Jamie bought the largest-sized Coke and trailed along behind them. The kids sat down on a log. Jamie walked up behind them and dumped her entire Coke over Morgan's head.

"She screams and she's like . . . They could have . . . Jumps up, she's like laughing. They could have killed me, you know, but Avi . . . I'm a fast runner, like chasing me, nobody can catch me, so they're like . . . Into the park? Oh my god, so much fun, and Avi throws a whole freakin' milkshake in my face and Dev throws his milkshake on Avi and we're like throwing chips at each other and tearing up pieces of sandwiches and like throwing . . . and the ketchup? I never had so much fun in my life."

"And after that you were part of the group?"

Jamie smiled for the first time. "Oh, yeah."

Erica thought the story was over but it wasn't. The kids were so covered with food that the driver wouldn't let them on the bus so they had to walk all the way up the hill to Morgan and Avi's mum's house. Luckily she wasn't home. They dumped their clothes in the wash and took a shower. Morgan and Avi gave them stuff to wear. They hadn't eaten any of the food they'd bought so Morgan and Avi made Kraft Dinner and then their mum and her boyfriend came home and made them go to bed, so all four of them got into Morgan and Avi's bed and they talked all night long. They were still talking when it was getting light outside. They told each other *everything*.

Morgan and Avi told Jamie they were sorry for making her cry. "Jamie," they said, "if you ever go off by yourself again like that . . . and won't talk to us . . . we'll kick your fucking ass."

"And Dev's like, 'You know what? I think you guys are our sisters,' and Morgan's like, 'Yeah, we know that, we already figured that out,' and Avi's like, 'and here we are together again after all these lifetimes. How cool is that?'"

ERICA WOULD KNOW BETTER when her grad students scored the inventory but she already had a good sense of these kids. They wanted to be identical, claimed to be identical? Fat chance of that. They were as different as chalk and cheese.

She was walking them over to the University Hospital. "Was that okay?" Jamie was asking, anxiety still radiating from her. She probably believed that she'd just been in a heavy therapy session. "That was fine," Erica said, "just great."

Erica was surprised at herself—that she wanted something so badly, that she wanted to solve the puzzle of this set of twins. It was fascinating to see the pieces of it coming together. At first glance Jamie looked like the driving force in their twinship, but all of the science fiction stuff, the manga and anime stuff, came from Devon. He'd pulled his sister into his story, and now they were living inside his mythology—and the Lynas twins were central to the myth. If Jamie and Devon wanted to be identical, the Lynas twins were the models for the identical they wanted to be.

"Erica?" Jamie said—and she'd loaded that single word with so much emotion that Erica stopped to look at her.

"Yes?" Erica said.

It was an odd moment. Erica had been so involved in writing her own personal narrative *about* the twins that she'd lost track of the live flesh-and-blood twins who were walking next to her. The fat golden light of late September was slanting across the campus, making everything glow, and Erica saw Jamie differently now, not as half of a twin puzzle but as a skinny little girl in a private school uniform who was looking at her with frightened eyes. "When we like . . . *promised?*" Jamie said. "We meant it. Did you mean it?"

"Like if there's an emergency," Devon said.

Erica was in the burn. "Of course I meant it," she said. "I don't care what . . . If it's a real emergency, you can call me *any time.* Yes, I meant it. Four in the morning, I don't care. But it's got to be real."

And *they're* real, she thought. What a bizarre thing to think—of course they were real—and the light was making her see them with an aching clarity. Maybe the crazy-ass shit she'd been doing with them had been worth it. Maybe she'd got exactly what she wanted. "But if it *is* real, you've got to call me. Okay?"

"Okay," they both said and smiled at her. Devon was the one with the stunning smile—he used it a lot—but Jamie's smile was rare, was brief, was bittersweet, and so it was the one that got to her.

Erica was the adult, the psychologist, the authority, so she should be talking now—saying anything to bring back the ordinary—but she didn't want to trivialize what had just happened. It was good that they were simply walking in the sun. They arrived at the lab at exactly the right time—no one was waiting. The nurse was leaning over the receptionist's desk, the two of them deep in a discussion of what seemed to be boyfriend troubles—"It's always the same thing. When it's *his* friends . . ." Erica used the requisition form to interrupt them.

She didn't want to say goodbye. She would see the twins one more time—when she got their blood tests back—and then there would be no reason to see them again. Did they know that? Did they think they'd signed on for something ongoing like counseling? If they did, it was cruel. Had she said or done anything to make them think that? Maybe she should say something. But no, it wasn't the right time. "Can you get home okay?"

"Sure," Devon said, "we've got a cab card."

Of course you do, she thought. "Listen. This is important. When we get the blood tests back, you'll have to come in again and your mum has to come with you. I'll fit my schedule around hers, but she *absolutely has to be here.* Have you got that?"

"Yeah," Jamie said, "we've got it."

"Hey, is this going to hurt?" Devon said, his voice too loud.

"It doesn't hurt a bit," the receptionist said, pointing at the nurse. "She's a real pro."

Erica waved goodbye. She stepped back outside into the beautiful fall afternoon—into the golden light. "You should have seen the light," she said in her mind—and then the bottom dropped out of the world. She'd been thinking about how to tell the story to Annalise.

WHEN THE LYNAS TWINS appeared a week later, they didn't look like crazy out-of-control bridge swingers. They looked cool and self-contained—and quite striking, like they'd been designed for high visibility. They were uncannily alike and then, as if that wasn't enough, were true redheads, flaming full-on carrot-tops with lots of hair—thick loops of curls falling past their shoulders and blunt bangs so long they completely covered their eyebrows. They were wearing identical

expressions—expectant, inquisitive and closed—their blue eyes emphasized with mascara and thick black liner. Erica was a grown-up kid from
Alberta and didn't approve of makeup on girls their age.

"Hi, I'm Dr. Bauer. You can call me Erica." They each took her hand
when she offered it. They didn't seem the least bit apprehensive; their
hands were dry and warm. They must have come straight from school;
they were still in their uniforms.

"I'm so happy to meet you. Jamie and Devon have told me a lot about
you. Which one of you is which?"

"I'm Avalon." That was the smaller twin. "I'm Morgan." That was the
one with the stronger face. Those were useful cues but if Erica ever met
them separately, she still wouldn't be sure.

"You don't have your mum or your dad with you today?"

"No, just us," Avalon said.

Oh my, Erica thought, another pair of inappropriately independent kids with who-gives-a-fuck parents. Was that a West Van thing?
"Your parents," she said, trying to hide the annoyance in her voice, "on
the consent form . . . Both of your parents agreed to have the interview
videotaped." That is, *somebody* had checked the appropriate boxes. "Is
that all right with you?"

"That's cool," Morgan answered for both of them.

"But we're not going to do that yet. I'll warn you before I turn on
the camera." Erica was more interesting in simply talking with these
girls than she was in running them through the interview. She wanted
to see how they fit into Devon and Jamie's mythology. "Let's just chat for
a while," she said.

Just as she'd guessed, they chose to sit side by side. Because of
the intake system in BC schools, they were in the same grade as Jamie
and Devon but nearly a year older and visibly pubescent. They seemed
unnervingly mature and ready for anything—Erica had the sense that
they were wearing their pretty faces like masks. Maybe that was how they
dealt with adults, but whatever that composure was, Erica felt it like a
forcefield around them. Yes, she could imagine them swinging the suspension bridge. She saw them as a version of the pain-in-the-ass "double
trouble" twins from the pop literature that Annalise had written about.

She didn't like them at all. She'd have to be careful or her dislike would show and she wouldn't learn anything useful.

Okay, the first few things she needed to do were get them relaxed and talking—any topic would do. "Jamie and Devon tell me you're dancers."

No response beyond a small affirmative nod from Avalon.

"What kind of dance do you do?"

Morgan answered, "Like everything . . . pretty much . . ."

"Ballet, lyrical . . ." Avalon said.

"Tap, jazz, hip-hop," Morgan finished it.

"Is one of you better than the other at anything?"

"Morgan jumps higher," Avalon said.

"Avi's better on pointe," Morgan said.

That was neatly done. Neither girl had said "I."

When singletons confessed to Erica—as they often did—that they found identical twins eerie, weird, unnatural or even a bit creepy, they meant twins like the Lynas girls. Earlier researchers had said that twins like that had "unit identity" but Erica didn't use that term because she didn't trust the theoretical framework behind it. She preferred to use the term "highly bonded" to describe the kind of MZ twins who were so strongly attached to each other that they functioned as a single unit and would presumably score high on her Twin Attachment Inventory. When they were children, highly bonded twins wore each other's clothes, became noticeably agitated if they lost track of each other on the playground, and sometimes spoke a private language. When they were in high school, they did each other's homework and still slept in the same bed. Because potential mates would never entirely understand the twin bond—and often didn't have the patience to try—highly bonded twins had difficulty forming intimate relationships. It was so hard for highly bonded twins to separate that some of them never managed to do it. Erica and Annalise had been highly bonded.

"Do you guys do everything together?"

"Pretty much."

She wasn't getting anywhere. If she wanted more than brief responses to a series of questions, she should try something else. Just like most thirteen-year-old girls, they obviously cared about their appearance.

"I love your bangs."

"Oh, thanks!"

"When I was your age, nobody wore bangs like that. It's nice to see them coming back."

"They're *Japanese* bangs."

"Really? I bet you like Japanese comics."

"You think? No!"

"Yeah, we're fans. Japanese culture is like . . ."

"crazy cool. We're in the anime club."

"We wish we could wear seifuku . . . you know, with the sailor flap . . ."

"and the bow," Avalon said, drawing an imaginary one over the loose knot of her necktie. "Kawaii."

"Too cute," her sister translated.

Erica had to smile at that. "So what else do you like . . . besides Japanese culture?"

Many kids their age answered questions like that with, "I don't know," or "not much," but Morgan said, "We surf?" the girl-talk rising inflection making it sound like a question.

That was a surprise. "Really? Where?"

"Tofino mostly?"

"Isn't the water cold in Tofino?"

"Crazy cold."

"Like frigid. Oooo. Terminal."

"You have to wear like a wetsuit or you will die literally."

"We've had hypothermia lots of times."

"Sometimes we go down to Point Roberts but not so much."

"We've been to Washington State and Oregon. When we're sixteen we're gonna buy an old beater . . ."

"and like chase the waves down the coast."

"You must be good swimmers?"

"Like otters."

"Like seals."

They were offering her small, sly, conspiratorial grins. They know they're funny, she thought—just as they know they're cute. Erica was amused in spite of herself.

"We're going to get our lifeguarding certificates," Morgan said.

With a shrug—"It's an easy way to make money?"

"We've already done some of the courses, but . . ."

"you've got to be like sixteen."

Now that Erica had achieved what she wanted—a laid-back unstructured conversation. The girls' parents were divorced. They were supposed to switch back and forth every two weeks but they mostly stayed with their mum because their dad was doing a house reno. Palmerston was okay, better than public school. They'd had issues in public school. No, they didn't ski or snowboard. They'd like to try snowboarding because it was like surfing, but they didn't have time. During the school year, they took a gazillion dance classes; some nights they didn't get home till after ten. In the spring they did dance competitions. In the summer they went to camp or hung out on the beach. At camp? Oh, swimming, canoeing, kayaking, hiking—like that. No, not surfing. If you wanted to do surf camp, you had to go to California. Their dad took them surfing every August.

At camp this summer, Jamie and Dev had gone with them; it was so much fun. They'd had a big dance on the last weekend; they'd never had so much fun. They loved coed camp, all-girls not so much. Did they like boys?— What? You think?— Sometimes they hung out with boys, grade eights, guys they'd known their whole lives, but they didn't really go out with any of them; they were just friends. Some grade nines kept asking them out but they didn't really like them. It was awkward. There were crazy cute twin boys in grade eleven, but they never talked to them. They saw something on the net about twins marrying twins. Did Erica ever know twins who married twins? Yes, she said, she did. They were very happy.

ERICA WAS GETTING a strong sense of these girls and would have preferred to simply keep on chatting, but the inventory was the excuse that had brought them into her lab, so it was time to run them through it. "Okay, so here comes the official part," she said. "I'm turning on the camera now. I'm going to start off by interviewing each of you separately. I would like one of you to stay and one of you to leave. Okay? Now one of you should go out into the waiting room and we'll call you when it's your turn."

The girls did not look at each other. They did not look at Erica. They did not hesitate. Avalon stood and walked out of the room, closing the door quietly behind her. The entire transaction must have taken less than fifteen seconds.

Neither girl liked being interviewed alone—she could see their tension—but even separated, neither girl lost her cool. They answered the questions quickly and clearly, often using the same words and phrases. They knew each other inside out, upside down and backwards—not surprising because they both liked exactly the same things, disliked exactly the same things, and did everything together. Even alone, each girl said "we" and never "I." They both identified Jamie and Devon as their best friends and Erica was relieved to hear it—she'd been afraid that they might not like the Oxley-Clark twins as much as they liked them. They didn't talk about "deep time" or "world stacks." Their mythology put a different spin on things. They both said that they and Jamie and Devon had been sisters in a past life.

Erica was afraid that her own experience—her observer bias—was preventing her from seeing them clearly. She'd lost her dislike for them. She didn't want to go there but she couldn't help it—they reminded her of herself and Annalise. Like Erica, Morgan was the stronger, more boyish twin—like Lise, Avalon the delicate, more feminine one. It didn't help that Avalon and Annalise both had names starting with "A"—one of those nasty coincidences that life throws at you all the time. But the Lynas twins were more similar, in most respects, than Erica and Lise had been. In fact it was hard to see any large differences between them—although there had to be some; no MZ twins were ever truly identical. The small differences had become clear enough; if Erica met them separately now, she would know which was which. She could understand why Jamie had a crush on Morgan—the one with more force, the one who always spoke first. Morgan's face was sharper, had more character. Avalon's face was rounder, closer to what most people would see as cute. Their relationship was deceptive. Morgan looked like the dominant twin but Erica was sure that Avalon had enormous power in the twinship—that Avalon was the foundation of it just as Annalise had been in theirs.

ERICA BROUGHT THE GIRLS back together and completed the inventory. She'd pretty much stayed on script the whole way through so there would be nothing for her grad students to worry about. She turned off the camera and told the girls that she'd walk them over to the University Hospital for their blood tests. "Are you going home in a cab?"

"Oh, no. On the bus."

"It's okay. We know how to get back."

For her own personal purposes Erica wanted to follow up on their mythology. "Do you really think you have past lives?"

Morgan answered first. "Oh, yes."

"Were you always twins?"

"No, but we're always like *related*."

"It keeps switching around. Sometimes we're married"

"or we're girlfriends . . . or boyfriends."

"Sometimes we're kids and parents. Like that."

"And you're going to have future lives too?" Erica asked them.

"Oh, yeah. Lots."

"We're going to stick around as long as any sentient being needs us."

"So we're going to have countless future lives."

The three of them had stood up and were walking toward the door. Morgan stopped, turning to Erica. "Dev and Jamie think *you're* a twin."

"Are you a twin?" Avalon asked her.

Shit. Erica felt like a spike had just been driven through her. She snapped into her disassociation trick. *I'm not really here, I'm somewhere else.*

"Yeah, it's true. I'm a twin . . . identical just like you guys . . . I *was*. My sister died last year."

A small round inarticulate cry came out of Avalon.

"We're sooo sorry," Morgan said. "That really sucks."

"How did she die?"

"She was killed in a car accident."

Erica might have been able to stay disassociated except that the twins' eyes were filling with tears. The moment she saw their empathetic response, her chest went into spasm. She caught it, bit down on it, choked it, but not before an unmistakable and mortifying sound had been torn out of her—a single sob.

Erica was stuck frozen in the middle of her interview room. If she moved a muscle, the worst thing that could possibly happen would be happening—she would be crying. *No, I'm not here. Really I'm not.*

Moving like a single unit, the twins stepped up to her and hugged her, one on each side. Erica drew them tight to her and cried.

When she could trust herself to speak again, she said, "I'm so sorry. I didn't know I was going to do that."

The twins had run their eye makeup. Morgan shook her head "no." No, what?

"We hope . . ." Avalon said and rolled her eyes upward. Her voice was still full of tears. "We hope . . ."

Morgan had to finish the thought. "We hope when we die, we'll die together."

ERICA WAS DRIVING—not bothering to play games with highway entrances but sending her Golf burning straight down the road toward Alberta and home. She was doing 120 on a stretch posted at 90 and she didn't give a shit. There was no possible way she could make it home in less than fourteen hours but she knew perfectly well that she wasn't driving to Medicine Hat; she was just aimed that way because it felt right. So much of our lives, she thought, are conducted exactly the way our ancestors conducted them—making irrational ritual gestures, dealing in sympathetic magic. Our mental apparatus is pretty much the same as it's always been for the last 200,000 years and we might as well be painting horses on the walls of the caves at Lascaux for all the good it does us. It was sappy useless fuzzy-minded anthropomorphizing to personify the dead and address them—when she caught herself doing it, she always stopped—but she was murmuring, "Annalise, Annalise, Annalise." Of course the Lynas girls had rubbed her the wrong way when they'd first walked into her office. They were highly bonded MZ twins.

Maybe the last thing in the world she should be doing right now was working with twins. Except that she couldn't imagine being interested in anything other than twins. She loved the Lynas girls. They were great girls. They had what human beings were supposed to have—empathy. Only MZ twins could understand Erica's heart.

59

Driving like this was crazy. Eventually she would have to stop and turn around. She got off the highway in Abbotsford and pulled into the first restaurant she saw. It was a just-off-the-highway joint with no surprises—the kind that served chips with everything—and that's exactly what she wanted. She should eat protein but her body craved sugar. She compromised, ordered tuna on brown; the soft bread would convert to sugar the moment it hit her saliva. She was ravenously hungry but she couldn't finish the sandwich. That happened to her all the time now; it was like coming up against something in her stomach that went *THUD, stop, I can't take any more.* She couldn't go on like this. All of her clothes were baggy.

By the time Erica stepped outside into the flat ugly parking lot, the light was getting squeezed out of the sky. She hated being on the highway in the dark but there was no way out of it. She drove back toward terrible Vancouver just as fast as she'd driven away from it. What was pushing her down the road was fury. She'd been angry at Annalise's death before but this was the first time she'd felt the full blowtorch intensity of it.

She was back on the Drive too soon. Her cheap apartment came with no parking. The workday was long over and everybody was home, so she had to drive around for ten minutes looking for a spot. Still riding her fury, she ran up the three flights of stairs, unlocked her door, switched on the overhead light. She always hated that moment when she first walked in. To get that moment over with, she pushed right through it, walked straight into her office just like she had something to do there.

She hadn't been able to face the contents of Annalise's memory box. The thought made her sick. Now she unfolded the interlinked cardboard flaps her mother had created so carefully, picked the box up and inverted it, dumping everything onto the floor. A lot of it was paper—but objects too. Annalise's first pointe shoes. The pain sent Erica to the floor right along with everything else.

The tortured prisoner who'd been floating in and out of Erica's mind since Lise had died—that metaphor for herself—appeared again, this time strapped down to a table on the cold morning when they'd decided to begin the systematic process that would destroy forever her ability to function as a human being—the day when they began using the salt and chili paste, the razor blades and butane lighters. My god, Erica thought, some of the things that go through my mind now are absolutely sick—and that sick fantasy had no function other than to distance her from the real pain, wordless and impossible.

She could attend to anything. The background murmur of the CBC. The way the streetlight made a pattern on the wall behind her computer. The buzz, or swish—neither word was right—of the traffic outside. The sounds from the apartment below hers, the TV, the voices—distant muffled unintelligible. She could even smell their cooking—or somebody's cooking. The smell of grease, burgers or fish. She told herself to stand up and she stood up.

She picked up Lise's pointe shoes and held them, stroking them. They'd once been a hopeful pink but now they were old and battered and grey. Oh, baby, she thought, what am I going to do on our birthday?

ERICA OFTEN USED the desperate hours between four and seven a.m. to grade papers or catch up on her university emails or write her research summaries but some nights she couldn't do that. Sometimes she hated her so-called discipline—too many studies with small sample sizes and slight-of-the-hand stats that got quoted in textbooks like they were gospel, too many studies, years and years of them, that hadn't controlled for genetics and so were junk. It simply wasn't science. What Stacey did was science. Stacey did everything double-blind, even something as unproblematic as measuring sample size. When Erica couldn't do anything useful in the night, she went on the net and played Tetris.

Nothing required Erica to go to the university on Fridays but she usually went in anyway because being at school was better than not being at school. That Friday she woke late. The last time she'd looked at her clock it had been 7:14 but then she'd managed to sleep soundly until 10:08. It had been a thick heavy dreamless sleep that left her feeling groggy and low. She made coffee and checked her emails. The lab sent their reports in batches and she'd received an electronic copy of the latest batch. The hard copy—the official record—would arrive in her office in a day or two. She wasn't surprised to see that the Lynas twins matched on all eight blood types but she was more than surprised—shocked actually—to see that the Oxley-Clark twins also matched on all eight. Oh, my god, she thought, they're MZ! How could that possibly be?

Well, no, Jamie and Devon weren't MZ. No way. DZ twins could match on that first round of tests—it was unusual but not unheard of. By coincidence they must have both inherited the same blood types—that was the simplest explanation. But what if they *were* MZ? They couldn't be Turner Syndrome—they looked too normal for that—but there were other ways it could happen too, some of them quite exotic. If they were MZ, they'd be the rarest of the rare. Well, they'd said in their emails that they were rare.

Suppose they were? How the hell did they *know?* Everyone would have been telling them their whole lives it was impossible, that they were fraternal. All they had to go on was what they looked like. But what about Jamie's dark eyebrows and Devon's pale ones? No way. They had to be DZ.

Too impatient for email, she called the lab. "Hi, this is Dr. Bauer from ITS . . ." Ordinarily she would have said "Erica"—the university ran on a first-name basis—but she was pulling rank. "Can I jump the queue on this one . . . like ASAP, like can I get it *yesterday?*" She asked them to check the logbook to make sure the samples hadn't been mixed up. She ordered the second round of tests—a karyotype and ten more blood types. She had to know what she was dealing with.

5.

"IF WE'VE GOT A double-X boy, we've got gold." Stacey was so excited she was actually trembling.

The results had come back from the second round of tests on the Oxley-Clark twins; the minute she'd got them, Erica had walked straight over to Stacey's lab. The twins had matched on ten more blood types. That meant that they were MZ just as they claimed to be—that they were right and the whole rest of the world was wrong. Then, to make matters even more bizarre, the karyotypes had revealed that they both had XX chromosomes.

"Oh, god, Stace, this is all too much. I'm just trying to imagine breaking the news to their awful mother—'I'm sorry to have to tell you this, Mrs. Oxley, but your twins are identical and they're both biological girls.'"

"Why did you think Devon was a boy?"

It wasn't just the question—it was Stacey's deadpan expression, the flatness of her tone. Erica didn't find much of anything funny these days but this was funny. She couldn't stop laughing. "I didn't take his pants off. I have absolutely no evidence that he's a biological boy."

"So he could be a biological girl?"

"Yeah, he could. For a while I even thought he *was* a girl . . . but he self-identifies as a boy. On the questionnaire, his mother identifies him as a boy, and she identifies the twins as fraternal, so *his own mother* thinks he's a boy. Of course his biological sex doesn't have to match his gender, but if he's transgender, everybody would have to be on board with it—his mum, his school, a doctor or two, and it just doesn't seem . . . We talked for hours and those crazy kids were really into overshare. If he's FTM transgender, I'm sure they would have told me, but . . . Okay, they do have something weird going on with sex and gender, but I can't make sense of it."

"Let's make it make sense," Stacey said. "What do we have to go on?"

"Could DZ twins match on all eighteen blood types?" Erica already knew the answer but she wanted to hear it from a molecular biologist.

"It's theoretically possible," Stacey said, "but the chances of it happening? Close to zero. They've absolutely got to be MZ."

This was the first time Erica had ever been in Stacey's lab—which was odd, given that they'd known each other for two years. Erica had always imagined it as an immaculate steel-and-plastic setting for a science fiction movie but it wasn't like that at all. It had a gritty, ad hoc, well-used feel to it—rows of battered benches with various complex constructions of glass tubing on them, a wall of what appeared to be industrial refrigerators, a squat square machine humming to itself, probably a centrifuge. A dozen people were working in there; they had the standard sleepless, overworked, jeans-and-runners look of grad students and not a single one of them was wearing a lab coat. This was the centre of Stacey's life—and Erica had never set foot in here before. How good a friend was that?

"So," Stacey was saying, "let's start with what we do know. Sex determination in mammals defaults to female, right? And it's the SRY gene on the Y chromosome that determines maleness, right? So what if Devon has a translocation of SRY? He would be one hundred percent phenotypically male."

"You mean absolutely normal?"

"Right. An absolutely normal boy."

Erica had never heard of this. "Really?"

"Yeah, really. I know it sounds weird but SRY1 is a regulator. All the sexual effectors are downstream of SRY1. Unless he had a karyotype for some medical reason, he could go his whole life and never know he was double-X. Cool, huh?"

Stacey was right in her element—fully engaged, her eyes sparkling. "But there's a problem. Devon *can't* be that type of double-X male because if Devon and Jamie are MZ, *both* would be double-X males. And there could also be another mechanism at work. The change that results in the translocation of SRY onto another chromosome doesn't have to be inherited. It could be de novo in either gamete as a result of a new mutation during gametogenesis. But even then they'd still both be double-X males. Are you following me?"

"Yeah, so far."

"Well, it gets even better. SOX3 has recently been identified as a double-X male sex reversal gene. Devon could have an SOX3 activating mutation that occurred after twinning. Over-expression of SOX3 could be driving a double-X male sex reversal. And you know what we've got then?"

"What?"

"Early promotion, tenure, a big splashy paper that everybody's going to cite and a whole shitload of grant money."

Erica was laughing again. "Stacey, you're too fucking much."

"No, I'm serious. Whatever type of double-X boy he turns out to be, it's bound to be good for us."

It was a cool concept but it didn't feel right to Erica. It didn't match the evidence. "I don't know," she said. "I don't think so. It still doesn't account for— Okay, what if he's not a double-x boy? What if he's an intersex biological girl who was raised as a boy? Wouldn't that be right up your alley?"

"Yeah, it would. But why do you think that?"

"Read their emails." Erica had printed them out.

LEFT TO HERSELF, Erica would never have thought of Jericho Beach and might never have noticed how sweet the day was. She and Stacey had stopped at the water's edge just short of getting their feet wet. "Okay," Stacey said, "they've always been told they're fraternal but they think they're a rare kind of identical. Where did they get that crazy idea? What evidence do they have? Just because they look so much alike? They want to know if they can be 'fixed' with an operation. What operation? You're right. Devon's probably a biological girl with sexually ambiguous genitalia."

"Yeah, that makes sense," Erica said. "It's the only thing I can think of."

If Stacey had noticed the suicide threat in the emails—and she'd have to be an idiot not to notice—she must have decided not to comment on it. Maybe she didn't take it seriously. Erica had read the emails a dozen times by now—and she'd met the twins and interviewed them—and she could see how someone, even their mum or dad, might not take it seriously. They were bright, imaginative, privileged kids who created their own drama and starred in it. Threatening suicide had been a great way to blackmail their parents—and it had worked—but that didn't mean that they might actually do it. Except that Erica believed that they might actually do it. She wished she could talk to Stacey about it but she knew that she couldn't.

The beach wasn't crowded—it was a work day late in the afternoon—so it was mainly moms with young kids and a random assortment of other odd people who didn't have regular jobs. The slanting light was sweet as honey; the sun was actually warm. What a glorious October—and Erica felt a tug at her memory, something at the back of her mind she couldn't pin down. It was so bittersweet it had to be attached to Annalise. "I'm glad you thought of this," she said to Stacey. "This is fun."

"Yeah, it is, isn't it? If I don't get out of my lab sometimes, I start feeling like a cell sample."

Off to their right a dog was frisking in the surf, shaking the water out of its coat—a big silly dog, a setter. He belonged to a young mum who was calling out to him—"Hey, Max. Come on, boy." Erica liked the young mum, liked her happy dog, liked her wobbly toddler so new to walking he hadn't quite got it down yet. They gave the day a bread-and-butter ordinariness, a sense of ongoingness, like that most clichéd of old clichés: "life goes on." But did it?

"It's ridiculous," Erica said. "We're trying to *guess* when all we need to do is get them into the University Hospital and then we'll *know*. But their mother . . . What if she says no way? I don't even know if she filled out the questionnaire. They could have done it themselves. They're perfectly capable of that. And we need to get their blood retested. It wouldn't be the first time the lab's screwed up."

The light above the sea was drawing Erica's mind out, smoothing it—almost a physical sensation. It wasn't Alberta's big sky but it had its own kind of expansiveness. This must be what BC people meant when they called it Lotusland. The light was as big as a promise.

"They're thinking about having an operation to make them totally identical," Stacey said, "so who was going to have the operation? Devon? And then he'd be a girl and then they'd be identical? But then in the next breath they say, 'Why should we have to do that? If people let us alone, we'd be happy.' So it seems to be okay with them whether Devon's a boy or a girl? Really? That doesn't make a lot of sense. Doesn't it matter to most people whether they're a boy or a girl? Isn't it fundamental?"

"Gender identity?" Erica said. "Fundamental? Yeah, absolutely. But you'll also notice that they said 'we.' How do we know it was Devon who was going to get the operation? It could be Jamie. Or it could be both of them. Although I can't imagine what those operations would be. You're right—if they're both XXs, what are they trying to fix? It's got to be Devon. We just don't have enough information yet. Why are we even speculating?"

"It's fun, isn't it? It's like a crime novel. What if we can add up a few clues and guess it right? So they were sending ambiguous gender signals when you first interviewed them?"

"Sure they were. And I think they were doing it deliberately, as a kind of . . . I don't know. A game? A joke? Part of some crazy drama they were staging for my benefit? I don't know, Stace. They're weird kids."

They sat down on a log. Erica had allowed Stacey to pick the sandwiches—grilled peppers and eggplant with feta cheese, a perfect mixture of flavours that Erica had forgotten she liked. The crunch of the fresh bread was wonderful. She'd even forgotten how much she enjoyed eating. That other old cliché, "the simple pleasures of life"—how long had it been since she'd allowed herself to experience any of them?

"You know, if Devon's an intersex biological girl with a normal MZ sister," Stacey said, "that would be an ideal situation to test the effect of sex hormones on all sorts of things. The problem is, it's getting so hard to get anything funded."

Stacey reached into her bag and took out two tiny wine bottles—the finest of airline Chardonnay, she said, saved from the flight back from her conference in Hawaii. She handed one to Erica.

They unscrewed the caps and drank. The taste made Erica's nose crinkle. "A surprisingly charming acidity," Stacey said in the tone of a wine critic and made Erica smile.

"It could be a lot of work to track this one down," Stacey said. "I'd have to pull my postdoc from his project and invest the resources to get it done . . . and that would mean we wouldn't be making progress on my CIHR project. That renewal's due next year and if we don't get it published, we'll be screwed to the wall. On the other hand, if this is really big, we can't just ignore it. A double-X male with an MZ twin sister? Of course we'd have to go after that. A pair of MZ twins, one normal and one sexually ambiguous? We'd have to go after that too."

"Yeah, we would," Erica said but her mind had already left the scene. She'd just found the bittersweet solution to "glorious October." It was from one of Lise's favourite poems—Erica could hear her sister reading it out loud. They must have still been in high school—and then the image came into sharp focus, Lise on their fifteenth birthday, the poem by Dylan Thomas, about *his* birthday—"Oh, may my heart's truth still be sung . . ." It was like a prayer for the next birthday, and the next birthday after that, and all of the birthdays forever, but Annalise was gone and Erica's heart's truth would never again be sung—

67

Oh, fuck. Wait a minute—her mind was looping back around on something. She'd always thought of Annalise as the softer one, the more fragile one, but was she? What if Erica had died and Annalise had been left? Why did that thought hurt so much she couldn't stand it? Annalise was married, she'd have Mark, and that was a consolation but *nobody* can replace an MZ twin—it wasn't like someone you love had died, it was like you've been chopped in half. How could you live with half of you gone? If one of them had died when they were in high school, the other wouldn't have lasted a month—and that was the simple truth.

The sun was dropping below the horizon and bluing out the sky. The colour and size of the world—the waves rolling in, the dog barking, the sounds of children's voices, the light going fuchsia and then blue—it was all painful, but it was the pain of being alive. How much of Erica's pain now had a self-dramatizing gothic quality? This particular moment didn't have that quality. Staring into the absence where Annalise would have been, Erica was trying to find a pain she could live with. What if Annalise was actually a separate person? It wasn't like they'd been together right up till the end. They'd been separated for seven years. Until Annalise died, their separation had been the most painful thing Erica had ever experienced. But she'd survived it, hadn't she?

Erica wished she could leave the chopped-in-half twin at home, that she could stop flattening her feelings, making them random and pointless, closing off windows and doors. What about the simple pleasures of walking on the beach on a beautiful day, a gourmet sandwich, a tiny bottle of abysmal Chardonnay, a fascinating problem shared with a friend? Was that enough to create the illusion of meaning so strongly that you might want to stick with it? "She was so full of life"—and there it was, another fucking cliché, something they *always* said about dead people—but Lise *had* been full of life. She would have loved being there on the beach with them; she would have loved Stacey. She would have said, "Get out of the space you're in now, Ricki. It's sick."

ON THE DAY when they were supposed to, the Oxley-Clark twins showed up right on time. They were dressed identically down to the finest detail and they were dressed as boys—baggy jeans, black Converses, plaid shirts

68

and black hoodies. Their identical hairstyles were equally a mess. They walked in with exactly the same hangdog apologetic *boyish* slouchiness they'd been radiating when Erica had first met them—but there was no sign of their mother. Furious, running on automatic, Erica said, "This is my colleague, Dr. Chou. She's going to join us today."

"Please call me Stacey."

"Your mother is . . . *where?*"

"She couldn't make it," Jamie said, looking at her shoes. "Like right at the . . . you know, at the last minute . . ."

"Like double-booked," Devon said. He gave Erica a brave try at a smile; his eyes told her how sorry he was about lying.

Erica was on the edge of losing it. "You're kidding me." She was trying to calm herself—*Okay, okay, okay.* She looked to Stacey for guidance—help!—but Stacey seemed just as stunned as she was.

"You guys, ah : . . make yourselves at home," Erica said. *Fucking little brats.* "Relax for a minute. I've got to confer with Dr. Chou."

Erica grabbed Stacey's arm and hustled her out of there. Stacey unlocked the door to her own office and they stepped into it. Stacey shut the door behind them. "What's going on?" she said.

"You think I know? This is the same shit I've been dealing with since—"

"Why didn't you *tell me*? They're *absolutely alike.*"

"No, they're not. You only saw them for two minutes. They're as different as a penguin and a panther. I know. I've run them through the inventory—"

"How do we know they're not *both* double-X boys?"

"Oh, for fuck's sake. We don't know. Where is their goddamned mother?" Erica was yelling. She had to stop it.

Stacey patted Erica's shoulders. "Breathe," she said.

They stood a moment by the window. *Focus,* Erica told herself. She stared out at the flat light. Miserable Vancouver. It was always raining. "Can we take them straight to the hospital?" Stacey asked her.

"Are you out of your mind? Not without their mother's consent."

"The bloodwork?"

"Yeah, we can do that. I have the signed consent for that. But . . .

What do we do with them now? What are we going to tell them? We shouldn't even be *talking to them* without their mother."

"Oh, but we're going to, aren't we?" Stacey said with a thin hard smile.

Back in the interview room the kids had drawn themselves up onto the very front edge of the couch—two tightly loaded springs. "Okay," Erica said, "we got your blood results back but we need to test you again. In a minute, we can walk over to the hospital—"

"Again?" Jamie said. "Why?"

"Dr. Chou wants to have a really good look at your blood. We were hoping that your mother could be here today—"

Jamie's voice was a high-pitched yelp. "What did you find?"

"All the results are preliminary," Erica said. "We don't want to give you a false impression so we'd rather not say anything until we *talk to your mother*."

Jamie's eyes were fiery and hurt. "That's not fair!" Devon was frozen.

Stacey was using a sweetly reassuring voice—talking down to these frustrating kids like they were six-year-olds. "We do have results, but we're not sure of them. We might have to do a lot more tests . . . or maybe not. We really do need to talk to your mum. About all we can do today is take new blood samples. Okay?"

Devon pushed at his sister's arm. She batted his hand away.

"I told you," he said.

"Shut up!"

Jamie flung herself back onto the couch, drew her knees up to her chin and wrapped her arms around them.

"Tell them," Devon said.

"Shut the fuck up."

Jamie was staring hard at the floor. "I like . . ." she said.

Everybody was looking at her, waiting for her, and she knew it. "I like gave both blood samples," she said.

"You did *what?*" Stacey said.

"I gave both blood samples."

Stacey had been standing. She sank into a chair. "You're kidding." She pressed one hand over the bridge of her nose, covering her eyes. Her whole body was shaking. Oh my god, was she crying?

70

No, she wasn't crying, she was laughing and it was exactly the right thing. The tension went out of the room—punctured balloon, whoosh!—and set off a chain reaction. Everybody was laughing. The twins were hysterical.

"Oh, my god," Stacey said, "how did you do that?"

"We were like amazed it worked!" Devon said.

"The nurse was talking to the other lady—"

"The receptionist?" Erica said. She remembered.

"Yeah," Jamie said, "and I just went and gave the first blood sample, and they like kept on talking, and then it's Devon's turn and he's like, 'I hate needles! I think I'm going to faint.' The nurse's like, 'It doesn't hurt, it's over in a minute, see how brave your sister was,' and I'm like, 'Oh, Dev, come on. It's nothing.'"

"And I'm like"—Devon imitated himself wailing—"Ooo, I can't stand needles! Ooo, I'm getting sick to my stomach! Ooo, I'm gonna throw up!"

"So I'm like, 'Let me talk to him a minute, okay?' So we go off in the ladies' room and change our clothes. We don't have to change that much 'cause Dev's already got my socks on under his pants, so we just switch his pants for my kilt and we switch our shoes, and I push my hair back like this, and we go back and I'm like, 'Okay, I'm ready. Can you do it really fast?'"

Jamie had actually altered her voice, turning it into a good imitation of her brother's. She'd even managed to reproduce his teeth-gritted tone of I'm-going-to-be-a-man-about-this. "Hey," Stacey said, smiling, "you're a great actress."

"And the nurse's like, 'Sit down, you won't even know it, it'll be so fast,' and I'm like, 'Hey, can you do my left arm? I'm a tennis player,' and she's like, 'No problem.'"

"You kids are amazing," Stacey said. "You really had us going there. We really thought you were identical twin girls. That's a pretty good joke." She glanced over at Erica. They were in Erica's territory and the kids were Erica's subjects. Erica nodded—go ahead, you're doing fine.

"So if you went to all that trouble," Stacey said, "you must know you're not really identical, right?"

"But we *are* identical," Jamie said.

"We know we're identical," Devon said.

Here we go again, Erica thought. "Okay," she said, "so we're going to have to take some new blood and find out—"

"But if it turns out you're fraternal," Stacey said, "what's wrong with that?"

Jamie had been laughing along with everyone else but now Erica saw her close up, her face going hard and wary.

"We're like *deep* identical," Devon said. "We were once a single entity . . . in deep time."

"Oh, yeah?" Stacey said. "That's *really* deep time."

"It's like—" Jamie said and stopped. She was staring at a random spot on the wall. Erica had studied the video of their interview. That was exactly what Jamie had done before she'd told the highly charged story of the bridge-swinging incident. It must be her way of detaching herself, of defending herself.

Stacey wasn't patient enough. "You feel that you're—"

"Stace," Erica said to stop her. Stacey gave her a sharp look—puzzled, annoyed.

For the longest time Jamie didn't say anything at all. Then she said, "It won't show on a blood test. That's why we did it. You've got to— It's like a freakin' trick, so you've got to— It's complicated but we *know* we're identical, like—" In an explosive gesture—one hand slashing the air—she gave up.

Devon had been watching his sister; now he entered right on cue. "You ever see *The Matrix*?" He was using the cheerful reasonable voice of a teacher who is about to make everything clear to a class full of idiots. "What if we're like in the Matrix? What if this is all like virtual?"

Stacey couldn't believe it. "You think us sitting here in this room right now is *virtual*?"

"Well, it could be," Devon said, grinning—and off he went into *Two from One Fire*, and parallel worlds, and simulated experiences like in *The Ghost in the Shell* or *Blade Runner*. He loved talking about this stuff. There didn't seem to be any science fiction story he didn't know. "Like a trick?" he said. "Like they planted memories in us? Or they can take memories away? And you can't see it from the outside unless you've had like a major consciousness morph. But what if me and Jamie were already fused? What if we've always been a single entity?"

Erica and Stacey exchanged a look.

"You know what?" Stacey said. "You don't need science fiction. Science is fantastic enough. You open up one little piece of the puzzle, there's always more to the puzzle. It's fascinating. But believe me, where we are right now . . . It might be mysterious . . . or scary, or a pain in the ass, or . . . whatever . . . but it's sure not *virtual*."

"But if it *was* virtual," Devon said, "you'd have to say that, wouldn't you?" He was thoroughly enjoying himself. He wasn't arguing with them; he was giving them a performance—a demonstration of how clever he was.

"Okay," Stacey said, "this is lots of fun but let's come back down to earth. Some things are true and some things are not, and you can't change what's true just because you don't like it."

To Erica's surprise, Jamie *could* make eye contact—she was looking directly at Stacey. "*You* don't like it," she said. "We're identical, *that's* what's true."

"Hey, wait a minute," Stacey said. "We're on your side, okay? All we want is what's best for you. Why don't we start with the facts, okay? We'll get another blood test and—"

"Fuck your blood test," Jamie said.

Devon was shocked. He actually changed colour.

Stacey gave Erica an oh-my-god look. Clearly it was Erica's turn. "We *are* on your side"—that was an easy thing to say and so was that other easy thing—"We *do* need to talk to your mother."

"Hey, listen, you guys," Stacey said. "You're *fraternal* twins. What's wrong with that?"

Stacey never got any closer to her human subjects than the identifying numbers on their cell samples, so she had no experience with this sort of thing. According to the university guidelines, she absolutely should not be counseling these kids, but she was too angry to pay attention to Erica's warning looks. "Why do you want to be so much alike? You're dressed the same way. You've even got the same haircuts. How much more alike do you want to be?"

73

Devon sighed. "We want people to *know* we're alike— We're MZ twins discordant for sex."

"Okay," Stacey said, "that's a claim that can be *tested*."

"Not with your test," Jamie said. "It's in a parallel world."

It took Stacey a moment to absorb that one. "My god, do you honestly believe that?"

They didn't answer.

"Okay, let's start over," Stacey said. "Let's look at the evidence. What evidence do you have that you're identical?"

"We don't know what you mean." Devon seemed to be talking for both of them now. "You mean like what made us think we were—?"

"Yes. That's exactly what I mean."

He considered it. "We like took one look at each other, and then . . . We just *looked* freakin' identical, you know? Then we started talking and it was . . . We were separated *for four years*. We didn't know anything at all about each other. But like every single thing we thought was *exactly the same*. Everything. Just, you know, like whoa! Like we're different on the outside. Like Jamie's a girl and I'm a boy, like she's into sports and I'm into computers and anime and stuff, but *inside* we're identical. Everything that happened to us . . . the way we feel about everything . . . The more we talked about it, the more it was like, *you too, huh?* We just couldn't freakin' believe it."

Now he was crying and Erica felt it like an inner blow—her own raw adrenaline responding—and then she was in the burn. Devon pressed his hand over his eyes and turned his face away. Jamie grabbed his arm protectively, sent Stacey a murderous look—*Now see what you've done!*

For the first time since she'd met them, Erica saw the twins as disturbed kids. The sunny optimistic twin—the bright happy show-off—had just been reduced to tears. His sister was furious and not bothering to hide it. Erica clicked into default and said what she was supposed to say: "We've got a great counseling service here at the university. If your mother agreed to it, I could arrange an appointment for you."

Devon's tears or not, Stacey was not about to let go. "You talked about an operation . . . in your emails. Which one of you was going to get the operation?"

"That was before—" Jamie was so angry her words were coming out choked, barely intelligible. "We didn't— Shit. Nobody tells you about any of this shit. Mum won't talk about it. You've gotta go over the whole fucking Google and you still can't— We thought it was the operation, *but it's not the operation, it's the hormones*— We just don't want to change any more. We've changed enough— When we were like reunited, we were the same size. Exactly. We could wear each other's clothes. But now I'm getting bigger than Dev."

Stacey actually laughed. "Oh my god, there's nothing wrong with that. You're growing up."

"You think we're retards? You think we don't know what freakin' puberty is? We just don't want it to happen to us. We want to stay the same. We want to take puberty blockers."

It took Stacey a moment to absorb that one. Then she said, "Puberty blockers! How did you even *hear* about puberty blockers?"

Devon was still leaking tears but he'd found his hopeful voice again. "We could always change our minds later. Do you think our mom would—?"

"Oh, my god," Stacey yelled at them, "that's utterly ridiculous! Nobody's going to put you on puberty blockers."

"Stace?" Erica said, trying to shut her up.

Now Jamie was crying too, fighting it, hating herself for it, her face tilted down toward the floor. "We're *identical* . . . and you're not . . ." She had to take long ragged breaths between words. "And you're not . . . going to . . . separate us . . . If you try to separate us . . . we'll kill ourselves . . . You think we're kidding? We're not fucking kidding."

DR. WILLIAM INGRAM, the Chair of ITS, was a clinical psychologist— although Erica tended to forget that because he was such a picture-perfect university administrator. Back in the '80s he'd written a big book on the psychology of twins and she'd read it because she was supposed to read *everything*. He'd used the case-study method—drawing, of course, upon his own clinical practice. His sample size had been less than thirty, and he hadn't bothered to distinguish between MZ and DZ twins because back in the day everybody *knew* that family environment had more impact on personality than anything genetic. For a while his book had been frequently cited, but no one was citing it now. How must it feel to live long enough to see everything in your groundbreaking work—the foundation of your academic career—utterly destroyed by the Minnesota Twin Studies?

Erica and Stacey were sitting in Dr. William Ingram's office, doing their best to explain themselves. So far Erica hadn't said anything inappropriate—or she was pretty sure that she hadn't. "They seem to think that if they're identical, they can't be separated," she said. "They're terribly afraid of being separated."

"And if they're separated, they'll commit suicide?" Bill was taking notes.

"Yes. The girl was the one who said it. Jamie Oxley-Clark . . . Do we have to report it to the Ministry? If I talk to their mother—"

"I'm sorry, Erica. We don't have any choice. The policy is absolutely clear."

Shit. "Give me a chance to warn her then," she said. "We don't want her to be blindsided. Can you imagine how she would feel if . . . you know, out of nowhere—"

"A pissed off mum is the last thing we want," Stacey said.

Thanks, Stace, she thought.

"I can hold off for a day or two," he said. "That's the best I can do. To the end of the week?"

"Thank you," Erica said.

She should be feeling something. This was the outcome she'd been dreading, so she should be feeling disappointed. But, on the other hand, she was no longer alone with the burden of the twins' suicide threat, so she should be feeling relieved— But what on earth was she thinking? She wouldn't call herself "disassociated," but she was getting there—drawn back and watching. The only thing she seemed to be feeling was a sick fear—that she might fuck up even worse than she had already.

"If one of you could write it up . . . ?" he was saying.

"I will," Stacey said. "I'll do it right now."

Stacey stood up to go so Erica stood up too. Was it over?

"Erica?" he said. "Could you stick around for a minute?" No, it wasn't over. She sat down again. She saw Stacey's startled eyes sending her a message. Alarm? Sympathy?

Bill walked Stacey to the door. Erica looked at the light fading at the window. There was a peculiar quality to the light in Vancouver at this time of day—not entirely dark yet. She hated it and it drew her. It made her want to drive.

Bill had pictures of his family all over his office—on his walls, on his desk. He had a son and a daughter, both older than Erica. He had four grandchildren. He liked to talk about them.

Erica heard the door shut. She heard him sitting down in his office chair. She turned to look at him. He'd kept much of his hair but it had turned white. "Your postdoc and several of your grad students came to see me," he said.

Of course they did, she thought.

"They're quite concerned about you. They have the greatest respect for you and your work . . ."

She didn't need to attend to what he was saying. Much of it was designed to soften the blow that was obviously coming. She was doing exciting work, he was saying, unique in the field, and her students felt privileged—blah, blah, blah. A great mentor—blah, blah, blah. But the two sets of interviews she'd conducted herself . . .

"It was an error of judgment," she said. "I've already decided there's no way I can use the data."

"That's right," he said. "There's no way you can use the data . . . Erica? I watched the videos."

"Oh?"

Just as she'd thought at the time, there was no problem with her interviews with the Lynas twins—"the little red-headed girls," he called them. She'd stayed on script. The Oxley-Clark twins were another matter. When she'd gone off-script with the boy, it had been fairly innocuous—although, of course, it had invalidated the data—but her error with the girl had been serious. "You encouraged her to reveal personal information," he said.

"Yes," she said, "I did."

She was required to say something more. "She seemed to be in some distress," she said. "I was concerned about her safety."

No, that was the wrong word. She should not have said "safety."

Now he might guess that she'd known about the suicide threat right from the beginning.

"I'm sorry," she said, hurrying things along. "It was a serious error on my part. I will never do anything like that again."

He was assessing her. She could see it on his face. "You know the policy . . . ?" He was waiting for her.

"I strongly suggested that she see a counselor. I will say the same thing to her mother." That elusive blonde bitch was going to see just how persistent Erica could be. If she didn't respond to phone calls or emails, then Erica was going to park in her fucking driveway until she showed up.

"I could report this to Ethics," he said, "but I'm not going to."

"Thank you. I appreciate that."

"Erica? Have you considered taking medical leave?"

Oh, god, so that's where this was going. "I missed some time right after it happened. At the start of the term. But I haven't missed any time since."

"Well, that's precisely the point, isn't it? Perhaps you *should* have taken some time off."

"Maybe. But . . . It's been getting better. It's been nearly a year."

"A year? Erica? Twin loss is devastating."

She took a deep breath and held it. If she let it out too fast, she'd be bawling like a baby. How fucking fragile am I? she thought. When anybody's nice to me, I burst into tears?

He was telling her how simple it would be. A doctor's note, that's all it would take. He was suggesting that *she* see a counselor—perhaps someone here at the university? Of course she must know about twin-loss support groups?

Oh god, she thought, *do not cry*—do *not* turn into a weeping mess in front of your program chair. She was exhaling carefully, a little bit at a time. It was making her light-headed. Okay, easy, she told herself, breathe in and out—that's all that's required—and think about something else. Watch yourself watching yourself.

He was telling her what a great hire she was, how much he valued her research. He was telling her that he and her colleagues had total confidence in her. "Medical leave would stop the tenure clock," he said,

78

"so you wouldn't have to worry about that. You need to take some time for yourself, Erica."

"Thank you." Yes, she could speak without crying. "I appreciate it. I'll consider everything you're saying."

That should be the end of it, shouldn't it? To signal that she wanted it to be over, she stood up. He stood up too, but he was smiling at her rather oddly. "With the girl twin," he said, "it looked for all the world like you were doing client-centred therapy."

There was absolutely nothing she could say to that—but she didn't have a choice; she had to come up with some kind of response. "I guess I was . . . I must have been taking some kind of therapeutic approach . . . or some . . ." She was in the office *of a clinical psychologist*. She was glad that he couldn't look directly into her mind. "I hadn't— I wasn't— I was *concerned* about her."

He was, thank god, walking with her to the door. "I was afraid," she said. "If those kids went into counseling? Maybe with a psychiatrist? A psychiatrist would probably want to medicate them, and that . . . wouldn't . . . A psychiatrist wouldn't understand . . . the, uh, the twin-specific—"

"Erica?" She heard the imperative in his voice. She looked at him.

Farsighted, he was looking at her over the tops of his glasses. His eyes were kind. "Those twins are not your responsibility."

6.

ERICA HAD FINALLY gotten around to doing what she'd been putting off for weeks—she'd jacked her pocket-sized digital recorder into her office computer and dumped her meeting with Karen Oxley onto her hard drive. Now she would listen to it, make notes, and dictate her summary into speech-recognition software—another of the terrific toys supplied by her SSHRC grant.

She'd met Karen in her home. They'd sat on the couch facing the windows but this time it hadn't been heavenly summer shining through; it had been Vancouver's more typical depressing metallic rain-light. Karen had served Earl Grey tea and whole-grain cookies from some famous West Van bakery. She'd been wearing another yoga outfit, all black—very dramatic with her blonde hair and golden eyes—and Erica had disliked her just as much as the first time they'd met. "Do you mind if I record you?" she'd said.

"Yes, I do mind," so there was no recording of Karen's initial reaction. The entry in Erica's notebook read: "Informed her that we had to contact the Ministry. Shocked and angry. Assumed correctly that Jamie was the one who made the suicide threat. Also angry about the faked blood test and the request for puberty blockers. She had never heard a word about puberty blockers. Again requested permission for recording. Explained university privacy policy. She gave consent for recording."

Erica clicked the play icon and the speakers reproduced Karen Oxley's voice with astonishing realism. The recorder had picked her up in mid-sentence: ". . . anything they don't like, they're just going to threaten suicide? We can't live with that kind of blackmail, and— I haven't— They want *what?* Some kind of drug that . . . something that would . . . what? Just stop their sexual development dead in its tracks? Eew! That makes me queasy just thinking about it. It's— Excuse me, I'm kind of upset."

Erica's highly sensitive omnidirectional mic had picked up the sound of Karen's footsteps as she walked all the way into the kitchen and then back again. "It's been twenty years . . . over twenty years . . . since I've smoked." Karen's voice sounded dry and ironic. "And suddenly I want a cigarette."

A ploosh from the couch as Karen threw herself back onto it. "Jamie was always secretive, but Devon . . . whatever he's thinking, I hear about it. So I'm . . . Shit. I'm surprised. Shocked. This is the first time— Would they really want to look like . . . what? Tall children? How could they date anybody? Can you think of a worse way to go through high school? Why on earth would they want to do that?"

"They'd go on looking like each other. That seems to be the point."

"And I thought they were over this suicide business. My god, do you think it's serious?"

Erica's response sounded pre-recorded—which in a sense it was: "All suicide threats should be taken seriously."

Karen said nothing. She went on saying nothing for so long that Erica's recorder kept boosting its gain until she was listening to the sound of the rain on the windows.

"Shit," Karen said, "you must think I'm a terrible mother."

IT WAS A GOOD THING that Karen had agreed to be recorded; once she got going, she was talking so fast that Erica couldn't possibly have taken adequate notes. No, the twins had no physical abnormalities, she said. Yes, of course, they'd had full physical exams and they were just as normal as could be. My god, there was none of this crazy twin crap when they were little. She'd tried her best not to gender-stereotype them. She'd bought them all kinds of toys—blocks and trucks, dolls and doll houses— let them play with whatever they wanted, but in day care, Devon played with boys, Jamie played with girls, and as for being twins and sharing things, forget it. The main thing she remembered was, "Mine! Mine! Mine!"

Gender-variant? That was a neat term. She'd never heard it before today. But just how variant was variant? Who made the rules? What? Kids were supposed to go on perpetuating gender stereotypes? But if gender-variant meant way over the line, then they'd never been gender-variant. Switching clothes for the blood test? That wasn't the twins being gender-variant, that was the twins being assholes.

Jamie and Devon had their own personalities right from the minute they were born, and they were as different as two kids could be. Dev was a sunny little character, never had any trouble making friends, but he never had any trouble being alone either. From the moment he realized that moving a mouse made something happen on a screen, he was attached to a computer, and he could go for hours entertaining himself. Jamie couldn't sit still long enough for any kind of quiet play. She needed to be moving all the time, and she needed to be with other kids, and she had terrible problems in school. She learned to read quickly, and if they tested her comprehension verbally, no problem, but she simply could not learn to write. She had trouble even learning the alphabet. She and Dev were so different that they didn't spend much time together.

"I'm sorry I separated them. You know, when you've got four kids . . ." Karen was having a hard time with this. "I thought of Devon as the easy twin and Jamie the difficult twin, and was she ever difficult! On top of that Paige was a very demanding child, and Cam was always in trouble at school . . . *always* . . . and I don't know what I was thinking. My marriage was falling apart."

This was the point in the interview when Erica stopped thinking of Karen as a West Van bitch with too much money and began to see her instead as a harassed mum doing the best she could. "Anyhow, the settlement. It made sense at the time. Rob adored Devon. The last thing I wanted to do was make a big court case of it. I'd done that with my first husband—

"Oh, I can't let myself off the hook. It was an utterly shitty decision. I asked Devon if he wanted to go to California to live with his dad, and he said, 'That's okay.' Rob and Dev were always close but— We'd always kind of split the twins up. Jamie had been my twin and Devon Rob's, so it was already— My god, but you don't ask a seven-year-old to make a decision like that. I must have been— It was the biggest mistake of my life. I'd read things that said you don't separate twins, but I thought it was *identical* twins you don't separate and my kids never seemed like twins. I wasn't sure they even liked each other very much. For a while Jamie would say, 'I miss Dev,' and then she stopped saying it.

Now Erica was listening to Karen starting and stopping as she tried to find a way through the tangle: "Jamie's so . . . I'm not sure secretive's the right . . . very protective of her . . . personal space? . . . difficult . . ."

Jamie got labeled "special needs" in grade one, and she absolutely hated that. It made her feel like a freak. ADHD was the first label they hung on her. "Okay, she *is* hyperactive, that's true, but attention deficit? She has very little patience with being bored—what's wrong with that? I was under constant pressure to medicate her, but I don't believe in medicating children." The other side of the coin was that Jamie's motor skills were way ahead of the other kids, and she took to soccer like she'd been born to play it. West Van has a fanatical soccer-mum culture, and

Jamie was getting lots of positive feedback. So there was something about herself she could be proud of.

In grade six it all started to fall apart. "There was this clique of snotty little bitches at Inglewood . . . exactly like the girls when I was there. Poor Jamie, all she wanted was to be a part of the group, and one day they'd pretend to be her friends, and then the next day they wouldn't talk to her . . . that same old shit that girls have always done to each other. She could never understand what she was doing wrong. It broke my heart. It was so much like what I went through, but I . . . I just couldn't figure out any way to help her. She didn't care what happened to me. She didn't want to hear about it. It was ancient history. It didn't apply to her."

Devon was having a hard time too but Karen wouldn't know about it until later because her ex-husband, Rob, "was not exactly forthcoming." He'd got married again, and they had a new baby, and they wanted to get Dev out of their hair for a while, so they sent him to Vancouver for a visit. Jamie and Devon hadn't seen each other since they were seven.

"Jamie was so depressed she didn't give a damn whether her brother was coming up or not. 'Ho-hum, big deal.' We drove out to the airport and waited for him to come through customs, and the minute he did, it was like lightning struck. When they were little, they'd looked like any ordinary brother and sister. No one would've said, 'Wow, do those kids look alike!' But Dev got off the plane and they were dead ringers for each other. It was eerie actually. They really did look like identical twins. They took one look at each other and went into shock."

Devon was only here a month but that was enough. "That's when all that crazy identical crap started." Dev went home, and then for both kids grade seven was the year from hell. Dev just dialed out. His school suspended him. Jamie quit playing soccer, and soccer had always been her salvation. Karen couldn't understand it, but Jamie kept saying, 'No, no, Mum, I just don't want to play anymore.' No reason, right? And then there was this . . . Cyber-bullying? And physical bullying too. Of course I went to see the school principal and he tried to convince me that what was happening was not happening. 'We have zero tolerance for bullying at Inglewood.' Right? Well, the kids have zero tolerance for ratting, and if you report anything to a teacher, your life's over. It was exactly the same when I was there."

Karen talked to the people at Palmerston Academy. That seemed the next logical move. But Jamie didn't want to go there.

"So what do you do? I had her tested. It's something I should have done years ago. Yes, she's gifted. And yes, she is special needs. She has a learning disability—'written output disorder.' She is *not* defiant, lazy, rebellious, inattentive, whatever, she's got *a fucking learning disability* and at least I've got it on record. Of course none of this fixes anything. She was getting more and more depressed. I could see it right before my eyes and there was nothing I could do about it.

"Just before Christmas she said to me, 'Mum, if I ever kill myself, please don't think it was your fault.' That's a hell of a thing to have to hear from a kid who's just turned twelve."

Karen's account of events matched what the twins had written in their emails. They became firmly attached to each other on the net. "I think they were each other's lifelines," Karen said.

Devon's father cut off his access to computers. The twins exchanged snail mails; Karen intercepted one of them, read the suicide threat. "It scared the bejesus out of me. What really got to me was how clearly they'd thought it through. I got on the phone to Rob and howled like a banshee. He said, 'Okay, you've got Devon for a while but he's on loan.'"

Karen put the twins in Palmerston. "I didn't ask them. I just did it." The change was instantaneous. Two miserable kids were instantly transformed into happy kids—getting good grades, making friends. "Dev had all these DVDs and comic books . . . *manga*. I'm not allowed to call them comic books."

"Yeah, they said the same thing to me."

So they joined the anime club and met the Lynas twins and attached themselves at the hips. "I've tried to like those girls but . . . You can't possibly tell them apart and they just *love it* that you can't possibly tell them apart. They look at you with those big spacey blue eyes and you can never . . . They're like cats. Just sort of silently appear. And they're fabulous liars, make up these incredible yarns. They're surfer girls from Tanzania, come from a long line of thieves and criminals, and they know karate. Of course my kids eat up every word. But no way am I going to interfere with my twins' social life. I'm just glad they've got one.

"The Lynas twins are into that anime stuff too, like a whole fantasy world. *Two from One Fire* . . . it's like the Bible or the Holy Grail. Kagami and Makoto are absolutely real people, and it's . . . I don't know. How can you argue with success? Everything's so much better. Their attitude. Their grades. Jamie can actually write something that you can read if you study it for a while. Everything's better. But I'm just afraid . . ."

"Afraid" was the key word. Karen kept repeating it. She was afraid of the twins' fantasy world. She was afraid that the line between fantasy and reality was getting a little blurry.

Listening to the recording, Erica heard herself not getting the subtext—not that she was saying anything wrong. "You did the best possible thing for Jamie," she heard herself saying. "You put her in a different school. You changed her social groups."

"Yeah, I guess that's right. Everything's so much better now. But I'm just afraid . . ."

Erica listened to Karen's long pause. She didn't remember that particular moment. She didn't remember if Karen had been looking out the window or staring into space or what she'd been doing. She didn't remember *hearing* what Karen said: *"I'm afraid they've already crossed the line."*

ERICA HAD STOPPED taking notes. She was lying back in her ergonomically correct office chair, her eyes closed, listening to the voices, hers and Karen's. It was raining in the recording—a steady background patter—and raining in real life, a hard rain slamming into Erica's office windows. In a curious bleak way, the double rain was unaccountably satisfying, a looping back, and that was probably why Erica had been putting off this work that should have been routine—she hadn't wanted to say goodbye to the Oxley-Clark twins. As long as they'd been part of her life, they'd created the illusion of meaning but now they were in the past and all that was left was duration. Time continually unwound itself and this was the first Monday in November, the month when Erica and Annalise had been born.

"It's *not* a suicide pact," Karen was saying. "They keep telling me that . . . 'No, no, no, Mum, it's *not* like that.' The best I can tell it's a— They talk about it as though they have no control over it . . . like a doomsday machine. If events push it beyond a certain point, it just goes into effect and they can't reverse it. Devon calls it— I can't remember, but it's like when you're approaching a black hole. When you cross a certain point, you can't come back."

What Erica should have said was nothing. She should have made encouraging sounds and allowed Karen to talk her way through it. Instead she'd commented, offering pithy useless statements like this one: "Children commit suicide because of their interactions with other children in groups." *Yes,* she said to herself now, *and your point is?*

"Don't all teenagers think about suicide at some time or other?" Karen was saying. "Well, maybe not boys so much, but girls. I know I did. But if you've ever played the suicide card and it's worked, how could you resist playing it again? I think it's just part of their fantasy world. I think most of these crazy things aren't meant seriously. They're just meant to push people's buttons and to get some kind of reaction. But a lot of kids actually do it. Every time you hear the news, there seem to be another one. Do you think . . . ?"

Do I think it's serious? How the hell should I know? But that isn't what she'd said. Erica listened to her own voice sounding so flat it was practically robotic: "All suicide threats should be taken seriously."

NO MATTER HOW SIMILAR MZ twins appeared to be, they were different. The major difference between Erica and Annalise had to do with a quality of mind. They'd both understood it but had never found a good way to describe it—the reason the world was a different place for each of them, the reason Erica had been drawn to Psychology and Annalise to English. Wallace Stevens had been Lise's favourite poet; Erica never quite got him. Lise used to quote him all the time, one line in particular: "Music is feeling then, not sound." For Lise lots of things were feeling, not sound, but for Erica they were sound. That became a shorthand joke between them. "That's sound, eh?" Lise would say.

"Yep," Erica would say, "pretty much."

86

There was nothing left of Lise now but traces in the untrustworthy assembly of Erica's memory—less than a ghost. Now that less than a ghost said, "The double rain's a metaphor for how depressed you are."

Screw that. It's not a metaphor. It's just the way it is. It just rains too fucking much in Vancouver.

My behaviour is no longer adaptive, Erica thought. I'm dying.

7.

THE NIGHT BEFORE their birthday Erica couldn't sleep much—or maybe she hadn't been asleep at all. She'd felt her consciousness warp—go wobbly—but her mind had never really shut down. Her apartment was at the top of the building and the sound of the rain was unrelenting. It was blowing hard too—a bit of cold spray striking her cheek from the partially open window by her bed. In a few hours people would start calling—her parents, her grandmother, both sibs—but she had nothing to say to them, nothing to give them. They would want to know if she was all right. What? All right? Are you out of your mind?

She got up and felt nothing. That was surprising. The darkness and rain and nothing—another of those dead-end moments. She'd hidden Annalise's purse in the back of her closet. Erica never carried a purse but Lise had used it as part of her costume as the conservative responsible high school teacher. Erica took everything out of the purse. Lise's wallet, her iPod, her cellphone. A granola bar, three scrunchies, a package of Kleenex, a tampon, some random scraps of paper. A hairbrush, four tubes of lipstick, one of mascara. Two eyeliner pencils, one with the tip broken off. Two flat scratched plastic containers, one of blush and one of eyeshadow.

Lise had done a hell of a lot of work to look *natural*—the effect she'd been trying to create—but Erica hardly ever wore makeup, only for dances and serious dates, and then Annalise had put it on her. There was no reason she couldn't do it herself; all she had to do was remember what Lise had done. Taking her time, Erica lined her eyes and feathered her lashes, added a touch of Lise's palest lipstick. She wanted to look in the mirror and see her sister.

She was on the road by five a.m. so she could be in the Hat by seven that night. The rain was utterly mad—the "pineapple express" they called it on the radio, rain carried in from somewhere, Hawaii maybe. They were using words like "torrential," but it was just Vancouver's usual rain ramped up to full kill—raining so hard it was bouncing up from the sidewalks. She had no idea when the sun would rise—although at this time of year it didn't matter whether it was up or down. Vancouver in November was darkness at noon. She was headed for the Trans-Canada.

She'd plugged Annalise's iPod into the stereo in the Golf, put it on shuffle. Annalise must have bought a lot of their old music—she heard AC/DC and Guns N' Roses and "Teen Spirit"—all that stuff they'd listened to on cassettes.

Her view was smeared into nothingness by the driving rain. A picture jumped into her mind—her windshield wipers stopping dead. She had to delete that image and pay attention to what was real. Her windshield wipers were working fine—although the rain was coming down so hard they couldn't clear it fast enough. All she had to do was drive slowly. She talked herself through every move. Rear-view check, shoulder check, change lanes. All she had to do was merge onto the Trans-Canada. She tasted the familiar hot metal of her own adrenaline.

She was in the burn. Easy, easy, easy, no need to hurry, lots of highway between here and the Hat—if she was going to the Hat. Her armpits were stinging. She forced her mouth open into a yawning position so she wouldn't grind her teeth. She was safe now—all she had to do was prevent her mind from turning the highway virtual. If she experienced driving as a video game, one small miscalculation— No, don't go there. The highway was straight. At that time of the morning she was sharing it with trucks. The rain.

The shuffle on Lise's iPod was giving her weird music she'd never heard—electronic shit with a heavy beat. When had Annalise started listening to that stuff? Their birthdays blended together now; that's what happened with memory—some things stayed, other things didn't. She remembered when cassettes were as cool as you could get, when they recorded from other people's cassettes or off the radio, made mix tapes. They rode around the Hat on their bikes and no one wore a helmet. That was a time she wished she could re-create—when they'd been Jamie and Devon's age. She wanted more of it than her sketchy memory. She wished she'd kept a diary, or someone had videotaped it, or there were more pictures—the street lights coming on as she and Lise rode their bikes home from school. They'd never been weird troubled gifted kids like Jamie and Devon; they'd just been ordinary kids. The big deal was to go to Earls or to Boston Pizza—nachos and French fries. They played Pac-Man. They made money babysitting. She wanted to walk into the house and find Mum talking on the old grey phone with its long cord attached to the wall, home to the light in the kitchen.

Annalise, the girly twin, danced. Erica, the tomboy twin, played softball. Every day practice—six to nine—she played with the older girls, sometimes even played with the boys. They played fastball, windmill pitching. Erica played third base—played quite shallow; she was good, the queen of the bunt. And now, catching up to herself, she was in Chilliwack, in the flat valley, driving past farmland. She couldn't remember driving. Maybe it wasn't dangerous for the highway to turn virtual. Maybe it was adaptive—you zone out and you drive.

She was entering the mountains, beginning to see the endless trees. She and Lise had rolled up their jeans at the bottom. Lise had worn Vans; Erica, Doc Martens. There was Pearl Jam on the iPod—Lise must have been nostalgic for the day. Later on they'd gone to bush parties—giggling about boys. Watching 21 Jump Street—Johnny Depp and Richard Grieco. They'd adored the stomach muscles on Richard Grieco. Annalise had a picture of him in her locker. Pretty in Pink, all the ordinary things. Madonna on the radio. They went to church every Sunday. She wanted it all back.

Yes, she could make it to the Hat. She'd be burnt out like a light bulb but she could make it. The sun was coming up, if you could call it the sun. She'd spent so much time on the Trans-Canada in the last few months that it felt easy and familiar—although the rain was making it worse—but making it worse made it more interesting.

No, screw interesting, the rain terrified her. All she wanted to do was get off the highway, get out of the rain, crawl somewhere wrapped in a blanket—and then what? She didn't feel like crying. That was a surprise. She'd thought she'd cry. She'd been afraid she was going to cry all day—their birthday. Erica had been born first but their mum had only one time to give them—they'd been born at 2:47 in the afternoon. That significant moment was a long way off. Would it be significant?

Nobody in their family had gone any farther than high school but education was the way you bettered yourself. Everyone said that. Erica and Annalise with their straight As were their two little geniuses. "Yeah, Mum," they said, sick of hearing it, "sure we are." They knew they were smart but nothing special. Going to Medicine Hat College was like two more years of high school—their mum didn't notice that they were growing up. They were *so* ready to leave home.

Calgary wasn't scary at all. What did Mum think—it was a big city? "Nice clean one bedroom apartment in Banff Trail area, ideal for student." It turned out to be just what the ad said—and, hey, great, the rent fit their budget. "It's, well . . . It's usually for one person," the puzzled landlady told them. "No problem," Erica said, *"we're twins."* Sure a double bed was big enough. They were small girls; they'd never slept in anything bigger than a double. It hadn't dawned on them yet that some people find identical twins creepy. Some of their happiest times were in that little apartment—their glory days, still co-authors of each other's papers, still double-dating. Gym rats, they peddled madly side by side on stationary bikes—the Spice Girls on the sound-system, the Macarena. They wouldn't know until later how sweet it was.

A real university—that's where you're supposed to get wonderful insights and sometimes you do when a professor says something that cracks your mind open. Lise's guru was Professor Cullen, strictly old-school, a Northrop Frye scholar, a grown-up prairie boy, bald and cheerful. Very much *Dr.* Cullen—it wasn't until grad school that they'd call their professors by their first names—and Lise thought he was just about as cool as a professor could be, the generator of a million fabulous insights. She came home starry-eyed from one of his lectures, wrote his words onto a notecard, and pinned it to their bulletin board. Erica never got it straight who said it—Montaigne?—but it was a good quote—NOTHING HUMAN IS STRANGE TO ME.

ERICA GASSED UP IN HOPE, her last chance before Merritt, sat in a Naugahyde booth, a truckers' place—what time was it? Ponchos and heavy windbreakers—men's voices—"Can you believe this friggin' weather?" She was hungry—she suddenly discovered—the last thing she'd eaten, a TV dinner the night before, and she hadn't been able to finish it. She needed sugar—ordered a bear claw and coffee—black, please. If she drank too much coffee, she'd have to pee.

Outside of Hope the highway started to climb. She was headed into the mountains. It was hard to maintain her speed. How could all those truckers still manage to do it—barrel-assing down the road? It was raining so hard she could see it bouncing off the highway like ping-pong balls. The steady lap of her windshield wipers. When the hell had Annalise got interested in electronic music? Erica didn't know who these bands were. The beat was hypnotic. It was good music to drive to.

The AIDS scare, people were terrified. Erica and Annalise had stayed virgins so long it was embarrassing—finally had given in and *done it* their second year in Calgary—both in the same week, although they hadn't planned it that way. Annalise, the girly twin, cooked—so everybody gave her cookbooks. For their twenty-first birthday Lise did rustic French—lentils with sausage, a good hearty meal designed to please their boyfriends. Memories. How random. She'd wanted to think about Annalise on their birthday, and she *was* thinking about her, but still wasn't feeling much. They'd told her in the hospital that she should not see Lise's body. "No, you don't want to—you really don't want to. If you do, you'll be sorry later." The road kept getting steeper. She was going so slowly that trucks were passing her in the left-hand lane.

If you date a highly bonded MZ twin, you'd better like her sister because you're going to be seeing a lot of her, and it's even worse than that—if you date a highly bonded MZ twin, you'd better like her sister's boyfriend because chances are you're going to be seeing a lot of him too. Just about the biggest, most dramatic, most incomprehensible difference between Erica and Annalise was their taste in boys. It just wouldn't compute—how could MZ twins like such different boys?

Lise's boyfriends were always regular guys like their dad or their brother. She liked strong boys with hard edges, boys who could take care of themselves—not the ones who got into fights but the ones who everybody knew not to mess with—boys who went hunting and fishing, who drove trucks to bush parties, who knew how to drywall, who could work in the oil patch. She liked to feel the charge of their sexual interest but she wanted to be treated with old-school gallantry and respect. When Lise's boyfriends had strong feelings, they washed them down with Molson Canadian.

Erica liked sensitive boys who would talk to her, who weren't afraid to cry in front of her, who listened to indie music or played the guitar or wrote secret poetry. Starting in high school, she'd had crushes on boys who turned out to be gay—like she could pick them up on radar. Daryl, her boyfriend at their twenty-first, wasn't gay—Erica knew that from first-hand experience—but he *was* a Theatre major whose main ambition in life was to play Shakespeare. Bob, Annalise's boyfriend, was a Poly Sci major headed for law school; his favourite book was *Atlas Shrugged*. They were both nice guys—and they'd figured each other out a while back—so the four of them made it through dinner cheerily enough. Then each twin went off with her boyfriend to his place. That meant Erica and Annalise were separated for slightly longer than a full day—pretty much the longest they could stand. By Sunday night they were alone again, telling each other everything—*"Okay, how was he?"*

SOMETHING WAS HAPPENING to the rain. It was getting fat—if that was possible. Erica slowed down. The trucks were roaring by her now. She shouldn't be on the Coquihalla. It was steep as all hell and the rain was turning to snow. It was smearing, slathering down, thick and wet and white. Well, of course it was snowing. It was the middle of November, wasn't it? She was down to fifty clicks. What if her Golf couldn't make it up? The highway was turning white in front of her.

Maybe she should pull off the road. But there was nowhere to pull off. If she stopped, she wouldn't be able to get started again, so she had to keep moving forward. She was still not feeling much of anything now—except a cold terror. Yeah, that was funny. She had to laugh at herself. It was a *cold* terror all right—more snow, more snow, more snow.

There really was a significant difference between them—that quality of mind. Lise had the feelings but all Erica ever had was the sound. "Were we born this way," Lise asked her, "or did we learn it?"

"If I could answer that," Erica said, "they'd give me the Nobel Prize."

Newborn twin girls. The one who was born second is an ounce and a half lighter than her sister, has slightly more delicate features, so you give her the girly name—Annalise—and everything follows from there. Maybe. If it all wasn't heritable— But look how it goes right from the start— You give Lise a doll, Ricki a softball. The little girls can imitate each other so well that no one can tell them apart except their mum—but they *want* people to be able to tell them apart—so Ricki wears loafers, Lise patents. One sister helps Mum in the kitchen, the other sister helps Dad do house renos. Ballet and softball. English and Psych. But they could still work on each other's papers—up until they couldn't. Stats, experimental design—the killers in Psychology—"I just can't go there," Lise said. Some of the poetry her sister loved, Erica couldn't make any sense of it. "It feels good as it is without the giant"—what the fuck did that mean?

In grade eleven they switched for a weekend just to see what would happen. Ricki wore the cute skirt and the touch of makeup, Lise the jeans and sweatshirt. They acted out each other's roles and fooled everybody—all of their friends, even their dad and both sibs—until, once again, their mum was the one who got it. "Just *what* are you girls *doing?*"

Their last year in Calgary they'd both worked on Lise's big paper, her honours thesis for Dr. Cullen—chasing down myths about twins. "The good twin and the evil twin" was a literary trope but it had no basis in reality. Thirty years of solid studies had demonstrated that MZ twins were much like each other in any trait you cared to measure, so how could one be good and the other evil? Incestuous twins was another myth. Sex discordant DZ twins were genetically no more closely related than non-twin sibs; the incidence of incest between them was no higher than that between non-twin sibs—that is, it was quite rare. In Psychology you learned to never say never, but sexual feelings between MZ twins were so rare as to border on impossibility.

Where did these myths come from? "Singletons project their fears and desires onto us," Lise said. That's when Erica and Annalise had come up with the idea of "singleton consciousness."

The most intense human bond that singletons ever experienced was a sexual one. That must be why they imagined a sexual element in the twin bond. But the twin bond was *not* sexual—and it was unique to MZ twins. Singletons couldn't even conceive of it. It was the first time that they'd seen themselves—well, if not as an *oppressed* minority, then a *misunderstood* one. The way the culture was built, singleton conscious-ness was not merely "normal" but "normative"—that is, everybody was supposed to be like that.

That's when Annalise got the flash that would change Erica's life. All of Erica's research interests would grow out of that flash; the work she was doing now was the result of that flash. Why did Annalise get it and not Erica? Because Annalise was the creative twin? Were they that different?

"We're outliers," Erica said, using the word as a metaphor just as Lise would have done. But Lise took it literally. Erica saw the flash go off in her sister's eyes. "If we're outliers from the bell," Annalise said, "what is the bell measuring?"

ERICA HAD SLOWED DOWN to a crawl. Some cars couldn't make it up the incline. They'd pulled over to the right and sat there, stopped, their headlights shining brightly into the smothering snow. Some trucks couldn't make it up either. Erica was hovering around thirty clicks but the Golf was a good car and kept on going. Yeah, right, she thought, I'm the Energizer bunny.

This was crazy, absolutely insane. The highway was nothing but white. There was the snow shed—whatever the hell it was called—and then she was working her way up a hill so steep she couldn't quite believe it. She passed another car that had got stuck. She really shouldn't be thinking about anything but driving. There was nothing to do but keep moving forward, keep her foot on the accelerator and just keep on moving, because if she ever stopped, she'd never get started again. She'd join all those other assholes, stalled in the white.

The dull ache of passing time and she was over the summit. It was snowing even harder and it was downhill. She could slide off this road. Maybe she should turn around, except there was nowhere to turn. It was daylight, for whatever that was worth, but she didn't know the road. The Coquihalla.

She wanted to continue mindlessly but she needed to stop—needed to pee and eat and think things through. She got off the highway in Kamloops. She went into a doughnut place, picked up a map from the front counter. Being inside was spinny, too hot; she felt displaced in there. She ordered a maple-glazed doughnut from the virtual waitress.

She spread the map open on the counter. She didn't really need the map—there was a map in her mind—but it was good to see it laid out in front of her like that. She was still a long way from Medicine Hat—impossibly far. She'd barely made it a quarter of the way. She'd driven out of Vancouver's crazy tropical rain—the pineapple express—and into prairie winter. What if she got to the Hat? If it'd be bad on the phone, it'd be a million times worse in person. There'd be nowhere to hide. Everybody would be so worried about her—worried sick—but what they'd really want was something for themselves. That's all singletons ever wanted. What could she say? "Hi, Mum, hi, Dad, wish us a happy birthday."

THEY HAD BOTH WANTED to get married and have kids—talked about it a lot. But in order to get married and have kids, you first have to have a boyfriend, and it's hard to have a boyfriend when you're still living with your sister, sharing everything with your sister, doing everything with your sister, sleeping in the same bed with your sister. Annalise finished her ed degree and went home and Erica was stuck in Edmonton finishing her doctorate. They got new Hotmail accounts to talk to each other. They emailed each other dozens of times a day. They talked on the phone every night. Screw independence, they said, this is just too hard.

They booked off from life to spend their twenty-fifth birthday in Calgary. Erica drove from Edmonton, Lise from Medicine Hat. Neither had much money—and they were both careful with money—but they dumped a fortune into the Fairmont because it was a special occasion, because they knew it was the end even if they weren't ready to admit it. That was only a couple of months after 9/11 and the whole world felt fucked up. Whatever next bizarre weird shitty thing was going to happen, they wanted to be together when it did. They kept saying, "Thank god we're both still in Alberta."

They didn't want to watch television—but they did anyway. That was when you kept seeing the same images over and over—how could they keep showing them over and over?—those planes hitting the Twin Towers. "The *Twin* Towers," Annalise said—another of her magical metaphors.

"It has nothing to do with us," Erica said.

They shared a queen-sized bed, called room service, felt wicked about the money they were spending. Erica even remembered what they'd ordered—turkey and steak. They shared everything just like they were kids again and then lay on that huge bed in that too expensive hotel. "Why is it so hard?" they said. Now they really did feel like freaks, like there was something wrong with them, like it was their fault—like it was something they should have solved years ago. Lots of MZ twins managed to separate—why couldn't they?

Annalise hadn't found a regular job in the Hat. All she was doing was subbing. The simplest solution was for her to move back to Edmonton. "Why is it always me?" she said. "Why am *I* always the one who has to compromise?"

ERICA WAS ON the road again. The LED lights were a brilliant smear coming up. What the hell were they saying? They'd closed the Coquihalla! Shit. Now she would have to go back to Vancouver on the Trans-Canada. It would take forever. Well, what else did she have to do? Other cars, slow as snails, in the thick snow, thirty clicks, no decisions, just keep moving. It was a matter of sheer duration.

Erica missed the burn, or maybe she'd been inside the burn for so long that she'd gotten used to it. Nothing was making her heart jump, making her sweat. Her mind had too much free space. Softball and weight training had changed Erica's body just as years of ballet had changed Annalise's. They'd stood in the front of the bathroom mirror in the Fairmont on their birthday and compared their bodies. They'd built themselves different bodies. They touched each other where they were different—the muscles in Erica's shoulders and arms, the muscles in Lise's calves and quadriceps. They were both sorry. "We could have done it differently," Annalise said. "We could have reversed it. You could have done ballet and I could have played softball."

It was true—the same genes had made them both natural athletes, fast and strong and agile. "Or we could have done everything together," Erica said. "We—"

Driving back to Edmonton, Erica was crying so hard she had to pull over. The same thing happened to Lise driving back to the Hat. "Maybe after I teach in the Hat for a year or two," Lise said on the phone, "maybe I can come to whatever city you're in and get a job."

"Maybe," Erica said.

A year later Lise called her and said, "Mark and I are going to get married"—Mark Bondaruk, the science teacher at Annalise's school. It shouldn't have come as a surprise. Erica had heard every detail of every date; she'd heard all about their sex life. But the pain was so sudden, so intense, that Erica had to push the phone away from her, afraid. When she could talk, she said, "Congratulations."

There was no way Erica could hide her feelings from her sister. "It hurts me too, Ricki," Annalise said. "Call me back in a couple of hours when you can talk about it."

Lise had been right. They could have reversed things. Sometimes in her dreams Erica danced on pointe.

ERICA HAD BEEN driving forever. She drove past the highway exit that would have taken her to East Van and Commercial Drive and home—not her home, the last place in the world she wanted to be. The exact moment, the anniversary of the moment of their birth, had come and gone, and Erica had missed it. It was over. She'd lost it. She had to get off the highway; she was falling asleep at the wheel. She got off in North Van and drove down Lonsdale. She didn't give a shit where she was, pulled over at the first restaurant she saw. She fell into a booth and ordered coffee.

Erica must have been asleep. Not just dozing, but sound asleep, deeply immersed in sleep. There was a huge hole in her consciousness. I'm blank, I'm nothing—that was sleep. Waitress was saying, "Excuse me, excuse me . . ."

"More coffee," Erica said, "please. Do you have carrot cake?"

From where she was sitting she could see that the daylight had been used up. It was black as pitch out there again and still raining—monsoon rain, pineapple-express rain. How could the sky have that much water in it? It was just short of five o'clock in the afternoon; Erica had been driving for twelve hours. It was stupid that she'd turned back. She could have made it to Calgary but she was on Lonsdale in North Vancouver.

She ate the carrot cake, got back into her Golf. The rain was so heavy she could have been in a car wash. She had to make it through the rest of the hours until midnight so their birthday would be over. She wanted the burn, had been hoping for the burn, needed to taste that awful metallic adrenaline, needed her mind to go away. I am alone and frightened, Erica thought. What a stupid sentimental thing to think. Annalise had been six weeks pregnant when she'd been killed on the highway.

It was simple. She would drive from North Vancouver to Horseshoe Bay and she would get off at every highway exit and then get back on again. And then she would turn around at Horseshoe Bay and do it all over again all the way back to East Van. Was that enough to take up the time until midnight? It didn't matter. After she'd done that, she would think of something else. She sensed that there was something icy and clear on the far side of the burn. She wanted to see what it was.

The Lonsdale entrance was too easy—she was on the highway before she had a chance to worry about it—but Cap Road was a bitch. It was black—like the entire world had forgotten the concept of daylight—but, in a way, that helped. She could see headlights from miles away—or what seemed like miles away—so she simply sat at the entrance and waited until there was nothing but black and then drove onto the highway. Getting back on at Taylor Way wasn't hard either. All she had to do was stay in the left-hand lane. There was hardly any traffic on the Upper Levels—most people had enough sense not to be up there on a night like this.

She was in West Vancouver now, the home of the Oxley-Clark twins. The Fifteenth Street on-ramp was a bit on the tricky side. She had to yield to cars coming down from both the left and the right—but their headlights gave them away. She got off again at Twenty-First, drove down to Marine, pulled over by the side of the road. Maybe she needed to sleep. That would kill some time. She lay back in the seat, her entire body shaking. She had a headache like a steel band. The foul taste in her mouth had been there for so long she was getting used to it. The last place she wanted to be was back up on the highway in the rain in the dark. Well, fuck that.

The entrance back on from Twenty-First gave her a long looping view of the highway before she had to get on it. No cars at all. The rain was absolutely insane—well, shit, it had been insane all day, what did she expect? She drifted down the long loop onto the highway, and there was a car in the left-hand lane, so she just let it go by. Visibility zero. She had to keep her speed up or she'd be a menace—although there were hardly any other cars on the highway, what was she thinking? She was doing fifty. Maybe she should get up to sixty.

She was overtaking a truck. The water was too heavy on the surface of the road; she couldn't see the lane divisions. It looked like the highway on the other side was part of the highway on her side. Crazy. Slow, she told herself. Careful, she told herself—the trucker's taking it easy. She was right behind him. Big fucking truck. He was in the right lane, spewing so much water behind him that she was drowning in it. If she wanted to be able to see anything at all, she had to get ahead of him. All she had to do was to move into the left lane and she could pass him.

Erica turned her wheel left—not hard, just drifting over into the left lane. Then she saw that there *was no left lane.*

Hauled the wheel hard right. Too late. Fuck. Her left front fender grazing something—median?—what?—hard, jagged, grating, concrete, and then she was spinning, spinning. Slamming the brake, automatic reflex, no, get off, it's like driving on ice *get off the fucking brake*—hydroplaning, going around and around, steer *into it* not *out of it.* How many times? Oh god steered hard at the spin, held it, held breath, pulled out of it—going straight way too fast. No, stay off the brake, Jesus, the median *the other fucking way.* Stay off, stay off, stay off—SLAM—explosion? Slammed back in her seat. Slammed in the face. Jesus, it hurts, oh fuck oh god, the airbag. Choking on smoke. Can you breathe? Can you—? See? Car stopped. Only one headlight.

Her right headlight was gone. Lise's iPod was still playing that electronic shit. A car was headed straight for her—headlights—*god, was she pointed in the wrong direction?* The car leaned on its horn, someone inside the car leaned on the horn, the horn yelled—to warn—anyhow, a warning, screaming, and vanished, Doppler effect and on down the road and passed her on her left. She had to get the fucking smoke out of the car. Rolled the windows down.

Everything skewed and screwy. Faced the wrong way, oh god, she wanted to live. Oozed the car around, making a U-turn. Sliding again, skating on the water, something wrong with her steering. This was fucked.

She got partway around, she had to reverse, headlights coming, she had to get off the highway. Mind chanting it—get off the highway, get off the highway—was turned, and another car passed her on the left, screaming horn, so she should move right, as far as she could get—yes, to the right. Oh fuck, watch for the concrete. Something there to the right—she couldn't see it. Rain pounding her through open windows. Steering fucked, she had to get off the highway. Was this the exit? Was the car falling apart? It sounded awful.

Coming down off the exit, she knew that exit, it was the twins' exit, off the highway, let her speed drop. Heavy into the burn now, she could feel it in every part of her. Untenable. What a weird word. She had to get the rain off her. She was fucking drenched. She hit the buttons but the windows wouldn't close. Broken. The rain was untenable, driving was untenable, stopping was untenable, living was untenable, dying was untenable. Their birthday wasn't over yet.

This was taking forever. She was driving. Wailing like an animal, she was driving in the dark. The rain in her eyes, in her hair. Their car was broken—horrible clanking, banging. Shit, it sounded like something just dropped off the car. Clunk, dropped and clanged away. When she turned the wheel, metal screamed. She could barely steer. Thank god she was off the highway. Why was she still driving?

She was climbing up some steep hill, steep as the Coquihalla. She had to get to the top—was this the top?—and stopped. Was she stopped? Engine kept on banging, rattling. She turned if off and it turned. It stunk, gas and oil and smoke. What if it burned? Could she get out? They had to cut Annalise out.

She was beaten. Broken? How was she supposed to know? Her ears were ringing. Where her seat belt grabbed her was like fire. Her collarbone? No, she could move her arms. She could move her legs. The rain was so cold. Where the fuck was she? Annalise, she thought, I wish I could have died for you. She was in the twins' driveway.

TWO

8.

THE GOOD NEWS and the bad news were exactly the same. This was Sunday night, family night, and everything was the way it usually was—and that was the way things ought to be, give or take an odd item here or there. There was nothing wrong with Karen's life at the moment—that's what she kept telling herself—so why couldn't she simply let it go at that? Why did she have that old familiar feeling of having screwed up somewhere? It felt like the recurring dream she'd been having for years—that she'd brought the groceries home but had forgotten the baby at Safeway.

The mere continuity of things was comforting, wasn't it? Well, it was supposed to be—the bright flicker of the TV, the homey glow of the fire in the fireplace, the beehive hum of a house full of kids, the pounding of rain on the windows to remind her that they were safe inside, and here was Drew, his hand falling onto her shoulder in his standard gesture of affection, patting her like a dog. "Is Cam coming home for dinner?" he asked her.

"Your guess is as good as mine."

"Are those Lynas twins here?"

"Probably. Nobody tells me. They just drift in and out like smoke."

Drew always cooked on Sunday nights, and he always wanted to know how many people he was feeding, and it was always impossible to tell him. "They don't eat much," she said.

"Are you kidding me? They eat everything in sight."

"Not the meat." That must be what was worrying him—did he have enough lamb chops?

"You don't expect me to cook a special meal for them, do you?" Why were they having this conversation? God, did the man have no memory? "Where are they supposed to get their protein?"

She said the same thing she always said—"Put some cheese out for them," and then, because he was on his feet and she wasn't—"Call Jamie for me."

He sighed, yelled up the stairs—"Jamie, your mother wants you," and then walked back toward the kitchen, blathering at her the whole way—something about what they'd just seen on the news. The kids were eligible to get vaccinated for the H1N1 virus starting tomorrow. He knew what she thought about that, but blah, blah, blah, as his voice faded into unintelligibility. "Drew," she called after him, "you *know* I can't hear you."

This open floor plan was supposed to do what? Create a sense of family? "Spacious" had been the realtor's buzz word, and all that space was supposed to make for "easy living." The kitchen, dining room, and living room flowed gracefully into each other—everyone on this floor able to see everyone else and smell the broiling lamb chops—but how about something as simple as a family conversation? Not a chance. They might as well be halooing at each other across a campground, voices diffusing into the airy zero below the eighteen-foot ceilings, while Karen, located in her favourite chair at the centre of all that easy living, was picking up everybody's background noise—Drew's clanging and banging, Paige's mindless TV, the twins' J-pop or whatever it was, those idiotic dance tunes that always sounded like an off-stage chorus of electronic mice—and then, as tonight's added bonus feature, the rain slamming the windows so hard the panes rattled. It was a truly gruesome night. It sounded like the entire Georgia Strait was about to land in her lap at any moment.

Karen had asked for Jamie, but in the twins' crazy fantasy world they were two halves of the same person, so either one would do, and the one she got was Devon. That was okay with her; he was easier to deal with than his sister. "Are Morgan and Avalon here?" she asked him.

"Yeah. Can they—?"

"Sure. We already counted them in." Those spooky little girls seemed to be around every weekend now. "Who's with Paige?"

"Lauren." One of Paige's dance school friends, the new BFF.

"See if she's staying."

He turned toward the hall and shouted, "Hey, Paige!"

"I can yell down the stairs the same as you can, Devon."

He gave her an excellent imitation of his sister's eye-roll and headed for the family room. Did the twins sit around and deliberately imitate each other, trying to pick up each other's mannerisms? She wouldn't put it past them. What other pair of twelve-year-olds would walk into the trendiest, most upscale salon in Vancouver and say, "Make us look identical"? Somebody must have told them that a stylist gets a twenty percent tip. To make sure they were doing things right, they'd given her twenty-five. Karen hadn't known the full amount of the damage until she'd seen it on her Visa statement—just short of a thousand bucks. Of course she took her credit card back. "That's consequences?" Drew said. "You ought to have their heads shaved."

When it came to giving Karen advice, Drew didn't hesitate. It was unnatural for a brother and sister to be so attached to each other. If they were his kids, he'd separate them pronto. Suicide? Are you kidding? That was a bluff, straight-on manipulation, and Karen shouldn't have fallen for it. She was making a serious mistake with her laissez-faire attitude. It wasn't just the twins—all four of her kids had a grotesquely overblown sense of entitlement. What she should do was get back to basics—lay down some laws, set some limits. Everything he said was just one cliché after another.

Well, you can set limits without posting house rules on the refrigerator—which is what Drew wanted her to do—and her kids were basically okay. Cameron was— oh, he was just Cameron. Even when he was being an asshole, there was always something likeable about him, and she was sure that he'd turn into a reasonable facsimile of an adult if she gave him enough time. Super-princess Paige could be annoying as all hell, but she was also as transparent as a window pane and easy to please—Karen thought of her as the *normal* kid. And then there were the twins—the central enigma. She hadn't told Drew about the visit from the social worker. She could just imagine what he'd say about that. But compared to the way they'd been a year ago, the twins were doing just fine. They never mentioned suicide anymore.

"Lauren's not staying," Devon told her. "Her mom's on her way."

Drew should be happy about that. "Call your brother," she said.

Dev always had his cellphone in his pocket. He took it out, flicked it open, poked at it. "His phone's off."

"Well, of course it is"—the irresponsible jerk. She didn't ask much of Cameron, but he knew he was supposed to be home for dinner on Sunday nights. "Don't count Cam in," she called to Drew, "and Paige's friend is leaving." That brought Drew to the living room, offering her another glass of the beautifully chilled bottle of whatever. She gave him a no-thanks smile. Get loaded before dinner? I don't think so.

"Listen to that rain," he said. "It's crazy."

But he would have no problem with another glass. He was allowed—he was a connoisseur, a collector of fine vintages. From his point of view, Karen was worse than ignorant—she was indifferent. She could tell a good wine from a bad one, and that was about it. At dinner, they would switch from white to red. Then they would be drinking the Chateau Whatever from that One Stellar Year when the Legendary Grapes of the Somewhere-or-Other Valley had achieved Utter Ecstatic Perfection, and ordinarily you couldn't get it for less than a hundred-and-sixty bucks a bottle, but Drew, because he was who he was—a special sort of guy—had been offered the rare chance to snap it up at ninety, though he had to buy two cases to get it at that price, so Karen better like it, and she did. She would have a glass of it with dinner, and Drew would drink the rest of the bottle and open another one. "Who's that?" he said to the doorbell.

"Probably Lauren's mum."

"One of the kids going to get it?"

"Are you kidding?"

Sighing, he headed for the door, and then Karen heard his hearty boardroom voice saying all the right things. Thank god, he even remembered Lauren's mum's name—"*Heather*, come in. What a terrible night! Sure you won't stay for dinner?"

Karen met Heather in the outskirts of the living room—"No, please, don't get up," Heather said, although Karen was already up. "I'm sorry. I should've been here hours ago," calling down to her daughter in the family room, "Lou-lou, honey. Come on, honey. Your dad's waiting."

Lou-lou? Karen thought, that's a good one. "I love your raincoat," she said—and meant it. Most West Van mums—Karen included—bought raingear that made them look like they were about to ascend Everest, but Heather was wearing an old-fashioned raincoat that belted at the waist—white with yellow daisies on it—and Karen felt a pang of jealousy. Heather was a young mum and could still get away with cute cheesy kitsch like that.

"Oh, thanks," Heather said. "I got it at Nordstrom's in Seattle," and Karen was picking up an odd signal—a social misalignment, a hesitancy. "I hope no one was hurt," Heather said.

What on earth was she talking about?

"Um . . . the car? In your driveway?"

"There's a car in our driveway?" Karen said.

Heather was so embarrassed it took her a moment to figure out what to say next. "Don't you know about it? It's in pretty bad shape."

What car? Karen thought—and then she got it. Oh. God. Cam. He must have wrecked the Lexus again. She sent Drew a warning look to keep his mouth shut.

"No, no one was hurt," Karen said—and then in a wry voice meant to carry just the proper amount of bitter parental humour, "We seem to have recurring problems with that car." She was hoping that would put an end to things—and added a small laugh to make sure it did.

"Oh." Heather was actually blushing. She really *was* young.

Okay, the awkward moment was over—let's forget it and move right along. "Boy, I sure don't envy you having to go out on a night like this," Karen said.

Because no kid ever comes when you call her, Heather had to go down and drag Lou-lou away from the TV, and that gave Karen the chance to bring Drew up to speed. "How the hell could he have got it out of the garage?" she said. "I'm going to kill the little bastard." Cam, of course, shouldn't have been driving at all. His license was suspended for his *second* DUI.

With Paige chattering behind them, Lauren and her mum were back upstairs, and now it was time for the long goodbye. Drew wasn't merely good at this stuff, he was *very* good at it—he even remembered Heather's *husband's* name. "We'll have to have you and John over for dinner one of these nights," he was saying just as though he and Karen were an ordinary couple who had dinner together every night—the impression he liked to give to the world.

Karen waited until she heard Heather's car driving away before she said, "He must have sneaked it out when I was asleep."

"When's the last time you had *your* car out?" Drew asked her.

"I don't know. Sometime yesterday. The rain hasn't been exactly—"

"What?" Paige said.

"If it was after I got here," Drew said, "he would've had to back around me."

"*What?*" Paige said. "Tell me!"

"Your brother's wrecked the Lexus again. And then he just took off and left it in the driveway."

Of course Paige had to go see for herself. "Coat!" Karen yelled after her and followed Drew into the living room. It wasn't fair how one trivial little thing could destroy that sense of continuity she'd been savouring— Sunday night, family night— Well, she'd been *trying* to savour it. Maybe there was no continuity and she should stop trying to pretend there was— except for Cameron. There was plenty of continuity to him. He'd always been a fuck-up, and he was still a fuck-up. But she was still his mother. She'd better get her head out of the sand and *do something*. Would he even graduate from high school? "This really is the end," she said. "I just can't take any more of his shit, I really can't."

"Mum!" Paige had skidded to a stop just short of the rug. Of course she hadn't put a coat on. "It's not the Lexus."

She was a little girl who enjoyed centre stage. Her eyes sparkling with triumph, she waited long enough to be sure she had their full attention before she gave them the next installment. "It's a *blue* car. It's like . . . *totaled*." And soon as she saw them get it, she took off—headed upstairs to deliver the news to Twin Central.

"Oh, for Christ's sake," Drew said. "Why would someone—?"

Now Paige and the twins were thudding down the stairs like ponies. Wonderful, Karen thought, let's get everybody involved. "Coats!" Karen yelled even though she knew it was a lost cause.

"There must be some kind of mistake." Drew had a great knack for stating the obvious.

"Well, yes," she said.

The kids had left the door standing wide open. The wind was blasting straight through the house all the way to the kitchen—another wonderful advantage of easy living in an open floor plan. "Look," Karen said, "if someone's left a car in our driveway, all we have to do is get it towed. Let's not get—"

Paige came shooting out of the night like a small wet rocket and slammed into her, throwing her arms around her, knocking her nearly off-balance. "Mum!"

Her bratty ten-year-old had just reverted to a preschooler. "What? What, sweetie? What's the matter?" Karen could practically taste Paige's fear.

"There's *a person* in that car."

Karen felt her skin prickle. "Drew!"

There was no time for him to react. Jamie had just followed her sister into the house. She was scared too. *"Morgan!"* she yelled.

Karen was hurt. What's the matter with *me?* she thought. *I'm* your mother.

The Lynas twins appeared so quickly they must have been waiting on the stairs. That's all we need, Karen thought. Her dislike of them had settled so deeply into her by now it felt visceral. That they doubled each other made them uncanny for starters—escapees from a Borges story— and then it was no joke, they really *were* like cats, came and went as they pleased and didn't give a damn for her. And why didn't their mother get their bangs trimmed? And how could she let them get away with all that tacky eye makeup? Karen knew that her feelings were irrational—it had gotten so bad that she even disliked them for their red hair—but she couldn't help it, and she certainly didn't want them here right now. They were annoying Drew too. "Wait a minute, girls," he said.

Wait for what? They weren't doing anything. They were clustering with Jamie, their voices going buzz, buzz, buzz. *"Jamie!"* Karen yelled louder than she'd intended. What she meant was, *Get your butt over here!*

Devon walked through the door leading a girl by the hand. Their entrance was so quiet and undramatic it felt like an afterthought. No, not a girl, a young woman—dark hair streaming down her pale face. She wasn't merely wet, she was soaked to the skin, and she was not all right—was far from all right—one look at her face would tell you that she was not all right. Her eyes were frozen, staring straight ahead. She didn't seem to register where she was—didn't seem to register anything at all. Devon let go of her hand, stepped to one side, and looked meaningfully at Karen. He had delivered her to the front hall, and so his job was over.

Okay, Mom, you're the grown-up. Do something.

Karen had automatically drawn Paige to her—a protective gesture. "It's okay, sweetie," she said under her breath—although it wasn't. Then one of the Lynas twins darted mysteriously through the open door and out into the night—doing what? And oh my god, Karen knew that woman from somewhere—and then it clicked into place. She was that pain-in-the-ass psychologist from the university—the one who'd reported Jamie's suicide threat to the Ministry. Why was she here? It didn't make any sense. "Jamie, did you do this?" Karen said under her breath.

Wide-eyed, Jamie shook her head.

"You didn't invite her or—?"

"No. Swear to god, Mum."

"Dr. Bauer," Karen said. "Are you all right?"

There was no change on Dr. Bauer's face—nothing. "Are you hurt? Have you been in an accident?" Nothing.

"What's going on here?" Drew said—not helpful.

"Oh, you must be frozen," Karen said. "Come in by the fire." Nothing. "Dr. Bauer?"

Karen was having one of her intuitive flashes, and now she sensed something shielding this woman, something that said, *Stay back, stay back, stay back.* How do you deal with someone who's like this—who's staring, who's motionless, who doesn't speak? It woke an ancient dread in her that felt archetypal, that frightened and froze her. She looked to Drew for help, but he seemed frozen too, his face fixed into a sickly half-smile.

Whichever of the Lynas twins had run outside had just come back. Karen saw her send her sister a signal. Karen's senses had been stripped raw, and she actually *saw* a meaningful communication between the girls, as clear as if it had been a flash of light.

The twin who'd stayed behind stepped directly up to Dr. Bauer. "For god's sake, *don't touch her!*" Karen wanted to yell. But why? Karen couldn't understand the depth of her own revulsion. It felt vestigial, peasant-like—you don't touch a mad woman or a leper.

The twin stepped forward until she was only a foot away from those terrible staring eyes. She looked straight into them. "Hi," she said in a bright chirpy voice, "do you remember me? I'm Avalon."

Karen couldn't tell if there'd been a slight change in Dr. Bauer's face or if she'd only imagined it. "Can you talk?" Avalon said.

The voice was flat and mechanical. "Yes."

"Oh, good! Do you know who you are?"

"Erica."

"Hey, Erica, that's *really* good."

Avalon took Dr. Bauer's left hand into hers, turned it over, and pressed her fingertips into her wrist. Oh my god, she was taking her pulse. How did she know how to do that? Then Avalon did something utterly bizarre. She reached around Dr. Bauer's head, linked her fingers together, pulled her hands into the back of Dr. Bauer's neck and left them there, holding on. "Do you know where you are?" she said.

"No."

"That's all right. That's just fine. No, no, don't turn your head, please, Erica. Just look at me. We're going to take care of you now. Everything's going to be all right."

The other twin, Morgan, was already unzipping Dr. Bauer's jacket. "We're going to make you more comfortable," Avalon said. Morgan peeled off the sodden jacket and threw it on the floor. Now she was unbuttoning Dr. Bauer's top.

"Wait a minute, girls," Drew said. "Just what are you doing?"

"Leave them alone," Jamie said, not to Drew but to Karen. "They're *lifeguards*."

Morgan had stripped Dr. Bauer down to her bra. She was skimming her fingers lightly over the woman's bare skin, over her collar bones, then down over her ribcage. There was a reddish bruise running diagonally down from her left shoulder—the exact shape of the seat belt that must have grabbed her and slammed her to a stop. "We're going to help you lay down now, Erica," Avalon said.

Morgan slid around behind Dr. Bauer, wrapped her arms around her, and took her weight. Avalon was still holding onto her neck. "That's it, Erica," Avalon said. "Everything's fine. Just relax. We're not going to drop you"—and the twins, as perfectly coordinated as if they'd rehearsed this maneuver a million times, tilted Dr. Bauer gently backward and lowered her to the floor. Once she was sitting, they guided her on down

112

until she was stretched out flat on her back. "Get some pillows," Morgan said to Jamie.

Both Jamie and Devon ran to strip cushions from the couches. Morgan slid two big ones under Dr. Bauer's knees, wedged two small ones on each side of her neck. Only then did Avalon ease her hands away. "Don't turn your head now, Erica. Okay?"

Morgan was pulling off Dr. Bauer's running shoes. Avalon had straddled her, was looking down directly into her eyes. "Can you wiggle your fingers, Erica?" she said. "Oh, that's so good! How about your toes? Hey, that's just perfect!"

Morgan undid Dr. Bauer's jeans, lifted her pelvis, and slid the wet jeans down and off. "Girls!" Drew yelled. "Just what *the hell* do you think you're doing?"

Morgan was running her hands over Dr. Bauer's bare legs. "Mrs. Oxley," she said, "we're gonna have to call 911," and she was already on her feet, headed for the portable in the kitchen.

"Now wait a minute," Drew said. He was moving to intercept her. "That's ridiculous. Nobody's calling 911. This is all just happening too fast. I don't— Who *is* this woman? We don't even know how serious the accident was. You shouldn't be taking her clothes off. What if she—"

"They're lifeguards!" Jamie yelled at Drew, darted past him, snatched up the portable, and threw it to Morgan. Then she planted herself directly in front of Drew, her dark eyes blazing defiance—if you want to get to her, you're going to have to move me first.

"Oh, for Christ's sake," Drew said. He was so angry he was panting. He shot Karen a murderous look.

Shit, Karen thought, I don't need this. It was no secret that Jamie and Drew hated each other, but why did they have to act it out *now*? That meant Karen would have to get involved, and even if Drew was dead wrong, she'd have to be on his side. They'd made an agreement that they'd never go against each other in front of the kids, so she didn't have any choice. She knew what he wanted. She was supposed to say something like, "Jamie, that's entirely unacceptable. Go to your room right now."

That would be ridiculous. A woman was lying in Karen's front hall, hurt and in trouble.

"Drew," Karen said. "Just drop it, okay? We'll deal with it later."

"My god, Karen," he said, betrayed, "what are you thinking?"

To get well away from him, Morgan had run all the way back into the hallway. She was already punching out the number.

"Emergency! . . . Car accident, like serious . . . like *really* serious, like total . . . One victim. She's in the house. Breathing okay, like her airway's clear. Her pulse is steady but we can't tell like . . . No, we don't know that . . . No external signs of injury. We've got her in recovery position, stabilized her head. She can wiggle her fingers and toes. She's like dazed and confused . . . . No, not so much. Her skin's cold, like *super* cold . . . Yeah, we're warming her." To Karen, "They're on their way. They want to confirm your address."

Karen recited her address, and Morgan echoed it into the phone. "Morgan?" she said. "What's wrong with her?"

"They don't— They're like— They can't say anything. They'll be here as soon as they can."

"What do *you* think's wrong with her?"

Morgan made a helpless gesture—why are you asking this? "Like hypothermia?" she said.

"Yeah," Avalon said, "she's too freakin' cold . . ."

"Like what you're supposed to do is take all her wet clothes off . . ."

"Even her underwear."

"Okay," Karen said, "let's do it."

Karen knelt by the injured woman—was she injured? And yes, she could touch her—not a nightmare spectre from the darkest bog-peasant memory of Karen's European ancestors, just an ordinary small woman wearing a sports bra. Seen up close, that seat belt–shaped bruise was really ugly. Karen worked her hands under the woman's back and undid the clasp—and oh my god, her skin was cold. She'd never touched anyone whose skin felt so cold.

"Paige, go get me some clean towels out of the upstairs bathroom." It probably didn't matter whether Devon was watching or not, but it wouldn't hurt to get him out of here. "Go outside and meet the emergency people," she told him, "and wear a coat. *I mean it* . . . Jamie," she said, "get the big comforter from the couch." It was near the fire and should be warm.

114

Karen peeled off Erica's underwear. Paige had brought the towels. Karen and Morgan patted her dry. They spread the comforter over her, tucked it in around her body

All that was left to do was wait. Our perception of time, Karen thought—how strangely mutable. In a crisis like this a few minutes could take several eternities—as though there was all the time in the world. The girls were looking at her. The Lynas twins' blue eyes no longer seemed spacey and alien—they seemed alert and concerned. The brown of Jamie's eyes was just like her father's—that connection, that continuity. The girls were looking at her because she was the mum and she was supposed to know what she doing—but forget any sense of continuity. No matter how much she tried to help them, her children would have a far less pleasant life than hers, and their children would have a life that was truly appalling, and that bleak truth was always there, just below the surface, as she floated along, telling herself, minute by minute, that everything was okay, that everything was the way it ought to be.

A shudder passed through Erica's body. Then she began to shiver. Her entire body was shaking. For the first time since she'd appeared in their hallway, she closed her eyes. Now her teeth were chattering so loudly they sounded like marbles shaken in a can. Tears trickled down from either side of her closed eyes.

"Hey, don't worry about anything," Avalon said. "We're going to take care of you."

"They're here," Drew said, his voice resigned and angry.

Devon was leading the Emergency crew in—a tall lean woman with short hair and a stocky dark man. They were wearing uniforms, the rain beading off their jackets. Drew was stepping right up to them as though he owned the situation. "An accident. We don't know how long—"

"Yeah, we saw the car," the man said.

"Stay out of their way, kids," Drew said. Karen wanted to smack him.

The lean woman went straight to Erica, knelt by her. "Somebody here has first-aid training," she said with an oddly cheerful grin.

"They're lifeguards," Jamie said.

"We're not certified yet," Morgan said with an apologetic shrug.

"Good girls." The lean woman took Erica's pulse, then wrapped a blood pressure cuff around her arm. At the same time her partner was fastening a broad collar around Erica's neck.

Erica was making a small keening sound like, "Ahhh, ahhh, ahhh . . ."

"It's all right," Avalon whispered, took Erica's hand and squeezed it. "I know it sucks, but it's gonna *protect* you." Still nobody had bothered to close the front door. Karen heard another car diving up.

Devon ran out to see who it was—"It's a fire truck!"—and here were four young guys in their Fire Department slickers, all of them trailing water all over the hardwood floor. My god, Karen thought, how many people does it take?

A million people were all talking at once. "When was the accident?" somebody was asking. "Where did it happen?"—and Drew was blathering on, making up a story out of nothing—he knew nothing—but the Emergency woman was taking Erica's blood pressure, and that's where Karen's attention ought to be. The woman had inserted some kind of gadget into Erica's ear; now she was checking its readout. She pursed her lips and exhaled. If a sound had accompanied that gesture, it would have been a whistle. "Let's move her right along," she said to her partner.

Time was suddenly collapsed—no longer lots of it, not much of it left at all. Maybe these people communicated like bees or ants—but they must be able to communicate somehow—because here were two of the firemen with a shiny chrome stretcher, or gurney, or whatever the hell it was, and they were moving Erica onto it, comforter and all. She began to wail like a child, "No, no, no!" They were strapping her down. She was reaching out blindly with one hand.

Avalon grabbed the hand. "We're right here, Erica. We're not going to leave you."

"Can we go with her?" Morgan asked the Emergency woman. "She's so scared."

The Emergency woman looked at Karen. *Sure*, Karen said with her eyes, with a nod.

"Okay. Come on, girls."

"You're gonna hear the siren," the stocky man said to Drew. "Sorry about that."

Out in that terrible night, the sounds of men working, their grunts and exhalations— "That's it . . . Okay, right . . . There you go"—and then they did hear the siren. It made several *oop, oop, oops,* and faded away. Wow, that was fast. The rain was still coming down hard—the steady sound of it had never let up.

The Emergency crew was gone, and the two firemen had come back, so now four of them were hanging around haplessly in Karen's hallway like leftover actors after the curtain's gone down. In their slickers and fancy gear, they looked like grown-up boys. For the moment, no one was saying a word. They were looking at her with expressions that were half apology, half sympathy—*We're the Fire Department and we love you*—and Karen felt the full force of how attached she'd become to Dr. Bauer—to Erica—in those few vital moments, but now she was gone, and the Lynas twins were gone right along with her, and she was sorry. She was suddenly angry and didn't know why.

"Don't worry," one of the firemen said. He seemed to be the one in charge. "We've called it in. They'll take care of everything."

Those strange and puzzling twins were all Erica had to help her through the labyrinth of Emergency, and they were just kids. "Is she going to have to—? The paperwork and everything. Maybe I should— It's going to take forever."

"No, it's not."

"They'll take her right in," another one said.

Karen couldn't let it go. "I've waited *for hours.*"

"No, no, she won't have to wait," he said, and Karen finally got it. No, of course Erica wouldn't have to wait. She might be dying.

IF YOU'RE THE MOTHER of four kids, you know all about Emerg—the home of calamity. There was nowhere to park near the entrance—at least nowhere you could leave your car for any great length of time, and you were most definitely going to be there for a great length of time. Karen parked where she always did, directly across the street from the hospital, and then, resigned, forced herself out into the rain and ran for it. That poor woman—how long had she been sitting in her wrecked car getting rained on? Why?

You would think that people would have enough sense to stay home on a night like this, but no—there was a whole row of sad wretched souls perched on chairs waiting to be admitted. Karen didn't want to see their pain so she walked quickly by without looking their way. Some people came here and died—what a happy thought. She knew the drill, bypassed the admitting nurse and went straight to the locked door that led inside where the sufferers were being treated. "I'm here for Erica Bauer," she said to the first nurse she saw, got a blank look. "She's got twins with her."

"Oh," with a grin of recognition, "the *twins*." Karen was buzzed through.

Miserable fucked-up sick people, injured people, maybe even dying people—and in spite of all that misery, the inner workings of Emerg always seemed to Karen maniacally cheerful. Maybe it was being busy busy busy in the middle of the night that did it, a shared camaraderie, a communal shield of denial against the downside of being human.

"Mrs. Oxley!" The twins were sitting on the floor in one of the little cubicles created with green curtains, but there was no sign of the patient. "Erica's gone to get X-rays."

"Here, kids. I brought you something to eat."

"Oh, Mrs. Oxley, you're so lovely."

"We're so hungry we can't even tell you."

Karen was getting the credit for it, but it had been Drew's idea to fill two Tupperware containers with rice, broccoli, and carrots and then nuke a layer of cheese on top. Drew was good at feeding people. He thought about it a lot.

"They warmed her up like really fast,"

"like wrapped all these things around her"

"and like dripped her full of warm stuff."

"They did it in front of you?"

"Oh, yeah. Like *right here*."

They were eating like they hadn't seen food in days, but they still managed to notice how uncomfortable she was. "We'll steal a chair for you, Mrs. Oxley," one said, and the other had already gone to get it. She really wished she could tell them apart.

Their dad was coming to get them, they said. It was taking him a while. He was all the way out in Langley or Ladner—someplace that started with an L. They were supposed to be at their mum's, but she never went out at night. What? Karen thought. Not even if your kids are stuck in Emergency? And what about Erica?

"She was so scared."

"She cried and cried."

"We filled out the forms for her."

"We had her purse so we knew what to say."

"They think we're like her relatives."

They were amazingly resourceful for girls their age. Maybe they didn't need Karen here, especially if their dad was coming. Maybe now that she'd fed them, she could just go home. But no, she knew perfectly well she was stuck—although she didn't know why. She hardly knew this annoying Erica Bauer person. A professor at a university—she must have friends or relatives or *somebody*. "Did you ask her if there was anybody you should call?"

"We tried to . . ."

"She can't really like, you know, answer things like that."

"What do you mean? She can't talk?"

"Yeah, she can talk, but it's like . . ." Neither twin seemed able to finish the sentence. Finally one of them said, "She's like dazed and confused."

That was exactly what Morgan had said when she'd made her 911 call. It sounded like a stock phrase, something they'd been taught to say. It could mean anything.

You weren't supposed to use your cellphone inside Emerg, but Karen did anyway, called Drew to let him know she'd be a while. Cam had come home, he said, so he was leaving. He had wall-to-wall meetings tomorrow, so he needed his sleep. He'd cleaned up the kitchen, the kids were all in bed, no problem. She didn't believe it for a minute. It wouldn't have killed him to spend the night. What was he thinking? Leaving Cam as the responsible adult? Utterly mad. The most responsible of the lot was Paige, but of course nobody would pay the least bit of attention to her because she was the youngest. Maybe that's who she should call next— no, she should probably call Jamie, although the one she'd get would be Devon, and he'd just say, "Sure, Mom" to everything. School in the morning. Monday. It was her turn to do the carpool. And here she was stuck in Emergency mysteriously responsible for someone she didn't know. Shit, it was all too much.

With no warning, a male attendant pushed through the curtain with a little bed on wheels. The twins leapt up, aiming bursts of high-pitched greetings at Erica—the kind of reassuring baby talk you'd use with a hurt dog or a child. Somebody had removed the protective collar from her neck, so at least that part of her must be okay.

Karen looked, and there it was again—that unsettling impression she'd had when Devon had first led this strange woman into the house—no way she could be an adult, she had to be a damaged girl. The rain had made Erica's dark hair spoing up into a tangle that framed her small valentine-shaped face. Her skin was appropriately pale for someone who might have been dying—had she been dying?—and her blue-grey eyes with startling black rings around the irises looked huge and sad. She didn't look out of it at all. Her eyes were fully awake, alive and alert.

"Dr. Bauer," Karen said, "are you feeling any better?"

Erica looked away, breaking eye contact—then, to make it even more emphatic, turned her head away.

Well fuck you too, Karen thought. You came in here stark mother naked, wrapped in a comforter. What if I just took the dry clothes I brought for you and went home?

"She won't talk now," one of the twins whispered into Karen's ear. "Except to us a little bit." Wonderful, Karen thought. It was just getting better and better.

The twins sat down on the floor. Now they were just as silent as the patient. The curtains were supposed to provide a little bit of privacy, but of course they didn't. The steady beehive hum of the whole place was clearly audible. I don't need this, Karen thought. Why didn't I bring a book? She closed her eyes and tried to lie back in her stiff nasty little chair. She could feel the muscles under her shoulder blades knotting up. Tomorrow she'd have to try to find time for a massage—

"Daddy!"—a man in a big thick industrial-grade yellow slicker with rain running off it. One moment he hadn't been there, and the next moment he was. He looked like one of the firemen who'd just been in Karen's front hall. "What's this?" he said, grinning.

The arrival of their father instantly transformed these calm resourceful girls into giddy children—talking so fast they were riding over each other.

"It's *our first rescue!*"

"We tried to do everything right . . ."

He had a big voice—not loud, but deep. "Good on you, girls."

"Nobody ever told us . . ."

"like what's normal, like we should . . ."

"she was going a hundred and ten . . . ?"

"You leave that to the doctors," he said and extended a hand to Karen. "I'm Bryan Lynas."

His mere presence seemed to have sucked all the space out of their little cubicle. To give herself room, Karen stood up. His hand was warm and rough, callused. He held hers a moment and then let go. He had bright blue eyes like his daughters, but a different shade—darker, with a glint like pewter—and he was checking her out in an absolutely open, unapologetic, unabashed way. Annoyed at him, and at herself, she'd instinctively drawn her shoulders back and tightened her stomach muscles. She was being subjected to the Male Gaze—as she'd learned to call it in university. She'd always thought that she was a bad feminist because there were times when she loved the Male Gaze—incited it and played to it—but other times she found it just as creepy as she was supposed to. It depended entirely on who was doing the gazing. She liked it better if it wasn't quite this explicit. "I'm Karen Oxley," she said—and maybe she'd made her voice a bit too cool. "Jamie and Devon's mother."

"You can see whose dad I am." He had a nice laugh. It sounded genuine.

When you're flustered, default to the weather, so she asked him if it was still raining. "Like pitchforks and hammer handles." Now she was checking him out, trying to find a niche to put him in. He had some kind of an accent, but she couldn't place it yet. She guessed him to be about her age—maybe a year or two older. Kids who go to fancy-ass private schools like Palmerston don't usually have tradesmen for fathers, but that's what he looked like—baggy khaki pants and battered workman's boots, the steel-toed kind. Full head of hair that hadn't seen a brush lately—like his girls, a ginger, but not their flaming carrot-top, darker, a ruddy near-brown with flecks of grey in it—and like his girls, freckled, but not their cute spattering across cheeks and noses, *seriously* freckled—little brown spots all over his face, even on his lips, on his hands. He had really attractive laugh lines around his eyes. Maybe she would like him.

"Fill me in, girls," he said. "Who's the victim?"

Stereophonic twins were falling all over themselves to tell him—"the lady from the university . . . you know, Dad, like the one . . . She studies *twins* . . . we went to see her . . . Dev and Jamie went . . . had *hypothermia* . . . no, in Dev and Jamie's driveway . . . like *totaled—*"

A very angry nurse suddenly rammed her head through the curtain. "Girls! Please! You've got to keep it down. There are sick people here."

They shut up as quickly as if somebody had hit an off switch. Their father dropped an arm over each, drawing them to him. He winked at Karen—meaning what? "I reckon we're going for a little walk," he said. "You right?"

It took her a moment to understand that what he'd just asked her was a serious question. "As right as I'm ever going to be."

"Yeah," he said, and she finally nailed his accent. Nobody said "yeah" like an Australian. Shit. Aussie men were the worst unreconstructed macho pigs in the universe.

They'd walked away and left her? Just like that? No, the kids' coats were still in a heap on the floor next to the dirty Tupperware. Karen had lost track of Erica for a moment, saw that she was simply lying there with her eyes closed. She might as well be sound asleep—although Karen knew that she wasn't—and somebody was being stashed in the cubicle to the left of them. From the sound of the wheezy dim voice, it was an old man. His wife must be helping him. He was saying something about pillows. It was a big deal—the pillows. He was having trouble breathing. He couldn't lie back too far—he needed more pillows. This is too sad, Karen thought. I shouldn't be hearing this.

Then Bryan Lynas and his daughters were back. They were so quiet now that she hadn't heard them coming. Each twin had a can of pop from the machine in the waiting area. He gave Karen a nod—a friendly acknowledgment—and leaned over Erica's bed.

"Cat got your tongue tonight?" he said. She didn't open her eyes or acknowledge him in any way.

He slammed his hands onto the mattress so hard the bed bounced. Erica's eyes popped open. Karen was shocked. What on earth was he doing?

He was bending so close to Erica that their faces were only a couple of feet away. It wasn't that he was staring at her; it was more like he was examining her inch by inch. Erica's eyes flashed—offended, outraged— but she said nothing. He studied her for a while longer, then straightened up and turned away. With a huge snorting laugh, he said, "She's lost the plot, girls."

"Who the hell are you?" Erica yelled at him.

"Who's asking?" he yelled back.

A violent emotion splashed across Erica's face but Karen couldn't read it.

"If you don't find your voice, my friend," he said to her in an ordinary conversational tone, "they're going to keep you here, and you won't like it one little bit."

He reached inside one of the pockets in his slicker, produced a damp business card, and handed it to Karen. "You need any help with her car, give me a call. I take care of things like that."

The twins had gathered up their coats. "Good night, Mrs. Oxley. Thank you, Mrs. Oxley," and then, with no more goodbyes than that, they were gone. So what had just happened?

She looked to Erica, prepared to start a conversation, to say something, anything at all, offer some kind of sympathy for whatever weird shit had just gone down, and Erica's eyes did meet hers for a moment, making genuine contact—but then she must have changed her mind. Her face blanked out. She turned her head away. You stubborn little bitch, Karen thought.

Karen looked down at the card in her hand. It was recycled paper, rough and beige. "Bryan Lynas," it read, "serving the North Shore since 1998," and there was his number. It started with 778, so it had to be a cell.

Nowhere on the card did it say what he did. What a strange rude man—but he'd sure got a reaction out of Erica.

The curtain in their cubicle flapped open again, and a nurse pushed through it—the same one who'd shushed them earlier. A small dark disheveled woman in a lab coat followed a step behind her and stopped abruptly. "I am Dr. Tomescu," she said, addressing no one in particular, and then to Erica, "You are feeling better." It didn't sound like a question, and Erica didn't answer.

The nurse was simply waiting, her face stripped of any expression whatsoever. She was holding two paper cups. The doctor was staring at Erica, obviously expecting a response. Then, giving up, she turned to Karen. "She is stable. Her X-rays are good. She have bruises and abrasions but no major trauma. When she come to us, she is in much distress. She have hypothermia but not severe. We warm her. She is normal."

"Okay," Karen said. "That's good news."

Now the doctor was talking to Erica. "I have no need to keep you longer here. I give you something to calm you, and then you may go home."

Erica still said nothing. "It is all good, yes?" the doctor said.

The doctor's jacket-like thing might not have been a lab coat at all but some non-medical piece of clothing that only resembled a lab coat. It was an unpleasant greeny-beige, clean enough, but looked like it had been slept in for a few nights running. She'd pinned her dark hair up with a series of clips, seemingly at random, and it was poking out here and there in unruly tufts. Now that Karen had a chance to take a good look at her, she was surprised to see that her thin weasely face was actually quite attractive.

The nurse was still just as silent as Erica, but she was offering her one of the paper cups. "What's this?" Erica said.

Hey, that's good, Karen thought, she's going to talk after all.

"You should not be alone," the doctor said. "There are people at home where you go?"

"No," Erica said. "I live alone."

"It's all right," Karen said, "she can stay with me." My god, she thought, what am I saying? But it didn't feel like she had any choice.

"You are the sister?"

"No," Karen said, "she's a friend of the family, but that's—"

Erica's voice rode over her—loud, sharp, and angry. "Wait a minute. What are you giving me?"

"Clonazepam," the doctor said. "It will make you calm."

"I don't want to take Clonazepam."

"Why?"

"It's highly addictive."

"Addictive? To be addictive, you must take every day for many days. I give you point-five milligram this one time. You will not be addictive."

Erica and the doctor seemed to be locked into a staring contest. "You are Dr. Bauer, yes?" the doctor said.

The question seemed to have startled Erica. She began to say something but stopped. In a barely contained fury, the doctor seized Erica's chart and poked at it with an index finger. "It says here you are doctor."

"They shouldn't have written that. I'm a psychologist, not a medical doctor—"

"My treatment," the doctor said. "You do not agree?"

It took Erica a moment to find an answer. "I don't want to interfere with my cognitive functions."

"When I first see you, Dr. Bauer, you are in distress. You are in *considerable* distress. You weep. You are incoherent. You speak of death. You say your accident is continually before your eyes—"

"That's not what I said."

"If you do not take this, Dr. Bauer, you will suffer needlessly. You will suffer pain. Your accident will continually before your eyes. This is a safe drug. It is good to interfere with your cognitive functions tonight, yes?"

The two women stared bleakly at each other. One thing that Dr. Tomescu and Dr. Bauer had in common, Karen thought, was an utter lack of the light touch.

"You take it now, it will last tomorrow. You take it now, you will be calm. You will rest. Your sister will take care of you. And then you will see your family physician. This is all good, yes?"

Erica held the doctor's eyes a moment longer. Then a slithery guilty look passed across her face. She scraped the pill out of the paper cup, popped it into her mouth, and chased it down with the water the nurse was offering.

Satisfied, Dr. Tomescu stepped back. "You do not drink alcohol. You do not drive a motor vehicle."

"I know what a benzodiazepine is," Erica said.

The doctor scrawled something onto a prescription pad and offered it to Karen. "You give to her this for pain as needed, yes? You also give to her vitamin D. You also take vitamin D." She snatched the paper back before Karen could take it. "Here, I write it for you. All Vancouver people have this deficiency. It can cause cancer. Please believe me this is true."

The doctor offered the revised prescription, and Karen took it. "Thank you, doctor," she said automatically.

"You are most welcome. I am most happy to meet you."

The doctor walked briskly out with the nurse following her. Karen was left with Erica. What if she doesn't talk to me? Karen thought. "I brought you dry clothes," she said.

Erica was sitting up on the edge of the bed. She didn't meet Karen's eyes. "I should go home," she said. She sounded exactly like a sullen teenager.

"I don't think so." Karen handed her the lululemon bag.

"I can get a cab."

"Forget it. Everything's fine. You're coming home with me, and you're getting a good night's sleep, and you can take it from there."

Erica got up, dumped the contents of the bag onto the bed, shrugged off her medical gown. She obviously didn't have any problem with people seeing her naked. The seat belt–shaped bruise had turned a spectacular rainbow of colours. She had the hard neat little body of somebody who worked out.

"Everybody wants me drugged, so I'm drugged," she said, not really addressing Karen. Then she seemed to register that none of the clothes were hers, gave Karen a look of recognition—like she'd met her before, might actually know who she was. "This is so kind of you. Thank you."

"You're welcome," Karen said.

Everything fit, even the shoes. "Oh my god, I've made so much trouble for you," Erica said. "So much trouble for everybody. I'm so sorry."

"It's okay," Karen said.

"Maybe she gave me a placebo. I don't feel a thing. I really am sorry. I can call a cab."

"Just come home with me, all right? It's late."

Erica didn't speak again until they were outside on the street. The rain was still hammering down like doomsday. "Oh god," Erica said, "I can't stand this." Karen walked as quickly as she could, glancing back to make sure that Erica was following her.

As Karen was unlocking the passenger door, Erica said, "This is way too much trouble for you. Way too much. Let me go back and—"

Karen said exactly what she would have said to Jamie if she was being difficult—"Get in the fucking car."

THEY WERE ON THE Upper Levels approaching the Caulfeild exit. Nobody else was on the highway—it was after one in the morning—but it was still like a monsoon up there, and Karen had to keep it down to sixty. Erica had been silent since they'd started driving. She'd pressed one hand over her eyes, contracted her body into a tight knot. She looked like she was trying to make herself motionless, or invisible, but now she made a sound like a throaty gasp. "What?" Karen said. "Are you all right?"

"Holy crap! This drug's not kidding."

"Not kidding how?"

"It's hard to describe. Like my whole body's been poured full of warm honey."

"That sounds delightful"—and presumably, if you're been poured full of warm honey, you won't make any trouble for anybody and you'll go straight to bed like a good girl. But Erica was suddenly talkative. "Everybody's being so nice to me, and I've been such a bitch."

I'm glad you noticed, Karen thought. She was finally drifting down the long sweet curve that would take her off the highway and lead her home. She was so tired that even the soles of her feet ached. If she went straight to bed, she could get almost six hours of sleep, but as she was pulling into the driveway, Erica said, "Wait. Please. Can I look at my car?"

Karen stopped behind the wrecked Golf, shining her headlights on it. Erica jumped out, paused a moment to glance back at Karen with a loopy somewhere-else grin. "Yow, am I ever sore!" she said and sounded almost happy. That must be some drug, Karen thought.

Erica had reflexively pulled up her hoodie, was now a shrouded figure, a lunatic image darting around the wrecked car in the brilliant white-yellow headlights, the rain straight silver lines drawn by hand, a surreal film clip that didn't belong anywhere in any life that Karen knew anything about. The sound of the windshield wipers was hypnotic, reminded her of something else—that steady swish-thud. Was it the surf? No, not the surf, but like something like it. Oh, hurry up.

Erica got back into the BMW, and Karen drove into the garage. "It's fucked, isn't it? My poor car?"

"Yeah. Toast. Drew was surprised you could even drive it." But of course Erica wouldn't know who Drew was. She should probably explain it, but she didn't have the energy—any more than she had the energy to ask why Erica had been parked in their driveway in the first place.

"It's sad, I guess. It was really hard to get that model in that year in that exact colour of blue. I thought it'd be fairly common, but it wasn't. I had to go all the way to Coquitlam to get it. Now how am I going to get to school? . . . I'm sorry, but . . . I don't want to be a bother. Any more than I am already. But do you suppose I could have something to eat?"

"Sure," Karen said, "no problem." So much for the notion of dumping her in the guest room and going straight to bed.

As they were walking across the open area on the main floor, Erica said, "My god, it's spectacular!"

What was spectacular? Oh, the view through the wall of windows— you could see from the Lions Gate Bridge across to Kits, the glowing jewels of the night blurred behind the rain. Yes, it was a fabulous view. It was sad how living with it made you stop seeing it.

Karen stared into the fridge. There was always something left over—usually one of the infinitely expandable wodge casseroles that Claire made on the days when she came in. "Mac and cheese?" she said. "Broccoli and carrots. How about a lamb chop?"

"That sounds lovely."

Oh, she wants *everything*, does she? Karen made up the plate, shoved it into the microwave. "The first time I was here," Erica was telling her, "I just couldn't believe it. It was like walking onto a movie set—"

Just to keep things interesting, here were the twins entering just at the edge of the kitchen light. For a moment they looked exactly like they wanted to—indistinguishable—but as they got closer, they resolved into distinct kids, Jamie the taller one.

"Erica!" Devon said. "Are you okay? We were so worried about you." Sometimes he sounded positively adult. When he'd first come to live with them, he'd worn pajamas, but now, like his sister, he slept in extra-long T-shirts—in fact, the pastel-striped one he was wearing *was* Jamie's. Did it matter? Probably not. Gemini forever.

Jamie seemed to be her standard sullen self, scowling and awkward, and Karen felt a pang. She wanted to wipe away the darkness from her daughter's face. Poor kid—she was so closed off. It couldn't be much fun being her.

To Karen's surprise, Erica hugged both kids. She was telling them that she was fine—telling them in some detail, actually. "You aren't leaving, are you?" Jamie asked.

"Go back to bed," Karen said because it was what she had to say.

"Don't leave till we get home tomorrow, okay?" Jamie said. It sounded like an order. Where did she get that stuff? Did she think the whole universe revolved around her?

"Bed," Karen said. "I mean it. Now."

The twins were gone, but they'd left behind strands of themselves—the adventure of something different, brand-new, in the middle of the mysterious night, and Karen had enough of the twelve-year-old left in her to feel it too. Her perfectly ordinary kitchen had been "defamiliarized"—a word she'd learned as an English major a million years ago. "They're wonderful kids," Erica was saying, "I'm very fond of your kids."—eating up the lamb chop, each carefully cut-up bit of it added to a forkful of macaroni, talking in between bites. "Haven't eaten much of anything for . . . god, I can't even remember."

The drug had turned Erica into an absolute chatterbox. "It all tastes *so good!* I've got to stop living on TV dinners—" and on she went, talking about food, about cooking, about how she'd never learned to cook—obviously stoned out of her mind. Karen wanted sleep like a drowning person wants air.

Erica suddenly stood up—or tried to—and sat right back down again. "Yow! I'm dizzy— It's weird, but I keep— Do you suppose I could take a shower? I feel absolutely grotty." She steadied herself on the table top and stood up slowly.

"Can you walk?"

"Yeah, I guess so. Everything's kind of . . . Shaky? Fuzzy? Wobbly? Blurry?"

"I get it," Karen said.

Okay, so she couldn't very well show her the downstairs bathroom and abandon her. She took her by the hand, led her upstairs into her own bedroom, lit the light, and deposited her on the edge of the bed. "Just stay there, okay?"

But instead of simply staying there, Erica shed her clothes. "Are all these yours? They fit me. And you're so much taller. Do you always wear this yoga stuff? Maybe I should buy some. It's so comfortable. Our feet must be the same size. You're being so nice to me. Wow, am I ever out of it. I can't even think straight."

Karen turned on the shower and adjusted the water temperature. She didn't want Erica to scald herself. She led her in and held onto her until she was safely under the water. "There's shampoo right there if you want it."

"I'm a little bit impaired."

"Impaired. Right. Not to mention that your cognitive functions are interfered with. Be careful."

Karen left the bathroom door open. How had she ended up with this wacko lady in her shower? She might as well sit on the bed while she waited, but once she was there, she simply fell over. Even as she was drifting off, she was still listening. She heard the water stop, but she couldn't pull herself together fast enough. She heard a loud clunk, jumped up, ran straight in, and found Erica hanging onto a towel rack. She caught her under the arms.

"Oh my goodness." Erica had partially dried herself, but her body was still moist and warm. She was trying to smile. Her eyes were enormous. "I'm okay if I don't try to do anything."

"You could say that about a lot of people."

Karen grabbed up another of the clean towels and began to pat her with it. She had to be careful around that nasty bruise. "All my emotions are stripped away," Erica told her in a small precise voice. "It's strange. It's a very odd sensation. It's dangerous. I've got a whole bottle of Clonazepam at my place. I've never taken one. It has some serious side effects."

"Is that right?"

"I'm so glad my birthday is over. It was so very hard for me. It was my birthday, you know. The fifteenth of November. It was my first birthday without my sister. She was killed in an accident. It's so hard for me. But I can't feel it now."

Her birthday? Her sister? Karen was so tired it was taking her a beat to catch up—but then she did. Oh my god, what could she possibly say? No wonder this poor girl was such a mess. "I'm so sorry about your sister."

"Thank you. You're being so kind to me."

Karen had her dried—or at least most of her dried—so now what was she going to do with her? The accident, the hypothermia, the stress, the grief—whatever—had smeared dark smudges under Erica's eyes, and her face was deathly pale. Some girls wore makeup to look like that—ethereal, damaged, exquisite. What an odd thing to be thinking at a time like this. Karen had to say something more. Any of the standard clichés would do. "It's really hard to lose someone that close to you."

"She was my twin."

Karen was too tired—too worn down—to be able to roll with that one. Her eyes filled.

Erica's eyes filled too. "I can still feel something," she said. "Isn't that amazing?" With careful fingertips, she wiped the trickle of tears away from Karen's eyes—first from her left eye, then from her right.

Everything normal was pretty much shot to hell. "What was her name?" Karen asked.

"Annalise. If you want to know what she looked like, look at me."

This strange woman couldn't possibly know how beautiful she was. "Oh, dear," Karen said, "let's get you to bed."

Jamie slept in extra-long T-shirts because her mum did. Karen gave Erica a clean one. The master bedroom was enormous—so big that Karen's king-sized bed didn't seem the least bit too much for it. On the nights when Drew had a bottle of wine in him—thrashing around and snoring up a storm—it still wasn't big enough. Had he slept in it since Claire had changed the sheets? No, he hadn't. She turned down the right side of the bed. Erica climbed in. Karen covered her up. "You're so kind." Then she was asleep. Just like that.

It was nearly three o'clock in the fucking morning. Karen was so wrought-up, she considered taking a zopiclone but then thought, to hell with it, stripped down to her tank top, threw her clothes anywhere, got into her side of the bed, and turned out the light.

9.

THE STORY WOULD GO racing around their little group like wildfire—"Karen fell asleep in Sunrise Yoga. She was even snoring."

"Come on, I wasn't really snoring, was I?"

"You were, actually."

Oh, for fuck's sake. Karen did not care at all for that image of herself—zedded out in a room full of stretching middle-aged ladies, demonstrating to the lot of them that she simply couldn't take it anymore. The only way to overwrite a story like that was to make it even better. "I'm utterly thrashed," she said. "I've got a psychologist asleep in my bed."

"In your bed?" Jen said. "You'll have to tell me about that one."

Yes, she would, and that was the point. Karen's role in their little group was that of the hapless person things *happened to*—"Oh, with Karen it's always something," they said—but it wasn't that her life was any more bizarre than anybody else's; it was that she, the most of any of them, loved to make her life into stories. She'd been doing it since high school.

She began with the most dramatic moment—Devon leading Erica into the house. "Otherworldly," she called it, "like a Gothic horror movie." She was pleased to see that Jen was all ears.

Karen and Jen were where they always were after Sunrise Yoga— in Delany's. Karen was drinking what she always drank—a skinny latte with a triple shot. They were two-fifths of their tight little group—Karen, Jen, Gudrun, Sandy, and Amy—a particular clique of grown-up West Van girls who had been playing an ongoing game of one-upsmanship with each other for— She hated to think about it, but yes, it really had been *thirty years!*

They had all been married—some of them several times—and they had all acquired children. Some were still married, and some were not. Jen was the only one who had no man in her life at the moment. She defended herself by repeating that ancient feminist joke—"a woman needs a man like a fish needs a bicycle"—and laughing heartily. She fooled no one.

Karen did have a man in her life, and from the outside, Drew looked pretty good. None of the ladies would ever be so crass as to talk about money, but that didn't mean they weren't aware of it, and Karen was doing okay in that category, too. She had clearly won the hot bod competition, the result of lucky genes and a ridiculous amount of work—power walking, yoga, Pilates, and torture sessions with her maniacal personal trainer—and she had the best house of the lot of them—well, that was debatable, but hers had the highest assessed value—and she had the most children, but with three fuck-ups out of four, she was definitely not winning the brilliant-and-successful-kids prize, although she still might have a chance with Paige who seemed determined to outshine all the stars in the firmament.

But in the overall score Karen was still losing to fabulous Gudrun who was hard to beat. Gudrun had the kind of blank Nordic good looks that dressed up nicely, and she'd recently undergone the most tasteful of facelifts from the finest of California cosmetic surgeons. Gudrun was married to a dazzling cinematographer who made, as Gudrun liked to put it, "an obscene amount of money." Gudrun's son number one had a full scholarship to the University of Michigan, and son number two, the charming witty one, was about to go off to LA to learn how to DJ, all expenses paid, of course, by Dad. Gudrun lived in a beautifully restored character home, did gourmet cooking in her custom-built kitchen with granite counter tops, and hosted legendary dinner parties at which you met minor movie stars, BC Liberal politicians, and Americans. Gudrun as top pussycat meant that the social order of their little group hadn't changed in any significant way since high school. Meanwhile, Karen and Jen had never entirely shaken off their reputation as the misfits, the come-latelies, the wannabes—and they were united now, as always, by the simple fact that they both loathed Gudrun.

Karen had known Jen longer than any of the other women—since kindergarten, actually—so she and Jen shared a lot of history. They might both have been accepted into Gudrun's little clique, but their years before that had been a hell they wished they could forget. If Karen remembered Jen as a fat, red-faced, blubbering nerd whose mother sent her to school in utterly *disastrous* outfits—corduroy dresses in various shades of purple—then Jen remembered Karen as a scrawny big-eyed rodent in baggy jeans, flat as a boy, trapped in a recalcitrant body that adamantly refused to get its period. Now, when they met alone for coffee, they talked like each was the other's best friend.

"There's just one thing I don't get," Jen was saying. "What was she doing in your driveway in the first place?"

"Now that's the big question, isn't it? I haven't got a clue. The twins swear on everything sacred they had nothing to do with it."

"Do you know anything about her?" Jen leaned closer across the table, her eyes sparkling. "I mean *really* know anything? What if she's crazy? What if she's stalking you?"

"Why would she do that?"

Jen shrugged. Karen shrugged back.

"I'll keep you in the loop," Karen said, which meant that she would be keeping *all* of the ladies in the loop. Karen had got exactly what she wanted. The next time they had one of their jolly girls-only dinners, she would be the star entertainment, proving once again that she had a hell of a lot more interesting life than they did.

The story that Karen had not told Jen, or any of the ladies, or *anybody*

134

for that matter, was about the visit from the social worker. Both Erica and a colleague had heard Jamie's suicide threat, so they'd had no choice. University regulations required that it be reported to the Ministry of Children and Family Development.

"Thanks a fuck of a lot," Karen had said to Jamie. "You broke it, you fix it. When the social worker shows up, she'd better think you're happy happy happy."

"I *am* happy happy happy," Jamie had said.

The social worker was quite young—a large woman, plain and earnest—and Karen could see by the stunned expression on her face that she'd never before set foot in one of West Van's high-end houses. Karen served tea and brownies and made an effort to be charming and down-to-earth. Of course she knew how much the twins wanted to stay together, she told the woman, but no, she'd never heard a single word about suicide.

The twins earned themselves a pair of Oscars that day. They wore their Palmerston uniforms, and Jamie was *immaculate*—her kilt straight from the dry cleaner's bag, even her knee socks pulled up. "It was a joke," she told the social worker.

"Yeah," Devon said, "like kids say all the time? 'Oh my god, I'm gonna kill myself!'"

"Yeah," Jamie said, "like kids say, 'Should I kill myself now or later?' That's the way we talk . . . you know, like a joke. If we really meant it, we wouldn't say it."

The social worker talked to each twin alone and then had a second chat with Karen. Things were going so well by then that they were on a first-name basis. Karen was able to commiserate with Margaret about the budget cuts and her insane caseload. They even shared a few wry anecdotes about what a bizarre place West Vancouver was—Margaret was from Surrey. "It's up to my supervisor," Margaret kept saying. She must have said it four or five times. But supervisor or not, Karen knew that it was highly unlikely that she would ever see Margaret again. It was a shame that she couldn't tell this story to the ladies. With a few choice embellishments and a properly timed delivery, it could have been one of her better ones.

KAREN LEFT THE BMW out because she would need it later. As soon as she walked into the house, she smelled bacon frying. Then she saw that Erica, the spectre, had at least made it out of bed. Still wearing Karen's lululemons, she was sitting passively at the kitchen table watching Cameron make breakfast, and that wasn't merely incredible, it was drop-down-in-a-fit incredible. "You want anything, Mum?" Cam asked her.

"No, but thanks for offering. Did you sleep okay?" she asked Erica.

"Haven't slept this well in months. Thank you."

Karen waited, her psychic antennae tuned for nuance. "I guess I must've been hydroplaning," Erica said to Cam.

"Awesome," he said.

Oh, right, they must have found the only possible thing they had in common to talk about—motor vehicle accidents. "How are you feeling?"

"I don't know. That crazy doctor was right about the Clonazepam. It lasts on into the next day. I'm barely functional." She sounded barely functional—flat as an ironed sheet.

"Are you planning on going to school today?" Karen asked her son.

"I've got a spare."

The hell you do, she thought.

"I'm sorry, Mum," he said with his usual self-deprecating smirk, "I'm failing life."

He was right on that one. Cam and his accidents. They'd ranged from the piss-ass stupid to the magnificently stupid—from the *two* times he'd brought the Lexus home missing its right-hand mirror to the night he'd managed to bounce it off half a dozen parked cars on their own street. And then, of course, there was the broken axle. How do you break an axle? He'd been just as puzzled as everyone else. "I don't know . . . Jeez, I just drove off a curb." That must have been one hell of a curb.

At seventeen Cam was taller than his father, taller than anybody else in the house, and still growing. No matter how recently he'd bought a shirt, the sleeves were always too short. He had an Adam's apple as prominent as if he'd swallowed a tennis ball and a light splatter of acne across his face. He always seemed to be sorry about something, and it wasn't an act—he really *was* sorry. Well, okay, he might be a bit of a disaster, but he never bothered anybody, and he didn't have a mean bone in his body. And he was handy—the only one who knew how to turn off the water when they had a leak, the only one who could be cajoled into changing light bulbs or plunging toilets. Now he'd actually made breakfast for Erica. From his point of view it must be the ideal breakfast—a fresh pot of coffee, a dozen slices of heavily buttered toast, and all the bacon that had been left in the fridge.

"I can't seem to find my cell," Erica was saying, looking at Karen with eyes like empty circles. "I guess it must be in my car? I need to call the university? It's hard for me to get started?"

Karen handed her the kitchen portable. No matter how old she was, Erica really did look like a high-school girl, and she was obviously in need of rescue. No wonder Cam had made her breakfast. "Do you need anything?" Karen asked her. "Have you thought about what to do with your car?"

Zero response. Okay, another problem for Karen. That rude Aussie had said he could take care of it. Where was his card? In the *other* lululemon top. It must be on the floor in the bedroom. "Be right back," she said.

Even in chaos, Karen always remembered where things were, and none of her clothes were where she'd tossed them. Oh, there they were—neatly folded and laid out on the cedar chest—and Erica had also raised the blinds and made the bed. Karen retrieved the card, and while she was upstairs, thought that she might as well have a quick look at her agenda book. She picked it up but didn't open it. The monsoon rain had blown through, leaving Vancouver with its standard November drizzle. The light was pearly, iridescent, and perfectly designed for someone who wanted to spend the day drowsing in bed with a pot of Earl Grey tea and her laptop—but that was not going to happen. Was Cam actually going to school today?

Striding into the kitchen with a purpose, she said, "Where's Cameron?"

"I think he's gone out." Erica was standing at the kitchen sink directly in front of the window, rinsing off the breakfast dishes and putting them in the dishwasher. "Somebody picked him up. Two boys in a silver Infiniti."

A silver Infiniti? Karen had seen that car before. Cam used to introduce her to his friends, but he didn't any more. Hopeless, Karen thought and sank onto a chair.

"Thank you for letting me sleep with you," Erica said in her computer-generated voice. "That was very kind."

"It's a big bed," Karen said. "Is there any more of that coffee?"

Erica poured her a cup. The milk was already on the table.

"Erica? Can I ask you—? Where on earth were you, that you—? I mean how did you manage to get hypothermia?"

Karen might as well have been looking into the eyes of a cat for all the reaction she got. "I was, um . . . just in my car. I must have been getting rained on. The windows were down."

"Why were the windows down?"

"I had to— It was full of smoke? I guess from the air bag. Once I got them down, they wouldn't go back up again. They were . . . you know . . . the mechanism must have broken."

How long had she been sitting in the car? But no, it was best to skip that one and move right along to the really big question. "Okay, but why were you in my driveway?"

"I was, oh, driving around randomly, trying to get through our birthday. And then I had the accident. I got off the highway, and I was in West Van. You're the only people I know here. I thought I could use your phone."

That bogus explanation had been thoroughly rehearsed. "Okay," Karen said, "but why didn't you get out of the car?"

"I don't know. Exactly. I guess I was in shock."

She's lying to me, Karen thought. Why is she doing that?

BACK UPSTAIRS in her bedroom, Karen knew what she was supposed to do next—sit down at her desk with her agenda book—but she was bleary-ass tired and irritable as a cat, an utterly lethal combination. She needed to organize her mind, and there was no reason why she couldn't do that lying down.

Yes, stretched out on the bed was better. Okay, what? Pay some bills, call her mother, get that squashed car out of her driveway— She had done the morning drop-off at Palmerston, so some other mum, probably

Lauren's mum, would do the run from Palmerston to Mal—as the kids called the Malveaux Academy of Dance—and then she would do the pickup. Did she have to get sushi for dinner? No, this was a Claire day, so they'd all get treated to another round of British poverty cooking. And the twins? Did Jamie have a one-on-one? No, they'd changed the day. Now it was Wednesdays. So the twins would get home on their own— and before she got any farther, Karen really should check her agenda because there was always something floating loose— Did she have a hair appointment?

Karen hated daytime dreams—especially ones like this one in which part of her was still awake and knew perfectly well that she was dreaming. Her house had become as elastic as chewing gum, and she had stretched out one side of it to look underneath, and there was a big lump like a pillow under a blanket— Well, no, it wasn't exactly like that; it had something to do with the earth under the foundation, but whatever, it was truly unpleasant, and she knew it wasn't real at all because she was also aware of herself lying flat on her back on her bed with a T-shirt over her eyes.

"Karen?" She had been so sound asleep she might as well have been smothered. She brushed away the T-shirt and looked. Erica, strange Dr. Bauer, was touching her lightly on the arm.

"I'm sorry," Erica said. "Your mother's here."

Oh for screaming fuck's sake. "Okay," Karen said. "Tell her— I'll be down. Just give me a minute."

"I'm making her tea. Is that okay?"

"Yes, yes, yes. That's just lovely."

Do not go back to sleep, Karen told herself firmly but then she did— awoke with a jerk, grabbing the bed to stop herself from falling. Her time sense told her that it couldn't have been more than ten or fifteen minutes. She levered herself upright, propelled herself into the bathroom, splashed her face with cold water, brushed her hair, popped two Advil, and picked up her agenda book.

It was her own fault. If you copy the entry that says "call Mum" from each day's undone list to the next day's to-do list, and you do that every day for five or six days running, you get Mum herself. "Erica has been telling me all about studying twins. It's fascinating." Her mother was using that faintly frostbitten voice she reserved for members of her immediate family when they were behaving badly—like still being in bed at noon, for instance.

Erica had settled Karen's mum in the dining room, of all strange places, and had even managed to locate Grandmother McConnell's Royal Crown Derby—well, that wasn't so hard; all she had to do was look in the china cabinet. She'd also managed to locate the Savary Island oatmeal-raisin cookies, and that implied a fairly thorough examination of the kitchen cupboards, but however Erica had managed to do it, she and Karen's mum were taking tea like two ladies. Mum had dressed for the occasion. She was very much of the pantsuit generation—today it was a pale blue one—and she was wearing the string of lapis that Karen had given her on her last birthday, a nice gesture meant to say, *You see, I do appreciate your presents*. Karen sat down with them.

Erica directed at Karen something that appeared to be a thin smile, and Karen sensed a diffidence to her now, a quality nearly apologetic—but no, that wasn't right. Karen didn't know what to think.

"I've just been telling your mum that . . . With my kind of research . . . Okay, variance is a very difficult concept to get. My students always have a hard time getting it. If we say that half the variation in most human behaviours can be explained by genetic factors, that doesn't mean to say that we're half the product of our genes and half the environment."

Karen couldn't find anything to say to that. Was she supposed to? Erica's smile wasn't really a smile, and it wasn't really apologetic. She and Mum had been talking for how long? Forty minutes? An hour? Did Karen give a shit? She felt spiteful, groggy, out-of-sorts—doomed to spend the entire day out of phase with the world, a cog that wouldn't mesh.

Karen poured herself a cup of tea. There was even milk in the Derby creamer. Karen began to eat a cookie she didn't want. It had way too much sugar.

"But if you're fraternal twins, you can't really learn to be identical," Erica was saying. "Being an MZ twin *is* genetic. It's not something you can learn."

"That's right," Karen's mum said, "but it gives them something to do. Devon's sensitive like his mother. What's wrong with that? He won't always need to cling to his sister."

"He doesn't exactly cling to his sister," Karen said.

"It's just a phase," Mum told Erica, "Don't you think so?" but she didn't give Erica a chance to answer—"Jamie's not so bad. You were just as bad," she said to Karen. "Worse actually."

Oh, really? Karen thought. At least I wasn't getting interviewed by university professors and threatening to kill myself. "You don't have to live with her, Mum."

Her mother turned back to Erica—"Mothers and daughters, hah! They're too close to see it, but Karen and Jamie are as alike as two peas in a pod. The only difference between them is thirty years."

"I thought you thought it was *Paige* who's like me."

"Well, she is, but that's different. She's going to give you a lot more trouble than Jamie, that's for sure. With this mother-daughter business there's always a year or two of sheer hell. *Sheer. Hell.* Boys are far easier at that age. If you had a man in the house, he could take some of the—"

"A man? What? Drew doesn't count?"

"Drew Thompson? Don't make me laugh."

A little on the forthright side today, aren't you, Mum? "How's Dad?" Karen said to change the subject.

"I've got him taking his ginkgo twice a day. It really does help."

"I don't really think he's got memory problems. He was always—"

"There's nothing wrong with Jamie. She's just a tomboy like you were. You and that little Donlevy girl—"

"Patsy," Karen said.

"Speaking of twins," Mum said to Erica, "Karen and that little Donlevy girl liked to pretend they were twins. I'd almost forgotten that. They actually went around telling people they were twins. They didn't look even remotely alike. Whatever happened to her?"

"Patsy? She went to McGill. We kind of lost track of each other after that . . . But I wasn't really a tomboy. I was just socially inept."

As usual, her mother wasn't listening—she was just waiting for her turn to talk. "Then when Karen hit high school and the hormones hit *her* . . . all of a sudden we can forget the tomboy phase. Boys coming out of the woodwork, a whole new crowd of girls, and—"

"*Patsy* was the tomboy," Karen said. She didn't know why she needed to hang onto her point so doggedly. "I just followed along in her wake."

"If you think it's bad with Jamie, just wait. Paige is going to get her period right around the same time that you're losing yours, and then, whoo! lots of excitement around here . . . Oh, and before I forget. The vaccinations. That H1N1 boondoggle. You're not going to fall for that one, are you?"

"No, Mum. I've already told them—"

"So if it's all in the genes, you don't have to worry so much. They're good kids. All your kids are good kids." To Erica— "This must seem like quite a menagerie?"

"Oh, no. I'm from a big family— I never said it was all in the genes—"

"What's your ethnic background, if you don't mind my asking? Bauer? Is it a German name?"

"Oh yeah, but so far back it hardly counts."

"We're mostly Scots . . . but, yes, so far back that it hardly counts. Speaking of genes, Karen really surprised us. Those golden eyes! Chuck and I could never understand where they came from."

They were both staring at Karen. "The genetics of eye colour is much more complicated than we used to think," Erica said. "You can get almost any variation."

"And when Karen was little, she was so blonde she was almost *white*. She looked like she'd fluttered in from fairyland." But then she couldn't help adding, "But everything's got a downside. Blondes don't age well."

"Thanks, Mum, I really needed to hear that."

Blonde, Karen was thinking, and the word continued to toll like a bell at the back of her mind— *blonde, blonde, blonde*—and she finally opened her agenda book. "Oh my god," she said, "I *do* have a hair appointment."

BLONDE WAS RIGHT—if it had been just a wash and a style, she would have canceled it, but it was a colour. With blow-dryer and brush, Dakila was finishing her off, murmuring little words of approbation designed to reassure her that she had come out, once again, as really really *really* beautiful. No one, Dakila said, would ever believe that Karen was in her forties. No, no, no one. No one would ever believe it. No one, no one, ever.

Karen's body felt like a lump of mud under the pink plastic cape. It could have been a perfect two hours of time out of time—a perfect two hours to sleep—but she hadn't been able to sleep, had drowsed ineffectually, sipping yet another triple-shot latte she didn't need as her mind ground out the same stupid repetitive bullshit it usually produced when left to itself. Ah, this wretched beauty business. She'd stopped getting Brazilians when she and Rob had split up, so why was she still expending time, energy, and money to transform a perfectly attractive dark honey—not yet a single grey hair in it—into an aggressive colour she thought of as "trophy-wife blonde?" Probably because her pubes were private, but the hair on her head was public and had become an essential element of the Karen Oxley brand—and then, to her surprise, she was struck by something that felt like the kind of unexpected thought you would tell your therapist—if you still had a therapist. The person she'd created, the one staring back at her from the big bright mirror, was the person she'd wanted to be when she was fifteen. Too bad she wasn't fifteen.

From inside the pocket of her Burberry trench coat her cell emitted that discreet little chime that told her she'd just received a text message. It had been chiming off and on since she'd got there, but she'd been ignoring it. "Can you hand me that, please?"

Four missed calls, one from Devon and three from Jamie and then, last of all, the text. Because of Jamie's learning disability, texts were usually from Devon, but this one, fueled by teenage outrage, had come straight from the heart of the trouble:

ty mum y do u evn on a sellfon????

After a moment's study, she translated the message into: "Thank you, Mum. Why do you even own a cellphone?"

She paid Dakila—and for making her feel beautiful again, tipped her wildly too much—stepped outside the mall to find the day turned dark, bleak, and clammy, the morning's drizzle replaced by steady rain. O fucking November, you're going to kill me yet.

She called Jamie, heard the sound of her daughter choking on her own fury—"Where *are* you?"

143

"Park Royal. I just had my hair done."

"We've been calling and *calling* you. You've got to come and get us. We missed the bus."

"There's always another bus, sweetie."

"Not for an hour—" and Jamie imploded into incomprehensible fragments.

"Slow down, sweetie, wait a minute, what?"

But now it was Devon on the phone, his tone saying that he would make everything all right, explain it all. "We wanted to see Erica before she left—"

"Oh, for god's sake, I've got to get your sister." Mal and Palmerston were in two entirely different directions.

"It's okay, Mom. You've got plenty of time."

Time? Oh, really?

Up on the highway in the rain doing thirty clicks over the speed limit. Why? Because her kids had a grotesquely overblown sense of entitlement, that's why—and because she felt guilty about not answering her cell—what if they'd been hurt?—and then, of course, they weren't in the turnaround. She pulled up in front of the sign that read with characteristic Palmerston clarity: ABSOLUTELY NO STOPPING EVER. It was where she always picked them up. Now she was just as furious as Jamie— punched in her number. "Where are *you*?"

It was Jamie's cell, but Devon answered. "We *see you*, Mom. We're coming. We're inside. It's *raining*."

She watched them walking toward the BMW, not in a hurry at all, entwined in some seriously twin conversation. Jamie wore pants to school much of the time now, but she occasionally switched back to a kilt—deciding for no apparent reason, obviously nothing to do with the weather. Today it was one of last year's kilts—too short—and last year's ballerina flats too, beat to shit. Her knee socks had fallen down, and she looked unutterably scruffy. Both kids got into the back, reducing Karen to the role of chauffeur.

Up on the highway, Devon said, "Sorry, Mom. The vaccination made us miss the bus."

"What vaccination?"

"The H1N1."

"Wait a minute. I never signed the—"

"It's okay, Mom. We signed for you. We know you don't like signing things."

Karen was sure that if she tried to say anything at all, she'd lose it. She rode her full-blown fury all the way back to the house, sent the BMW rocketing up the driveway, and nearly hit an old grey panel truck that was parked next to Erica's squashed Golf. Erica herself was standing there in the rain, and so was the weird Australian. Erica waved, and the twins were already jumping out of the BMW, not bothering to say goodbye or thanks or a single fucking thing. I hate all of you, Karen thought.

But at least somebody was taking care of the Golf—that was a start—and she shot back down the driveway, headed for the highway where she'd just been. She was so angry she made it to Mal with a few minutes to spare, added herself to the long row of parked cars with waiting mums. Oh god, she thought, I can't cope—folded her seat back to nearly horizontal.

Karen woke with a crash as the door of the BMW slammed open. In a cloud of giggles half a dozen interchangeable skinny long-legged bunheads in pink tights were piling into the back. Karen knew the ones Paige's age—Megan, Ashley, Madison—and of course she knew Lauren—Lou-lou—who had recently achieved BFF status, but she couldn't keep the older girls straight. They changed from night to night. So maybe it was Emily, Emma, or Sydney in the back of the BMW. Or maybe it was Amanda, Kayla, or Mackenzie. She had to depend on Paige not to leave anyone behind, but that was okay because Paige knew every Mal girl on the North Shore, had befriended them all on Facebook and knew exactly where they lived right down to the most improbable twisty turn in the most remote cul-de-sac.

There must be some intelligible pattern in Paige's mind—drop the ones farthest away first—although Karen sensed immediately that something wasn't quite right. The day had undone her, and all she could do was drive like an automaton through the wretched rain. The first one—was it Kayla?—dropped all the way out beyond Eagle Harbour, jumping out of the BMW to chants of "Good night, good night," the girls making *call me* gestures. Following instructions, Karen went shooting back up above the highway for the next one—Mackenzie? Paige had created an ingenious pattern that must have its own strange logic, but it wasn't the way Karen would have done it—and then, at the end, it all became clear. They were nearly home and Lauren was still in the car. They should have dropped her right after they'd dropped Megan. "You know there's no visits on school nights," Karen said.

"She can go straight home after dinner," Paige said in the voice of Little Miss Innocence. "Isn't it a Claire night? Dinner will be all ready. Please, Mum, it's just this once."

"You manipulated me," Karen said. "I don't appreciate it."

But why should she bother with this—or, for that matter, why should she bother with anything? She piloted the BMW straight up her own driveway. "Lauren," she said, "call your mother."

ERICA'S SQUASHED CAR was gone, and so maybe Erica was gone too, but no such luck—she'd been enticed upstairs and into Twin Central. Whatever they'd been talking about—Karen had heard their animated voices—the conversation stopped dead when she walked into the room. All three of them turned to look at her. "Claire says we can eat any time we want," she told them—yes, you insufferable brats, it's *me*, your mother.

Nobody said a word. Erica, sitting on the edge of Devon's bed, had assumed what appeared to be her default position—an eerie cut-flower stillness that made her look lovely, mute, and helpless. It was unnerving actually. Then Jamie said to Erica, "Mum won't let us get a tattoo."

What a wonderful opening line. Did it relate to an ongoing conversation or was Jamie just dropping it in now apropos of nothing? "That's right, I won't," she said.

This was not a new topic. The twins had been talking about it for months, and every time Karen was sure they'd forgotten it, they brought it up again—they wanted to get the Gemini sign and each other's names tattooed onto themselves. Maybe it was a function of being twelve, but they seemed to have no ability to imagine a future. Karen had tried to paint them a vivid picture of how awkward it would be explaining to a boyfriend/girlfriend why they had their brother/sister's name tattooed onto their shoulders, but it didn't compute. Now she said what she always said: "No way. Tattoos are forever."

Jamie said what *she* always said: "*Twins* are forever."

"How about the Gemini sign without our names?" Devon said.

"What? You want to permanently brand yourselves as twins?"

"Why not? We're *permanent* twins."

"As hard as it might be for you to believe this, there's going to come a time when you won't want—"

"Just a *small* Gemini sign. Lots of kids—"

"No way. Look, I don't care if—"

"We want to get pierced too, and Mum won't even let us do that. Lots of kids have piercings."

The mere thought of piercing made Karen queasy. "What is this?" she said. "Body modification night? I'm sure Erica doesn't—"

"Maybe we should get our earlobes pierced . . . big deal."

"You've got to get it done with a needle, like—"

"*Everybody's* got their earlobes pierced—"

"If you do it with a gun, you can get HIV."

"Mum? You always said I could get my ears pierced when I was twelve, so can we?"

"You can get your ears pierced any time you want, sweetie. You know that."

"What about Devon?"

"He has to ask your dad."

"That's not fair."

"Of course it's fair."

"Ask Dad?" Devon said, laughing. "That'd be like a one-way ticket back to California."

"On some topics, your dad's never left the fifties," Karen said.

"Lots of boys have their ears pierced," Jamie said.

"Oh, really? Boys your age in West Van? Name me five of them."

"Are you pierced?" Devon asked Erica.

"Name me *one* of them," Karen said, refusing to give up.

Erica pushed the thick curls back from either side of her face to show them simple gold studs. Her eyes looked more engaged than they had all day, and she'd acquired the beginning of a genuine smile. She must find the kids amusing, or entertaining, or something. "My sister and I pierced each other," she said. "Strictly old school, a darning needle and a potato."

The twins exchanged a look.

"Don't even think about it," Karen said.

"Why'd you do it?" Devon asked Erica.

Erica had a real smile now. "Why? The same reason most kids do it. Because everybody else was doing it."

WHY THE HELL was Drew here? Straight from work, still in one of his high-end bland grey suits—although he'd loosened his tie and hung up his jacket. This didn't make any sense. Monday was the night when he did something cheesy and old-school with the boys. Playing cards? Getting loaded at the Legion?

He'd been poking in the fireplace, but he straightened up when he saw her. "Karen," he said, "we have to talk."

"Sure," she said, meaning *later*.

Amazing. Everybody seemed to be here for dinner. Last night was supposed to be family night, and this was nowhere Monday, but here they were nonetheless—even Cameron who was headed straight for Erica, the attractive nuisance. "Why is that woman still here?" Drew was asking under his breath.

What business was it of his? "Your guess is as good as mine. They drugged the hell out of her in Emerg. I think it's just wearing off."

Enough of this, Karen thought. Let's move it right along. "The mince is in that one," Claire told her, pointing to the larger casserole. "The *organic* mince." Claire was certain that the only difference between organic and non-organic meat was the price. "Tofu," she said, pointing with distaste at the smaller casserole, and now that she had Karen's attention, launched into one of her famous complaints, pissed off that Drew was here on *her* night—"He wants a sit-down dinner on a school night?" said in one of her hissing whispers, "Incredible."

"Boy, am I sore!" Erica was telling Cam. "I guess it's kind of a—" and Erica drew a large spacey loop in the air. Meaning what? And Karen seemed to have picked up a shadow. Jamie had been trailing her since they'd left Twin Central. "Mum?"

"What, Jamie?"

An angry demanding jerk of her head. God, twelve was a terrible age, every thought flagged as urgent. Karen followed her daughter out of the kitchen and through the dining room and across the living area until they were stopped by the far wall. "What?"

Jamie took a deep breath. "We want to take puberty blockers."

This was worse than piercings. Karen was smacked by a queasy I'm-going-to-be-sick feeling at the mere thought of puberty blockers—it hit her right between the legs and smeared up into her stomach. "I don't want to talk about this. I told you—"

"Please, Mum, just listen, okay? Don't go like all weird. Erica says there's this doctor at the university who'd talk to us."

Fucking Erica— Karen didn't trust herself to say anything. She could see that Jamie was sad and scared, her dark eyes trying to cut through some membrane, some mask that separated them. This might be the first time that Jamie had talked to her alone since Devon had come to live with them—but Karen saw Jamie exchange a look with her brother across the spacey distance. Devon had already filled his plate and was standing at the edge of the dining room, watching.

"Oh, god, Jamie," Karen said.

"We want to go on being identical."

What was *wrong* with these kids? No matter where they started out or how many twists or turns they made to get there, all streams flowed to the same place, the drain at the bottom of the bathtub, the one-way black hole called *identical*. Karen couldn't find anything to say.

Jamie seemed to have written a bit of the missing dialogue—imagining what her mum must be thinking. "Devon doesn't really care—"

"What? He wants to stay a little boy forever?"

Jamie looked away at nothingness—that focusing gesture she'd used since childhood—then back at Karen. "Mum?"

Karen could sense how hard Jamie was trying to invoke that lost time when she and her mum had been best friends. "I don't want to get my period."

Karen knew that she shouldn't try to trivialize this one. She'd heard it before, but never this clearly. It was hard for her to imagine what that must feel like. She'd been just the opposite; she'd prayed for her period— had actually got down on her knees by her bed and *prayed* for it. "Oh, sweetie, you shouldn't even be thinking about it yet. By the time you get it, you'll be ready for it. You're probably going to be late like me."

"Late? How late?"

"I was fifteen."

Jamie's face said that was nowhere near good enough. "Mum, it's— No— I'm changing *already*. I'm taller than Dev. My feet—"

Easy, Karen told herself. Don't blow up. If it was about Jamie's period, she could stand there and talk about it as long as it took, but it wasn't— it was about fucking *identical*. "You're a girl," she said. "Girls grow up and turn into women. That's just the way it is. Women get their periods. Listen, sweetie, we all have to deal with it. It's okay. It's just a part of life—"

"But I don't have to deal with it. Erica says there's this doctor—"

Karen felt something inside her snap. It was as clear as if she'd heard a twig break. "I don't want to hear another word about puberty blockers, you got that? Not another fucking word. I've already told you that. That's not just crazy, that's bat-shit crazy."

Karen saw a splash of pain in Jamie's eyes—and then a closing up. Jamie turned and walked away.

KAREN WAS SITTING in her usual central spot in the living room, drinking tea. Drew was well into his third glass of wine. Even though she wasn't in sight, Jamie was still centre stage. "At the very least she owes me an apology," he said.

Last night, he was talking about. Drew, she thought, you are such an asshole I can't even find the words to express it.

Erica still showed no signs of leaving—the twins kept insisting that she had to stay to see Morgan and Avalon—so she was probably back upstairs in Twin Central hearing how mean Mum wouldn't let them get their puberties blocked, and mean Mum herself was feeling teary and exhausted and trying not to show it. She'd made a terrible mistake with Jamie, and she didn't know how to fix it. She could feel a dark anxious pressure in her chest—a swelling, a sorrow. Why couldn't she have just stood there and listened? But no, she hadn't, so the least she could do now was keep Drew off Jamie's ass. "There's no way in hell that Jamie's going to apologize to you," she said. "Let's just move on to the next act, okay?"

"You saw what she did," he said. "It was open defiance."

"Oh, for god's sake, it was an emergency. A one-off. Everything turned out okay. Why don't we just let it go?"

"Karen. Come on. We had an agreement. If it falls apart the minute there's an emergency, it's isn't much of an agreement, is it? It would have only taken you a few seconds, but— It was unacceptable."

A flurry of movement in the distance— now what? Devon had just appeared at the far end of the living room and was waving his cellphone at her. "Mom!"

She sent Devon a shooing motion—*go away!* "Somebody dying in our front hallway would have been fairly unacceptable too," she said.

"Nobody was going to die. That's just— Karen, it's always something. You keep making excuses for her. You're not doing her any favours, you know. Why do you think she has so much trouble at school?"

"Mom," Devon yelled, "come *here*. It's *important*."

I can't stand this, Karen thought. What are they doing, double-teaming me? "She's not having any troubles at school *lately*," she said to Drew. "Oh, for god's sake. Wait a second," and she jumped up to see what on earth Devon could possibly want. "So it's your turn now, eh? What?"

He offered her the cellphone. "I just asked Dad if I could get my ears pierced. He says, 'It's up to your mother.'"

Karen couldn't believe it. "You called your father?"

He nodded.

"He's on the phone?"

He nodded again.

"You called your father on the most top-secret of his top-secret numbers? The one that's supposed to be *for emergencies?* To ask him if you could get your ears pierced?"

Once again Devon was demonstrating his conviction that his smile could fix anything.

"You idiot," she said under her breath and took the cell. She was in no mood for small talk—"Rob, did you just say, 'It's up to your mother?'"

She had no trouble decoding her ex-husband's deceptively self-deprecating chuckle. "Yes, I guess I did."

"We're talking about your *son* who's about to turn *thirteen* getting *his ears pierced*."

"My sentiments exactly. But, um . . . it's a judgment call, Karo."

Rob was the only person in the world who called her "Karo." That ridiculous pet name was the only tenderness left of their marriage, but every time he said it, she thought of syrup.

"You're the one on the ground," he said. "I don't want to undermine your authority."

Oh my god, he thinks it's a management problem. "So it's really up to me, eh? I don't believe it for a minute. You're setting me up."

"What are you doing, Karen? Trying to put me in the position of the bad guy?"

Here was a perfect example of why she was no longer married to Rob Clark. "God forbid you should ever be the bad guy," she said. "You have a good night, Rob," and handed the phone back to Devon.

This had to be the latest round in some ridiculous skirmish she seemed to be fighting with the twins, and up until that moment she hadn't even known she'd been fighting it. She could see the pattern—tattoos to piercings to puberty blockers and then back to piercings. Maybe she'd set them off when she hadn't answered her cellphone, but whatever, they couldn't simply let it drop. Devon might be the one standing in front of her, but Karen could feel Jamie's presence behind him, and no, they weren't going to stop—not until they'd won *something*. "Get out of here," she said.

That left her alone standing in the hallway looking into the living room where Drew was staring at her, doing nothing whatsoever except waiting, his foot-tapping impatience clearly visible across the airy distance of the open floor plan designed for easy living. Oh, god. She'd always thought of Drew as a *comfortable* man, and she'd gotten used to him— But what?

He was only nine years older than Karen, but she thought of him as a refugee from somebody else's generation. He was proud of his big thick head of hair without a speck of grey in it, was "not in bad shape for a man my age"—as he liked to say, sucking in his gut and giving it a couple of energetic slaps—but he was already showing signs of the grumpy old fart he seemed destined to become. *A man my age*—how could he say that? What was wrong with him? For a man, your fifties is supposed to be *young*, the prime of your life. But his politics—his entire worldview—was an old fart's, so far from Karen's that the only way they could talk about anything serious was to make a joke of it. What was she doing with a man like that?

THE HOUSE WAS FULL of kids, and Claire was getting paid, but Karen was helping to clean up because she didn't want to talk to Drew. He shouldn't be here anyway because it was a *Monday* night, damn him— The doorbell. My god, now what? Couldn't she ever get a break?

It was Bryan Lynas, grinning and even more freckled than she remembered—it gave him a dangerous fox-like look—and he had his carrot-top daughters with him, one on either side. They were still wearing their pink tights. They must have come straight from Mal. "We've come to see the patient," he said.

Was Erica a patient? Karen stepped back so they could come in, and the twins greeted her with a "Hi, Mrs. Oxley," darted by as quickly as fish, but this outlandish man stopped her with a cautionary wait-a-minute gesture. She hesitated, and he grabbed one of her hands. They obviously never taught Australian men not to touch women they didn't know—but she stifled her annoyance and allowed herself to be led outside. His hand was rough with calluses—and warm. He shut the door behind them. It was a miserable night, and she didn't have a coat on. This better be good. "My ex and your son seem to be getting their blow from the same fellas," he said.

She followed his eyes to the silver Infiniti. It had come back, and with this bit of news, her perception morphed it from a mundane everyday West Van car into some thug-like gangland vehicle, and she'd understood him at once but didn't want to. He must have misread the look on her face—"Coke," he said to make sure she got it.

"Oh, god," she said.

"Great pair of dickheads. They supply a lot of the West Van kids." He opened her own front door for her.

"Thanks for telling me . . . I guess . . . What should I do about it?"

She'd meant, *Should I call the cops?*—although that was a truly terrible idea, one she dismissed as soon as she had it—but he laughed and said, "Stop paying for it," and still grinning like the court jester, walked on ahead of her, leaving her standing in her own front hallway.

"*Drew*," she said, slathering the name with honey so this Bryan Lynas asshole would get the point, "look who's here. It's Morgan and Avalon's dad."

Just as she'd thought he would, Drew flipped instantly out of his sulk and into his role as Man of the House, the CEO of the whole works—leapt to his feet, and the two men went straight for each other, hands outstretched, each pronouncing his own name as though it was a magical incantation.

To Drew's braying invitations to partake of the household hospitality, Bryan was saying that he reckoned his girls might not mind a bite. No, he wasn't much of a bloke for the vino, he said. Not to worry, Drew said, but he was betting that a nice cold lager might not go amiss? Yeah, mate, that would go owright, and Claire was sending Karen a look of pointy-eyed distress because everything she'd just finished putting away was now coming out of the fridge again as Drew slammed item after item onto the kitchen table—the veggie casserole, half a loaf of bread, the butter, the ketchup, mustard, and pickles—and then the lager popped and poured. Brian took a long glug, rewarded Drew with a satisfied sigh and a toothy grin. "I've got to run?" Claire said dubiously.

Working-class Brit to her toenails, Claire worked to the minute, and the hands of the kitchen clock were nailed exactly on nine. If Karen wanted her to stay longer, that would require a negotiation which, in turn, would require the utmost delicacy so as not to hurt Claire's feelings. Karen would offer to double Claire's already insanely inflated hourly wage, and Claire would say, "No, you don't have to do that," but they would both know that Karen would have to do that. Tonight Karen simply didn't have the energy for it. "It's okay," she said. "The kids can take care of it," although they both knew how ridiculous that was—and Karen was

154

thinking, I've got two teenage dope dealers downstairs in Cam's room. Oh god, I have to *do something*.

Cameron had left the lights on just as he always did, and he'd left the door standing open to reveal the same ungodly mess that was always in there, but Cam and the dickheads were gone. Karen must have missed them only by a minute or two. She didn't know whether to be pissed off or relieved. What could she have said to them? "Don't ever come back here or I'm going to call the cops?" The unfortunate thing about the location of Cam's room was that if you wanted to leave the house, all you had to do was walk through the door conveniently placed at the back of the garage. Karen could never understand why she'd never thought of that when she'd moved him down there.

Even for West Van, Karen's house was high-end. With an assessed value of four and some change, it was, by anybody's standards, a luxury house. It had six bedrooms, four up and two down. You would think that in a house like that, there would be no problem finding the right place for everybody to sleep, wouldn't you? Jamie had blithely assumed that Devon would simply move into her room with her. "Are you out of your bloody mind?" Karen had said. But then, when Karen had dared to suggest that Devon go downstairs, Jamie had wept like Ophelia—"You're trying to separate us, Mum!" Oh, sure—by two whole flights of stairs. The only person who thought that Paige should go downstairs was Paige who envisioned taking over the entire bottom level and inviting a dozen of her friends for a permanent sleepover, so Devon had moved into Cameron's room, and Cam was the one who went downstairs. Of course it took Karen, Claire, a cleaning crew, and two professional movers to actually accomplish it.

Karen had loved the guest room too much to give it to Cam who was never there anyway, so she'd moved him into the smaller room that used to be her office, and that had actually been a good thing because it had given her the chance to redecorate the guest room, but it was, unfortunately, right next to his. An infrequently cleaned locker room used by ten beer-league hockey teams couldn't have smelled any worse than Cam's room.

Karen picked up an armload of ancient pizza boxes. Why was she doing that? Why hadn't Claire done it? What was she paying Claire for?

She'd been aware of the TV the entire time she'd been downstairs; now she followed the sound into the family room. Paige and Lauren were sprawled on the floor, and even though no one had made them do it, they were actually doing their homework. With no warning at all Karen's eyes stung with tears. Oh, Paige, she thought, you nice sweet *normal* kid, I've got to stop neglecting you. "Get your act together, Lauren," she said. "I'll take you home."

"Aw, Mum."

"No sleepovers on school nights. Come on, girls, you know that."

"HAVE YOU TRIED to talk to her?" Drew was asking. "She's completely out of it. She should be hospitalized." He was going home, thank god. His jacket on, tie pulled up, he was now delivering his closing statement as the CEO. Everybody seemed to leaving—the speckled Australian and his twins saying goodbye to her twins, all of them milling around in the kitchen—but Erica didn't seem to be leaving. Paige and Lauren had followed Karen upstairs, and Paige was offering Lauren the Häagen-Dazs, for god's sake, and Karen seemed to have run out of the ability to say any of the right things, do any of the right things—she couldn't even go through the motions. All the voices were just so much babble. She let the pizza boxes fall onto the counter. The kitchen was a mess—instant pigsty. She almost didn't care.

"You've got to get her out of here, Karen. That crazy woman is not your responsibility."

"Yeah, I know. Yeah, I will. Could you drop off Lauren on your way? She's just down in Lower Caulfeild. She'll show you."

He was thinking about it. What was there to think about? "Aw, Karen, that's kind of— I've got to get to bed." She knew perfectly well that there was nothing waiting for him at his place but a bottle of Chateau Whatever and Letterman. "We've got one of those awful working breakfasts. Crack of dawn."

She didn't believe it for a minute. This was Drew's revenge for being ignored, for not getting his way. They both knew it was his revenge. Maybe that was the wrong word. It was more like *if you want me to scratch your back, scratch mine*. It was probably the way the boys ran things. He wasn't even bothering to cover it up the way a woman would.

Driving again. A bloody awful rainy night. Paige and Lauren in the back rehashing the social complexities of kid-level West Van, of dance school and grade five. A notion that had been floating at the back of Karen's mind for some time now was coming into sharp focus—that her life had become unmanageable. No, that wasn't strong enough. It had become *incomprehensible*.

Rob had been Drew's boss at Wayne Energy, and Karen had always known that Drew had a thing for her. He was the kind of guy who radiated lust out of his eyeballs. Shortly after she'd divorced Rob, Drew's wife had divorced him, and then he had stealthily insinuated himself into Karen's life—a dinner here, a gift there, a series of nice thoughtful little gestures. She had appreciated them— Okay, so she'd been lonely, and Drew had been somebody to talk to. It wasn't as though they had hot passionate sex. These days they had hardly any sex at all, and when they did, it was yawn ho-hum sex with Karen lying on her back worrying that the friction was going to give her a yeast infection. So why didn't she just tell Drew to go away? Well, because if she'd been Rob's trophy wife, she was Drew's trophy girlfriend, and it really mattered to him. It was all for show, and if she split up with him, it would look bad for him out in the world where it counted, and she liked him, and she just couldn't do that to him. Sigh.

The car radio was playing Paige's station, The Beat—as the insanely cheerful girl announcer kept informing her—a station just as straight-forwardly Top Forty as Paige was. The rules must be that you walked your BFF to the door even in the rain because that's what Paige did, and then, remembering that Mum didn't like being treated like a chauffeur, she got into the front seat. "I love you, sweetie," Karen said.

"I love you too, Mum," Paige said automatically.

Fucking November, slap of the windshield wipers, just drive—and Karen's mind was going where it had already gone a million times before— no, she didn't like Drew all that much, had stopped liking him a while back. In fact, she liked Drew Thompson somewhat less than she liked Rob Clark, and she'd *divorced* Rob Clark. Maybe she should have stuck with Rob—the original, not the copy.

"You okay, Mum?" Paige asked, and Karen's eyes stung again. Paige was the only one of her kids who would ever ask her if she was okay. Karen could feel her unshed tears like a river pushing against a dam. I've got to get to bed, she thought. "I'm just tired," she said.

The house was finally quiet. Karen gave her daughter a pat on the bum. "Bed, sweetie." Erica, that strange girl, had left, thank god. Maybe Bryan Lynas had taken her. Karen had to do something with the kitchen. She couldn't simply go to bed and leave it like that. Claire wouldn't be back until Thursday.

That nasty startle effect—heart thump and squirt of adrenaline—when you think you're alone but you're not. It was like a reveal in some cheesy melodrama—Erica, in her immobile cut-flower pose, was sitting at the far end of the kitchen table.

The kitchen was immaculate. The pizza boxes were gone. Every surface had been scrubbed clean. Even the inside of the sink was gleaming. Oh, Karen thought, you've been one busy little bee, haven't you? Erica looked up, her face as blank as a clean plate. "I'm sorry," she said, "but I just—"

Karen waited, but the sentence obviously wasn't going to get finished. This isn't fair, she thought.

Karen lit all four of the small lamps in the guest room. Erica had stopped just inside the door. "What a beautiful room," she said but remained where she was, unmoving.

Karen hadn't been able to re-create her earlier life exactly, but the guest room was as close to it as she could get. She'd hung the high windows with the same kind of plain cream-coloured drapes she'd used in her quirky little apartment in Kits Point so many years ago. She'd framed the best of her posters from readings with her writers. All of her signed first editions were displayed in her old white bookcase. The simple crystal vase was a genuine artifact from back in the day and stood waiting for a spray of flowers. Her original Ikea computer station had vanished somewhere along the way, so she'd bought a new one that looked like the old one. She'd kept the first bed she'd ever owned. Cameron had been conceived in that bed. Now, for guests, it had fine linen on it—Egyptian cotton, 500 thread count.

Erica took one step into the room and paused again, taking it all in. Karen had to make the offer—and it was a genuine offer—but a polite person would read the subtext and go home. Erica was looking directly at her with her huge lovely eyes that were just as impossible to read as they had been all day. "Thank you," she said. "This is so kind of you."

10.

BANG! The *front* door. Why didn't Cam come in through the garage?— he had no problem going *out* through the garage. Stumbling thud of his feet down the stairs—pissed out of his mind again. How long had it been since she'd actually *seen* Cameron?—since his physical body had actually been present in front of her eyes? That had been Erica's first day at the house, Monday, and this was Thursday night, so that meant it had been *four days ago.*

Karen hadn't been quite asleep—had been in one of these nasty irritating states in which you keep trying to convince yourself you're asleep when you know perfectly well you're not. No, sleep is not fragments of conversations that don't make any sense folding in and out of images that don't make any sense, a long and meaningless movie punctuated with spasms of worry, with occasional dots of unconsciousness thrown in just to fool you, and Cameron's drunken arrival had really done it—she was wide awake now at fucking one in the morning. Cam's stinky little room was right next to the guest room, so Erica would have heard it with excruciating clarity when he'd slammed his bedroom door and fallen over onto his bed with a gargantuan crash. Cam, I am going to kill you.

It was obviously a zopiclone night, but instead of sitting up and reaching for the pill bottle, Karen lay there fuming. She was listening to squeaks and rustlings from downstairs. It had to be Erica. Poor thing— of course it was Erica, probably on her way into the kitchen, looking for her own insomnia cure—maybe a glass of milk. So why was that strange sad woman still in Karen's house after four days? Good question. "What are you," Drew had asked her, "the SPCA?"

Erica was still there because every time she'd tried to leave, Karen had talked her out of it—"Oh, no, wait till you're feeling better"—and she'd even given Erica the keys to the Lexus, and that meant, of course, that whenever Erica went anywhere, she had to come back. None of this was exactly what you'd call rational. It wasn't as though Erica was an old and valued friend—she hardly knew the woman.

If alone at one in the morning wasn't truth-telling time, when was? From her years of therapy Karen knew all the standard questions, and now she asked herself one of them—"What is this doing for you?"—and she didn't even have to search for the answer. If Erica was there, Drew wasn't. Could it be that simple? Meanwhile she'd been tracking the minute noises from downstairs, and now Erica was in the living room, or possibly the dining room—the open floor plan made it hard to tell—but one thing for sure, she wasn't in the kitchen.

What could she be doing? Maybe Karen should go see—that would be a good way to end her endlessly recycling ruminations—and that was enough to finally get her to sit up and turn on the light. She never wore a robe unless there was company in the house, but there was, and so she did, and crept quietly downstairs—not too quietly. She didn't want to be a scary spectre appearing suddenly out of nowhere.

Erica was a slender figure—in the dark, in the archway between the dining room and living room—and appeared to be doing nothing but standing there. Karen cleared her throat as a warning—yes, there's somebody here with you—and said, "Can't sleep? I don't blame you. Cam made a hell of a racket."

For a moment Karen was afraid that Erica hadn't heard her—although that didn't seem possible. She was only a few feet away. Then Erica turned to look at her—the motion strangely slow and deliberate—said, "I'm sorry."

She heard me coming, Karen thought. "There's nothing to be sorry about."

The main level of the house was dotted with recessed night lights—an odd design feature. When it was a dark night and there wasn't much light coming in through the windows, the living area was transformed into an otherworldly vista that looked like interlinked airline runways seen from a vast distance. The glow from the nightlights was localized—cold and greenish. Erica's eyes were catching glints of it and seemed to be enormous, as big as a manga character's. This is all a bit too science fictiony, Karen thought, and turned on a table lamp.

Lit by the warm tungsten, Erica was transformed into something ordinarily human. She'd never looked like an adult to Karen, but tonight, barefoot, wearing nothing but a big grey T-shirt, she could even be Jamie's age. Her curly hair was tousled from sleep—or from an attempt to sleep. It was a colour very similar to Jamie's—a brunette with not a trace of warmth in it—but darker, like hair that had been on its way to black but had given up just before it got there. "I was going to have some warm milk," Karen said. "Would you like some?"

Erica was looking directly at her but didn't answer. What was she doing—a reprise of her willful silence in Emergency? But then she said, "I'm sorry. It's hard for me to talk."

"That's okay. You don't need to talk. It's the middle of the night."

Erica looked in the direction of the windows where distant lights were scattered across the darkness, then back at Karen. "I seem to have all the symptoms of clinical depression."

Oh, what a lovely bit of overshare, Karen thought. She needed to say something comforting, or if not comforting, at least sympathetic—or *something*. "My therapist used to tell me . . . I was in therapy for years. It really helped . . . When I was depressed, Helen told me to go inside the depression and see what's in there."

"I've done that. I know what's in there."

Karen's mind stopped working for a moment. Then it kicked back in. Erica had spoken like someone who had to tell her secret quickly before she ran out of courage. Erica hadn't named it, but Karen knew what Erica had found inside her depression.

I've got to get this poor woman to a doctor, Karen thought—or get her to somebody. Helen would have been perfect, but Helen was dead. Hadn't Jen been talking about some wonderful counselor one of the ladies was seeing? But no, that was ridiculous. Erica might need long-term therapy, but right now what she needed was a quick fix—and Karen had to say something more. "Symptoms?" she said.

Erica's face tilted toward her with an expression of polite inquiry.

"Okay, so . . ." Karen's mouth had dried up. She cleared her throat and swallowed. I don't want to be doing this, she thought. "So what exactly are the symptoms of clinical depression?"

Like an expert contestant on a quiz show, Erica responded immediately. Her voice was unnerving—clear and precise with no emotion at all. "Loss of pleasure in . . . just all the ordinary things that used to make you happy. In almost anything, actually. Insomnia. Loss of appetite and weight loss. Loss of sexual desire. Slowed thinking, restlessness, inability to concentrate, indecisiveness . . . I should have left here days ago, but I just can't . . . focus? Feelings of worthlessness. Why are you being so nice to me? It must be like having a zombie staying with you."

"No, it's not." Although it was kind of like that—except that Erica was a helpful zombie. "The kids adore you."

"That's good. I take it back. There *are* things that make me happy. I like being with your kids . . . and with the other twins, Morgan and Avi. I like being here. It's like a sanctuary. I can't tell you how much I appreciate it. Thank you. You've been so very kind to me."

"You're welcome."

"But it's worse tonight. It's different. I'm really sorry."

"Have you taken anything?"

"No. It's all just *me*. I seem to be depersonalized. Nothing feels real. Everything feels . . ."

"Feels what?"

Erica said nothing. Helen had told Karen that a therapist is someone who waits. Helen had been able to wait forever, but Karen couldn't. "Come on, tell me," she said.

"Dreadful."

That surely required a response, but Karen couldn't find one.

"I'm scared," Erica said and hesitated, making a small ambiguous gesture with her hands. "I'm not having hallucinations or anything that extreme. I can remember what I'm *supposed* to do. Or I think I can remember. I'm not sure of that. My ability to test reality seems to be impaired.

I'm afraid that my behavior is bizarre and inappropriate."

Again Karen tried to play therapist. "What does bizarre and inappropriate look like?"

"I shouldn't be standing here talking to you in the middle of the night, should I? I should have left on Monday."

Erica was looking at her closely, studying her. She's trying to see if she can trust me, Karen thought. "Do you have anything to take?"

"No, not here. I've got a million different . . . Clonazepam and Valium . . . but they're all over at my place. I must be frightening you. I'm sorry."

"No, you're not," Karen said, but she was sweating through her thin bathrobe. "Okay, why don't we start by just getting you through the night? One step at a time?"

Again that odd inquiring look. Almost as though it was saying, *Are you the same species as me?*

"Okay?" Karen said. "Is that okay?"

"Yes."

"Is there anything I can do to help?"

"Yes, there is. If you don't mind. This might sound strange, but . . . it helps if you talk."

Talk? Talk about what?—and then she got it. Karen had four kids. At one time or another every one of them had awakened her in the night to say, "Mummy, I had a bad dream." Talk meant something like *tell me a story*.

KAREN HAD BEEN SAYING anything that came into her mind—trying to sound adult, self-assured, and serene—but the real solution, of course, was zopiclone. Karen took those clever little blue pills more often than she should, so now they weren't as effective as they used to be, but when she'd first tried them, they'd snuffed her like a candle. "You'll be gone in ten minutes," she told Erica.

"I don't know," Erica said. "I'm just not sure."

Oh, just take the damned thing! Karen thought.

Karen had arranged everything the way she used to do it for her kids—the way she still did it for herself when she was having a bad night. She and Erica were in Karen's bed, each with her own bed table and cup of hot milk. The pillows were freshly fluffed and the covers pulled up. Four of the smaller lamps lit the bedroom with a dim amber glow that was not too bright—just enough to dispel any pockets of darkness that might generate monsters. The clock radio was tuned to an FM station that played nothing but light classics, the volume turned down to barely audible. The windows were open a few inches to create a nice contrast between the cold chilly night *out there* and the safe warm haven of the bed. The sound of the rain was perfect—a soothing patter. It was nearly two in the morning, everything was cozy, and Erica wouldn't take the fucking sleeping pill. "They don't do anything weird," Karen told her. "All they do is knock you out. They don't even leave you groggy."

"Okay," Erica said in a firm little-girl voice, "I *will* take it. Just not yet. I'm sorry, but . . . Let me get used to the idea. Things are getting better. Gradually. I'm feeling more real. You're really helping. You're so kind."

There were two things that Karen was sick of hearing from Erica— "I'm sorry" and "You're so kind."

"You want me to go on talking?"

"Yes, please."

Talk about what? Her mind had been flipping through memories of her kids and their bad dreams. Cam had been the worst. Right after she and Ian had split up, Cam had terrible nightmares. He woke up scream-ing night after night. He nearly drove her crazy. He seemed inconsolable. She didn't want to tell Erica that.

As always, Erica's face was impossible to read, but she must be waiting for the next installment. Okay, Karen told herself, say anything. "This has always been my room ever since we bought the house. Rob's room was where Jamie's room is now."

It was odd—Karen and Rob had never been able to sleep in the same bed. Eventually she'd realized that Rob was a little afraid of her—that his fear was related to sex in some obscure way that she never understood. When her body was near his, it always meant sex to him, so when he wanted to sleep, the person she was in the dark—the body in the bed— didn't feel safe or comforting. It made her sad.

"Rob showed me this house," she told Erica. "It was a total surprise. He hadn't said anything about looking at houses. We were supposed to be having brunch. It was part of his . . . I'd just split up with Ian, and I was in my to-hell-with-men phase. Rob was trying to convince me to marry him, so he . . . The day was just spectacular, that golden light you can get in the late afternoon, and the house looked just amazing. The view, oh, my god, and six bedrooms. 'Rob,' I said, 'what would we do with six bedrooms?' 'We could have lots of kids,' he said."

"Did you want to have more children?"

"Yeah, I did."

Later, working with Helen, Karen had realized that she'd been bribed—or bought. She didn't like that. But West Van real estate had shot up just the way it was supposed to, and here she was, the proud owner of the house. Some people thought she'd been clever. She didn't feel clever.

Erica was still waiting. It was bloody hard to keep on talking to somebody who wasn't responding. "I was in therapy off and on for years," Karen said. "I already told you that, didn't I? I had a wonderful therapist. Helen. But she died. Breast cancer. I really miss her."

Are you going to speak? she asked Erica with her eyes. No, she obviously wasn't.

"She was trained in classic Gestalt but put her own spin on it . . . a little bit of James Hillman, a little bit of Marie von Franz, lots of Jung."

Erica's expression changed—something appeared on her face that was like a smirk or a secret smile. "Is something funny?" Karen asked her. "Is *that* funny?"

"The textbook I use . . . doesn't even have Carl Jung's name in it. Annalise read him. When she was writing her honors thesis. She thought he was . . . a kind of literary figure."

"Your sister? What was her thesis on?"

"I . . . can't talk yet? I don't think I can talk about this."

"Okay."

Now what? "Do you like the sound of the rain?" Karen said.

Once again Karen found herself looking into Erica's eyes, but this time she felt a spark of wordless communication. She knows how hard this is for me, Karen thought. She wants to help.

"Your mum said . . ." Erica paused, looking away to the far end of the bedroom, and, for a moment, Karen had the illusion that she could see it through Erica's eyes—long reaches of empty space, the graceful curves of the cherry wood highboy catching the light, and then, receding beyond it, planes of various shades of rose. It must look alien to her, she thought, exotic—but was it comforting? Then Erica was looking at her again. "She said there was another little girl? When you were little? You pretended to be twins? Tell me about her."

"Oh. Patsy. We went to camp together. Every summer from the time we were eight. That seems awfully young to be away from home for the first time, but ... Yeah, the first year was scary, but we loved it. Summer wouldn't have been summer without Camp Kingcome. Patsy kept on going right through high school and actually became a counselor."

When they were little, it was pretty much a summer friendship. Every August they'd stand on the dock weeping, vowing that this year they'd stick together no matter what, but they lived at opposite ends of West Van, went to different elementary schools, didn't see much of each other during the school year—except for the occasional sleepover when they'd stay up all night long, talking. They couldn't wait to get to grade eight so they could go to school together.

"Patsy had a huge impact on me," she said. "I didn't realize how much until later. I wrote ... I took Creative Writing in university, and I wrote about her. They were pretty good stories. I think they were, anyway. Everybody in the workshop seemed to like them. They told me I had a real talent for writing kids—"

"Are you still friends?"

"No, we lost track of each other in high school. I never understood what happened ... exactly. We drifted into two different cliques. I guess they were our boyfriends' cliques. Patsy started going out with this scary badass, Big Mack Mackenzie, and the guy I was ... the absolute opposite, captain of the soccer team, old West Van money. What a bore! And the boys utterly detested each other, and there wasn't a lot of room for us to ... That was kind of the end for us. It was sad, actually. I still feel bad about it. But the friends you have when you're a kid—" Karen wasn't sure how to complete the thought. "They're special, charmed, magical? Uncanny? But you'll never have friends like that again. Do you know what I mean?"

"No, I don't."

Lovely. And what did *Erica* mean? That she didn't have any friends as a kid—or she just didn't want to talk?—but then Erica said, "MZ twins make friends differently from singletons."

"Oh?"

"If you're a certain kind of MZ twin, you don't need to make friends. You've already got your best friend."

Karen felt that on her skin like a spray of electrical sparkles. Okay, here she was, finally arriving—*the dead twin*. Was she something Erica wanted to talk about, needed to talk about, or a topic they should avoid like the plague?

"It's interesting . . ." Erica said, sounding unfinished. Karen waited.

"Your mum said you pretended to be twins?"

"Yeah, we did. That was after we saw *The Parent Trap*—"

"Amazing." Karen was startled. It was like somebody had pushed Erica's come-to-life button. "So many singletons have told me that. They and their best girlfriends saw that movie and wanted to be twins—"

"Yeah, that's right. That was us. For a while we dressed alike. I mean absolutely all the way down to our shoelaces."

"What was she like?"

"Patsy? A super tomboy."

"Like Jamie?"

"On, no. Not like Jamie at all. No, Patsy was . . . She had a huge personality. Open, sunny, brave, optimistic—"

As opposed to what? All the words Karen would have uses to describe her daughter—secretive, closed off, fragile, edgy, dark, moody, melodramatic? Karen had never thought of Jamie as a tomboy.

"Patsy was . . . Before the boys got their growth spurt, she was stronger than any of the boys our age. She could run faster. She could swim better. I don't think she ever thought of herself as pretty, but I thought she was beautiful. Lean and wiry. Long legs. Big happy smile like the sun coming up. She didn't give a shit. Whatever she wanted to do was fine with me. We were always in trouble."

One of their crazy stunts—it was funny, actually. They'd almost been sent home for it. They'd been caught spying on the boys when they were

167

peeing. Patsy had found a chink in the boy's bathroom—an open space between two logs just big enough so they could take turns looking in. "Oh, did we ever catch hell for that!"

They'd been best girlfriends from the first, but then, later, Karen's feelings turned into hero worship and she saw Patsy as invincible and would have followed her anywhere. She was convinced that nothing bad could ever happen if they were together. One of their stunts had been truly dangerous. It made a great story—in fact it was the first summer camp story that Karen wrote in her creative writing class. They'd decided to take a rowboat out in the middle of the night and row it to Bowen Island. Patsy had a crumpled-up map that showed where it was, and she had a compass so they would always be going in the right direction. What more did they need? Patsy was sure that they could get there and back by moonlight, long before the dawn. They were eleven.

They waited for a night when the moon was full. It was clear, too, and just as bright as could be. They snuck out of their cabin sometime after midnight, got the rowboat out with no trouble, and simply started rowing. It was glorious. "There are conversations you can only have once in your life, and you can't be much older than eleven when you have them. 'What do *you* think about the moon?'"

Thank god it was a long inlet. They never did make it to open water, and eventually Patsy had the good sense to turn back. She was a fabulous risk-taker but always practical. The amazing thing was that they got away with it—were back in bed in their cabin with minutes to spare.

They'd known that they had to keep it dead secret, and their grand moon-soaked adventure became woven into the legend of themselves, as though they'd been on a pilgrimage or a quest. They vowed to continue keeping it secret, holding it tight to themselves forever—till death. "Nobody knew where we were," Karen would say. "We could have drowned, and nobody would have found our bodies for days."

"No," Patsy always said, "it was a still clear night, and we knew what we were doing." Yes, even at eleven they knew. An essential part of the larger secret was that kids can know more, be far better, than adults ever give them credit for—at least if those kids are that legendary duo, Karen Oxley and Patsy Donlevy.

Karen was surprised at how much she was feeling. "I've never loved anyone in my life in the simple easy way I loved Patsy. It made me happy just being around her." She was embarrassed to hear the quiver in her voice, but Erica's voice was as flat as a breadboard. "Girls often form intense one-on-one bonds in childhood and early adolescence."

What an odd cold thing to say—it was almost a put-down—but maybe it had been meant to be kind, meant to give her a way to pull back from the emotion. That was probably how Erica dealt with her own emotions. "Not the boys though," Erica said. "They tend to run in packs. They don't—" and stopped herself.

"It would be interesting to do some longitudinal studies," Erica said. "I'll bet that those intense twin-like relationships between girls don't usually last longer—"

Once again Karen found herself waiting for something that was not coming. She glanced at her clock radio. Oh my god, it was after four—and there, on Erica's saucer, was the little blue pill that would fix everything. Erica looked at it too, then back at Karen. "Can I tell you about Annalise?"

KAREN WOULD NEVER AGAIN think of Annalise as "the dead twin." Of course Erica had needed to talk about her—she'd been talking steadily, and Annalise was a real person now, someone who might look like Erica but who was quite different from her—a bright sunny girl with a quirky sense of humour, somewhat shy, who'd loved sunsets, cats, ballet, and poetry. Not just a friend, but Erica's sister, and not just her sister, but her twin—and Karen couldn't conceive of such a loss. Erica had cried more than once, and Karen had cried with her. "You're so empathetic," Erica had said, surprised. Hadn't anyone ever cried with her before?

It was nearly six, but Karen had stopped caring about the time. She knew that what they were doing was important, was a vital human contact—and she'd had far too few of these in her life lately. She'd already written off the coming day. After she delivered the kids, she'd cancel life and sleep. It would fuck up her routine, but so what? Maybe it needed to be fucked up.

"If I had a sister," Karen said, "and she was allowed to wear pretty dresses and I wasn't . . . wow, would I have ever been jealous. Weren't you ever jealous?"

"Oh, no. We . . . If Lise was pretty, she was pretty for us. *We* were pretty."

Karen had been trying to get it, but she still couldn't get it. Did identical twins really have *a different consciousness* from everybody else? That's what Erica thought. She seemed to have as much trouble understanding what it was like *not* to be a twin as Karen had understanding what it was like to *be* one. Erica kept talking about singletons as though they had some essential knowledge that she didn't. Karen was a singleton, so Karen should know, but she didn't know either. What did Erica want from her?

"If she'd died when we were in high school, I couldn't have survived it," Erica said.

So what would she have done—simply killed herself? She talked like she and Lise were two halves of a single person— "If you want to see what we were like, just look at Morgan and Avalon"— and that was exactly the kind of identical bond that Jamie and Devon were trying to create, but it was impossible. The MZ twin bond wasn't something you could learn—Erica kept saying that. It was purely genetic.

"I just don't know how you can . . . Like the major life events, life decisions? How can you do everything *alone?*"

In Jungian typology, Karen was an intuitive type. All of her life she would have sudden flashes of insight—moments when she knew something without knowing how she knew it—and now she knew what Erica wanted. It was really quite simple. Erica was trying to figure out how to live without her sister.

"Look," Karen said, "we singletons . . . we're never as alone as you think we are. I was always . . . First there was my family. And then there was Patsy. And then a bunch of friends in high school, and a series of boys, and . . . oh god, two husbands, and then kids. I don't know. There was a . . . I lived alone for two years. It was a wonderful time. Sometimes I think it was the best time of my life. I lived in this bizarre little apartment in Kits Point. I went out with guys, but they weren't important. I was going to become *a writer.*" Karen couldn't help laughing at herself.

"Later. When I'd had enough experience so I'd have something real to write about."

But she was working *in the industry*, a publicist for McFarland and Hall, and that got her close to the source. They didn't pay her a lot, but she loved her job so much that sometimes it astonished her that they actually paid her at all. She did media mail-outs, made a million phone calls, had coffee with key people, wrote ad copy. She was in charge of authors promoting their books, picked them up at the airport, drove them to their hotel, and then escorted them around town for readings and interviews. She loved every one of them—even the dreadful assholes who tried to hit on her. She got them to sign their books for her, and all of those signed first editions were on the shelves down in the guest room where Erica was staying. Some of the best writers in Can Lit were on those shelves.

"I loved being alone," she said, "although it was scary, although I was lonely sometimes."

Erica was listening, watching. Her interest was so intense that it was almost too much, too bright.

Those two short years—that was the only time in Karen's life when she'd actually supported herself. Even now, how she was living— She didn't like being the kind of woman who lived off her divorce settlements. "Oh, I know I earned it in a crazy sort of way, but still—" When she was working at M&H, there was no question about who was in charge of her life. She didn't remember the men very well. She refused to get seriously involved with any of them. "Nobody was going to take this away from me."

It was hard to put into words. "Most of my life I felt like I was missing out on myself. I didn't feel whole. Does that make sense?"

"Yeah, it makes sense . . . intellectually . . . but I can't really— Okay, but there's like a bubble around singletons, and Lise and I had always—"

THUD—a hard slamming sound, then a metallic snaggle, and it was the bedroom door pushed violently open. "Mu-*um!* What are you *doing?* We've got to *go!*" Oh my god, the kids. Karen hadn't set her alarm.

Jamie had been moving at full speed but stopped so suddenly that she actually slid on the hardwood floor. Her face—staring eyes, open mouth—shocked. Seeing—yes, of course—her mother in bed with Erica.

What to say now? Jamie had been in a kilt mood all week, and she hadn't begun her daily disintegration yet. Even her knee socks were pulled up. And then, as Karen was trying to assemble something in her mind, Jamie began to smile. It was more than just a smile—it spread slowly across her face to become the most open, warm, engaging smile that Karen had seen in months. "Oh, sorry, Mum," she said. "We'll be in the car."

Jamie backed out and closed the door. "Oh," Erica said, "I'm so sorry."

"Stop saying that! There's nothing to be sorry about. Did she look like she was upset? She really likes you."

Karen forced herself to sit up. Before that, she hadn't known how tired she was. It was going to be one bitch of a morning. "Oh, god, I've really got to go."

"Wait," Erica said, "do you want me to do it?" How had this living breathing sparkling-eyed girl replaced the zombie of the night before?

"Oh, no," Karen said, "that's—"

"I'm wide awake. I couldn't possibly sleep now. I go for days without sleeping much anyway. Let me do it. It'll be fun."

"Okay . . . But there's some kids you've got to pick up. Take the BMW. They won't all fit in the Lexus. Paige will tell you what to do. She's utterly reliable."

Karen fell back into the bed. Sleep was already sucking her down like warm oatmeal.

KAREN SENSED a reason to wake up. She opened her eyes and saw Erica looking at her. "Everybody delivered." Erica pressed the keys to the BMW onto the bed table. "Sorry if I woke you. I thought you'd want to know."

Karen had no sense of lost time. She was as wide awake as if all she'd done was push the "pause" button in herself. "I did want to know." The too bright light at the edges of the drapes told her that it was mid-morning. "Everything okay? Are you all right?"

"Oh, yeah. But I really do have to sleep now."

"Wait," Karen said. As she'd been drifting off, she'd kept right on talking to Erica in her mind, and she'd found another story to tell her—had a superbly clear vision of it—and she knew that if she didn't talk it through, she'd lose it. She was certain it was a story that Erica needed to hear. "Can you stay up just a little— I have to tell you something first. Is that all right?"

A movement on Erica's face—a suggestion of a smile. "Sure," Erica said, and then, without being invited, got back into the bed.

"It was— Okay, so when Rob and I started having our affair, we didn't— I was about to say that we didn't give a shit, but that's not right. A big part of the sex, the energy of the sex, was pushing the edge. It was like . . . Yes, it really was like we wanted to get caught. It would be . . . I don't know, the ultimate thrill. We went out in public. A million lunches and coffees and dinners. We got out of West Van, of course, but . . . Rob was something of a bon vivant, and he knew lots of great places. Downtown. Kits. Granville Island. East Van. It was just a matter of time."

The minute Ian came home from work that day, Karen knew that something was up. She didn't get to hear any of his funny anecdotes about clients or colleagues or quirky twists in the law. He waited until she put Cam to bed, waited until they were certain he was sound asleep, and then he said, "Are you having an affair?"

"Oh, god, no. Whatever made you think that?"

Karen went on denying it. It never crossed her mind that she could do anything but deny it.

Ian got out the fancy-ass whisky he kept for company and poured two shots and shoved one across the table to Karen. He downed his. She never drank whisky, but she thought, what the hell, and downed hers. "Great idea, eh? You're about to have a discussion with your husband about the affair you say you're not having, and you kick it off with a shot of whisky."

After a while, neither of them could sit still. Keeping a good healthy distance from each other, they paced up and down in their pokey little kitchen. Karen was willing to say anything to move the conversation away from the hypothetical affair, so she started complaining about how empty she felt—unfulfilled, bored, like she'd lost her authentic centre, all that crap. And Ian was saying, "But Karen, for god's sake, you can do anything you want. We could hire a nanny to look after Cam. You could get out more. See your friends. *Anything*. You don't have to stay stuck here in the house with a two-year-old day after day. God, that would drive anybody crazy. I'm not asking that of you. Just don't have an affair on me, okay?"

Karen had stopped with the one shot, but Ian hadn't. He was working his way through the bottle. No matter what she tried to talk about, he kept coming back to the affair, and every time he did, he had a few more details of what somebody-or-other might possibly have seen, until, eventually, they were down to one particular night in one particular restaurant—an East Indian place on Fraser—and what that hypothetical woman had been wearing—high heels with ankle socks, for Christ's sake, something that *nobody* was wearing any longer—a sick little kinder-whore bottom-feeder look from Karen's high school days that she'd revived because it really got Rob going.

Ian was a lawyer—not a courtroom lawyer, but a lawyer nonetheless. She should never have lost sight of that. But she had an advantage—she was sober, and he wasn't. She could see him controlling himself—the iron grip he had on himself—and she finally understood how carefully he'd guided her to that restaurant on Fraser, how carefully he'd been manipulating her. The entire time they'd been talking, he'd known perfectly well that she'd been having an affair. He had piles of evidence. Probably a lot more than he'd told her yet. He'd been giving her plenty of rope to hang herself with. When she understood that, she felt a white cold fury.

"Yeah, okay," she said, "you've caught me. I've been seeing Rob Clark"—and then, immediately, started lying about it. "No," she told him, "not for long. Only a few times. It doesn't mean anything. I was bored, and it was just something to do. It really doesn't mean anything at all."

Once she admitted it, that changed everything. She could see him starting to lose it. Both of them were furious and not bothering to hide it. "Fuck, Karen, what were you thinking?"

He kept drinking whisky. Pacing. "That fat bald old fucker? Just *what* were you thinking? What did you think *I'd* think? What do you think *of me*?"

It had been hours since her single shot, and she was sober as ice. She and Ian had switched roles, and it scared her. Usually she was the emotional one, the hysterical one, while he was cold and rational, the bloody lawyer. Yes, his *emotion* scared her. She hadn't seen much of it before.

She knew that she had to take things easier than easy. She knew that they had to stop. She kept saying, "Come on, Ian, we're not going anywhere with this tonight. Let's sleep on it, okay?" but it was like he hadn't heard her. It was like she hadn't said anything at all. He kept throwing out words about the affair—*the affair*—how he just didn't get it. Trapped inside the iron cage of his words was an energy that didn't give a shit for words, and she couldn't understand it—the level of his outrage. She thought it had something to do with being a man—that a woman's outrage would be very different. "Does that make any sense?" she asked Erica.

"Sure it does."

Karen was talking about something serious, something subtle, and she wanted Erica to really understand. She would try it a different way. "It was like something we don't usually see, something that goes on all the time *but we just don't see it*. Does *that* make sense?"

"Yes."

"Ian was telling himself a private story, and later I could remember some of the words but not how they fit into the story. I never could get the story straight. All these years later, I still can't. 'Jesus, Karen,' he said, 'you let that fat old asshole shove his cock up you,' and then there's a slice of time missing from my memory. I mean *gone*. Maybe I said the wrong thing—or maybe I didn't say anything at all."

He slapped her. Or he tried to. She ducked and twisted away—an absolutely instinctual reaction, something her body knew how to do even if her mind didn't. The slap didn't land full on her face, but it drove her head to one side, sent her reeling backwards into the wall. "Jesus, Ian!" she yelled at him.

They were both stopped. They were staring into each other's eyes. The look in his eyes was something she would remember forever. She was looking through the iron bars of his mind to that thing that was trapped inside it.

He turned away from her, grabbed up a plate from the table, and threw it against the wall.

That wild gesture set him off, and he started jerking cupboard doors open, hauling things out and smashing them. She stood, frozen, her cheek blazing where he'd hit her, and stared at him until she understood what he was doing. The only things he was breaking were wedding gifts—the china, the crystal. She knew that if Ian wasn't breaking the wedding gifts, he'd be breaking her.

There was a terrible sound. Karen realized that she'd been hearing it for a while but hadn't been able to pay attention. It was Cameron screaming. He was standing just inside the doorway screaming. She didn't know how long he'd been there. She didn't know if he'd seen Ian hit her, but he probably had. She couldn't imagine what else could have stopped him in the doorway. Ordinarily he would have run straight to her. "Come here, sweetie," she said. "It's all right," and picked him up.

Ian stopped breaking things. He stared at his son and his wife. He had no expression on his face. He walked out. He walked past them like they were two pieces of furniture and walked through the living room and out the front door. She heard his car start, and she heard him drive away.

SO HER MARRIAGE WAS over just like that. Gone, smashed, destroyed—absolutely nothing of it left, not even a lonely little fragment. It was probably her fault, but that didn't matter because she knew she could never be alone with that man again, not even for five minutes. Okay, so when things are that bad—seriously bad, really fucked—there's only one place to go.

Her parents had bought the house on Eighteenth the year Karen was born. They still lived there, and Karen still had the key. She tried to come in quietly, but that wasn't going to happen, not with Cam. The minute he saw his grandmother hurrying down the stairs in her old terrycloth bathrobe, he started crying again—"Nana! Nana!"

Her mum didn't ask her what was going on because that was obviously not the first order of business. "Oh, you poor little guy," she said, "let's get you to bed." They'd already turned the room that used to be Steve's into Cam's play room. It was a safe familiar place to him. He'd had naps there lots of times.

After Cam was asleep, Karen sat in the kitchen with her parents and told them everything. Of course she had to tell them about the affair. They drank chamomile tea— "just like Peter Rabbit," her mum said with her loopy sense of humour. Her dad seemed to be focused on the slap that hadn't quite connected. He wanted to know every detail of it. "What do you mean, you ducked? Do you mean you dropped down or you moved back?" She described it as clearly as she could.

Then she saw how angry her father was—actually trembling. "Karen," he said, "it doesn't matter what you did. This isn't a three-strikes-you're-out situation. That son of a bitch hit you. He doesn't get another chance."

"Yeah, I know, but . . . Oh, Dad, he'd had too much to drink."

"What? You held a gun to his head and made him drink that whisky?"

They talked for a couple of hours, and her parents said what they always said. "This is your home. You can stay here as long as you want. You know that."

Karen went to bed in the room that had always been hers, and she was glad to be there, but she couldn't sleep. She hadn't cried yet, and that surprised her. Her husband had hit her. Her marriage was ruined, wrecked, destroyed beyond repair. She was supposed to be devastated, but she wasn't. The main thing she was feeling—and it was embarrassing that she was feeling it—was relief. The stupid lies were over. Thank god for that.

She got up, crept quietly out of the house, and walked down the hill to Marine. Her mind was a chaos—so many things to think about, none of it making sense. She'd been in some sketchy situations with men before, but this was the first time she'd been deeply afraid of a man—*physically* afraid. She knew that all over the world, right at that very minute, men were beating the crap out of women, and they'd been doing that forever, but it had never occurred to her that somebody might beat the crap out of her. Okay, but Ian had stopped himself just in time—she had to give him that. So then all of this drama was about *a slap?* How pathetic. What real problems did she have?

She walked down to the seawall, then west to Dundarave Pier, and sat on a bench and listened to the waves. It was a dark night, overcast. When she looked out, there was nothing to see. As she let her mind drift, she began to understand why her father had asked her all those questions. He was a structural engineer. He was thinking about lines of force. What if she hadn't ducked or twisted away or whatever her body had done on its own? What if she had simply stood there? She saw it clearly—the uncoiled torque of Ian's body—the force of his entire body. She saw his open hand landing smack in the centre of her face.

Fuck, she thought. Yes, she had a real life with real problems. How could she have married a man like that—a man she hardly knew? She had stopped seeing Helen when Cam was born—Ian had talked her out of it—but now she had to go back.

In her very first session with Helen, Karen had tried to explain why she was there—just what exactly had brought her into a therapist's office. It was hard to pin down. It was a kind of malaise. She felt like she'd taken a wrong road somewhere. It was exactly like the two roads that diverged in the Robert Frost poem. If she could figure out where those roads diverged, she could walk back and take the right road.

Helen told her it was an archetype—that image of diverging roads. "We create our lives with the small individual decisions we make minute by minute. We face those diverging roads every day."

That was all well and good—that was all quite poetic—but Karen was never entirely convinced. That image in her mind didn't feel like an archetype or a metaphor. It felt like exactly what it looked like—two roads diverging at a specific time and place. What if it had been that simple? Marrying Ian? Had that been the wrong road? No, it must have been long before that. If she hadn't been on the wrong road, she wouldn't have even considered marrying someone like Ian. She saw the light beginning to turn the sky in the east into a lucent indigo above the mountains. She walked toward the light.

It was weird, but now she was thinking about Jane Austen. She adored Jane Austen—had written a paper on her. She had argued that the eighteenth century idea of "companionate marriage" suffused all of Austen's work, and that it was a very simple idea—a husband and a wife should be friends.

Karen walked in the dark, listening to the ocean. Ian MacLachlan is not my friend, she thought, and neither is Rob Clark. They could both go fuck themselves. When she divorced Ian, she would go back to her maiden name, and she would keep it for the rest of her life. Difficult as she could be at times, Karen Oxley was a familiar bundle of self, but Karen MacLachlan had always remained incomprehensible. If Karen had learned anything in therapy, it was to ask herself the difficult questions she usually directed at other people. Okay, if Ian had been telling himself a private story, one that she didn't understand, what was *her* private story?

Beginning with the man she'd chosen, she had designed everything about her marriage to be seen from the outside.

She walked toward the dawn. Because the mountains were in the way it would take a long time before she would see the sun come up, but she watched the sky change, and then on the pier at John Lawson, looking east toward the light, she experienced one of the most remarkable moments of her life. It wasn't gradual, and she couldn't remember exactly what she'd been thinking just before it happened, but it struck her like a religious epiphany—sudden and total and real. It was all so simple. She was *whole*.

She didn't need men in her life—maybe later, but not now. She needed to take care of Cam, and to do that, she needed to take care of herself, and that's exactly what she was going to do. She'd live with her parents. There was no shame in that. She was twenty-eight, but so what? She knew that people would talk—she knew exactly the kind of vile, petty, small-minded, hurtful things they'd say about her—but what if she stopped caring about any of that? Then she could do what she wanted.

Yes, she *had* taken the wrong road, and all she had to do now was get back on the right one. Her mum would help her look after Cam. Karen was young. She still had time. She could get a job again. She'd loved her last one, and there had to be a place for her somewhere in the publishing industry. She might even go back to university and get another degree.

All the time that Karen had been talking, she'd been aware of Erica, and now that she'd come to the end, she was intensely aware of her. She turned to look. The corners of Erica's eyes were pinched with fatigue, and for the first time Karen didn't see her as a teenager but as a mature woman. She'd been afraid that Erica might have been only half-listening, that she might be drifting, but no—she could see that Erica had been with her the whole way, was still with her—and oh my god, it was nearly eleven. Karen had slept for an hour, but Erica hadn't slept at all.

Karen had never told the entire story to anyone before—not straight through like this, not as clearly as this—and there was one more thing she had to say. "I knew exactly what to do, and it felt absolutely right. And then I didn't do it. Why didn't I do it?"

11.

TONIGHT WAS SUNDAY NIGHT, family night, so that meant that it had been exactly three weeks since Erica had driven the remains of her squashed Golf into Karen's life. Something about the situation didn't compute—something uncanny, even a bit goose-bumpy. When Karen imagined telling it as a story, all she could find to say was that a door had opened and she'd walked through it. That wouldn't be enough for most people—not for gossip-hungry Jen and the ladies, certainly not for Drew—but she didn't feel like trying to explain herself. When she and Erica had talked all night long, they had exchanged mysteries—and that exchange, itself, had become a mystery.

Erica spent much of her time at the university—she was, after all, an assistant professor—but when she wasn't at the university, she was at Karen's. She fit into the household routine as easily as if she'd always been there. She had taken over some of the driving—the pickups, the deliveries, the shopping. She did the kitchen clean-up. She helped the twins with their homework. She was a neat-freak, walked around the house tidying things up. She referred to herself wryly as "the guest who never leaves." Karen always said, "Don't worry. Stay till you're feeling better," and Erica always answered with her standard phrase, "You're so kind."

They didn't need to pull another all-nighter because they talked whenever they were together, and they were together a lot. Karen took

Erica to the gym with her, took her for walks on the seawall. She showed her the spot on the pier at John Lawson where she'd had her epiphany. Karen heard all about the torturous process of getting a PhD just as Erica heard all about the torturous process of delivering four babies. But they didn't just talk about the big things—they seemed to be trying to dump their entire memory banks into each other's minds, and nothing was too trivial. Karen knew that Erica was phobic about wearing rings on her fingers, probably from playing softball. Erica knew that Karen always sneezed when she brushed her teeth because she was allergic to mint.

Karen was haunted by the image of Erica and Annalise standing naked in their hotel room in Calgary looking at themselves in the bathroom mirror. It was like a fragment from a dream that stood for nothing but itself—any attempt to interpret it would diminish it. Karen told herself to do what Helen, her therapist, would have told her to do—stay with the image, deepen it. The two girls were studying themselves to see how they had changed their bodies, how softball and ballet had made them different. They were sorry they were different.

As fascinated as Karen was by the story of Erica saying goodbye to her sister in Calgary, Erica seemed just as fascinated by Karen's moment on the pier at John Lawson—that sense of wholeness, completeness. She repeated the question Karen had asked herself— "And if you knew the right thing to do, *why* didn't you do it?"

It frightened Karen how easily she could lose track of herself. "You have to understand how everybody saw me. I'd been the golden girl who could do no wrong, but now I was a fuck-up. I'd had a messy affair and wrecked my marriage. And I'd broken up Rob's marriage. And I had a kid, and Rob had a kid . . . a little girl not even two yet. Now I can't understand how I could have done it . . . jumped into that crazy affair. What was I thinking? I *wasn't* thinking. I hated myself. Marrying Rob offered me a way out. Safety, security, all those things women are supposed to want, I guess I wanted them. It was too easy to say yes."

She tried to tell Erica again about that subtle thing she'd seen, or felt, the night that Ian had hit her, but every attempt at definition dissolved into nothing. No, it wasn't quite that all of us have a secret life, a private story—although it was *almost* like that. It was obvious to everyone, yet no one ever saw it—a feeling, a continuous presence, an energy. One way to talk about it was with that old Shakespearian metaphor—like theatre, we walk onto the stage and assume roles that are already written for us. At the same time we're writing our own story, trying to make a different story—but it wasn't like that at all. The theatre metaphor was too solid, too substantial. It was more like a ripple in a force field, the tug on a strand in a spider web—but it wasn't like those things either. She wanted Erica to understand something she didn't understand herself.

She was sure that if she ever dropped even the faintest of hints, Erica would leave, but she didn't want Erica to leave—and even said it: "I'll be sorry when you go." Erica replied with her grave smile and said what she always said: "Thank you. You're so kind." But she had to go back to Medicine Hat for Christmas, and that should provide a natural end to things—but would it?

Family night had been built around a routine. Drew usually came over on Saturday, spent the night, and then on Sunday cooked the dinner, but since Erica had arrived, he wasn't doing that. He made occasional forays into the house, stayed just long enough to see that Erica was still there, and stormed off in a huff. It was absurd, but he was the only one who knew how to cook a real meal from scratch, so family night had become take-out night. The first Sunday without him had been sushi night, the second Chinese night, and this was Thai night. Because Karen was going out with Drew, Erica was in charge of it.

Karen couldn't remember the last time she'd bothered dressing up—she'd been living in yoga-wear for what seemed like forever—but back in the day dressing up had been one of her major pleasures. She was in a dark teal mood tonight—tube skirt and off-the-shoulder sweater designed to show off her gym-trained shoulders, and they were very good shoulders, too. She hadn't bothered with jewelry—that would have been tacky, would have interrupted the simple elegance that was her trademark—and had finished off her look with the sleek black Louboutin boots she'd bought on impulse and had never worn before. Karen walked into the dining room to show off. Everyone was impressed, Paige especially. "Wow, Mum, you look like a celebrity!"

"If I didn't know you," Erica said, "if I'd just met you at a party or something, you'd scare me to death."

Karen felt unaccountably hurt. "Is that a compliment?"

She walked away from them, toward the living room where Drew was perched stiffly on the edge of a chair waiting for her. Erica followed. They stopped in the hallway. Karen hadn't put on her peacoat yet—she'd wanted everyone to see her dark teal mood. Erica took the coat from her, held it for her, helped her on with it—what a strange gesture. "I didn't mean that you don't look good. You look great. It's like . . ." She drew an empty space with her hands. "Annalise wore heels. I never did."

In a moment that was like a fragment dropped out of time, Karen was caught by Erica's beautiful eyes. "That thing you keep talking about," Erica said, "that you can't define? Private stories? Whatever? Okay. We're not what people see."

KAREN COULDN'T BELIEVE IT—Drew was *still* talking about Jamie. "You're not doing her any favours, you know. You're letting her run over you roughshod." More than merely preoccupied, he seemed to be running on some obscure default mode that didn't require much power—not quite hibernating but not fully functional either. He pressed his hand into the small of Karen's back and escorted her into the dining room.

The maître d' appeared in a flash—"Ah, Monsieur Thompson, how nice to see you again," with an honest-to-god French accent. Drew didn't say a word but made a rude chopping gesture that could be translated into, *Shut up, you pretentious jerk, and get us a table.* She remembered why she hated going out to dinner with him.

Drew liked to be known for his taste in fine dining, and this was the highest-end of Vancouver's high-end French restaurants, a discreet little place where he often brought visiting American oil executives. It required reservations days in advance—unless, of course, you were Drew Thompson—and attracted a clientele who didn't mind dropping a thousand bucks onto their expense accounts. The dining room was not large; Karen could see everyone in it, and every man in it was checking her out. She felt a response so physical it was like being washed with a tingly pleasure beam.

It had been years since she'd worn heels this high, and that, she supposed, was a sad commentary on her current life. She used to enjoy the sensation of walking in heels, the height they gave her, the sense of being poised and ready for things distinctly interesting—and they'd been Rob's number one fetish, so she'd had plenty of encouragement to wear them while they'd been married. Karen's sexual response was, as she'd told Erica, so stereotypically feminine that it was embarrassing. Getting dressed up turned her on, and her male companion was supposed to get turned on just by looking at her, and that was supposed to turn her on so that they'd both be swept away into a positive feedback loop that would lead, several hours later, to a lovely time in bed. Looking at Drew, she saw that he didn't give a rat's ass.

That, however, was not true of the gentlemen at the table to her left—five of them, young guys in banker-style business suits. They'd polished off a whacking big dinner and several bottles of wine along with it, were well into their brandy and Irish coffee and crème brûlée, and there was no doubt that Karen had *their* attention—every bloody one of them. The consensus from their table, obvious from their eyes, was that they wouldn't mind adding her to the dessert menu. She sent them just enough of a conspirator's smile for it to register. Oh. My. God. She was forty-three years old. If she could still get that kind of reaction from a table full of thirty-somethings, then life wasn't so bad, was it? The maître d' held her chair for her, and she sat in it. Drew had not observed the mini-drama, but the maître d' had. He and Karen grinned at each other like Cheshire cats. "You know what?" Drew said. "I feel like escargot tonight. How about you?"

"I don't think so, sweetie." How long have you known me? she asked him in her mind. And why don't you know by now that I don't eat snails?

DREW HAD EATEN his snails and Karen the lightest thing she could find—the Coeur de Laitue with Vinaigrette Maison. He was now working on the Escalopes d'Agneau Grillées, while she was dining on Saumon du Pacifique. He was eyeing the roast potatoes she was neglecting, ready, the moment she was finished, to whisk them off her plate and onto his. They were drinking a bottle of wine that cost twice as much as both of their dinners, and he was drinking most of it. She was thinking about how similar he was to Rob and how different. They were both men whose moods improved the minute you threw a meal into them. They both had expensive tastes in alcohol—Rob loved his single malts, Drew his fine wines. They both considered themselves gourmets, but cheerful expansive Rob was loved by the staff wherever he went while Drew treated waiters and waitresses with cold sneering condescension and made up for it by tipping their asses off. Rob would never in a million years have eaten anything that had been on Karen's plate.

Drew and Rob had worked together for years, and Drew considered Rob to be one of his best friends. Things had been a little tense between them when Drew and Karen had first got together, but as soon as Rob found Christine, the men were back on excellent terms. The last time Drew had been in LA, he'd actually met Chris—he called her "stunning" and "a sweetheart." She was perfect for Rob, he said—she shared his values. Like Karen, she was a blonde. "Rob has a thing for blondes," he told Karen just as though she might not have noticed.

Then, as Karen looked up, looked at Drew methodically consuming his medium-rare lamb, she experienced one of her utterly convincing inner clicks. It was over. It had been over for quite some time. The only question was whether to tell him now or tell him later.

"I don't know if you've considered this, Karen," he was saying, "but the situation you're in is fairly dangerous."

He'd finally arrived at the point of this dinner—*his* point, at any rate. "The thing about stalkers is that they're not rational. She's obviously deeply depressed. She's badly in need of psychiatric care. She lost her sister, and now she seems to have attached herself to you. God knows what she really wants. She probably doesn't know herself."

It wouldn't do any good to argue with him. If they were breaking up, it would be pointless anyway. She should probably tell him tonight, but it was going to be a bitch of a week, and she just didn't need the extra aggravation.

"Wrecking her car just to get an entrée into your home?" he was saying. "That sounds fairly desperate to me. And then pretending to be so out of it she couldn't even talk . . . Well, what a performance!"

"Now wait a minute, Drew. She had hypothermia. The doctor in emergency—"

"Hypothermia doesn't take away your powers of speech, Karen. It just doesn't work that way. Stop and think about it a minute. What kind of mind works out a plot that complicated? If you ever bothered to actually talk to her—"

"*Talk* to her!" This was useless. How could she steer the conversation in some other direction? "I've talked to her plenty, and she's not the least bit dangerous. The kids like her, and she's actually been quite helpful, and . . . Oh, the twins are turning thirteen on Saturday. Did you remember?"

Of course he remembered, he said—she didn't believe him—but he wasn't about to be sidetracked. The problem with stalkers, he told her, was that they didn't fit into any predictable pattern, each was different. Some were annoying but relatively harmless, others made people's lives absolutely miserable. Some were psychotic—if they were rejected, were capable of anything, even murder. God, she thought, he's been reading too many Stephen King novels.

Karen sent a covert smile to their waiter. He arrived instantly. She asked for jasmine tea . . . and something light? Oh, lemon sherbet with biscotti sounded delightful.

Drew was still talking, but she tuned him out. There was a lot on her mind. This was the first year Devon would be home for his birthday since he'd turned seven, which made it a special birthday, and the twins saw it as doubly special. Their childhood was ending. They were becoming *teenagers*. They'd actually used the phrase "a life milestone," and Dev must have impressed his father with the significance of the occasion because Rob had sent each of them a cheque for a thousand bucks with a note attached saying, "Don't spend this on anything useful." Well, Rob had got off easy. Okay, she'd said, so what do you want? Their hair done again, they said, and some new clothes, and their ears pierced, and a big party for their friends. They wanted to invite the entire Anime Club—and, no, not to some cheesy restaurant—"to our home." Karen felt the deep mystical significance they attached to the notion of "our home."

"And not just pizza and paper plates either," Jamie said. "A real dinner. You know, Mum, like you do for *your* friends."

"*My* friends? There's never more than five of us. And what? You mean with your great-grandmother's silver and china?" Yes, that was exactly what Jamie meant. "Full on," she said.

Okay, so the full-on dinner was Saturday night, and then the next night was the traditional family birthday dinner at Karen's mum's. For the past four years Drew had been at every one of those family birthdays—by now it must be part of *his* tradition—so it wouldn't hurt to have him at another one, would it? And then there was Christmas— should she tell him before or after Christmas? She didn't want to spoil the holidays for him. God, she hated hurting people. Sometime in the new year, maybe.

"Don't forget," she said, "the twins' birthday dinner. You know, at Mum's."

"Karen, seriously, I don't see how you can expect me to behave just as though everything's perfectly normal. The first thing we've got to do is get that crazy woman out of your house. You want me to talk to her? Give her an ultimatum? I have absolutely no problem with that. And then you and I have to sit down with Jamie and have a long talk—"

That was it. "Drew?"

"Establish some rock-solid ground rules this time, and—"

"Drew!"

He hated being interrupted—she knew that—but he did stop. He must have sensed that something was up. His face had fallen into that expression she thought of as "CEO neutral."

"*You and I*," she said, "that's not going to happen, sweetie. It's over."

"WOW, MOM," Devon said in a half whisper, "this place is seriously gay!" It didn't sound like that nasty teen put-down "so gay"—it sounded amazed or even delighted.

They had just arrived at this weird little shop mysteriously named "Excalibur," and he was right—it *was* seriously gay. The mannequins in the window were multiply pierced males dressed in menacing outfits— leather jackets, motorcycle boots, cop-style caps. One of them was not only pierced but had metal clips attached to his nipples. Another was kneeling with his arms strapped behind his back. And then, if you kept on looking, you found the one near the back wearing a studded collar and a leash. Karen, Erica, and the twins were standing in the rain outside this display of unabashedly gay S&M because Jamie and Devon had insisted on getting their ears pierced at exactly the same place where Morgan and Avalon had theirs done. Bryan and his girls were supposed to meet them, but they hadn't shown up.

"Maybe we should go in?" Erica said.

"Maybe we should go home," Karen said.

"Mum!" Jamie managed to make that single syllable sound both whiny and threatening.

That morning—the morning of their big life-changing birthday—Jamie had got out of bed in the worst of all possible moods, and she'd been foul and inscrutable ever since. Now Vancouver was doing December in its dank pissy familiar way—steady rain and clotted darkness in the middle of the afternoon. The umbrellas were in the car, of course, and Karen was chilled to the bone.

"This sucks balls," Jamie said—pushed through the door and walked into the shop. I love you too, Karen thought. All she could do now was follow Jamie, but she was stopped by a loud whoop. Bryan Lynas appeared as unexpectedly as if he'd dropped out of the sky. He and his girls must have hit the ground running—they were in full gallop, all three of them wearing cheery yellow rain slickers. "Happy birthday!" the girls chanted at Devon.

"Sorry, ladies," Bryan was saying, "time got a bit buggered up on me." As he went by, he caught Karen and Erica, one arm around each, and propelled them through the door. "How you going? Owright?"

Catching up to Jamie, the Lynas twins exploded into squeals—"*Happy* birthday!" Karen saw Jamie smile for the first time that day.

The proprietor of the shop matched the window display—was huge, had dense mosaics of black tattoos on both arms, half a dozen steel loops and studs riveted through his ears and face, a neatly trimmed full beard, and a shaved head. He and Bryan were wrapped up in a muscular embrace—"Hey, Lynas!"—accompanied by ritual yelps and slaps on the back. Okay, Karen thought, at least Bryan isn't homophobic.

"Here's the mum," Bryan said with an inclusive gesture.

"Karen Oxley," she said, offering her hand to the paw of this cliché character whose name turned out to be *Arthur*.

"He's the best," one of Bryan's twins was telling Erica. "He's lovely. He pierced *us*."

Devon stepped forward to shake Arthur's hand, but Jamie was hanging back, her eyes fixed on her shoes.

"Today's their birthday," one of the Lynas twins was telling Arthur, "and you're a birthday present."

"Awesome. I love being a birthday present. What's the big number?"

"Thirteen," Devon said with his brilliant smile.

"Ah, it's good, it's good, it's all good," Arthur was murmuring. "Okay, Karen, can I see some photo ID?"

Exasperated, she jerked her wallet out of her jacket, but before she could open it, he said, "So sorry, dear, had to ask. Could you fill out these forms? One for each kid, eh?" He snapped two pieces of paper onto a clipboard and offered it to her, but Devon intercepted it. "We'll do it, Mom. You just have to sign."

"You must think I'm crazy to let them do this," Karen said to Erica.

"No, I don't."

Arthur was showing the twins his autoclave—"Sterile's the name of the game." That was good to hear, but he and Bryan seemed to have wandered off into a side conversation about a large round table in the centre of the shop. It was used to display leather underwear and a few other steel-and-leather items whose use was not readily obvious. Arthur gave it a push, and it teetered dangerously. "Wonky is it?" Bryan said. "You got some scrap leather?"

"Mom," Devon was calling to her, "what kind of studs do we want?"

"The best."

"The best's titanium," Arthur yelled at her. "We use pure medical grade. It's the easiest on the body, but it's kind of pricey."

"I don't care how pricey it is, use the best you've got"—and leave me out of it.

189

"Just the thought of piercing makes me queasy," she told Erica, "like drop-down-in-a-faint queasy. I've always been that way . . . Needles, bodily fluids, blood. Eeeew."

"Our older sister's like that," Erica said. "Trina's actually a fainter, so we teased the living daylights out of her. The minute we got cut or anything, we headed straight for her."

Karen was glad to hear Erica talking about her twin. Annalise could drift in and out of the conversation now without the sense of the world coming to an end. Erica did seem to be getting better, although of course it was bound to take time. "I was the queen of bloody knees," she was saying, "then when Lise started pointe, she'd come home with her toes bloody—"

"Stop it with the bloody toes, please. I actually have fainted. It's worse when I think about it."

"You can desensitize yourself to phobias, you know. It's not hard to do."

"Really? Not today."

Karen turned to look out the steamy window at the rain. She didn't want to see it done even at a distance.

"Do me first, please," she heard Jamie saying. That was a surprise.

"Okay, son, no problem."

"I'm a girl."

"Well, of course you are, darling, of course you are."

"Is it over yet?" Karen asked Erica.

"Not even close," Erica said. "He's marking her earlobes . . . . Okay, I think he's going to do it now. Yeah, there he goes."

Karen held her breath until she heard movement. She turned to see Jamie walking toward her with a genuine smile. "Does it hurt?" Devon asked her.

Jamie gave him her best eye-roll. "It was like the most excruciating pain I've ever experienced in my life." She lifted her hair to show off a bright flicker of titanium, and Karen turned away immediately. "Don't," she said. "Jamie, come on. You know how I am." Jamie laughed.

"After the holes are healed up, you can wear anything you want," one of the Lynas twins was telling Jamie—and lifted her hair to show off a shiny black teardrop running down her earlobe. Her sister simultaneously exposed her earlobe to Karen and Erica. "Onyx," one of them said.

"How cool is that?" the other one said.

Karen risked a glance back into the shop. Bryan had crawled under the round table and seemed to be working on something. Now in a voice like a cartoonish parody of his own Aussie accent he yelled out, "Strewth, I've cut it four times and it's still too short!" Arthur rewarded him with a high-pitched cackle—and then Karen saw that Devon was sitting in a chair in front of Arthur—and Arthur was wearing *surgical gloves*. No, she shouldn't have seen that. She turned away immediately. She held her breath again.

"Hang on," Erica said, patting her on the shoulder. "It's almost over."

THE TWINS PIERCED, the forms signed, the bill slapped on the plastic, they were out on the street. Karen felt emotionally exhausted, needed her caffeine level boosted, badly—and spotted a Starbucks in the next block. "Catch you later," Bryan was saying, gathering his girls to him. Like a chorus, his twins echoed, "Catch you later." The father-daughter team did look cute in their yellow slickers. "Come early, okay?" Jamie yelled after them.

"Coffee," Karen said and began walking toward it.

"I can't begin to tell you how happy this makes me," Devon said, touching an earlobe.

"It means something important to you?" Erica asked him.

"Oh, yeah . . . It's like . . . just so cool."

"He's saying fuck off to his old school," Jamie said.

"You would have got in trouble for pierced ears?" Erica asked Devon.

"Trouble? I would've been snuffed in like five seconds."

Erica had a real talent for getting people to talk—probably because she seemed so genuinely interested in them. "A lot of bullying . . . ?" she was saying to Devon.

"Bullying? Oh no. We had a zero tolerance policy. Bullying was absolutely unheard of." He laughed. "No, everybody bullied everybody all the time. Like constantly. I tried to stay like below the radar, but it didn't always happen."

The inside of the Starbucks smelled like wet wool and winter misery, but the customers seemed to be happy enough—a collection of twenty-somethings with knapsacks, books, and laptops. Karen found an empty table near the washrooms. She was grateful to Erica for doing all the talking. That might give her what she wanted—a few minutes to herself, a few minutes to sit there simply doing nothing. God, it was going to be a long day.

But she had to take drink orders. She kept waiting for the right moment but didn't want to interrupt Devon. Erica had really got him talking—telling bullying stories, laughing like it had all happened to somebody else, some hopeless pathetic loser kid, not him. Boys pinned him to the ground while others took turns spitting on him? They took his shoes? "Yeah . . . Like, 'Hey, faggot, who told you you could wear Nikes?' I had to go to the freakin' lost-and-found to find something I could wear home."

Karen had never heard any of this before. She was stuck there, hovering at the side of the table with no coffee, afraid that if she walked over to the barista, she'd miss something. "Wait a minute," she said. "What school was this? In the Valley?"

"No, no, no. This was after Dad married Chris . . . after we moved."

"Didn't you tell your father about any of this stuff?"

"Oh, yeah, sort of . . . like not so much. He wasn't . . . He's like, 'That's terrible, Dev. You want me to talk to the principal?' No, I did not want him to talk to the principal. If he talked to the principal, I would've been Purina Puppy Chow. And he's like, 'Have you thought about Anderson Hill?' That's the freakin' boys' school they want to send me to. Can you imagine me at a boys' school? *Me?*"

Karen had seen Erica get up and walk over to the barista, but her mind was so numb she hadn't really registered the significance of that. Now Erica was back with a tray of drinks, handed one to Karen. "What's this?"

"A grande skinny latte, triple shot. Isn't that what you wanted?"

She'd got caramel macchiatos for the twins—"Decaf," she told Karen under her breath. Wow, Karen thought, she's better than any boyfriend I ever had.

Grateful for the dark bite of the espresso, Karen sank into one of the fat leather chairs. Devon was telling Erica about the freakin' boys' school, but Jamie interrupted him. "Tell them about what they did to Consuela."

Startled, Devon studied his sister. Identical or not, he must sometimes find her just as puzzling as everybody else did. "Yeah," he said, "they just fired her. How can you just fire somebody like—"

"Consuela?" Karen said. "She was your housekeeper—?"

"Yeah, Mom, she was our housekeeper! You know that. You met her when you took me down there, remember? You talked to her on the phone like a million times. I used to hang with her and her kids . . . Luz mainly."

Of course Karen knew who Consuela was—what was wrong with her?—but that ghastly trip to LA was an untrustworthy haze in her memory. She could remember how shitty she'd felt but not many of the actual events. She'd wanted Jamie and Devon to think that everything was just fine, so she'd been forced to act like everything was just fine, and it had taken a toll on her. She didn't know how she'd managed to get through it, actually. "Did I meet Luz?"

"No. Probably not. She's like shy."

Erica gave Karen a significant look—meaning what?—and then began to ask Devon more questions. Yeah, Luz was a year older than he was but they got along great. Luz and her mom lived in Devon's house—it was a big house, a rancher—and sometimes Dad wasn't around that much anyway. He had an apartment downtown, and when he was working on something, he'd stay there for like days. Consuela had a husband and two older kids, boys—they were a lot older—but they didn't live there. No, Consuela wasn't separated—she got along fine with Carlos. Sometimes Devon would hang out with their whole family. It was a huge family. "Luz's cousin got married, and . . . Wow, do Mexicans ever know how to party! They taught me how to dance. I even learned some Spanish. I bet you didn't know that, huh?"

"Say something in Spanish," Jamie said.

"*Que tranza, guey?*" he said, happily showing off. "That's like, what up, dude? *Aquí cotorreando.* Just chillin'."

He'd just rolled his R like a native speaker. "My god," she said, "that's amazing, Dev. Why didn't you tell me you could speak Spanish?"

He shrugged apologetically. "It's just kid Spanish."

"Did you hang out with the Mexican kids at school?" Erica asked him.

"Oh, no. They went to public school. I was in this like rich kids' elementary school . . . Crawford House . . . we called it Crawfish House."

"Did you like it?"

"I don't know. Yeah, it was okay. It was like . . . enriched? They put me in the geek program. Teaching us code and stuff."

As Erica kept asking more questions, Karen finally understood what was going on. Erica was *a psychologist*. She must have conducted hundreds of interviews before, and she was conducting one now, right here in Starbucks.

Devon hung out with a couple of the kids from the geek program, he told them. They'd go to each other's houses and play World of Warcraft or just goof off on the computer. "You think *I'm* a geek. Josh was a super-geek. He could like hack into things."

This was the most that Karen had heard out of Devon since he'd come back. He was *her son*, but she didn't know him very well. She'd been imagining him as an awkward solitary kid alone in his room playing video games, but that picture was fading away. He did have friends—if not a huge number of them, at least some close ones. Now he was talking about somebody called Taylor. Was that a boy or a girl? Karen had never heard of anyone named Taylor.

"Josh's sister," Devon explained to Erica. "She was like into manga and anime, *Sailor Moon* and all that stuff. Shōjo stuff. *Revolutionary Girl Utena. Neon Genesis.* She lent me all her stuff. She was like three years older than us? Four maybe? A teenager."

Josh's mom took them to Anime Expo. "Whoa!" he said, "it was . . . I just couldn't believe it. It like blew me away."

"So you were friends with Taylor?"

"Friends? I don't know. I was like this nerdy little fanboy. 'Hey, can I hang out with you? You're awesome.' She put up with me."

As Devon had been talking, Jamie seemed to have sunk back into her foul mood. She was stirring the foam at the bottom of her cup with her index finger and licking it. Without looking up, she said, "So tell them how they fired Consuela."

"Oh, yeah, so after Dad marries Chris, she's like . . . She's into horses. She has all these . . . They're some kind of fancy horses. She does this . . . what's it . . .? Yeah, dressage. You know, where you get all dressed up and get the horse to jump over things? So he buys like this humongous house, with all these stables, like a million acres, way out in the freakin' middle of nowhere, and Chris decides she wants her own staff, so they just fire Consuela and get a bunch of new people—

"How can you . . .? I was like . . . She was like a mom to me . . . I mean I know you're my mom, Mom, but like when I first moved down there, I missed you guys and all, but . . . Yeah, Consuela was great. When somebody works for you *for years*, how can you just fire them like that?"

The quiver in his voice made Karen afraid that he was going to embarrass himself by crying in Starbucks, but he didn't. "Me and Luz are still friends on Facebook," he said.

"Tell them how you got totally grounded," Jamie said.

"Yeah, I was. Dad's like . . . He's like totally whipped. Anything Chris wants, that's what's happening, and she's like, 'This anime stuff isn't healthy for kids.' Yeah, somebody in her church told her all about it. Un-American. On the gay agenda. Jeez, can you believe that shit! Josh and Taylor like invited me to go to Anime Expo again, but . . ." He shrugged. "No way.

"Our freakin' house. It's not like somebody's house you can live in, right? It's like a freakin' hotel. And I'm supposed to go outside and *get fresh air* . . . but I'm not allowed to go near the horses and I'm not sup-posed to bother the staff."

"That's when they sent him up here," Jamie said, "like, 'Just get him the fuck out of here.' And then when he got back, they thought he was talking to me too much, like online. They wouldn't let him near a computer."

"Yeah, I was totally cut. We had to write snail mails."

"Tell them about Chris going through your room," Jamie said.

"Yeah. She did. She found all these . . . She's like, 'Why are you reading this—?' Like *Shojo Beat*. That really got to her."

"It's a manga magazine," Jamie said.

"Yeah, and Chris's like, 'This is a *girl's* magazine! Like for *little* girls! You have no business reading this.' Oh my god, and it's got great things in it—*Nana, Crimson Hero*. And she found *The Ghost in the Shell*, she hated that, and . . . But the one that really got to her was *Two from One Fire* and it's like perfect. It's like *for us!* But she's like, 'Devon, this is pornography! Absolutely disgusting! I will not have Avery growing up in a household filled with pornography,' and Avery's a little baby! We never even get to see Avery because Valentina takes care of her. Chris goes in and picks her up for like ten minutes a day, and that's it for Avery . . . And anyhow why would you name your kid after *a label?*"

Karen had to laugh at that, but Jamie was not amused. "She took all his stuff," she said.

"Yeah, she did," he said.

Erica was wearing that expression Karen had come to think of as her "house cat look"—hyper-intelligent, fully engaged, and not human at all. "Is that when you first started thinking about suicide?"

Karen felt her heart miss a beat. It wasn't a metaphor; she actually felt it—thump, pause, ka-THUD—but Devon seemed to be taking it in stride. He was frowning slightly, thinking about it.

"There was this kid," he said. "I didn't really know him. He was a lot older than us. Taylor knew some kids that knew him. His name was Andrew Warrenton, and he killed himself. It was . . . They had a big celebration of life for him, and lots of kids went to it. Taylor went to it. Everybody was like, 'He looked so normal. His family was so normal.' He was . . . He went to this private school. He hanged himself with his school necktie. And everybody's like, 'Why would he do this?' Some kids thought he was gay, but nobody knew for sure. And they said he was like . . . picked on? Or maybe he was on Prozac or some shit like that. Or maybe he was into street drugs? And I didn't think about him much, but . . ."

He took a breath. "And then it kinda hit me, you know what I mean? There probably wasn't just one thing. It was like *everything*."

"That must have been a hard time for you," Erica said.

"Oh, yeah. Hard? Yeah. Yeah, it was hard." He looked at his sister. "Things were pretty hard for you too, huh?"

Jamie was staring at the table top. "Oh, yeah. Can we go home now?"

HOME HAD BEEN utterly transformed—all too shiny bright, all too bloody much, and Karen was supposed to be in charge of it? She was trapped inside a kaleidoscope—voices and lights and reflections of lights on the windows polished by the cleaning crew, the daylight outside gone to a pissy nothing but here inside every lamp turned on— Oh, and Jamie was lighting the tapers on the beautiful tables— and all of these realistic human bodies were in motion, striding purposefully through the light, all of them talking, all of them wanting something from her— "Excuse me, Mrs. Oxley—"

What if she became bedazzled and simply stood there, doing nothing, exhausted and non-functional? "Mrs. Oxley— Mrs. Oxley—" The servers seemed like nice kids, university kids—Erica had already learned their names—unpacking all of that insane amount of food. They seemed superbly self-confident, taking up the entire kitchen to be self-confident in, and Bryan Lynas was asking her, "You had it *catered?*" a tickle of amusement in his voice. Are you laughing at me, you speckled asshole?

She handed him the microbrewery lager she'd poured for him. "You only turn thirteen once."

Now he was laughing out loud. "You only turn *any age* once."

So if it was excessive, so what? The twins were ardent meat eaters, and this was, after all, their party, but the Anime Club had quite a few vegetarians in it, at least two vegans, and a few kids who were lactose or gluten intolerant. Fuck you, Bryan Lynas, of course it's catered.

It had taken Karen, Claire, and Erica all of yesterday afternoon to create this movie set for a nineteenth century period drama. Twenty-seven of the anime kids had responded to the RSVP on Facebook. The open floor plan designed for easy living actually did make things easy for once—there were no walls to get in the way—so they'd added four small tables to the dining room table. Each was covered with ancient fine linen provided by Karen's mum and set with Grandmother McConnell's silver, china, and crystal. Karen had managed to grow up without bothering to learn one fork from another, so Erica had done the settings. "Oh, I know where everything goes. Lise and I used to set the table for Christmas."

Dinner plate, butter plate, dessert plate— appetizer fork, salad fork, dinner fork, dessert fork— water glass, beverage glass— oh my god, it was insane— pink roses at the centre of every table, and then the lovely white taper candles that Jamie had just finished lighting.

"You'd think this was a party for golden-agers," Karen said, "but it *is* pretty. We've got to get some pictures."

Erica was offering her the camera, but Bryan, that handy guy, said, "You want me to take some?"

"Sure," she said, "take lots. Get some of the twins."

"No worries. Twins!" he called out, attracting both his set and Karen's.

It hadn't been Karen's idea for the twins to dress up for their party, it had been theirs. She'd thought it would be fairly simple—she'd buy Devon a few nice shirts and some dress pants, and Jamie a pretty dress—but no, they had to be *identical.* "You *know that*, Mum!" So they'd done their shopping in the boy's section at the Gap. Now they were wearing identical white shirts and grey pants. They cleaned up well, she thought. Yeah, they were good-looking kids, both obviously boys—until you got to the too-cute hair and the studs in their ears, and then you might have second thoughts. "Do they know how ambiguous they look?" she asked Erica.

"Yeah, I'm sure they do. It was one of the first things I noticed about them—that ambiguous gender presentation."

"Is that what you meant by 'gender variant'?"

"Yes. But I don't think they'd think of it in the same terms we do."

"How would they think of it?"

Erica gave her an edge of a smile and shrugged.

"You're supposed to be the psychologist," Karen said—but then realized that she'd just set Erica up to say what she always said. "No. Forget I said that. I *know* you're not a *clinical* psychologist. But you must have a personal opinion."

"I think for them 'identical' means some kind of compromise gender."

That made sense. Camera flash going off—Bryan photographing both sets of twins together. Morgan and Avalon always wore too much eye makeup, but tonight, with cherry-red lipstick and too-short dresses, they were even more teen-nasty than usual. Her kids were dressed like boys, so when you put them all together, they looked like two couples. Could Devon be sweet on one of the Lynas girls? She'd never thought of that before.

Bryan was taking his photography assignment seriously. He sent his twins out of the picture to concentrate on hers. Now he was directing them to face each other. They'd just had their hair redone, so that was a dead match, but not much else was. The enchanted period when they'd been exactly the same size was long over, and Jamie was growing fast, already an inch or two taller than Devon. Her adult face was beginning to show. They didn't look like identical twins any longer—they looked like brothers, one a year older than the other.

Something was bugging Jamie. She made a dismissive gesture and walked out of the photo shoot.

"What's the matter, sweetie?"

"I don't feel right. Dev looks awesome, but I'm not—"

"You look awesome too—"

"No, I *don't*. Should I wear a dress? You wanted me to wear a dress."

"I don't care. It's your birthday. Wear anything you want."

Jamie made an inarticulate sound in the back of her throat and took off for her room. Devon followed, but his sister turned back to him in the hallway, said something dark and conclusive, left him standing there, distressed. "Did I just see what I think I saw?"

"Yeah," Erica said, "he just got cut. So much for the twin bond . . . She's probably anxious about cross-dressing in front of her friends."

Karen hadn't wanted to go there—feel the full weight of it. "She really *is* cross-dressing, isn't she?"

"Of course she is."

"You must think I'm crazy."

Erica looked her straight in the eyes. "No, Karen, I do *not* think you're crazy. But you are driving her nuts, you know. You're supposed to tell her what to wear so she can blame it on you."

Erica was so right it was actually funny.

"What's with your sister?" Karen asked Devon.

"I don't know." She could see that he was hurt. "She's like weird. She's been weird all day."

"You can't always fix things for her, Dev," Erica said.

"Yeah," he said, "I know that. But I want to . . . She usually tells me, like whatever . . . Jeez, in Starbucks? She was—?"

"Mum!"—that horribly awkward moment when you've been talking about someone and they suddenly reappear—*have they heard you?* Turning to look up the stairs, they saw Jamie exploding into motion, throwing something. It opened, fluttered, turned into a navy blue dress that landed with a ploosh at Karen's feet. "Why don't I own a dress that fucking fits?"

I've had just about enough of her, Karen thought—and yelled back, "When I wanted to buy you one this morning, you told me you'd rather shove pins in your eyes."

Erica picked up the dress. "God," Karen said, "you know what people always say? How having kids gives you the chance to relive your own life? Thirteen is such a ghastly age. Such a wet, drippy, miserable, pathetic, utterly disgusting age. You couldn't pay me enough to live through that... Sorry, Dev, I didn't mean you. I'm talking about girls."

The doorbell chimed. Panicked, he glanced at the empty space where his sister had been. "I'm going to kill her."

A whole cluster of girls was arriving at once—five of them. "Happy birthday, Devon!" and the flash notified everyone that Bryan was capturing the moment. Just as though they'd rehearsed it, the girls flipped themselves toward the camera, mugging and raising their hands in V signs. "Take their coats, Dev."

How could someone who surely couldn't weigh a hundred pounds make so much noise coming down the stairs? Jamie had changed into her standard slouchy outfit—boys' baggy jeans and an old plaid shirt.

"Oh, Jamie!" This was no longer infuriating or funny—it was just sad. "Sweetie? Do you want me to help you find something?"

"It's okay, it's okay. I don't care." She batted Karen's hand away.

Stung, hurt, Karen drew back. Don't react, she told herself. She was supposed to be one of the adults around here, so she should be able to take things as they came, but, unfortunately, her feelings didn't agree with her. For the length of a gasp, she was the same age as her daughter, stuck in the horror of *now* when everything is a crisis and the entire world teeters on the edge of disaster.

Jamie was wound as tight as a mousetrap—one touch and she'd go off—but Erica said, "Hey, we can do better than that," and patted her lightly on the shoulders. Miraculously, Jamie didn't explode. "Breathe,"

Erica said. "Come on, let me help you. I was a tomboy too, you know." Karen didn't know whether she wanted to kiss Erica or strangle her.

"Twins," Erica called to the Lynas girls, "we need you."

Devon started after them. "Sorry, Dev," Erica said, "this is girls only," then added, "It's a fashion crisis, and that's serious business."

There were too many hurt feelings here, so Karen decided to forget about her own. "It's okay, Dev. They'll figure it out. Answer the door. People have to feel welcome."

More girls—didn't the Anime Club have any boys in it? As soon as this bunch was inside, the bell chimed again, and Devon was nowhere near, so Karen jerked the door open to find not another gaggle of girls but rather—silent and poised—the image of perfection, the coolest of the cool, the fabulous, the one and only Akime Kimura, the president of the club—*and her mother.*

"Karen," Mrs. Kimura said, "you are good to us. You have the entire club for dinner. What a big job!"

Oh my god, what was Mrs. Kimura's first name? Karen had met her before—several times—but she didn't have a clue. "How nice to see you again—"? "Please come in."

Akime was carrying a large rectangular present wrapped in colourful paper splashed with anime characters and tied with an enormous pink bow. She handed it to Karen. "This is for Jamie and Devon. It is from the *entire* club."

The purpose of the Palmerston Anime Club—as stated on their Facebook page—was "to celebrate and promote Japanese culture," but Akime was the only member who was actually Japanese. She'd been born in Japan, spoke Japanese, had dozens of relatives who still lived in Japan, and often returned there for visits. And if that wasn't enough to elevate her to the level of a deity, she was also a genuinely nice girl. When she'd run for president, she'd won by acclamation because no one would stand against her. Now, upon her entry into the hallway, a hush fell over the kids, a reverential awe. Devon had turned to stone. "Take their coats!" Karen hissed at him.

Akime was wearing a simple forest-green dress. It looked like a Banana Republic and was exactly like what Karen would have bought for Jamie if she'd been allowed to buy anything.

"Happy birthday, Devon," Akime said so gravely she made it sound like a blessing.

"Sure," he said stupidly, "thanks."

Akime and her mother were looking across the living area to the table settings where the slender tapers were burning. Mrs. Kimura pressed her hand over her heart. "Your home," she said, "it is so beautiful," and Akime echoed her, "Oh, so beautiful! So very beautiful!"

Karen, the grown-up, had been frozen into speechless idiocy just as hopeless as her son's. Where the hell was Jamie?

Bryan Lynas had not been photographing this particular scene, but now he seemed to have sprung up at the centre of it. Tonight was the first time Karen had seen him when he didn't look like he'd come to dig a ditch in her backyard. He was actually dressed up—well, sort of dressed up—in black corduroy pants and a flannel shirt in an unfortunate plaid with so much green that it made his freckles glow like hearth fire. This must be the way he liked to do things—sudden, quick, and unexpected—but what on earth was he doing? His entire manner had been transformed; he was moving in a strangely formal way, actually bowing. He couldn't be making fun of Akime and her mother, could he? Bizarre sounds were coming out of his mouth. With a lurch, Karen felt the niceties of her party being sucked down a wormhole. Oh my god, was he imitating Japanese?

For a moment Mrs. Kimura was so shocked she looked like someone had thrown cold water on her. But then she answered him. She was speaking Japanese, and he must be speaking Japanese too. Several exchanges went back and forth. Mrs. Kimura was smiling. She shook her head in amazement and looked at Karen. "He speaks good Japanese!"

Bryan laughed and kept on going. He said something that got Akime giggling so hard she had to press her hand over her mouth. Now even her mother was laughing.

What an asshole, Karen thought— but no, he was turning out to be hilarious, a perfect icebreaker. All the kids were laughing too. He sent Karen a sideways wink. Now she had his number. A bad boy, a grown-up brat, he must love shocking people. Maybe it was an Australian sense of humour.

With a thudding of feet, his daughters were back downstairs, squealing, "Akime!" People were milling around, everyone talking at once, and that seemed to have cued the servers, who appeared with trays of appetizers, each labeled *meat, fish, vegetarian*, or *vegan*.

"Your dad is so funny!" Akime was saying.

"Oh, yeah, is he ever."

"Like sometimes way too funny."

"How did you learn to speak Japanese?" Karen asked him.

He laughed just as she'd known he would. "Ah . . . lived there for a while. A few years actually. Teaching English. Last thing you'd think, wouldn't you, hearing what comes out of my mouth? . . . No, I wouldn't mind a bit," offering his empty beer glass to Karen.

"Oh my god, Jamie!" one of the girls yelled, and they all began chanting, "Happy birthday!"

Startled, Karen turned to look and for a moment didn't recognize her own daughter. She would never have thought that Jamie was capable of making an entrance, but that's what she was doing—walking through the hall, taking her time about it, walking more gracefully than she ever walked anywhere. "Oh, Jamie," Akime said, "you are so beautiful."

Was she beautiful? Karen had never seen Jamie wearing makeup before. The Lynas girls must have put it on her—eyeliner and mascara, just as much as they wore—and it made her dark eyes look huge and luminous. But they'd only done her eyes—not a trace of anything else on the rest of her face—and with her nearly black hair and pale skin, she looked otherworldly, spectral.

Erica had appeared at Karen's side. "Whew, what a transformation," Karen said. "How did you do it?"

"I was just the facilitator. Morgan and Avi did it."

Then Karen got the full impact. Black straight-leg lulus with a dark blue yoga top and a black beater under it—oh my god, she thought, *every thing she's wearing is mine!* Jamie usually hid inside baggy clothes, but with all that stretch fabric, there was nowhere to hide. She wasn't even slightly developed yet, poor kid, but what was revealed was an athletic straight-up-and-down elegance—she even looked taller—and where on earth could she have got the shoes, black patent tuxedo flats with broad bows on the toes? Then Karen remembered—of course they were hers, too. They were real patent, and they'd been bloody expensive, and she hadn't worn them for years.

"Yeah, the shoes were the key to everything," Erica said. "Wow, do you ever have a lot of shoes! Avalon found them in the back of your closet, and the minute they saw them, it was like a flash went off, and they all thought of the same thing. They were going to make her into some kind of anime character. What do you think?"

"I don't know. I don't like that much gunk on her eyes, but . . . Okay, it's her party. Hey, Dev, who's your sister supposed to be?"

"A bishonen," he said, grinning, and then translated it for her—"a pretty boy."

KAREN AND ERICA were finally collapsed on a couch at the far end of the living area—she hoped that they were far enough away from the action so the kids wouldn't feel spied on. The handful of parents who'd stuck around for appies and drinks had left long ago. For the first time that day Karen was getting what she wanted—a chance to do nothing. "Success, eh?" she said.

"Oh, yeah."

The cake had been presented, the birthday song sung, the candles blown out. Karen had consulted the Lynas twins about the cake decoration. "Kawaii," they'd said, which must mean "excessively cute." They'd drawn a sketch of what they wanted, and the decorator in the bakery had followed it, so running around the sides of the cake was a sugar ribbon set with thirteen sugar bows. On the top were thirteen red roses and thirteen white ones, each with a candle in the centre. The candle-roses surrounded a baby-pink circle emblazoned with baby-blue lettering—the name the twins used on their email account, the logo they'd wanted to have tattooed onto themselves: GEMINI FOREVER! Everybody loved the cake. The kids had got hysterical over the cake. Now they were cutting it up and passing it around—and drinking Japanese green tea. "Doesn't it strike you that this is an amazingly decorous party for a bunch of teenagers?" Karen said.

"Yeah. I was just thinking the same thing. If these are the twins' best friends, you've got no worries. When Lise and I were thirteen, all we wanted to do was get pissed at bush parties and make out with strange boys."

That made Karen smile. "You grew up faster than I did. When I was thirteen, I was still a little kid. All I remember from that year is hanging out with Patsy Donlevy."

It felt great just to sit, not to have to worry about the next demanding detail—too much going on, too many things to process. Rob's new wife sounded like an absolute horror. Could Devon—sunny optimistic no-problem Devon—have actually been thinking about killing himself? It didn't seem possible. He seemed so stable, but Jamie—? Anyhow, disaster had been averted. For today at least. Happy birthday, twins.

"This is an interesting group," Erica was saying. "Eighty percent girls. A wide age range for kids in a voluntary group—extremely unusual. I'm guessing the youngest to be around twelve, the oldest seventeen. The mean age must be around fourteen."

"You're funny. Is that what you do to amuse yourself?"

"Sure. Why not? That's what I did as a postdoc . . . observed groups in late childhood and early adolescence. This is a fun group to observe. The Caucasian kids are in a minority."

"Yeah, they are. The school's mainly white, but I think the Anime Club attracts the minority kids. Lots of Asian kids. A few Persian kids."

"Do you see the Lynas twins making a move on the Korean boys?"

"No. Are they really?"

"Yeah, they are really. Just watch. Really cute boys. Home-stays. Grade tens. They're not related, but they're the same age and look a lot like each other, and of course they stick together because they're the only Korean boys in the school—"

"What? You talked to them?"

"Yeah, a little bit. They're just twin-like enough to attract Morgan and Avi. If you're interested in the Lynas twins, you can't just ask out *one* of them, you've got to approach them as half of a pair. Lise and I weren't that bonded. We went out with boys separately . . . although we felt strange about it. Okay, and you can see that your twins are *not* functioning as a unit. Jamie's hanging out with that cluster of younger girls, and Devon's glued himself to Akime . . ."

"Oh, everybody loves Akime."

"No, but look at him. He doesn't just love Akime, he *adores* her . . . Do you want another glass of wine or something?"

Karen shook her head. One glass gave her a lift, a second made her sleepy. Much of the drinking she'd been doing for the last couple of years must have been to keep Drew company—and then she realized that she'd gone the entire day without thinking about him. She hadn't been making an effort; he'd simply never appeared in her mind. That was sad—or it was supposed to be. Her announcement had fucked up the rest of their night out—so what else had she expected? The important thing was to keep the lines of communication open, he'd said—followed by an endless series of emails and voice mails. By Wednesday, she'd had it, collected everything of his and packed it up. Cam, her normally useless son, had wandered home at exactly the right moment to say, "Drew's toast, eh?" so she and Cam had loaded the boxes, the wine racks, the whole works into the BMW and delivered it to Drew's front porch. The calls and emails had stopped abruptly that night, and then, on Thursday, Drew had sent her house key back by courier—with no note—and she'd finally allowed herself to cry.

"OH MY GOD, oh my god, oh my god, oh my god!" That was Jamie shrieking at the top of her lungs. What? Oh, the present opening. And here was Devon, running over to say, "Hey, you guys have got to see this. It's freakin' incredible."

Karen and Erica exchanged smiles, followed Devon to the candlelit tables. The present that had flipped Jamie into ecstasy looked like the ultimate in coffee table books—big and thick with a brilliant cover. The image on the cover was the very same one that hung on the wall in Jamie's bedroom—the *Two from One Fire* twins, Kagami in her leather catsuit, dangling from her rope, barefoot Makoto in his floral pajamas, the two of them staring at each other through a window with identical expressions of astonishment on their identical faces. The kids had piled up around the end of the table to get a look. The title was in Japanese. Akime translated it—"*The Art of Kaneshiro Mitsuko.*"

Jamie was almost too excited to talk. "It's every one of her colour illustrations . . . For every one of her manga . . . *It's from Japan!*" The text was in Japanese.

"Not so much to read," Akime said, turning the pages. "Mostly pictures. You see, here are drawings from when Kaneshiro Sensei is still in high school, and here is painting from her first manga ever." A soft-focus watercolour of two schoolgirls in their sailor-style uniforms standing under a willow tree, one looking sadly at the other who was looking away into the rainy distance. The image was soaked in melancholy, and the girls gathered around the table all went "ah" at the same time as though they'd rehearsed it.

"Many things here. Her *name* for her manga." That must mean storyboards—they were rough sketches of panels with the figures roughed in.

"And this is from her butterfly manga. She is famous for this." It was a full page of a sparkly-eyed girl lying on her stomach, propped up on her elbows, holding an iconic tube of gleaming red lipstick. Her golden blonde ringlets were gathered into an enormous pink bow. A semi-circle of flounced crinolines rose up behind her, and one leg was raised to show off a pink patent pump with a high stiletto heel. Above her a butterfly was unfolding its wings on a flowery branch, its empty cocoon hanging to one side. Karen saw the painting as high kitsch, but it too got lots of ooohs from the girls.

"We don't know these early ones," Devon told her. "*Two from One Fire* is her only manga that's been translated into English."

"All the covers for *Two from One Fire* are here," Akime said, turning the pages. The painting she was showing them now couldn't have been more different from the last one. It was sooty and dark, featuring inky blues and nasty dim reds—a bombed-out city of ruined and burning buildings, piles of the dead lying about, black smears of birds circling overhead, and, in the distance, the silhouettes of two bodies hanging from lamp posts. "Eeew," Karen said.

"Yeah," Devon said, "we told you it's heavy." Yes, they had, and they'd also told her it was awesome, cool, incredible, and "sick"—which to them meant "great." It was a work of genius, Jamie said. It was the best manga ever, Devon said. It was *for them*, they said, as though it was the magical key to their lives. Most kids their age wouldn't want to share their fantasy life with their mother, but they'd begged her to read it. Why hadn't she?

"And here is interview with Kaneshiro Sensei."

Karen had never thought much about the author of *Two from One Fire*. It had always seemed to her like a natural phenomenon that had simply appeared one day out of nowhere—like an earthquake or tornado—but when she'd imagined someone writing it, the figure that had appeared in her mind was an ancient venerable Japanese gentleman in a Zen rock garden. But no, the author in the photograph was a young woman who could still be in her twenties. She was wearing a black dress so plain it was almost ugly, seated at her drawing table looking sideways at the camera with mistrustful eyes. Her hair was skimmed back into an unflattering ponytail, and Karen saw her as a pretty girl doing her best not to look pretty.

"Oh, my god," Jamie said. "What does it say?"

"Oh, it is very long. Sometime I will translate it for you."

"Give us a hint," Devon said.

Akime took a moment to read through the opening. "So much! He asks her about her life. She was born in 1976 in Iwate Prefecture. She comes from a big family. He asks her how she begin to draw manga. She says she is not good in school. She does not play sports. She very much likes to draw. All the time she is drawing, drawing, drawing. Her teachers, her parents say, 'You foolish girl, you will never amount to anything.' When she graduates from high school, she studies for a year fashion design in Tokyo. Then she works in a shop in the Harajuku district . . . . Oh, this is so much to translate!"

"Okay," Devon said, "you don't have to. But tell us about *Two from One Fire*. What does she say about that?"

Akime turned the page and studied the Japanese text. "Okay. Her butterfly manga is very successful. Many kids like it very much. They dress up like the people in her manga. Kaneshiro Sensei is on television many times. They give her many cute clothes to wear. They put her picture in magazines. She likes cute clothes, but she does not . . . She says, 'I do not want to draw another manga like *Butterfly Reversal*.' She likes very much the old school shōjo, Hagio Moto, Takemiya Keiko. She likes also very much the American science fiction. She thinks that next she will draw science fiction manga. She says, 'I do not want to draw manga just for girls but for everybody.' She goes to a new magazine. She is very worried about this. She is afraid that nobody will like her new work."

Everybody had stopped talking. Akime looked up, saw that she was centre stage. She sighed.

"Okay. This part is very interesting. When Kaneshiro Sensei draws manga, it must be . . . She cannot draw just for fun or because someone ask her. She must feel it very much. She is thinking about her new manga, and she cannot sleep. She is having bad dreams. She sees terrible things in her mind. She talks to her editor. She says, 'I cannot draw these terrible things I see in my mind.' He says to her, 'You must draw these things. If you do not draw them, they will never leave you. If you draw them, they will leave you and you will feel better. You will not disappoint your fans. This will be a good manga.' So she begins to draw *Two from One Fire*.

"Kaneshiro Sensei draws the first chapters, and her fans like them very much. But what she sees is so terrible, she is afraid to draw more. She is very tired. Her manga goes away from her. Nothing is left. She is very sad. She is empty. She thinks always about the impermanence of human life. She cannot go on.

"Her girlfriends are worried very much about her. They take her on holiday. They take her to Izu. Kaneshiro Sensei likes very much to listen to the sound of the sea. There . . . Oh, I cannot translate this! My English is not good enough."

"Just a bit?" Devon said.

Akime stared at the text. "This is very hard for me. After many days she looks . . . No, that is not right. She *sees*. I do not know this word in English. She sees into the sunyata. Then her manga comes back to her. She returns to Tokyo and she is drawing, drawing, working very hard, doing her best, until she finish it. Then she wins a big award. She does not think that she deserves such big award. They are making *Two from One Fire* into anime. She is famous. But she wants only to live a quiet life and draw her manga."

12.

KAREN AND ERICA often ended up in Karen's bedroom now in the late afternoons. Erica sat at the desk, Karen stretched out on the bed, and they worked on their laptops. Karen liked these shared moments at the end of the day—they gave her a chance to reflect, gave her a sense of continuity, of permanence—although, as she reminded herself, nothing is permanent. The dim blue worry-light at the windows was fading away. "You okay?" she asked.

"Oh yeah," Erica said, "sure. This time of day makes me restless."

"Me too. The sneaky in-between time. If it bothers you, why don't you close the drapes?"

"No, I like to see it coming . . . Unless you want to."

"No, I like it, too."

Karen heard the twins—the sound of their voices—and looked up. Erica's eyes met hers. These moments of silent communications were becoming as important as any of the words they said to each other. She finds the twins amusing, Karen thought—no, it was even stronger than that; Erica was genuinely fond of them—and here they came, drifting into the room with a haphazard out-of-focus air as though they were merely passing through and didn't actually want anything, although obviously they did. "Hey, Mom, can Jamie wear your shoes?"

"Of course she can," Karen said.

Why wasn't Jamie the one who was asking? But instead of saying anything, Jamie threw herself down on the bed next to Karen. That's what she used to do back in the day when she and her mum had been the best of friends, and Karen was surprised—even a bit shocked. It had only been a week since the twins' birthday, but she could sense a subtle change in them as though the number thirteen had worked some obscure magic.

"Dev's dressing me up for Bryan's party," Jamie said. She was lying flat on her back, talking to the ceiling. "You guys are going, aren't you?"

Another fucking party? "I thought it was just for kids," Karen said.

"No, it's for everybody."

"He even told us," Devon said. "Make sure your mom and Erica know they're invited."

"Come on," Karen said, "we haven't recovered from your parties yet."

"*You* come on, Mum!" With a moan of exasperation, Jamie grabbed one of the pillows and flipped it over her face. "You've totally got to go."

It was unfair that the twins had been born so close to Christmas—it made the entire month of December utterly gruesome—and Jamie was a traditionalist. It wasn't that she expected to have a wonderful time at Nana's—she called it boring, actually—but everything had to be done the way it had always been done, especially this year so Devon could fit back into the pattern that, from her point of view, he never should have left. So after you celebrate the actual day of your birth with your friends, you celebrate again with your family the next day. Nana cooks your favourite meal and bakes you a cake, and she and Grandpa give you a present that's always a little odd—exactly the kind of thing you call "random"—but you tell them you love it anyway. Without the dinner at Nana's, your birthday wouldn't be your birthday.

The family party had been just as satisfyingly boring as it was supposed to be. Paige and Cam were required to be there, and they had been. Still weary from the friends party, Karen had immobilized herself on the couch in the living room while Erica had helped out in the kitchen. As she'd listened to her mum asking Erica endless questions—"drawing her out," as her mum would have put it—she'd finally understood the slightly formal, slightly strained, slightly walking-on-eggshells feeling coming from her parents. They thought that she and Erica were *girlfriends*. Well, okay, if you show up to the family birthday four years in a row with Drew Thompson, and then, with no explanation, you show up with the mysterious woman who's been living with you for the past month—what else are they supposed to think?

She'd followed along into the basement when her dad had offered to show Erica his stereo—state of the art, circa 1975—the huge cabinets that held the woofers and sub-woofers, the little cabinets that held the tweeters, and so forth and so on, a million components that always seemed to her like an objective correlative of her father's mind. He'd never switched to CDs. "A boondoggle," he called them. Of course vinyl was coming back—with analog you're not just sampling the sound wave, you're *reproducing it.* He spent much of his time down there now, patiently using a nineteenth-century technique to refinish antique furniture and listening to his record collection—over a thousand albums, all of them classical, all of them gems. He gave them a sample—the ancient burnished sounds of Monteverdi—and Erica said exactly the right thing—"It's so realistic, the musicians might as well be right in the room with us."

So her parents had made it clear that it was all right with them if she had a girlfriend, and that had been amusing enough, but the little chat with Jen in Delany's after Sunrise Yoga had not been the least bit amusing. Drew, apparently, had been talking. "He's saying that you broke up with him over that girl. He says you're in love with her."

Erica was a stalker—that's what Drew was saying—seriously disturbed, blah blah blah—potentially dangerous, blah blah blah. "Oh my god," Karen said, "that's utterly ridiculous. She's not the least bit dangerous. She's sweet and kind of lost. I'm just helping her out."

The conversation meandered around a few other topics, but Erica was always floating along just below the surface. "Oh," Jen said as though she'd just remembered it, "Amy said she saw you and, um . . . that girl—"

"Her name's Erica. She's *a woman.* She's got her PhD, for Christ's sake."

"Okay. *Erica.* Okay, I get it. She said she saw the two of you in Whole Foods. She was going to say hi but she was all the way over on the other side of the store. She said she was very pretty." That, of course, translated into: *The ladies are talking about you.* It also translated into: *Come on, Karen, you can tell* me.

"Yes, she is," Karen said, ending the conversation.

RELIABLE VANCOUVER was giving them pissy December, and all of her children were accounted for. Cameron was wherever he was on a Saturday night, and if anything went wrong, she'd surely hear about it. Paige was safe at Lauren's. Jamie was lying next to her on the bed, and Devon was sitting on the floor. By five it would be as dark as it was ever going to get—and more rain. The last thing Karen wanted was to go anywhere—although it looked like she was going to have to drive the twins to Bryan's. Maybe she could send them in a cab. "I think Erica and I will just order in some sushi?" she said and sent Erica an inquiring look. She should try to remember to give Erica some money for all the take-out she'd been buying.

"No, Mum," Jamie said from under the pillow, "you've got to go."

"If you don't go, Bryan will be distraught," Devon said.

"Yeah, it's like his Christmas party."

"Morgan and Avi really want you guys to come."

"They got inspired by the candles at our party so there's gonna be like candles everywhere."

"And there's gonna be like a shit-ton of food. You don't have to eat freakin' sushi."

"And you guys can get dressed up, Mum. Everybody's getting dressed up."

"I don't know," Karen said.

"That's it," Devon said, "you're so going," and vanished into the walk-in closet. She heard him rummaging around in the obscure depths at the back. "What on earth are you looking for?"

"Um . . . black high heels. Old school."

High heels? For *Jamie?* "You mean dress shoes?"

"No no. *Old* old school. Like in an old movie."

"What? You think I run a fashion museum? I may have something. Look on the right, way way in the back. Don't make a mess."

"Hey, awesome!"—the clunk clunk as shoes landed in the middle of the floor.

Karen sat up to see what they were—round-toed black patent heels, retro-'40s. Rob had bought them for her when they'd been married, and they were quite high, actually. "Aren't those a bit much?" she said.

"Is it a costume party?" Erica asked. She had been silently watching.

"Not exactly," Devon said, "but definitely dress-up."

"Yeah, Mum," Jamie said, "go for it. Full on. Like the night when you went out with asshole."

"Jamie! That's not nice. Be gracious in victory."

"You like—? Victory? You think I like *won* something? *You* be gracious, Mum."

Devon grabbed one of Jamie's bare feet and tugged on it. "Come on, twin."

Jamie rolled the pillow down onto her chest and hugged it. "I don't feel like it."

"Feel like it."

"I feel like it." She tossed the pillow at Karen and then, in a single amazing motion, bounced herself off the bed and onto her feet. Devon handed her the shoes. She looked at them and laughed. "I should make *you* wear them."

The twins wandered away the same way they'd come in—with that air of, oh, there's no purpose to this, it's all just sort of vaguely happening.

"Curtain," Karen said. "Next act."

Erica met Karen's eyes, smiled, closed her laptop with a decisive snap.

"Do you want to go to this party?" Karen asked her.

"If you want to." Erica was on her feet and walking. "I get so twitchy sometimes. When Lise and I were kids . . . Oh god, it was hard for us to sit still! If we'd been big-city kids, they would have put us on Ritalin."

Pacing through the rose-coloured spaciousness at the far end of the bedroom, Erica allowed her fingers to trail along the curves of the cherry-wood chairs. "When I first saw this room, I didn't like it. It seemed so . . . I don't know. It took me a while to see how it all fits together. It's beautiful."

"Thank you."

"Are *you* okay?"

"I'm kind of sad," Karen said.

"Why?"

"Oh, god," she said, "where to start? Copenhagen, I guess. It just all seems so hopeless."

She'd been on the net, reading about the UN conference on climate change. Despite all their fine words, they'd accomplished nothing, a fucking joke actually, nothing binding on anybody. Canada had been utterly contemptible. The Harper government was making Karen ashamed of being Canadian.

"Yeah, I read about it too," Erica said. "I hate all of them."

"You're not okay, are you?"

"No, I'm not."

She walked slowly back until she was standing by Karen's bed.

"I'm . . . I don't know . . . frozen . . . I can't make decisions. I have to go home for Christmas, and the airfare from Calgary to the Hat is just insane, but I don't want to drive, and I haven't even booked my flight. Everybody wants to know when I'm coming, and I still don't know. I've left it so late, I'm not even sure I still can get a flight. I really don't want to go."

"Stay here. Stay with us."

"I can't do that. You know that."

Erica made another circuit of the room, still pacing in a deliberate way as though she was measuring the distance with her feet. "It's the anniversary of . . . Annalise died on the twenty-second. That's Tuesday. I can't decide if I want to be in the Hat on Tuesday or not, so I can't book my flight."

For a moment Karen didn't know what to say—but of course there was only one thing she could say—"If you wanted to stay here, we could have a . . . like a memorial or something." My god, what was she committing herself to? Thursday was Christmas Eve. She'd bought most of the presents early the way she always did, but there were still a few things on her shopping list, and the tree wasn't even up yet.

"We could walk in a park or light candles," she said. Well, that certainly sounded pathetic. "We could do anything. Or you could be alone or whatever feels right. Then you could go home on Wednesday. We could book your flight right now. I could do it for you. Then it'd be done."

"Thanks. That's so nice of you. But I should probably be home on Tuesday even if . . . I'm not the only one . . . My poor dad, he's just—"

They both heard heels hammering the hardwood floor. They both turned to look. "You thought I couldn't walk in them, didn't you?" Jamie said. "Ha!" and she strode mightily in—clomp, clomp, clomp—and spun around grinning, making her skirt swing. "Ta-da!"

Talk about bad timing, Karen thought. "Jamie," she said, "maybe if you kids . . ." but Erica stopped her with a small hand gesture, a signal from her eyes. Meaning what? Don't make a big deal out of this? We'll talk about it later?

"What are you," Erica asked, "a manga character?"

"No," Jamie said, "just a Harajuku girl."

"Not full on," Devon said. "We haven't got all the stuff to do it full on. She's like Harajuku light."

"It's Avalon's dress," Jamie said.

"Yeah, like Morgan and Avi gave us all their old clothes."

It was a child's dress, something a nostalgic mum might have put on a twelve-year-old—which is what Avalon had probably been when she'd worn it—an old-fashioned dress, black, prim, with long-sleeves, a prissy little collar, and a flaring skirt that hit Jamie just below her knees. "It's Australian," Devon said. "Avi's grandmother sent it to her." With the retro heels, it was fairly startling—not to mention the black lace gloves and the black-and-white striped knee socks—but the main thing that was startling was that it was *Jamie* who was wearing it. She showed herself off to Erica with an awkward pirouette.

Erica has a better relationship with her than I do, Karen thought. Ouch. Could there be a tiny grain of truth inside Drew's crazy rants? Was Erica taking over her life? No, of course not, but it was eerie how quickly and easily she'd blended into it. Okay, so Karen might be a little jealous, but she didn't want Erica to leave, and that was the strangest thing. She'd Googled "twin loss" and "post-traumatic stress disorder," and that had helped to explain Erica, but she didn't know what to Google to help to explain herself.

Dev was in costume too—well, sort of in costume—in distressed skinny jeans, rolled at the bottom, old scuffed work boots, and a baggy black T-shirt with the white silhouette of a manga girl on it. Wings spread, she was floating downward with a caption that said, "Take me somewhere far from here."

"It's all Morgan and Avi's stuff," he said.

"You guys are wonderful," Erica said, and pointing at his T-shirt—"Is that from *Two from One Fire*?"

"No, it's from CLAMP. She's like a four-leaf clover. She has so much power she could destroy the world . . . Mom? Can you show me how to put makeup on Jamie?"

Makeup? On Jamie? And here was Jamie herself, offering a hand. "Come on, Mum, we've got to get going." Karen allowed herself to be pulled onto her feet and dragged into the bathroom.

"Do huge eyes on her," Devon said, "like mega-sparkle."

"Sorry. Don't have any mega-sparkle. I was too old for mega-sparkle twenty years ago."

The twins had lined up in front of the mirror. Erica had followed them in and come to rest behind them. "Hey, Mum, look," Jamie said, "I'm taller than you are."

"Yeah," Karen said, "almost."

"What do you do first?" Devon said. "Liner?"

How strange, she thought, he really wants to know. "Yeah, liner." She rummaged in the drawer for a pencil that still had a usable point on it. "Don't do it the way Bryan's girls do it, okay? That's just crude . . . Jamie, just look straight ahead. Try not to blink."

"Awesome!" Devon said. "Let me do the other eye."

"It's easier if I do it. I can just—"

"No, come on. I really want to."

Karen handed him the pencil. "Try not to stick it in her eye."

"No? Seriously? I was planning to ram it right through her cornea."

"Eew! Don't even make jokes like that."

Karen was showing *her son* how to put makeup on *his sister*—was this appropriate? Probably not, but what the hell. She could see how hard he was concentrating. He had a knack for it—patience and a steady hand. Jamie had made her face as blank as a mannequin's, but she was watching herself in the mirror—and behind her, Erica was watching Jamie watch.

"No, no blush," Devon said, "she's got to look pale and ghastly."

"Ghostly?"

"No, Mom, *ghastly*. Do you have any lipstick that's like, um . . . real dark? Like burgundy or plum?"

Karen met her son's eyes. She didn't understand what was going on here, but she could feel the intensity of it. "There're a million in the drawer," she said. "Find one you like."

He checked out several, chose an old one the colour of port wine, coated Jamie's lips with it. "That's a bit much," Karen told him, "even for a ghastly girl. Blot it." She showed him how.

Finished, Jamie turned and directed an ominous Addams Family stare at all of them. "Sick!" Devon said, grinning back at her.

"Okay, your turn," Jamie said and pushed Erica toward the mirror. "You gotta dress up. If I can do it, you can do it."

Karen was surprised that Erica didn't resist, allowed herself to be guided into place, was standing now where Jamie had been. Karen was looking into those huge blue-grey eyes with the determined black rings around the irises. For a moment she couldn't imagine what to do next. Poor Erica, what must she be thinking? "Do you want to play?" she asked her.

"It might be fun," Erica said.

"YOU CAN LIVE in West Van your whole life, and there's still parts of it you've never seen." Nobody in the car replied, and Karen was left with the scratchy feeling that she'd been talking to herself.

Bryan's house was a modest old wood-and-stucco split-level nearly all the way out to Horseshoe Bay, several blocks up the hill from the water. Scanning for a place to park, Karen saw nothing but bumper-to-bumper cars so she kept on going. When she did find a space, it was on some obscure road where the municipality had apparently forgotten streetlights. She turned off her headlights, and that left her with a view of precisely nothing. She slid halfway out of the driver's seat, felt for the ground—there had to be something substantial down there somewhere. She felt like a prime idiot. What was she doing playing dress-up with her children, out on a night that might be the nastiest of the winter? Not stormy, not gruesome, not grotesque, just nasty—an endless dank blah blown sideways out of the void.

Erica had already climbed out and was offering a hand. Easy enough for her—she wasn't in extreme heels—but the twins had insisted that Mum dress up like the night when she'd gone out with Drew, so here she was in her Louboutin boots—in the dark, in the rain, hanging onto Erica. "My hair's going to be a mess," she said. Oh god, she thought, I sound like such a ditz.

"Mine too," Erica said. "It curls up like a Brillo pad."

Jamie was already far ahead of them, clomping along like a pony. She must be operating on radar. "Watch your step, sweetie," Karen called to her.

"You watch your step, Mum. I'm *an athlete.* I can walk just fine!"

That was interesting—Jamie still saw herself as an athlete even though she hadn't played any sport since last year. She stopped now and waited for them to catch up. "Do *you* ever wear heels?" she asked Erica.

"No, not really. I tried at my high school prom, just ordinary pumps. As soon as we started to dance, off they came, and that was the end of me and heels."

They were getting close enough to Bryan's house to see the yellow lights of the windows, and Karen could hear the music—the beat of it, anyhow, a steady four-four slammed out as solidly as if somebody was chopping down a tree. "Do you like feel weird in a dress?" Jamie was asking Erica.

In the far depths of her closet, in the area she thought of as "archival," Karen had found an adult version of Jamie's dress, a Laura Ashley that dated back to her marriage to Ian. The skirt had been a touch too short on Karen, so on Erica it was just right. "Not that weird," Erica said. "It's kind of fun."

"Do you ever wear dresses?"

"No, not really. A woman professor can wear pants all the time. They have to be *nice* pants, but nobody in a university is going to expect you to wear a dress if you don't want to."

"But do you like feel *okay* in a dress?"

"Oh, sure. Annalise used to dress me up all the time . . . you know, for dates."

"How about shaving your legs?" Oh my, Karen thought, you're persistent tonight, aren't you?

"Yeah, I do *that.*"

"Why?"

Erica laughed. "Because that's what we're supposed to do. Because all the other girls do it. Because it's a habit now. I'll be sitting in the bathtub thinking about something else, and I'll realize that I've automatically shaved my legs."

"I'm never going to shave my legs," Jamie said. "That would *so* not be me."

They were hardly inside before they were pounced on. "Jamie, you're *wearing a dress!*"—and that was either Morgan or Avalon, the other one right behind her. If this was a costume party for the kids, they were certainly in the spirit of things, in long flowing gowns that fell almost to the floor—one in lime and the other in peach—and pink ballet slippers, real ones with elastics across the instep. They'd gathered up their fiery orange hair into sloppy birds' nests tied with ribbons, and they'd traded colours—the lime ribbons with the peach dress and the peach with the lime. They'd painted their eyelids a swimming-pool aqua and their lips and nails a tail-light red. "Oh my," Karen said, "you girls are certainly colourful." Did they actually have a mother?

"Do you want me to take your coat, Mrs. Oxley?"

"Sure." She should probably give up—no matter how many times she told them, they were not going to call her "Karen."

The music was so loud that she could hide her voice behind it. "Which one is which?" she asked Devon.

"Jeez, haven't you figured them out yet, Mom? Morgan's in green."

Good—now she had them colour-coded. Avalon was helping her off with her coat, and Morgan was taking Erica's. A gaggle of noisy girls had suddenly blown in from a side room to check out what must be the most amazing sight they'd ever seen—"Oh my god oh my god oh my god *Jamie!*"

So what *was* going on with Jamie? A kind of progression?—transforming herself into a pretty boy on her birthday had enabled her to be a Harajuku girl tonight? She seemed to be looking for ways to define herself—exploring ways to be a girl. Maybe by the time she got her period, she'd be ready for it. Erica was a good role model for her, actually.

Jamie was giving Erica a manic grin. Devon said, "Wow, do you guys ever look alike," and it was true. Their hair was nearly the same shade of brunette; makeup made Jamie look older and Erica younger. Their little-girl black dresses were obviously a deliberate match—a sister act, cute times two. With Erica in flats and Jamie in heels, they were nearly the same height. "Yes!" Jamie shouted, pumping her fist in the air. "It's the revenge of the tomboys!"

The main action was in the side room—squeals and giggles. Morgan was tugging on Jamie to drag her there, and someone else was trying to get by, another spinny girl who'd come shooting out of nowhere, careening into Karen—"Oh, sorry." Erica reached out to steady her, and Karen caught her hand. Then the girls were blown away as quickly as they'd come, and Bryan Lynas was revealed at the end of the hallway. Could he have been there the whole time? It looked like he'd been waiting for them. Karen was acutely aware of herself in her own little black dress.

There was a basic rule about clothes—if you wanted something elegant but plain and simple—something classic, symmetrical, undecorated, with not a single clever designer touch to distract the viewer—with no shiny belt to break up the line, no leather piping to add a hint of irony, no amusing bow to reference an earlier era, no cheesy slit up the skirt or tacky cut-out on the torso—if, in short, you wanted nothing but a plain black dress, then you were going to have to pay for it. The dress Karen was wearing was an Italian brand from a little shop on Robson—a black wool sheath with a deep V neckline. It fit her like a dream, and it cost so much that she'd decided never to mention the figure to anyone. It was obvious from the way he was looking at her that Bryan deeply appreciated her little black dress.

Then in his utterly unabashed Aussie asshole way he was also checking out Erica, and Karen felt—oh ridiculous!—a ping of jealousy. How could she compete with an ethereal thirty-something who looked like she was seventeen? But why? What a thought! Who was competing? And then he stepped forward so they could hear him over the music, said, "Ladies, you honour us," pressed the palms of his hands together and bowed—namaste—a gesture so odd she was left with nothing to say—but he was already in motion, leaping away to thrust his head into the side room. "For the sake of sweet bleedin' Jesus, turn that fucken shit down!" The music dropped noticeably. "More!" he yelled. It came down again.

"That's better. No matter what I do, the volume keeps sneaking up on me. Mysterious, isn't it? What are you ladies drinking?"

Leading them to the drinks table, Bryan morphed into a tour guide, addressing not only them but the room at large, pointing out the brilliant features of his kitchen reno. "Old reclaimed tile. Beautiful stuff. And vintage farmhouse sinks."

In two quick bounds he was at the archway leading into the dining room, his sweeping gesture indicating where he'd knocked out a wall. "Opened it up so it flows better." Then, with another leap, he was back to the countertops, his fingers caressing them. "If it was my house, I'd use soapstone, but everybody wants granite, so granite it is."

Agile as an acrobat, he was shooting from feature to feature. "Faux drawers hide the dustbin . . . Cabinet doors slide instead of swing, saves space . . . Check out the waxed ceiling beams . . . And *there's* what's going to tie it all together!"

Karen followed his pointing finger up to an unfinished circular hole in the centre of the ceiling. There was another hole just like it in the second floor ceiling, and above that a distant third hole in the roof, covered by dull gleam of what must be a tarp. "Give us some sun, the whole house will glow. The Americans will love it."

But what was that? In the darkness at the very edge of the nearest hole—two small lights, two greenish-yellow specks. As Karen was trying to figure out what they were, they vanished. Then they reappeared. Oh, she thought, it blinked. "Look," she said to Erica. "There's an animal up there."

"Where? Oh, I see. Yeah, you're right."

Beer must be the thing to drink; a whole table was piled high with it—most of it from local microbreweries—but there were a dozen bottles of wine on the side. She allowed Bryan to pour her a glass of white and didn't even bother to look at the label. It was far from drop-dead delightful, tasted massively of oak, but it wasn't half bad either. Erica was drinking bubbly water.

Usually Karen could read a strange crowd in a matter of minutes, but not this one. A few predictable West Van types—men in neutral cashmere sweaters, their wives styled by Holt Renfrew—but also young guys in toques and work boots, their girlfriends in cheap tight dresses. The majority of the crowd looked like the kind of people you'd see lined up on the street for an art movie—young—in jeans, runners, and those stupid plaid shirts on the girls as well as the boys. And Bryan must know every Australian in the lower mainland—she could hear Aussie voices all around her. Now what? "I guess we circulate."

Girls were darting in and out of the side room, making runs on the food table, and Karen got a glimpse of Akime and another girl from the anime club. If Jamie was Harajuku light, they must be full on—as outlandish as Edward Gorey drawings. She wanted to get a better look at them, but they were already lost in the crowd—and here were Morgan and Avalon swooping down as unexpectedly as blown seagulls. "Erica! Come on. We've got to show you something." Then—and Karen felt it very much as an afterthought—they included her: "Mrs. Oxley. Come on with us. Please."

Avalon took Erica's hand, and Morgan took Karen's, and they were being led to the far end of the hall, away from the crowd, and then up a set of recently built stairs—bare unpainted wood. "Awesome boots, Mrs. Oxley," Morgan said, looking down at them, amazed.

"Thanks. They're kind of impractical."

Morgan giggled, let go of Karen's hand—leaving her momentarily alarmed and unstable—then quickly wrapped an arm around her waist, caught her hand again, and began to guide her upward, step by step, into what looked like total darkness.

They were climbing away from the maddening electronic music, but it persisted as a steadily pulsing background. "Who's the band?" Erica was asking. "I really like them."

"Right now?" Avalon said. "That's Miss Kittin and the Hacker."

Karen wouldn't have noticed Morgan's strength if the girl hadn't been holding her so tightly. Morgan was slightly sweaty. Maybe she'd been dancing. "We made the playlist," she said proudly.

"We'll send you the link if you want," Avalon said.

As Karen's eyes adjusted, she saw that there *was* light up there—insubstantial and guttering, a fat candle in a glass mantle resting on an upended crate. "Watch your step, Mrs. Oxley," Morgan said. "There's all this shit on the floor."

"Like screws and nails and shit," Avalon said.

"And you don't want to get too close to the hole."

"You'd end up in the kitchen."

"You wouldn't like it."

The candlelight was behind them now. As they made their way down the hall, they were casting long opaque shadows. Karen was picking up the strong scent of something—musky, like flowers mixed with wood smoke. "You want to see our room?" Avalon said.

Karen heard the click of a switch and the room sprang up out of nowhere—a truly dizzying sight hotly lit by half a dozen yellowish paper lanterns. Karen was used to seeing the pile-up of images in Twin Central, but this was even more intense—every wall densely layered with graffiti and clippings. The Lynas twins obviously liked boys—especially boys with their shirts off, displaying ripped abs—and they also liked girls in crazy clothes, twins of both sexes, and, of course, manga and anime characters. They hadn't merely taped things up; they'd doodled all over their walls with coloured Sharpies. "It's gonna get like sanded down and spackled and painted," Morgan said, "so Dad lets us do what we want."

The walls were so hectic it took Karen a moment to notice the road signs nailed up everywhere—real road signs that must have been borrowed from real roads—a series of negatives: No Parking, No U-turns, No Loitering, No Exit, No Trespassing, and No Entry. Erica bent down to study the one that said "Electrical hazard! Keep out!" The message was emphasized with a cartoon of a man being electrocuted. "This one's really scary."

"It was easy, actually," Morgan said.

"Yeah, like just four phillips heads," Avalon said. "*That's* the one that was hard." She pointed upward to a sign near the ceiling that said simply "Marine Dr."

Oh my god, Karen thought, these girls are a menace—they're just as nuts as their dad. But then she saw that the room was amazingly tidy—no random heaps of clothes tangled up in corners. Through the open door of the closet she saw a rational pattern—pants, then skirts, then dresses—and the shoes lined up carefully on the floor. "You girls are sure a lot neater than my twins."

"Oh, we like have to be. If we don't keep it neat, we don't get to *eat*"—pronounced to emphasize the rhyme. That's fairly severe parenting, Karen thought. Maybe she should try it.

"It's totally different when we're at Mum's, like random."

"Totally."

"Random."

"We'd like to live with Dad all the time, but it's just not—"

"Sometimes he takes off."

"Like for days."

"And Mum would be really hurt if we never went back there."

"I'll bet she would," Karen said.

"When Jamie and Dev stay over, we like roll out the other futon." Avalon was poking it with the toe of her ballet slipper.

They're actually proud of their space, Karen thought. They're showing it off to me—Jamie and Dev's *mother*. It must never have occurred to them that it wasn't appropriate for Devon to be sleeping in the same room with them—and what? Dev and Jamie slept together? Was this one of those dire disturbing things she would be better off not knowing?

"Come on," Avalon said, "this is just a sidebar."

The lights went out, and Karen followed the girls back into the dark hallway. She felt Morgan's arm wrap around her again and allowed herself to be led. They were approaching a large rectangular patch of warm light—a rice paper screen. Avalon folded it back so that they could step through. Erica went first, and Karen heard her sharp intake of breath. Karen followed and stopped—more than surprised. Whatever she'd been expecting, this wasn't it. Thick white altar candles lit the small closed-in space, and she was facing the Buddha, a statue a good four feet high. He was resting on a wooden packing crate—a classic image of him, seated, one hand raised and the other pointed downward. The twins pressed their hands together and bowed.

"Oh, my goodness," Erica said, "it's so beautiful!" The dusky scent Karen had been picking up was incense burning in a brass brazier. How strange, she thought. This looks like it's serious—maybe it's even sacred space for them.

The wall behind the Buddha was hung with a large curtain or rug—circles of oranges and reds pushed to their full intensity by intertwining designs of blue, black, and green. Off to the left was another statue of the Buddha—polished wood with a golden sparkle—this one lying on his side, eyes shut, head propped up on one hand.

"This is Japanese," Morgan told them, patting the seated statue.

"And this is Tibetan," Avalon said, pointing at the hanging.

"And this is Thai," Morgan finished it, smoothing her fingers over the curving hip of the reclining Buddha.

This small glowing space might be the entry to a mythic world, but Karen couldn't let go of the real one—if you put rice paper near candle flame, you get potential disaster. She was still the mum, so she had to say something. "It's lovely, girls, but, it's really dangerous to leave all these candles burning."

"We only lit them for you."

"We'll blow them out like after."

The twins seemed to be waiting for something to happen. So what were the guests supposed to do now? Say something, offer words of thanks and appreciation? Looking for guidance, she turned toward Erica, but her lovely face had never been more inscrutable—and Karen was struck with the miraculousness of colour.

We forget about it, she thought—moving through the ordinary, we stop seeing how forcefully light breaks up into colour. It was vivid now—the visual heat of the wall hanging, the rainbow of the twins, the golden sparkle on the reclining Buddha, the metallic sheen on the seated one, and the warm flush of Erica's skin, the clarity of her exquisite eyes. "Do you guys know the story of the Buddha?" Morgan said.

"Well, sort of," Erica said. "Not really."

Avalon was looking at Karen. "I guess I know what everybody else knows," she said. "He sat under a tree and got enlightened."

"Can we tell you the story?" Morgan asked.

"Don't worry, we'll give you like the super-short version," Avalon said.

"Sure, okay," Erica said.

"There was like this beautiful young prince, and his name was Siddhartha," Morgan said.

"His dad was the king, and the king didn't want Siddhartha to see anything sad or depressing," Avalon said.

As they always did, the twins were taking turns talking. "So Siddhartha's dad built this beautiful palace, and he got these beautiful young kids for Siddhartha to play with, and he made sure that Siddhartha never saw anything sad or ugly."

"But one day Siddhartha went out for a ride, and he saw this old man by the side of the road, and he asked the dude who drove his chariot, he's like, 'What's his problem? He doesn't look too good.'"

"And the charioteer's like, 'Oh, that happens to everybody. If you live long enough, you're going to grow old and then you'll be all wrinkled up like that, and you won't be able to get around too good.'"

"Siddhartha's like, 'Everybody? Does that mean me too?'"

"And the charioteer's like, 'Hate to tell you this, prince, but yeah, you too.'"

"So in a day or two Siddhartha went out again, and this time he saw a man with some horrible disease, like his skin rotting off him and shit like that, and Siddhartha's like, 'Hey, that's fairly horrible. What's with this guy?'"

"And the charioteer's like, 'Well, he just got sick, you know. People get sick all the time. Horrible diseases go around, and they're real easy to catch.' So that gave Siddhartha more heavy shit to think about."

"Well, the third day he went out, Siddhartha saw a dead man."

"He's like, 'What the fuck! He's not moving around or anything. He might as well be a stick of wood.'"

"And the charioteer's like, 'Yeah, that's death. Everybody dies in the end.'"

"And Siddhartha's like, 'Me too, I guess,' and the charioteer's like, 'You got it, prince.'"

"Siddhartha's like, 'Hey, this is some real heavy shit.'"

"Okay, so the fourth day when Siddhartha went out, he saw a monk, like a dude wearing robes and carrying a begging bowl and just walking around with nothing, right? And he's like, 'Who's that dude?'"

"The charioteer's like, 'He's a monk. He's trying to figure out all this heavy shit.'"

"Siddhartha's like, 'Oh my god, well, I'm gonna do that too.'"

"So he left the palace, and all his cool stuff, and all the beautiful kids he hung around with, and he put all that behind him, and he went out into the world to try to figure everything out."

"Siddhartha tried all kinds of stuff, but that's a long story so we're just going to skip over it, okay?"

"Yeah," Avalon said, "we'll tell you another time if you want."

"But anyhow, nothing worked. So one day Siddhartha sat down under the bodhi tree. And the king of demons came and threw all kinds of heavy shit at him, just the most horrible shit you can possibly imagine, like to fuck up his mind, but Siddhartha saw it was all just illusion."

"And you see that hand pointing down? That's Siddhartha pointing down to Mother Earth, and he's like, 'Okay, Earth, you know I've gone through a gazillion incarnations and accumulated a shit-ton of merit, right? Okay, I swear by the earth I'm going to sit here until I get perfect enlightenment.'"

"And he got it! And after that, we call him the Buddha, because that means enlightened."

"And 'enlighten' means to wake up. Cause we're all zoned out, right? And we've gotta wake up."

"You see that other hand, with the open palm? That hand's like, 'Come here! You can do it too, and I'll tell you how. Everybody's welcome.'"

"*Everybody*. And that means us."

"And that means you."

"And you see the other Buddha?" Avalon asked, trailing her fingertips over the reclining figure.

"That's the Buddha after he's entered into nirvana," Morgan said.

"He's gone. That's why we call him *sugata* because that means good and gone."

"Like there's nothing left. Like there's not even anything left where there used to be something. Like nothing. Like *gone*."

Avalon picked up a candle and held it out to them a moment like an offering. Then with a small puff she blew out the flame. "Gone," she said.

KAREN AND ERICA were back downstairs now, hidden away in this lovely niche while the party roared on without them. Karen was keenly aware of how they must look, arranged on either end of the shabby couch flanking the fireplace—off to themselves like this, unfriendly, unsociable—but she didn't care. The Buddha had disrupted her mind, which, she supposed, was exactly what the Buddha was supposed to do. "Can I get you anything?" Erica asked, her eyes indicating Karen's empty wine glass.

"Can you drive home?"

"Oh sure." Her new-moon smile.

Erica collected their dirty plates. Then, as Karen watched her threading her way through this crowd of strange people, she saw that the party wasn't as far away as it seemed—merely bracketed off—and Erica appeared to be perfectly at ease in her strange costume. "I don't think I've ever worn a petticoat before," she'd said. How odd—Karen would have thought that all girls must have worn a petticoat at least once in their lives. As Erica moved, edging around a cluster of plaid-shirted kids, smiling at them, the candlelight glinted off the flowered brocade of her Laura Ashley dress, glinted off her patent flats—the same ones that Jamie had worn on her birthday—Karen thought that she looked like a girl retrieved from a dream.

One side of their niche had been created by another of those Asian screens, set in place to hide a dark chasm where Bryan had knocked out another wall, and Karen couldn't stop imagining disaster—someone staggering stupidly around the screen to vanish into oblivion, or a touch of flame at the wrong place and everything going up in a whoosh—too many candles burning on crates, on the mantelpiece, and this radiant little fire blazing happily in the fireplace—and oh my god, rice paper, rice paper. The smell of wood was everywhere—burning wood, freshly cut wood— and wafting through these spaces, reflected in the echo chambers of her mind—the fairy-tale lights, the Buddhas upstairs, these peculiar people, their various voices, the disruption of the usual, the shredding up of something— Karen couldn't get a handle on what she was thinking. This was all too strange, and she was drinking too much.

She liked being stashed away in a corner, liked the fire, the crackle of it. She'd almost come to like the throbbing electronic music that Bryan's girls were playing, and she certainly liked whatever was going on in her mind—mysteriously out of kilter—and here was Erica coming back, bringing her another glass of white wine and a slice of carrot cake. There'd been a dozen different desserts to choose from. How could she have known that carrot cake was Karen's favourite? "Oh, thank you."

"You're welcome." Erica's voice was so grave it seemed a mockery of politeness. Karen had realized recently that Erica actually did have a sense of humour—although a dry one, understated, easy to miss.

A titanic *thunk*—and then, as Erica stepped out of her line of sight, Karen saw that Bryan Lynas had fallen into the ratty overstuffed chair directly in front of them.

"Ladies," he said, toasting them with a ridiculously large mug of dark beer. "I hear my girls have been giving you the Dharma. Good on them. They wouldn't do that if they didn't think you needed it. But don't get the wrong idea. They're not bodhisattvas yet."

Just as he'd done in the piercing place, he suddenly switched into a parody voice. "I get the call, right? Some bloke." She heard it now as a comedy shtick—you want Australian, I'll give you Australian. "Is this Bryan Lynas? Yes, yes it is. This is Constable so-and-so of the RCMP. We have your daughters in custody. Bugger, what have they done now? Inebriated, are they? No worries, I'll be right over. Inebriated? Hell, they're laid out flat as a pair of lizards."

Like father like daughters? Karen wouldn't have called Bryan drunk, but he was certainly flying. "And that's not the half of it," he said in his normal voice. "Reckon you saw the road signs?"

"Oh, we did indeed. It's quite a collection."

"Yeah. I told them, 'One more bleedin' road sign, I'm shipping you straight back to your mum.'"

He took a long pull on his beer. His eyes were glittering with amusement, and he had never stopped looking at her. She was getting that tingly sensation of being washed by a pleasure-beam, waves of heat licking her skin—a sensation that had been missing from her life too much lately. She could actually feel her face flushing.

"Aw, but they're great girls," he said. "Sometimes they just can't help themselves . . . afflicted with that crooked Lynas gene, goes all the way back to Jonathon Praisegod Lynas transported to Van Diemen's Land for having his hand in the wrong bloke's pocket. Oh, and by the way"—now he was addressing Erica—"I got your car."

Car? Karen thought. What car?

"Said you wanted safe, so you've got safe. 2003 Volvo. Single owner.

Ace condition. Plenty of go if you need it. Red, if the colour means any-thing to you. New set of tires. Not a steal, but fair."

Well, of course. Erica was not going to go on driving the Lexus forever because she was not going to stay at Karen's forever—as obvious as obvious could be—but Karen felt stung and disappointed. What on earth had she been thinking?

"It's out in Langley," he was saying. "I go out there all the time, could give you a lift."

Erica's eyes met Karen's for a moment, sent her a message—wry and pointed but unintelligible.

Erica, in her childish dress, had drawn her knees up like a child, her patents on the couch. Bryan was telling her that Volvo parts were hard to get, but he had a mate out that way who worked on Volvos. "If I were you, I'd dump another thou into it right off the bat. Then you'd be right as rain."

"I don't mind doing that," Erica said. "I want to be right as rain."

Bryan was looking at Erica in an entirely different way than he'd been looking at Karen. Appreciative, yes; sexually interested, no—that's how she read him, and she was glad to see it. "Cash is always best," he was saying.

He stood up, lifted his beer mug first to Erica, then to Karen—a fare-well gesture. This must have been merely a stop on his rounds—working the crowd at his own party—but his eyes were back on Karen, and the heat was still there. Everybody knew by now that she and Drew had split up, and Bryan must know it, too. Oh my goodness, she thought, what if he isn't just fooling around, what if he's actually interested in me? "Bryan?" she said. "What exactly is it that you *do?*"

He laughed, allowed himself to collapse back into his chair. "You've been dying to ask me that, haven't you, Karen? I fix things for people. Got a wrecked car in your driveway and you want it to vanish—it's gone. Your mate here wants a safe reliable car—she's got it. But those are just the little problems. I take care of the big problems, too. I'm in the network with the right people—you understand what I'm telling you here?" He gave them a beat to absorb that.

"Works by word-of-mouth. You've got a problem? Talk to that crazy Aussie, Bryan Lynas. Yeah, let's sit down and have us a pint or two. I do my Crocodile Dundee imitation, and they're going, oh my god, a genuine wild man from the underside of the world! He's crazy as a shit-house rat. The ordinary rules don't apply to him. Maybe he can actually *do something*. I gaze soulfully into their eyes, say, 'Tell me all about it.' They pour out their bleedin' hearts to me. I tell them, 'No worries, mate, it's taken care of.' And then I go and take care of it. The kind of bloke I'm talking about, they don't mind reaching for their wallet—"

His daughters distracted him. They had just come sidling in, Jamie and Dev following, all of them wearing that unmistakable I-want-something look.

"Yeah, and I flip houses," he said, turning his attention back to Karen. "Been doing that for a while. Most of my energies these days are going into the reno on this one. I was ahead of the game until my ex and I came to our parting of the ways. The ladies always get the houses—isn't that the basic rule of divorce law? So she's left me one flip behind."

He tried to take a pull on his beer, but his mug was empty. He rose to his feet now like a man with a mission. "Pops?" Morgan said.

"*Pops*, is it? Sweet Jesus. Yes, my dear."

"Can Jamie and Dev sleep over?"

"There's their mum."

"Yeah, can we, Mom?" Devon asked her. "We'd help them clean up."

Don't do this to me, Karen thought. Of course she had to say no— but then again, maybe she didn't. What if she knew nothing about the sleeping arrangements—what if she'd heard nothing, seen nothing? If she played it that way, she'd be a terrible mum, but it was probably better than making a scene and embarrassing them. She'd have to have a serious talk with them sometime, but not now. "All right," she said, "but if you say you're going to help, you've really got to help."

"Of course we're going to help." Jamie at her pissiest.

Bryan was definitely leaving now, was already in motion, but then he stopped. It was as though he'd pressed the pause button so he could take everything in. How odd. She'd seen him do that before—simply stop and look. What was he looking at? Erica and Jamie dressed up like sisters? Devon wearing his daughters' clothes? Karen in her little black dress? He'd already seen plenty of her little black dress.

His twins seemed to be tuned in to him, must have picked it up from him—they were inside the same pause. "Hey, Dad," Morgan said, "did you see the soles on Mrs. Oxley's boots?"

In case he hadn't, Karen lifted a foot to show him. "How cool is that?" Avalon said.

"It's the Louboutin signature," Karen said, "the shiny red soles. They're trademarked. When the cognoscenti see them, they're supposed to think, 'Oh my god, she's wearing Louboutins just like Kate Moss or Kylie Minogue.'"

"Yeah," he said, and then, smiling, "the cognoscenti."

Looking directly into Karen's eyes, he pronounced the word again as though he was savouring it bite by bite—"Cog nos cen ti."

IT WAS LATE NOW, the party winding down. Karen hadn't been out this late in years. She'd known that Bryan would come back, and he had come back—although he'd taken his own sweet time to do it. She was distinctly buzzed. White wine.

"Already burning the heart out of my country," he was saying. They were talking about the climate change conference, and she still couldn't get over it—how amazing it was that she'd found somebody in West Vancouver who actually agreed with her.

Erica was following the conversation, but she wasn't saying anything. Her costume made her look like a little girl fascinated by the grown-ups, hanging onto their every word— But no, that was too easy, wasn't right, wasn't even close to right. Another view of Erica flickered in and out—subtle, ambiguous, illusory, incomprehensible—all those fuzzy words that stood for *who the fuck knows?* Language was inadequate. Yeah, it often is. Karen should stop drinking. Now. She set her glass down on the floor. "That senator from Australia," she said. "She really gave them shit."

"Right! That was our girl, Christine . . . Christine Milne. The Greens started with us, you know? The first elected Greens were in Tasmania. She gave a press conference when she got home, and the Tassie press didn't even cover it. Fucken idiots. Some local carry-on was more important. The world leaders finally agreed, that's what she said. They agreed it's bad and they're not going to do sweet fuck-all about it."

"That little island that's going to get drowned—"

"Tuvalu," he said, "yeah. You talk about being out in the middle of nowhere—"

Suddenly Erica came springing into the conversation. "They wouldn't even consider their proposal! Did you read his speech? The whole world's waiting on a bunch of US senators . . . and Obama—"

"Bugger. Don't blame us, it's all China's fault."

"That poor man from that little island," Karen said. "He was actually crying."

"And he was absolutely right," Erica said. "We should at least be trying for one-point-five. Two would be a disaster. Four, it's game over." She was talking quickly as though she'd stored up a whole night full of words. "I read *Heat* right after it came out. It really fucked my mind. Then I read *everything*."

Erica's words weren't as important as her energy—and with that thought, Karen was drawn further out into the subtle web she'd been discovering—or creating—and then, with an internal flare, she knew that the cut-flower stillness, the passivity Erica usually wore, was her depression, not the real her. What Karen was seeing now, flickering in and out, was Erica as she'd been before her sister died.

"The science is absolutely rock solid," Erica said. "Where we're headed . . . We can't adapt fast enough. There hasn't been this much carbon in the atmosphere since the fucking Pliocene. We're headed into a mass extinction. Even if we survive, we're going to lose billions of people."

Back home in Alberta she kept her opinions to herself. "People believe what other people in their groups believe, and anything that contradicts that, they'll simply deny it. We call that 'confirmation bias.'"

There was no point in fighting a war she couldn't possibly win. She was sick of hearing about the oil sands and the economy. She was sick of hearing, "Okay, Ricki, if that's what you believe, why are you still driving a car?"

"Everybody thinks we're a bunch of redneck assholes in love with Ralph Klein, but we're not. When everything's great, why vote for change? And when anybody who wants a job can get one, then everything's great . . . Yeah, that's how we like it . . . My brother's not in love with the tar sands. The *oil* sands, he'd say. He's in love with working for a living and making decent money. He's a steam engineer. He's got his ticket. He'd be just as happy to work on renewables. What we've got to do— If we want any chance of survival, that fucking filthy bitumen has got to stay in the ground. Alberta's economy does *not* need to be tied to oil. Jesus, billions of dollars of subsidies. We've got to stop that shit, start subsidizing renewables. It's that simple, but you can't get past the lies, the propaganda—"

"The miserable bastards," Bryan said, "they're trapped by their own fear and greed."

"They probably don't believe it," Erica said, "can't let themselves believe it. If they did, they'd have to change their lives."

Karen saw Erica lose focus, look away at nothing. It must be the depression settling back down on her again. "Or maybe they do believe it," she said. "Maybe they believe it and think, so what? Why should it matter what happens to the world after I'm gone? That's a good question, you know. When you're dead, you don't know anything, you don't *exist*. So why should it matter?"

13.

IT FELT ODD to be riding in the passenger seat of the Lexus. While they'd been hidden away in Bryan's house, the rain had morphed from dank blah into the kind of cold steady Vancouver downpour that felt ancient and indifferent. The quiet hum of the engine, the steady slap of the wiper blades, the fragmented lights moving across Erica's face, her exquisite profile—unhappy girl. Karen wished there was something she could do for her.

"Do you want me to go up to the highway?" Erica had certainly learned her way around West Van in a hurry.

"No," Karen said, "just stay down here. It's more scenic." That was meant to be a joke. There was nothing to see.

It must be depressing to be convinced that nothing survives after death—although it might very well be true. Whatever. Brooding about it didn't change anything. All Karen had was that old therapy motto—"Be alive while you're alive." Sometimes it felt like that was enough, but other times it didn't.

What could Erica be thinking—silent girl, snaking along these twisty roads in somebody else's car in the rain? Karen had been right not to worry about lending her the Lexus—she handled it with great authority.

"The soul is convinced of its own immortality," Helen used to say, quoting some noted Jungian, and Karen had run across that bright little flicker of conviction in herself more than once—in dreams, in those strange moments when the real felt tilted and permeable—although how the soul might possibly survive she had no idea. Maybe we become other people. It mattered to her very much what happened to the world after she died. She wanted so much for her kids.

Erica drove into the garage, pressed the clicker to close the door behind them, and, yes, it did feel distinctly odd to be on the passenger's side. Karen got out, unlocked the door to the downstairs, stepped aside to allow Erica to go first. She'd been planning to take off the Louboutins the minute she got home, but she didn't. She did pause to wipe their soles on the doormat. What had she been thinking to wear them out on a night like this? They were works of art, collector's items.

She pressed the light switch just inside the door, and Erica appeared out of the darkness. She was simply there, waiting, and Karen knew that they were far more intimately connected than they had any right to be. It was that old elusive sense of a secret life running below the ordinary—another tug on another strand. She had to try to remember.

They walked past Cam's room, then past the guest room, and she saw Erica hesitate. "I should hang your dress up?"

"Oh, yeah, come on up," Karen said. "Let's debrief." She was far from ready to say good night.

Still not speaking, they climbed the stairs, crossed through the living area with its greenish Star Trek night lights, and Karen wished that she could see the world again as her children saw it—as magic. They continued on up into Karen's bedroom where she turned on one of the small lamps, brought up the rose-coloured warmth. The windows were partially open, the rain a steady sound. Karen couldn't think of a thing to say.

Following the no-shoes house rule, Erica was carrying the patents. Karen turned on another lamp for her so she could see her way to the closet, then sat on the edge of the bed, unzipped the Louboutins, and pulled them off. Standing, she was acutely aware of her feet once again flat on the floor, of the rug under her feet—the sensation of the nap. "Unzip me," Erica said.

Karen stepped forward to do it, but Erica didn't turn around.

Karen didn't know that she was going to kiss Erica until she was already kissing her. Erica didn't seem to mind—didn't even seem surprised. She wrapped her arms lightly around Karen and held on.

Karen must have been poised inside an enormous suspension as fragile as a soap bubble because, now that the bubble had burst, her mind was chattering again—Hey, wait a minute, you idiot, what are you *doing?*

Erica stopped, stepped back, but still held Karen, her hands on her shoulders. "I like you so much, Karen. You're just lovely. But I'm straight."

Karen jerked away. "I'm sorry." She couldn't remember ever having been so embarrassed.

"Oh, don't be *sorry.*"

Karen felt her face burning. She must be as red as a sunset. That hadn't been a friendly kiss between girlfriends. "Oh my god, what was I thinking? I'm *so* sorry."

Erica caught Karen in a fierce hug. "Don't be sorry, don't be sorry, don't be sorry."

Karen freed herself, backed away, put a good four or five feet between them. She couldn't imagine anything she could possibly say. She couldn't even look at Erica.

"I knew you were going to kiss me . . . just before you did. I could see it in your eyes. I could have stopped you, but I didn't."

Tangled and unhappy, Karen said, "I don't know what I'm doing. I've had too much to drink." Great, she thought—the standard excuse for behaving like an asshole.

"I *liked* kissing you. Couldn't you tell? But it's—"

One of Erica's unfinished sentences—but it's what? Not right? Fucking weird? *What?* Then Erica finally found the word she wanted, said it apologetically—"It's enough."

Then Erica exploded into motion—too much energy to handle—walking away, walking back, her arms swinging. "You singletons sexualize everything!"

Karen was— distressed? rattled? mortified? Anyhow, frozen to the spot, voiceless, as Erica flung words at her. "Sexual feelings are the strongest feelings you guys ever have, so you think the twin bond has to be sexual, but it's not."

No sign of depression now, Erica was all force and fire—look at her eyes! "The bond between MZ twins. It's the strongest attachment one human can have for another. Stronger than between lovers. Than between husbands and wives. Stronger than between parents and children. *And it's not sexual.*"

So this was who Erica actually was. A small-town Alberta girl doesn't work her way up to becoming a professor in a major Canadian university by being sad, passive, unassertive, indecisive, and resigned—no, absolutely not. "I'm probably hard-wired for it," she was saying. "I keep doing it to people. To singletons. I'm an MZ twin. I get too close, too fast, and I want too much. Are you okay?"

"Embarrassed," Karen said. "I guess I'm embarrassed."

"Don't be. Everything's okay. For me, it's okay," and stepping closer, turning around, "Unzip me."

Karen unzipped her. Erica shed the dress.

"Here. Let me," Karen said, taking the dress.

"It was fun wearing it." She stepped out of the petticoat, handed it to Karen. "Thanks."

Despite what she'd just said, Erica seemed now just as embarrassed as Karen—well, she was standing there half dressed, wasn't she?—and they'd been caught in one of those sticky impossible moments the twins called "awkward."

"Good night," Erica said.

"Don't go. Stay with me."

Oh god, what was she saying? "You've told me a million times how much you hate sleeping alone. Why should you have to sleep alone?"

All Karen could see was Erica's sentient housecat look that communicated nothing.

"This isn't just a—" Karen couldn't find a dignified way to say it. "Isn't just another—"

"*Stop it.* I know that. You don't have to say that."

"I want you to stay."

THE WINDOWS WERE exactly the way Karen liked them—open just enough to allow a breath of chill into the room. She wanted to experience the night and at the same time feel safe from it—warm under the covers—and she wanted to hear the rain as a steady background, that primal sound of falling water. Thank goodness they seemed to have survived the kiss. Thank goodness they were still able to talk the way they had before—freely and easily with no agenda. They were even able to talk about sex.

"No MZ twins are ever absolutely identical," Erica was saying, "but when it came to the boys we liked, we were just . . . Lise was very conservative. She liked traditionally masculine boys, old school. Mark's like that. The guy she married. But I'm much more experimental than she was. I always liked oddball guys with a little bit of girl in them."

Erica sighed. "But I haven't . . . When she died, all my sexual feelings died, too. It's . . . It goes with being depressed, standard textbook shit. No sexual feelings. Zero."

Now Erica was telling her about the relationship she'd left behind in Madison. He was a sessional in Poly Sci, just finishing up his PhD—Gerald, and you were not allowed to call him Gerry. How they met—Erica was watching the World Series in a student watering hole in the Memorial Union, and she started chatting with this cute guy sitting next to her. "You know anything about baseball?" Of course Karen didn't.

"Okay, a game can go on forever with nothing happening. I mean *forever.* I mean *nothing.*"

They were both baseball nuts, so they were exchanging statistics and factoids, and Erica segued into stories about playing softball. "I used

239

to be something of a star, actually, and he seemed fascinated by that. I looked like shit. Old T-shirt, ratty jeans, hadn't washed my hair in a week. I could tell he wanted to come on to me, and I kept waiting, but he didn't, and I thought, oh god, why didn't I at least take a shower this morning?"

Then Tim Salmon smacked a homer in the eighth, and a huge adrenaline rush went around the room, and that gave Gerald the kick he needed, and he asked for Erica's number. "Was he ever nervous! Wow. Like sweating. I never knew there are guys who get turned on to tomboys. Naïve, eh? But there are, and he was one of them. He liked me to dress like a boy, to be rough with him. Not kinky just *rough*. The aggressor. I'd never had sex like that before. It was fun . . . although I would have liked more variety."

That was interesting. Maybe now nothing was off limits. "Erica? Do you think Jamie and Dev are attracted to each other . . . ? I mean sexually?"

"Absolutely not."

"Really? How can you be so sure?"

"They were raised together until they were seven, right? If they'd been separated at birth, then you'd have trouble, but they weren't. They're protected by the Westermarck effect. That seems to happen to kids naturally if they're raised together. They've internalized the incest taboo. The thought of having sex with each other would seem ridiculous to them . . . or even repulsive."

"That's what they . . . I caught them in bed together. I blew up. I told them if I ever caught them again, Devon was going straight back to his father. They were just as mad at me as I was at them. 'What do you think we're going to do, Mum? Get with each other? We're not going to do that. We're *twins*.' "

"That's right. They understand the twin bond. They see it with Morgan and Avalon. They know it's not sexual."

Talking about it was a relief—things always seemed worse if you kept them to yourself. Maybe now she could ask Erica how she'd ended up in her driveway, sitting there immobilized in her wrecked Golf getting hypothermia. But how could she ask her that? Erica had already given her the canned story, phony as it was, so if she said, "What were you *really* doing?" it would imply that she thought Erica had been lying.

That might sound accusatory, or even hostile—might destroy this new level of intimacy they were sharing. It's okay, Karen thought, I don't need to know. She'll tell me the truth when she's ready.

Neither of them had said anything for a while, and sleep was beginning to paw gently at Karen's edges. She thought that Erica might have drifted off, but no. "After Annalise died, Gerald sent me the nicest letter. Not an email, a real letter. It was just beautiful. Thoughtful. Straight from the heart. And I never replied. I never even sent him a one-liner thank you."

"Don't beat yourself up. You've survived a major life trauma. You'll catch up to your friends later."

"I don't know. I got, I don't know, twenty or thirty cards and letters and emails, and I didn't answer any of them. Not one."

"You ask too much of yourself. Give yourself some time to heal. Everybody understands that." Karen couldn't deal with too much more tonight. Sleep was pulling her down.

VOICES BACK OF the rain. That was all right. Mum and Dad. Way far away. In their own room. So everything was safe. Karen turned over in bed, and the sensation of wearing pajamas dissolved—and then the dream dissolved. Oh my goodness, how real it had been. Somebody was in bed with her. Erica. She was glad it was Erica.

There were no voices now—the sound of the rain had nothing in it but rain. What an eerie dream, almost metaphysical. Helen used to say that in the psyche all times exist simultaneously. "Erica?" she whispered, "are you awake?"

"Like an owl."

"Did you sleep in pajamas when you were little?"

Erica actually laughed at that. "Yeah. Did you?"

"Yes. I just had the . . . I was dreaming, and it was absolutely real. I was back in my bed in my parent's house. A little kid. I had the absolutely real sensation of wearing pajamas. Isn't it weird that they'd put buttons on something you're supposed to sleep in?"

"I don't remember. I don't think we had buttons on our pajamas. When we were . . . I don't know, ten or eleven . . . we decided to sleep in

241

long nightgowns. We wanted to feel like the girls in *Little House on the Prairie*."

"That's cute. I was remembering . . . oh, all this childhood stuff. Night, rain. My parents in their room down the hall. Feeling safe and eternal."

On many of those safe and eternal nights Patsy had slept over. Maybe that's what had triggered the dream, the feeling of being in bed with a girlfriend. Maybe that's what this was—a girls' sleepover—so there was nothing strange about it, nothing to be afraid of. "You're getting better," Karen said. "You're healing."

"I don't know. Do you think so?"

"I can feel it. Can't you?"

"I don't know. Maybe. Karen, I'm so fucked up, you don't even know. I've been trying so hard, but I still think about suicide."

Well, that was fairly chilling.

"You've been so nice to me, and I'm such a . . . I've attached myself to you like a leech. And you're a singleton. So I knew better, but I did it anyway. Of course you'd feel it as sexual."

Karen was surprisingly angry. "Listen. Forget that crap, okay? Stop beating yourself up. You're so fucking self-effacing. You're nothing like a leech. A leech sucks blood and gives nothing back. You give far more than you take."

"Thank you."

Karen heard the pause, waited.

"But I *am* so fucked up. I can't even . . . Some things I just can't do. I should be in the Hat on Tuesday. I owe it to my family, but I just can't do it."

Karen felt for Erica's hand, took it, held it. We *are* connected at some mysterious level, she thought. Maybe I am a little bit in love with her.

"You said you get too close too fast . . . that twin thing. What if it's not too close too fast? Do you want me to go with you?"

14.

ERICA CAME BURSTING into the restaurant like someone who was desperately late—which she was—and flung herself into the booth so hard the table rattled. "Sorry!" It was nearly eleven. She looked even worse than she had the night before—pinched and white. "Everything took forever. Dad didn't want to lend me his car, but he did." She slammed the keys down on the table.

"It's okay," Karen said, although it wasn't. She'd been up, dressed, and waiting since eight.

"I'm so glad you came. It's so good of you to do this."

"Don't think about me," Karen said. "This is your day." That was a standard line from therapy workshops, and she hoped that Erica wouldn't hear it for what it really was—automatic bullshit. Karen was not in the world's greatest mood. She'd had too much time to ask herself too many questions—interminable scratchy scads of time—but she hadn't found any answers. All she knew for certain was that if she hadn't kissed Erica on Saturday night, she wouldn't be here in Medicine Hat, Alberta, on Tuesday morning three days before Christmas.

Their waitress must have read Erica's frantic entrance as hunger—or at any rate as a need to order. "Just coffee," Erica said to her, "black," and to Karen: "I can't eat anything."

"You didn't have breakfast?"

Erica shook her head.

"You've got to eat. You've got a difficult day ahead of you."

"I don't know. Do you have a bear claw?"

"A bear claw is not breakfast," Karen said. "How do you like your eggs?"

They'd arrived the night before in the cast-iron dark, flying from Calgary on a prop plane the size of a school bus with wings on it. They'd agreed that it would be a terrible idea to let Erica's family know that she'd brought a friend with her. "It'd change everything, turn into a big fucking deal. We'd have to have you over for dinner, everybody on their best behaviour. It'd be absolutely ghastly." Yes, it would, Karen had thought, and she had no intention of intruding on their grief. She was coming to help out Erica with *her* grief, and that was more than enough. They'd taken a cab in from the airport, and Erica had dumped her at the Travelodge.

"Travis just took off," Erica was telling her, "the asshole. Just pissed off with his buddies. Yesterday. One of them has a cabin somewhere. He'll be back tomorrow. I guess they're doing whatever boys do when they're by themselves. Riding around on a snowmobile, drinking too much. Playing poker. Whatever. If I'd known he was going to do that— You were right. I should have stayed in Vancouver."

Erica was wearing a dirty old parka that used to be sky-blue—it looked like something she'd found at the back of a closet—and a black toque pulled down over her curly hair. At first she'd seemed brittle, ready to break, but now Karen was picking up anger vibrating beneath the surface like a low constant static. "Anyhow, Trina's having us all over to dinner tonight. 'The family has to come together,' she says. Yeah. Except for Trav. He's the only one who has any sense."

The way Erica liked her eggs was over easy. "I'll go to Trina's after I drop you at the airport. That'll be enough. I told them I want to be alone today. I told them I'd be late. I told them I'd come for dessert. Fuck."

Erica picked at her eggs, cut them up, moved them around on her plate, and actually ate some of them while Karen watched her do it—and she was *still* waiting for Erica. It had been one long difficult night. The room had been just fine, spacious and clean, but there must be a pool somewhere because the whole world smelled of chlorine. She'd tossed a few books into her flight bag but hadn't been able to concentrate on any of them. She'd channel surfed, looking for a talk show that would hold her interest, but hadn't found one. She'd paced up and down and stewed, worrying about her kids, worrying about herself. This was by far the most quixotic stunt she'd pulled in years, and, yes, it had begun with the kiss. And then the kiss had turned into something like a dare. You think you can get as close to me as a twin? Well, I dare you.

But it wasn't just the kiss. If she wanted to work her way back along the chain of events, it had started even before that. Egged on by her charming children, she'd dressed herself up in exactly the sort of costume that Rob used to encourage her to wear—an honest-to-god come-and-fuck-me outfit complete with five-inch heels—and because it was specifically designed to get men going, it had got Bryan Lynas going, and he'd directed a million volts of sexual energy back at her, so he'd got *her* going, and there she'd been, inside the old demonic feedback loop—and then, on top of that, she'd sipped her way through most of a bottle of white wine—goodbye, impulse control—so she'd gone home and taken it out on Erica, poor girl. What other choice did she have other than flying to Medicine Hat?

Erica checked the time. She was wearing what looked like a man's sports watch—huge and silver. Karen had never seen it before. "Your flight's at eight," Erica said. "I'll get you to the airport around seven, eh? Plenty of time."

"Yeah, should be. It's a small airport."

This whole thing was, of course, utterly insane. Was that distressed scruffy little waif sitting across from her the same eerily magical person she'd kissed on Saturday night? The same person who had been sleeping in her bed ever since? The same person she'd thought she might be a little bit in love with? Karen, she told herself, you're too old for this nonsense. Grow up.

Right, so what about the kids? They were fine. Probably fine. She was only gone for one night, and Paige was safe at Lauren's, and the twins were with Bryan, and Claire was at the house to keep an eye on Cameron. Okay, and there were some things you could ask Cam to do and he would actually do them—anything that needed to be moved, fixed, nailed up, torn down, taken apart, put back together—all the boy stuff, so she was sure she could count on him. By the time she got back, he would have bought a nice comely tree, carted it home, and planted it in the living room in a good solid stand complete with water. No matter how quixotic and impulsive she'd been, everything would work out fine. She would be home late tonight, and tomorrow she would gather the entire family together, and they would eat pizza and decorate the tree.

Erica checked her watch again. "I'll bet you've never been here before. Come on, I'll give you a tour."

"Don't think about me. What do *you* want to do?"

Erica gave her a hard level look. "I'm not hoping for any great revelation, Karen. I'm just trying to get through the day."

"YOU WERE EXPECTING bald-headed prairie, weren't you?"

"Yes," Karen said, "I probably was."

"You thought it was going to be flat as a cutting board with twenty feet of snow, right? Thirty below with the wind chill making it feel like forty, right?"

Erica must still have her sense of humour—or at least she was able to pretend that she did. "Yes," Karen said, laughing, "that's exactly what I thought."

Erica was right—Medicine Hat was not what Karen had expected. Built into the valley of a substantial river, painted white with snow and decorated for the holidays, it looked like the kind of model Canadian city you'd find on a calendar. It was cold today but far from bitter—about the same as Vancouver at its coldest. Although snow was piled up everywhere, the roads were clear, the sidewalks shoveled right down to the concrete. It was a city that liked its trees; they were stripped bare for winter, but in the summer they must make the streets look green and neighbourly.

"Nice to see the sun," she said. It was a big fat winter sun, dominating the sky, lighting up aisles of mackerel clouds.

"We're the sunniest city in Canada," Erica said.

They were driving down what appeared to be a main street, passing a twenty-foot Christmas tree, and it didn't seem entirely real, could be a special on the CBC—"Christmas on the Prairies."

"Annalise was a timid driver," Erica said, "a cautious driver."

Karen sensed that Erica was letting her in on a conversation she'd been having with herself. "Just like anything else, if you want to be good at something, you've got to practice. We were MZ, so we had the same natural abilities. She could have been just as good a driver as me, but when we were together, I did all the driving— There's her ballet school." She pulled over so Karen could see it—although there was nothing to see but a door in the side of the building.

Driving again, Erica flowed seamlessly into the light traffic. "She did everything—jazz, tap, lyrical—just like the Lynas kids. But ballet was what counted. We never thought she was going to be a dancer, but she threw her whole heart into it."

There were not many cars in this part of town. Maybe everyone was at work. "No, I wouldn't call her a good driver, but she was careful. That's how she made up for it."

Karen's job was to keep her talking. "So you did all the driving?"

"Yeah, I did. That's one of the ways we split things up. We split up a lot of . . . She did the cooking, I cleaned up. I paid our bills, she bought our clothes. Some things we shared. The housework. I was much neater than she was."

"She bought your clothes? Really? For both of you?"

"Oh, yeah. I hated shopping, but she was the girly twin, so it was fun for her. She went with her girlfriends. We were . . . I was a touch taller, less than half an inch, and I weighed more, but never more than three or four pounds. The main difference between us was ballet versus softball, but she knew how to pick tops that would fit me, and from the waist down we were absolutely identical. Size anyway. She had dancer's legs."

Erica pulled over again. "There's our softball field. I spent half my life there." Nothing to see except for a big empty rectangle of snow with a fence around it.

"But how did she know—?" Karen wasn't sure how to frame the question. "If she bought your clothes, that meant that you had to trust her to decide what you wanted to look like."

"Oh, it wasn't a matter of trust. We knew what we wanted to look like."

"Okay."

There it was again—that inexplicable twin bond—but if they'd been ordinary sisters, Karen might have read it differently. Annalise had dressed her sister like a boy—what a nasty controlling thing to do—so Annalise could really shine as *the girl*. But maybe that was entirely wrong. Maybe that didn't apply at all.

Erica had been driving uphill for a while, and now they were in a residential area looking down over the valley. She slowed down. "There's our house. I don't want to hang around in case somebody sees me with you in the car, but I wanted you to see it."

It looked like a nice enough house—wood frame, well maintained.

"I'd already been home for most of the month. Once I finished up my term, got all my grades in, there wasn't anything to keep me in Vancouver.

247

Annalise and I spent a lot of time together. Enough so it was a real test on Mark . . . whether or not he could handle the twin bond. If somebody marries one of us, they have to be able to handle the twin bond. And we were pushing him right to the limit. She stayed over with me for three nights, in our—" Erica's voice broke.

Karen didn't know what to do. Should she tell her to pull over and cry? That's what a therapist would tell her. They were headed back down into the valley. Erica was driving a little too fast for comfort.

"We still had our room at Mum and Dad's." Stopping herself from crying had made her voice flat and formal. "If you've got a house with four bedrooms . . . and if all your kids have moved out, you're not lacking for space . . . so they left the room for us. When we were in University . . . and came back . . . that's where we stayed. It's where Annalise stayed when I was in Edmonton and she came back to the Hat. It's where I stayed whenever I came back to the Hat. We thought it would always be our room . . . well, maybe until I got married, too. But it felt like . . . Just to get in bed with Lise and spend most of the night talking. She was so excited about the baby. That's mainly what she talked about."

Karen was grabbed by the sudden twingey pain between her legs that hit her sometimes when she'd just heard something she didn't want to hear—something she *really* didn't want to hear. "A baby? Was she pregnant? You didn't tell me she was pregnant."

"Yeah, she was six weeks pregnant."

Not speaking, staring straight ahead, Erica continued to drive. Breathe, Karen told herself. Just look out the window and watch the world go by.

"Her death," Erica said, "that's what I kept recycling. The classic PTSD symptoms, the obsessive . . . The nightmares. But the baby? That was different somehow. A different order of things. It was . . . I try not to think about it. It's just too fucking sad."

"MANDATORY DESTINATION," Erica said with a wry smile. "Absolutely required. I have to submit a report later."

Karen tried to return the message, a co-conspirator's smile—yes, I understand the mask you have to wear—but she was still trying to pull

248

herself back together. *Annalise had been pregnant.* It *was* just too fucking sad.

Erica parked in the lot by the office, and they walked into what looked like the most compulsively well-maintained cemetery Karen had ever seen in her life. The headstones were identical and arranged in neat rows that receded like formal equations toward distant vanishing points. Sterile, she thought. The Romantic in her wanted a resting place of the dead to be wild and gothic—dense overgrowth, dark willows, ancient monuments, stone angels—but she said, "It's a beautiful cemetery."

"Yeah, if you like cemeteries."

Out in the open air, Karen lost her illusion that this was no worse than a cold winter's day in Vancouver. The fat disk of the sun seemed flat and distant now, no warmth to it at all. Cloud cover was piling up, and the light had gone as dull as tarnished silver. Oh fuck yes it was cold. She put her gloves on. She didn't own anything designed for a winter like this, but she'd thought she'd be okay if she went layered—a T-shirt, a Banana Republic top, her warmest hoodie, and a North Face jacket. It wasn't enough.

"The last time I was here was when we buried her," Erica said. "I think I must have been totally disassociated. I have images of it in my mind like a movie, but I don't remember from . . . This is hard to describe. I don't have any memories of it from being inside myself. I know I couldn't talk. I couldn't say a word."

Yes, seeing your twin sister buried must be the worst kind of nightmare—and Karen told herself to stay away from that feeling, stay detached. It wouldn't do either of them any good if she got as emotional as Erica. Then they'd both be lost in messy chaos, and she wouldn't be any help at all.

"This is our part of the cemetery. These are all Bauers." They must have walked into an earlier section. The headstones weren't identical any longer and the rows not as compulsively neat.

"Here's the little tree that Travis had planted for her. He didn't ask anybody, he just went ahead and did it. He's like that, he just . . . I have to be able to say that I've seen his little tree. He did it for me as much as for Annalise. Oh god, we got into a huge argument. Everybody!"

Now Erica wasn't bothering to hide her anger. "That's really what you want to do when somebody's dead—get into a big fucking argument about what to do with their body, right? Trav was the only one who agreed with me. We wanted to have her cremated, and then they could work her ashes into the topsoil in the memorial garden and put up a plaque for her. But nobody else wanted to do that. They wanted to bury her with the Bauers—you know, three generations of Bauers. I should have had the say because I was her twin, but everybody else thought that her husband should have the say, and Mark didn't want to get into a big fight with Mum, so he just said okay to anything she wanted. So there's Annalise's body absolutely useless to the environment for several hundred years. That's why Trav had them plant that little tree—so something would be growing. And there's her headstone. I have to be able to tell everybody how nice her headstone is."

Annalise Elisabeth Bauer Bondaruk
Beloved wife, daughter, sister
1976—2008

Karen didn't know what to say. She had to find a neutral ground where they could both retreat. "What's *your* middle name?"

"Rose. Named after Dad's big sister, Rosa. She died when Lise and I were four or five, and we didn't even remember her. I never use it, never think about it. There's absolutely no fucking way I'm Erica *Rose*."

Not much of the sun was left, and the mackerel clouds were darkening up at their edges, making them look like a sculpted ridgework. Occasional flakes, brilliant as diamond chips, were beginning to float down around them.

"Snow," Karen said and held out a hand to catch the sparkles.

"Yeah, I checked the weather report. We're supposed to get a light dusting but nothing serious. Not enough to cancel your flight."

Oh, fuck. Karen didn't want to hear that a flight cancellation was even a remote possibility.

"Aunt Rosa isn't buried here," Erica said. "She's buried somewhere else with her husband's family," and began to walk back toward the parking lot. Karen practically had to run to catch up. "What about *Calgary?*"

"Calgary?"

"The weather in Calgary."

"I didn't think to check. Let me see." Erica dug her smartphone out of her parka. "Um . . . snow. Light snow."

"Fuck."

"It says *light* snow. You'll fly out okay. If there was going to be a problem, they'd say so."

Karen wasn't so sure of that.

"I was the first one to get to the hospital," Erica said. "These two RCMP officers, a man and a woman. Showed up at our house. Boy, they sure didn't want to be there. What a fucking miserable job that must be. There's this—take-up time, I guess—the time that it takes you to compute it, understand it, and I was quicker than anybody else, and I started yelling, 'The keys. The car keys.' At my dad. And he was still totally stunned—he was the last one to get it—and he just reached into his pocket and handed me the keys. People were yelling at me, 'Ricki, what are you doing!' but I was already out the door."

Forget about playing therapist, Karen thought, I'm not the right person to be doing this— But maybe it would be all right if she could stay detached. All she had to do was listen. That's what Helen used to call "a fair witness"—someone who listens, and pays attention, and believes.

"So I got there ahead of everyone else, and I was the only one who saw her body. I came out of the room where they had her, and Mum and Dad had just got there. And Travis. Trina and Reese hadn't got there yet. 'You don't want to see her,' I said, 'you really don't,' and I just took off walking. And I just walked. I suppose I must've walked around for hours. I don't remember. A police car pulled up next to me—I don't even remember where I was—and they must have been looking for me because the cop said, "Erica?" and I got in and let them drive me home."

They had made it back to the parking lot. Erica unlocked the driver's side, then walked around to unlock Karen's door. She even opened it for her.

Karen got in and fastened her seat belt. Erica started the car but didn't drive away. "Trav had been out looking for me, too," she said. "I made everything worse for everybody. I was no help to anybody."

"WHAT'S THE NAME of the river?"

"The South Saskatchewan."

They were walking by the South Saskatchewan River—walking fast. Erica was the only person Karen knew who could keep up with her. None of the ladies could—she always had to slow down for them—but when she and Erica had walked the seawall, they'd been perfectly matched, stride for stride, and they still were. Even as fast as they were going, Karen was still freezing her ass off, but she didn't want to say so. This was too important.

"I had classic PTSD," Erica was telling her, "right out of the textbook. Whenever I'd try to go to sleep, I'd see Annalise. Or I was driving furiously to the hospital, sure I could save her. It was absolutely vivid, like I was right back . . . I went for . . . oh, I don't know, *days* without sleeping. Everybody wanted to drug me. Doctors kept pushing pills at me. My family. Everybody. But I was not going to fuck with my brain chemistry.

"I cried for hours. I didn't think it was possible for somebody to cry as much as I did. I kept thinking, okay, that should be enough. But it wasn't. I cried so much I got exhausted and dehydrated. Other people must've been having a hard time, too, but I wasn't really paying any attention. I couldn't really pay any attention.

"I had to be outside. I just kept walking . . . around and around. I walked here a lot. I thought about suicide. Constantly. When I was rational, I thought, okay, if you don't do something, you're going to get sucked into that black hole, and that's going to be the end of you. So I started . . . It was like a research project. I was going to find out exactly what happened to her. *Exactly.*"

SHE SET OUT to do it in a very methodical way—made a list of people who knew things she needed to know and opened files on them. Some of what happened was public record—the police report—but other things weren't. Some people had no problem talking with her, but others weren't allowed to—or said they weren't. She was insanely persistent, and some people got super pissed off at her. The paramedic who'd been with Annalise was a key player. When she caught up to him, he didn't say, "I can't talk to you," or "I won't talk to you." He said, "I'm not supposed to talk to you." Erica heard the loophole and went for it.

His name was Lucas. He was a tall skinny guy in his forties with a sad worn face and a little potbelly. He didn't look healthy. He met Erica "for coffee," but after a while, the coffee turned into beer, and then the beer turned into shooters. As soon as he started to talk, Erica had his number. Annalise was the third person he'd lost in the last six months, and he had PTSD big time—and a serious drinking problem. She knew that he badly needed to talk and if she waited long enough, he would.

She wasn't drinking, but she had to look like she was. She kept moving the glasses around on the table, going to the ladies and dumping her beer in the toilet, and he didn't seem to notice. Eventually he said, "What is it you want to know?" and she said, "Exactly what happened . . . that's all I want to know. *Exactly*. In as much detail you remember it . . . It would really help me to know that. I might feel some kind of closure if I knew that."

Erica never carried a purse, but she'd found an old beat-up one of her mum's. She'd put her little Sony recorder in it—the same one she'd used to record Karen. She'd wrapped the external mic in a piece of black tights so you couldn't tell what it was, cut a slit in a corner of the purse, and taped the mic into the opening. She set the purse down on the table with the mic pointed toward Lucas. She reached into the purse to get the money for the next round and turned on the recorder. She'd been planning to transcribe the recording, but she didn't need to. She played it over so many times that it got transcribed into her brain.

EVERYBODY THAT NIGHT did what they had to do, and they did it well. That's how Lucas remembered it. They closed one lane of the Trans-Canada, put out the barriers. As soon as Lucas and his partner arrived on the scene, they knew it was a bad one. The one driver, the boy, was dead, but the other driver, the girl, was still alive. She was trapped in her car. They couldn't take her out on the passenger's side because she was jammed in tight—like the whole front end of her car was crumpled up around her. So they conferred, and the cops decided to take the door off.

They've got one of those Jaws-of-Life machines, and they start working on the door on the driver's side. They can get the passenger's side open, so Lucas climbs in to check her out. Yes, she's breathing, and there's nothing obstructing her airway. He asks her if she can talk, and she says yes. He asks her what her name is. It's a standard question. She says, "Annalise Bauer." Not her married name . . . She says "Bauer." It's hard for her to talk. She's panting. But she says, "We live in Crescent Heights."

"It about broke my heart when I heard that," Erica said. "She was a little girl again. She gave him Mum and Dad's address and phone number. When we were little, that's what they told us to say if we ever got lost."

The window had exploded from the impact, and there's pieces of glass lodged in her face. Blood. But Lucas thinks that's superficial. The serious shit is the broken bones—left clavicle, left humerus. And her pelvis is broken. He can't tell how bad it is, but he knows she has a pelvic fracture—and probably broken ribs. She's panting, oxygen hungry. She isn't getting nearly enough oxygen—the number's way too low—and her heart rate's elevated. Irregular. Her blood pressure's low, and it's dropping. She's dying right in front of his eyes. One of her broken ribs must have punctured her lung. That kind of injury is called a pneumothorax. Yeah, he's thinking, that's what it is, a fucking tension pneumothorax. He would have to stick a needle into her to let the pressure off.

Oh, fuck, Karen thought, I'm going to faint. She had all the nasty symptoms swarming over her—sweating, light-headed, the world gone wobbly. It didn't make any sense. She was outside in the cold. She was walking. She didn't need to faint. *Keep walking,* she told herself. *Walk fast.* She could still hear Erica's voice, but it sounded like it was coming from the other end of an echoey tunnel.

Annalise was in some distress. Probably from oxygen hunger and the pain catching up to her. But Lucas can't think about that. If he thinks, oh, the poor girl, she's so fucked, he won't be able to do his job, and if he doesn't do his job, she's going to be dead before they can get her out of the car. He yells to his partner, tells him what he needs. They've been working together for a while. They're a good team.

254

They get the cops to shine one of their big spotlights through the window so Lucas can see what he's doing. He's already got oxygen on her. He wishes his partner could fit into the car with him. Annalise is in considerable distress now, and he needs somebody to stop her from trying to pull the oxygen mask off. But then she starts to lose consciousness.

He puts on gloves and a mask and eye protection in case he gets sprayed. What with her wedged into the seat like that, there's no way he can get her clothes completely off, but he unzips her jacket and cuts off the front of it. He cuts off her bra. He preps her chest and feels for where the needle should go.

"I Googled it," Erica said. "It's the second intercostal space along the mid-clavicular line. You've got to get it in exactly right. You don't want to hit a rib, and you don't want to hit blood vessels, and you sure as hell don't want to hit the heart. But Lucas had done it before. He knew what he was doing."

Lucas uses a two-inch needle catheter. His partner has it ready for him. Okay, so here goes. You can't be wishy-washy, eh? It can't go in at an angle—it's got to go in straight.

Karen was going down. Fuck, no she wasn't. She just had to get her head down. She spread her legs and bent forward, letting her head hang almost to the ground. The world was spinning—Jesus, fuck.

"Karen! Are you all right?"

"Yes, yes, give me a minute."

Breathe slowly, she told herself. Don't pant. She was cold. She was freezing. That should help. To be out here in the cold.

She felt Erica's hand on her shoulder. "Oh my god, I'm so sorry. I forgot how squeamish you are."

"It's all right."

Karen stood up slowly. The world had stopped moving. "I'm not going to faint. I thought I was, but I'm not going to. Tell me the rest of it."

Erica was looking at her with eyes that were huge pools of nothing.

"Come on," Karen said, "you've got to tell me. That's why we're here, isn't it?"

LUCAS PUSHES THE needle in. He's leaning close, and he hears the whoosh when the air comes out—the pressure coming off—and he kind of grins to himself. He's always amazed when some fucking procedure works the way it's supposed to. He tapes a square of rubber over the catheter to act as a one-way valve. Yeah, it is working—not as fast as he'd like, but her heart rate's dropping. She's back in sinus. Her blood pressure is coming back up. Her oxygen level is coming back up.

By now the cops have got the door off the car. They did it really fast, less than ten minutes—that's how good they were—and Lucas and his partner can get Annalise out. Because she's so badly injured, it's a tricky maneuver. They've got to use a scoop stretcher because they can't roll her. You can't roll somebody with a pelvic fracture. But they get her out and into the ambulance, cut her clothes off, and make like these quick improvised slings for her arm and shoulder and pelvis. They've got to stabilize the fractures as much as they can. Lucas puts a ventilator in her nose and a large-bore IV in her hand—the doctors are going to need that. She's doing a lot better. She's stopped fighting for breath. She's crying. She's trying to say something. That's a good sign. Pretty soon she's going to need morphine for the pain.

They're burning along the highway with the siren going. The hospital's alerted. They're ready for her. If they can get her stable, she's going to Calgary. The helicopter has already landed on the roof to do the medevac. Lucas is saying all the automatic things—"Don't worry about a thing, Annalise. We've got you now. We're going to take care of everything. Everything's going to be all right."

She's trying to talk. She says, "Please call my dad."

He says, "Don't worry, Annalise, we're going to call him. You just hang in there."

That's the last coherent thing she says. And then—oh fuck—her blood pressure's dropping off. Her heart goes into arrhythmia. He checks the catheter. It's still working. Shit, he's thinking, she's got internal bleeding. They're going to have to do a FAST scan to see how bad it is. But they're almost at the hospital. She's drifting in and out of consciousness. But he keeps talking to her. "Hang in there, Annalise. You just hang in there."

They're in emergency, and the doctors have got her. Doc Meyer—Lucas has worked with him before—and some new young guy, an intern. And fuck, the minute Annalise hits Emergency, she goes flatline. They zap her, but there's some states when the heart just doesn't respond. Lucas isn't responsible for her any more. He doesn't have to follow everything they're doing. All he can do is watch. They zap her more than once. The new guy wants to keep going, the intern, but eventually Doc Meyer says, "No. It's pointless. She's gone."

It's like all the energy drains out of everybody, and they're all just standing there looking at each other. For a few seconds nobody can say anything, but then they all get busy again because they've got procedures they've got to follow when somebody dies. There's no way Lucas is going to go out and complete his shift. Nobody expects him to. He's going to go home and watch television and get shit-faced.

Erica stopped walking so abruptly that Karen shot on ahead of her for a few steps and had to turn back. Erica was staring out over the South Saskatchewan River.

"He said it would probably sound strange, but it didn't sound strange to me. He said, 'When you're working on people, you love them. You don't know who the fuck they are, you don't know a fucking thing about them, and you're just trying to do your job, like step by step, and you're not thinking about who they are, but you love them. And when they die, something in you dies too.'"

KAREN FELT UTTERLY BATTERED, but she was finally getting warm. They'd been sitting in Tim Hortons for close to an hour. The pot of tea was helping—and the doughnut. Erica must be feeling battered, too; she hadn't said more than a few choppy sentences since they'd sat down. She'd finally got the bear claw she'd wanted that morning. What was it about stress that made your body cry out for sugar?

Thank god it was over. Karen was congratulating herself that she'd turned out to be tougher than she'd thought. She'd come close to it, but she hadn't fainted. She must actually have some inner resources—who would have guessed it? She'd done what she had to do—been a fair witness. But oh my god, what an ordeal. "I could take a cab to the airport, you know," she said. "Then you could go to your sister's."

"I don't need to be at Trina's." Erica's voice was flat and sullen. She sounded like Jamie. "It'd be better for everybody if I'm not."

What could Karen say to that? She couldn't very well say, "Think about *me*." The whole point of this exercise was that Erica shouldn't have to think about her. Oh, but she needed to sleep—half an hour, even twenty minutes. She simply couldn't take any more. Maybe she could suggest that they *both* go back to the Travelodge and have a nap. No, that was crazy—she'd already checked out.

"I don't know how long I was with Annalise," Erica said. "The intern came in with another doctor—that older doctor, Dr. Meyer. I could tell they were just dying to inject me with some fucking sedative so I better not give them any grief. So I left her there."

She's repeating bits of the story, Karen thought. She'd watched other people doing that in therapy groups, so she knew that Erica would have to keep on repeating things until she got clear—until she'd exhausted all of the emotion—and that meant that Karen would have to keep on listening to it. Well, okay, she could do that. The hard part was over, and by midnight she'd be back home in her own bed—well, unless it was snowing in Calgary. What a disaster that would be—to be stuck in fucking Calgary three days before Christmas.

"They let me out into the hall, and there were Mum and Dad and Travis. Mark wasn't there yet."

Karen had never thought about it before—it was one of those perfectly obvious things you somehow skimmed over and didn't notice. After her sister had been killed in a car accident, Erica had been in a terrible accident herself. It must have seemed unbelievably cruel to her—like the ultimate "fuck you" from the hand of fate. It was odd, though—she never talked about it.

"Mark had been doing some last-minute shopping, and his cell-phone was where he left it all the time . . . on the table by their bed. So he didn't know there was anything wrong until he got to our house. They'd left Samantha with the kids. She was the one who had to tell him. Poor Sam. He went straight to the hospital. Trina and Reese were there by

258

then. Nobody had seen her but me. He wanted to see her, but they talked him out of it. It must have been Dr. Meyer. He said, 'You don't want to remember her like this. You want to remember her the way she was.'"

It wasn't even four yet. It'd be worth paying for an extra night just to be able to sleep for an hour. Maybe Erica could use a nap, too.

"I didn't want the doctors to drug me, so I told myself to behave. I said to everybody, 'You don't want to see her. You really don't.' And then I just walked outside and walked away from the hospital and kept on walking."

After this, Karen thought, we should probably see a little bit less of each other. That's right, when they got back to Vancouver, they both would probably need a break from each other. That was absolutely normal for people who've gone through enormously stressful events together. Erica would need a break just as much as she would.

Erica looked at her big silver watch. "Come on, we've got to get going."

"ON FRIDAY EVERYONE got out early for Christmas break," Erica said, her voice flat and hard, "and everybody just wanted to leave and get out of there, and that's exactly what Annalise did, too, so she had to come back on Monday."

They were parked in the lot in front of Annalise's school. Oh god, Karen thought, now we have to go over the accident. All she could think about was getting to the airport, but she was trapped in the car with Erica. She surely wasn't required to say much of anything. But the daylight was fading away, and those horrid little sparkles of snow were falling steadily now. What was it doing in Calgary?

"She had to go back to the school and . . . I'm not really sure what all, but put things away and tidy up her classroom, some paperwork . . . I'm not sure what, but she had to go back to school on Monday. After she did that, she'd be free for the rest of the break.

"So she comes out, and she's parked here in this lot. It's about 4:30, getting dark, a bit of a snowfall like tonight, that in-between stage, not quite night. Not so miserable so you'd have your guard up but definitely a bad time of night . . . It wasn't too cold, but below freezing. Yeah, a lot like tonight."

259

Erica put the car in gear and drove out of the lot. She followed the road back the way they'd come, drove all the way to the Trans-Canada but instead of turning onto it, pulled over and killed the engine.

"I parked here so you can see where it happened. You see, it's double lane highway, and there's no stop light, and if you want to take . . . want to turn left, you've just got to wait. Sometimes the highway is totally empty. And the visibility's pretty good. Okay, she stopped at the stop sign right there . . . waiting to turn left onto the Trans-Canada. She looks to the right, and there's no one on the road as far as she can see. That's a long way. She looks to the left and there's a truck in the right-hand lane—a huge truck, a semi. So she's obviously going to wait for the semi to go by.

"But the semi signals that he's going to turn. Okay? He's going to turn in here. I know her, and I know how cautious she is, so I know that she waits until she sees him actually begin to turn. She doesn't just automatically believe his turn signal. So the semi really is turning, and she looks to the left into the twilight—the little bit of snow—and there's nobody. What she doesn't see is that out in the left lane there's a hotshot kid doing about 120 K. But the semi is blocking her view. So from what she sees, she can go. The most cautious possible thing would be to let the semi complete his turn so she can see the road clearly in both directions, but it's Christmas break, everybody's at the house, and she wants to get home. As far as she can see, she's got the highway to herself.

"Would I have sat there and waited for the semi to get out of the way? I don't know. It's what you're supposed to do. I probably would have waited. I just don't know.

"She pulls out from the stop sign and starts onto the highway. The trucker sees the hotshot in his mirror, coming up fast, insanely fast, coming in the left lane, so he hits his air horn, gives it a good one. Annalise does what almost anybody would do—slams on the brakes. She's on black ice.

"I've gone over this a million times, and the only thing that might have saved her— if instead of hitting the brake, she'd gunned it. She probably wouldn't have got clear, but she might have taken the impact in her left rear quarter panel, and that might have saved her. Or maybe she wouldn't have any traction on the black ice, I don't know. I keep asking myself if I would have gunned it, and I don't have any answer. I might have. The time to react—we're talking nanoseconds.

"Okay, so her brakes didn't slow her down at all, and she's spinning on the black ice, or just beginning to, so she doesn't take the impact directly on the driver's side—she takes it slightly at an angle, slightly ahead of where she's sitting. If she hadn't been spinning, it would have been a perfect T-bone, and she would have been killed instantly.

"The hotshot was doing at least 120 K, maybe more, and his air bag—? I don't know. It either didn't deploy or if it did, it didn't do the job. Maybe he was just going too fucking fast. No seat belt. Insane. The impact takes him through his own windshield, and he's toast. He was only twenty-four—a nice kid, apparently. He had a lot of friends. They had a big funeral for him.

"So the impact sent Lise into a spin the other direction, but there's nobody on the road, and it doesn't roll, and it doesn't hit anything, and it just comes to a stop on the far side of the highway pointed west. The trucker's on his cell to 911."

Erica checked her watch. "It was right about now."

She started the engine, pulled out, stopped at the stop sign, and then shot the car onto the Trans-Canada.

Karen's heart was in her throat—oh my god, *did she look?*

Well, of course she must have looked. They were across, they were safe, they'd made the left turn. Karen's heart was hammering so hard it felt like it was going to break right out of her chest.

Now Karen looked. She hadn't bothered before. They seemed to be alone on the Trans-Canada—no sign of headlights. The little flickers of snow were falling steadily.

"They closed this lane," Erica said and slowed down, pointed to the right. "Her Golf was right over there."

"Okay."

"Right *there.*"

"Okay, okay. I see. Her Golf was right there." Her *Golf?*

Erica had fallen silent. There was nothing to hear now but the hum of the engine, the slap of the windshield wipers. All Karen wanted to do was get to the airport, but it was way too early for that. Odd that Annalise should have a Golf—that's what Erica had. Two wrecked Golfs. Yes, it really was odd. It must have been a twin thing. They'd probably bought them at the same time, maybe even from the same dealer.

Keep her talking, Karen thought. That's what you're supposed to do. "Did you get your cars at the same time?"

"What?"

"I thought maybe you got your cars at the same time. You both had Golfs."

"Oh, no, no, no. I had a Camry. She got the Golf in the Hat. Trav got it for her."

"But then—? But you had a Golf."

"I *told you*, remember?"

Why did Erica sound so angry? "After I got back to Vancouver, I— It was a bitch. To get the same model in the same year in exactly the same colour of blue. With all the same . . . you know, like, all the . . . I thought it'd be easy, but it wasn't. I had to go all the way to fucking Coquitlam."

Karen was hurt. If she's going to yell at me like that, she thought, then I'm not going to say another word.

Erica drove back into town, pulled over and parked on what looked like an ordinary residential street. They were directly across from the hospital. A big sign said EMERGENCY. "We're early," Erica said.

"Early?"

"For when I got here . . . but that's okay. We don't have to wait for when I got here. They were having a rough night in Emergency, so that's probably how I got to see her. Emergency was a zoo, and I was angry. Angry and persistent. At that point I was just cold, and nobody was going to say no to me. The doctor they had on that night—one of the doctors, the one I saw, the intern—he looked just frazzled. Fried. Like he hadn't been asleep in a week. I kept saying, 'She's my sister—my *twin* sister—I have to see her.' I was convinced that being a twin gave me more rights than anybody else.

"So a nurse went in to try to make Annalise a little more presentable, I guess, and then they let me in with a nurse, and the minute I saw her lying there on that whatever it was—a gurney I guess it was—it was like somebody hit me behind the knees with a bat and I just went down. I howled like a fucking animal, and I just went down to the floor.

"The nurse stares at me—oh my god, was this ever a mistake! And she tries to get me to leave, but there is no way I'm going to leave, and we got into a bit of a tussling match, and here's the intern and another guy—an attendant or somebody, I don't know what he was, maybe a male nurse—and something goes click in my mind, and I think okay, if I don't calm down, they're going to haul me off and forcibly sedate me. So I go cold, and I look the doctor right in the eyes and say, 'Leave me alone with my sister. She's *my twin*.' He doesn't know what the fuck to do. He's a mess. He just wants to get out of there. 'Okay,' he says, and then they do it, they actually leave me alone with her.

"Looking at your twin is like looking at yourself. They must have cleaned some of the blood off of her, and they'd pulled a blanket up so all I could see was her face. I took the blanket off. She was naked. Except for . . . sheets wrapped around her. Like a sling for her left arm, her left shoulder, and around her . . . around her hips. Wrapped tight all the way down to her knees. Like a mummy. I didn't know why till later, till I talked to Lucas. He'd been trying to stabilize her pelvis, the pelvic fracture. That's what you do for a pelvic fracture. There was this little . . . It looked like a puncture wound in her chest. It was where the catheter had been, but I didn't know that. All I could see was that something had made this puncture wound in her. Not in the centre. Over to the side where she was broken. Her eyes were closed, but her mouth was open. Maybe your jaw drops open like that when you die, I don't know. Her face—her forehead and her cheeks—were cold. But her hands were still warm. Her hands were still perfect, nothing wrong with them. They were still usable, useful. They could have been my hands. Maybe they *were* my hands.

"I don't expect anyone to understand this except for a twin—a twin would understand this. I didn't know who was dead, her or me—"

Karen heard Erica swallowing, swallowing. The effort to tell this story without crying—it had to be unbearable. Erica had wrecked her Golf on her birthday—on *their* birthday. There was no way in hell that could be a coincidence.

"I picked pieces of glass out of her face. I was getting her blood on me. I *wanted* to get her blood on me. At that point I couldn't cry yet. It was too intense to cry. I kept touching her. I wanted to make everything all right. I knew she was dead, but I wanted to make her body all right. I wanted to fix her where she was broken. I wanted to take those sheets off her. I didn't want to leave her. I wanted to stay with her for hours, for however long it took. I wasn't absolutely sure we weren't both dead—"

Karen jerked the car door open, jumped out, and walked. "Sorry, sorry," she yelled back. "Going to faint. Got to walk."

But she wasn't going to faint—she was running away. She didn't have any choice—it was instinctive. Panic was chasing her—or terror, or whatever the fuck she wanted to call it. It was too big, too dark. Erica had reproduced her sister's Golf so she could kill herself in it.

THREE

15.

DEAR ERICA,

Are u ok? We havent heard from u for awhile & hope ur ok. Did u get our Xmas present? We hope u like it. We miss u & think about u a lot& we hope u miss us too.

We are writing to u from sydney australia. We are so excited to be in sydney australia. It is me Devon writing but Jamie is here too. We do not have time to do spell chex, we hope this is not too hard to read, LOL.

Do u want to know why we are in sydney australia? We will tell u. Every body in west van left town for the olimpics, it is ironic. u know Morgan & Avalon, there dad was taking them to australia for the olimpics, hes like u can take ur friends if u want, so they invited us!!! We even got out of school a few days early cuz Australia is so far away.

When u are flying to australia u are flying forever, they give u dinner & then u watch a movie & then they give u a snack & then u go to sleep & then u wake up & they give u breakfast & ur still flying!!! We stopped in Hawai but we did not get to see it, all we did was change planes. We finally got to sydney, we have been at the beach, IT IS SUMMER HERE!!! we luv it, we did not know we were going surfing, we got off the plane & went sufing, it is crazy. I grew up in California & never once did i go near a surf board, i'm like are u kidding me, i can not do this, i am a total geek, show me to the nearest computer, but everybodys like come on Devon get with the program.

Jamie says to tell u she can stand up on her board, no body can do that their 1st day, everybodys amazed, like wow Jamie u are a born surfer! She realy likes it, I stay in white water cuz I do not want to drown! it is actually kind of fun, i am surprised. Morgan & Avi are teaching us, they have been surfing since they were 5! We have to be careful not to burn, the sun is so hot. like every 5 min we put on sunscreen or we wear t shirts, we are in culture shock.

Mom left town for the olimpics too, she went to palm desert with Paige. Mom does not like the united states but our Dad picked palm desert Bcuz hes a crazy golfer. He is coming to meet Mom & Paige, he hasnt seen

266

Paige since she was little, she is scared to see him, he is bringing Chris, u know wife#3, I am not a fan. They are going to take Paige to Disneyland. Mom is like thank god for disneyland, she has many books to read. The only 1 left in west van is Cam, Mom bought him tickets to the hockey games in the olimpics, they cost a fortune, Cam never gets excited about anything but he is excited about the hockey games!!! Claire is staying at our house so Cam & his asshole friends will not trash it.

We have to keep a journal for language arts, that is our assignment for the olimpics, we are supposed to write everything down and LEARN SOMETHING, LOL! can u be our journal? Can u please save our emails & when we get back can u send them to us & we will fix them up & run them through spell chex. It is more fun to write to u than to write a journal cuz u can write back. That is a hint ☺

Is it ok to write to u? We were major sad when u left. We hope to see u soon. Maybe u can come & visit us when the olimpics is over? Please do not forget us.

Your friends forever,
Jamie & Devon

16.

THE CARTONS HAD been arranged in a double row along an entire wall of Mark's garage—plain everyday brown cartons, at least twenty of them methodically stacked to take up the least amount of space. They looked so orderly and mundane, absolutely innocuous, like the leftovers from somebody's house move. It had been over a year. "I took you at your word," Mark told her. "You said everything. That's everything."

It was bitterly cold in the garage—well, it was February. Erica ran her fingers over the edge of one of the cartons. It was dusty. She should say something but this was not a standard situation that came with a set of stock phrases attached, so what was she supposed to say? She couldn't very well say, "That's nice."

"I don't . . . I guess I don't really want to see any of it again," Mark said. "I could put it all in the truck and take it over to your mum and dad's . . ."

Did she want him to do that? She didn't know if she wanted him to do that. "I could hook up a space heater and you could go through it all here . . ."

That would be a fairly dismal exercise but at least no one else would have to see her doing it. She saw him studying her, trying to read her silence. "We could just leave it all here for another year. I really don't care."

Why couldn't she give anything back to him? It was getting awkward. She had to say something.

"I know you don't want to ship it all to Vancouver," he said.

"No, no, no," she said, "that'd be crazy." Her voice sounded husky and unused. She cleared her throat.

"I told them. 'When Ricki said everything, she meant *everything*.'"

"Thank you. That *is* what I meant."

"I couldn't touch anything. Trav and Trina did most of it. Mum helped them out." He made an apologetic gesture—abrupt and violent— open hands punching the empty air. "I just couldn't," he said, "you know, touch anything."

"That's normal," she said. "Most people feel like that."

A tarp was draped over something. "What's this?" she said.

"Her desk. You said you wanted her desk."

Erica lifted a corner of the tarp. As soon as she saw it, Erica knew that she didn't want the desk. It was just a cheap ordinary white computer station. But she did want the computer—or the data on it. Maybe she could dump it onto a flash drive.

"Some of the furniture," he said. "I gave some of the furniture to the Sally Ann . . . her dresser . . ."

"That's okay."

She pulled back more of the tarp and saw the bulletin board propped behind the computer. It had been screwed to the wall above the desk in Annalise's little office. The first thing she saw was that old notecard pinned near the top: NOTHING HUMAN IS STRANGE TO ME.

She let the tarp drop. "I really have to get out of here," she said. "Okay? Is that okay? I want to see the sky."

ALTHOUGH SHE WOULDN'T have thought of it immediately, where Mark took her was an obvious choice. They were standing on the hill above Echo Dale Park and that gave her precisely the 360 degree view she'd wanted. "Just, you know, drinking myself shit-faced every night," he was telling her. "It didn't help. If anything, it just made things worse." He was talking to her without looking at her—probably the only way he could do it.

Erica rotated slowly, trying to take it all in—the big Alberta sky—but she'd grown up here and had always known that you could never take it all in—looking away to the rolling hills in the distance, looking in any direction, looking away for miles. The sun was falling toward the end of a brilliant February day, drawing cirrus clouds to itself, a speckled highway of them. Later the sky would smear purple, then red, then sink into a smoky dusk, creating the images that the human brain—in this case, Erica's human brain—would connect to other remembered images to create the illusion of meaning. The hills were covered with snow but the trees stuck up like blackened sketches. The ruts in the road were brown. She was cold. Wherever they were, Erica and Annalise had always liked looking at the sky.

"Did you feel . . . ?" Should she be asking him this? Why not? They'd both been through it. "Did you feel like the whole world's smeared with pain?"

He nodded. He still wasn't looking at her. "Like every object is smeared with it, like Vaseline?" she said. "Like you really can't *see* things. And nothing's real? You've got to remind yourself how people are supposed to act because you can't *feel* it."

"That sounds about right." He produced a thin laugh and she tried to laugh too—the cheerless humour of fellow survivors.

"Did they want to put you on some kind of mood stabilizer?" she asked him. "An antidepressant?"

"Oh, yeah. I tried, ah . . . I don't know what it was . . . for like a day or two? Just made me feel like shit. I thought, hey, anything's better than this."

A good man, she thought—Mark Bondaruk, the science teacher at Lise's school, solid and responsible. Not Erica's kind of guy but a good choice for Annalise. He would have made a great family man.

"I don't know," he said, "it's been a year. Nothing's ever going to be the way it was." Again he made that angry gesture like trying to throw things away. "Some days it's okay. You've got to get on with your life, eh? You can't just give up."

No? she thought. Why not?

She'd been hoping that she could talk to Mark. She'd thought that their shared grief might make it possible but she saw now that it didn't. It was sad—well, sad for her anyway—but she had to be careful. Her judgment was badly off. She'd burned out Karen even more badly than she'd burned out Stacey and she didn't want to burn him out too.

She couldn't stop thinking about that horrible time back in December when she'd brought Karen home with her. Remembering the worst of it, that moment when she'd realized what she'd done—when they'd been parked across from the hospital, across from Emergency, and Karen had suddenly jumped out of the car and taken off. Erica had been so shocked that she'd been incapable of doing anything, had sat there for whole minutes watching Karen walking away, walking fast, turning into a small distant figure that was in danger of vanishing in the blur of falling snow, in the dark. She'd said that she was going to faint. Why had she said that? Erica had been telling her about touching Annalise's body—the way Annalise's mouth had dropped open, the way her face had been cold but her hands were still warm. Nobody wanted to hear things like that. For the longest time Erica had sat there, watching Karen walk away, not able to do anything, not able to make her mind work, until she understood it—*oh, she had to get away from me.* Far too late she followed, stopped for her, drove her to the airport. Neither of them tried to talk. It was snowing in Calgary, but the planes were still flying. The flight from the Hat was going to leave on time. They were early, but Erica didn't wait with Karen because she knew that Karen didn't want her to. She knew that she had ruined everything.

Well, okay, so now what? She was supposed to say something hopeful to Mark. Wasn't that how you had to play the game? "We're social animals," she said. "We live in groups. I'm trying not to let my groups down . . . my family, my colleagues, my students."

"How about you, Ricki? You can't let yourself down either."

That really pissed her off. Everybody said things like that. She was sick of hearing things like that. "Oh, I know," she said. "I'm doing okay. I'm getting . . . You're right about work. I can get lost in my research." No, she couldn't. She'd hadn't been able to do much of anything.

"I've been going to the gym," she said. No, she hadn't—not since she'd been living at Karen's.

"I try to keep busy." Fuck, she thought, I hate myself.

After she'd screwed up so badly with Karen, Erica had stopped pretending that she might ever get better. Now she was asking for something more modest—that she could get through day to day and do what she was supposed to do. She wanted to be able to live the rest of her life in a way that would do the least amount of damage to other people. It was the only thing she could think of, the only way she could function, but she couldn't tell Mark that—it sounded too fucking bleak. Okay, so why not give him the oldest cliché in the book? "I guess time heals everything."

"That's what they say. We'll have to go on faith, eh?"

Alerted by the tone of his voice, she turned to look at him. He was smiling.

She'd never thought of him as a handsome man but she saw him now as better than handsome. His broad, thick-featured, stubbornly masculine face was dependable—a face you'd want to grow old with. She liked his small brown eyes. She understood why Lise had loved him, had married him. "Ricki," he told her, "she was happy. I never saw her so happy."

She looked directly at him so he would know she was listening.

"You know how they say being pregnant makes a woman glow? Well, it really does. All the hormones. Like she had a light shining inside her. Her colour . . . She was just so beautiful, so so beautiful, and she was like—"

She waited for him. She had all the time in the world.

"She had everything she ever wanted," he said, "a good job, and . . . She loved her kids at school, and we'd got to the point . . . There's a point when you know you're really married, eh? Like it's not a novelty, or something you're trying out, playing house, but really married. You wake up one morning and say, 'Hey, I'm really married,' and that's just fine,

271

and . . . She even said it to me. 'Mark, I'm so happy, I'm just so happy.' She was so happy about—"

God, it must be so hard to be a man like Mark who's not allowed to cry. She tried to let him know by the way she was standing, the way she was not looking at him, that he had all the time in the world.

Finally he was able to say the words—"*The baby* . . . she was so happy, you know, about the baby. And Christmas, you know, and you were home. She missed you so much, Ricki. You see, that's what she needed to make everything perfect, that you were home."

Erica had thought that she'd gone numb, that she could no longer be hurt, but it wasn't true.

"She was on her way home and she never knew what hit her. She died instantly."

Oh, good, she thought, that's what they told him. That was a good thing to tell him. She was glad they'd told him that.

"When she drove away from school that day," he said, "she was coming *home*. It was Christmas. Her whole family was there. You were there. She had her whole life ahead of her, and— She had the baby— She died instantly. She was happy, Ricki. I never saw her so happy."

FRESH IN FROM the cold, Erica felt assaulted by the heat of the house. It was overwhelming, actually—and welcome because it gave her a new set of stimulae to focus on. Her entire family was there by common con-spiracy—Christmas had been pretty fucking insane, but here she was back home again so everybody could have another try at normal. *Okay,* she told herself, *get here, be here, participate*—but seeing Mark had been too intense and she knew that she couldn't participate in any real way, that the best she could do was pretend. She hung up her coat and walked straight back to the kitchen where her mother, her sister, and her sister-in-law were. That was okay so far. There was surely nothing strange about walking straight back to the kitchen. Her mother gave her a quick hard look, checking her out. "How's Mark? Did you have a nice visit?" meaning: *Are you okay?*

"He's fine. Yeah, it was nice," meaning: *I'm okay. I'm not going to melt down.*

Erica's crazy dog-like nose identified every hot dish they would be having. Three grandchildren in the house seemed to require that everything be kid-friendly—Trina's tuna casserole, Samantha's broc and cheese, Mum's meatloaf and then, just to make sure that the men got enough starch, mashed potatoes. What a menu. Maybe she could make a joke about it? But no, that wouldn't be appropriate.

"He didn't want to come for dinner?" her mother said.

"No. He's sorry. He sends his regrets."

"Well, he's certainly welcome."

"He knows that, Mum."

Just like always, the kids had been banished to the basement where the old TV was supposed to keep them quiet, and the adults were split along gender lines—the women in the kitchen, the men in the living room. This arrangement had been going on for years and Erica could depend on it. Her mum didn't need to say what she always said—"You're useless in the kitchen, Ricki." Her brother, Trav, must have been watching out for her. As she passed him in the dining room, he handed her a glass of pale ale—that's what she always drank—and he, too, was giving her an apprehensive look. "I'm okay," she said and wished it was true.

She went to her room to get her laptop, stopped on her way back to pour most of the pale ale down the sink, and joined the men. Her dad glanced up at her, smiling, started to say something but stopped—and she saw a look of raw anguish pass across his eyes. Oh, she thought, he must have forgotten for a moment that there's only one of me. Now she was supposed to give him something—some gesture, some sign of warmth. "Dad," she said and patted his shoulder. She hoped that was enough.

The dinner tonight was supposed to be for her, but nobody was talking to her, not really—they were just tossing around stock phrases. She'd been such a hopeless basket-case at Christmas—so bizarre and inappropriate—that they were walking on eggshells if they came anywhere near her. Annalise had left a hole in the family the size of the Milky Way—but they were all going to try to have a good time because they didn't have any choice. They had years and years and years of this to get through, so everybody had to try.

Mum at least had her belief that Lise was safe in Heaven, looking down on everybody. She envied her mother. It wasn't that Erica wanted a big stupid childish story to believe in—it was that she wanted *anything* to believe in, just the possibility that things might get better.

She settled onto the couch next to Reese, her balding mumbling brother-in-law. The men allowed themselves a moment to acknowledge the arrival of tomboy Ricki exiled from the kitchen—nodded in her direction, smiled at her. Then, in a collective panic, they jumped back to the fascinating subject they'd been discussing—Team Canada's goalie. Luongo was solid, the right man for the job. No, he wasn't, he leaked like a sieve. The problem with Luongo was you couldn't depend on him. Sometimes he was a genius, other times he wouldn't be picked for a ringette team.

Erica was a hockey fan too and knew the right things to say but she couldn't work up the energy. She flipped her computer open. How inappropriate was that? She couldn't tell. Maybe it wasn't inappropriate at all. It might be a relief for the guys. Then they wouldn't have to rack their brains to come up with things to say to her.

She had a new email. It was from Stacey in Hong Kong, a long one. Stacey must have intended it to be amusing—it read like a travelogue. Erica would read it carefully later and try to answer it.

Then there was the one from the twins that she still hadn't answered. She read it again. That brief stretch of time when she'd lived with Karen and her kids—five weeks—seemed like a dream now, a magical time lit with hope. She'd actually thought that she might get better—that she *was* getting better. Jamie and Dev had accepted her into their family, had treated her like a friend. She'd thought that she could help them, protect them, keep them safe. How sad. How ridiculous. She couldn't help anybody. But she absolutely had to answer their email. She'd never thanked them for their present, and that must have hurt them. She could not let them down or hurt them any more. That would be terrible, the worst thing she could imagine. "Hey, Dev and Jamie, it's great to hear from you," she wrote. Okay, and now what?

"I miss you too," she wrote. "It must be lots of fun to be in Sydney. I've never been there, but I hear it's a great city." God, that sounded lame.

Come on, Erica, she told herself, you don't have to be profound, just write ordinary stuff. "Yes, I did get your Christmas present," she wrote. "Thank you so much." They had sent her, neatly wrapped, what she imagined was the most precious thing they had to give—the first four volumes of *Two from One Fire*. "That was very thoughtful of you, the perfect present. I haven't had time to read it yet. I want to set aside the time so that I can read it straight through without distraction, and I have been super busy. I am so sorry I never thanked you. Please forgive me. I got you a present too. I will give it to you when we see each other again." That was a lie—but a white one. Now what on earth could she give them? A book maybe—something about twins.

"You're right about the Olympics," she wrote. "It's supposed to be ours so it is ironic how many people have left town. You remember my colleague, Dr. Chou? She's in Hong Kong. And I'm in Medicine Hat. It's really cold here but that's fine with me because this is where I grew up. It's home and it's good to be with my family again. I hope Paige and your mum have fun in Palm Desert."

Karen. It was so painful to think about her. It had been far worse than what had happened with Staccy, and it was exactly what would go on happening if Erica didn't get her shit together. When she'd first met Karen, she'd seen her as a spoiled rich-bitch blonde, and that was a perfect example of how wrong surface appearances could be. Nobody sees anyone else as they really are, and that's the way it is—the way it has to be—in the world of singleton consciousness where everybody's alone and isolated, where nobody knows anyone else's heart.

Karen's hard shiny surface was designed to protect her, but she wasn't like that. She was a kind person who had what humans were supposed to have—empathy—worrying about her kids, trying to see things through their eyes, juggling a million practical details of their lives—and she still had enough of herself left over to be kind to strangers. Nobody can replace your twin—nobody can even come close—but that hadn't stopped Erica from trying. It had felt instinctive, beyond her conscious control. Maybe I'm hard-wired for it, she thought—and even while she was doing it, she knew how wrong it was. She should have known that Karen would read it as sexual—singletons can't even begin to conceive of the twinship bond—and how could she have brought Karen home with her? What had she been thinking? She *hadn't* been thinking—crazy, sick, bizarre, inappropriate—stupid and selfish, obsessed with her own grief—not able to see anything outside of her own grief.

Annalise, she thought, you would be so ashamed of me. I can't keep doing this. Singletons can only take so much. That was true of all of them, even the best and kindest of them—you could burn them out and then they would have to get away from you just to protect themselves. If they didn't get away, you could pull them down right along with you. She had to find some way not to hurt people, maybe even some way to be kind to them. It was the only thing that mattered. She had felt so close to Karen and then look what she had done to her.

"Yes, of course, you can use me as your journal," she wrote. "I'm honoured that you asked me. I'll put your emails in their own file and send it to you when you get back. I'll even correct your spelling if you want. I'm sorry this is so short but we're about to have a big family dinner. I'll write more later when I can."

Some part of her must have wanted to live. She could have pulled over at any out-of-the-way place far from streetlights and then she would have died sometime in the night—but no, she'd driven onto Karen's drive-way. Forcing herself to sit motionless in her wrecked Golf as the icy rain pounded her had been one of the hardest things she'd ever done, but it was true what they said about dying of exposure—eventually it stopped hurting. She'd already gone through the worst of it. She couldn't remem-ber how they'd brought her into the house. If no one had found her, it would be over and she wouldn't be here. Everybody would be better off without her. If she borrowed her dad's car and drove somewhere out of town and lay down in the snow, she wouldn't last an hour.

"I'm your friend forever too," she wrote and hit send before she had a chance to change her mind.

17.

PAIGE GOT STUCK in mirrors. Not just distracted but absolutely stuck. It wasn't anything as simple as mere vanity—and Karen should know because she'd been there. It began with an astonishment at your sheer physical presence in the world but then evolved into a continuing assessment of what you've got and what you can do with it. "Stop staring at yourself, puss," she said, "you're just as spectacular as you were ten minutes ago."

Paige did not stop. She was watching Karen watching her. She made her face blank and then turned on a parody of a beauty-pageant smile. "Oh, *stop* it!" Karen said, laughing.

Paige was laughing too, but she said, "Hey, Mum, how do you know if you're hot?"

"You're ten years old, sweetie. If you're hot, you're in big trouble."

"I know that, but . . . I'm almost eleven. I mean like when you're . . . you know. Were *you* hot, Mum?"

"What? At ten?"

"No, no, no. Come *on*. In high school."

"Not particularly. I was a late bloomer like your sister. A beanpole. It took me forever to develop."

Hot? She wished she could delete that one from Paige's hard drive, but she knew she couldn't. As much as she appreciated Paige's good points, there were times when she was truly annoying. Of all of her kids, Paige was the one most like her.

After one last lingering look, Paige disengaged from her reflection and continued what she'd been doing before she'd been sucked into the mirror—checking out their villa. She was still at an age when little things pleased her. She was delighted that she was allowed to take over the entire living room for herself. "Wow! Mum! This is the best place you've ever taken me. We've each got *our own TV*."

As she always did, Karen forgave Paige for everything. "It's you and me against the world, sweetie."

"Can I watch TV, Mum?"

"Why would you want to do that? The sun's shining. Your dad's going to be here any minute."

"What if I don't like him?"

That wasn't the first time Paige had asked that, and Karen said the same thing she'd said the last dozen times. "Of course you're going to like him. He's a likeable man. There's nothing wrong with him. He and I were just not right for each other, that's all. Everybody likes him."

Because of that likeable man with nothing wrong with him, Karen was in the belly of the beast, trapped for a week inside one of the most peculiar fantasies the United States of America had about itself—at a bloody *golf resort*. It was on *Dinah Shore Drive*, and you got there via *Bob Hope Drive*. Their villa was just as nice as Paige thought it was—clean, bright, high-end, and spacious. Their patio looked out onto the eye-searing green of the golf course with palm trees and cactus-like things sticking up here and there. The Something-or-other Mountains were rumpled up on the horizon. They'd traded in Vancouver's winter drizzle for the constant and dependable desert sun. Rob and wife number three would appear shortly. Then, after everyone became comfortable with everyone else, Rob and wife number three would take Paige away to Disneyland, and Karen would be left to herself. She would have a nice easy workout in the gym every day so her body would feel alive and useful. She would lie in the sun long enough to get a honey buff but not long enough to encourage skin cancer. She would eat anything she pleased any time she felt like it, not at some prearranged mealtime. She would get a facial at one of those deliciously decadent high-end spas—and maybe more than a facial, maybe even the whole bloody works. For a few days she would not be responsible to anyone—*she would not be the mum*.

"But how do you *know* you're hot?"

Oh, for god's sake, couldn't she leave it alone for a few more years? "Okay, you want to know? Hot means the boys are chasing you. And if being hot is the most important thing in your life, that means you're letting the boys *define* you, and that means you will be one miserable kid." Paige had heard this speech before—or others much like it—and she never believed a word of it. Paige knew that it was essential to use your looks to get things from people. She'd been doing it since she was two.

Wherever she went, Karen needed to settle in, create a sense of order, so she was hanging up her four good dresses. Two would probably have been enough, but she had to have a choice, didn't she? And yes, something was bothering her, something more serious than Paige obsessing over being hot. Leaving Cam with Claire was probably not the greatest idea in the world, but what could go seriously wrong? Cam was a fuck-up and Claire was as thick as a board, but it was unlikely they'd burn the house down. And then there were the twins, but she quite liked Bryan Lynas, con artist that he was, and everybody said the same thing about him—yes, he was eccentric, crazy as a coot, but a good father and absolutely reliable— but *Australia!* It was so far away. "Have you heard from the twins?" she said.

"Yeah," Paige said, "they're in Sydney."

"I *know* they're in Sydney." She'd received the required one-liner from Dev, but she was hoping that they'd been a little bit more forthcoming with their sister.

"They've put some pictures on their wall. You want to see them?"

"Of course I want to see them."

"What don't you get your own Facebook account, Mum?"

"It's a matter of principle. Come on, show me."

Paige already had the laptop open. Karen peered over her shoulder. She couldn't imagine why the twins would have posted that cliché postcard image—a perfect aquamarine wave caught just as it was cresting, the top bending forward toward the camera, a slender girl surfing across its face. "Look," Paige said, "it's Morgan."

"Oh, no, it's not. It's an ad, one of those tourist—" Paige clicked on full-screen, the girl zoomed up, and my god it *was* one of the Lynas twins. Crouched, staring intently toward where she was going, her distinctive carrot-coloured hair blowing out behind her, she was riding her surfboard like a pro. Wearing what? Not a swimsuit—must be special surfer gear, powder-blue shorts and a long-sleeved jacket. The picturesque wave was towering over her, threatening to fall right onto her head. The caption read: "MORGAN THE GIRL IN THE CURL!"

"Oh, my goodness," Karen said, "they really are surfers."

"Yeah, Mum. You ready for the next one?" Ready or not, Paige had already moved on. It was a group shot—Bryan with his twins, and with

279

her twins, the lot of them grinning at the camera like fools. The Lynas girls were both wearing those pretty powder-blue surfing outfits and looked quite cute, but her kids looked appalling—in bleached-out board shorts and the rattiest of Jamie's old T-shirts. They'd been adamant that they would pack their own freakin' suitcases, thank you, but why hadn't she at least pruned their clothes beforehand? Jamie was shooting up like a weed. Both kids had pushed their bangs out of their faces, and they both looked like boys—and then standing behind them were men. Lots of men. At least a dozen or more men, packed into the picture like sardines and receding into the distance as far she could see. They were raising big foaming mugs of beer in a toast to the camera—bare-chested men, all of them deeply tanned, some sporting beards. Who were all these *men?* "What," she said, "they don't have any women in Sydney?"

Paige giggled. The image vanished, replaced by a message pane. Paige was typing into it. "Wait. What are you saying?"

"Mum wants to know if they have any women in Sydney."

"Don't say that! Bring the picture back. I wasn't finished looking at it."

The picture popped up again. All the caption said was "US IN SYDNEY." The sun in Australia was supposed to be murderous—were the twins burnt? Their skin had a ruddy glow, but no, they didn't look burnt. Bryan Lynas, she thought, if you let my kids burn, I will bloody well kill you. And my god, Bryan, shirtless, was a fairly spectacular specimen. She could even see his stomach muscles—amazingly ripped for a man his age. His chest was just as freckled as his face. He was absolutely unsuitable for her, of course, not even worth thinking about—and besides, after that intense sexual crackle at his party, she'd been sure that he was going to make a move on her, but he hadn't, so piss on him.

"Okay," she said, "next."

"That's all," Paige said.

"Tell them Mum hopes they're having fun. Tell him how nice our villa is."

THE SUN WAS STILL high in the sky, the warmth was lovely, but it was February after all, and even in the desert she would need a sweater later. "Come on, sweetie, don't get sucked into Facebook. Get out in the sun."

She should stop worrying about the twins—they were perfectly all right—but she had to worry about something, didn't she?

Well, okay, she wasn't anticipating any problems with Rob. She'd always liked him, and she still liked him, and now that he'd acquired wife number three, his bitterness toward wife number two should have vanished, shouldn't it? But what *about* wife number three—Christine the horse lady, the X factor, Devon's evil stepmother? God, she sounded like an absolute horror, but Karen was planning to make a real effort with her. That's right, and everybody would make an effort, and they'd all get along fine—wouldn't they?

Karen went back to the bedroom to finish unpacking her suitcase. There wasn't much left in it now but books. She'd brought too many, but just like clothes, too many was better than not enough—her required escape reading. Oh. Dear. Erica. She didn't have to add her to the worry list because she'd never left it. Yes, it *was* sad, but what else could she do? That ghastly moment across from the hospital in Medicine Hat—too big, too dark. Walking away in the snow, fleeing, Karen had known that her spooky intuition had been right. When she'd first seen Erica, mute and soaking wet, pulled out of death and delivered into the front hall, something in her had said, *Stay back, don't touch her!*

Karen had walked so far that her fingers and toes were screaming with cold. Okay, how was she going to get to the airport? Take a cab? What about the suitcase in the car? She didn't really need anything in it, did she? And then Erica pulled up next to her. What could they possibly say to each other? Nothing. Erica was mentally ill. Seriously. Karen had to protect herself and her family, didn't she? Don't they always tell you to put your own oxygen mask on first? Oh my god, that death-obsessed girl had been *driving her kids around*—every time Karen thought about it, her blood froze.

It was inconceivable the trauma that poor girl had lived through, and she badly needed help—*professional* help. Helen would have been perfect, but Helen was dead. There was no way Karen could help. Erica wasn't the only one who should be seeing a therapist—it was utterly sick how she'd attached herself to that poor girl. The night of Bryan's party—oh my god, the kiss. She could blame it on the three glasses of wine, but that was bullshit. She'd been as bad as a man, and Erica had been so gracious about it— Stop it, Karen. She was going around in circles again.

Time for it to end anyway. People were talking. So easy to misinterpret. Erica must have known it was over, too. She simply hadn't come back to the house after Christmas. Well, yes, she *had* come back—once—to get her things—and that had been awkward, but it had been okay, friendly enough. Had it been okay? No, not really. Karen hadn't called her once since she'd left, and that was definitely *not* okay. What's wrong with me? she thought. I haven't even called her. That was unnecessary. That was *cruel.* But what could she do? Really? What else could she *possibly* do? But she missed her every day. It felt exactly like the break-up of a love affair. Whenever she thought about Erica, she felt like crying.

"HEY, KARO"—his voice from the next villa over.

"Here's your dad," Karen called to Paige who was still inside, probably still lost in Facebook.

Karen walked around the fence that separated their two villas, saw her ex-husband striding toward her across his patio. He was wearing baggy khaki shorts and a ridiculous orange shirt. Had he shrunk? No, he'd always been this short—her treacherous memory must have made him taller. "Rob," she said, and he caught her up in a big sweaty hug.

Stepping back, looking into his amiable brown eyes, she felt herself default to grin mode—a mirror image of what he was doing—and then she was stopped by a reality glitch that made her mind race to catch up. He'd always been—well, "soft" was how she'd thought of him, but now he was beginning to resemble the Pillsbury Doughboy. He still had that lovely sunshine smile he'd passed on to Dev, but his skin had gone greyish, and fine dry lines had crawled all over his face. He'd always been bald on top, but he used to have at least *some* hair. How sad. But he was, she had to remind herself, just a year off sixty. What on earth did she look like to him?

Appearing at an angle behind Rob, a flare of a blonde—wife number three—a small-waisted, long-legged trophy-wife blonde—but Karen was distracted because Paige had caught up to them, saying, "Hi, Daddy," like a good girl. That's what she'd always called him on the phone—but she and Rob hadn't seen each other since Paige was five, and Rob seemed stunned. "Hey, honey, have you ever grown up!"

Yes, Karen thought, she *has* grown up. Yes, she *does* look like me. Don't I deserve to have at least one kid who looks like me?

Rob crouched to hug his daughter, and the flare of blonde materialized into a woman who was the same height as Karen, probably close to Karen's weight, wearing a face remarkably similar to Karen's—"Oh, aren't you adorable!" the woman was cooing to Paige. "Rob you didn't *tell me*. He said you were pretty, but he didn't tell me you were *this* pretty!"

This was too much even for attention-sponge Paige; her eyes said, *Mum! Help!* but as Karen was searching for a useful line, she saw that wife number three was now staring at her in a bizarre, impolite, zombie-like way. "This is Chris," Rob said. How odd, Karen thought, he's *presenting* her to me.

Christine had to be somewhere in her late thirties, but her face had hardly a line on it. Very tasteful eye makeup—not overdone. Nice sandals—simple, elegant. Nice shorts and top combo too—Banana Republic? Some designer brand?

Then Karen's mind broke down into something like an inner stutter. She didn't seem to have enough processing power to handle everything that was going on. Looking at Christine was like looking at a photo of herself from years ago—met her eyes, saw her thinking the same thing—*oh my god, she looks like me!*

Chris had gone into shock one beat ahead of Karen, and now they were frozen into a pair of decorative patio ornaments. Move or something, Karen told herself, or at least *say something*. "How was the drive?"

"Oh, no probs. Rob does the driving, and I just sit there and watch the countryside roll by." Chris had a light fluting laugh that was like a grown-up version of a giggle. "Your flight okay?"

"Just the way I like them—uneventful."

It was true—Christine couldn't have looked any more like Karen if she'd been her little sister. Rob, you son of a bitch—how could you have done this? It was like some kind of a sick joke. "Getting out of Vancouver was a bit of a hassle," Karen said. "The whole city's in lockdown for the Olympics."

"Terrible about the luge guy," Rob said, "the Russian?"

"No, he was Georgian. Oh, yes, just terrible. What a terrible way to start the games."

"That track was way too fast. They should have known better. So I imagine Vancouver's high security?"

"Oh, yes. We're getting a good idea what it'd be like to live in a police state."

Chris was giving Karen a wan smile. "We stopped at Trader Joe's. They uh . . . don't have much of a deli section."

"Good meat though," Rob said and walked back into his villa like a man on a mission. Chris followed him, and Karen followed Chris, and Paige followed Karen. They piled up in the kitchenette. Rob produced a bottle of whatever single malt he was favouring at the moment. Chris was already popping ice cubes into a glass for him, fluting to Paige, "We got some ginger ale for you, honey. Do you like ginger ale?"

"Yes, please."

"So Devon's not here," Rob said. "I thought he might come with you."

"I *told* you. He's in Australia with the Lynas twins."

"I didn't give you permission—"

"You said you'd get back to me on that. You never got back to me on that, so I wrote the permission letter."

"Oh?" annoyed, "but you don't—"

"It must have worked. He's in Sydney."

Rob turned abruptly and walked back out into the sun. Whew, Karen thought, we're going to have a delightful time.

"I was going to make a pitcher of margaritas?" Chris said.

"Lovely," Karen said although she hadn't drunk margaritas since one dim night in university when she'd got barfing pissed on them.

Chris was still focused on Paige. "So your dad tells me you're a dancer . . . What do you take?"

"Um . . . mainly ballet. Jazz, tap, lyrical, hip-hop . . . but mainly ballet."

"Are you going to be a great ballerina?"

Paige wrinkled her nose. "I don't know. I guess." It must have been a puzzling question for her. She took ballet because it was the thing to do. If she was planning a dance career, Karen had never heard about it.

Moving fast, with an alarming efficiency, Chris was depackaging nacho chips and dumping them into a bowl. "I took a little ballet . . . but not like you. We just had one dumb old lady in town. We all went to her. But I was a cheerleader though."

Chris had a trace of itsy-bitsy in her voice—too much for Karen—and a strong regional accent. At first Karen had thought it was southern, but no, it wasn't. She didn't know the States well enough to be able to pinpoint it.

Chris doused the nacho chips with packaged shredded cheese and popped them into the microwave. "Here, let me help you," Karen said and pried the lid off the five-layer dip.

Chris opened the salsa. Her nails were works of art—a classic French manicure so bright and shiny they had to be gels. When Karen had been a trophy wife, her nails had *not* been bright and shiny. Rob had been on her constantly about her ratty nails. That utterly trivial little thing had become a major point of conflict. How bizarre.

Chris was still focused on Paige. "You looking forward to Disneyland?"

"Oh, yes!"

"We thought we'd swing by the house so you could meet your little sister . . . and maybe we could go for a ride. Do you like horses?"

"Oh, yes, I love horses!" Not once in her life had Paige ever expressed the faintest interest in horses.

Christine didn't have Karen's golden eyes. Nobody had Karen's golden eyes. Christine's were an undistinguished hazel—and she coloured her hair, a hint of roots showing, dirty dishwater, and the blonde a bit too much, a bit too Marilyn. Oh, cute, cute, cute. She was what?—older than she looked. But she had to be a good twenty years younger than Rob. You hang in there, blondie, Karen thought, and you're going to be one rich widow.

THE FIRST TIME they'd gone to bed, Rob had been astonished that Karen's pubic hair was blonde. She was astonished at his astonishment—"What colour did you think it was going to be?" He confessed that he'd always had a thing for blondes. His wife was a brunette.

When she and Rob had been in the midst their liaison dangereuse, Karen hadn't understood how she could possibly have gotten herself into a situation as absurd as that, but now she could understand it easily enough. Ian had been working his ass off to become a partner at Blair, Haydon and Fitzpatrick while she'd been stuck at home with a difficult two-year-old. Sex had never been the main thing on Ian's mind; after Cameron was born, it was even less on his mind. Karen had an eager babysitter ready at a moment's notice any time she wanted to call her mother. But why that chubby, balding, relentlessly cheery American goofball, Robert Clark? If she said that his power and money hadn't meant a thing to her, she would be lying—and then maybe because it *was* dangerous, maybe because some bratty part of her wanted to *be the blonde*.

The first time they'd tried to have sex, he was limp as a noodle. He said he was too turned on to get turned on—"if that makes any sense." It didn't. The CEO of Wayne Energy Canada had a mortified smirk plastered across his face—not far off the sickly ingratiating grin you get from a dog you've just smacked with a newspaper for shitting on the carpet. It was the same sickly grin he would wear nine years later when she would tell him she wanted a divorce.

Rob's sexuality wasn't hard to understand. His fantasies were old-school and generic. He got turned on by a woman's willingness—*eagerness* was even better—to transform herself into a sex toy. The distaste wife number one felt for that sort of thing was probably the main reason that Karen became wife number two.

Karen hadn't been particularly aware of her own sexual fantasies before that—certainly not as coherent narratives with specific details—but she could never claim that the crazy night at the Bayshore was entirely Rob's creation. He'd been the lead writer, but she'd had considerable input into the script. The cute little made-to-order corset and the patent stilettos were courtesy of Rob Clark; everything else she'd bought herself.

She was supposed to look like a very expensive hooker—"whore" was the word Rob preferred because it sounded dirtier—and her dress was very expensive indeed, an Anna Sui. Of course Rob had picked up the tab for it. She was blonder than usual—"Swedish," her stylist called it—and she'd plastered herself with tons of makeup. Her dress was a babydoll, cut low, and the skirt was quite short. Except for the corset, she wasn't wearing any underwear. All she had to do in public was walk across the lobby of the Bayshore.

The danger was not the least bit virtual. Friends of Ian's, or of Karen's parents, or, for that matter, friends of hers could very well have been at the Bayshore—it was a popular hotel. All Karen had to do was get out of the cab, walk inside and across the lobby, take the elevator up to the seventeenth floor, and walk down the hall to Rob's room. She should have tried the heels beforehand, but she hadn't. There's no heels so high that *I* can't walk in them, she'd thought—well, okay, sweetie, think again. It was good that the script called for her to "walk slowly" because that's the only way she could walk. She couldn't imagine anything more ignominious than falling off her heels in the lobby of the Bayshore.

Rob was sitting in a nice big leather chair in the lobby pretending to read the *Financial Post*. She saw him see her the minute she stepped inside. It was mid-evening, and everyone in the lobby froze and stared at her—*everyone*—the bellboys, the concierge, various guests in various stages of arrival or departure. She made sure to walk close to Rob's chair. She got a flash of his eyes. He looked exactly like a sweaty middle-aged perv in an expensive Italian suit. The heels were so high that she was getting cramps in her calves. She made it into the elevator. The door swooshed shut. It was blessedly empty, and she sagged against the wall.

She let herself into Rob's room, turned on every light. She checked herself and found—surprise surprise—that she would need no lubricant. She arranged three pillows on the bed, blindfolded herself with the clever little black velvet blindfold Rob had left for her, lay on her back with her legs spread open and her pelvis elevated on the pillows. Rob had said that he'd make her wait as long as he pleased—maybe he'd even have dinner.

He told her later that he'd only been able to stand it for twenty minutes, but Karen experienced it as longer than that. She heard the door open and close. She heard a man taking off his pants. When he thrust into her—as big and hard as it should be in a fantasy—she knew that it had to be Rob, but it could have been anybody. After all that fabulous buildup, the sex might well have been anticlimactic—except that it wasn't.

"YOU DON'T ACTUALLY believe that Barack Obama was born in Kenya, do you?"

"We have no way of knowing, do we? The way they can do forgeries now . . ." Chris shrugged eloquently. "And if you have the entire resources of the federal government behind you . . ." There was, obviously, no more that needed to be said.

They'd arrived at that particular thorny little knot in the conversation far too easily. Chris might be an old-fashioned girl—that's how she'd described herself a few beats back—but her mommy must never have told her that good old-fashioned girls do not discuss politics with strangers, because her opening gambit had been, "So what do you think of our president?"

"Us Canadians or me in particular?"

"Oh, you in particular."

"I guess I'd have to say that I'm disappointed in him."

Karen had chosen her words carefully. That line could go either way, and Chris had grabbed it and run with it straight to Kenya. Now Chris was talking about Obama's *socialist agenda*, and a thought came sailing into Karen's mind—a thought she hadn't known was there before, and not a helpful thought—*You nearly killed my son, you ignorant little bitch.*

"Your president," Karen said, "yes . . . Okay, let me tell you a story."

Karen saw Rob send her a signal—an angry flick from his eyes. They'd been married for eight years and knew each other well, so she was most definitely getting his message. She smiled sweetly at him. She was sure that he would get her message, too.

"Let's go back to the summer of 2007," she said. "I check up on my money from time to time, and I called my brother, and I said, 'Forgive me for bothering you with this, Steven. You're the banker, and I'm just your ditzy little sister, but it does appear that I am losing roughly sixteen thousand dollars a day."

That one got a gasp out of Christine. Good, Karen thought. I've got your attention now, don't I? Of course I do—I'm talking about *the money*. "Steve said, 'Good grief, let me get back to you on that,' and he did get back to me on that, and it turned out that I was right. I said, 'Fine. So get me out of the market.' He said, 'Well, it's a bit of a bear market at the moment . . .' and I said, 'I don't give a fuck if it's a frog market, get me out of it. Put everything in money.'"

The "fuck" had got to Rob. He was so annoyed that he didn't bother to keep the sound of it out of his voice: "I *told* you to keep most of it in T-bills—"

"I know you did, Rob. I always pay attention when you tell me things, believe me I do." She smiled again and saw that Paige was staring at her wide-eyed—*Oh my god, Mum, don't do it!*— but Karen was already too far along and was enjoying it too much.

"I always kept a huge whack in T-bills," she said, "but I started to worry. At night when I should have been sleeping, I began sniffing around on the net, and I kept reading about this stuff called 'commercial paper.' The word I kept running into was 'toxic.' I asked Steve to see if I had any of this toxic crap in my portfolio, and guess what? I had quite a bit of it."

Nobody else was saying a word. It was so quiet that she could hear the crack of the clubs on the golf course.

"How could that be?" Karen said. "I thought I was buying T-bills. Well, okay, Steve had put some of my money into a fund run by the MacArthur Davis Asset Management Group. They're worth billions. They seem to be specialists in buying and selling debt—"

"I know who they are," Rob snapped at her.

"I know that you know, Rob. Your name is listed on the board of directors."

They exchanged looks. He was beyond angry now. Putting on his CEO mask, he smiled faintly and shook his head.

"So MacArthur Davis was offering mortgage-related securities," she said. "They were supposed to give you a nifty little return and be just as safe as money. In Canada, the conduit they were using was the Kensington Capital Group. I'd never run across the word 'conduit' used in quite that way. I was really adding to my vocabulary . . . Oh, and by the way, we're talking about the same Kensington Capital Group that's currently under investigation by the Ontario Securities Commission."

Karen took another sip of her margarita. Now she could afford to take her time. "By the end of the summer the entire financial system seemed to be hitting a logjam. You might remember that I called you up?

The problem wasn't credit, you said, it was *liquidity*. 'Don't worry, Karo,' you said, 'it's pretty much business as usual.'

"Thank god I didn't believe you. I started trying to figure out just what this asset-backed paper was. And you know what? A lot of other people were trying to figure it out too, and everybody was having just as hard a time as I was because it was locked away inside these black boxes, and god knows what was in them . . . some of the most worthless pieces of shit the world had ever seen. But a lot of it was being treated like money because it had received a triple-A rating from various bond-rating agencies . . . and those fucking bond-rating agencies were all crooked and being paid off by the boys at the top."

"Karen!" he said, "that's not—"

"Okay, okay," she said, waving him silent, "I do have a point, and I'm nearly finished. I had many long conversations with my brother, and he had many clients who were in the same boat that I was, and he knew a lot of other money managers who had clients, and how he did it I'm not sure . . . Maybe the right people went out and played a round of golf together, who knows . . . but guess what? All of a sudden I'm not in MacArthur Davis any longer, and I don't own any asset-backed crap. Instead I own GICs and a few other delightfully safe items. So he did save my ass . . . although I had to push him . . . and somebody else had to eat that asset-backed paper. So I saw the shit coming, and I had enough time to do something about it . . . and I took a hit but I came out okay, but what about all the people at the bottom? Out of work, losing their homes, fucked over good . . . so the clever boys could walk away with their million-dollar bonuses?

"Okay, this brings us back to your president. He kept the same bunch of crooks and idiots who caused the problem in the first place. *Bankers.* Geithner. Oh my god. Citigroup should have gone down. AIG should have gone down. They all should have gone down. The criminals who packaged that toxic crap should all be in jail. Disappointed in Obama? That's an understatement."

"We all took a hit, Karo."

"What? You couldn't buy another hundred-thousand-dollar horse?"

Even as dumb as she was, Christine got that one. She looked away, her face flushing.

"Chris, honey," Rob said. "Why don't you take Paige over to the concierge and sign her up for some activities? Yeah, and you should probably hurry. They're going to close any minute."

THERE IS NO TWILIGHT in the desert. The sun is either up or down. Now it was down. The warmth of the desert was misleading—it wasn't really summer, it was February. Not even six yet, but it was already dark. The silence was monumental. Finally he said, "That was uncalled for, Karo."

I am not going to apologize, she thought—but then, after a moment's reflection, she decided that she had to give him something. "Maybe it was," she said.

Rob sighed, stood, walked inside. She could hear the tinkle of ice cubes. "Another margarita?" he called to her.

"Do you think that's a good idea?" she called back and tried out a little laugh. "No thanks. I'm switching to water." Was that as good as an apology?

He returned, deposited his glass on the patio table with a clink, settled into his chair, and presented her with one of his famous looks. He probably scared their asses off in the boardroom with looks like that. "Drew called me," he said.

She felt a nasty zap of electricity licking her skin. "Oh?"

The roads and the little paths into the golf course had all lit up at nightfall, and the sudden illumination was supposed to make the resort look cheery and safe, and of course it *was* cheery and safe. The boys on their golf carts were still rattling by, stopping to pick up residents and transport them from place to place. A nice-looking middle-aged couple was out having a stroll on the road in front of Rob's villa. Yes, it was a pleasant night. It wasn't even chilly yet.

"I'm not sure I appreciate that," she said.

"Why not? Drew and I have been friends for twenty years. He was very upset. He needed to talk to *somebody*," and she got the look again, intensified—and now she understood it. Oh my god, he thinks I've defected to the enemy.

Drew was still telling anyone who cared to listen that Karen had ditched him *for that crazy girl*, and that was almost certainly what he'd told

291

Rob. When it came to matters of sex and sexuality, Rob had not evolved one iota from the appalling middle-class suburb in Cleveland where he'd grown up. Groups of women made him nervous. Even when Karen got together with her high school friends, it made him nervous—"*The ladies*," he called them, underlining the words with a waspish buzz. "I'd never say this to anybody but you," was the way some of his more dreadful statements opened. He liked to go on about "the kind of feminist who spells it with an L." He'd once referred to Gudrun's younger son, the charming artistic one, as "that fearsome little fairy." If Karen had a live-in girlfriend, the last place in the world where Rob would want his son to be living was with Karen. He would never say so in public, but it would be the elephant in the room. "So what did Drew have to say?" she asked him.

"Oh, just . . ." he shrugged, "the kind of things you say to an old friend when you're suffering through a major . . . when your long-term relationship has just broken up. Things you'll probably regret saying later. I wouldn't want to repeat any of it."

You son of a bitch, she thought. He'd run this game on her before, but this time she would not get sucked into it. Her curiosity was supposed to overcome her good sense, and she was supposed to introduce the topic of Erica, and the moment she did, she'd be guilty. She couldn't very well open with, "We weren't really lovers," or "She's moved out" or "She had nothing at all to do with it." She couldn't even mention Erica.

"Drew and I never had a long-term relationship," she said. "That was the problem. He thought we did, but we didn't."

Okay, Rob, I've declined your opening gambit. If you want me to play, you're going to have to sacrifice a pawn at least. She watched him thinking about it. "What's this about the identical haircuts?" he said.

Drew. Shit. How was she to know that he'd turn out to be a secret agent? He must have given Rob an earful. She'd been absolutely right not to tell him about the faked blood test or the request for puberty blockers or the visit from the social worker. Thank god he hadn't been around to see the *second* installment of the identical hairstyles—or the pierced ears.

"They did it themselves," she said. "They just took the credit card and did it. I didn't know a thing about it until it was over. I wasn't even—"

"Devon got his hair dyed to match his sister?"

"Yes. Yes, he did."

"Does that strike you as healthy?"

"Not particularly. But it doesn't strike me as a big deal either. They were just being assholes. I yanked their credit cards."

"So it's okay with you if Dev wants to *look like his sister—*?"

It was astonishing how quickly they could evolve from a series of careful feints to all-out war. "It's not like that. They want to—"

"Drew said Jamie's firmly in charge. She might as well be leading Dev around by a ring in his nose."

"Oh, for Christ's sake, it's not like that at all."

Rob would be super pissed off about Erica, but the way the game was being played, her name would never be mentioned. He was talking so fast that Karen couldn't get a word in edgewise, and he had inexplicably flipped back a year to Jamie's letter that he'd intercepted. "Deeply disturbing," he called it, and he meant more than the suicide threat. "At first I thought it was in code. A third-grader could have done a better—"

"She's got a learning disability! I had her tested—"

"Jesus, and the sick fantasies. *Reunited by death* . . . not the kind of fantasies a girl should be having about *her brother.*"

"Oh? But it'd be okay if she was having them about *a boyfriend?*"

"Come on, Karo, get serious."

It wasn't just her letter that he found deeply disturbing, he was saying—Jamie *herself* was deeply disturbing—"I don't believe in medicating children either, but sometimes—"

All this crap was straight from Drew. Jamie had issues—was hopelessly out of control, a fucked up Goth girl who was obsessively attached to her long-suffering brother. She should be dumped full of drugs and shipped off to some girls' boarding school on the Island. Drew knew somebody whose kid who was really a mess, and they found a good psychiatrist who put her on antidepressants, and they sent her to Saint Somebody-or-other's— "Oh," Karen said, "I know who he was talking about. Bev Sommer's kid. Yeah, she really was a mess. A cutter. She ran off with some disaster of a boy, and they didn't even know where she was for months. Jamie's not like that. She's not even remotely like that. There's nothing *wrong* with Jamie."

Rob was so agitated that he couldn't sit still any longer. He jumped up and started banging around with the barbecue. "I'm sure Dev's done all he can for her, but now it's time—"

"What?" she said, "you think it's all Jamie's fault." The saddest thing was that he was talking about Jamie as though she wasn't his daughter. "So you sent Dev to Vancouver to rescue his poor sick sister? Jesus, Rob, that's not what you said at the time."

"I know what I said at the time. I've never said anything different. *He's coming home for high school.*"

When Americans said "high school," they meant grade nine. No, he's not, she thought. Dev's absolutely *not* going back to California for grade nine. "Okay, I read *his* letter too," she said. "I never would have opened Jamie's mail if you hadn't opened Devon's—"

"Wake up and smell the coffee, Karo. It's your laissez faire attitude—"

"Shit! You sound exactly like— Dev had it all worked out. Clear as could be. Like an instruction manual. Step by step. The cars, the hoses, the duct tape—"

"You didn't believe that suicide crap, did you? They weren't going to—"

"The hell they weren't!"

That shut him up. He was staring at her. He might never admit it, but it had scared him too. She could see it in his eyes. "He was just as depressed as Jamie," she said.

Now it was her turn. He and Chris had turned Devon's life completely upside down, cut him off from his friends, dumped him into a new school where he was bullied horribly, isolated him in a house way out in the country, fired the nice Mexican people who had—

"Now wait a minute. I did *not* fire Consuela. She received a generous pension, I mean *generous*—"

"Screw your generous, Rob. She wasn't around any more. And Chris took his things, his manga and—"

"Wait a minute. What are you talking about? You mean that *Japanese pornography?* For Christ's sake, Karo, you should have seen that stuff. Absolutely disgusting. I can't even— I mean graphic. Jesus, have you seen any of it? Men screwing boys. Boys in drag. And the violence! My god, it'd turn your stomach."

Was that *Two from One Fire* he was talking about? She didn't know what to say—but it looked like she didn't have to say anything. He'd stopped in mid-flight. She followed his gaze, saw Paige and Christine approaching on one of those little golf cart things—a tall blonde and a short blonde, two smiley faces. Rob sighed. As they got closer, Karen could hear the sound of their voices, high and girlish, and then a teenager's laugh from the boy driving the cart.

"Yes, I made some mistakes," Rob said. "I'd be the first to admit it."

What was this shit? She'd forgotten how quickly he could change positions, and she sensed a trap. She should never allow herself to believe, not even for a moment, that he'd ever give up on anything—oh no, he was indefatigable.

"When Chris and I were getting together," he was saying in his newly acquired deeply sincere voice, "yes, Dev did get neglected, I have to admit it." Had he actually been as angry as he'd been playing it? Maybe so, maybe not, but there was no doubt how angry *she* was—shaking with it. She told herself to keep her mouth shut.

"I had a lot on my plate," he said, "and I simply wasn't paying attention. Believe me, Karen, that's not going to happen again. You've got to trust me on this. Devon means the world to me."

ROB DID NOT COOK, but he was one of those men who considered themselves to be masters of the barbecue. If you described to him *exactly* how you wanted your steak, that was *exactly* how you were going to get it. "I don't know," Paige was saying, "like not as bloody as Mum!"

"A little bit of pink," Karen said. "If it's any more rare than that, she won't eat it."

"I'm on it," Rob said.

The steaks were sizzling away—top quality, as he'd made sure to tell them—porterhouse. Paige was helping Chris set out the predictable deli food—potato salad, coleslaw, and one of those packaged salads with the nuts and the blue cheese. The requisite carb—garlic bread—was heating up in the oven. It was all just lovely lovely, but Karen's stomach had clenched itself up into a fiery fist. Swallowing your anger is not good for you—would she be able to eat a fucking thing? She was drinking tonic and pretending it had gin in it. When in doubt, don't drink anything at all, and she was in deep doubt. How could she have thought that if they all made an effort, they'd get along fine? How could she have thought that anything good might come out of this fucking freak show?

Paige, miss sociability, was trying to hide her disappointment. Unless you were from Vancouver shut down by the Olympics, this was not your spring break, and there were not a lot of kids here, nobody her age. A handful of teenagers had been playing poolside volleyball—that was about it—but sports was most definitely not Paige's thing. She was nonetheless doing her best to find something to like—it was so *warm* here, so *nice* here, the pool had such a *nice* waterslide.

"You know, there's *two* malls," Christine said.

Paige lit up. "Oh, really!"

Oh my, yes, Karen thought, now you've found the right button to push—we've flown all the way to the Great American Desert so Paige can go shopping in the bloody malls. Perfect. Yes, there surely had to be some American brands that hadn't made it to Canada yet. ". . . leave your silly old dad to his golf," Chris was saying, "maybe we'll get our nails done . . ."

Rob at the barbecue was chuckling along with them. "Quite the young lady," he was saying. Oh my god, Karen thought.

She should be making an effort—doing her best to keep things easy peasy, light and breezy—but she simply couldn't do it. Her mind was still off on its own tangent, and she couldn't turn it off. All those years when she'd had a sense of agency— That was the buzzword, wasn't it? It was a feminist word, wasn't it? It was one of those words you'd never heard in your life, and then, all of a sudden, you're hearing it fifty times a day. What was it supposed to mean—*agency*? That you were actually in charge of something? Hey, lady, you got *agency*? Oh, yeah, sure, I've got agency all right.

"Oh, the stars!" Karen said, and they were indeed magnificent, a big sky full of them, but what she wanted was an excuse to turn her back on everybody and walk away. It didn't have to be far away—just a few steps would do it.

Drew, she thought, you fucking bastard—you traitor, you turncoat, you fucking *mole*. All those nights sitting around with you, drinking some fine vintage and watching the news and then hashing things over in our jolly ineffectual Canadian way—agreeing to disagree—and I get to play the far-left bad girl, and you get to play the old-school Tory—but ha ha, no one could possibly believe anything I'm saying, could they? No, of course not—we're all grown-ups here, and grown-ups understand *the economy*. Global warming? "For god's sake, Karen, people have been predicting the end of the world for thousands of years, and it hasn't ended yet!"—and maybe we'll go to bed and have the tepid dishwater sex we have on those rare occasions when we still have it, or if you're that kind of three-quarters loaded you like to call "dog tired," maybe you'll dribble off homeward to get yourself ready to do whatever it is you do to get paid the staggering amounts of money you make which are never quite as staggering as the amounts of money that Rob makes, but you've got yourself Rob's wife, don't you, sweetie? And this is called *agency*?

Patriarchy—there was another good one. It had been part of the standard vocabulary when Karen was in university, and she'd used it herself often enough, but she'd never entirely believed in it—how could she when her own father was the sweetest man in the world? But what do you call it when your ex-boyfriend calls up your ex-husband to discuss you? Two former colleagues from Wayne Energy, two old boys still operating in the same bloody network, two good buddies from way back, *two men—and they're talking about you*.

My life was not supposed to be like this, Karen thought. It didn't have to be. She'd made some lousy choices somewhere along the way. Agency? What a fucking joke. A corporate lawyer and two oil executives—talk about sleeping with the enemy, Jesus!

Paige, she thought, my poor little pussycat, you're too pretty, too smart, too cute, too privileged, and *too much like me*—you're utterly doomed.

God help me, she thought, I'm a terrible mother. Well, maybe she didn't have to be—but what about Cameron and the dickheads? And poor Jamie, the difficult daughter. Everybody was down on Jamie—what could she possibly do for Jamie? Or Devon, for that matter? And what was wrong with the twins anyway? Erica was right—there was *absolutely nothing* wrong with the twins as long as they were together.

KAREN AND HER first husband had made their lawyers rich. It wouldn't have been proper for Ian to get someone from his own firm, but he knew all the young hotshots in town, and he got himself a very bright boy. Karen asked around, and everyone mentioned a prominent feminist lawyer whose specialty was family law. People described her as a Rottweiler. She didn't look like a Rottweiler; she was a well-dressed lady in her fifties who wore a touch of makeup and favoured old-school power suits. "Okay," she said at their first meeting, "he's offering you child support that ends when Cameron turns nineteen, and what else? He wants you to buy out his half of the house?"

"I don't want the house," Karen said, "but some of my dad's money went into the down payment."

"Yes. Right. You brought your own assets into the marriage, and you gave up your career to stay home and take care of Cameron while your husband finished articling and began *his* career? And he thinks he can offer you a pissy little child support agreement and walk? I don't think so."

Neither Karen nor Ian had budged an inch. She'd been getting even for the slap, and he'd been getting even for the affair. The bright boy and the Rottweiler fought it all the way down to the wire, but the bright boy was new to the game while the Rottweiler had been playing it for years. Karen skinned Ian good. Of course the Rottweiler got a huge chunk of it. And what did Karen get—besides the money? Ian's enduring hatred. They couldn't even manage a civil ten-minute conversation. And he took it out on Cameron—who was now a total fuck-up—and that appalling scorch-and-burn bitterness had been one of the main reasons Karen had settled things so amiably with Rob. Oh, and he had been extremely generous, too, and that had certainly helped.

The three big things that are supposed to split couples up are children, sex, and money—well, she and Rob had never fought over sex or money—and no one ever mentions politics, but if George W. Bush and his pals hadn't decided to invade Iraq, it was quite possible that Karen and Rob might still be married. She'd never known exactly what it was that Rob did for a living—couldn't even begin to describe what one of his work days might look like—but she did know that he wore more hats than the one that said, "CEO, Wayne Energy, Canada." Eventually he was flying back to the States so often that he might as well be living there, and he'd never seen his stay in Canada as anything but temporary anyway. There was no doubt in his mind what he was going to do next—simply move his family to California.

Karen had been expressing a rising crescendo of *her* doubts, but Rob was not hearing them. Karen's therapist, the all-knowing Helen, had been diagnosed with breast cancer and had retired from practice, so Karen was left with nobody to talk to but herself. The whole preposterous business came to a head as Karen watched Rob watching George W. Bush descending onto an aircraft carrier to announce: "Mission accomplished!" Rob was chortling and drinking Scotch. "What are they doing," Karen said, "channeling Leni Riefenstahl?" Rob didn't get it, of course.

"Rob," she said, "listen to me. I can not live in that crazy country. I do not want *my children* growing up in that crazy country." That was the opening round in a long series of complex and exhausting negotiations that would eventually lead to Karen signing one of the oddest divorce agreements in the history of Canadian family law—the one that Jamie described, uncharitably, as "trading Devon for the house and a whole bunch of money."

Okay, that was long ago. Karen didn't know the law exactly, but she was pretty sure that no judge would make a thirteen-year-old live where he didn't want to live. She'd have to talk to the Rottweiler again. But did she want to get into a custody battle with Rob Clark? Across an international border? Oh my god, no.

USING HER THUMBNAIL as a knife, Karen snapped a zopiclone tablet into two unequal parts and swallowed the smaller one. I must be desperate, she thought—here I am using a sleeping pill as a tranquilizer—but she'd done it before, and it had worked. Tonight she needed to take the edge off just enough so she could read. That had been her great escape ever since she'd been a kid. If you don't like your own life, try somebody else's.

Paige had fallen asleep on the sofa bed in the living room. Karen rummaged around in the covers until she found the remote, clicked off the TV, and walked back out onto the patio to take one more look at the stars. They were supposed to make you feel the insignificance of your own puny little human life, but she didn't need stars to make her feel that. How many more starry nights before they packed Paige into their car and drove off to Disneyland? One? Two? It probably depended on how many holes of golf Rob wanted to get in.

The zopiclone was hitting her—she could feel it blurring her edges. She hoped the twins were okay—thousands and thousands and thousands of miles away. She hoped everybody was okay. This was like the praying she'd done as a child—dear God, please make sure that everybody's okay. The stars—brilliant enigmatic scattering of cosmic debris—were swooping her mind out as big as the sky. It was interesting how no picture of stars could do the job quite like standing out under them. If she was alone here, she could like this place.

It was time to find something to read. What? She stepped back inside, slid the doors shut, checked a second time to make sure they were really locked. Yes, she could definitely feel the drug now—lapping at her footsteps, threatening to tangle her up. Carefully, carefully, she padded into her bedroom to look at the books she'd lined up on the desk.

She'd brought mostly Can Lit, and the obvious choice was good old Alice Munro, the queen of the short story, but she owed it to Alice not to be stoned when she read her. None of the other books looked very appealing, actually. She and Jen were secret chick-lit readers, and Jen had passed her this one across the table at Delany's—"Pure escape, you'll love it"— but would she actually love a book titled *Lust, Loathing, and a Little Lip Gloss*? Was it possible that she'd hauled all of these heavy piles of bound paper to the desert and now didn't want to read any of them? But then, finally, there was her assignment from the twins. When Jamie had seen Karen packing the books, she'd tossed the first volume of *Two from One Fire* into her suitcase. "Come on, Mum, you know you've gotta read it."

Okay, so maybe it was the perfect thing to read stoned—maybe the cartoons would meld together into one fantastical blur—and besides, she wanted to see what bothered Rob so much. She grabbed the manga, dropped herself onto the bed, and began flipping through the pages. Oh, there was the violence he'd been talking about—a bombed-out city, fragments of it burning under a smoky leaden sky. Dead people were flung about like refuse. Some were lying in pools of their own blood, pieces of their bodies blown off. In a close-up drawing, the corpse of a young man had strings of intestines spilling out. Two rats were gnawing on them.

Karen looked instantly away. She'd actually felt her stomach lurch. Yuck. She turned the book over to see if anyone has bothered to warn parents, and yes indeed, they had: PARENTAL ADVISORY: MATURE TEENS 16+ and then, the warning spelled out in small print: "Violence, strong language, some nudity and sexually suggestive scenes." Oh god, maybe Rob was right.

Karen had always believed that children should be allowed to read whatever they damned well pleased, but now she was having second thoughts. Drawings are not the same thing as stories in prose, and did she actually want her kids looking at these disturbing images? There wasn't much she could do about it—they'd already read *Two from One Fire* over and over until they were saturated in it. Why hadn't she bothered to look at it before?

She began flipping through it again. Surely there had to be something in there besides this sickening violence. Did it really have gay pornography? Ah, but here was a different sort of drawing, a whole series of kitschy little girls who seemed to be hanging out in a huge hall, sipping tea and chatting with one another. Diamonds couldn't sparkle any more than their huge eyes—and oh my goodness, look at the enormous skirts, the seas of petticoats, the flounced pantelettes, the lace-trimmed ankle socks, the gauzy little gloves, the patent mary-janes trimmed with bows and ribbons—and everything was drawn in crazy detail.

A pretty little maid was bowing before one of the girls, offering her a rolled-up parchment on a silver platter. "Forgive me, my Princess," she was saying, "but I have been tasked with delivering this missive to your hands alone," and Karen's BlackBerry chimed. Fuck, now what? For one wacky moment she'd thought it was a sound effect from the manga.

It was nearly midnight. The display told her that it was Robert Clark calling. Jesus, Rob, what's with you? I thought you had an eight a.m. tee-time. She considered not answering, pretending to be asleep, but no—she was too curious. "What?" she said.

"Um . . . It's me? Christine? Did I wake you?"

"Well, not quite."

"Do you want to—? Um. We got off on such a bad start today— Do you want to chat for a little bit?"

When Karen stood up, she discovered that her room had become mysteriously too big for her. Oh well, she thought, go on force of habit—that should work. Outside again—easy does it. There she was— Christine—sitting on the little bench across from their villas. If Karen simply walked forward one step at a time, step step at a time, yes, she would get there.

Christine flicked a single panicked glance in Karen's direction and then stared down at her pretty manicured toes and burst into a breathless torrent of speech—"I'm so glad that you . . . that it doesn't have to be this way. We got off to a really bad . . . Unfortunate! But we don't really know *anything* at all about each other. People always . . . Our thoughts and fears, our hopes and dreams. But we always make assumptions. We do that all the time. But it's . . . It's just so darned important to look into each other's hearts, to see what's in there, deeply . . ."

Oh my god, Karen thought. "Yes," she said, "you're right about that." She sat down carefully on the bench. The drug was doing more than blurring her edges—it was filling her mind with blob.

Chris met her eyes. Behind all the rattling words she was terrified. "Rob warned me that you're liberal . . ."

"Liberal?" Karen said. "I'm farther left than that!"

"My dad thinks the same things you do about the banks. He wanted to see all the banks go down, and all those financial . . . He was absolutely furious with Obama. He was . . . You'd love my dad. He's outspoken. 'Free-market means *free market*,' that's what he says. He doesn't trust the government either."

Yes, this was a genuinely bad idea. A sleeping pill is not a tranquilizer. A sleeping pill is supposed *to put you to sleep*. Karen was having a bitch of a time following what Chris was saying. Focus! she told herself.

Oklahoma—that's where Chris was from. That's what she was talking about. "I've never been there," Karen said, "but I've seen the musical."

That surely must be one of the most ridiculous lines ever to come out of Karen's mouth, but it was a big hit with Chris who leaned toward her, giggling, and briefly pressed her fingers onto the back of her hand.

"I'm a born peacemaker," Chris whispered like a conspirator.

Now what on earth was she talking about? Rob, it seemed, had entirely lost track of Brittany. Who the hell was Brittany?

Christine thought it was just terrible. "Paying for things is not the same thing as being a good dad. I told him that more than once. I contacted Joyce. Of course she was dubious, *very* dubious, but she met me for lunch. She married again, did you know that? She married a . . . I forget what he is . . . a city planner or something. A very nice man."

Who the fuck were these people?

"And Brittany's a lovely girl. It's absolutely uncanny how much she looks like Rob. Of course we want Avery to grow up knowing Brittany. And Devon and Jamie and Paige, of course. Of *course*. They're brothers and sisters! Oh, I just have to tell you what a lovely girl Paige is, what a sweetheart! You must be so proud . . . I gather that Jamie's a bit of a problem?"

"She's okay. She's a teenager."

"Oh, I know! The kids today have been absolutely ruined by social media. It's turned them into a bunch of lazy couch potatoes. Don't even want to go out of the house. Walk around texting each other and staring down at their cellphones, don't even look up. And the video games! Hopeless! And the . . . You know, the role of parents . . . I think we have to moderate this, um . . . ration it. I think if we cut them off from all electronic . . . Well, that would go a long way toward solving the problem, don't you think?"

"I don't know. It's maybe, ah . . . foggy . . . I mean, more fore . . . What's the word I want?"

"Oh, I do that too!" Christine said, giggling again.

There was no way Karen was ever going to find the word she wanted.

"Rob's just as bad sometimes," Chris was saying. "I keep telling him to stop and smell the roses. He gets so sucked into this stuff. He's never unplugged. Never! Sometimes I just take that darned BlackBerry and put it on the shelf and say, 'Okay, honey, now we're going to be free from all that for an hour.'"

"Yeah, you can sure taste a lot of wime." Oh fuck.

"Rob, that silly old bear . . . You know how he is about his only son. But it's such an impressionable age, decisions that will affect the entire rest of their lives . . . And you know older boys prey on younger boys, and then once they're drawn into that sick lifestyle, they're so ashamed! And then they just sink down even farther. We have to be so vigilant. We can't let our guard down for a minute . . ."

Ah, the stars. The night seemed to have turned into something painted by Van Gogh.

"Christine," Karen said, "this is, ah . . . sweet. Really sweet of you. But I've got to, ah . . . go to sleep."

"Oh, I know it's late, I've kept you up too late, you poor thing. Come on, let's walk back."

Chris stood up, and so did Karen. Chris offered her arm, and Karen took it. They began walking back together like sisters. Karen appreciated the support.

"When I was carrying Avery," Chris was saying in her conspiratorial voice, "that was such um . . . but such a blessing, I can't begin to tell you. But I wasn't really there for Devon, nowhere near the way I should have been. When he comes home, we're . . . Oh, kill the fatted calf! But I know it's good for him to be away. Another country. Broadening. Get to know his biological mother. Karen, you've been such a good scout about all this. We've got to pull together."

Here was the point at which they should part. To the right was Christine's villa, to the left Karen's—how symbolic. But was anything as significant as it seemed? Probably not, but if Karen didn't get inside soon, they would have to pick her up in one of their little golf carts.

"The way our life is," Christine was murmuring, "it's like that old story, do you know the story? It was back in one of those old kingdoms, and the king and all of his men were feasting in the big hall. They were drinking ale or mead or whatever and eating all this food and yelling and banging on the table, and there was a minister of our Lord staying in the Castle, and the king invited him to join them and tell them about this strange new religion. And while they were feasting, a tiny little bird flew in the back window, and then flew down the length of the table, and then flew out the other window. And the minister said, 'That's what our life is like. We fly in from the terrible hard cold winter, and we fly across the room, and then we fly out again into that terrible hard cold winter, and that's how brief our life is,' and the king and all of his men converted to Christianity right there on the spot."

"Nice story," Karen said. She'd heard it somewhere before. "Good night, Chris."

"Good night! Oh, but . . . You know, that *is* how our life is, so brief, so brief, it's over so quickly. All we have is faith! And love. Without love we are as tinkling brass. Oh, Karen, I'm so glad I had a chance to talk to you. I knew we'd get along just fine if we could only be alone for a minute."

18.

HI, ERICA, we are supposed to write every day for language arts but we have not, we will try to catch up, we have so much to tell u. we are staying with David, he is Bryan's mate, they were BFs back in the day. David has a BF, his name is Mat. David & Mat are a gay couple, we never met a gay couple before, they are really nice. There place is small so we sleep on the floor, it is fun. Mat gets up too early, chex to see where the surf is up, then we jump in the van & go. Bryan is the best surfer, when he rides the wave he is like a movie but mostly he chills with David & they talk bout back in the day. The boys on the beach go nuts over Morgan & Avi, like wow twins!!! like wow they can surf!!! ossie boys are assholes, like the things they say, OMG are you kidding me! M&A mostly blow them off, this is so boring, yawn, let us go hang in the lineup, but some are nice, some of the girls are really nice, every body thinks it is cool we are from Canada.

We do not understand why people can not tell Morgan & Avalon apart, they are very different. Avi is a pretty surfer, every body says that, she is amazing, she can not fall off her board, she is so pretty every body turns to look at her. Morgan is not so pretty but she is crazy, she is not afraid of any thing, she does things u can not believe, David got a great pix of her in the tube, we put it on Facebook, hes got an awesome camera, he also got sick pix of her wiping out big time. Bryans like Mo if u don't get some sense u are not going to live long. Morgan is a mondo shredder, every body says she surfs like a boy, Jamie wants to surf like a boy too, she is trying, ha ha. Jamie says to tell u she did not like the ha ha i just wrote. Every body is so much better than me, Bryans like this is not about competition, its about having fun. I wish I was a better swimmer, i get too scared, i do not go out to far. Avi helps me & shows me stuff.

We love Sydney!!! it is the best, we are outside all day, there are restaurants that have tables outside, there are people selling things every where so u can just buy things to eat any time u want. When we are not surfing we walk around & talk to people. David & Mat know every gay bloke in Australia, David is famous in Gay Rights in australia, every where we go people know him, it is dope. we put a pix up on facebook & moms like dont they have any women in Sydney, ha ha! u would not believe how much beer they drink!!! Every body is like gday mate, they all talk like Bryan, if we stay here long enuf we will talk like that too! People always think we are both boys, Jamie is like hey Bryan can i be a boy while we are in Sydney & hes like whats that u say son? So now Jamie is a boy & sometimes we go around with no tops. Jamie says to tell u she loves being a boy. We have never seen a city as beautiful as sydney, we could live here forever!

Ur friends, Devon & James ☺

Hi, Devon and James,

You guys sound like you're having a wonderful time. It feels odd to be writing to you from the middle of winter here while you're in the middle of summer there. Enjoy being a boy, James. It must be lots of fun, especially so far away where you won't run into anybody you know.

Remember I told you how my sister and I split up the gender roles? Morgan and Avalon are a little bit like that, but Lise and I took it to extremes. I was the tomboy twin and I could go for months without ever putting a skirt on. Once when I was about your age we were playing softball somewhere and I went into the girls' and ran into this much older girl who was freaked out. She was yelling at me, "Get out of here. This is THE GIRLS!" and I was yelling back, "I AM a girl!" I was really upset but I was also secretly proud that someone would actually think I was a boy.

Here's what I secretly thought. If I was a girl who could do anything that a boy could do, and if I was so good at being a boy that people sometimes actually thought I was a boy, then that made me BETTER than a boy! I don't think I ever told anybody that. Except Annalise. She and I always told each other everything.

I'm glad to be with my family again. I'm sorting through my sister's things. It is very hard for me and I will be glad when it's done. I never tried surfing. We have no surf in Alberta, ha ha. Maybe I would like it. I used to like snowboarding. I am really looking forward to hearing the next installment of your adventures.

Take care,

Erica

Hey Erica, tomorrow we have to leave sydney, sob, becuz we are going to Tassie where Morgan & Avi were born, they are so excited! also to see their grandmother, she is dying of cancer, it is very sad. Bryan is like OK James i can not pass u off as a boy to my family, so James will have to be Jamie again.

Hi, this is me James, Dev is typing for me cuz u know i have a learning disability. i liked what u said in ur letter, u know about being BETTER, it made me smile. Tomorrow i will be Jamie again & i am alrite with that. i also liked what u said about not running into anybody u know. When u were the tomboy twin did the kids give u shit?

This is me Dev again, we want to tell u some thing important. All the time u lived with us we were sad about ur sister but we did not know what to say. We hope u finish sorting thru ur sisters stuff real soon, is it alrite to write this to u? We really want to see u when we go home. We hope u want to see us to!!!

Your friends, D&J

Hi, Devon and Jamie,

Of course it is all right to write what you are feeling. These are emails between friends and we can say anything we want. Yes, I would like to see you too. Talk to your mum about it and maybe we can get together for a walk or lunch or something. I enjoyed living at your house and will always appreciate how kind everyone was to me.

No, I did not get shit for being the tomboy twin. I think there are a number of reasons for that. One is that MZ twins don't really need other kids so much because they already have their best friend, and that protects them from group pressure. Two is that sometimes there is a social advantage to being an MZ twin because kids often think that twinship is cool in itself. Then in the southern Alberta culture where we grew up we had lots of room for girls to be tomboys. Also, I was half of a twin unit and Annalise was quite feminine, and so the two of us together made a social statement. The kids would go, "Oh, it's the Bauer twins. Ricki is the tomboy twin and Lise is the girly twin." It's like we came as a package and that made everything all right.

Thank you for your kind thoughts. I really appreciate them. Yes, it is hard to sort through my sister's things but I know I have to do it and I will feel better when I get finished. I look forward to your emails. They always cheer me up.

All best,
Erica

Hey, Erica, we are in Tassie, it is amazing, we flew on a plane named VIRGIN BLUE!!! M&A have many relatives, like we had this humongus dinner. Bryan has two older brothers, they are way older than Bryan & they are married and have kids & some of their kids have kids, so M&A have a gazillion cousins but none our age, they are either grown up or they are babies, we cannot possibly remember every body's name! Bryan's mom is very nice, all her hair fell out cuz she had radiation & she wears a scarf, she was only supposed to live a few months but shes already fooled them, every body keeps telling her to take it easy, she does not want to take it easy, she was so happy to see Bryan & M&A that she cried! She has not seen M&A since they were babies.

For Bryan they got all these different kinds of tassie beer, like from MICROBREWREYS it's a big deal, everybody had to try them, we even got to try them, they were all way to bitter for us! Bryan's mom & Bryan's brothers wives made this huge dinner, it was roast beef with yorkshire puddings, they knew Bryan & M&A were vegitarians but it did not compute, like they thot that meant u didnt eat meat most of the time, ha ha, they could not imagine any one who would not like roast beef!! Bryan ate it OK but M&A could not. Afterward he gave them a talking to in private, hes like if u were out with a begging bowl u would eat whatever u got, it wouldnt matter if it was meat, even the budda did that & theyre like we tried dad we just couldn't do it! Jamie & i have no probs with meat, bring it on! Bryans mom loved us!

Bryan says he will take us surfing every day, his mom has to lie down lots so thats OK, there are good beaches around Hobart, Tassie has some of the best waves in the world! The water is so cold u have to wear wet suits all the time, M&A brot there old suits for us, they did not fit them any more but they fit us, mine is a bit to big but Jamies fits fine. We r so happy u want to see us when we r home, did u finish sorting thru ur sister's stuff?

Your friends, Jamie & Dev

Dear Jamie and Dev,
What a great email you sent me! You painted a really vivid picture of Bryan and his family. I think it will be great for language arts.

No, I am not finished with my sister's things. I did a rough sort in her husband's garage and we sent a lot of it to the dump but everything left is now jammed into the room that used to be ours in our parents' house. I have all of Lise's clothes. It is very painful to me to look at Lise's clothes. I am sorry, I probably should not be writing this to you. Do not feel that you have to respond. It is making me feel better to write it down. Please don't worry about me. I will be okay.

Your friend, Erica

Erica we r going surfing & every body is waiting 4 us but we just got ur emal & we want to write back fast B4 we go. we r so happy u answered our emails, u can rite depressing shit to us all u want, we r so glad u r going to see us in Vancouver. The thing we told u about language arts is totally true but mainly we just wanted u to write back & u did!

did u & mom have a fight? we were afraid to ask u that B4. we were so happy when u & mom were GFs, it was perfect for us. we were hoping that u would become part of our family. we do not know what happened, what ever happened, we are your friends forever even if u & mom r not GFs any more u will always be part of our family.

J & D

Dear Jamie and Dev,

Thank you so much for your email. It made me feel so much better. I can't tell you how much it means to me that you think of me as part of your family. I am looking forward to seeing you in Vancouver.

Things are always worse in the middle of the night. It is okay. I will be finished soon. My brother Trav and his wife are having us over to his house for dinner tomorrow. I have a little nephew named Cory. He is four and very cute. It is always fun to see him.

Please don't worry if I don't answer your emails right away. I might not be able to answer emails for a while. But don't worry, I will always answer eventually. Please tell me more about your trip. I love hearing about your stories.

With much love, Erica

Hi Erica,

we are glad our email made u feel better, we wrote it in like10 sec, we thot
it was retarded but we sent it anyway, did you see Cory? was it fun? do
u have any other neeces or nephews? we have to go home in a few days,
it is sad. Morgan & Avi are not ready to leave the wheel yet & we are not
either, so we are stuck here in the world of forms & need to figure many
things out. we have too many questions, because we are identical it is
very complicated. we hope u are feeling better, we will see you soon!!!

Your friends J& D

Erica had been so deeply asleep that her mind had shut down and left
her with no sense of time passing—the first honest-to-god real sleep since
she'd been home. She checked her alarm—it was nearly eleven, so that
meant five or six hours. She had to be in pretty sorry shape for that to
count as a good night's sleep but she actually felt rested. When they'd
been little kids, she and Annalise had wondered why, when you woke
up, you always ended up in the exact same spot in the same life you'd
left behind. It felt like it would be so easy to wake up in some other place.

She forced herself get up. It was cold in their room but that was
okay. It would keep her moving. She remembered writing an email in
the night, remembered that her eyes had been burning, remembered
thinking that she should lie down for a while. She poked a random key
on Annalise's computer to wake it up.

Dear Jamie and Devon,
It is nearly five in the morning and I cannot sleep. I find it very
oppressive to be awake in the middle of the night when my
mum and dad are asleep and I have to be careful not to make
any noise. I feel very isolated and sometimes I feel that nothing
is real. This is a condition that psychologists have studied and

written about so at least I know what it is. If it wasn't the middle of winter I would probably be walking a lot but it is bitterly cold at five in the morning and I can't stand to be outside for very long. I don't know whether I should send this email. I can remember what I used to think was appropriate but I cannot feel it. I guess all I have that keeps me going is

Great unfinished sentence, Erica. All you have to keep you going on is *what?* She Xed out of the document, deleting it. If she'd been planning to send an email like that to the twins, she must have been out of her fucking mind. Lack of sleep, she thought. There've been studies on this. That's why sleep deprivation is a standard feature of all intelligently designed torture regimes.

When her unsent email vanished, it revealed her inbox. While she'd been gone, she'd received another message from the twins.

Dear Erica, are u not amazed, this is the 2nd email in 1 day! we went to bed but can not sleep cuz we can not stop talking & we thot we would write to u. Jamie is growing so much faster than me it is really depressing, the time for her to get her puberty blocked was when we were first reunited & were exactly the same size, that would have been the best time. If she did it now, how long would it take for me to catch up to her? Is there something i could take that would make me catch up to her? Is it estrogen that is making her grow? i know i should not take estrogen cuz it turns u into a woman. Inside we are absolutely identical & we do not want to turn into women so neither one of us should have estrogen in us but we prob should not have testosterone either, isnt there some other choice? Every body has a little bit of both in them dont they? Are there any other hormones? We google it but it is way too complicated. Is there a mix of hormones we could take that would make us grow but still stay the same & end up the same size? We are afraid that medical science is not ready for us, LOL.

312

Amazing. Nothing could be any clearer than that. Devon had told her exactly what he and Jamie wanted, and they were right—medical science wasn't ready for them. It was a million miles outside her own field but they were raising some interesting questions and she could probably find some tentative answers for them. That's exactly what ITS had been designed to do—facilitate dialogue between scholars from diverse disciplines. She could get some input from Dr. Nitzberg from Medicine—he was an endocrinologist—and Celia Gergess from Women's and Gender Studies. Stacey would probably have some interesting things to say too. Erica could actually set up a meeting. She could even invite Bill—he was a clinical psychologist—and get some brownie points— Well, no, she couldn't. He'd told her that the twins were not her responsibility.

IT WAS LIKE there were two Ericas, the nighttime one and the daytime one. It wasn't that she couldn't remember the nighttime one—it was that she had a different set of feelings. The nighttime Erica had sent a series of increasingly inappropriate emails that had led the twins to this intimacy. They'd lost their censor because she'd lost hers. They'd thought that she and Karen were girlfriends. They'd wanted her to become part of their family. She *had* become a part of their family and she'd got what she wanted—they trusted her. Now she was responsible for them—in some weird way even more responsible than Karen. She couldn't carry the weight. How could she help anybody else if she couldn't help herself?

How to get through the day? She needed coffee but her mother was home so she would have to talk to her. "Is there any coffee?"

"Yes, but it's cold now. I never know when you're going to get up, Ricki. You can heat it up in the microwave. Do you want me to do it for you?"

"No, I can do it."

"Do you want some eggs?"

"No, it's okay." Wrong response—her mother was giving her a bleak accusatory stare. "I'll eat something in a minute. I just need coffee."

Mum was the origin of the genes that had made Erica and Annalise small girls, made them look younger than their age. She was even smaller than they were—barely over five feet. She was sixty-seven and looked fifty. In their twin-private world they'd seen her as a small annoying dog that sometimes got so upset it couldn't stop barking. In their twin-private language, a faint suggestion of a bark meant, *Watch out. Mum's being yappy.* Erica could see that Mum, given half a chance, was going to become very yappy. She had to get outside.

In her huge poofy winter coat and Ugg boots—both Christmas presents from her family—Erica carried her coffee around to the back of the house so she could look out across the valley, across the river, to the highway where Lise had been killed. It was unfortunate that she could see that exact spot from the back of their house. The Hat did not have to be this cold in February—it often wasn't—and it was clear by now that Erica had a major depressive disorder. If she could only get through the rest of the school year, survive until May, then she could think about what to do next.

When she came back inside, she found her mother standing in their bedroom doing absolutely nothing. She didn't turn around when Erica came in but she must have heard her because she started talking immediately—"My goodness, Ricki, it's no wonder you're having a hard time, crammed in here with your sister's things and you just shut yourself in here night after night and you don't sleep—just *crammed*. Most of it should go to Goodwill so somebody could get some use out of it, what are you thinking? No way you have to do this all by yourself. I called Trina. She's going to come over tomorrow and we're going to get all this packed up—"

"Trina!"—their impossibly bossy pain-in-the-ass big sister.

"Yes, Trina. You may not like it but we'll get it done. Do you have any place to store all this? In Vancouver? You shouldn't just pile it up in your apartment."

"I've got a storage locker in the basement."

"Good. Store it in there and don't look at it for a year. I mean it. An entire year. What on earth are you writing in the night?"

"What?" Erica felt like she'd been caught in the midst of some unspeakable act.

"In the night. I hear you. You dad can sleep through anything but I hear you, what are you writing?"

"Emails."

"Emails? About school?"

Erica shook her head. In a minute she was going to start screaming but Mum was only trying to help—in her own way, the only way she knew how. The infuriating thing was that she was right. "People want too much from me," Erica said. "I don't have anything left to give them."

"I should think not." Her mother pointed at Annalise's computer. "Turn that thing off."

Could it be that easy? Erica hit the power button. She couldn't have predicted her own reaction—oh my god, it was such a relief. And it was okay. She'd warned the twins that she might not answer for a while.

"Ricki? I know you don't believe in Christ but you must believe in something."

"What? A higher power?" No, she thought, there's no one here but us, and we're not doing a very good job. "What am I supposed to do, Mum? Pray? Dear God, you know that I don't believe in you but help me anyway."

"That's a start."

Erica was far from happy but right at the moment she was not crazy. She gathered up her laptop and her phone and gave them to her mother. "Keep these for me, okay? Until I go back to Vancouver. I'm dialing out. I'm unreachable."

"Good for you."

"Thanks, Mum."

"You're welcome. Take a bath and put on something nice. We're going to Ralph's Texas and have a steak and then we're going to a movie."

"What movie?"

Her mum's thin dry smile—"It doesn't really matter, does it?"

19.

LOOKING AT HERSELF in the mirror—the same one that had caught Paige—Karen could understand why, as bat-shit crazy as it might be, teenage girls posted naked selfies on the net. She'd been waxed from toes to chin, and she'd had a deep-cleansing facial and an eyebrow shaping.

Nobody but Dakila would ever cut or colour her hair, but she'd had a shampoo and style. In honour of her stupid fights with Rob, she'd declined polish on her fingernails, but they'd been buffed so highly they might as well have been shellacked. She'd picked a neutral grey for her toenails, and they'd come out the same metallic colour as a flying saucer fuselage. She'd refused a spray-on tan—no, no, no matter how bloody *natural* it might look—but she'd had a deep tissue massage in which they'd laid heated black basalt stones onto her back. She'd sweated in the steam room and melted in the whirlpool. Her entire body had been smoothed with rare oils. Then, as a special complimentary gift to a client who'd spent the entire afternoon and a rather staggering number of American dollars in the place, her makeup had been done for the evening, and if the person looking back at her from the mirror didn't quite match the Karen Oxley brand, she was certainly attractive enough to have broad appeal to the general public. Overall, Karen was pleased—in fact, for someone who was soon to turn forty-four, she looked just fine. Maybe she could take a few selfies strictly for fun. It would be easy to do. She had a camera on her BlackBerry. The selfies would go nowhere but onto the hard drive of her Mac. But she imagined the ladies—she'd absolutely *have* to tell Jen— "Oh, did you hear the latest? Karen was taking *naked pictures of herself* in a resort villa in Palm Desert!" Well, screw the ladies. Who was it for anyway? I'm pampering *me*—yes I am, isn't that what I'm supposed to do?

She seemed to be stuck in the mirror as badly as Paige. It was sad how few times in her life she'd been able to look at her own naked body and like what she saw—without a million sorry reservations, destructive criticisms, dire warnings, endless comparisons, plans to do better— prayers to God, for god's sake!—all the endless mind crap that girls do to themselves, trying to be girls. But where had she ever got the idea that she was like Paige or Paige was like her? Paige was a natural-born beauty, super sociable, and considerably less than a brilliant student. Karen at the same age had been a scruffy skinny uneasy little kid made of piecemeal fragments that would take forever to add up to anything. When grown-ups wanted to compliment her mother, they didn't say, "She's so pretty," they said, "She's so clever." Scraggly unwashed nothing blonde, dirty feet, big dog-coloured eyes, and silence—that's what grown-ups would have seen. School was easy. She got straight As and was always reading. She was not popular. Her only real friend was Patsy Donlevy.

Naked now, but when she was dressed and assembled, her social mask in place, she could become another person, someone who could be intimidating—what a strange thought. "If I met you at a party," Erica had said, "you'd scare me to death." Then Erica had said something else. What? Something about the things we can't define. "We're not what people see"— that's what she'd said. How do you take selfies anyway? Karen retrieved her BlackBerry from the table by her bed and deliberately approached the mirror. No, she thought, you do not have to tell Jen about this—or anybody. No, she thought, you do not have to smile. All you have to do is look at yourself carefully.

"HI, HONEY, are you alone?"

This man, this perfect stranger with an American accent, had just called her *honey*. Karen was not in the mood to do any of the usual polite maneuvering. "Yes," she said, "and I want to stay that way."

He might as well have been dressed to go on safari—in a khaki shirt, open to show off the grey hair on his chest, and a pair of those Tilley Endurable shorts with the million zipped pockets. His eyes narrowed to slits. His mouth formed the word without sound, but she got the message anyway—"Bitch."

Karen was far more shaken than she should have been. She'd done everything she could to create a clear-cut boundary around herself. She'd chosen a table off to one side, far from the other guests. She'd worn the most neutral outfit she could imagine—loose top with a sports bra, jeans, and flat sandals—and she'd brought a book with her. She'd even been reading it. So where did men get their colossal arrogance—their conviction that no matter who a woman was, where she was, what she was wearing, or what she was doing, what she *really* wanted was male attention? She could still see the safari man. He was sitting at a distant table drinking alone. Fuck you, she said to him, go drown yourself in the pool.

Her waiter appeared, and she ordered the chicken and artichoke-heart salad. Did she want a glass of white wine? She was surprised at herself, but no, she didn't. And in the length of time it had taken her to order, the desert had switched from spectacular sunset to starry night— just that fast, like a magician's trick, *presto chango*! She should have brought a sweater. She'd been in a great mood, but now she wasn't.

The items on her worry list were fighting for her attention. She and Rob were obviously locked into a long-range battle over Devon, so she'd have to consult the Rottweiler, but there was nothing she could do about it now. She'd heard from the twins. They were in Hobart, wherever that was, Bryan's hometown apparently—they'd had to fly there—and Devon had actually answered her email. Yes, of course they were being careful not to get burnt, and they had *not* got burnt. Rob had called from some fancy-ass hotel near Disneyland, and she'd talked to Paige, and everything was fine there, too. She'd called Claire. Cameron had invited a few friends over the other night, but they'd all been nice kids, mostly gone by midnight, and there hadn't been a single fight— My god, that was Claire's working-class Brit yardstick for a successful teen party?—*not a single fight?* But the house was fine, yes yes yes, *everything* was fine, and all that was left was Karen—was *she* fine?

Meanwhile, hidden inside her BlackBerry, there were—not merely one but *four* naked selfies. Okay, all she had to do was delete them and no one would ever know. What would people think of her if they knew? That she was hopelessly vain? Or lonely? Sex starved? Pathetically insecure? But if she said that she'd taken them simply because, for once, she'd liked the way she looked, nobody would believe her, and then, in one of her intuitive jumps, she knew who they were for. Just as though she was doing an exercise in Gestalt Therapy, she addressed the girl she had been at fifteen. "Here. These are for you."

FIFTEEN. Grade ten, oh my god, that was close to *thirty fucking years ago*. Much of it was a shifting blur, but she did remember some of it so vividly that she might as well have filmed it. There, forever in her memory, was Patsy, just back from summer camp, waiting for her at the end of the Dundarave pier. The summer sun had turned her dark gold, and the dazzling light off the water was making her glow like she was lit from the inside. Maybe it was because Karen had missed her so much, but she remembered that moment as heart-stopping. She'd never in her life seen a girl as beautiful as Patsy Donlevy.

"I've done it," Patsy told her. "I'm a certified camp counselor." Next summer when she was sixteen, they would actually pay her—and Karen could remember fragments of what they'd talked about, all the usual camp memories, the food fights and the sneak-outs, and the magical nights around the campfire, and of course the night they'd tried to row to Bowen. Camp Kingcome was still going strong, Patsy said. Her campers had loved her; they'd cried when they had to say goodbye. It was so strange—Karen and Patsy had not been model campers. A few times they'd come close to being sent home. "We were bad girls for sure," Karen said. "I can't believe you're a Christian camp counselor."

"Well, I am and a damned good one too. Anything the little shits could dream up, we did worse, so I was always one jump ahead of them."

Talking, they'd walked to the pier at John Lawson. Patsy usually made a joke out of everything, but that day she'd been serious. "We're Anglicans and we don't push Jesus down their throats like at some camps. You know that. But the closest to God . . . You know that hymn about God holding you in the palm of his hand? Didn't it feel like that sometimes? At night around the campfire, or at the outdoor chapel? That's the closest to God I'd ever been."

"Yeah," Karen said, "me too," and she meant it.

IT WAS THE FIRST YEAR since they'd been eight when she and Patsy hadn't gone to camp together. Karen could have done the counselor training too, but she hadn't wanted to. She felt bad about that, but she'd had her own reasons for staying home. She'd spent the summer trying to worm her way into Gudrun Eklund's little clique.

As far back as grade eight, their class had been split into winners and losers, and Gudrun had always been a winner. She was a natural beauty and a natural blonde—as blonde as ice, as a matter of fact. By grade ten she'd matured into the pink-and-golden elegance of a young Swedish model and had scored the ultimate victory—she'd got herself a grade-twelve boyfriend. Karen had known better than to even try to talk to Gudrun, but Gudrun had approached her first. "James Wellman's interested in you." Oh my god, a grade-twelve, one of the cool boys, the captain of the soccer team! "He likes younger girls," Gudrun told her, "and he thinks you're just about the cutest thing he's ever seen."

Younger girls? Karen thought now. *Oh, really?* But at fifteen she'd been flattered down to her toenails, and if James Wellman was interested in Karen, that meant that Gudrun was interested in Karen.

"Who'd want to go out with James Wellman?" Patsy asked her. "He's just a beachboy jock." Patsy didn't think much of Gudrun and her little clique either. "Why would you want to hang out with them? They're mindless idiots. Why be in *any* clique? Just be yourself." That was great for Patsy to say—she was hanging out with the badass kids.

SANDY COVE, what a memory that was. The moon was shining on the ocean, Karen couldn't believe how bright. "God, it's beautiful," Patsy said.

Just like everybody else they'd come to check it out, to see if there really was a party. It was a tiny beach, but there must have been a hundred kids crammed onto it and more coming all the time. You don't have a beach party in October—that was crazy—but all week they'd been sweltering under a rerun of summer, and Karen had felt that collective craziness building up. Nobody knew whose idea it had been, but the word had gone around, kids saying, "Yeah, Sandy Cove on Friday night if it's not raining." Maybe whoever had started it thought it was a joke, but if it was, then the joke was on them. When a hundred kids show up, they *are* the party.

A lot of the kids had beer, and Karen could even see somebody passing a twenty-sixer around. Some kids had ghetto blasters, so on one end of the beach there was Loverboy and on the other Blondie, the music mixing in the middle. Wild. The kids were milling around, yelling at each other, the grades dissolving into each other. She felt what everybody else was feeling—fuck school.

Patsy led Karen into a knot of badass girls, older girls, totally chill. Patsy knew all of their names by now. "Pats," they called her. Their lipstick was so dark it looked black in the moonlight. One of them offered Patsy a bottle. She took a big drink and passed it to Karen. It was so sweet it made her teeth go fuzzy, but she felt the heat. Alcohol.

They kept on going down onto the wet sand because that's where the badass boys were. Big Mack McKenzie met them, and then he and Patsy walked right down to the edge of water. They might not have made it official yet, but they already looked like a couple. "The tide's going out," Patsy said.

"Awesome." He pulled a mickey out of his jacket and offered it to Patsy. She took a drink and handed it back to him. "Want a smash, Karen?" he asked her.

Karen knew better than to take a big drink of straight vodka. She wasn't that dumb. She did a tiny sip, and it burned like white-cold electricity right down her throat.

She looked around to check the scene, and there was James Wellman. She was surprised. She would have thought he'd be way too cool for something like this, but there he was with a pack of other grade twelve boys, standing there drinking cans of beer. Of course James was watching her. He was always watching her. She turned her back on him.

Big Mack passed the mickey again, and Patsy and Karen did another hit. Karen took a bigger hit this time, ablaze. She'd been buzzed before. They'd borrowed some of Patsy's mum's vodka one night, mixed it with ginger ale, and got pretty buzzed. Tonight she wanted to get totally buzzed.

"Whew," Patsy said, "look at the chop on the water." Then she grinned at Karen and whinnied.

Karen couldn't believe she'd done that. It was something they'd done when they were little kids. She whinnied back at her, and they took off running right along the edge where the waves were breaking. They were nine years old again. They'd never pretended they were ponies, no way. They were *wild horses running in the surf,* and they were doing it again, galloping and whinnying at each other. It felt wonderful. Patsy was way faster than Karen, but Karen caught up to her on the other side of the beach. Some grade eleven boys thought they were a riot. They were shoving beer at them. Karen hated beer, but she chugged some of it, and then they ran back, whinnying.

Big Mack thought it was a riot, too. "You girls are too fucking much." He pulled out the mickey again.

James was watching her. Karen always knew exactly where he was, just as he always knew exactly where she was. She was so sick of his shit—why didn't he just call her? She took a good big hit on the vodka, and it burned like a flashbulb. She was so sick of herself. The good girl, the nice girl, the straight-A girl, the little nothing girl—she wanted her gone, she wanted her dead.

She walked straight over to him. She did not smile. "James Wellman," she said, his whole name just like that, "want a smash?"

The other boys went "ooo!"—a boy-sound that meant *heavy!* Patsy and Mack were laughing. James took the mickey, did a hit, gave it back. His eyes were locked on Karen's. She turned her back on him and walked away. The clouds were rolling in fast to cover the moon.

PATSY AND KAREN AND MACK were right down at the edge of the water when the cops came. No way they could drive their cop cars down to the beach—they had to walk down the stairs the same as everybody else—and there was a motion moving down from where they were coming, ripples down through the crowd, kids going, "the cops the cops the cops."

It was dark now, but the cops had insanely bright flashlights. They didn't seem in a bad mood, just going, "Come on, kids. Party's over. Get off the beach. Go home."

One cop was kind of chuckling. "Well, if it isn't Big Mack Mackenzie," he said and shined his light right on Mack's face.

The minute Mack had seen the cop headed their way, he'd passed the mickey to Patsy, and she'd stepped off to one side. Now Mack spread his hands open, giving the cop a grin. Then, somehow, Patsy must have known what was going to happen next. She fired the mickey at Karen, and it wasn't that Karen was a great catcher, it was that Patsy was a great pitcher. It landed right smack on Karen's chest; her hands came together like a clap, and she had it. She was backing off when the flashlight hit Patsy—"You too, girl. Come here." Just like Big Mack, Patsy walked toward the cops with her hands spread open, and Karen was getting out of there, the mickey in her jacket.

Karen pushed through the kids to get to the stairs, and she saw that James was right behind her. He was all by himself. He'd left that pack of boys. She looked back at him and laughed. She took a hit on the mickey so he could see her doing it.

322

She was a lot smaller than he was, could snake through the kids better, so she made it up to Marine way ahead of him. Two buses were just sitting there on either side of Marine facing in opposite directions, the drivers yelling at each other, probably complaining about all these crazy kids, and there were three cop cars and more cops herding kids toward one bus or the other. She looked back and saw that James had just made it up to Marine. She made sure that he saw her; then she took off.

She didn't know where she was going, just looking for the dark. James was right behind her. She was giggling. She offered him the mickey, but when he reached for it, she snatched it back and took off again. He was the captain of the soccer team, so he caught her in nothing flat. He pinned her up against a tree, grabbed the mickey, took a drink, killed it, threw it away. Then he was kissing her. She could feel the whole full forceful weight of him on her, and she didn't exactly mind. She didn't know where they were. Behind somebody's house, she guessed. He had one of his legs between hers, and he was grinding his hips into her. It was the first time she'd ever felt a boy hard like that. It was inside his pants, but it was still hard.

Some part of her mind said, "Karen, you've got to get on that bus."

She pushed James away. If he hadn't let her do it, she wouldn't have been strong enough, and she could feel that. "The bus! I've got to get on that bus."

"I've got a car. I'll take you home."

She had got ahead of herself somehow, but now she was catching up—this was fun, this was exciting, but now she wanted it to stop. Besides, she couldn't let him take her home—she was way past her curfew—and she couldn't let him take her to Patsy's either. That wouldn't look good. "The bus!" she yelled at him. She squirmed free.

She had just started to run across Marine when a cop grabbed her. "Wait, wait, just wait." There were a whole bunch of kids. When the cops were sure it was safe, they let them cross. She looked back, and James was standing on the other side of Marine, staring after her.

The bus driver was so disgusted—all these laughing screaming out-of-control kids piling onto his bus. "Move to the back. Move right on to the back." Karen moved right on to the back and fell over into a seat by a window. She imagined what they must look like from the outside—the magic blue bus that she saw sometimes, drifting through the night, lit up yellow, bright against the blue night, packed full of crazy kids, so mysterious, and now she was on it.

By the time they got to Horseshoe Bay, there was nobody left but her. She stood up and, whew, was she ever buzzed! Holding onto the seats, she made her way to the front, saying, "Thank you," politely, and then she was on the sidewalk way too fast. Just walk. Slowly and carefully. With every step her whole body rattled.

The clouds had thickened up, and nothing was left of the moon but a big pale smear. It was dark and cold, *she* was dark and cold, her feet wet, her runners mucky with sand. All she wanted was to fall over onto Patsy's bed. She got to her house and tried the back door. It was locked. She tried the front door. It was locked, too. I'm an idiot, she thought. She wasn't just buzzed; she was fucking drunk.

There was a light on in Patsy's bedroom window. How had she got there ahead of her? Somebody must have given her a ride. Karen did that trick they'd done for years, found a pebble and bounced it off the window, but nothing happened. If Patsy had gone home with Big Mack, Karen was screwed. But no, that wouldn't happen. Patsy knew that Karen was coming back to her place.

Somebody touched Karen's shoulder, and she jumped about a foot and let out a little scream. It was Patsy. Karen was so stunned she couldn't do anything. "Is she up there?" Patsy said.

"Who?"

"Patsy." She pointed up at her bedroom window.

Karen started to giggle.

"Did you try throwing a pebble or anything?" Patsy asked her, perfectly straight.

"Yeah, I tried that."

"Let's try it again." She bounced a pebble off the window, and they waited. "Maybe she's asleep," Patsy said.

"What are we going to do then?"

"I don't know. I guess we're screwed."

Then they fell into each other's arms, laughing like idiots.

20.

Karen had written the heading in big block grade-school letters. She'd meant it to be funny, but who was she trying to amuse?

Zopiclone had put her to sleep, but she'd only slept for a few hours. Lying in bed wondering what to do with herself, she'd decided to keep a journal again. Her first journal, begun when she'd been twelve, had been a standard drugstore item for kids—lined paper in a cheap spiral-wire binding—so she'd never used anything else. She'd kept those spiral-wire journals religiously until she'd married Ian, and she'd started a new one each time she'd gone into therapy. The last one must have been in 2002, and here she was, starting again. "I feel like warmed over dog shit," she wrote. So there!

She'd driven over to one of the malls to buy the notebook and then had pissed away several hours doing shopping therapy. *Just looking*, she'd told herself, but of course she had to buy something. Kohl's was just a big department store much like the Bay, but there were plenty of fun little high-end specialty shops tucked into the corners of the mall. She'd bought skinny jeans that were too tight for someone her age, but what the hell—and then leggings that were disguised to look like skinny jeans, and they were even tighter—and then a pair of cowboy boots. Why? Don't ask.

Disgusted with herself, she'd come back, forced herself through the training circuit in the gym, and finished off her punishment with forty-five minutes on the treadmill. Now she was collapsed onto a patio chair, drinking San Pellegrino with lime in it, and her body felt just about as useful as mud. Well, at least she'd probably be able to sleep tonight. Should she write about any of this? The journal didn't seem like such a good idea now.

The cowboy boots. The owner of the shop—a sweet-talking ruggedly attractive southern gentleman in his fifties—had played her like a fiddle. He'd laughed with her over the pink boots and turquoise ones with stars. Yeah, he had to keep those tacky things in stock for the kids, he'd said, for the silly teenagers who wanted to be cartoon cowgirls, but what she should see—oh, just to admire them because she might never get the chance again— Canada was a lovely country, by the way, he visited there often, did a little trout fishing— but what she should see were these hand-crafted boots because she would never again find such superb workmanship at such reasonable prices, many of them one of a kind, made by artisans of the old school. "Oh, my," Karen had said, "they certainly are beautiful" and they were, too. The ones that seemed to have her name on them were a gorgeous dark blue—real indigo, he'd said—try them on. Not what she'd expected—snug but not stiff or recalcitrant, exquisitely supple, and exactly her size, how lucky. A lifetime investment, he'd said. Year after year they would only get better, fit themselves perfectly to her feet, acquire *a rich patina*. No, you should never use shoe polish. You should use this specially compounded oil, massage it lovingly into the leather until it glowed. Ah, the blue. She'd never seen anything like it. She had just dumped twelve hundred US dollars into a pair of midnight-blue cowboy boots.

Karen liked to think of herself as progressive, one of the few socially aware left-leaning people in all of the entire benighted Tory miasma of West Vancouver. She was supposed to be engagé. Oh. Dear. God. The real-life Karen obviously didn't give a flying fuck. "It seems like a lot, but it isn't infinite," her brother told her from time to time—Steven, the banker. Karen was slowly but steadily eroding her capital. "As outlandish as the idea might seem to you, Karen, it *is* possible for you to spend it all." Yeah, but who saw the meltdown coming? Not you, Steven. But another meltdown? An even bigger one? It could kill her. Okay, she could always sell the house—if there were buyers for high-end properties—but then, if she wanted to switch into long-term projections, there was the problem of the planet getting hotter. If it got hot enough, it wouldn't matter how much money she had. It wouldn't matter how much money anybody had.

Once a year, as tax time approached, Karen sat down at her desk and wrote cheques. The recipients varied from year to year, but the stable core of them were the NDP, the Green Party of Canada, the Council of Canadians, Greenpeace, and the Sierra Club. They all sent her tax receipts, and she gave them to her accountant. Big fucking deal.

KAREN HAD QUIT SMOKING when she'd been working at M&H. It had taken her four or five tries, but eventually she'd succeeded, and she hadn't smoked since. She never missed it, never thought about it, and absolutely loathed the smell of cigarettes. Except that every few years something went wrong—it didn't have to be a major event by any means, just something truly nasty—and then her dead habit woke up and bit her. This bloody resort was not designed for walking, but you could walk if you wanted to, and that's what she was doing—past villa after villa in the starry night. All she needed was one cigarette. Surely there had to be some smokers left in the world, and if they were smoking, they had to be *outside*—and yes, there were people on their patios, but none of them were smoking. Fuck the fucking desert, she didn't want a cigarette anyway. It would just make her dizzy and sick.

"I don't understand it!" she'd once cried out to Helen during an absolute disaster of a therapy session, and Helen had said, "No, it's not that *you don't understand it*—it's that *you don't like it.*"

Once Karen was out of high school, all she wanted was to forget it, but it was something she couldn't ever forget—it used to come up with Helen in therapy all the time—and she'd tried to tell Jamie about it, but Jamie wasn't interested in the miserable things that had happened to Mum back in the dark ages. Even after thirty years, she could still reproduce that endlessly repeating cycle of crap that ran through her mind.

Stupid little girl, she called herself. She was afraid of everything. She couldn't believe how mean the kids were in high school. Everybody picked on everybody, and that's just the way it was. It all seemed so pointless. She'd got Gudrun to talk to her, big fucking deal. She'd got James Wellman to make out with her, but what if it was all a joke? "Ha ha, surprise! The laugh's on you, you stupid little girl. You didn't think I could actually like you, did you?" Probably everybody at school knew that there was something wrong with her. She'd got her period a whole year later than everybody else so maybe there *was* something wrong with her, she meant *physically*, something that affected her brain. Maybe she could never grow up or do anything right. She couldn't stand high school—everybody else could stand high school—she was a fucked up stupid little kid, flat as a breadboard, no way James Wellman could possibly like her, and probably nobody else liked her either. Nobody would ever ask her out. She was even worse than Jen, and Jen was hopeless. She would be stuck with Jen at the losers' table forever.

Then she'd made it even worse. You don't mess around with a grade twelve boy when he's been dating a grade twelve girl. Pushed, shoved, tripped, whispered about, laughed at, her books ripped out of her hands and thrown down the hall, everything in her locker pulled out and dumped, and she couldn't report any of it, because if you rat to a teacher, your life's over. She simply had to get into Gudrun's clique or she was going to die. Then there was that big drunken party Dave Cogan threw just before Christmas when his parents were out of town. James Wellman had mysteriously enticed Karen into one of the bedrooms, and just as mysteriously he'd talked her into giving him a blow job. The thought of it still made her skin crawl. A whole bunch of kids had seen them go into the bedroom together, and a whole bunch of kids had seen them come out. Nauseated, Karen had spit that slimy phlegmy blob onto the floor, and they'd just walked out and left it there by the side of the bed. Oh. Dear. God.

On Monday morning Karen had told her mum that her cramps were really bad and she should probably stay home, but in her mum's mind it was perfectly clear—Karen had violated her curfew on Saturday night, then had moped around all day Sunday with a hangover, and now she was trying this ridiculous number. "Don't give me that crap," Mum said.

Karen had been calling Patsy all weekend, but Patsy's mum had told her that she was staying over on Bowen with a girlfriend, and that meant that she'd been with Big Mack. Karen always met Patsy outside the school entrance that faced down the hill, but she wasn't there on Monday. Karen asked the other kids, but nobody had seen her.

Their lockers had grillwork on them, like slots, and Karen had never been able to figure out what it was for—like if you had some little animal living inside and you needed air for it to breathe? And somebody had folded up a piece of paper and shoved it through the grill on her locker. She took out the paper, opened it up, and her heart stopped. Somebody with a black Sharpie had written one word across that whole piece of paper—SKANK.

She went through the morning in a daze. She couldn't concentrate on anything. The pains in her stomach were really bad. The more she thought about it, the worse it got. How could she have been such an idiot? When the grade twelve girls caught up to her, they were going to fucking kill her.

It got to be noon, and the hall was full of kids, and two older boys walked past her. She didn't know them, didn't even know what grade they were in. As one of them got next to her, he went, "Skank!" He'd made it sound like a cough, and the other boy laughed. She knew that she should never react to shit like that, but she couldn't help it. She stopped dead. All it took was one person to put a piece of paper in your locker, but if some boys who didn't even know you were in on it, then it was all over the school.

The last thing she wanted to do was go in the caf. She poked her nose in there, but there was still no sign of Patsy. She dawdled around out in the hall thinking about how every day from now on was going to be hell. She didn't think she was strong enough to take it, but what choice did she have? She knew that her dad couldn't afford to send her to private school.

Then she thought that she might as well get it over with, so she went inside and stood in line. The smell of the food was making her sick. She looked up, and there was James Wellman rushing over to her with a big stupid grin on his face. "Karen," he said, "where have you been?"

The whole caf went spinny, almost like it wasn't *her* getting spinny, it was *the room* getting spinny. Right there in front of everybody James gave her a big hug. An insane giggle was coming out of her mouth. She sounded totally demented.

He paid for her lunch, and he picked up her tray. She followed him like a puppy. They were on their way up to the second level where the grade twelves hung out. The grade twelve girls looked death at her, but they couldn't do anything because she was with James. He put her tray down next to his. She sat down next to him, and she still couldn't believe it. Everything was going to be okay. She was not some disgusting little grade ten skank who'd sucked off James Wellman at a party. She was James Wellman's girlfriend.

She tried to eat something, but she wasn't sure she'd ever be able to eat anything ever again. She was where she'd always wanted to be, up with the cool kids looking down on everybody. She should feel great, but she didn't. She was sitting next to James Wellman, and everybody could see them sitting together, and suddenly she hated him. She absolutely hated him. She was thinking about yesterday. Sunday. All fucking day Sunday, and he hadn't called her.

Down on the lower level Jen was sitting at the loser table where Karen usually sat. Patsy should have been there, too, but if she wasn't there by now, she was probably still with Big Mack on Bowen, blowing off school. So Jen was there by herself, and nobody wanted to be the first person to sit with her, not even the hopeless dork boys who usually sat with them. The dorks walked over toward the table, and when they saw that there was nobody there but Jen, they kept on going. It was like Jen had leprosy.

Of course Gudrun and the other girls up on the second level were watching. Gudrun nudged Karen like, "Isn't this a riot?" Every time somebody else walked toward Jen, and looked around, and checked things out, and decided not to sit with her, it got even funnier.

Gudrun wanted to make sure that Jen knew they were watching, that *everybody* was watching, so she took a French fry and rolled it up into a little ball and flipped it down onto Jen's table. Jen saw it but didn't quite get it, so Gudrun did another fry. Jen looked up. Her whole moon face went beet red. Then she just stared down at her tray. That was just too good, so the grade twelve girls all started firing fries down on her.

The boys didn't get what was going on, but if the girls were firing fries down on Jen, they were going to do it, too. Pretty soon there was all this food sailing through the air, fries and baby carrots and even scrunched up bits of burger, like it was totally raining food, and right there in the caf with everybody watching her, Jen started to cry.

It made Karen sick. She was thinking, come on, Jen, isn't it time to run to the girls' room? Just get out of here! But Jen dropped her head and started going boo-hoo-hoo, and the kids couldn't throw food fast enough. All except Karen. Gudrun saw that she wasn't throwing anything and gave her this evil look, like, *What's with you?*

Oh my god, then here was Patsy with her tray. She must have just got to school. She saw what was happening to Jen. She put her tray down, walked directly over toward the grade twelves, and looked up. She was furious. "What do you guys think you're doing? That's the meanest thing I ever saw."

Come on, Patsy, Karen thought, don't do this to me. Then she saw Patsy register that, yeah, it really *was* Karen up there, sitting with the grade twelves. Patsy's face changed.

Nobody said anything, but nobody was throwing any more food either. In a reasonable voice Patsy said, "What's with you guys? She never did anything to you."

James went, "Did you hear somebody say something?"

Gudrun went, "No, I don't think so. Nope. Nobody said anything."

Gudrun was still staring straight at Karen. "Isn't it a friend of yours?" she said.

Karen's heart was beating so hard she could swear to god it was going to come right out of her chest. Her mind was racing to find something to say, but then she'd already said it—"Come on, guys, give her a break. She's a camp counselor."

That one got a big laugh, and the laugh gave Karen an awful ugly kick of pleasure. Before she could think about it, she said, "It's a *Christian* camp." That one got an even bigger laugh.

Patsy looked like Karen had thrown something in her face. She straightened up tall, and she turned and walked away. Karen could see by the way Patsy walked how hurt she was. She didn't look back.

21.

DEAR ERICA,

I have started this email a dozen times and deleted it. I'm going to let this one stand and send it no matter what. I am writing to you from Palm Desert, of all strange places. The twins are in Australia with Bryan Lynas, Paige is at Disneyland with her father, Cam is at home with Claire watching over him, and I'm here alone. It seems forever since I've been alone. It has given me a chance to think.

I must have seemed distant to you the last time we met, and I want to apologize for that. As we headed into Christmas, I felt scattered in a million directions, but it was more than Christmas preparations. Our trip to Medicine Hat deeply disturbed me. What you experienced was so traumatic that I couldn't deal with it. In therapy we were told that we should not get "confluent" with others while they are working. That means that we should not share their emotions so deeply that our own emotions are activated. The ideal is to be a "fair witness." That means to be fully engaged but detached. A fair witness should be someone you can trust, a solid ground, a landing point, and I'm sorry that I could not be that for you as much as I wanted to be. I hope that you did feel at least some sense of closure, or maybe the beginning of it. I know that it must take a long time to heal from trauma as severe as yours.

The last thing I want to do is create some impossible burden for you like all of those condolences you never answered. You don't have to answer this email, but please at least send me a line or call me so that we can get together. You are very important to me, and I don't want you to vanish from my life.

Coming back to this after an hour – I thought I was finished, but I'm not. I don't want this just to be "me me me," but I do want to tell you what I have been thinking and feeling. I didn't want to look at Annalise's death because then I would have to look at my own, or my children's, and I couldn't do it. And then I have to admit that you scared the shit out of me. If I am misreading you here, please tell me, but I felt that you reproduced your sister's car so you could kill yourself in it. That was just too big, too dark, too crazy, and I couldn't deal with it. All I wanted to do was run away, go home, lose myself in Christmas, and forget all about it.

I was in therapy off and on for years, and one of the things I learned is that we hardly ever know the real reasons why we do anything. We are like sleepwalkers, or like people walking around under the influence of a post-hypnotic suggestion, and we can come up with all manner of clever excuses and rationalizations for what we are doing, but as to gaining any insight into what's really going on, that is excruciatingly difficult. I didn't know what I was doing with you while you were living with us, and I still don't know, but only now am I beginning to see the size of it. Huge.

What were you doing in my driveway? I know you gave me an answer to that, but it wasn't the real answer. What scared me so much in Medicine Hat, what I was thinking about on the two planes back to Vancouver Let me start over. It was a wrong way to put that question. I kept asking myself, "Why did she pick me?" Now I realize how wrong that was. You didn't pick me, you picked my twins. I was worried that you had some sinister purpose, that you were some kind of a stalker, but then I thought, okay, what did she actually do while she was living with us? She was kind and helpful. She answered all of the twins' endless questions. She was a great role model for Jamie with her gender issues. And then I knew why you ended up in our driveway the day you tried to kill yourself. It was Jamie's suicide threat. On some level you must have wanted to protect her. Does that feel even remotely true or am I off in outer space?

I don't know what I did for you while you were with us. You kept thanking me, telling me how kind I was, but I didn't feel all that kind, and I didn't need to be thanked. I was fascinated by you. You were giving me something important, something that had been missing from my life. You were like the BFF girls have when they're kids. You were like my friend Patsy. I felt like I was being offered a choice again. I'm trying to talk about that mysterious thing we know but don't often see and have no way to explain.

Erica, I am afraid for you. Please do not hurt yourself. You are so important to me. Please, when we get back to Vancouver, can we get together and begin again? I miss you every day.

All best,
Karen

Hi Erica, today was like the most amazing day, Bryan took us to Shipstern Bluff & it was awesome!!! He did not tell us where we were going, we just got in the car & we drove forever & then we got out & he is like we are going for a little walk watch out for snakes, every snake u see in Tassie is poisonous! we are like what do we do if we see one??!! he is like we will pursuade it to go away, we did not see a snake.

Jamie says it was just like a hiking trail in BC Xcept some of the trees & stuff looks way different & we saw parrots! & we saw a eshinida, it is like the weirdest thing u ever saw all covered in spikes with a skinny little nose, Bryan says they lay eggs, we would of walked right by it Xcept Bryan saw it, we looked at it for a long time!

little walk, ha ha, it took like two hours, i was not a fan, Bryan kept making me go first cuz i am the slowest, finally we get to Shipstern Bluff, it is one of the most dangerous waves in the world, no way we could surf it, he just wanted us to see it. We got to these high cliffs over the ocean & ate our lunch, OMG we were starving & the wave does not look to bad from up there but we climbed down the cliff to the beach, it was very steep & Bryans like just sit here & tell me what u see

the wave is humungous, unbelievable, like taller than a house & it makes this huge gigantic roar & goes slamming up against the big huge chunk of rock like a cliff. the wave does not fall straight down but comes down in chunks. Bryans like the water is cold enuff to freeze a brass monkey & it has great white sharks in it & if u screw up u are a million miles from anywhere. when M & A were babies he heard that some bloke had surfed it so he came out here, like he carried his board all the way here, and he sat & watched it & hes like fuckin hell & he picked up his board and went back to Hobart.

Bryans like this is good for language arts, your teacher said u should learn something, okay NOW YOU ARE GOING TO LEARN SOMETHING, he made us take notes!!! Hes like surfing should not be to prove something, the old Hawayans who invented surfing were not trying to prove anything, they became one with the wave & that is why they could go out for miles threw all these little reefs and islands. You can not conquer the wave, Ossie's are the worst for that, they are going to conquer it, beat it, overcome it, slice it dice it cut it up, to prove how shit hot they are but that is not the right way, u have got to watch the wave until u are the wave & then u have nothing to prove & then u can ride it.

Bryan's like i want u to know where u are, write this down. North is Sydney where we came from. South is Antartica. if u go east for fifteen hundred miles across the Tasman Sea u will hit New Zealand & then u will hit nothing till u get to Chilli in South America! If u go do west u will pass underneath Africa and keep on going till u bump into Argentina! That is why the western winds blowing into Tasmania are the purest ever recorded on earth. They have got nothing in them but salt! u are at total nowhere at the bottom of the world, write that down.

The rich ppl are burning up the world, u got that? They are making it hotter & hotter with carbon & many species will die, including us. The problem is ignorance, write that down. Out of ignorance arises fear and greed. They are like hungry ghosts, whatever they have it is never enuff. They think they own the wave. Nobody owns the wave. We have got to become one with the wave like the old Hawayans. Here in Tassie the bastards wanted to dam the Franklin. The green movement started here in Tassie. Thousands of people were ready to get arrested. We stopped them & they did not dam the Franklin. When u get home u google it & write it into language arts. Now the whole world is Tasmania cuz the whole world is nowhere at the total bottom. U tell ur teacher i said that.

This is all the notes that Bryan made us take. It took us 4ever to write it down!! but we are happy cuz now we have all this stuff for language arts, we think this is all we need for language arts

we are so tired goodnight
Jamie & Dev

Hi Erica

Guess what, yesterday Jamie told every body what they did to her at inglewood, like she never told ANY BODY before except me, NOT EVEN MOM, she always said she could never tell ANY BODY BUT ME!!! but she told Bryan & Morgan & Avi. She says to tell u she does not know why she did it, ppl always say it will make u feel better if u talk about it but she did not ever want to talk about it, shes like woa why am i doing this? This is what she said. u know how Jamie is a tomboy like u, she was always good at sports, she was an ace soccer player, all the soccer moms were like OMG Jamie is so good, she is the best, she thot she was pretty good, she was happy, then she went to inglewood and there was this bunch of girls like always giving her shit. some body took a picture of her after a soccer game, she played real hard, it was raining, she was a mess. some body put that picture on facebook & wrote JAMIE HAS A PENIS.

they thought it was a big joke. it went all over facebook, people kept posting on her wall, they would post a picture of a penis or the definition of penis & like that, somebody put a picture of a penis in her locker, she would open up a book & find a picture of a penis in it. It was not just the girls, the boys did it too, they were the worst, Jamie would walk down the hall & the boys would wait till she got by and then theyd be like PENIS! she got horrible pains in her stomach, she did not want to go to school, they put gross shit on facebook, some grade 10 boys tried to get with her, she could not go on, evey body was making fun of her, she was going to commit suicide, she googled it, she was going to hang herself, she thot that was the best way, its the same thing i thot, i bet i even read the same google, see we told u we were identical!

Hi, this is me Jamie. when i run into those dooshbags from inglewood like in the mall they are like oh hi Jamie THEY DO NOT EVEN REMEMBER WHAT THEY DID TO ME!!! i hate them.

Hi, this is me Devon again. u told us at the university every thing is confidential please make this confidential, Jamie does not want to put this in language arts, she does not want any body to read it but u.

Your friends,
Jamie and Devon

336

Hi Erica

this is Jamie i want to tel u wat hapend 2day. evrybdy is aslep even Devon is aslep so he can not tipe 4 me but i want to tel u Bcuz this is th most importnt thin that evr hapnd to me in my life & i want to rite it down. u no i have a lerning disbilty plese dont laf at my speling, I am tri ing reely hard, i want to rite this down Plse save it for me & plese fix it for me. it wold be relly nice if u cood fix it for me thanx

u no yestrday i told evbody wat happnd to me at inglwod, so 2day we went to a good beech, it was rite arond hobrt, & it was reel nice wen we got ther & we all cot some gt waves evn Devon cot sum ridz & we wer havin a gt tim but th wethr in Tssie is reel changabl, like 1 min it was reel cam and suny but then it got narly all of a suddn, like instat, & Bryans like its gettin narly lets pack it in thats enuf for u kids, but i thot i cod cach 1 more, i went ot anywy, Bryans like yllin at me Jamie u arshol

I dont know wat I was thinkin, it was reel retrdd, i see ths fuckin wave & im like OMG im gonna get cot insid, im gonna get killd 4 sur, & ths big wave fals on me, it wuz as big as a howse!!!!

th wave comes down & kix the shit out of me. i do not no whiche way is up like i can not evn figur out wher to try to get to. i can not tell u how scared i was i thot i was goin to die!!! i even bownsed off th botom of the see

i did not no wer i was but i got bruses all over me i can see them now i am sor all over but im like just thron evrywere & holdin my breth. i did what Bryan told me wen i saw i was going to wip out i took the bigest breth in th world, im like OMG my bord, wer is my bord, I do not want 2B hit by my bord

im bownsing off the botom of the see & i feel som bodys hands on me!!! it is Morgan. th minut she saw me go out she dove rite in after me & she got to me evn wen i was all the way down at the botom. i feel her hands on me & it makes me feel so good & then we come up & im so scared i can not tell u

Morgans like dont fite me Jamie were in the rip

& then Bryans rite there 2 i do not fite them & we have to go sidewaz cuz were in the rip & they get me back up on the beech & im like OMG

337

OMG that was th most horrble thing ever i can not tell u how horrrble it was!!!

we get up on th beech & im getting my breth back & we jist sit ther & watche the waves. the skys like gettin reel dark the wind like crazy the waves r big as howses, but thn we sit ther & it changes agan, th wind stops & im like hay th waves r brakin cleen

Bryans like ya there brakin cleen & i dont no wy but im like i can do this. hes like don't be a fool & im like no no i meen i can do this

i dont know wy i thot i could do this. im like i wont leev this beech i refuse to leev this beech i will stay here all nite but i will not leev this beech

hes lafing at me hes like ur reelly crazy uve only been surfing a week & thn he looks at me & he nos i can do it

Bryans like ok but i will not take u out 2 far. im like i dont want to go out 2 far. i just want to do this. so we get on owr bords & start padling out. u can heer the see so freekin lowd OMG the waves r reelly big & im like wy am i doing this? i will B killed 4 sure

were out there lookin back at th beech like a millon miles. Bryans like yellin at me, ther is no time so i gotta tell u fast. some ppl go there hole lives & do not no this. u think this is all reel but it is not it is all mind. the see is mind the sky is mind the bord ur on is mind & u think ur a person but ur not ur mind

im like ya whatevr why r u teling me this but then im like

& im like wy did not any body tell me this B4

Bryans like u gotta do what i tell u. when i tell u to go u got to go do not hesitat & im jist watchin it

hes like theres ur wave girl & i do not hesitat

u know whats weerd? i turn th bord rite & i stand rite up.

i can not stop thnking abot this. i dont no how lots of ppl do thins they dont reely want to & thats wy they fuck up. or they dont Bleev they can do thins so they fuck up. do u no what i meen?

i turn th bord rite & i stand rite up

i can feel th see under my feet its like a car on a bumpy road & i am movin so fast

anothr weerd thing i am not scared not even 1 little bit i am riding

338

th wave & i cannot fuck up it is so wondrful i can not tell u. M & A & Devon r all yelling for me go Jamie go u can do it & i ride it all the way in

then Bryan rides his wave in he wipes out at th end but not 2 bad & he dos not care he is lafing he gets up on the beech & he is so glad he picks me up & swins me arond & hes like Jamie u can tell those fuckin west van pussees theres nothin they can do to u. uve surfed the waves in Tasmania!!! This is the hapiest day of my life!!!!

Ur frend 4evr Jamie

FOUR

22.

WAS THAT THE door knocker or the rain? Karen was alone in the house. Maybe she'd heard a car engine, too, but it was hard to tell with the rain as talkative as it was tonight. Oh fuck, now what? She'd already planned her evening—a quick omelette and a slow glass of wine and then to bed with a pot of tea and a good book. Her cure for melancholy. It had been over a month by now, so it was obvious that Erica was not going to answer her email. Why was she having so much trouble coming to terms with that?

Listening, she heard the unmistakable chime of the doorbell. She had to see who it was—it could be something about her kids. She closed her laptop, hurried downstairs. Bryan Lynas was on the other side of the door, his yellow slicker beaded with water, a plastic-wrapped bundle cradled in his arm—tulips. Seeing him there was so unexpected that she didn't know what to do next. "Oh, my goodness, are these for me?"

"Yeah," he said, "Safeway's finest."

"Thank you so much," she said automatically. "What a nice surprise."

She must have clicked into a default mode that was like an old-school etiquette manual. "Please come in. Can you stay for a minute?"

"Maybe this is a bad time?"

"No, no, not at all."

He hesitated, giving her a slow careful look that she read as a check to see if she meant what she was saying. Then he slid out of his slicker and shook off the rain.

She felt absurdly shy. "Here, let me take that. Would you like a cup of tea? Or maybe a beer?"

"I'm right. Unless you're having something." He seemed tentative, grave, even cautious. He didn't seem like himself at all.

He knelt and began to unlace his work boots, a newish pair with some shine still left on them. "Good heavens, Bryan, you can leave your shoes on."

"Aw, no. Your floor's shiny clean. You could eat off it."

She hung his slicker in the hall closet. He followed her through the living room and into the kitchen. He was remarkably quiet for such a big man, and the rattle of the rain masked everything.

"Nasty night," she said, not really meaning it—actually liking it because it matched her mood. The first time she'd met him, it had been a nasty night, too. Was this one of those synchronicities Helen liked to talk about? She could feel a flickering connection, not quite a déjà vu but something like it—an enigmatic trail leading away into the rain.

March was better than November. They were through the worst of the year. She should turn on some table lamps, make things warm and welcoming, but she liked the light coming through the windows—tarnished silver—and didn't want to dilute it with tungsten yellow. Daylight savings had kicked in over the weekend, so that cool light would be hanging around for a while.

She snipped the plastic off the bouquet, clipped the stems, and settled the tulips into Grandmother McConnell's best cut-crystal vase. The window light was making the colours blaze—pale yellow, blood orange, scarlet. Then she felt a cold muddy contraction at the top of her stomach. She must have left her common-sense mind at the door. How had she let this happen? She was alone in her rain-quiet house with a man she didn't know very well at all. That was how women got themselves into serious trouble. It happened all the time.

She looked directly into his eyes, saw him looking back at her. This was nothing like the way he'd looked at her at his party—as though she was a chocolate éclair and he could eat her up in five gulps. He was standing well back from her. All she could see was a clear steady regard. Even with her psychic antennae fully extended, she couldn't find anything sinister about him. Of course she was safe. She'd trusted her children with him, hadn't she?

"It's that time of day," he was saying, "when I get to feeling a little peckish. Reckoned you might be feeling the same way, too."

"I might be. Is that a dinner invitation?"

"Yeah," smiling, "I reckon it is."

She wouldn't have thought that he was a man to wear scent, but she was picking up a crinkle of lime. He'd shaved recently, brushed his thick hair, put on clean jeans and a newish plaid shirt. She recognized one of the authentic Scots tartans—greenish yellows, orangish reds, and a deep mumbly green, oh, which tartan was it?—her mum would know in a flash. It matched his colouring. She forgot from time to time how ginger he was, how astonishingly freckled. His eyes matched the silver light. She'd always known that he was interested in her. It might have taken him a ridiculously long time to get here, but here he was. "Sure," she said. "Okay. Did you have any—?"

"Anywhere you like. You got a favourite place?"

"No. No favourite place."

Was it accidental that she was kid-free? No, of course it wasn't. Paige was at Lauren's, and the twins were with *his* twins at their mum's. Nicely done, she thought, I have been set up. "You've got to give me a minute to change," she said.

"Aw, you're right the way you are."

"No, not really."

All the things she'd thought about him—a macho Aussie asshole, a grown-up bad-boy brat, a manipulator, con artist, maybe even something of a crook—none of that mattered and maybe none of it was true anyway. He annoyed her, and she had always liked him. Then, in one of her intuitive flashes, she saw how he could bring all of himself to bear in a way that most people couldn't. Did she want all of his attention focused on her? "Bryan?" she said. "Get me out of West Van."

"You know, that's exactly what I was planning to do."

IT HAD BEEN YEARS since Karen had sat in the passenger's seat of a truck—not an SUV but an honest-to-god working man's *truck*. With the windshield wipers blapping steadily away, he was shooting them east on the Upper Levels. In her current incarnation as Mum the Chauffeur she didn't trust anybody's driving but her own, but she would make an exception for Bryan. His driving was more than assured, it seemed like second nature. She could relax into it. "You get much rain at home?"

"Depends on where you are. Not like this. Hobart's in the rain shadow so it's pretty dry. The east coast gets some gnarly weather off the Tasman Sea."

She was still in etiquette-manual mode. The twins and their trip to Australia was a safe topic. "You sure made a hit with them. They put a map of Australia up on the wall in Twin Central."

He laughed. "Did they now? It was great having them along. They're great kids."

Looking for a container to hold this strange night, she had decided to call it *going out on a date*. The last time she'd been out on a date had been with Drew when he'd still been courting her, but dates with him had been predictable, pleasant enough but "mature" in the worst sense of the word. This was different. She had wanted an escape from her miserable soggy mood, and this was it—a girlish back-in-high-school feeling, butterflies in the stomach. She didn't know how things were going to turn out, didn't even know where they were going—she'd thought maybe North Van, but no, he blew right on by the Lonsdale exit.

He was talking about Jamie. "I was just like her. If you sat me down and tried to *tell* me something, you might as well be speaking Bulgarian. Anything I ever learned, I learned by doing. She thinks with her body."

That had never occurred to her, but the minute he said it, she knew it was true.

"She's having a rough time now, but she's going to make a great adult."

"I hope so. I gather she took to surfing?"

"Took to it? Sweet Jesus, nobody learns as fast as she did. It's like she was born on a surfboard."

It was raining harder now, and they were crossing the Second Narrows. She was still worrying about what she looked like. She'd left him in her living room far too long while she'd put herself together. Something had told her that the little black dress and the Louboutins had created a magic she could only use once. So? Something fun. How about the skinny jeans she'd bought on impulse in Palm Desert? They might be a touch too young for her, but they did contrast perfectly with the midnight-blue cowboy boots. Add a nice top and a touch of makeup and you're there. Now she was thinking that she would have been more comfortable in lulus—but being comfortable wasn't the point, was it?

Bryan had taken the Hastings Street exit and was shooting them south into the darkest reaches of East Van, an area that Karen didn't know at all. *Inquire about his mum,* the etiquette manual told her.

"Tough old bird. Fooled the doctors so far. Responding well to the chemo. They're not saying she's beat it, no way, but they reckon she's got another six months to a year. Just glad my girls got a chance to know her."

Breast cancer, full stop. A horrific disease, it had snuffed Helen, her wizard of a therapist, had taken her at seventy, far too young for anybody to die. Karen should probably get herself checked more often than she did, but she hated tests and hospitals, hated doctors, hated *her* doctor, actually, the condescending asshole. But she didn't want to think about any of that tonight.

Bryan had driven them so far south that the land had begun to get flat. He turned onto a broad blank street, slowed down to tourist speed, and drifted past a weedy vacant lot with a mesh fence collapsing around it, then past Wang's Heating and Plumbing, Aardwolf Auto Parts, and a boarded-up brick building that seemed to have only one shop left in it, the Black Medallion Tattoo Emporium. He pulled over and parked. This couldn't possibly be where they were going, could it? She heard the door to the passenger's side open, saw that he was offering his hand like a gentleman of the old school. Like a well-schooled lady she allowed herself to be assisted down to the sidewalk.

He didn't say a word. Wherever they were going, he obviously wanted to surprise her. She hated feeling this clueless, but another part of herself was saying, "Isn't this what you wanted?" The daylight had faded away sometime ago, and a single streetlight was not doing much. No one should be out and about at night in a desolate spot like this, but she saw half a dozen hooded figures obscured by shadows and rain. They were just standing on the sidewalk, smoking, and her mind said, *Oh my god, a street gang.* The way Bryan was leading her, they were going to pass directly in front of them. She was actually frightened, but then one of them said, "Hey, Bryan, what's up?"

No! Did he really know everybody in the universe? "Going for a bite," he said. "Who's spinning tonight?"

"Inoperable."

Now that she was close to them, Karen could see that they were just kids in hoodies, some of them not much older than Cameron, at least half of them girls. "He any good?" Bryan asked, and one of the girls answered with a slight smile, "Sick."

"Yeah," he said, laughing, and led her across the street toward another brick building, this one heavily plastered with posters, an inexplicable design painted next to the door— but it wasn't inexplicable at all, a crude kangaroo that looked as though like it had been created by a manic six-year-old with a can of green spray paint. Rough letters on an unfinished board told her that they were entering The Billabong.

Bryan led her in and up a long flight of narrow stairs between dim Tuscan-red walls. She could hear voices and smell the food before they got to the top, so here was the surprise, an improbable little restaurant tucked away in this obscure part of town. With Bryan's hand on the small of her back urging her forward, she saw a crude sign screwed into the brick wall at the top of the stairs, an arrow pointing the way to "Alice Springs – 12,901.6 km" then an archway opening into a trendy interior buzzing with people. "I did the reno," he was murmuring in her ear. "I'm pretty proud of it."

It must have been a warehouse once. Massive timbers supported the ceiling. Nothing was disguised as anything else—pipes were pipes, wood was wood, metal was metal—but the brick walls had been painted in mossy muted colours that could have come from one of Bryan's shirts— dun, ochre, russet, forest-floor green. He was pointing up at the pendant lights, glass cones the colour of beer bottles. "Beauties, eh? From the twenties or maybe even the teens. When you're designing a space for people, you start with light and you end with light because, you know, light is what we see by." His grin said he was kidding her, just a bit, but the wash of nostalgic amber did make everything glow like an early colour photograph. "Old hotel in New West, getting demolished. The price was right. Haul them out of here, boss, and they're yours."

"Whoa! Bryan. You sorry old bastard."

"Hey, Dusty, how you going, owright? This is my friend, Karen."

Karen felt her hand seized, looked up into the laughing face of a tall rangy woman with neon-pink hair and tattoos running up both forearms. She and Bryan were trading cheery blasts of words, and her accent was just as down-under as his. Oh my god, Karen thought, I've been transported to Australia.

The Billabong was split into two levels, the serious diners at tables up here on the top and the beer-and-burger crowd down on the lower level—mostly kids like the ones she'd seen on the street outside. Some of the men on this top level knew Bryan—leapt to their feet, thrust out their hands. He made the rounds, embraced some of them, slapped them on the back. "My friend, Karen," he kept murmuring. She felt heat in her face. It was happening too fast—he had put her on display. Her ski jacket wasn't long enough to hide her, and what on earth had she been thinking? No way these teen-nasty jeans were anything but too tight. She'd been planning this as a private game, or at least semi-private, a flashback to adolescence, but not a rerun of high school with half a dozen asshole males staring at her ass.

"Open up the top room," Dusty was yelling at somebody, "Bryan's here with *a lady*." Oh, for Christ's sake.

Dusty led them up a few steps and through an archway into a small dining room that overlooked the street, pulled out a chair so Karen could sit in it. "Love your boots! What a beautiful colour."

"Oh, thank you. It's real indigo." Shut up, Karen, you ditz.

Another Australian had arrived, this one short and dark wearing a food-spattered apron—the cook, "Bev" apparently. "You folks eating sentient beings tonight?"

"Yeah, I reckon this is the night for it."

"Then I'd say the tenderloin is what's happening."

"Bring it on," he said, and to Karen, "medium-rare?"

"Yeah, but . . ."

"You a wine drinker?" Bev was asking her.

"Well, sure. Maybe if . . ."

"No worries. We'll take care of you."

The cook was gone. Dusty lit the small gas fireplace next to their table—whoosh—and pulling the doors partway shut behind her, left them alone in this pathetic little dining room. Karen was wondering why she was so angry. Shouldn't this be funny? Wouldn't it make a great story?

Yeah, maybe, but not yet. "The last man who ordered dinner for me was my father, and I think I was nine at the time."

"Aw, Karen, it's not like that. We're not customers, we're guests. Bev is going to give us her very best."

"Tenderloin? I thought you were a vegetarian."

"Yeah, I am. But you've got to relax sometimes. You hang onto something too hard, it makes you rigid, turns you into a fanatic."

"What's the difference between that and calling yourself a vegetarian and then eating meat whenever you feel like it?"

He was laughing at her. "Nothing. Nothing at all."

She wasn't ready to forgive him yet. She was seated facing the high windows that overlooked the dismal street. "You know, Bryan, this may be the most unprepossessing view I ever saw in my life."

"Aw, no. It's a great view. That's Charlie's warehouse. It's a legendary place. See, they've opened it up, and the kids are going in."

Here was Dusty again, bringing them a green salad, a loaf of sourdough, and a plate of oysters—"Fanny Bay, fresh." Bryan was getting what looked like a pint of dark ale, and Karen had just been presented with the smallest glass of wine she'd ever seen. "Sauvignon blanc," Dusty said, showing Karen the label on the bottle—New Zealand, Saint Clair. "Bev's proud of her wine pairings."

After the pucker of the oyster, the wine was big and bright. "Is that all I get?"

"No worries," Bryan said. "Try the bread. It's hot."

Her anger seemed to be dissolving as quickly as it had appeared—as though it hadn't been a real feeling but something she'd manufactured for the occasion. Maybe she'd just been hungry, and what was the point of being here if she didn't allow herself to experience it? Everything could be new if she wanted it to be.

"Ah, there he goes," Bryan said. Karen felt the beat as much as she heard it—the slam against the windows directly in front of her. Bryan was laughing. "Yeah, that's it. And we're all the way over here with walls in between us. If you're in there, you can . . . the energy! Fuck me dead. You see, when you're walking into Charlie's, you're not just going in there to dance. You're walking into another world." He actually winked at her.

349

"So I had to see for myself, right? I asked around who was the best, and one night when the best was spinning, I walked in there. At first I was regarded with considerable suspicion. 'Who is that old dude, somebody's grandfather? A friggin' cop?' By about one in the morning, they reckoned I was okay . . . barking mad but otherwise okay. By about two or three, they decided I was better than okay, I was, you know, one hell of a cool dude."

He speared the next-to-last oyster and ate it. Looking into his moony grin, she thought, oh, you fucking conman. He'd hooked her. She wanted to hear the rest of it.

"By dawn," he said, "I'd picked up a little posse, and we were all of us deeply in love with each other . . . in the most elevated spiritual way. I was running on nothing but my naked mind, but those kids were flying under the wings of that big dark bird they call 'E.' When Charlie's packed it in, the daylight was too fucken much. I brought those sweet kids over here and fed them Eggs Billabong and drove them home."

Nicely done, she thought. Now what was she supposed to say? There were a dozen ways to play this game. If it was mainly for the thrill, she could reproduce a much younger Karen—the one who'd decided to wear these jeans—could metaphorically bat her eyelashes at this big brave man and his adventures, but she didn't want to do that. Luckily Dusty had come back, bringing a bowl of ceviche, a small platter of tostados, and another New Zealand white to fill Karen's tiny glass, this one called Fire Road.

The ceviche had a flavour in it more than the usual lime, chili, and cilantro—just on the edge of bitter—but Karen couldn't identify it. "Lovely," she said.

The constant thud of the bass was the main thing she could hear from Charlie's. It laid the bottom on a music made from busts of rain in the windows, but here, sheltered in the magic of the new, she realized that Bryan was the latest incarnation of the dangerous-edged bad boys she'd never allowed herself to date, afraid of losing control—although with men, control was an illusion—but here, in this beer-bottle amber light that made the colours punch up like exclamations— almost feverish— ah, there was no conclusion. She hadn't been right since Palm Desert— Fuck it.

Pointing at the window, at Charlie's, she said, "Would you want your daughters going in there?"

She'd thought he'd laugh, but he didn't. "No. No, I wouldn't. But they're going in there anyway. When they're old enough. They love that EDM shit. It's the music they hear in their souls. Sure they're going in there, Charlie's or some place like it. That's why I had to see it for myself."

Now what? "The ceviche . . . There's a flavour that I can't . . . on top of the lime."

"Yeah. It's bitter orange. You know, those buggers they make the marmalade out of."

"Oh. Yes. Yes, it is."

"I do a lot of cooking— Aw, Karen, you know what? Being a dad's the hardest work I ever did in my life."

YOU SEE, THE TWINS' MUM— Tracy, the terrible— Well, that's a bit of a story. The bubble burst in the Japanese economy in '91, and money was tight as a tick on a cat, and Bryan was getting the message that it was time to go home, so that's how he ended up back in Tassie at loose ends. He did a little work for his brothers—when he bothered—and he chased the waves just the way he used to when he was a kid, and who should he meet on the beach but this darling Canadian girl in a hot pink bikini. Tracy had one of those visas that allows you to work in Oz for a year, was a receptionist for a dentist in Hobart. She was not terribly keen on Tassie, could hardly wait for the dentist's regular girl to get back from vacation so she could go to Sydney or maybe Melbourne.

Well, nature had her way with them. Tracy had an ultrasound and discovered that she was carrying not just a single lone baby but twin girls. She took this as a sign from the Goddess. Returning to Canada with twin girls and no husband was most definitely not on her agenda. "Bryan Lynas," she said, "it is time for you to become an honourable man and marry me," and who could argue with that? She was reading this big fat book about the magical ladies back in the days of King Arthur— it was her bleedin' bible—and that's how the girls got their names. "She was going to spell Morgan with an 'i' in it, and I told her, 'No. No, you're not,' and that's the only input I had in the matter."

351

"Oh, *The Mists of Avalon*," Karen said, laughing. "We all read it. Did you read it?"

"Had a go, but it was too misty for me."

Their first year was not noted for marital bliss. Crammed with two babies into a dingy flat no bigger than a saucepan, and Bryan was working steady for his brother—a fucken disaster, that was—and the famous Tassie wind rattling through the walls, and pretty soon Tracy was longing to return to the clement green rainforest she called home. And meanwhile Oz was not looking too good. The brilliant Australian electorate had put that miserable dickhead, John Howard, in office, and Canada seemed like a reasonably progressive country.

You talk about culture shock going from Tassie to Japan, well, that's nothing compared to arriving in West Vancouver. "Tracy's dear old dad . . . sweet Jesus, what a nasty bit of business he is, so far to the right you need Hubble to find him."

Bryan noticed immediately that dear old dad might have many problems, but money was not one of them. "And what line of work do you suppose he was in? Why, *Real Estate*. I thought, hmmm, Lynas, there must be a way for you to get into this game, and by god, there was. The word goes around about this bat-shit crazy Aussie who can fix things, and guess what that makes me? A bleedin' *handyman*. In West Van, if you've got a reliable handyman, he's gold by god, and before you know it, I've got more work than I can handle, booked weeks in advance, had to hire a couple of fellas to help me out, and I pick up a fixer-upper on Lower Lonsdale, do the sweetest little reno you ever saw, and there's my first flip. Cheers," and he toasted her with the fresh pint that had just arrived on the table.

"As a species," he was saying, "we're just bigger smarter monkeys, and monkeys learn by imitating other monkeys, so I'm just doing what the old man did. The male goes out and makes a living, and the female stays home and takes care of the kids, right? Well, no."

He was getting to be known as a man who can fix more than just your house. Some of the things he had to fix were taking him away for weeks at a time, and Tracy the tempestuous was not the kind of girl you can leave alone for very long. So there's wankers with electric guitars coming around, and a shit-ton of blow, and Bryan hardly knows the twins. Then one day he gets a call from the principal at Inglewood. Seems like his darling daughters have got themselves suspended. Seems like they gave some boy a concussion, sent him to the emergency ward. Seems like they hit him over the head *with a chair.* Fuck me blind, he thought, the poor little buggers have inherited the short Lynas fuse, so he said to himself, owright mate, you're good at fixing things, let's see you fix this one.

The principal was going on about how Bryan should be happy they're not bringing in the cops and the social workers, how the twins need counseling for impulse control, how they've got to make public apologies and write action plans and all that other horseshit, and the concussion hadn't been that bad. The boy never even lost consciousness, all he got was a nasty goose egg, and he was a mean little bastard anyway, picked on the younger kids, and the twins had warned him plenty.

"So I've got a mate on the Board of Directors at Palmerston—"

"Oh my god, Bryan, is there anywhere you don't have a mate?"

"That's how I make my living. Making connections."

So Bryan expressed interest in the fine educational opportunities available at the Palmerston School, but he was also forced to point out that the tariff there was a little on the steep side. "To tell you the truth, my friend, I'm making pretty good money but not *that* kind of money." His mate said, "Didn't I hear that your twins are award-winning dancers?" It turned out that Palmerston was keen on fostering excellence in the arts, so the arrangement was made that as long as the twins got decent grades and kept on bringing home those silver and gold medals from the dance festivals, their tuition was taken care of.

Then, after he got the girls into Palmerston, he reckoned it was time he made some effort to be a halfway decent father. "Just like anything else, you put your mind to it and you figure it out, right? Well, no. You can't let your guard down for a minute because . . . well, being a father is one of these games where they keep moving the goalpost on you."

Bryan-as-Dad was this miraculous dude who dropped in from time to time, took the twins surfing every summer, but they didn't really know who he was. Whatever he'd learned in life, he should try to pass on to them—that's what a father does, right? "But sweet Jesus, *fourteen!* That's one hell of a year for girls. I can still teach them something . . . maybe. They'll still listen to me . . . maybe. But pretty soon they won't. Then it's gonna be boys, boys, boys, and Dad will be this ancient dipshit who doesn't even know enough to tie his own shoelaces."

"It doesn't have to be like that!" she said, laughing, but it probably did have to be like that.

TINY PLATES OF APPIES kept arriving—triple-berry bruschetta, scallops with mango salsa, grilled eggplant with feta—each with a wine-pairing, and those little white sips were beginning to add up. She was getting lightly buzzed. She liked being here with him, liked the pounding bass line from Charlie's, liked the appies, liked the buzz. Now it was her turn to talk. Most men weren't good listeners, but he was, and he kept encouraging her.

She'd been trying to give him her standard summary of herself— the well-polished story of Karen Oxley, a bemused naïf to whom bizarre things inexplicably happened—but he wasn't entirely buying it. He wasn't merely listening, he was *paying attention*, and he kept urging her off into places where she hadn't planned to go. Of course they were talking about their kids, and he actually got her to tell the whole complicated story of Jamie and her miseries. "'Mum, if I ever kill myself, please don't think it was your fault.' Jesus, Bryan, she'd just turned twelve!"

"Yeah, the rat pack at Inglewood gave her a good run for her money. She told us something about that . . . when we were watching the wave at Shipstern."

"Did she? That's more than she ever told me. I don't think I've had a serious talk with her in over a year."

"Yeah? Sometimes kids will tell other people stuff they won't tell Mum. But no worries, you guys will be friends again. Sports is her ticket. Keep her aimed that way. As long as she keeps her body moving, she'll be okay."

My god, he was observant. He had a good read on *all* of her kids. She wouldn't have thought that Cameron had been around enough to make much of an impression, but he obviously had. "Yeah, he's a boy. Totally old school and *totally boy*. Little heavy into the blow, is he? Why don't you try cutting him off? 'Look, old son,' you tell him, 'you've got to man up here. End of your free ride, time to move it along.' Not enough credits to graduate, so what? If it ever matters to him, he can go back and finish high school . . . distance ed or whatever."

"His school counselor said the same thing."

"Yeah? Well, the bugger's right. What Cam needs right now is a job. It's one thing to be snorting Mum's money, but it's another thing to be snorting your own. Still might do it, but if he's busting his arse to get it, at least he's gonna think about it. Likes working with his hands, does he? Want me to get him on at Kiewit? You know, those are the folks that build your roads for you."

"Don't tell me. You've got a mate . . . ?"

"Yeah, as a matter of fact, I do— Eh? What's this?"

It was Dusty bringing the main—a plate of tenderloin steaks, the grill marks on them, steamed new potatoes with parsley and dill, carrots and broccoli. "Madagascar pepper sauce," she said, presenting a bowl of it. "It will fire things up pretty good if you want to go that way."

THE ELECTRONIC MUSIC from Charlie's wasn't any louder, but the quality had changed. She could feel the heat of it—or maybe it wasn't the music, maybe it was what she was making of it— Oh my god, it was all vibrating together, on and on— ginger speckled Bryan Lynas on the other side of the table, whoever he was, and how easily they were talking now. A full-sized glass of wine had arrived, finally, an Australian Merlot, and some asshole like Drew might want to argue with the pairing, but she didn't. She was more than a little buzzed.

"Aw, Karen," Bryan said, toasting her with a fresh pint, "we should have done this a long time ago."

This was how these extended dinners were supposed to work but hardly ever did—you kept eating, and kept drinking, a continuous flow of small amounts, and you didn't get pissed, you got transported to some lovely elevated elsewhere. Her body was registering the change— she was so hot now she had to take off her sweater. This was what she'd wanted— the new, shifting and unpredictable, enticing and a bit dangerous. The steak might be the best she'd ever eaten in her life. "It took you long enough," she said. "I was beginning to think you'd forgotten me."

"No way. It's just that . . . Well, I didn't want to interfere with anything you might have going."

Okay, so now it was out in the open—this really was a serious date, and they didn't have to play it any other way—but what had he just said? "Anything I might . . . ?"

"There are guys who don't give a damn if a lady's attached or not, but I'm not one of them. My experience is, if a lady's attached, it always gets messy, and that's like . . . You get to a certain age, who needs the drama, right?"

"That's, ah, very principled of you—" Where had that ridiculous language come from? "Drew and I split up before Christmas. I thought you knew that."

"I'm not talking about Drew."

"Oh."

The beat from Charlie's pounded on and on and on. She couldn't find a thing to say. She looked into his eyes. She hadn't understood before— behind the rough edges and the macho bullshit, he was a kind man.

"It's okay," he said, "we don't need to go there. How's the steak?"

"You thought we were girlfriends?"

"Karen, I never in my life saw two people . . . The night of my party, I never saw two people who looked so much in love as the pair of you."

She looked away from him, looked through the partially open doors to the restaurant where people were milling about.

"I'm sorry," he said. "Let's try something else, eh?"

"No," she said. "No. I don't mind talking about her. I know what it must have looked like, but—"

But what? Why did it seem so important to be honest? She was just having dinner with some guy, *why* did she have to be honest? But if she didn't start talking soon, it would seem like a big deal, and she didn't want him to think that it was.

"Life's always got its little surprises," he said.

BRYAN'S OLD MAN was an electrician, and his brothers were in the building trades, and he had three uncles in the building trades, and everybody
reckoned that's what he was going to do, too. Bryan and school could
never agree, so he grew up on a surfboard, but he always liked working
with his hands, so he got his certificate in building and construction,
and then he was supposed to get some kind of job or apprenticeship, and
find a nice girl and marry her, and that would take care of the rest of
his life, but he thought, fuck that shit. He didn't want to spend the rest
of his life with Mount Wellington hanging over his shoulder, so he got
himself a one-way ticket to Sydney.

It was like a shit-ton of rubble had been lifted off his back. In Sydney
he was nobody, and that suited him. He's always been a sociable fellow, so
he got hired on as a busboy in a hotel, and back in the day beach bums
could rent little holes for practically nothing. When he wasn't working, he
was chasing the waves, and he reckoned that's exactly how life ought to
be. He was not always the gnarly old bastard she saw before her—wasn't
a half-bad looking kid when he was nineteen—and there was this older
bloke he kept running into. David. Yeah, her twins met him. They stayed
with him and his boyfriend when they first got to Oz.

David was twenty-six, educated, came from money. Had a degree
from the uni, had taught English in Japan, and he was going to have to get
serious about his life some day, but not quite yet. Right then he was doing
the same thing Bryan was—chasing the waves. And David had the most
perfect man's body you ever saw. He looked like a fucken Greek statue.

So one night David invites Bryan out to dinner, takes him to this
posh restaurant, says, "Don't worry, mate, it's all on me. Order anything
you want." The lager is flowing, the food is coming, and David keeps
asking questions to get Bryan talking about himself, and all of a sudden
this thought leaps into Bryan's mind. Hold on here! I don't like the way
this is going. He's treating me like a sheila. "You see, I kind of knew the
bloke was gay, but it was something I'd never let myself think about."

As soon as Bryan got wind of what was up, he reckoned that what
he should do was enjoy the dinner, and then, when they got outside, he
should thump the bastard one. But here comes the twist in the story.
Somewhere inside Bryan there was this other person who said, "Why

would you want to do that? This bloke's never been anything but good to you. He's helped you out a million times, taught you some tricks on the board, bought you a few rounds, lent you money and never asked for it back. Why would you want to hurt him?"

So the ordinary Bryan started arguing with the inside Bryan. "Everybody knows that faggots are the scum of the earth and that they deserve to be pounded out." That was just common knowledge. Bryan didn't know the law in New South Wales, but back in Tassie, if they caught two men in bed, they could do jail time for it.

"But I've always been a contrary bastard, and the minute you tell me not to do something, I'm gonna contemplate doing it. I don't know, but my whole life was balanced there for a moment just like on a wave."

He kept arguing back and forth in his mind. And the inside Bryan said, "You're in Sydney. Nobody knows you, and nobody gives a fuck." And it said, "Isn't he a good-hearted guy? Isn't he a friend of yours? Isn't he a fine specimen of a man? Why don't you give it a try, you might like it." And god knows why, but the inside Bryan won.

"I was going against every fucken thing I'd ever been taught in my life, you know what I mean? But I decided to give it a go, so I looked across the table and said to him, 'Hey, mate, you didn't have to work so hard,' and we had us a good laugh. We were lovers for the rest of the summer."

It was David who kept telling Bryan to go to Japan. "They're desperate for native speakers. They'll hire anybody. They pay pretty good. You ought to give it a shot." Bryan had never had a single thought about Japan, but the great thing about it, the thing that really got to him, was that it was *not Australia*. That was even better than *not Hobart*.

So David Xeroxed his transcript from the uni and painted over his name with that white typewriter paint and typed in "Bryan Edward Lynas" and Xeroxed it again. It was pretty crude, but it worked in Japan, and Bryan got a job offer. David and his mates passed the hat to pay Bryan's airfare, and the next thing he knows, he's "sensei," and he's thinking, Jesus, Lynas, you can't let these kids down, and that's how he learned to teach English.

"So it all came down to that moment sitting in that restaurant—when I was balanced on that wave in my mind. And that's all I can tell you. When a wave like that comes along, you've got to ride it."

A CHILLED BOWL—real silver!—with fresh raspberries. A platter with small blocks of Gorgonzola, Roquefort, and well-aged Gouda. Belgian chocolate, both dark and white, broken into chunks. And the rare treat to tie it all together, Canadian ice wine served as cold as a prairie winter. Bryan had even switched from his dark ale to try a glass.

His maneuver hadn't been subtle at all. In fact, it had been fairly crude—I'll tell you about my gay experience so you can tell me about yours—and if she'd been in some other frame of mind, it might have annoyed her, but things were so magical tonight that it didn't.

"I don't know," he was saying, "David keeps telling me that I'm the B in LGBT, but— I reckon we're in too much of a hurry to put labels on things. If you sit on it, it's a chair. If you put it on your head, it's a hat."

Oh my goodness, did he ever have a strange mind. She'd thought that by this time in her life she'd become unshockable, but still she was a bit shocked. She couldn't imagine Bryan in bed with a man, even as a one-off. He seemed so *masculine*. "I'm not in any great hurry to label myself either," she said, "but whatever it was with Erica, my god was it ever intense!"

Of course she hadn't actually had *a gay experience*—unless you counted the kiss—but it felt good to be able to talk about Erica openly and easily. How odd that it should be with him and with none of her women friends. And there was another odd thing—knowing that he'd had sex with a man made her like him better.

Here, pushing the doors wide, were Dusty and Bev. They each took one end of a cabinet on wheels, lifted it up the steps, and rolled it over to the table. Bryan was applauding. "Beverley, you're still number one, the best in the business!"

"Absolutely true," Karen said, "a culinary genius."

Bev was arranging glasses and bottles on the top of the cabinet. "Aw, thanks," she said.

"Bev's been to culinary college," Dusty told them.

"Right," Bev said. "We usually call it, 'cooking school.' It's been a real pleasure, folks. Mostly what I do now is crank out burgers for hipsters."

Dusty closed the doors and turned out the lights, leaving them only the ruddy glow of the gas fireplace. Bev was pouring out brandy and liqueurs.

Bev had a silver wand? No, it was one of those skinny electric lighters, the kind you use on a barbecue. She lit the fluid in a glass—WHOOF. The flame was blue. She poured the flame from one glass to another. With silver tongs she drew up some mysterious ingredient, long and curly. Oh, it was an orange peel cut into a continuous spiral. She lit it, and the blue flame rose up to the tongs. "Ah," Karen said involuntarily.

"I'll tell you a secret," Bev said, whispering, "the show's better than the coffee."

She poured the results of her fireworks, steaming, into two demi-tasse cups. Dusty lit the candles on their table, and they were alone again. Karen had almost missed the last shadowy sleight of hand when Bryan had slipped Dusty his credit card.

The coffee was super-pungent with spices and brandy. Karen loved the candle light. The dinner had worked the way it was supposed to—she wouldn't have called herself drunk, but she had certainly been transported.

"Erica was so open," she said. "She brought the mystery back for me, made me think that things were possible again, and maybe that was enough. Maybe we weren't meant to be friends. I don't know, I'm probably working out unfinished business with my childhood girlfriend. That's what it feels like—that super-intense feeling girls get for each other when they're eleven or twelve."

"Aw, no. Now you're just talking it away. You guys made a karmic connection the same as I did with David. You shouldn't let it go at that. Why don't you go see her? You know where she lives, right? She teaches at the university, right? You can find her if you want."

Karen was brimming over with feelings, and she didn't know what to do with them. She was in touch again with what she'd known as a child—that there was a mystery to the world. The moment she tried to put it into words it sounded so cheesy, but it was something that children knew right down in their bones. And then—oh my god, becoming an adult, the narrowness of it—when you're cynical about everything, when everything's become ironic. Just as she'd wanted, Bryan had taken her somewhere new, but now she had no profound words to give back to him—only the usual ones. "What a fantastic meal! What a great night! Thank you."

"Karen, it's been my pleasure. I always wanted a chance to get to know you better."

Were they reduced to formula pleasantries? No, they didn't have to be. She'd thought of a curtain-line a while ago—it was kind of obvious, actually. She'd been saving it, and this felt like the right time to deliver it. "Hey, mate," she said, "you didn't have to work so hard."

23.

"JAMIE! Keep after it!" Jesus, the man had a voice like a bloody air horn. He'd played soccer as a kid, so he seemed to think that gave him social license to be an asshole. Karen could see the dirty looks he was getting even if he couldn't. "Come on, Bryan, you're not in Tasmania anymore."

He was laughing at her again. "She's gotta know we're with her. It'll give her a lift."

They had all turned out for Jamie's final game. Bryan had brought his twins, and Devon was his sister's number one fan so he never missed a game. He was so into the play that he kept bouncing up and down and waving his arms in the air—"I get more nervous than she does." Paige, very much under protest, was cutting a ballet class to be there. She kept asking, "Is it nearly over yet? When's it going to be over?" Cameron was the surprise. Karen wouldn't have thought he'd give a shit one way or another, but here he was, yelling, "Jamie, go, go, go!" The Ambleside soccer fields with their state-of-the-art artificial turf might be great for the players but were not exactly spectator-friendly, so Jamie's fans were lined up outside the mesh fence, staring in at the action, as the cold persistent rain drifted over them. Paige was the only one who'd had enough sense to bring an umbrella.

Karen hadn't known that she'd missed the overheated world of girls' soccer until she'd been plunged back into it again—back to the gossipy mums, the specialized language, Jamie's razor-wire nerves, the right stuff you had to have, and the sheer silly heraldry of it all. Inglewood was the home team, dressed in immaculate white. The Palmerston girls were in their navy jerseys and navy striped socks. Jamie had used ProWrap as a hairband to keep her scruffy fly-away manga bangs out of her eyes, and she was wearing the shoes she absolutely had to wear—Copa Mundials. "Come on, Mum, you know I can't play without them."

Jamie, my difficult daughter, Karen thought, what happened to you? The girl who'd come back from Australia was different from the one who'd left. She hadn't been home a day when she'd announced that she wanted to play soccer again. She wanted to go back to her club—she'd thought it would be that easy—but no, it was impossible—that's what they'd told Karen. Jamie could not just take off for a year and then come back whenever she felt like it. She'd have to try out all over again, and then, if they let her back in, she could register in September, but there was absolutely no way she was going to start playing for her club in the middle of the season. "Fuck them," Jamie said, "I'll play for Palmerston."

Their school team was a joke—less than mediocre, it was utterly inept, but the Palmerston girls were stoked. They'd got themselves a striker. Jamie's job was simple—to score whenever Palmerston had the ball—but the defensive pressure on her had been fearsome, and her team hadn't been much help. You can't play one against eleven. So far, she'd managed to score only once.

Jamie had the ball now, was working it. Feinting, faking—that's what she was good at—an aggressive flashy player. Compared to the other girls on the field, she looked like a scrawny little kid, but she was faster than any of them—although that wasn't doing her much good at the moment. Inglewood had three players on her. One of them—the huge hulking thug who'd been shadowing Jamie the entire game—got control of the ball and booted it back the way it had come, down toward Palmerston's goal. "Aw!" from Devon—a small cry of pain.

Karen could see how badly Jamie wanted to go after it, but she couldn't do everything everywhere. Her coach must have given her a stern lecture, so she was sticking to her position—attacking midfield. If she got sucked into the defensive end, she wouldn't be in the right spot for a pass or a breakaway. Panting, she collapsed forward, elbows on her knees, grabbing at this fragment of a moment to catch her breath. Except for that short time when she'd been subbed out, she'd played the entire game—constantly in motion—and she must be beat to shit. Poor kid, Karen thought, but then she amended herself. Jamie wasn't a poor kid at all. She was exactly where she wanted to be. The rain was coming down hard now, but in West Vancouver if you don't play soccer in the rain, you don't play it.

Nobody had expected Palmerston to have a chance. It was a pathetic little private school, after all, and they were playing Inglewood, a public school with a huge pool of girls to draw from. The only question was how badly they'd get trashed. At the moment they were down three to one. For Jamie it was a grudge match. She'd suffered so much at Inglewood that she absolutely loathed the place—for her, it might as well be Mordor—and she'd been too keen, too eager, and had been called offside twice. Her coach had even subbed her out for a few minutes, but he couldn't leave her on the bench because without her, Palmerston had no team at all. Well, no, that wasn't fair—there were two other club players on the team, Emily and Rachel, and they weren't half bad when they got a chance to do anything.

There was less than ten minutes left to play. Only a short while ago Palmerston had seemed to be picking up momentum, but now the ball was stuck in their end, down by their goal. Karen couldn't see clearly what was happening—a roiling tangle of girls—but the defence must be working hard to try to get the ball back up the field to Jamie.

"Palmerston!"—another of Bryan's air-horn blasts—"Move it, girls!" and his twins providing a high-pitched echo—"Palmerston! Palmerston!"

Emily, a big strong girl, seemed to have got control of the ball and then—wham!—sent it in a long looping kick high above the Inglewood girls, aimed directly at Jamie. This must be exactly what Jamie wanted. She ran hard to meet the ball, to control it in the air. Bam! she took the hit smack in the middle of her chest—ouch! Karen thought—and put the ball on the ground exactly where she wanted it, directing it away from Inglewood's thug who was coming straight at her. This was Jamie at her best—dribbling, fancy footwork—around the thug, and around another defender, and then, oh my god, scooting quickly away from yet another.

That's how she'd scored before. She was looking to see if she could do it again. Maybe she could.

But tall lanky Rachel was in the perfect position at the top of the box, yelling, "Jamie! Cross! Cross! I'm open!" Jamie looked, saw her, lobbed the ball up and over the defenders, sent it perfectly to Rachel who controlled it with her thighs, got it on the ground and drove it hard for the net. But Jamie hadn't stopped. She'd followed her kick into an all-out sprint. It was uncanny what happened next. Rachel's shot had gone wide, but Jamie was running into the perfect spot to finish it. With her first touch, she drilled it home. The keeper hadn't been able to do a thing but watch it go by. "Owright!" Bryan yelled.

Jamie jumped into the air, landed with that classic teen gesture—that jerked-down fist that said YES! Rachel was running up to her. They hugged, still in the box, and then began jogging back, swamped by teammates. They all wanted to hug her, and her coach was yelling, "Great play, girls." Less than two minutes left in the game, so that was it—Palmerston down three to two, but a respectable loss, not too shabby for the team everybody said was the joke of the North Shore. As Jamie jogged past her family—all of them calling her name—she sent a small bright flame of a grin directly to Bryan.

"GET SOME PLATES," Karen told Paige.

"Why doesn't Jamie do it? They're her friends."

"And some glasses and silver."

"Why do I have to do it?"

"Because you're a nice kid who wants to be helpful?"

"Ha ha, Mum," but she began hauling out plates and banging them down on the kitchen table. "Can Lauren come over?"

"No. It's a school night."

"That's not fair. Jamie has her friends over."

"This was Jamie's last game. She scored two goals."

"I missed a ballet class."

"End of conversation."

"Mum!"

"*End* of conversation."

The front door banged open—Bryan, his twins, and Devon, all of them carrying pizza boxes. "Hey, Mom, it's clearing up."

She looked to the windows, saw that Dev was right—the fat ball of the sun completely cloud-free, blazing its last sideways rays across the full length of the ocean. The girls were coming back downstairs from the grand tour, Emily and Rachel oohing and aahing over the view—of course they would, the whole house was built around the view—and Devon neatly intercepted his sister at the foot of the stairs. Karen thought for a moment that he was going to hug her, but no, he simply stopped directly in front of her and smiled. Startled, Jamie stopped, too, then smiled back at him. Their eyes locked, and Karen saw energy flare between them so intensely it seemed to change the light values in the room. Whoa, if you wanted a twin moment, there it was.

Then it was Bryan who was hugging Jamie. He picked her up and swung her around. "Hey, darlin', great play!"

She was actually giggling. He set her down, grinned at the others. "Yeah, girls, great teamwork. Like something you'd see in a World Cup match, and I'm not kidding you."

Jamie liked this so much she was flushed and beaming like a little kid. "You were tempted to try it yourself, weren't you?" Bryan asked her.

"Oh, yeah," Jamie said.

"Why didn't you?"

Jamie glanced at the other girls. "Soccer's a team sport."

"Good on you. Life's a team sport, too, by the way. And after you crossed to your mate here, you kept on running. Why'd you do that?"

"I don't know."

Karen would have left it at that, but Bryan seemed to want an answer. "What were you thinking about?"

"I wasn't thinking anything."

"Yeah." He laughed, smacked her on the shoulder—exactly the gesture you'd use with a boy. "You got that right. You arouse the mind without fixing it anywhere."

Jamie was the perfect age to take Bryan's Zen bullshit for the depth of profundity, and there was nothing wrong with that. Karen was glad his heart was big enough for a third daughter, and he was right about

Jamie—sports seemed to be her salvation—but there was a tangle of subtext here, too. Karen hadn't known how badly Jamie needed a dad until she had one, and Bryan was a pretty good dad—when he was around, but he could vanish without a trace for days at a time—and the one person Jamie didn't seem to need at the moment was Mum, and that hurt. She remembered telling the ladies—and meaning it in all seriousness—"Jamie's not just my daughter, she's my best friend." Well, that was over. Stop it, she told herself. Don't go there.

Jamie had taken over the hostess role from Paige, was pouring out the milk and bubbly water. It was wrong to think of her as a sullen teenager who didn't give a shit—she gave *more* than a shit, actually. This was the same Jamie who'd invited the entire anime club to a sit-down dinner with Grandmother McConnell's china, and now she wanted to show the soccer girls that she had a nice home, a nice family. Karen could see how hard she was working to look merry and bright in her natural habitat.

From their chatter Karen gathered that the soccer girls played field hockey in the fall. "You should try out," Emily was telling Jamie.

"Yeah, you should," Rachel told her. "You'd be great."

"Okay," Jamie said, "maybe I will."

Field hockey? Oh my god. And if these girls were going to be Jamie's friends from now on, Karen would have to get to know them better. Both were much farther along in their growth spurts than Jamie. Emily, the author of the mighty kick that had enabled Palmerston's goal, was a big healthy happy almost-blonde. "What a beautiful home you have, Mrs. Oxley," she was saying. "I love your bedroom. All the, um, rose colours . . . and the antique furniture. It's like a room in the provincial museum."

Don't laugh, Karen told herself. "Thank you. I put a lot of effort into it."

Emily could not possibly be anything other than nice, but tall Rachel was the interesting one. Right at the age when she was all legs, dark hair cut into a short pixie, midnight blue eyes, and a handful of cute freckles splashed across her nose. There was something not fully formed about her—kiddish, coltish, not at home in her body yet. She probably needed a soccer field to give her enough room to move, to test herself. She didn't smile much, but when she did, Karen guessed why—her mouth was full of metal.

Oh my goodness, *braces*, adolescent hell. Poor Rachel. Poor *Paige*. The twins didn't need them, but Paige did. She was supposed to start this year. By the time her teeth were as perfect as everything else about her, it would have cost as much as a new car bought straight off the lot. Yes, girls really were harder than boys.

Paige had seen Karen looking at her, was whispering, "Mum, it's *not fair.*"

"One law for the lion and the lamb is oppression."

"What? Jamie's the lion and I'm the lamb?"

"Forget it, puss. Eat your pizza."

Bryan's twins and the soccer girls weren't an easy or natural mix, but everybody was making an effort—trying to make small talk like the adults they were on their way to becoming. After a number of false starts, they'd located a topic that interested all of them, and they were working it for all it was worth. "You *never* eat meat?"

"No," Morgan said, "like seriously never."

"We try sometimes," Avalon said, "but it makes us like sick. Literally."

"We can't eat anything that could of ever looked back at us."

"I'm a semi-vegetarian," Rachel said. "I eat meat sometimes, but not a lot."

"We try to avoid red meat," Emily said dubiously.

"Like there's some kind of vitamin you only get in meat—"

"Yeah, but you can get it somewhere else—"

"Seaweed?"

"Me and Dev are like serious carnivores. Rowrr!"

"We'd like to be vegans, but it's too much work."

"Totally."

"Absolutely no way *pizza* could be like vegan."

"*No* way."

"Vegan's like a thousand fascinating things to do with tofu."

"Totally."

Things were all rolling along cheerily enough, and what if Jamie really *was* merry and bright? She'd thought of herself as an athlete even when she hadn't been one, and here she was back in the thick of things. Field hockey? That strangely violent colonial game for young ladies that you had to play in a skirt? Sure, why not?

Now Bryan seemed to want something from her. He'd just checked his watch. "Come on, Kay, let's go for a little walk. I've got a surprise for you."

KAREN GRABBED HER JACKET, but she didn't really need it. Outside in the world the sky had blown clear. The pavement, wet from the rain, was gleaming in the last of the sunlight. It felt almost like summer.

"Want me to come back tonight after I dump the twins?"

"Yes. Please do."

"Right. We got a date then. I'll be back around . . . I don't know, nine or ten."

That was all well and good, but where were they going? Bryan surely hadn't hauled her outside to make a play date. They were walking west onto that part of her street she hardly ever saw because she never had any reason to drive that far. Skyview was one of West Van's many odd little no-exit streets, and there was nothing at the end of it but the small circle of a turn-around—but they weren't going that far. He was leading her toward an old house that was only three down from hers—a boxy wood-and-stucco construction with a shake roof that could use some work—quite a bit of work, actually. It must have been a nice home when it was built, but now it looked seedy, run-down, out of place between the glassy sci-fi structures on either side of it. "Must be the last house on our street that's left from the original development."

"Yeah," he said, "exactly. Early '60s. If everything works out right, it's gonna be my next flip."

"You're kidding."

"Why would I be kidding?" with his big laugh, and he was already poking the doorbell. A middle-aged gent jerked the door open so quickly that he must have been waiting right behind it—tall and bearlike, white-haired, baldish, in an old man's blah-brown cardigan.

"Hey, Bob, how you going? Owright? This is my friend, Karen Oxley. She's your neighbour, you know. Three houses over," pointing, "the big one."

"The one that's set way back? The one on the double lot?"

"That's it," Karen said apologetically, "with all the glass."

"Oh, my, is that ever some house! Come in, come in. I'm Bob McKee."

As soon as they were inside, Karen heard the TV howling away at a monstrous volume. Bob McKee was leading them down the hall toward the kitchen—well, continuing on past the kitchen, actually, and into a small dining nook where an ancient lady was lying back in a battered La-Z-Boy with a floral comforter spread across her, watching an enormous old-school box. Up close, it was so loud it bordered on the ear-drum-shattering, but a younger woman popped up from some hidden corner to retrieve the remote from the old lady's lap and kill the sound. Then the silence had a ringing, problematic, oh-my-god quality as though they had all been suddenly stripped, left unprotected, to stare awkwardly at each other.

"This is Bianca," Bob McKee said. Karen read her as Filipina, or maybe Hispanic. "She helps us out. And this is my mother."

The old lady grasped the walker near her chair and tried to lever herself up. "No, don't get up, Mum," patting her, "It's okay."

"I'm Maggie!" the old woman shouted at Karen, "Maggie McKee!" Her small blue eyes were bright and happy. How sad, Karen thought, she wants somebody to sit down and talk to her—but that wasn't going to happen. "Come on, folks," her son said, "I'll give you the tour."

Old people had a certain smell, hard to identify but distinctive—medicinal with a touch of eucalyptus, a bit soiled, a bit pongy. "This is the dining room. We, um . . . had to make it into Mother's bedroom. She has trouble with the stairs."

The living room was crammed with a dizzying amount of crap—pseudo-antique furniture with ragged upholstery—and lots of kitsch, too-cute porcelain figurines and framed muddy watercolours of what West Van might have looked like before there were people. Embarrassed by the human drama they were supposed to be ignoring—poor bright-eyed old Maggie left alone—Karen was trying to find something to like. "Oh," she said, "Wedgwood."

"Yeah, Mum collected a lot of that stuff. Over the years. Funny about the human memory, isn't it? When you get old? She won't remember you've been here, but ask her about the Depression—"

369

"Got a bit of a leak, do you?" Bryan was pointing at a dark streak running down one of the walls.

"Um, well. Only if it rains real hard."

"Like it does all winter, eh, Bob?"

Upstairs there was a master, ensuite, and two more generous bedrooms. The paint dated from the day when everything was supposed to be white or cream, and it hadn't aged well, looked smeared and dirty, but there was a sizable bathroom with good light. Bryan was poking at the cracking green tile around the tub. "Got much of a drainage problem, Bob?"

"No. Not so I ever noticed. When Dad was alive—"

Bryan twisted both taps to full on. Bob stared into the torrent of water with sad eyes. Bryan gathered him up with a hand on his shoulder, guided him forward. "Reckon we'll just let her run for a while, eh? Let's show Karen the rec room."

That, of course, was the finished basement with '70s teal-blue wall-to-wall and a collection of old Ikea furniture. Drapes were drawn over two squat windows with a plain wooden door between them. Bob fiddled with the lock, worked the door open, and then, grinning like a game show host, gestured for them to step through it. That blank door had been hiding a small patio and a magnificent garden. Karen wasn't ready for it—"Oh, Bryan, the roses!"

"Yeah, Dad loved his roses. There's every colour you can imagine."

As though timed for their visit, the sun had sunk to exactly the right spot to throw the long slanting golden light that always struck Karen to the heart. The day's rain was sparkling on every petal of every rose. It was all just too fucking perfect for words.

"You missed the daffodils. That was all daffodils." Bob pointed to the beds where the stems had been clipped and tied off. "Mother's got a couple of boys come in and take care of it now. Just the basics. You should've seen it when Dad was alive."

"Your dad was a keen gardener, was he?" Bryan asked him.

"Oh, yeah. After he retired. He loved it back here."

They followed Bob along a stone walkway, turned with him to look back at the house. "Um. Bryan? I'm kind of worried about the bathtub."

"Then you better check on it, eh?"

He gave Bryan a bleak stare. "Okay, folks, you just look on around. Take your time. Look at anything you want."

Karen waited until Bob was out of earshot. "That was mean of you."

"Aw, no. I reckon it's not overflowing yet. But any house this old is bound to have drainage problems. If he'd had any work done on it, he would have told me."

As they strolled back, Karen discovered a lovely herb bed—lavender, thyme, rosemary, mint, and some others she couldn't identify. Bryan crushed a leaf between his fingers, smelled it, offered her a sniff. "Some kind of sage," then looking up the house, "Bob's been dreaming of two, and I want to get that notion out of his head. Even in your posh neighbourhood, it's not worth two. Not as is. Roof, drainage, wiring, kitchen . . . sweet Jesus, and that's just for starters. I'll offer him a fair price. Closer to one."

"One's about right . . . Oh my god, Bryan, I just can't get over the garden. You know, the weird and wonderful thing about West Van is you can walk two or three houses up the street and find a totally different ecosystem." There was nothing behind Karen's house except a huge stand of drab Emily Carr rainforest.

"Yeah?" he said, "and you've lived here how many years now? And I'll bet you don't know a single one of your neighbours. Am I right? . . . But I'm a nosy bastard, like driving around to see what I can see. Spotted this place, walked up, knocked on the door. Bianca let me in, and Maggie and I had us a nice cup of tea and a little chat. Told me all about her life. Bianca gave me Bob's number. Yeah, he was gonna put it on the market one of these days. Now he's talking about this summer. Perfect for me."

He paused to look back at the garden and the lawn behind it. "Wasted space up there. See how sunny it is. Put in a vegetable garden, you could feed twenty people."

"And your solar panels on the roof." He was always talking about solar panels.

"Yeah, if it was mine. Not to flip . . . Vegetable garden, solar panels . . . you go too green, you make it too much of a niche product. Could sit on the market for a couple of years waiting for the right buyer . . . So what do you think, Kay?"

"It's a sweet old house. It's a lot like my parents' house. But in this neighbourhood, most people would think it's a teardown. The land value alone must be in the eights or nines."

"Yeah, but not everybody wants a house like yours, and after *my* bleedin' reno, nobody's gonna want to tear it down. I like old houses. I got a feeling for them. You get all the crap out and just sit with them for a while, they tell you what they want."

The house must have already been telling him a few things. "You see, run a balcony along there," his pointing finger traced the line of it below the bedroom windows on the second floor, "yeah, looking down over the garden. How pretty would that be? Gotta redo the roof, so while we're at it, why not slap up another room over the garage? You see, it wouldn't break the line, and everybody loves lots of rooms. Needs a big spanking new kitchen with all the bells and whistles. French doors on the basement so you walk right out into the garden with your morning coffee, in the summer give you that . . . you know, that back-to-nature feeling like you're on vacation. Put in . . . I don't know, maybe a sauna, but I reckon a full bathroom down there, anyhow. Sea-blue tile. Yeah? I like to do a reno so the right buyer will take one look and think, fuck me, mate, I could move right in here, not have to do a thing. West Van market keeps going mad, I could get three for it."

"Yeah, you probably could."

"Why don't you go on back, Kay? I'm going in and have a little chat with Bob."

SOMEBODY HAD CLEANED UP the kitchen. Paige or Jamie? Not a chance. It had probably been Bryan's twins and Devon—she'd seen that helpful triad at work before—but whoever, they'd left her with nothing to do. She felt oddly discombobulated, walked back into the front hall. She could hear girls' voices upstairs and the TV downstairs, and then, standing there pointlessly, she finally realized that she was pissed off at Bryan. If he was going to buy that house, it was his deal to make, but she'd lived here her whole life and knew a thing or two about West Van real estate, and she'd been dismissed.

But that wasn't all of it. It's not that he needed her permission to buy that house, but— Hey, wait a minute. Yes, in a strange kind of way he did. He was barging uninvited into her neighbourhood, wasn't he? And maybe she didn't want him as a neighbour for the next year or so? Or maybe it was his spooky daughters she didn't want, dropping in even more than they did already? She'd tried, but she couldn't quite warm up to them. Or maybe—what? Oh, right—she didn't want Bryan living so close merely because he'd found another house to buy—*his next bloody flip*—she wanted him living there because that's where he wanted to be. Were they in a relationship or not? He seemed so enlightened some-times—yeah, that was the right Buddhist word—but other times he could be just as blinkered and annoying as any other man she'd ever known.

So now what? She shouldn't just stand there fuming—might as well see what the kids were up to. She walked upstairs, found Jamie and the soccer girls piled onto Jamie's bed, deep in the midst of some fervid rapid-fire conversation, but the minute Karen stepped through the door, they all shut up. "You girls want anything? Some tea or anything? Ice cream?"

"No, Mum, we're cool."

Okay, Karen thought, I've got the message. She withdrew into the hallway, but Jamie leapt up and was coming after her—was right in her face, blasting her with a furiously hissing whisper—"Don't say *anything*, Mum. I mean *seriously*."

"What? What was I going to say?"

"We *know* it's a school night. They *are* going home. Rachel's mum's coming."

Karen spread her hands in a peacemaking gesture. "Come on, sweetie. Don't pick a fight with me over nothing. They can stay as long as they want."

Jamie didn't look the least bit mollified, stared at Karen a moment longer, then turned and marched back into her bedroom. For Christ's sake, Karen thought. You expect Mum to show up for every bloody game, but if she tries to exchange a few pleasantries with your teammates, you bite her head off. Lovely child.

And where was Devon? Only a few months ago he would have been sitting on the bed with his sister, and if the soccer girls found that weird, it would have been their problem. Twinship had been the centre of the universe then—Gemini forever—but not now. Erica had been right. "If you don't separate them," she'd said, "they'll eventually separate on their own," and that's exactly what was happening. When Jamie joined the soccer team, Devon could easily have gone back to nerdland to goof off on the net, but he hadn't. Mysteriously, he'd joined forces with his *little* sister.

Karen went downstairs to see. Yes, there they were. Bryan's girls were sitting on the couch, Devon and Paige on the floor directly in front of them, all of them watching a dance movie. The Devon-Paige alliance was so improbable that Karen would never have predicted it. At first she'd thought it was a matter of convenience—you hang out with whoever's available—but no, it was more than that. Devon and Paige genuinely liked each other. She could see how being friends with her smart, funny, sympathetic older brother would be fun for Paige, but what was Devon getting out of it? Did he actually enjoy watching endless dance movies? And talking about what? How Paige wanted to be hot? What the cool girls were wearing in grade six?

Paige had only been five when Dev had gone to live with his dad. Did she remember him? She said she did, but Karen wasn't sure she entirely believed her. Paige probably remembered *something*, but not as much as implied by, "How could I ever forget Devon!" *Full sib*, is what Dev said about Paige, and that genetic relationship seemed to matter a lot to him—although it certainly didn't to Jamie. She and Paige had so little in common that they might as well have been running on two parallel tracks accidentally located in the same house. To Jamie, Paige was "a spoiled little West Van snot." To Paige, Jamie was simply "mean." There was some truth to both of their points of view.

"What are you watching?" But she could see what they were watching—oh my god, it was *Flashdance*. "Where on earth did you get that?"

Devon took her literally: "London Drugs."

"No," laughing, "I meant where did you even hear about it?"

"Googled dance movies." So they were adding to Paige's collection. Her favourite was *Center Stage*. Karen could see some of the others spread out on the coffee table—*Fame, Dirty Dancing, Chicago, Moulin Rouge, Billy Eliot*. On the screen Jennifer Beals was walking through the industrial landscape of some gritty American city. Karen hadn't thought about

Flashdance in years. It didn't matter how preposterous the plot was, it had nailed the psyches of adolescent girls bang-on while providing plenty of eye candy for their boyfriends, so it was no wonder it had been a big hit. "This the first time you've seen it?"

"No. The second."

Second time or not, they were all glued to the screen. "Wow," she said, "this is giving me a major nostalgia flashback. It's from my last year in high school."

"Watch it with us, Mum," Paige said.

Karen settled onto the couch next to Bryan's girls. "God, Jennifer Beals was *so* beautiful. I'd forgotten. She put us all in leg warmers and black leather miniskirts."

Was the universe unfolding as it should? It seemed to be for Jamie, but Devon? She wasn't so sure. She wished she could talk to Erica about it— Ah, Erica— Yes, it was exactly like the breakup of a love affair. At first it hurt a lot, and then it hurt less and less, and then it drifted away until it got stashed in a mental file-folder labeled "Regrets."

KAREN HADN'T BEEN fully asleep, but she'd been drifting like a soap bubble—not a metaphor but a visual image. She could actually see herself as the bubble, floating back toward the surface of a cloudy viscous fluid. Now she was breaking through, popping up into the air, and vanishing— and that meant that she was awake again. Strange the pictures that your mind shows you sometimes. She sat up, rearranged the pillows behind her. Bryan was farther down than any soap bubble. He was deeply asleep, even snoring. This happened to him a lot after sex—no transition—one moment bright-eyed and chatting and then, *bam*, gone. She knew from past experience that he would be out for some time. He could sleep through anything.

Whenever she and Bryan had one of their play dates, she always left several small lamps burning for precisely these moments—so that when she woke up, she would be connected back to herself. She was tempted to retrieve her laptop from her bed table, but no, that would be too depressing. She didn't want to read any more about the BP oil spill. The containment dome had failed. Underwater plumes of oil, miles long, were washing ashore in Louisiana. What really got to her, what seemed so unbearably sad, was that dead sea turtles were washing ashore, too.

No, she was going to stay where she was for a while—detached from the world, enjoying the warmth, the coziness, the sense of being in a safe burrow. Once again she and Bryan had fucked each other senseless, and the distinctly animal smell of it wasn't all that unpleasant. She'd read somewhere that women in their forties were at their sexual peak, and that seemed to be true for her—she was having the best sex of her life. Well, it took two, and she and Bryan fit together beautifully. Unlike most other men she'd known, he seemed to have nothing to prove.

She'd been in an utterly foul mood before, but now things were better. Amazing what good sex could do for you—she actually felt calm and relaxed. Was he going to buy that house up the street? Would she see any more of him if he did? Did she want to see more of him? She heard his breathing change—a snag on a snore, then a deep inhale. She looked down and saw that his eyes were open. Sometimes she remembered them as bluish grey, but there wasn't anything the least bit blue about them. They were as grey as tarnished silver. "Hey there, Kay."

"Hey there, Bryan."

He shifted under the comforter, stretched himself like a big cat. "What a great way to wake up . . . in bed with such a lovely lady."

It was nice to hear it even if it was standard old-school bullshit. "How sweet of you."

Karen always loved this easygoing time after the sex—when they had no agenda, could talk about anything. "So . . . did you and Bob McKee come to any arrangement?"

He laughed. "You're a funny one. You've had your fun so straight back to business, eh? Bob McKee? I reckon we made it through the first round anyway. He wants to sell, and I want to buy, so we're dancing. I'm low-balling him, and he's not talking two anymore. We'll get there. No hurries. I've got to sell my place before I can buy his."

He stretched again, sitting up—seemed to be working the kinks out of his shoulders—and then his grin morphed into one of his deeply inquiring looks. "Kay? I don't always think things through, and it's occurred to me . . . maybe you don't want me living right down the street from you?"

She didn't know what to say. She wasn't sure what she wanted, but she was glad—even relieved—that he was thinking about it, too. He was more sensitive than she'd taken him for. "I'd be there at least a year," he said.

"Yeah, I know. Do you want to be there? Do you want to be so close?"

"Yeah. I reckon I do. How about you? Do you want me so close?"

"Yeah," she said, imitating his accent, "I reckon I do."

He laughed—"Owright then, let's see if we can make it happen," and then, to her amazement, he actually was telling her about *his plans*. His mum was running out of time, he said, and he wanted to be with the old gal when she passed. He'd already bought his ticket—did it back in January when he could get a seat sale—so he'd be gone for about a month at the end of the summer. "Talk about your arrogant bastards. Okay, Mum, please don't die till I get there, and then once I do, you've got thirty days."

He had to make some arrangements—didn't have much furniture and household stuff, so all that would go in a storage locker, and he'd leave the twins with their mum, and would Karen mind if he parked his truck in her driveway? He kept a lot of valuables in that truck. Oh, she finally got it—he was telling her about his plans because she was included in them. "Sure, you can," she said. "Why don't you just leave your truck in the garage? In the summer I can keep the BMW out. I'll be using it all the time."

"Thanks, Kay. That's a big help."

He'd flopped back down into the bed and pulled the cover over himself. It was nice to feel the warmth of his leg resting against hers— and maybe this was an easygoing drowse time for him, too. He seemed to be thinking out loud. He'd considered taking the girls with him, but it was probably better if they remembered their nana the way she'd been in February, not to mention the cost of *three* bleedin' airline tickets. Twins were ungodly expensive sometimes—oh, right, she likely knew all about that. Aw, he wished he could give his girls more of a stable life. Tracy the tumultuous was a disaster of a mum these days—yeah, and if he and Bob McKee could do a deal, that would expedite matters, would be good all round. Yeah. And he had to get his fucken house on the market before he went back to Oz. He was starting to max out his credit cards.

377

"If it gets too tight, I could always help you out until you sell it."

"Aw, no, Kay. That's a nice offer and all, but I don't take money from women."

Wow. Zinger. She was hurt to the quick. "Oh. Sorry."

"No, no, no, *I'm* sorry." He was giving her another of his checking-you-out looks. "That came out wrong. Didn't mean it to sound like that."

"That's okay."

"No, it's not. I hurt your feelings, I can see it. Problem with me is things don't always come out the way I mean them. But . . . okay. You see, the way I grew up, blokes don't take money from women. If I did that, I'd be just like that miserable wanker sponging off my ex."

"It wouldn't be like that at all!"

He didn't say anything—flipped back the covers, got up, pulled on his boxers and jeans. "Reckon I'll have a cold one. Can I get you anything?"

She was annoyed with him, and it probably showed in her voice. "I don't know. A glass of white wine? Oh, and while you're up, can you check on the kids?"

Why was he laughing? "Is there any time you're not thinking about your kids?" he asked her.

"You just saw me. A little earlier tonight. When I wasn't thinking about my kids."

"Yeah," grinning, "I reckon I did, didn't I?"

When he came back, he brought her not only a glass of wine but a pear neatly cut up on a plate, several slices of Jarlsberg, and some whole-grain crackers. She knew it was a peace offering, and what else could she do but accept it? "How nice!"

"Yeah, that pear had your name on it. Paige's light's out, Jamie's light's out, but Dev's still up, banging away on his computer."

"The little jerk. Okay, if he wants to go to school on four hours sleep, that's his problem."

Bryan sat down on the edge of the bed on her side, set his glass of ale down on her table. That meant that he was getting ready to leave. He never spent the night. She'd stopped asking him. He was a restless bugger, he said, slept in short bursts like a bush animal. If he stayed, he'd just drive her up the wall.

"My girls," he was saying, "since they decided to save all sentient beings, they've become a bit of a pain in the arse. Yeah, like a pair of Buddhist Girl Guides. I tell them, 'You don't have to work so hard to find right action. It's usually right in front of your nose.' So they take me at my word and start with their mum, but Tracy the terrible doesn't want anybody saving her, especially not her bleedin' kids. Poor little buggers come back to my place and cry their eyes out. I tell them, 'No worries, girls, she's got to hit bottom, and I reckon she's still got a little ways to go.' Problem with Tracy is life's always been too easy. Work? What the fuck's that? Well, Jesus, Kay, I'd do anything for my girls, but bugger me if I'm gonna support her coke habit *and* her wanker boyfriend. She gives me any grief, I'll take my girls and go home. Let's see how she likes trying to collect alimony from Tasmania."

That was a fairly chilling thought. "You wouldn't do that, would you?"

"No, not really. Unless I got forced to. But it's always nice to have Plan B, isn't it?" He gave her his finest conspirator's grin, set his empty glass decisively down on the table. "Well, old gal, I reckon I'll be moving it along."

"You're not really going to get any work done at this hour, are you?"

"Oh, sure I am. It's nice and quiet. I'll get a couple of good hours in. Do some drywalling."

"You're bat-shit crazy."

"Reckon so."

He stood up to go. "Love you."

That was fairly amazing. "Me too," she said.

The sound of his truck starting up left her with that mixture of annoyance and affection that seemed to be her default with him lately. She wouldn't be seeing him again for a few days. Love was a pretty strong word, but she did like him—she liked him a lot—and she trusted him.

KAREN HAD JUST COME BACK from Iyengar yoga. She usually didn't do Iyengar, but she'd wanted something so demanding that it would transport her from afternoon to evening—the worst time of day when she was alone—and it had worked. Now she had nothing on her mind more serious than a long hot bath, but the house seemed too quiet and empty, too glassy and too big, and what was that? A soft furtive sound, a tapping or a scurrying—Karen couldn't identify it. Not quite like a mouse. Whatever it was, it had stopped. A poltergeist? Don't be ridiculous. A murky Queen Anne in some rural small town might have a poltergeist, but an upscale West Van house built in the '90s? No way. There simply wasn't enough history to attract a self-respecting ghost.

There it was again—that discreet sound. She should stop telling herself that she liked being alone in the house because she didn't. The sound was coming from Twin Central. "Devon?" she said.

Of course that's who it was. He was seated in front of one of the twin monitors, his fingers flickering on the keyboard. "Whew," she said, "did you ever scare me! I didn't know you were here."

"Oh, sorry, Mom."

If her house was haunted, she was doing it herself. She sat down on the edge of Devon's bed. His fingers feathered out another pass over the keyboard. She was glad he was home. "Dev," she said, "when you first came back . . . ? Did the house seem strange to you?"

He turned to look at her, his eyes puzzled. "Yeah, it did, kind of."

"How?"

He had to think about it. "I don't know . . . Like I'd dreamed it?"

What could she say to that? "I thought you were doing something with Bryan's girls."

"I was, but they blew me off. They've got a date."

Yeah, a *real* date, he told her. Morgan and Avi liked boys, but they had problems with boys. They used to hang with the Koreans—"you met them, Mom—Ji-hoon and Min-soo, you know, like Joe and Michael"— but as soon as school was out, they went back to Korea, and that left a boy-vacuum. A lot of the boys at school thought Morgan and Avi were hot, and boys kept asking them out, but *one at a time*, and they always said no because they didn't want to be separated. Okay, two of the guys must have figured it out because they asked them out *together*, so they had to say yes. "Grade tens. Andrew Fairfax and James Littleton."

"I know the Littletons . . . if they're old West Van. James? Is his father Ken Littleton?"

"Come on, Mom, how would I know?"

Bryan was the coolest dad in the world, Dev was telling her, except when it came to Morgan and Avi *and boys*. Andrew and James had to show up early and have a little chat with him—like it was a major police interrogation—and then Bryan drove them to North Van where they were going to that Vietnamese restaurant and then to the movie. Now Bryan was at home, doing some drywall or shit, so if they called him from anywhere, he could jump in his truck and be there like instantly. He was driving Morgan and Avalon crazy. They appreciated the ride and all, but the bus would have been fine, and they could have used a little extra alone time with the boys. Devon had heard all about it because the twins had been texting him. They felt bad about blowing him off.

Yes, it was funny. Karen even managed to laugh. But why hadn't she heard any of this from Bryan? She was trying to argue herself out of her feelings—don't be so sensitive, you ditz—but no, she had a right to be just as sensitive as she pleased. If Bryan was alone tonight, he could have spent it with her. Well, maybe he *wanted* to spend the night alone, working and worrying and waiting for a phone call. She felt sorry for the boys. He'd probably scared them shitless.

Paige was at Lauren's. She'd been there so much lately that Karen was beginning to owe Lauren's mum big time. She'd have to insist that Lauren stay over and then do something special for them, take them to a movie? And Jamie was sleeping over at Rachel's again, so she'd have to meet Rachel's mum pretty soon. And Dev had been left out, poor kid. "Come on," she said, "I'll take you out to dinner." It wasn't just for him. She badly wanted his company.

"No, it's okay. I was just going to make a sandwich or like—"

"No, you're not. I'm hungry and you're hungry, let's just go get some sushi."

"Sushi?" He sounded so affronted that it took her half a beat to realize that he was kidding her. "I don't know about that, Mom. I'm an *American* kid. How about a cheeseburger?"

"Sure," she said, laughing, and stood up. She wasn't intentionally looking, but she managed to see him type "GTG" into a window before he shut the computer down.

His eyes met hers. "It's just like a chat room, Mom. I know it makes you nervous, but I can see the trolls and pervs coming from a mile off. I just block them."

"I don't know, Dev. It still—"

"Seriously. And anyhow I'm like running dark. Nobody can even find my IP address."

"How on earth can you do that?"

He smiled. "I could tell you, but I don't think you'd get it."

Devon—this boy she didn't know very well, this complicated boy with his secret knowledge—was her son. How strange was that? "Come on," she said, "let's just go."

Since their birthday, both he and Jamie had refused multiple offers of haircuts—god knows why—so now they both had big unruly mops that they were constantly pushing out of their eyes. Dev's solution was wearing a toque. He snagged it from the computer table and jammed it onto his head.

She followed him downstairs and into the front hall. He shoved his bare feet into Cons—yuck, what a creepy feeling that must be. What was it with the kids these days—they hated socks as a matter of principle? And where had he got the deeply distressed jeans he was wearing? Probably from Bryan's twins. They kept passing on their too-small clothes to her twins, and those skinny jeans did look good on him—were a good fit—although there was something about their cut that bothered her, how tight they were to the leg. "Take a jacket," she said. "It's still chilly at night." He reached up to get a big plaid flannel shirt. Where had *that* come from? And then she read the little leather rectangle on the waistband of his jeans. It said *"dollhouse,"* and she had one of her intuitive flashes. Oh my god, she thought, he's gay.

IT WAS A PRETTY NIGHT—warm for this early in the summer and not raining—and kids on their Saturday dates had taken up all the tables outside on the patio, so they were lucky to get a booth inside. Dev had ordered his cheeseburger, but Karen was still staring at the menu without actually seeing it. Whenever she had one of her intuitive flashes, she always had to test it out in her mind. Her intuition was right most of the time, but it had also been known to be wrong, some-times disastrously so.

Seeing Devon as gay was one of those things that once she'd seen it, she couldn't stop seeing it. He and Jamie had been great at creating the guess-my-gender look. They'd polished it to a fine art. But since they'd hit the end of identical and gone their separate ways, Dev had drifted over the line. Tonight somebody who didn't know him—their impatient waitress, for instance—might check him out, register the cut of his jeans, move up to the messy hair sticking out of the bottom of his toque, and then, finally, take in the bits of titanium twinkling on his earlobes, and read him easily as a scruffy preteen girl.

Ah, their poor waitress. She was just a kid trying to make a few dollars, and Karen wasn't being fair to her. The restaurant was packed. "Um . . . a scafood salad?" Karen said. She was guessing they must have something like that on the menu.

"The *grilled* seafood salad," the waitress said. "Good choice."

Okay, so that took care of that. Now what? She never had trouble getting Devon to talk—any topic would do. "I'll bet you're glad the school year's over, eh?"

"Totally."

Gay, she kept thinking. Really? Devon wasn't like Gudrun's son, didn't have any of the obviously gay mannerisms. Devon seemed like—well, exactly the way he defined himself, like a computer nerd. But there were lots of clues. "Wow, this place is seriously gay!" he'd said, delighted at that weird piercing studio, and he'd been the one who'd wanted to get pierced—Jamie could have cared less. Then there was the meticulous way he'd dressed up Jamie for Bryan's party, and his fascination with makeup, and his alliance with his little sister. Since he'd come back to Vancouver, he hadn't made a single male friend, and now there was his new-found passion for *the dance*. And here was the clincher, the final detail that had triggered her flash. What straight boy would willingly walk around with "dollhouse" written on his ass?

Christine and Rob must have figured it out ahead of her—Rob had been going on about *gay* Japanese pornography, and Christine? Karen had been so stoned on zopiclone that she couldn't remember much more than shredded fragments, but what she did remember— "only son, impressionable age, sick lifestyle, constant vigilance, yattata yattata yatta." Yeah, they'd figured it out all right, but the idiots thought that there was something they could do about it. They wanted *to fix him.* Well, fuck you, Robert Clark, she thought. I've talked to the Rottweiler, and I know the law in both countries. There's no way Dev is going back to California.

Karen and the other ladies had heard every detail of it when Gudrun's son had come out. Of course Gudrun had known about it long before Ryan told her, but you can't very well ask your son, "Hey, are you gay?" No, your son has to trust you, has to come out *to you.* Meeting Bryan's gay friends in Sydney must have been great for Devon, must have made him feel validated, and now he needed to know that he had support at home, too. So if she couldn't ask him, maybe she could guide him gently in the right direction. "So how did you get so interested in dance all of a sudden?"

He smiled. "Like seeing Morgan and Avi at the festival competition."

She should have known that. "They think I should take classes," he said.

"Oh?" She should have seen this coming, too.

"Yeah, they're like, come on, Dev, if you don't do something, you're gonna turn into one of those ET slugs with nothing but a big head attached to a computer. And maybe I'd like to do jazz. They're like, go talk to Miss Malveaux."

"Sure," she said, "that sounds like a good idea. Go talk to her."

She could see his relief. He must have been worried about her reaction. "Yeah, maybe I will. If Dad knew, he'd freakin' kill me."

"Yeah, probably. Your father's notions of—"

"It'd be like a one-way ticket back to California."

"No, he couldn't do that. You're old enough now—"

"Yeah, I know! I *know* what the Rottweiler told you. You *told me* what she told you—"

She saw him abruptly lose the ability to speak. Wow, that was fast. He turned his eyes away from her to stare out into the crowded restaurant, blinking. What on earth had just happened?

He was still looking away, but he'd found his voice. "None of you guys know how hard this is for me. Everybody's down on Dad, but he's not so bad. He's *my father*. Like he's not Jamie's father, like he doesn't give a fuck about Jamie, and she knows it. She fucking hates him. She doesn't even call him 'Dad' any more, she calls him 'Rob.' She wants Bryan to be her dad. She was stoked when you guys got together, it was like perfect for her."

Karen had a million things to say, but she told herself to shut up and listen.

"I like Bryan just fine. He's awesome. But *Dad's* my dad. How do you think it would make him feel if I stood up in court—"

"It wouldn't be in court. It wouldn't be as formal as that. More like us just sitting around—"

"Oh, yeah, us sitting around with some freakin' judge. And I've got to say, 'Yes, your honour, I want to live with my mother.' How do you suppose that would make Dad feel? He's supposed to have custody of me."

Then fortunately—or maybe unfortunately—their dinners arrived to take the emotional level down a click. Did Dev want vinegar? Yes, surprisingly for an American kid, he did.

His dad had been calling him up lately, he told her—like calling him on his BlackBerry—and they'd been having these endless conversations. Mostly Rob did all the talking. "Like he didn't talk to me that much when I was living with him."

This was the first she'd heard about it. Oh, so her long-distance chess match with Rob Clark wasn't over, was it? No, not by a long shot. It was wishful thinking to imagine that it had been. Rob, the grand master, had merely changed tactics.

Dev could do a great imitation of his father's voice. "He's like, 'I don't have a problem with you staying with your mom for another year or two. I know you've made a good adjustment to your new school and all, and you've made new friends.' He's like, 'I'd never make you come back if you don't want to, and that's a promise. But you shouldn't close your mind to other possibilities.'

"He keeps talking about Anderson Hill, that freakin' boys' school. They've got like this whole program for geeks. I'd be able to write my own shit, maybe do a start-up later on, and like that. And they're like . . . like they absolutely guarantee you'll get into some hot-shit university. He thinks I ought to go to Yale. Fuck, Mom, *Yale!* I don't know what I want to do. I don't even know if I want to go to university. Why am I supposed to know what I want to do? I'm just going into freakin' grade nine!"

"That's right, Dev, you don't have to know."

Only a teenager could eat a cheeseburger like that—"fully loaded"—enough bacon on it to make an entire other sandwich. She was poking at her salad. *Grilled* had turned out to mean *GRILLED*, and what she saw before her was a massive amount of well-cooked seafood on a few lettuce leaves when what she actually wanted was sashimi and a cup of green tea. She ate a scallop.

"He wants me to come home for a couple of weeks . . . later in the summer, like after co-ed camp. He's like . . . He wants to have this big conference about *my life*."

Karen had no idea how to play this one. This was complicated, this was a mess. The only thing she knew for sure was that she shouldn't make a move until she'd had a chance to take a long, hard look at the chessboard. "So what do you think? Do you want to go down there for a visit?"

"Not without Jamie."

24.

ERICA WAS RUNNING out of time. The store was closing in fifteen minutes and people were already lining up at the checkout. She was staring at the "self-tightening webbing straps." She'd never thought of strapping before but a ligature is a ligature. She'd been caught by the words "self-tightening." They implied that once the process had begun, it could not be reversed.

She could see how it would work. As the strap pulled through the buckle, there would be no way to loosen it without letting off the weight.

If she kicked the stool well away from her, there would be no way to let off the weight. It had been a long time since she'd been in full burn, but that's where she was now—sweating, her heart pounding with a dim splashy echo. It would be unbearably slow. The increasing inability to breathe would create a mindless animal panic. She would be kicking, screaming, clawing at her throat but there would be no way to stop it. Eventually unconsciousness would snuff out the panic. When she died, she wouldn't know it. Well, yes, but that was true of dying no matter how it happened, wasn't it?

She kept playing out the sick fantasy in her mind. She imagined kicking the stool out from under herself and then realizing that it was a terrible mistake. She would pull herself up the strapping until she got to the pipe where it was tied. Then she would hang onto the pipe until her strength gave out. If she was in the basement of her building at night, no one would hear her screaming. Maybe if she wrapped one arm over the pipe and hung from that, she would be able to work the strapping loose with her free hand. Stop it, stop thinking about strapping.

Now she was looking at black steel wire. That would work too—yes, absolutely. No way you could knot it though, you'd have to run it through something—a pulley maybe. If you rigged it right, steel wire running through a pulley could be very fast. What size pulley? Did she want "double sheave swivel eye pulleys"? 1 inch or 2½ inch? Oh, screw that. Just use what everybody else uses—rope.

She was walking faster. It was worse than the burn. Non-ordinary mental states got scholarly labels attached to them so clever people could talk about them but that was so much bullshit. A fizzing or buzzing in her mind made it hard to think—it was like a mental clumsiness—but at the same time her actions were as purposeful as if she was being run by a computer. She didn't trust nylon. She didn't think it would be flexible enough to work quickly. "Three strand twisted Manila" would probably be better. Did she want it in ⅜ inch, ½ inch, ⅝ inch, or ¾ inch? The thinnest would cut but the thicker ones would be hard to knot and slower.

Somebody was talking to her. It was one of the guys who worked there—a big gawky kid in his twenties. He had an enormous Adam's apple. "Excuse me. Can I help you find something?"

"No, it's okay. I'm just looking."

It was still daylight, a little after nine. When she had walked into the hardware store, she'd been killing time but now it didn't matter. She would drive to Kits and walk on Jericho Beach. She had all the time in the world to walk on the beach. She was on medical leave.

SHE HAD TRIED TO CONVINCE Bill that going on medical leave was a terrible idea but he hadn't bought it. If you have totally lost the ability to do the research you're paid to do at a research university, what good are you? Andrew had been running her lab with no supervision. She hadn't been able to give her thesis students any kind of feedback. She had lost her ability to either read or write so of course she hadn't been able to finish either of her papers. Then, as the last straw, she'd melted down in front of a classroom with two hundred undergrads in it.

She'd been lecturing on biopsychological research in stress-response theory. It was a lecture she'd written her first year at the university and it wasn't bad. She been so spaced-out that she probably sounded computer-generated but everything was going okay until one of the keeners in the front row wanted to discuss an odd little paragraph in the textbook—the notion that you could stress-proof your children by giving them a warm and supportive family environment. What she could have said was, "Maybe so and maybe not. After thirty years of twin studies we know that most human traits are heritable. So how could we test that hypothesis?" but that's not what she'd said. He was arguing with her—something she ordinarily encouraged—but he made a fatal mistake. He said, "But it's in the textbook."

She was miked and it was a new classroom with an excellent sound system. When she talked in a normal voice, she was perfectly audible all the way to the back of the room, so when she'd yelled at them, it must have been earth-shattering. *"I did not choose the textbook!"* She had warned them *over and over again* to mistrust studies over twenty years old because they had almost certainly not controlled for genetics and were, therefore, so much junk. Then she must have been going on for a while about research methods and confirmation bias—she didn't remember—but she did remember yelling: "The truth is so repellent to

388

human consciousness that it takes something as powerful as the scientific method to find it."

When she came back to herself, she saw two hundred frozen undergrads staring at her with terrified eyes, probably thinking, oh my god, is this going to be on the exam! Instead of apologizing, she'd walked out without saying another word, leaving her TAs to clean up the mess. The unfortunate student who'd triggered her meltdown felt publically humiliated and said so at the Equity Office.

Bill had been very nice about it—everyone had been very nice about it—but it was the end of the road. All she'd wanted to do was survive until the first of May—when exams would be over, when the dismal Vancouver rain would be over. She'd given it her best shot, but it hadn't been good enough. It was the worst outcome she could imagine. They hadn't even allowed her to finish the school year.

Erica had been passed from one part of the university to another part of the university. Dr. Julia Abramov was a warm, sympathetic, motherly lady in her mid-fifties who was doing research on depressive disorders. She spoke to Erica as an equal—professor to professor. Erica found that approach refreshing and told her some of the truth but nowhere near all of it. Dr. Abramov signed off on Erica's medical leave and then wrote her a prescription for Cipralex.

"Let's start here," she said. "We'll try various things until we find what works for you." She talked about the possibility of monoamine oxidase inhibitors. She'd had very good success with some of them. Her central message was that Erica had come to the right place, that they would most definitely find the proper therapeutic modality for her—although it might take some time. She made Erica an appointment with another doctor, one who offered cognitive behaviour therapy, and signed her up for a support group where she would meet other people who were recovering from major depressive disorders.

Erica had no intention of taking Cipralex or any other selective serotonin reuptake inhibitor. She looked at the literature again and confirmed everything she already knew. Using SSRIs to treat depression was a hit or miss affair. With a few people they worked, with most people they didn't, and with some people they actually made things worse. When they did work, nobody knew why. In the world of real science, Stacey's world, no one had yet demonstrated a solid link between serotonin and depression.

· Within a day of her first missed appointment, she began getting phone calls from various parts of the university. She never answered her phone but listened to the messages on her answering machine. She knew that she was protected by federal privacy legislation that prevented the various parts of the university from talking to each other about her or from giving any information to her family. She guessed that she had anywhere from a month to six weeks before the RCMP would show up to see if she was still alive.

DSM-IV REQUIRED at least five of their listed symptoms for a diagnosis of major depressive disorder and Erica had all nine of them. Any idiot with an MD could see that she fit the category called "severely impaired." The question was, what to do about it? There were a number of ways to think about this. Because she had plenty of time she thought about all of them.

Dr. Abramov was no idiot. She was an intelligent, highly educated scholar who kept up on the latest research. She was also a warm empathetic person who cared about her patients. Erica could go back to her, apologize for having vanished, promise to do better, and comply with treatment. She could take whatever drugs Dr. Abramov told her to take and do whatever Dr. Abramov told her to do. Some people actually did recover from major depressive disorders and Erica could be one of them.

On the other hand, what if the vast majority of humans were deluded, including Dr. Abramov? Even though she hadn't been able to answer Karen's email, Erica had read it over dozens of times and the phrase "like sleepwalkers or like people walking around under the influence of a post-hypnotic suggestion" stuck in her mind. What if only a small number of people were able to face the truth about human life? That small number would, of course, not behave in a way considered "normal." To the deluded majority, they might appear to be severely depressed.

Then, switching back to where she'd started, Erica could see that her belief that she was one of the elite who understood the truth could very well be a symptom of her mental illness. She had spent years of her life studying that large body of continually evolving knowledge called

"Psychology" and it had formed the way she saw the world. She shouldn't abandon it now. A major depressive disorder often produced suicidal ideation and that could prove fatal. She was in serious danger. It wasn't enough to go back to Dr. Abramov. She should check herself into the University Hospital.

Viewed from another angle, however, it didn't matter whether she committed suicide or not. She would not describe her pain now as "unrelenting" the way it had been right after Annalise had died. It came and went, sometimes receded to a considerable distance, but she was never free from the shadow of it because she knew that no matter how well she might be feeling at any given moment, it would always return. She had read interviews with MZ twins who had lost their co-twin and most of them said that they did not get over it no matter how much time passed. That, of course, was anecdotal but it matched her growing conviction that nothing was ever going to get any better.

Being born with your best friend seemed to protect you from more than social pressure. The suicide rate for MZ twins was lower than the suicide rate for the general population—that is, as long as both twins stayed alive. The suicide rate for MZ twins who have lost their co-twin was higher than the rate for the general population. That made perfect sense.

If Erica lived long enough to perfect her Twin Attachment Inventory, she would have a way to measure the bond between twins. A good hypothesis would be that the higher the bond, the higher the suicide rate after twin loss. Compared to the general population, highly bonded MZ twins did appear to be a special case. What if, just as Annalise had suggested, it was like being born with a birth defect? What if *both* twins were required to maintain the organism? Then if one twin died, that would create a situation exactly analogous to organ failure and it wouldn't matter what the surviving twin thought or did, eventually she would die too. Perhaps suicide was a mechanism built into the system—but no, that surely was a crazy thought, the result of suffering from a major depressive disorder.

Erica never answered her emails or phone calls but she kept track of them because they were a good indicator of how much time she had left. Stacey had been a problem for a while but Erica had told her that she was on Cipralex and was feeling much better. Later on, she'd told her that she was doing quite well actually and was going back to the Hat for the rest of the summer. That had taken care of Stacey but lately her mother and her brother had been calling every day. She knew that was dangerous. Trav was perfectly capable of flying to Vancouver to look for her. She kept telling herself that she should call him and try to convince him that she was okay but she couldn't force herself to do it. He knew her and she couldn't imagine being able to lie to him. Then there were all of her missed appointments at the university that were still dangling in the air like pieces of cut fishing line. People had stopped calling but so much time had passed that the RCMP could be showing up any day now, and if they did, she would have to convince them that she was not a danger to herself.

If it had been Vancouver winter with the rain hammering down, she probably wouldn't have been able to get out of bed but it was July. September felt like a cut-off point but she didn't know what it would cut off. All she knew was that school would start without her and she couldn't imagine any future after that. There were only two mental states that counted now—those that she could stand and those that she couldn't. All nights were bad because she couldn't stand to be in her apartment. Her ability to watch TV had vanished along with her ability to read. The nights were short but she had to fill them up somehow. All-night restaurants didn't work because men kept trying to hit on her. She did her shopping at the 7-Eleven or at a Chinese market that stayed open all night. Sometimes she walked on beaches but she felt desperately lonely there at three or four in the morning, exposed and vulnerable. When she couldn't think of anything else to do, she gave up, went back to her apartment and played Tetris.

She could usually sleep in her bed for an hour or two after the sun came up but in the afternoon she had to be outside again. Even though she didn't want to talk to anyone, she liked to be surrounded by people. She could often fall asleep in public spaces. The university Aquatic Centre was good for that because it had a long tradition of being a refuge where exhausted students could sleep between classes. She could lie on a bench with her rolled-up hoodie under her head and a towel over her eyes and no one would bother her. Beaches were good too. It was socially acceptable to lie on the beach and sleep—at least in the daytime. Night was another matter.

KITS POINT HAD BECOME one of Erica's favourite places. She had been deeply asleep, was waking but still drifting—unstrung, reluctant to move—when her phone played the little tune telling her that she had just received a text message. She decided to ignore it. She wanted to imagine the world before she looked at it—the grassy hill sloping down in front of her, the sedate trees, the long view of the rolling ocean. Her Volvo was parked on one of the little residential side streets a short walk behind her.

She opened her eyes. To her left, the sun was setting in a show of violet and gold so vivid it could easily create the illusion of meaning. She had successfully killed off the day, walked all the way to Spanish Banks, then up to Fourth where she'd eaten a grilled triple-cheese sandwich, then back down to the beach and here again. Just as reputable studies had demonstrated, exercise seemed to be good for depression— she didn't feel too bad— although if she looked for it, she could always find the shadow. If the sun was setting, it must be around nine-thirty. In an hour it would be fully night, and dawn would be a long time coming. She didn't know what she would do with that time. She hadn't planned anything. She wondered who had texted her.

She dug her phone out of her daypack. It was from Devon.

Hi Erica u said if there was ever an emergency we could txt u. this is an emergency. please txt us. Dev & Jamie

The hard kick of the burn shocked her fully awake. How strange it was to be human—a few words appearing on a tiny screen had triggered a hormonal cascade and now she was ready to fight off an attacker or run if she had to. She considered doing nothing but there was no way she could not respond. "I'm here," she wrote. "What's up?"

Instead of answering, Devon replied with the standard teenage question: "where are you?" and then they went sliding off sideways into what seemed to be an amorphous chat about location. "The museum with the crab," she wrote to nail it down and he texted back, "o the planetarium."

She could have told him that it was where his mother had lived when she'd loved being alone. That's what had drawn Erica to Kits Point in the first place—she'd wanted to imagine Karen living here.

Erica had walked every residential street, studying the houses, trying to see something that could be Karen's "bizarre little apartment." She'd found two or three good candidates but there was no way to know for sure. Whenever she thought about Karen, she felt guilty and ashamed. All it would have taken to answer her email was one line, something like "I miss you too."

"Where are you?" she asked Devon and he told her that they were in Jamie's room. She could see it in her mind—pale violet with white accents, the framed poster of the *Two from One Fire* twins on the wall. Because he seemed in no hurry to tell her about the emergency, she told him how sorry she was that she'd never answered their last round of emails back in February.

that is ok. u told us u were going dark. Akime helped us for language arts. we got an A ☺

Going dark? she thought. That's a good one. Have I gone dark? "I'm glad you got an A!" she wrote.

we r going to California tomorrow. dad sez we will be back for Van An no prob but we r afraid he is going to pull some weird shit & we will get separated & then we will cross the event horizon

The event horizon was the deadly ring around a black hole. If you crossed it, you were gone. So that must be the emergency. What could she say? The next text appeared.

we do not want to cross the event horizon, we r having a big fight about this we r distraut!!!!!

This could not be happening because of mere coincidence and certainly not because of the "synchronicity" Karen liked to talk about—that Jungian voodoo. It was happening because a perfectly logical chain of events had brought them here. It had begun when Erica had first read their emails

394

and decided that she understood them better than any trained professional would—a colossal arrogance on her part. She'd been certain that she had specialized knowledge because she had been where they were. She too had heard that lethal repetitive voice saying, "You want out of this shit? That's easy. Kill yourself."

r u still there?

Yes. I'm here. I'm thinking about it.

we never had a fight B4, we always agree cuz we r identical, this is horrible we do not know what to do. here Jamie wants to txt u

ths is me Jamie. dev will not stik up 4 hmslf. mum tlkd to th rotwiler & she sez all dev has 2 do is tel th juge he wants s liv with mum he will not do that i do not want 2 go 2 calif but i am goin any way if dev will not stik up 4 himslf wat am I sppsed to do??? it is al fuckd!!!

hi its me Dev again. I should not have to talk to a judge. it is not fair. it is easier for Jamie. she does not understand how hard this is for me. she is mad at me

OK, so you're both going to Calif? You think your dad will separate you? What does it mean to cross the event horizon?

all information from us will be lost

Why is that? Because you will be dead?

yes

So those of us left behind will see two dead kids but once you've gone down the black hole, what will you see?

we do not know for sure. our souls will fuse.

That was pretty much what she'd expected. She did not know of any reputable studies on this but she was sure that adolescents did not understand death. They might have some ideas about it but down in the core of their being they just didn't get it—which probably accounted for their sometimes insane risk-taking behaviour. Even when they were considering suicide, even when they *did it*, they weren't thinking about death the way an adult would.

> Your souls will not fuse. You will not see anything. You will not think anything. Your brains will be dead. You do not have souls.

> if u do not have a soul u r not human

> That is false. We are only bodies.

> energy can not be lost

> That may be true but death is the extinction of the human personality.

> our knowledge only Xtends so far & no farther. Jamie and I were once a single entity. because of quantum superposition we will always Xist as a whole system with all of our possible states

> That's science fiction. I'll tell you how far our knowledge extends. We are hard wired to protect ourselves and pass on our genes. There is no meaning besides that, and that is no meaning at all.

Erica felt like she was being brushed with hot static—a million prickles on her neck and her arms. Annalise's death had taught her the truth. Now she knew that she had to write it.

> When we're dead, we won't remember anything, so life has no meaning. We can't stand thinking about it. Anybody can be tortured until they want to die but what they want is an end to pain not an end to consciousness. To understand human life is to hate it.

It was taking them a while to respond. Maybe they had simply had enough of her and were shutting down. But no, here was their text.

life has no meaning?

Erica had spent hours walking on the beach considering exactly that question and she had found the perfect metaphor to answer it.

To say that life has no meaning is like saying that there are no feathers on a cow.

She waited. The ocean was rolling in—dark, blank and meaningless. The sun was gone, leaving a last bright stripe of colour—meaningless. Come on, kids, she thought, don't give up now. But maybe she'd gone too far. Maybe she shouldn't have sent them her perfect metaphor. But here was their response.

any system collapses into a single state the moment it is observed. so all we see are a series of collapsed outcomes. in the whole system a cow with feathers is a possible state.

She must still have a sense of humour—she was actually laughing—but then, just as suddenly, she was crying. She heard her sister's voice as clearly as if Annalise had materialized next to her: "Stop it, Ricki. What you're doing is wrong." Looking up, she saw that the sky had been ripped in half like an old photograph.

She was crying so hard she couldn't see. It wasn't something she had to think about—it *was* just fucking wrong. I'm sorry, she thought, please forgive me. She texted them.

We wish with all our hearts that things aren't the way they are.

Were they still there? She tried again.

We always secretly admire the crazy people who refuse to believe that things are the way they are.

No response.

> You can't learn to be an MZ twin. You've got to be born that
> way. So it's impossible for you and Jamie to be MZ twins. That's
> why we're all secretly rooting for you.

No response.

> We wish you could do the impossible.

The distance seemed hopelessly far now, much farther than from Kits
Point to West Vancouver. It felt like one of Devon's science fiction stories.
The communication had been a fragile thread stretching across light
years of emptiness and now it was broken. She had to keep trying.

> Do the impossible.

Just when she was about to give up, their message came back.

> ok we will

25.

IT HAD BEEN MONTHS since Erica had heard her nasty door buzzer. Her
alarm clock told her it was just after ten. She'd been asleep for nearly
three hours, a fairly long stretch for her. The buzzer snarled again. The
RCMP? Her brother? Person or persons unknown?

Maybe if she did nothing, they would go away. She stank of yesterday's sweat—and not just yesterday's. A responsible adult would wash

her bedding every once in a while. Through her open window she heard voices down on the street. A man and a woman? Then footsteps coming up the stairs and somebody hammering on her door.

She'd been sleeping in the same clothes she'd been wearing for the last few days so she didn't have to get dressed. All she had to do was act like someone who was not suffering from a major depressive disorder. She slid out of bed, opened the door a crack, just enough to see who it was. Bryan Lynas, his freckles and grin. "How you going, Erica, owright?"

Before she could react, he was inside. He hadn't pushed her out of the way, exactly—well, yes, he *had* pushed her out of the way. She wasn't sure how he'd done it. "Saw your car so we knew you were home."

His daughters were inside too, shooting through the passage he'd made for them, Morgan saying, "Hey, Erica, we brought you breakfast."

"Little organic cafe on the Drive," Bryan said. "You probably know it? About two blocks up?" Just like he owned the place, he was opening the drapes, flooding the room with sunlight. "Lady downstairs let us in the building."

Erica didn't know how to react. Wouldn't most people be angry? Wasn't that the appropriate response? If she wanted to appear normal, maybe she should pretend to be angry but she couldn't very well manufacture an emotion on demand, could she? None of this was making any sense, and all she felt was a wordless alarm. She hardly knew this man but she'd always liked him and she liked his carrot-top daughters a lot. "What are you guys doing here?"

"Beautiful day. Reckoned you might want to take a little walk with us." He looked like *he* was ready to take a little walk. It was the first time she'd seen him wearing shorts.

Morgan had found a clean saucer and was putting a sandwich on it. Avalon had found the stopper for the sink, added a squirt of detergent and was running hot water over the piled-up dishes. Erica hadn't done her laundry either, not for weeks, and her dirty clothes were everywhere. She wasn't fooling anybody. Any idiot could see that she had a problem. "You got a good pair of running shoes?" Bryan Lynas was asking her.

She escaped into the bathroom, sat staring at the closed and locked door. Her ability to test reality seemed to be shot to shit. No, reality seemed to be testing *her*—but if this was a test, then who had designed it and to what purpose? Why the Oxley-Clark twins on one day and the Lynas twins on the next? The two events had to be related but she couldn't see how.

She came back cautiously, found that the twins had wiped down her little table and laid out breakfast for her—sandwich, glass of juice, even a napkin. She hadn't eaten anything since yesterday afternoon. Tomato, lettuce, cucumber and cheese on a buckwheat bun. She liked buckwheat. "You need nice clean socks," Morgan was telling her.

"Like good ones."

"You don't want to get blisters."

The sandwich tasted great. "Seriously," she said, "what are you guys doing here?"

"We don't eat eggs," Bryan said, grinning at her.

What? Eggs? He must mean the sandwich. "It's okay, I like cheese."

Avalon had found a pair of clean socks, was handing them to her. "I don't . . . What's going on? Are we actually going somewhere? Where are we going?"

"A bit of a walk," he said.

"You'll like it," Morgan said.

Okay, Erica thought, it's not like I've got anything else to do. She finished the sandwich, put the clean socks on and the running shoes. Then they were out on the street on one of Vancouver's tourist-attraction summer mornings that could almost make you forget how terrible the winter was. "Tell me where we're going and I'll meet you. I like to have my own car."

"Aw, no," Bryan said, "that's boring. Stick with us, we're interesting."

The twins were walking close to her, on either side of her, just like they thought she might try to escape at any moment. "I feel like I'm being kidnapped."

"Oh, you are," Avalon said, giggling, "totally."

Didn't they know that what they were doing was bizarre and inappropriate? Or maybe in their world it wasn't. What if she had drifted so far from the generally accepted guidelines that she couldn't tell anymore what was appropriate? Bryan was unlocking his truck.

Avalon slid into the back and Morgan directed Erica into the front seat—pushing her a little bit more than was necessary. "Fasten your seat belt," Bryan told her.

"I don't like this," she said. That was true enough. It was a clearly identifiable feeling. She could believe in it. "I get kind of claustrophobic when I'm not driving. Where are you taking me?"

"No worries," Bryan said and pulled out into traffic, "it's a short drive."

He'd lied to her. It wasn't a short drive at all—across the Second Narrows and up the Cut—and now they were on the highway headed west. She was slightly panicked—had a touch of the burn—although she couldn't imagine what there was to be afraid of. She wasn't really being kidnapped, was she? Well, maybe she was. Once the first bizarre thing happens, what's to stop even more bizarre things from happening? To lower her heart rate she closed her eyes and slowed her breathing.

She felt the truck stop, opened her eyes and saw that they were in a parking lot somewhere. Morgan jumped out and motioned for Erica to follow. "Wow," Avalon said, "look at all the American plates."

"Yeah," Bryan said, "tourist season."

They crossed the parking lot. They weren't following the crowd. Bryan was leading them to a vertical slab of grey concrete labeled "Grouse Mountain Grind Timer."

"What's this?" Erica said. "Is *this* the Grind?"

Nobody answered her. Morgan checked her sports watch. "Some of my students have done this," Erica said. "Isn't it supposed to be kind of hard?"

"Hard enough to be interesting," Bryan said.

It didn't look so hard—just an uphill walk on a wide path, steps cut into the ground. Now that they were actually here, she couldn't refuse to do it, could she? What would be the point of that? Maybe none of this was bizarre at all. Maybe in Australia this was normal. Morgan had already taken off at a good clip. Erica jogged a bit to catch up. No, this shouldn't be hard, not really. She'd been walking all summer. She could walk from Jericho to Kits Point like it was nothing. "Hey, Mo," Bryan was calling after them, "don't burn her out."

"I'm not going fast."

"The hell you're not."

It was already getting steeper. More steps, stones set into the trail, winding and narrowing. "The first time Dad took us up here," Avalon said, "was when we got suspended at Inglewood."

"We couldn't believe it," Morgan said.

"He wouldn't even talk to us till we got to the top."

"We thought we were gonna *die*."

"Yeah, well," Bryan said, "I was royally pissed."

Erica was getting a sense of a trail that had been cut out of a landscape that didn't necessarily want it to be there. On her left was a massive pile-up of BC's repetitive green trees, on her right a steep bank that was pretty much aimed straight down. The landscape itself was creating its own reality—was solidifying things around her. She sure didn't want to stumble and slide off. The fall would be real.

"They hit this fuckwit kid over the head with a chair," Bryan was telling her. "*With a fucken chair.* How crude can you get? You better believe I was pissed."

"Every time we tried to say anything—"

"Dad's like, 'Just shut up and walk.'"

"We get to the top, we're like crying—"

"Like, 'Oh my god, we're *soo* sorry—"

"Sorry, sorry, *sorry!*"

"Dad's like, 'Fuck your sorry. And you guys are *dancers*. You're supposed to be *graceful*. And you hit him *with a fucken chair*. Crude, stupid, unskillful, ridiculous, pathetic. Okay, girls, you're gonna learn the martial arts.'"

"Yeah, that's pretty much what I said."

"So . . . did you learn the martial arts?" Erica asked.

"A little bit."

"We'll show you when we get home."

"What's the purpose of the martial arts?" Bryan yelled in the preposterous voice of a gung-ho high school coach.

"For self-defence," the girls yelled back in unison.

"What else?"

"For the defence of women, children, and the venerable aged."

"There you go," Bryan said. He and his girls were laughing. Was it funny? If it was funny, why was it funny?

The trail was getting steeper, had more steps cut into it—way more steps. If this was normal—if going for walks with friends was just something you did—she might have said, "This is kind of fun but a bit of a challenge." Could she say that now? Yes, it was probably an appropriate thing to say, but nothing would explain why they'd turned up that morning out of nowhere.

"Good for your calf muscles," Avalon was saying, "Can you feel it?"

"Yeah," Morgan said, "and your glutes. Do this a couple of times a week—"

"—you get buns of steel."

"What I always wanted," Erica said, "buns of steel."

It was so steep now that it really was like a staircase. Not a straight path but winding around the side of the mountain first one way and then the other. This section had wooden steps. Human agency. Must be some significance to this. "Must take a lot of work to maintain this," she said.

"Yeah," Bryan said, "but they keep it up pretty good. Lots of daft people hike this trail."

They were climbing over huge rocks. Then more steps and more rocks and *more steps*—it seemed to go on forever. There was nothing to see, just the steep incline going up, and up, and a million trees. "This is kind of monotonous," Erica said.

"Yeah," Bryan said, "the charm kind of wears off, doesn't it?"

"There's two thousand eight hundred steps," Morgan said.

That was actually funny. It wasn't something she had to think about—she could actually feel the humour of it. "I'm glad you told me that," Erica said. "I really needed to know that."

She was working hard, sweating. Her T-shirt was soaked. She felt nailed into the particularity of the physical world in a way that she hadn't for a long time. She'd been living in some rarefied artificial luxury. The university was paying her a substantial amount of money so she could wander aimlessly around Vancouver at the height of summer and engage in all kinds of morbid airy-fairy mental bullshit, but this was work, this *was* a grind, and she wanted it to be over. Surely they must be near the top. But then, posted on a tree:

ATTENTION TO HIKERS
YOU HAVE REACHED THE ¼ MARK OF THE "GROUSE GRIND TRAIL"
THE REMAINDER OF THE TRAIL IS EXTREMELY STEEP AND DIFFICULT.
PROCEED AT YOUR OWN RISK

Fuck, Erica thought, one quarter! And it gets worse? She felt as disappointed as a little kid who's just been told that, *no, we're not there yet.*

"Depressing, isn't it?" Avalon said.

"Come on," Morgan said, "we're losing time."

Bryan, at his easygoing pace, was catching up to them. "No worries, girls. *Now* is the only time you've got."

"Go, Pops, give us more of your ancient wisdom."

"Gleaned in the faraway temples of mysterious Asia."

Laughing, "Where did I get such smart-arse kids?" and to Erica, "Drink some water."

"Come on, come *on!*"

"You wanna go for it, Mo," he said, "then fucken well go for it."

Morgan took off, and Erica took off right behind her. Wow, huge rocks. A climb, by god, not a walk. Morgan was far ahead, bounding over the rocks like a monkey. "She's trying to break fifty," Avalon was yelling after them. "You don't have to keep up."

True, but this was bringing out the tomboy twin in Erica and she *wanted* to keep up. If she didn't think about it too much, she could jump from rock to rock like Morgan.

"Hey, you're good," Morgan yelled at her. "You're really fit. You're gonna break an hour! Yay!"

Bryan's voice drifted up from somewhere below them. "Aw, she's not gonna break an hour. You gotta be stepping right along to break an hour."

"We *are* stepping right along!"

Yeah, they were—going faster than Erica wanted to—but this was better than thinking. She was sick of thinking. If she allowed herself to think, she might be scared out of her mind.

"On your left!" Morgan yelled. They were passing people, a knot of them, some middle-aged fit-looking folks who stopped, made room for them to get by. "Go girls!" one of the men shouted after them. The trees ahead seemed endless.

She wouldn't have guessed that one of the Lynas twins would take off and leave the other behind. She'd thought they were more attached than that. Maybe Morgan was doing it for both of them—Erica could understand that—and now with Avalon so far behind, Erica and Morgan made a twin unit. What an odd thought.

At the halfway mark a sign told them that the Grouse Grind was a smoke-free environment. "Well, duh," Morgan said.

Morgan was still going way too fast but Erica was keeping up, jogging right behind Morgan's bobbing ginger ponytail. She hadn't stopped thinking but whatever these mental fragments were—these ideas or sensations or blobs of useless shit in her mind—they were racing by so fast she couldn't keep track of them. *This* is what the burn should be, she thought, working your entire body, not driving a fucking car. What a crazy idea—activate your HPA axis to the point that you're ready to take on a mastodon and then use all that juice to pilot a steel box down a highway at 150 clicks.

My god, there was a limit to how much she could ask her body to do. She looked up to see if there was an end in sight. "No," Morgan said, "don't look up. It's depressing."

It *was* depressing. Some of these rocks were enormous—then concrete steps, then more rocks. Why was she racing a super-fit four-teen-year-old up the side of a mountain? More steps. And ropes—stretched along the side of the trail to help you on your way. She grabbed and hauled herself up.

More steps. She was falling behind now. Another blue sign on a tree: the ¾ mark. "The last quarter's not so steep," Morgan said. She'd stopped to wait for her—and probably to catch her breath—so Erica stopped too. Both of them were panting and raining sweat. Erica could feel the deep stroke of her heartbeat. She hadn't worked so hard since she and Lise had been gym rats together in Edmonton. "You okay?" Morgan asked her.

"Yeah. Sure."

"I'm gonna go for it. You can do it. Break an hour." Grinning like her dad, she squeezed Erica's shoulder, then started scrambling up the next pile of rocks.

Oh no, Erica thought, you're not going to lose me that easily, and took off after her. She wasn't halfway up the rock pile before she knew it was futile. There was no way she was going to catch Morgan. Every time she looked up, she could see her farther ahead, receding. All right then, she thought, go for it, you smartass *teenager*.

More steps, and all she had to do was keep going. Why should it matter whether she broke an hour or not? She didn't even know what that meant. Probably it meant better than average. The tomboy twin wanted to be better than average. The tomboy twin *knew* that she was better than average. With physical things like this, she always had been. Now she just had to prove it.

More steps. There was another rope to help her, a yellow one this time, and then a big sign: DOWNHILL TRAVEL PROHIBITED. Perfect, you either make it up or you die. But Morgan had been right—it wasn't so steep now—and here was something that looked like a cobblestone pathway. In her memory the voice of her high school softball coach— "Go for the burn, girls!"

More steps. And then— What was this? Wooden steps, wide ones, just like on a house. Was the trail over? "Erica!" Morgan was yelling at her, "Erica, come on! You're under. You're *way* under."

Out of the trees at long last and smacked by the sun. Looking up, she saw Morgan waiting for her next to what must be the timer at the top, a slab of concrete just like the one at the bottom. She forced herself to sprint.

If Morgan hadn't caught her, she would have fallen—splat—like a dumped bag of garbage. "You're under, you're under, you're under!" Not enough air in the world. "Fifty-three, seventeen!" Hanging onto Morgan. Two bodies—hot, wet and slippery. Sky, impossible blue, pulsing with her heartbeat. Morgan was holding her, walking her. "Not too shabby."

Her oxygen debt. Just breathe. "Sweet holy fuck. Did you break fifty?"

"No. We like fooled around too much at the start. Fifty-one, thirty-two."

Erica's hormonal cascade had carried her up here but now that she'd arrived, she was spinning out and wasted, useless. Her legs were shaking, every muscle in them shaking. "Oh god, I'm not going to be able to walk tomorrow."

"Hey, there's Avalon! Avi, Avi, come on, you're under!"

Erica yelled too—"Avalon Avalon!"—and she came jogging up to them, a big smile on her face.

"You did it," Morgan said, "fifty-eight, forty-seven."

"Cool."

"Dad can go fuck himself sideways," Morgan said, "we're all under an hour."

The sun was insane, painfully bright. Erica wished she had sunglasses. But the heat was good. She gathered her hair in the back and held it up so she could feel the sun on her neck. "Okay, now you've got to tell me. *Why* did you guys turn up this morning?"

For a moment she thought they weren't going to answer her. Then Avalon said, "Dev and Jamie texted us—"

"They said you were bored."

"Like crazy bored."

"They said you might want to go for a walk with us."

Oh really? Erica was pretty sure that "bored" was not the word that Devon and Jamie had used. They'd texted late last night, the girls told her—close to midnight. That had been long after they'd texted her, so that would have given them plenty of time to think things through. It was all making sense now. So what was the appropriate reaction? Annoyance? Gratitude? Fuck the appropriate reaction. She was glad to be here.

Bryan Lynas was walking up to them at his easygoing pace. "Sixty-eight seventeen, old man," Morgan told him.

"We were *all* under—"

"Yeah, Pops, everybody but you."

"No probs, I'm one of the venerable aged. Bit of a hike, eh, Erica,?" He dropped one hand onto her sweaty shoulder, gestured with the other—look.

She did need to do that, didn't she? She had just climbed a mountain, hadn't she? The sudden awareness took her by surprise—that she was alive and could see. The city of Vancouver was laid out as a glittering miniature, the blue ocean going on forever, the distant mountains etched clear on this clear clear day. Whether it meant anything or not didn't matter.

"**YEAH, GRAB THEM**! Go get them, go after them, *come on!*" Chasing Morgan and Avalon around the empty living room in Bryan's house was not something Erica wanted to be doing, but here she was, doing it. It was impossible to lay a hand on the girls. They were as slippery and elusive as fish. Bryan was laughing at her. "Okay, girls, you've made your point. Now let her catch you."

All Erica wanted to do was take a long hot shower and go to sleep. Fresh sweat on top of a week's worth of old sweat—she stank so badly that people had moved away from her in the gondola riding back down the mountain, and she was so exhausted that she'd fallen asleep in Bryan's truck. She had tried to talk him into taking her home, but he'd had none of it—"Aw, no, that's boring. Stick with us. We're interesting." Now, whether she wanted it or not, she was getting the promised martial arts demonstration.

Avalon slid to a stop and waited for her. This was frustrating. Feeling a touch of real anger, Erica grabbed the girl by the wrist. Avalon made a quick sinuous motion and was free, easily, was turning to confront Erica in a low defensive stance. In an eerie moment that was like hitting the pause button, they were staring into each other's eyes. Then Avi demonstrated in slow motion the short neat kick that would have nailed Erica smack between the legs if she'd delivered it.

"See how everything's circular?" Bryan said. "Let's say you got a big strong bloke coming at you, and you're just a skinny little girl, then what? The bastard is a fuck of a lot stronger than you are. He'll just punch right through your blocks, eh? But let's say he's taking a swing at you—" and with no warning at all he was taking a swing at Morgan, his fist aimed directly at her face. But his blow landed on nothing. She was gone. She'd dropped instantly into a low crouch and was aiming her fist at his testicles.

"You guys are serious, aren't you?" Erica said.

"The unfortunate thing about the world," Bryan said, "is that it's filled with arseholes. Okay, girls, what's the best way to win a fight?"

They answered in unison—"Not get into one."

"Right. Suppose you can't do that, what's the next best way?"

"Run like hell and scream like a siren."

"Right again. But suppose you have to fight the son of bitch. Then what?"

Morgan answered first. "Never meet force with force."

"Use your opponent's force against him," Avalon said.

"There you got it in a nutshell," he said. "Okay, Erica, I want you to go after Morgan. Full tilt, no holds barred." He poked Erica in the ribs. It hurt. "Yeah," he yelled, "go after her. Get mad. *Kill her!*" He poked her again.

In a flash Erica *was* mad. She leapt forward, went at Morgan with both fists swinging—and then she was rebounding, airborne—a sensation like running into an enormous rubber band that had simply contracted and thrown her away.

Bryan caught her before she hit the wall. "Good one, Mo," he said. "You see, Erica, that was all *your* force. And what she did was fairly advanced. Take you a while to learn that one. But let me show you something I can teach you in five minutes."

He grabbed her by the throat and slammed her up against the wall. "Jesus, Bryan! You're scaring me."

"Yeah. That's the right reaction. You should be scared. Okay, if the bastard is stupid, he might go for your windpipe, so you drop your chin." He released his hold slightly so she could do it. "Yeah, that's right. The minute you see the bastard coming at you, you drop your chin. That'll protect your windpipe. But let's say the son of a bitch knows what he's doing. He's gonna want to close off your carotid arteries on both sides, cut off the blood to your brain, right? Choke you right out. Poof, you're gone. You've got less than a minute to react. So what do you do? Okay, Erica, try to pull my hands away."

She tried, couldn't budge them. "See," he said, "that's using force against force. Not gonna work. Okay, now what I want you to do is raise both your arms straight up to the sky. This is not a strike, not a block, takes no force, just *up* as quick as you can do it. There you go. Now turn . . . *the turn is the key* . . . yeah, *your whole body* . . . just *turn* and walk away."

She did what he said, and she was free. "Neat, huh? And then you run like the wind."

Bryan and the girls were looking at her, grinning madly at her. How could they be enjoying this scary awful play fighting? How could they have enough energy to climb a mountain and then come home and do this crazy violent shit? Her three hours' sleep was not doing much for her. If she had to stand upright any longer, she was going to die. "Bryan," she said, "I've got to go home."

"Yeah, Erica, you're looking a little bit knackered. I do listen to you when you tell me things. I did catch your drift a while back. What you need now is a nice hot bath and a lie-down, am I right? Yeah. You're gonna love the reno I did on the upstairs bathroom. It's state of the art."

NO, DON'T WAKE UP—no, not yet—the kind of silence that's filled up, charged, strong smelling, flowery sweet and smoky. Oh fuck, she thought, I've lost it this time. I do not know where I am, not even the time of day. I've really honest-to-god *lost it*. Panic like ice. Shuffle through memory, frantic, where could she be? Tried to place herself in her bed in her rotten little apartment, couldn't make that work, so where? What would it be like to lose whole chunks of your memory? For one horrible moment she'd thought that Annalise was still alive, had imagined her in the next room.

Something moved and her entire body jerked rigid. A bug, a spider, a rat, some horrible nameless thing? She absolutely had to wake up, absolutely had to look. Her eyes popped open and she was staring into the inhuman green eyes of a lean grey cat.

A cat was a cat was a cat. "Where did you come from, you weird thing?" She could see it with frightening clarity, the vertical slits of its eyes, every white whisker clear and distinct. She ran her fingers over its head, over its back, felt its soft fur. Alive, she thought. A live cat purring. It must have been here for a while.

She usually had a clock in her brain to let her know how long she'd been asleep. It was usually fairly accurate. But she must have lost her clock. She could have slept all the way through the night and on into a new day or it could have been only an hour or two. She was remembering everything now—the Grouse Grind, the scary play fighting, her bath in the huge blue tub. She was as clean as a whistle. She'd even washed her hair. And she was lying on a futon inside a cubicle made of rice paper screens, brilliant sunlight at an angle, so it must be late afternoon. She was in the space Morgan and Avi had created for themselves down on the main floor. All the rooms on the second floor were empty because they had to be painted.

She had to plug herself back in to where she was. She sat up. The cat sent her a sharp accusatory look—pure anthropomorphizing, but she read it as, *You disturbed me, you idiot!*—and leapt up, bolted through a sliver of space where one of the screens had been left open, and was gone.

Morgan and Avalon must be the most well organized teenagers in the universe. Their clothes were carefully folded and arranged in neat piles with no indication of who owned what—of course not, everything belonged to the twin unit. Between blocks of raw wood used as bookends they had quite a manga collection—including the first four volumes of *Two from One Fire*. Jamie and Dev had sent those same four volumes to her as a Christmas present—and that was making her think of the twins and Karen, of the unanswered email. Inexcusable, she thought. I am a truly shitty person. I don't deserve to have any friends.

She forced herself to stand up. It took some effort. God, was she ever sore! It would be a while before she hiked anywhere again. The rice paper screens created a clean bare little space—quite Japanese, actually—and she hesitated, unsure what to do next. She probably should go home now, but she didn't want to move, didn't want to do anything. She was wearing the shorts and T-shirt the twins had lent her.

The charged silence of the house created its own energy and— Oh, *that* was what she'd been smelling—they were burning incense. This was all so strange that she wanted to tell Annalise about it, but of course she couldn't. She needed to go outside where she could see the sky, sense the day, but she had to move slowly so she wouldn't disturb anyone. Aware of the waxed surface of the new hardwood floor under her bare feet, taking one careful step at a time, she crept out of the rice paper room and into the larger space where the late afternoon sunlight was streaming down through Bryan's skylight. Except for the screens, there was no furniture anywhere—not even a chair. Bryan must be getting ready to sell the house.

At the far side of the living room was another rice paper cubicle, a bigger one than the twin's bedroom, one panel slightly open. That's where the incense was coming from. She peeked inside. There were the Buddhas she'd seen before. Bryan and his girls were sitting cross-legged on cushions.

Morgan must have seen her through the opening. "Erica, you're awake!"

Bryan didn't change position but he sighed and made a shooing motion. "Out with you, girls."

The twins darted out of the cubicle, pushed the screen shut behind them.

"I'm sorry if I . . ." Whispering seemed like the appropriate thing to do. "Sorry to disturb your . . ." She didn't know what to call it. Meditation? Ritual?

The girls were *not* whispering.

"No worries."

"We can't sit long anyway—"

"Dad can sit for like hours—"

"But we have monkey minds—"

"Guess what?"

She was following them into the kitchen. "What?" she said

"While you were asleep, Jamie and Dev texted us."

"Like their dad's new wife, what's-her-name, Chris,"

"like took their phones."

The incense was so strong that it had been masking everything else but now that Erica was so close to the stove, she could pick up the cooking smells—peanuts and something spicy and pungent. Cumin? Coriander? Then she caught up to what Avalon had just said. "What do you mean she took their phones?"

The story came out in a rush. When Jamie and Devon had arrived in LA that afternoon, they'd fired off a series of texts. Morgan showed her the last one.

WTF Chris is taking our phones! we knew dad was gonna pull some weird shit!!! fuck fuck fuck!!!! TXT you again when we can

That was fairly ominous. Why would they take the twins' phones? Easy answer—so they couldn't tell anybody what was happening. So what *was* happening? Their dad's weird shit—whatever that was. And then there was the crucial question—how close were they to the black hole?

26.

ERICA FIT EFFORTLESSLY into the twin unit. It didn't require words—Morgan was picking everything up, Avalon putting the dishes in the dishwasher, and Erica washing and drying the chopsticks. It all seemed so orderly here, one thing following another. She could smell the paint from upstairs where Bryan was working.

They'd eaten dinner sitting on a tatami mat on the floor. "Just a nibble for medicinal purposes," Bryan had called it but it had been far more lavish than that and she was pretty sure it had been in her honour. Peanut butter stew—the twins' fave. She hadn't known how hungry she was until she'd started eating. "You want to go to Johnny's and get some gelato?" Avalon asked her.

"Sure." How were they going to get there? She didn't have her car.

It was the kind of evening that Annalise used to call "singing" and tonight Erica understood exactly what she'd meant. The evening was full, fat and oddly personal, touching her with a soft breeze through the open doors and windows. A good hour of daylight was left, and, yes, it did sing, made her feel like a little kid. It would be nice to be outside under the sky, going somewhere special with friends. "Can we walk?"

Morgan laughed. "Well, we *could* but it'd take us like hours."

"We'll just grab the bus," Avi said, "easy."

Erica was glad to be here. Bryan and the twins had crashed into her deadly routine and disrupted it—and this was better. Even as she'd been doing it, she'd been aware of isolating herself, and now that she was with people again, it was a relief to be able to worry about somebody other than herself. Maybe everything was easier than she'd imagined. If she wanted to know something, why shouldn't she simply ask? "Do you guys understand the black hole?"

The twins looked at each other. They didn't do that very often because they didn't have to. Maybe they hadn't understood the question. "You know," she said, "Jamie and Devon's thing about the black hole . . . Do you know what they mean?"

"No," Avalon said, "not exactly."

"What would make them go down it?" she asked them.

"Being separated . . . and you know, like that."

"And it's real?"

Yeah, it was real all right. Devon had a weird mind, they told her. He was seriously into that quantum shit and he's like, if you go down a black hole, you'll bubble up in some totally different universe, but if he and Jamie went down the black hole, their souls would fuse. "And it's true," Morgan said, "they probably would because they're a split incarnation like us."

"Oh?" Erica said. "I've never heard of a split incarnation before. Do you want to tell me about it?"

"It's like . . . Okay, if for some weird reason, somebody splits . . ."

"Devon says it's like a quantum event . . ."

"just before they're going to get reborn, they split . . ."

"like Kagami and Makoto. You've read it, right?"

"I hate to admit it. No, I haven't read it yet."

"Come on, Erica, you've got to read it!"

THE DRAWING WAS so perplexing that Erica couldn't figure it out. It was almost entirely black. "I don't get it," she said.

Avalon pointed to an image in the lower right-hand corner. "Look, it's Kagami." Yes, there was the girl, gazing upward. It was like a visual test—once you've seen it, then the entire rest of the picture falls into place. A brutal light was shining directly behind Kagami's head, transforming her hair into a white halo, while her face, in shadow, has gone inky dark. She was almost a negative image—with a dangerous grin, points of her teeth showing, and sparks in her eyes. Stylized white characters floated down from the left—NO MOON.

"Kaneshiro Sensei loves black," Morgan said.

"A lot of mangaka don't," Avalon said, "but she does."

On the next page Makoto was just as much about light as Kagami was about darkness. His workstation was a curving wall of radiance that encircled him as his long white fingers moved at the centre. He was surrounded by shimmering images like projected holograms—texts, graphs, charts, tables, and a continuous flow of mathematical symbols. Greyed out by the glare, Japanese characters floated near his head. "They have given me access to the Arcanic Memory Bank. Incredible!"

He was staring into a sun-point so bright that it was the nothingness of bare paper. Light rays were streaming outward toward him—some pencil-sized and others thin as needles—and he was gathering them, twisting them, twining them. His concentrating eyes were enormous, the pupils contracted to pin points. He was weaving light. "This is insane!" he was thinking. "We're sucking the holy light of the sun and transforming it into deadly black anti-matter!"

"Great drawing!" Erica said.

"Oh, yeah, she's good," Morgan said.

Makoto has left his workstation to pace restlessly around his room. Behind him the endless flow of information is still raining down through the brilliant air. "Our population is declining. We're ravaged by neo-hermetic diseases. The flower of our youth is being slaughtered in the Disputed Territories. It's utterly hopeless!"

Far below, Kagami is gazing upward at the gleaming glass towers, her mouth an amazed oval—"Holy shit!" Her meticulously drawn leather catsuit is a work of art—set with studs, crisscrossed with zippers and straps, hung with neatly folded packets that look like tiny knapsacks. She's got what looks like a personal rocket strapped to her back. She steps forward into a clearing.

Seated at his workstation again, Makoto is surrounded by thick tangles of mathematical formulae with "$E = mc^2$" radiating at the centre. "Oh, dear Gods, it's worse than I thought. There are errors in The Great Foundation!"

He stands abruptly, makes an angry dismissive gesture, and the system shuts down.

"O, Dark Mother of Chthonic Reversals, come to my aid!" Kagami prays and takes off.

Overlapping panels show her rocketing upward, her hair skinned back by the speed. Then in a long shot she's a tiny black dart shooting up the glassy face of a tower, the perspective narrowing toward a distant vanishing point.

A soldier in battle fatigues is staring at his monitor. "Incoming on E-28, vector 47."

An older soldier has joined him. They both bend forward to study the screen. "You need to give your eyes a rest, Corporal."

Kagami has made it to a narrow ledge partway up the building. Poised there, she bends forward, panting, resting her hands on her knees. The view below her is a dizzying canyon of concrete and glass.

Makoto's bedroom is a small bare cubicle that looks entirely Japanese with its rice paper panels and futon unrolled along one wall. Barefoot, he has just changed into loose white pajamas with a faint floral pattern on them. He is buttoning the final button on his jacket. "We need the Progs! We need their wild genes and memes."

He's lying on his bed, staring at the ceiling. "We have to make peace. But how? The Progs have sunk so low into foul barbarity that they've lost all vestiges of the human."

He presses one of his smooth white hands over his eyes. "If they knew how weak we were, they could overwhelm us."

Outside, Kagami hurtles by, still on her way up. She's moving so fast she's a smudgy blur. How did the artist do *that*? It looks like she's taken a moist sponge and wiped it down the drawing.

Kagami has landed on the very top of one of the towers. The sparkles in her huge eyes are drawn exactly like the stars behind her, and she's grinning like a girl who's won the race. The pitch of the roof is so extreme she can't stand upright so she's clinging with one arm to the needle-like shaft that rises from the centre.

She ties a rope around the shaft, pulls it tight, tests it to make sure it's secure, and then, holding onto the rope, begins to walk backward down the steep pitch. She's off the roof now and dangling down the glassy face of the tower. She's so high that all lines converge.

Descending, she's beginning to encounter balconies, the walls of windows behind them dark. The sound effects say, "SKRITCH SKRITCH."

Makoto, puzzled, sits up in bed. With a flick of his fingers, he turns on a light.

Kagami, looking down, sees the light shining out from the balcony below her. She smiles.

"SKRITCH SKRITCH." Makoto is on his feet, striding into the next room so fast that his loose pajama pants are flapping behind him.

Erica turns the page, and it stops her—actually makes her skin tingle. It's the image on Jamie's wall—the image on the precious poster that one of Akime's relatives had sent from Japan. Coming upon it now, in context, seeing it in black and white and not in colour, makes it new for her.

The twins are staring at each other through the window. Kagami is suspended with that rocket strapped to her back, one of her broad flat boots pressed tight against the glass, the treads on the sole carefully drawn. Her tight black catsuit has the dull sheen of leather. Makoto has been stopped and stunned. His loose white pajamas shine like silk. Their shocked faces are drawn as exactly the same.

Makoto's eyes dart to the open French door. Kagami sees it at the same time, but she's faster—lands on the balcony in a crouch and springs up to leap through. She's inside. In a blur of lines she whips out her knife, aims it at him. "Make a sound and you're dead."

With open spread hands Makoto backs up. He looks more astonished than frightened. "You're a Prog!"

"Well, duh."

"But you're not allowed to— You're in violation of the Summer Accord."

"Screw that shit. Just keep quiet."

"Who are you?" he asks, looking at her curiously.

"I am Kagami the Cat."

She gives him a hard cold stare. "I am a scavenger. I steal from the living and the dead."

In a single jump she's close, the point of her knife grazing his throat. "The dead are easier."

Beads of sweat on his forehead, he closes his eyes.

She's so close she's practically whispering in his ear. "Do what I say and I won't hurt you. You got any small electronics?"

He's eyes pop open. "What? Like—"

"You know, like SKROKs."

"SKROKs? That's crazy. We haven't used SKR technology for a hundred years!"

In a small tight panel, she's looking at him with no expression at all.

417

"Please," he says. "The knife— You're frightening me."

This panel is almost identical to the last shot of her—she's still looking at him.

"I won't give you away," he says. "I promise."

She's *still* looking at him.

She shoves her knife back into its sheath. "Let me see your hand," she says.

For a moment Makoto doesn't know what she's asking him to do but then he extends his hand. She reaches for it. As the tips of their fingers touch, they generate a brilliant spark.

The spark swells into a blinding flare that's washing out the details from everything around it.

The light is so intense that Kagami and Makoto are drawn as outlines with their skeletons visible like they're being X-rayed.

Outside the tower. A huge burst of light is blasting out of Makoto's apartment.

From a view high in the night sky, the glass towers of the city are illuminated by an immense fireball where Makoto's apartment used to be.

From outer space, the earth is like a crescent moon, partially illuminated by the sun, but from the dark section of it, a fierce column of light is blazing upward.

The entire Milky Way galaxy is illuminated by an impossibly bright ray from somewhere inside it.

A single star explodes on a black pane—or maybe it's the creation of an entirely new universe—clouds of debris blown out from its fiery centre.

Everything has returned to normal. Kagami and Makoto are staring at each other, their eyes huge and wide.

"What did you do?" Kagami yells.

"Nothing! I did nothing!"

She's much more frightened than he is. Small shaky lines show how hard she's trembling.

"Don't be afraid," he says. "That was a rare arcanic event—a singularity. It's over now."

He reaches out to her. She hesitates, then extends her hand toward his. A panel shows their hands just as they're beginning to touch—his white and smooth, with oval-shaped nails polished to a high gleam, hers rough and callused, with torn ratty nails and black grime ground into the knuckles.

For a moment they're holding hands, staring at each other. Then she lets go, holds up her hand, presses hers against his. They're a perfect match.

Her forehead and cheeks are smeared with dirt, but otherwise their puzzled faces are identical. "You got a mirror?" she says.

He begins to lead her into the next room but she stops him. "Wait! Who's that?" She's pointing at a picture on the wall.

"That's— the Venerable Tanaka," he says, "my father."

Kagami's eyes well up with tears. She's pressing her hand against her chest. "When were you born?" she says.

He hasn't caught up to her yet. His mouth is been drawn as a stupid oval. "Born?-- In the fourteenth cycle of the eighth generation— in the seventh luno—"

"On the twenty-third day," she finishes it for him. "He's my father too."

His expression shows that he's finally getting it. "We're twins!" he says.

He bursts into tears. "You're my sister!"

He flings his arms around her.

Kagami allows him to cling to her, to weep onto her shoulder, but her face is stunned and blank, her arms are spread uselessly outward as though she doesn't know what to do with them.

Her face softens, and she allows herself to hug him back. "What's your name?"

"Makoto."

"Ah, Makoto, this is some pretty heavy shit."

"WOW," ERICA SAID, "Jamie and Devon must have— *Two from One Fire* must have blown their minds. So how do they read it? Is it just a good story for them, or is it more than that?"

Morgan and Avalon were wearing identical expressions she couldn't decode. Puzzlement? Apprehension? "What I want to know— Okay, do Jamie and Devon think they're like Kagami and Makoto in real life? . . . I want to know how they think."

419

"That's like kind of hard," Morgan said. "The first thing you've got to know is, Jamie and Dev don't think alike."

"Totally," Avalon said. "They're not like us. They don't think the same things."

She was afraid that she was going to keep poking at them to get anything more, but suddenly they were talking at breakneck speed, hitting her with a torrent of words—

"Like Devon always has this quantum shit going"

"and Jamie could care less."

"She's like, whatever."

"She really *is* like Kagami."

"And we told them about the Buddha and all that—"

"they thought that was really cool—"

"we told them about past lives and how—"

"Dad doesn't believe in past lives, by the way, or any—"

"He sort of believes in it, like maybe there's past lives, maybe not, it's not important."

"He's like, that's *peasant* Buddhism, superstition—"

"He's really pure—Rinzai Zen—"

"Like he doesn't think *anything* exists!"

"Pretty much."

"He took us around to see all the various Buddhist groups in Vancouver"

"so we could see who else was in the Sangha with us"

"and whoa, have you seen the big Chinese Temple in Richmond?"

"Incredible!"

"Totally."

"We like the Tibetans too, they laugh a lot."

"They told us to mediate on the Green Tara."

"She's kind of like Kannon Bodhisattva in Japan, or she's got another—"

"So anyhow if life is like a dream or a lightning flash or something in your eye, who's to say what's real?"

"The *Tibetans* talk about past lives—"

"We think we might have been miko in past lives."

"Like the girls who . . . Temple maidens. They were spirit mediums."

"You went to see them when you wanted to talk to the dead"

"and we have a little bit of that—we can see into Deep Time"

"and we know that Dev and Jamie were our sibs in a past life."

"*You're* related to us, by the way."

"Not like a sib, a little farther away than that, like an aunt or a cousin."

"So anyhow, we told Jamie and Dev about split incarnations, and that was exactly—"

"Like Kagami and Makoto were once a single entity"

"and if they can complete their karmic task, then their world will pop and replicate"

"and they'll like *fuse*."

"Totally."

"But they don't know any of that until the priestess tells them—"

"As soon as they meet each other— Well, no, Makoto has to escape from the Meritopolis first—"

"It's really complicated!"

"But anyhow Makoto escapes disguised as the Nameless Princess and then they have to go to the Temple of Intermittent Reality to find out who they really are"

"and it takes them all the way to *Book Four* to get there."

"The Temple of Intermittent Reality is crazy cool"

"like sometimes it's there and sometimes it's not"

"and when you're inside, sometimes you open the gates and there's the world you came from but other times it's a totally different world"

"so you can't depend on anything."

"So anyhow, that's when they find out about world stacks and replications and like that."

"The priestess tells them. The Venerable Namiko Sensei."

"She tells Kagami and Makoto who they really are."

"And who are they?" Erica asked.

"They're Two from One Fire, the eternal twins who have existed since before the creation of the world."

"Oh. Okay. So they're some kind of eternal beings, and— Okay, so they have a karmic task, and if they complete it, they'll fuse, turn back into the single entity they were in the beginning. Have I got that right?

And Devon and Jamie told me that if they commit suicide, their souls will fuse. Do they actually believe that?"

Again she'd asked them a question that stopped them cold. After a moment Morgan said, "Yeah, sure they believe it. They were once a single entity, so like . . ."

"Yeah, they would fuse," Avalon said. "That's why they don't think of it as suicide."

"That's just what's gonna happen if they get separated."

"That's what they told me too," Erica said. "But just how separated would they have to be? And then what would they do about it?"

They were simply standing there looking at her. "You don't know either," she said.

ERICA'S BRAIN WAVES must be changing—images in her mind were forming, then dissolving, as she watched. Soon she would be asleep and aware of nothing, but now she was seeing someone—could it be a girl? Before she could recognize it, the face tilted to one side, melted, became inhuman, turned yellow and then into a glowing orange blob that splattered droplets of red into her peripheral vision. She heard herself talking to herself. *Why do you care so much about Jamie and Devon? Once they're dead, it won't matter if they committed suicide. That's true for anybody. So it doesn't matter if it's now or later. Nothing's ever going to get any better. Why not now?*

No. Stop. Her heart racing, she sat up in bed. Even though it was a soft grey darkness, it didn't have any shapes to it, but she knew exactly where she was. She fumbled for the light, turned it on, and a savage stroke of brilliance nailed her back into the world. With their clever rice paper screens the twins had made a little room for her—white and bare and Zen-like. She had her own futon and pillow, her own white comforter. A small table lamp stood on the floor, close enough so she could reach it. Her clothes—the twins' clothes, actually—were folded neatly in a corner. The four volumes of *Two from One Fire* were laid out there in case she wanted to read any more of it. Everything was solid and comprehensible. She'd had that long nap in the afternoon so of course she couldn't sleep.

Thoughts were not voices. If thoughts became voices, you were in serious trouble. But what were you supposed to do with thoughts you didn't want to have? They studied things like that in the areas of psychology she'd always dismissed as voodoo but nothing she'd studied, and believed in, seemed to be of any use to her right now. There had to be some way for her to get through this night, step-by-step, and that way did not have to be supported by years of robust research—all it had to do was work. Okay, she could go on reading the manga. In *Book Four* the twins finally arrive at the Temple of Intermittent Reality to find out who they really are. She hadn't read that part yet. It could be interesting.

Erica wished that *Book Four* had a picture of the artist in it, but it didn't, so she had to rely on her memory of the big coffee-table book the anime club had given to Devon and Jamie. The picture of Mitsuko Kaneshiro was the first thing that had caught Erica's attention—that dark complicated look the artist had aimed at the photographer—and then the more Erica had learned, the more she'd felt an irrational connection to this Japanese woman. Of course it was an illusory correlation but knowing that hadn't diminished the intensity of *the feeling*. The artist had been born the same year as Erica and Annalise; just like Erica, she seemed to be suffering from a major depressive disorder. She had bad dreams. She couldn't stop thinking about the impermanence of human life. She saw terrible things in her mind. "You must draw these things," her editor told her. "If you do not draw them, they will never leave you. If you draw them, they will leave you and you will feel better," and that had sounded like a kind of therapy. Her girlfriends had been so worried about her that they'd taken her to a resort by the sea. There she'd seen something that Akime couldn't translate and that had given her the strength to go back to Tokyo and finish her manga. Erica wished she knew more of the story—but all she needed now was something that would hold her attention, so she flipped through the pages.

There was the temple, perched high on a craggy mountain with heavy snow blowing over it. The upwardly curling eaves of the roof extended out over broad verandas, the ridge on the top adorned with what looked like two half moons facing each other, or maybe like cat's ears. Using tall walking sticks, Kagami and Makoto were hooded figures trudging up the path, leaving deep dirty tracks in the whiteness behind them. They passed through a gated archway, pushed their hoods back, shook snow off themselves, stamped it off their heavy boots.

They were met by two little girls wearing white blouses, high-waisted skirts bound with wide sashes and ribbons in their hair. They must be the temple maidens. It was uncanny how much they looked like Morgan and Avalon—another quirk in Erica's mind, just more confirmation bias. "Come in," the temple maidens were saying. "We've been waiting for you."

Kagami and Makoto exchanged a look—surprised and puzzled. It was a dim twilight inside, shadowy. A tall slender figure, a dark figure, was stepping forward, only partially revealed. "This is our priestess," the temple maidens said and bowed to her. "The Venerable Namiko Sensei."

Erica had been expecting a middle-aged woman, or even an old wrinkled crone, but the priestess was a stately girl with a torrent of long black hair. Her eyes were brilliant, penetrating, intimidating. She looked very much like the artist—the way Erica remembered the artist. It could even be a self-portrait. "Eternal Twins," she said, "you honor us. Welcome to the Temple of Intermittent Reality."

Erica wasn't ready to read the text; she just wanted to look at the pictures. Buddha-like statues rested in alcoves, candles and incense burning in front of them. Temple maidens sat in meditation. Sections of the temple were closed off with rice paper screens. She turned the page. Kagami was sitting up in her bed, her eyes frightened. She was in a small room made of rice paper screens. Erica felt the image in her chest. She felt it as a terrible bang in her chest.

Erica's heart was a lump of contracting meat the size of a fist. It was never allowed to stop contracting—but of course it would eventually. How disgusting to have to depend on something like that. She was chilled, gasped for breath. The back of her neck had gone cold. It had to be another freaky coincidence—unless Erica was delusional, it couldn't possibly be anything other than a coincidence—but the screens enclosing Kagami looked exactly like the screens enclosing her. She was sitting partially upright, resting on one elbow, in exactly the same position as Kagami. Her plain white comforter was folded back in exactly the same way that Kagami's was. The light in the drawing was coming from a small Japanese box on the floor and Erica's from was an ordinary table lamp, but both lights were in exactly the same positions near the identical futons.

What could Kagami possibly do now? Erica badly needed to know because then she might be able to do it too, so she turned the page and saw that the girl was wandering through the temple at night—a hazy darkness lit, here and there, with candles.

Kagami stopped abruptly, her mouth an O. A tall slender figure had separated from the darkness. It was the priestess, Namiko Sensei. She gestured for Erica to follow her.

Now Kagami and the priestess were facing each other, kneeling in that impossibly uncomfortable Japanese position—knees together, buttocks resting on their heels, backs perfectly straight.

Namiko Sensei struck a flame from between her thumb and index finger, used it to light two candles, one on either side. Her eyes were burning as fiercely as the candles.

Kagami dropped her gaze.

"You are silent tonight, Kagami-san."

"Yes, sensei."

"Are you resting in your silence, Kagami-san?"

"I am not resting, sensei."

Using her magical flame, the priestess lit incense in a brazier between them. Thick smoke bellowed out.

The priestess moved her hand through the smoke. Images began to form, sooty and dark—a bombed-out city of ruined and burning buildings, piles of the dead, black smears of birds circling overhead, and, in the distance, the silhouettes of two bodies hanging from lamp posts.

The priestess passed her hand through the smoke again, swept away the ruined city, and now Erica saw a girl bound to a table. She had been tortured—cuts and burns all over body. It was unclear whether or not she was still alive. Her eyes had been gouged out.

Erica couldn't look anymore. She couldn't breathe. But she forced herself to look and saw that Kagami hadn't been able to look either. She'd dropped her head forward, trembling, taking her face in her hands.

The priestess gestured again and the images were gone. Now the smoke was just smoke.

Kagami looked up.

Namiko Sensei's eyes were burning into hers.

"Sensei?"

"Yes, Kagami-san."

"Sometimes, just at the edge of sleep, death whispers to me like a lover."

"That is illusion, Kagami-san. Death has nothing to say."

GONE. Slam rattle of a screen falling, but she was out, she was running, shiny hardwood under her bare feet, through the living room—Move! The only thing she knew, their old cure for terror—both she and Annalise had done it—GET OUTSIDE. Pause, unsure—thoughts catching up, her mind catching up to her, saw herself as a fluttering bird trapped indoors—and Bryan was sitting at the far end of the living room, cross-legged. KEEP GOING.

"Erica!" He jumped up and came after her.

She darted sideways to avoid him. Ran the through the kitchen and got stuck on the door. Crying, hammered it with her fists. He could catch her easily now, she couldn't avoid him now—and there he was, he had caught her—but no, he hadn't, he didn't touch her. His eyes—reading her eyes. He knew she wanted out. He reached past her, jiggled the doorknob, pulled the door open, and she was gone.

Out. In the yard. Running barefoot where? She stopped then to stare up into a overcast night sky, heard the wailing noise coming out of her. It was all catching up—I can't take it, I can't take anymore, I can't take it. She hurt her foot on something, a stone or something. There was absolutely nothing to do except fall onto the grass. Crazy girl, crazy girl—she couldn't live and she couldn't die.

He was offering a hand to her. She could take it or not. If she didn't want to be caught, he wouldn't catch her. Why was she still wailing?—thin fibre of sound unwinding out of herself like string.

She could think of her fear as death if she wanted to, or think of it as nothing at all, it didn't matter how she thought of it. Like a child, she was afraid that if she disturbed it, it would come after her. Their mum used to tell them, "Stop it, girls, you're just scaring yourselves," but sometimes they couldn't stop it—the shadow in the closet, the thing under the bed. Annalise, Annalise, I miss you so much.

She took his hand and allowed herself to be pulled up to her feet. She wrapped her arms around him, hung onto him. She could feel how real he was, how substantial. The way she could feel his solidity was like an energy emanating from him, an electrical charge. There weren't enough words for smells, but they were clear, vivid. Bryan smelled like her father, like her brother Trav, but he also smelled of wood, of paint—even a faint suggestion of lime like Stacey. Everybody in the world had their own distinctive smell. Bryan smelled like Bryan.

She was squeezing him so hard she must be hurting him. He was patting her, stroking her like she was some wild terrified animal—which she was—like calming a dog or gentling a horse—patting her, hugging her. "I can't—" she said. "I can't manage it— I can't— I can't find any way—"

"You'll be right, Erica. You will. You'll be right."

Holding onto him seemed to be making her shaking go away. Thoughts were forming—complete thoughts like a normal person has. Escape? Where? There was no escape. A bird, a dog, a horse—all those thoughts about animals and *she* was an animal. It was simply a matter of duration. Time. Future. She would not be joining Annalise. She would cease to exist and then the world would cease to exist. If they tortured her too much, she could always do it. Right now it was best not to think about it.

She let go of him and stepped back. Here were Avalon and Morgan, the temple maidens. How long had they been out here, watching? They must have seen how bizarre and inappropriate she was. Act normal, she told herself. You can pretend to be normal. "I'm sorry I'm such a basket case," she said.

"No worries," Bryan said, "you've got lots of company."

"I woke everybody up. I'm so sorry."

"It's okay," Morgan said. "We shouldn't of put you off all by yourself."

"You should of been in with us," Avalon said.

The night was overcast but warm. With his hand between her shoulder blades, Bryan was guiding her back inside. "I reckon we could use a cup of tea."

"Oh, I knocked your screens down. I'm *so* sorry," but the girls were already picking them up, moving them. "It's okay," one of them said, "nothing's broken."

Bryan was filling the teakettle. "That's good," he said. "Repairing rice paper's a bitch. You had a bit of a scare, eh?"

Could she talk about it? "I guess I did. I thought—" No, she couldn't talk about it.

The girls were disassembling Erica's room, constructing an entirely new room, a bigger one, where theirs had been.

"A bit of a nightmare, was it?"

"I guess you could say that."

The girls were dragging Erica's futon into their newly created room "You want to be in the middle or on a side?"

"On a side. I get claustrophobic in the middle."

"We knew that."

With a stuttering thump the ghostly grey cat arrived out of nowhere to land on the kitchen counter. "G'day, mate," Bryan said to it. "Reckoned you'd join the action, eh?"

Erica saw the cat with a terrible newness like she'd never seen one before in her life. How bizarre that something that was so absolutely *not human* should come and live with people. It had to make its way through the world with no hands. It had a long tail that it could move all the way out to the very tip. There was no warmth in its eyes. "She wants somebody to feed her," one of the twins said.

"You feed her," Bryan said. "She's your cat."

"Ewww. No."

"You do it, Dad."

"They don't mind opening a can of tuna," he told Erica, "but a piece of chicken's a bit much for them." *His* eyes caught Erica's eyes and held for a moment. It was a human communication. Now he was addressing the cat—"There are no vegetarian cats. Right, you old assassin? It's not the cat nature."

He got a piece of cooked chicken breast out of the fridge and began to cut it into small pieces. "You know, girls, if you can't touch dead things, you'll never grow up."

Oh my god, Erica thought, he knows it was no nightmare. How did he know? How did *she* know that he knew? What if she could no longer distinguish between what was real and what was not? She couldn't imagine anything more frightening.

SLEEPING AND WAKING—that's what made up the world now. Erica did her usual wake-up check on herself. It wasn't one of those devastating moments of forgetting and then remembering—as soon as her consciousness had returned, she'd known that Annalise was dead.

Her night might have begun in the Temple of Intermittent Reality but it had ended with a girls' giggly sleepover. The eerie temple maidens had morphed into ordinary fourteen-year-olds obsessed with boys and clothes and she'd heard all about it. She knew now that she couldn't be sure that anything was real but there was nothing wrong with taking things at face value. This was a lovely place to wake up—sunlight diffused through rice paper. Her inner clock had come back and she guessed it to be nearly noon. She pushed on one of the screens and stepped out into summer.

The back door and all the windows were open and there was a light breeze blowing through the house. Memory was what made these connections work. Summer meant no school, meant sun and heat and time, the feeling of living inside your own body, a feeling she would remember and call "being young." She was in her thirties and she could still feel it. These connections were meant to create the illusion of meaning and why shouldn't she let them?

She could smell paint. "Hey, Bryan," she called out, "good morning."

"Erica. How you going?" Coming from inside the empty room he was painting, his voice reverberated like it was in an echo chamber. "Have some buckwheat cakes. Applesauce, sour cream, maple syrup, take your pick. Maybe the coffee's still hot. I don't reckon you want kimchi for breakfast?"

The clock on the stove told her it was 12:46. Wow, she'd slept for a long time. She and the twins had probably drifted off around three—

so this was the longest single stretch of sleep since Annalise had died. How strange.

She chose both applesauce and sour cream, carried her plate upstairs, found Bryan on a ladder painting the upper edge of a wall. "Nice colour," she said. It wasn't quite taupe—darker and warmer than that—but whatever it was, it made a lovely companion for the sunlight. There were no chairs so she sat on the floor, leaned against an unpainted wall. The buckwheat cake had an odd nutty texture. "What's the crunchy stuff in here?"

"Fooled you, didn't I? Grated broccoli stems. How'd you sleep? Any more nightmares?"

"No," she said, "no more nightmares. Where are the girls?"

"Pissed off to the beach. Yeah, they were going to the beach today and the old man could go fuck himself for any other opinion he might have."

"That's what fourteen-year-old girls are supposed to do. Go to the beach."

"Beach, hell," he said. "They're going to meet a pair of fuckwit boys."

She laughed. When it came to the twins, he really was an old-school Australian male. He'd taught them how to break a stranglehold, but she would bet that he hadn't taught them a thing about safe sex or birth control. "That's what fourteen-year-old girls are supposed to do," she said. "Meet a pair of fuckwit boys."

"I reckon." His eyes met hers and she felt another of his wordless communications. Oh, and there was something else going on too. He had just given her a way to be here. If she wanted it that way, everything could be ordinary. He turned back to his job. He was a deft painter, just as good as she might have expected. "I'm a bit under the gun," he told her. "Got to get this fucken house on the market."

Right, she thought. Reality could be moved around like rice paper screens. "You want me to help you with that?" she said. "It'd go faster with two people."

"That's a nice offer, Erica, but it's got to be a professional-looking job."

"I can do a professional-looking job. I was the tomboy twin. I've painted lots of rooms."

"Okay," he said, "you roll it."

27.

KAREN WAS DOWNSTAIRS in the guest room, sipping Earl Grey tea, tasting the evocative flavour of bergamot, her version of Proust's madeleine cake. She'd done such a good job of re-creating the ambience of her odd little apartment in Kits Point that all she had to do was walk into the room to reconnect to the feeling of it. If she was going to spend much time down here, though, she would have to get some flowers—yellow snapdragons maybe—but she still didn't know what she was doing. Her latest spiral notebook lay open on her desk. She'd been planning to fill it up with the kind of notes that filled all of her other notebooks—quickly jotted, freely running accounts of anything on her mind—but this one, so far, had only its pathetic title, KAREN ALONE IN THE GREAT AMERICAN DESERT, and only one entry: *I feel like warmed over dog shit.*

Great stuff, Karen, very profound! Now, while she had a free moment, she should be making lots of notes. Her life was changing—that was for certain—but she wasn't sure how. Always before she would have talked it over with the ladies, but she hadn't. Ah, yes, the ladies. It was about time for them to have another of their jolly little dinner parties. Karen had missed the last one. It had been at Gudrun's, and everyone had said that it had been one of her best. Karen had been all dressed to go, but then, somehow, hadn't been able to go. She'd called Gudrun to say that she'd come down with something, a flu bug or something, that she didn't want to give it to anybody. They would have wanted to hear more of her amusing stories—about her breakup with Drew, about whatever had been going on with Erica, about hooking up with Bryan—and she simply hadn't been able to face that.

It was strange—and significant—that she hadn't wanted to talk to any of the ladies since she'd got back from Palm Desert. She hadn't even been able to talk to Jen—well, not until a few days ago. That had been fairly heavy. In Delany's, of course, after Sunrise Yoga, of course—and Karen hadn't planned on saying it—it had just come popping up out of nowhere—had anybody ever heard what happened to Patsy Donlevy?

Somebody had seen her in Montreal, Jen said. She couldn't remember who. It must have been somebody at their class reunion. If Karen had bothered to come to the reunion, she could have caught up on lots of interesting gossip. The anonymous somebody had said that Patsy was married and divorced and living in Montreal. She was the director of some artsy thing—a theatre company? No, not a theatre company, something else, but something artsy. Jen couldn't remember. But they said that Patsy spoke French like a native. What a monumental achievement—to actually learn French so well that you could live your life in it. But then Patsy had always been capable of doing anything she decided to do. "Any children?"

"I don't know. Nobody said anything about children."

She and Jen had been sitting in their usual spot near the back of Delany's. They'd been drinking the same things they always drank—Karen a skinny latte with a triple shot and Jen a London Fog, half sweet. Everything was so as-usual it hurt. They'd been doing this for years. It was appalling. "Jen," she said, "do you remember in grade ten . . . when Gudrun and the kids were throwing food on you in the caf? And Patsy stuck up for you and I didn't? . . . I'm sorry."

She hadn't planned to say any of that either. Jen's face fell. "Ah," she said after a moment, "that was a long time ago."

Then Karen saw Jen put her mask back on—the big wide goofy grin of the lady who is everybody's friend. "What's with you, Karen? Are you back in therapy or what?"

Therapy? Karen thought. *I wish.* And now, perfectly timed, the phone began to ring. There were portables all over the house, one right in front of her on the desk, but she didn't have any intention of answering it. She waited to hear the machine in the kitchen answer it, but it didn't. The ringing simply stopped. She heard Paige calling into distant parts of the house, "Mum? Mum! Where are you?"

Karen didn't move a muscle. The scent of bergamot in her nose, she felt as useless as the piece of Kits Point driftwood that decorated the top of the dresser. Paige appeared, still in her pink PJs, thrusting the phone at her. By what convoluted shuffling of the genes had Karen managed to give birth to such a cliché version of a blonde blue-eyed angel? "Oh, *here* you are! It's Cam."

Karen had no desire to talk to Cameron, but she had to sound like a good mother—cheery and positive and bright. "Hi, sweetie, what's up?"

"Sorry, Mum. The freaking asshole landlord wants you to cosign the lease."

"Me!" So much for cheery and positive and bright. "What's the matter with Zach? I thought he was signing the lease."

"Yeah, he thought he was, too," and Cam listed all of Zach's good points—great credit rating, two years at Kiewit, got a letter from his foreman saying he was a hot-shit dude, but it wasn't working. "I don't know, Mum. The asshole just won't rent to him. All you have to do is sign the—"

"What? Zach doesn't have parents?"

"Yeah, but— That's just not going to work, okay? Mum? Can you do it?"

"When? Maybe tomorrow. I've got to get Paige off to theatre camp. She's got to be at the dock tomorrow morning at some ungodly—"

"Today at one?"

"Oh, for Christ's sake. Drive to fucking Langley?"

"Jeez, we're gonna lose it! It's a great place. We've been looking all over."

That seemed to have left them with a thick spikey silence. She had just said no, hadn't she? So what more could she say? She felt terrible.

She heard him inhale. "Okay, Mum like . . . Look, I've done everything you asked me to do. I moved out. I got a job. I'm actually making good money. After a couple more paycheques I'm gonna buy my own car and give you back the Lexus. Now I just want to get my own place, okay? Like can you work with me on this?"

Cameron—the most neglected of her kids. She hadn't seen much of him when he'd been living here, and now she wasn't seeing him at all. Was it possible that she could simply forget him? How appalling was that? And the poor guy had never had a decent break, not once in his entire life. "Okay, give me the address."

IT WAS TRIVIAL, shouldn't matter at all, but Paige hadn't even started packing. She had taken what appeared to be the contents of her entire closet and dumped it onto the floor of her bedroom. The big green canvas bag that was supposed to hold her camp gear was still deflated, lying flat

433

in a corner with not a thing in it, not even a pair of socks. Karen couldn't keep the disappointment out of her voice. "Oh. Paige."

"But Mum. You said you'd *help me*."

"Help you, not do it for you."

"I was *waiting* for you. The lights are supposed to go on the bottom because they're *the heaviest*."

"What lights?"

"My *wall* lights. You know, Mum, they're like round, they've got batteries—"

"Where are they?"

"Lauren got hers at Home Depot."

"Oh my god. You mean you haven't even bought them yet?" Karen couldn't take any more. She walked away from her daughter and down the hall and into her own bathroom. What an appallingly upcoming day—maybe a bath would help. She turned on the taps. Paige had followed her. "Can we go to Home Depot?"

"Yes, yes, yes, we can go to Home Depot!"

The phone was ringing again. "Don't answer it!" Karen yelled, but Paige was already running for it. She was worse than a dog with a stick.

The water was nowhere near hot enough, but she sank into it anyway. Paige was back, waving a portable. Karen made a muting gesture—hand over her mouth. Paige covered the mouthpiece of the phone. "It's a man. He says his name's Bob McKee."

"Oh, for Christ's sake. Why's he calling *me?* Tell him I'm in the bath. No, don't tell him that. Tell him I'm out. We've got to go to Langley."

"Langley?"

"Just tell him I'm not here!"

Paige unmuted the phone and sang cheerily into it. "I'm sorry. She's not here . . . Yeah, okay, let me get a pencil."

The problem with the tub in the master was that it took forever to fill. Karen turned off the cold completely and lay back in the water, kicking, as the hot flowed down. Her body felt stiff and stupid. Tomorrow she was going to have to find a yoga class—and here was Paige back again. "Why are we going to Langley? Who's Bob McKee?"

"To help out your brother. Bob McKee's the guy who . . . His mum owns the house up the street. The one that Bryan wants to buy. I don't know why he's calling me."

"Why do *I* have to go to Langley? Can you drop me at Lauren's?"

"No, I can *not* drop you at Lauren's. You're not even packed yet, and you've got—"

Paige was still carrying the portable. The monstrous thing was ringing again. "Don't answer it!"

"But Mum! What if it's im*por*tant? Hi. Okay, just a sec." She was offering the phone to Karen. "It's Bryan."

"**WHAT DO YOU MEAN** she's painting rooms?"

"I told you, Kay. I didn't get the bugger done. There's two rooms left."

Erica! Where the fucking hell had she come from? Like two bad actors in a very bad sitcom, Karen and Bryan were confronting each other in her driveway. Her BMW was aimed down, his truck aimed up. Paige, curious as a cat, was standing right next to her, taking it all in. "Why didn't you tell me she was there?"

The son of a bitch actually had the gall to be laughing at her. "I *am* telling you. I'm telling you now."

Until she'd heard about Erica, Karen had been prepared to be warm, sympathetic, helpful—everything your partner is supposed to be. Bryan had got a call from his brother telling him to get his arse home ASAP— their mum was going into palliative—and there were a whole bunch of annoying mundane things he wanted Karen to do for him—something about the real estate agent—and he'd even handed her the keys to his house. She was standing there holding them. She felt like throwing them in his face. "How long has she been there?"

"I don't know. A few days—"

"And she got there, *how?*"

She could see that he was getting angry, too. "*I told you, Kay.* Your kids texted my kids—"

"And it was what? Some kind of intervention?"

"I reckon you could say that. She was . . . She'd lost the plot a while back. Didn't expect her to be there more than a night, and then— Bugger!"

435

Should I leave my truck somewhere else?"

"No. You're going to leave it here. We've *discussed* this. Jesus, Bryan, why didn't you *tell me?*"

She walked away from him, trying to collect herself. She needed some distance. Even a few feet would do. Sometimes she absolutely hated *emotions*—they made everything so messy. "Get back in the fucking car," she said to Paige.

You could not think straight when you were this angry. Nobody liked volatile crazy screaming angry weeping women, and she was absolutely not going to do that. She turned back, saw Bryan staring at her. He looked tired—drained and grey. Oh, he had *so* wanted to get his house on the market before he went to Australia.

Okay, she thought, start from another angle. "I'd take you to the airport, but I've got to drive to fucking Langley."

"No worries. I can take a cab."

She walked up to him—to confront him—but confront him with what? "Go down and see her," he said.

"Oh? Really?"

"What's stopping you, Kay? She'd be glad to see you, I know she would. The pair of you made a karmic connection. It's rare. It means something. Don't let it go. And she could use a little help. It's going to take her another day or two, so just go down and see her."

"I don't get this, Bryan. I really don't. I just don't fucking get it."

"Screw your bleedin' ego, Kay. Just go down and see her."

SLOW DOWN, Karen, you've got a kid in the car. She was too upset to be driving anywhere—certainly not to Langley. She pawed around in her jacket pocket, located her phone, and shoved it at Paige. "Call Devon. His number's on there."

"I know his number, Mum," and after a moment, "His phone's off. It clicked right into voice mail."

"Call Jamie."

"Um . . . Yeah, okay . . . Same thing."

"Where's the fucking paper with Cam's address?"

"Right here." Paige retrieved it from the floor and held it up. She was looking at Karen with the condescending expression she always wore when Mum was stressing. Her eyes were saying, *I'm so sorry for you, Mum, you poor insane thing!* Karen wanted to kill her.

"Do you know how to program the GPS?" Karen asked her.

"Sure."

"Then program it."

But instead of following the GPS onto the highway, Karen turned the wrong way, into Caulfeild Mall, parked in front of Safeway, and got out of the car. She couldn't have asked for a nicer goddamned beautiful picture-postcard-perfect lovely fucking summer day. She wanted a cigarette.

She got back in the car, retrieved her phone, scrolled through her address book until she found Rob's home phone number, and clicked on it. Christine's shiny bright voice—"Hi. We're not at home right now, but—"

Shit. She located Rob's super-secret for-emergencies-only cell number and clicked on that. He answered with her name, or his version of it—"Karo! I'm in a meeting."

"Where the fuck are the twins?"

"They're with Christine. Call her cell."

"You want to give me the number?"

A voice answered on the fifth ring. She knew that it wasn't Christine, but that's where she had to start. "Hi. *Chris?* This is Karen."

"Hi, Mum. It's me. Dev. Chris can't talk to you right now. She's driving."

"Oh." Was that really Devon? His voice sounded strange. "That's okay. I didn't want to talk to her anyway. I wanted to talk to you. Is everything all right?"

"Yeah. Totally."

"Okay. Did you—" She wasn't even sure how to put the question. "I just talked to Bryan, and . . . Did you and your sister . . .? He said that you guys sent Morgan and Avalon to see Erica. Did you actually do that?"

"Yeah, we did."

"Why?"

Devon didn't answer. Karen was listening to what sounded like the whoosh of a highway.

"Perfect," Dev said suddenly. "Totally. Yeah, Mum, it's all good. We're having so much fun."

What the fuck? Then Karen got it. "You can't talk, right?"

She could hear the relief in his voice. "Yeah. That's absolutely right."

"Okay, just say yes or no. You guys thought that Erica was . . . in danger or something like that?"

"Yes, that's right."

"So you wanted Bryan and his twins to . . . stage an intervention or something like that?"

"Totally."

"Well, they did. She's okay."

"Cool."

"Will you call me when you *can* talk?"

"No problem. It, um . . . might take us a while."

"That's okay. Are you guys really all right?"

"Totally. Christine says hi . . . Jamie says hi, too. We love you, Mum."

Even though it was no longer transmitting any information, Karen continued to hold the phone in her hand, feeling the small particular weight of it. The day had weight, too, and she could sit here forever in front of Safeway, transformed into zombie-mum. Dev's voice had sounded like—what? Stiff. Alien. It had been close to his voice all right, but it was like somebody had made a clever analysis of it and then reproduced it through a talking computer—and if she didn't get going, there was no way she could get to Langley by one. Paige was staring at her. "Mum? Can I play the radio?"

"You can just play the hell out of it."

AS SOON AS Karen arrived at the apartment Cam wanted to rent, she understood what the problem was—Zach was First Nations. Cam had never mentioned that. He must surely have noticed.

The landlord's name was purported to be Emil Harbard. That had to be a pseudonym or a joke—no one could possibly be named Emil Harbard—but there it was on the lease Karen was signing. By the luck of the draw, she and Emil had arrived simultaneously. As soon as he'd seen the BMW—and the blonde mum in her lululemons, and the

438

blonde angel little sister—a big fat grin had spread across his sleazy little face. The West Van address, of course, had nailed it. He was so happy to have such great tenants. Now he was handing her his business card, and there was that ridiculous name again, so it must be for real— HARBARD REALTY. "Great to meet you, Mrs. Oxley. Call me if there's any problems."

I'll be sure to do that, you racist asshole. "Nice to meet you, too, Emil. You have yourself one spectacular day."

All the way to Langley Karen had been stewing about Bryan and Erica, and now it was a relief to have something else to think about. The boys were showing her and Paige around the apartment. For a cheap-ass place, it wasn't half bad—one big bedroom and a living room that flowed into a kitchenette. Working on a road crew seemed to be doing good things for Cameron—he'd gained weight, looked stronger, not so gangly. Maybe Bryan was right; maybe now that Cam had to pay for it himself, there would be a lot less blow going up his nose. He was opening the standard fake oak cabinets in the kitchenette to show her how clean everything was.

"We've even got our own little balcony," Zach told her, "overlooking the scenic strip-mall." He'd said it so deadpan that for a moment she'd thought he was serious, but then he and Cam exploded into laughter.

Yeah, it was funny. "You need anything?" she asked them. "Furniture?"

"No, Zach has a bunch of stuff. Maybe I can take my bed?"

"Where would you sleep when you came back? No, just buy a bed. I'll come out here sometime and help you fix everything up. I love decorating."

"Cool, Mum."

"Thanks for driving all the way out here, Mrs. Oxley," Zach said. "That's pretty great of you."

Zach was a few years older than Cam, a tall good-looking boy with dark eyes. We Canadians don't have any problem with racism, do we? she thought. No, of course not—it's our benighted neighbours to the south who have the problem. What a bad joke that was. Residential schools. Jesus. "My name's Karen," she said, smiling. "It's not a bad drive."

"Yeah," Cam said, "highway the whole way."

Cameron, her neglected son. She really didn't know him at all. "How's your road?" she asked him.

"Road?"

"The one you're building."

"Just fine," he said, shrugging. "It's a fine road."

"You really want to know, Karen?" Zach said. "It's the best damned road since the Romans," and the boys exchanged glances and cracked up again. There was a good rapport between them. Then Karen got a series of little intuitive sparks, like phone camera flashes going off in rapid succession. She could stop worrying so much about Cam. She didn't really know him at all. Maybe she would end up liking him.

KAREN'S PHONE WAS singing in her pocket. "Fuck." She shoved her armload of wall lights at her daughter. "Get a basket or a cart or some—"

Paige grabbed the phone. "Oh, hi, Dev! Mum *really* wants to talk to you. We're in Home Depot . . . Wait a minute . . . It's Dev."

"Okay, okay, okay." Karen dumped the lights onto the floor. "Get a cart. How many bloody lights do you need anyway? . . . Dev! Where are you?"

"Venice Beach. Hi, Mom."

"Venice Beach?"

"Yeah, you know, like on the boardwalk. It's so cool, all these bizarre people, like a guy on a unicycle, like a freakin' fire-eater. We're with Brittany."

"Brittany?"

"Come on, Mom. Our *sister.*"

Oh. *Brittany.* "Okay." Easy, she told herself. Don't lose it. Just take it as it comes. "What on earth are you doing with Brittany?"

"Chris just dumped us at her mom's place, you know how Chris is, totally random, and Brittany just got the restrictions taken off her license so she took us to Venice Beach. It's so cool. I grew up in LA, and I've never been here before. Bizarre, huh? Anyhow, we couldn't call you before because Chris took our phones, and like there was no way we could call you. Like we tried. Jamie says we're under house arrest. There's a guy who does . . . They're like fake tattoos. They look really real. We're going to get like these huge spiders. Chris is going to shit!"

"Slow down, Dev, you sound positively manic." But at least he sounded like himself and not like some cleverly programmed bot.

"Brittany's really nice. She's a junior at Alliance, she looks so much like us it's scary. We're all just staring at each other, and she's like, wow, I've got goosebumps. She looks a lot more like us than Paige does, weird, huh? And she's like our *half*-sib. Hey, you want to say hi to her?"

That was an interesting thought but not the world's greatest idea. Hi, Brittany, it's me, Karen Oxley—you know, the evil blonde bitch who split up your parents. "Please tell Brittany I'd love to meet her sometime but not on the phone. What are you talking about—*house arrest?*"

"She took our phones. She's like, suck it up, buttercup, while you're here, you're going to be here. Like *be here now.* Did Jesus say that?"

"No, it was some pop guru back in the '60s."

"Yeah, we didn't think Jesus said that. We couldn't Google it cuz she took our phones. Anyhow, we snuck around the house looking for a landline, and guess what? We found all the . . . you know, like the holes where the jacks go in, but they'd taken all the freakin' phones, and the iMac that used to be in my room is like gone, and the door to Dad's office is locked, and . . . I told you how big our freakin' house is, right? And zero computers, zero freakin' phones. Jamie's like what the fuck, we're under house arrest."

"Shit! What is your father—? I'm going to be on the next plane."

"No, no, no, Mom, don't do that, everything's cool."

"Did your father say anything? Like any explanation—?"

"Not so much. Like I can go back up there for grade nine if I want, but he's like— You know, that freakin' boarding school. He wants me to talk to the headmaster. He's like, at least check it out. Sure, Dad, I'll check it out. No probs. We're actually having a good time in a weird kind of way. Everything's cool. Seriously."

Paige was back. "Couldn't find a cart." She'd brought two plastic baskets.

"Oh, for Christ's sake. Hang on a minute, Dev." Karen pawed through her jacket for her Visa. It had to be somewhere—oh, there it was in the *upper* pocket—shoved it at Paige. "Dev! Are you still there?"

"Where did you think I'd be?"

"Don't be a smartass. Okay, just slow down and listen to the question. This thing with Erica. Did you really tell Bryan's twins to . . . what? Rescue her? Stage an intervention?"

"Yeah, we did. She was like . . . We're texting, and she's like life sucks and then you die. It was depressing. And I'm like, oh my god, she's *seriously* fucked, isn't she? and Jamie's like, well, duh, so we sent Morgan and Avi to rescue her."

She still didn't get it. "Why were you texting her in the first place?"

"She always told us if there was an emergency we could text her— Hey, Mom, we gotta go."

"And there was an emergency? What kind of emergency?"

"Wait a minute, Mom."

She could hear voices but couldn't make out what they were saying. He must be having a conference with his sister. "Dev!" she yelled into the phone.

"Yeah, I'm back."

"Texting Erica? The emergency?"

"We, um . . . We were afraid Dad was going to pull like some kind of weird shit."

"And he *has* pulled some kind of weird shit!"

"Yeah, but it's okay— Mom, I'm on Brittany's cell!"

"Fuck. Give Brittany some money. Dev, I am absolutely not getting this. Why didn't you talk to *me*?"

"We did talk to you. You're like whatever, you guys decide. We're like . . . We're just kids, Mom. We don't always know what we want."

"Can I get that in writing? Dev? Are you coming back up here?"

"Are you kidding me? An all-boys boarding school? That's just not gonna happen. Yeah, *of course* I'm coming back. Chill, Mom, everything's cool. I really gotta go, okay?"

"Dev, Dev, Dev, wait a minute. Let me talk to your sister."

"Okay, just a sec." She heard another buzz, buzz, buzz—twin conference.

It was her daughter now—"Hi, Mum."

"Jamie? Are you guys all right?"

"Sure, we're all right. We're fine. Everything's fine."

It was startling how different the twins' voices had become. Dev's hadn't broken yet so they were still in the same register, but the quality was entirely different. He had sounded like a spinny little kid, but Jamie could be ten years older—a nearly adult voice, dark and guarded.

"Jamie," she said, "tell me why I shouldn't fly down there."

"Because you'd fuck everything up, that's why. Everything's fine, Mum. I mean it. I mean *seriously*. You've got to trust us. Just chill, okay?"

"Jamie?"

"I love you, Mum. Got to go."

"Jamie!"

"Dev says he loves you too. Bye, Mum."

28.

KAREN HADN'T REGISTERED much of Bob McKee when she'd first met him, but now that he had immobilized himself in one of her deck chairs, she was forced to see him as a real-life person. Closer to seventy than he was to sixty—a florid, blue-eyed man with sparse white hair and red veins in his nose, wearing a rumpled dress shirt and the kind of generic beige pants he could have bought at the Bay at any time in the last thirty years. "One one," he was saying. "That's the figure that Bryan and I were discussing. I expect he told you that, eh? But everybody says . . . Well, the market's supposed to be cool at the moment. One even?"

He was squinting against the sunlight, a haze of moisture on his forehead. "Not having any agents' fees . . . now that makes a big difference. Bryan and I discussed that. And the timing . . . now that makes a big difference, too. If I could get this done in . . . oh, I don't know, inside of a week? Ten days? I could come down. A little. You know what I mean?" He gave her a hopeful look as though there was actually something she could do about it.

"I do know what you mean, Bob, but Bryan's in Australia."

"He would've bought the house back in the spring if he could."

"I know. He told me the same thing."

She wasn't sure why she was even having this conversation, probably because she felt sorry for him. As he'd told her in the countless messages he'd left on her answering machine, his mum was in the hospital. She'd fallen and broken her hip. He had to sell the house ASAP. And here he was now on Karen's deck, explaining it all to her. "Tried to keep Mother there as long as we could. It was her home. Forty-seven years. It doesn't seem possible. Dad's been gone now . . . I don't know. It must be eleven years. Funny isn't it, the way time flies?"

He was telling her far more than she wanted to know about his kids, all grown up, three boys and a girl. He was a grandfather, too—it didn't seem possible. Dear god, how much longer was she going to have to put up with him?

She'd been in an utterly foul mood ever since she'd got Paige shipped off to camp. So much had been happening so fast that she hadn't been able to process it, but now that she was alone, it was catching up to her. She was still hurting from Jamie's "because you'd fuck everything up, that's why." Well, okay then, you overprivileged self-obsessed little snot, whatever weird shit your dad is up to, you can deal with it yourself—and what *was* Rob up to? "House arrest" Jamie called it, but it didn't sound too far off "unlawful confinement," and that was illegal, wasn't it? Karen had considered calling the Rottweiler but hadn't been able to do it because she'd be too embarrassed. She could just imagine what the Rottweiler would say—"Oh, so you sent *both of your kids* to visit your ex-husband *in the United States?* What? You were seized by temporary insanity?"

The unanswered email—she'd thought she'd forgiven Erica a long time ago, and maybe she had forgiven her—just as long as she remained filed away in some pastel-misty remembrance of things past—but suddenly it had become stingingly real again. Karen had poured her heart out—she'd practically bled all over the keyboard—and Erica could have sent any kind of a response. One line would have been enough. But no, nothing. There were probably perfectly good reasons, but— Jesus, she was tired of being reasonable.

The twins texting Erica—oh my god. Why had they kept it a secret? If they'd been so fucking worried about going to California, why hadn't they said anything *to her?* And Erica had been at Bryan's—for how long? That wasn't really clear. Several days? Painting rooms? Oh, really? You have to allow yourself to feel whatever it is you're feeling. Everybody knows that. That's Therapy 101. But what if you were a mature woman in her forties, the mother of four children, and you were feeling like a sixteen-year-old who has just discovered that her boyfriend has been sleeping with her best girlfriend? Of course that was ridiculous, of course things weren't remotely like that at all, but still— "Just go down and talk to her." Fuck you, Bryan Lynas.

Meanwhile she had to deal with tedious Bob McKee. "You *think* they're all grown-up and on their own," he was saying, "but then they fool you."

What was he going on about now? Oh, right, it was his youngest son. He'd just moved back in with them. Matt had a degree from UVic, but he couldn't seem to find anything. He'd got on at Starbucks. It was better than nothing. When Bob sold the house, things would get better for everyone.

"I'm sorry, Bob, but there's nothing I can do about it. Absolutely nothing. Bryan's in Australia, and I can send him an email. That's all I can do. And he's got to sell *his* house before he can buy yours."

Bob looked away at the sky above the ocean. "We, um . . . took out a reverse mortgage. That's the only way we could've kept Mother there. She was having a little trouble with her memory, but everything in the house . . . It was *all familiar*, you know what I mean? She was there forty-seven years."

Now he was talking obscurely about banks and payments and god knows what, and she suddenly got the picture. It was quite simple actually. The bank wanted its money, and he didn't have it. "Sounds like you need bridge financing."

"That's it!" He smiled for the first time. "Bridge financing. Yes. That would solve everything, but none of the banks will give it to us. The credit unions won't either. Makes you wonder, doesn't it? They're supposed to be there to help people—"

"You're sitting on a million-dollar house, and the banks won't give you bridge financing?"

"Well, you see, we're carrying a lot of credit card debt."

"There must be equity in *your* house."

"Oh, we don't own. We did for a while . . . in North Van. Nice little place. But you know how it goes."

No, Karen didn't know how it went.

"You see, I retired last year, and the wife hasn't been able to work for some time. She has some health issues. Nothing serious, but . . . I don't know. I guess we could've been better with our money."

Their eyes met. She felt it before she understood it—a sick, squirmy, pathetic feeling—and then she found the right word. He was *ashamed*. "You're in trouble, aren't you?"

He looked away. "The agent I talked to says if we put it on the market for nine-eighty-five, we'd sell it the same day. I thought I'd talk to you first though. I know Bryan wanted it."

"THAT'S ACTUALLY A GOOD IDEA," Karen's brother told her. She could hear the amazement in his voice. He couldn't believe that his ditzy little sister was thinking of doing something intelligent with her money for a change. Her phone call had caught him in the midst of a party, but he didn't mind chatting for a few minutes. It wasn't *a dinner party*—they just *had some people over*. She wasn't sure she understood the distinction. She could hear music in the background—Mick Jagger requesting that someone start him up. Steven's taste in music had frozen in time. After the Rolling Stones there was simply nothing worth listening to.

"Damn sight better than parking your money in GICs," he was saying. "West Van real estate is going nowhere but up. Rental accommodations are practically non-existent, so you could charge anything you wanted. The rent pays the mortgage, sit on it a few years, you're laughing. Wait till the market's hot, flip it."

She imagined him out on one of his many decks with *some people*. Bathed in the same golden afternoon light that Karen was enjoying, they would be nibbling hand-crafted appies and sipping chilled white wine while Mick Jagger helped them to maintain the illusion that they were still young.

Steven hated to hear his Lions Bay property described as a "monster house," but that's what it was. Contemporary West Coast architecture at

446

its most hallucinatory, it looked more like the headquarters for some phantom organization that secretly controlled the global economy than it did like somebody's home—a glassy curvilinear million-eyed Argus staring down at Howe Sound. Incorporating various enormous rocks into itself, it had a stream running through it, an outdoor hot tub and an indoor sauna, a gym that would have pleased an Olympian, a cute honest-to-god little theatre, and two full kitchens because Steve and Barb had entirely different cooking styles and didn't like to get into each other's way. A dozen people could have lived there easily, but now that the last of the kids had moved out, the house was occupied by a middle-aged couple and an amiable German shepherd named Gretchen.

"You doing anything, Karen? You're welcome to drop over."

What he hadn't said, what they both understood, was that she was welcome just so long as she didn't have any kids attached to her at the moment. "I'll take a rain cheque, Steven. I've got a date with Netflix."

"We really should get together, it's been too long. So? What's the assessed value?"

"I haven't got a clue."

"Do you want Larry to take over?" Larry was the real estate agent in Steven's network.

"No, I don't think so. I wouldn't mind some *information* from Larry, but I'm going to do the deal myself."

"That's never a good idea." His tone of voice had changed. Little sister had reverted to type. "You need some professional—"

"No, I don't. The whole thing's based on the premise of a private deal."

"Well, Karen. Okay then. Anything in your neck of the woods, the land alone's worth a fortune. You could make a killing. The market's not cool at all, it's just the summer doldrums, but the poor bastard doesn't know that. He's desperate. Perfect for you. But you do have to move fairly fast or he's liable to go fire-sale and you might lose it. But don't make a move without talking to Larry first—"

"If you could get Larry to—"

"Remind him how much he's saving with no agent's fee. Shit, kid, you can probably get him down into the eights. Easy. Larry will call you in the morning."

WAS SHE REALLY going to buy the McKee house? Yes, it looked like she was. It was for Bryan if he wanted it, but what if he didn't? What if he thought she was meddling, or worse, what if it came under the heading of "I don't take money from women"? They'd been in some kind of a relationship for five months now, and she still didn't know him well enough to predict his reactions. She still didn't even know him well enough to know if they actually *had* a relationship. If he wanted the McKee house, she'd sell it to him for what she'd paid for it. If he didn't, she'd do exactly what Steven had told her to do. Buying the house was a smart move, absolutely, but that wasn't why she was doing it. She didn't know why she was doing it.

She was getting that panicky Palm Desert feeling again—probably because she was alone again. Still on her deck on a gorgeous afternoon—one of many gorgeous afternoons that were going to come rolling along, day after day for the rest of the summer. If she waited long enough, she would get to see another splashy sunset over the water. If she didn't want to be alone, she could go over to her brother's and sit around with *some people*. A few of them were bound to be amusing. They weren't going anywhere, so she had plenty of time to get there. The sunset would be just as splashy when viewed from Lions Bay, and Barb's appies were sure to be yummy—and white wine, lovely stuff, chardonnay, pinot blanc, white zin, the best of California, the best of France, who the fuck cares. In seven years Paige would graduate from high school, and then what? All of her kids would be gone, and Karen would be alone in *her* multi-million-dollar house. She would have a life just as inflated, expensive, and pointless as her brother's.

No. It didn't have to be that way. "You're not in charge of anybody else," Helen had always told her. "You're only in charge of yourself." If she hadn't been so angry at Bryan, she might actually have been able to hear what he'd been saying. Okay, Karen, she thought, you can just take your precious ego and shove it. She jumped up, hurried into her bedroom, pulled on her sandals, and picked up the key to Bryan's house. She took the highway and was there in ten minutes.

As soon as she stepped inside, she knew that there was no one home—she could feel it—but she called out "Hello!" just in case, heard the emptiness echoing back at her—bare rooms with no furniture, blank walls with nothing on them. Out of respect for the floors, she stepped out of her runners and walked slowly toward the kitchen. The entire centre of the house was glowing.

Bryan had always said that his skylight would sell the place, and he was right—it was stunning, like walking into a cathedral. The walls he'd knocked out, the spaces he'd created, all invited her into somewhere new, opened out into farther interesting spaces, implying more room to move. What had been a straight whack of stairs was gently curving now, reaching upward to spiral around the emptiness at the centre, that shaft of light. "An open floor plan designed for easy living"—those puffed-up words from a realtor's ad copy—*this* was what they should have meant. Even the colours were perfect, odd and muted—taupe and old ivory, a greyish violet. She wouldn't have believed those colours could work if she wasn't seeing them with her own eyes. She felt the soul of the house. It touched her at a level below words.

She looked up. The skylight was so broad that it would catch the sun from mid-morning to mid-afternoon, and then the western windows would get into the act, bathe everything with gold. If it was raining, it would be that cool tarnished-silver she loved so much. Who would not want to live here? He'd bought the house right after the meltdown when the market had been in the basement, had got it for something in the nines, mainly land value. Everybody had told him it was a teardown. "Aw no," he'd said, "they built them solid back then." He couldn't have put more than twenty thou into the renos, maybe forty, tops. He was hoping to sell it for two and some change, and he probably would, and that was not bad for what he'd put into it. But he'd also put a large part of himself into it. He'd made the house into a work of art. It was cruel that he should have to sell it.

She'd been smelling the fresh paint ever since she stepped inside. Now she followed the scent upstairs to the room that used to be Morgan and Avalon's. The windows faced north, so Bryan had chosen a daffodil yellow for the walls. Someone, probably the real estate agent, would have to take away the drop cloth, the ladder, the paint cans, and the carefully cleaned brushes and rollers, but the room was finished. Bryan was right— Erica was good. A professional couldn't have done a better job.

Bryan had never defined himself, but Karen had thought of him as her boyfriend, sometimes even as a possible life partner, and Erica had been living with him for what? Several days? That wasn't clear, but now it didn't matter. The unanswered email didn't matter either. She tentatively touched the wall with her index finger. The paint was still tacky. Karen, you idiot, she thought. She knew she'd been late, but it hadn't been by a day or two. She'd missed Erica by a matter of hours.

FIVE

29.

ALL ERICA HAD TO DO was merge onto the Trans-Canada and before she'd even bothered to think about it, she'd already done it. Driving had become an automatic cognitive process again, as it should be, and the burn was nothing more than a wispy memory from an old nightmare. Lise's iPod had survived two crashes that had totaled the cars. Now, plugged into the Volvo's stereo, it was flooding her with Lise's memories that were also her memories. Here was Alanis Morissette with one hand in her pocket—a voice from their difficult second year at the college. They'd burned through earlier versions of themselves but they'd still been trapped at home in a world that had become too small, so tight it pinched. What Alanis had to tell them had been exactly what they'd needed to hear.

Erica was sharing the highway with trucks but they had their own job to do, slid over into the left lane to put her behind them and she was glad to see them go. No need to hurry, all of it was easy. She was reconnecting with the young Erica who had loved driving so much that she used to do it for fun. She'd got a late start so there was no way she could get to the Hat tonight but everything was going to be fine fine fine—she would stop at a motel when she got tired. She was aimed east with the sun blazing behind her.

Set on shuffle, the iPod was jumping randomly through time. Now, with "Teen Spirit," they were back in grade ten. Boys—oh my god. And softball, ballet. The leap across the stage, that uncanny moment when you could swear Annalise was hanging suspended in the air—grand jeté. "Your sister's got steel in her legs," Miss Catherine said, "she jumps like a boy." What an odd thing for her teacher to say about the girly twin, that *she jumps like a boy*. And Ricki, the tomboy twin, played softball *like a girl*—that is, with care, with delicacy, with her brain fully engaged. You want a suicide bunt, no problem. Ricki will get the ball on the ground one hundred percent of the time. The sneaky bunt, though, was her fave. Check out the pitcher, get to know her number, come to the plate vibrating with energy, let it crackle through your fingertips so everyone can see it. That's Ricki Bauer, she's gonna smack it—adjustments all across the field. When the pitch comes, slide the bat in your hands—she can feel it now in memory, a loosening and a squeeze, a fraction of a second—and she turns, hears that satisfying little click and she's gone.

After she'd dropped off Bryan's twins at their mum's, she had driven straight to the beach. "Small-town Alberta girl" was one of the ways that she and Lise identified themselves, so the ocean for them had been little more than a pretty myth, but Karen had taught her to feel the power of it. Karen needed the ocean the way Ricki and Lise needed the big Alberta sky. Sitting on a bench near the pier at John Lawson, Erica had watched the waves, listened to them, and tried to sort out her feelings. She had never been great with feelings—that had been Annalise's department. She was surprised at how much she loved Morgan and Avalon. She wanted them for little sisters, wanted to keep them, but she had nowhere to put them short of cramming them into her tiny claustrophobic apartment. Then, listening to the surf, she'd realized that something major had changed inside her while she'd been at Bryan's. She could call it the Temple of Intermittent Reality if she wanted to, but it didn't matter what she called it. If she wanted to go on being alive, she had to do something. She had to do the impossible.

She should gas up in Hope. It was her last chance before Merritt, and besides, she wanted to reconnect to their birthday, to that terrible drive that had almost killed her. It had been nine months since then and if she wanted a number so resonant that Annalise would have called it a metaphor, nine months was it. She found the same truckers' place, walked into the same spiderweb of male attention but today it was different. She was pretty in pink. She and Lise had still been kids when they'd seen the movie—they must have been ten or eleven. They'd adored Molly Ringwald, she'd seemed so *mature*—how funny was that? Erica had never worn pink before in her life but here she was wearing Lise's pink top, her pink runners and even her pink lipstick. Being noticed for being pretty in pink was different from being noticed for simply being female. She didn't know how to define the difference but she didn't like it.

She sat in the same naugahyde booth. She was wearing Lise's wedding ring—a social symbol that was supposed to create a force field around her—but she didn't have much faith in it. These could have been the same men as the last time—truckers checking her out. Their voices could have been the same voices—except that today they were complaining about forest fires in the interior. Lightning. "Hotter than hell, eh? Not a friggin' cloud in the sky."

She couldn't tell if her waitress was the same one. She hadn't eaten anything since breakfast with Morgan and Avalon. Her body wasn't begging for sugar the way it would have been if she'd been chasing the burn but she still wanted something sticky-sweet—instant rush. "A bear claw is not breakfast." No, and it's not lunch either—thanks, Karen. There was nothing hopeful on the menu so she ordered tuna on brown, please, no fries. Outside of Hope the highway started to climb. She was headed into the mountains.

FINDING A MOTEL in Revelstoke wasn't as easy as she'd thought it would be—she'd forgotten about tourist season. This was her third try, and yes, they did have a vacancy, although it was a double queen. Was that all right? "Sure," Erica said. She was tired. She had used up the daylight.

It was more of a hotel than a motel, a bit pricey, but there was a restaurant attached and she was starving. She'd planned to stop high in the mountains, halfway to the Hat, so she was right on time. The girl behind the desk was about Erica's age, maybe a year or two younger. Her nametag said, "Jessica," and she was wearing a wedding ring. She seemed to be having a problem with the cash Erica was offering her. "You do have a credit card?"

"Oh, sure. But it's peaked."

Erica hoped to god she had a credit card. She was improvising. She hadn't planned for any of these details. She flipped open Lise's wallet, found a Visa, laid it down on the counter next to Lise's driver's license. "I didn't plan to . . . I was in Vancouver and, you know, just doing a little shopping and . . . Well, there went the credit card."

"Vancouver!" Jessica said. "Oh, I know. I've done the same thing."

Their eyes met. "We don't usually take cash," Jessica said, "but . . . I won't charge anything to your card but I do have to take an impression. If I didn't, my manger . . . It wouldn't be pretty. How long will you be staying with us, Mrs. Bondaruk?"

454

She hadn't thought about being Mrs. Bondaruk. She didn't like it. "Just one night. I'll be home tomorrow."

"I'll bet you'll be glad to get home, eh? I'm from Lethbridge."

"You're kidding!"

From here on out it was easy, all good feelings and no further evidence required—two small-town Alberta girls, young and married, talking about whatever—about the Cariboo burning up, about Vancouver, a great place to visit but you wouldn't want to live there, about the stores on Robson Street. "You have a great night, Annalise."

"Thanks. You too."

Her room had a balcony. With not a plan in her mind, Erica walked out onto it and allowed herself to feel the relief of not having a road to watch. She couldn't account for the immense presence of the mountains. The night, using various shades of purple and black, had solidified itself into massive shapes and she was simply seeing them—but no, there was more to it than that. If they were merely pictures on her retinae, that wouldn't account for the weight she was feeling. Describing them to herself didn't add up to much. "It feels good as it is without the giant"— Annalise might have said, and now that unintelligible line of poetry wasn't unintelligible any longer. When she and Annalise had switched identities in grade eleven, they weren't being actresses. Not once had Erica ever had to ask herself what Annalise would do. Anything that Annalise thought, Erica should be able to think. Anything that Annalise felt, Erica should be able to feel.

It was late for dinner and only a few people were left scattered around the dining room. Erica sat at a table at the back where she could see them all. She didn't want to talk to anybody but she liked having people around her. What she wanted was a roast turkey dinner with stuffing and gravy just like Christmas but it was the middle of the summer and it wasn't on the menu. She ordered a sirloin. She was so hungry she ate all of the bread the minute it arrived. She'd been hoping that she could outrun the shadow but now she thought that she might have done it one better— maybe it couldn't find her because it was looking for the wrong person.

She wasn't used to carrying a purse and it took her a moment to find her phone. Morgan and Avalon weren't like Jamie and Devon with their individual BlackBerries. All they had for the two of them was a single old flip phone. She texted them.

> Driving back to Medicine Hat. Stopped for the night in Revelstoke. I'm halfway home. It feels good as it is without the giant.

Within seconds their text came back.

> yay!

While she'd been painting rooms at Bryan's, she'd regained her ability to fall asleep at night like a normal person, so she did drift off. Then later, sometime in the awful night, she woke with her mind icy and fast and her body as rigid as a spike. Who was she kidding? It didn't matter how many wonderful memories she'd made, she was going to lose all of them.

It was 5:14. She had to do something to break out of this unbearable state, leapt out of bed, turned on all of the lights, turned on the television—but pixelated talking heads did not help so she turned it back off. The tomboy twin would have thrown on her clothes, run to her car, and driven away in it, but she was no longer the tomboy twin.

She'd had a bath the night before—the tomboy twin would have had a shower—and she'd used Lise's moisturized makeup remover pads to clean her face. Now all she had to do was put Lise's makeup back on. She still had to take her time and think about it but if she did it every day, it would eventually become automatic just the way it had been for her sister. When she got home, she was going to have to replace all this stuff. It was getting old and ratty. The mascara had probably grown a billion microbes by now.

She should eat something but if the dining room didn't open until seven, she absolutely could not wait for it. She checked the hotel brochure, saw that it was a twenty-four-hour restaurant. Oh you wonderful people, she thought, I love you. Fuck cholesterol, saturated fats, trans fats, refined carbs and sugar—she ordered French toast with sausage, washed it down with black coffee. She got a maple Danish to go and was on the road before six.

She'd read somewhere about driver's ecstasy—not a scholarly work, just a literary essay in some magazine—but it had stuck in her mind. You needed music and she had that, and you needed a challenging drive through a breathtaking landscape, and she had that too—mountains and lakes unfolding before her, endless and unfathomable, and the risen sun burning through her windshield hard on her right. Americans came up here every summer to drive this highway. It would take her to places she'd never seen—names, dots on a map—and it would make them real for her. Glacier National Park. Lake Louise. Banff.

Annalise had hours and hours of music on her iPod. Erica hadn't heard more than a fraction of it. Set on shuffle, it kept presenting her with more tunes, voices out of the past, more of that hypnotic electronic stuff Annalise had grown to like after they'd separated. She turned up the volume. The flash that would change Erica's life—of course it had come to the girly twin, the creative twin, but if they hadn't been reversed, it never would have happened. Erica, for once, had been the poet. "We're outliers," she'd said, using the word as a metaphor just as Lise would have done. We're mavericks, she'd meant, we're strange. But Lise had become the psychologist—nothing human is strange to me. Erica saw the flash go off in her sister's eyes. "If we're outliers from the bell," Annalise said, "what is the bell measuring?"

They'd built themselves different bodies, touched each other where they were different. Could MZ twins ever misunderstand each other? Her mind was chanting along with the music, "What *is* the bell *measur*ing, what *is* the bell *mea*suring?" She turned the volume up even higher. Listening, driving, she heard that the music was feeling, not sound.

"Why is it so hard?" Freaks, outliers. The words she was chanting had stopped having any meaning, were just rhythm—bell *mea*suring, bell *mea*suring. No, the words hadn't stopped having meaning, they'd stopping having their usual meaning. Lots of MZ twins managed to separate—why couldn't they? "Why is it always me?" she'd said. "Why am *I* always the one who has to compromise?" The mountains, the sun, the flash of water in deep valleys, the bell. There should have been a better way.

Ricki came out of the womb raring to go—that's what Mum always said—but it was like Annalise hadn't been ready to be born yet. Even when they were apart, they were always inside the twin bubble—thousands of emails attested to that—and they always checked their decisions with each other except for the one time when Annalise had decided all on her own—when she'd decided to get married.

"What do you girls have to say for yourselves?" That was in the principal's office in grade five, and Ricki answered for both of them.

"Okay," he said, "and how about you, Annalise?"

Ricki had all the words but she didn't have any. Words were just meaningless sounds, blank blocks tumbling down around her. Words came tumbling down in great heaps and piles and meant nothing, nothing, and all she had was feeling, not sound. Ricki was looking at her, trying to help her with her eyes, and she felt a tear run down her cheek because she wasn't ready to be born yet. She could see how much Ricki loved her. "Annalise," the principal said, "one of these days you're going to have to learn to stand up for yourself." Yes, she would have to learn how to do that. Ricki had always been strong for her and now she would have to be strong for Ricki.

THE DRIVE FROM CALGARY to Medicine Hat was the opposite of the drive through the mountains—it was the most boring stretch of road in the world, straight as a drawn line, nothing to see, nothing to break the monotony unless you got nailed by a bit of southern Alberta's freaky weather, a hail storm for instance. Erica had come down from the ecstatic high of the mountains and felt flat and exhausted. The music wasn't doing anything for her now so she switched to the CBC. Keeping her eyes on the road, she ate the maple Danish.

It was crazy to drive straight through from Revelstoke to the Hat but except for pulling off twice to pee and stretch her legs, that's what she did. She parked on the street outside the house. Even after all these years she still thought of it as *her* house. She'd made good time—the sun was still high—and she should be happy but she couldn't quite manage it. She felt like every fibre in her body had been ground to wood pulp.

She got out of the Volvo, drew back her elbows, stretched her chest muscles, then allowed herself to fall forward, slack-kneed, and felt a couple of vertebrae snap between her shoulder blades. Duration might be the worst of all punishments but now it was over. She straightened up, amazed at this street so familiar that it almost erased the rest of the world. Luckily she remembered Annalise's wedding ring, slipped it off and into a pocket in her jeans. Ordinarily she couldn't stand rings for more than a few seconds but she'd almost forgotten that she had it on.

You don't knock on the door of your own home, so she walked in and down the hallway past the living room and saw her mother standing in the kitchen with a flare of sun behind her. "Hi, Mum."

Something shiny in her hands, her mother turned toward her and froze—a crystal vase released into the air, hanging a moment—too long—catching light and then blowing itself apart on the kitchen floor. A reedy alarming sound, a wail, almost a whistle—her mother's knees buckling and she was going down into a million sparkling shards of glass. Erica ran to catch her. "Mum Mum Mum!"

As soon as Erica felt the tense little body coiled up in her arms, she started to cry. So did her mother. "Ricki, I swear to god, if you ever do this again I will kill you, I will kill you with my own hands, I swear I will! How could you do this to us? Your father— His health's not good, you know that, I swear I will kill you, I mean it!"

"I'm sorry, I'm sorry, I'm sorry."

"Your brother was going to— Any day now. He was going to take off and fly to Vancouver. It's true. He was. I swear to god, Ricki, you put us through hell. We thought we'd lost you— Damn it, stop. You're stepping in all that glass. Don't move. No, back up. Watch out. Let me get a broom."

Erica stepped back out of the glass shards. She couldn't stop crying.

"I thought you were your sister. I thought, it's a vision or a visitation or I don't know what. I thought you were Annalise. I was praying. I prayed— You're wearing your sister's clothes!"

"Yes. Yes, I am."

"Does that make you feel closer to her?"

"Yes, it does. Mum, I'm so sorry."

IF YOU WANT TO GO OUT for coffee in Medicine Hat, Tim Hortons is where you go. There are several to choose from. "Are you seeing anyone?" Mark was asking her.

"No," she said, "not really." He wouldn't have asked her that question unless *he* was seeing someone. "How about you?"

"Yeah, I have, um— Heather Wallace. Remember her? She remembers you."

"Bob Wallace's little sister?"

"Yeah, that's her."

She couldn't believe it. Heather? The youngest of the Wallace kids? She remembered her as a weed-thin little thing with dirty feet and stringy blonde hair hanging in her face. Wasn't she a million years too young for Mark? "How old is she now?"

"Twenty-seven."

"You're kidding."

"No. Not kidding. Been a while since high school, eh, Ricki? Time zips by like a jackrabbit."

Yes, it does—life goes on. While Erica had been gone, her family had erased every trace of twinship from the room that used to be hers and her sister's—transformed it into what they now called "the guest room." Her dad had painted the walls; her mum had hung new drapes, bought a new comforter and a new throw rug. The double where she and Annalise had slept had been replaced by a single. That's okay, she thought. It's better, actually.

Erica liked the idea of being a guest. She liked hearing the sound of the fan in the hallway when she went to bed, liked sleeping naked with nothing over her but a sheet. She liked waking to the heat of the day. Then one morning, lying in bed with her mind clear and no need to get up, she finally understood something that should have been obvious all along. When most people are dead, they can't pass on their genes but Annalise could because her genes and Erica's were identical. That's what she wanted to tell Mark but things weren't going well. "So—?" she asked him, "is it serious?"

"Don't know about that. Too soon to tell. Might be. She's a sweet girl."

They seemed to be acting out some ancient prescribed ritual. Even their language sounded formal and she couldn't find that elusive point of contact from last winter, the bleak camaraderie of fellow survivors. She hadn't wanted to do to him what she'd done to her mother—look so much like Annalise that she'd frighten him or creep him out. She hadn't brought any of her own clothes with her so she'd chosen the most neutral things of Lise's, hoping they'd be so generic that Mark wouldn't remember them—a white top and jean shorts and flat suede sandals. She wasn't wearing makeup. She had wanted him to see the tomboy twin's scrubbed face. "Mark?"

He must have heard the tone in her voice. He stopped what he was saying and looked at her. She took Annalise's wedding ring out of her pocket and laid it down on the table between them. She saw the shock in his eyes. He picked the ring up, closed his hand around it and held it.

This was a ceremonial moment and would last as long as it lasted. To give him a kind of privacy she looked away from him, looked at the sunlight streaming through the windows. Some kids came in and ordered coffee and donuts—teenagers bored out of their skulls in the Hat in the summer. She remembered that boredom.

"I thought you must have it," he said, "but I didn't want to ask you."

"I'm sorry," she said. "I should have given it to you a long time ago. Grief made me selfish. I'm sorry."

"It's okay." He put the ring into the pocket of his shirt. "Yeah, I thought you must have it."

The ring had broken through the barrier—she could feel it—but there was nothing more she could accomplish in Tim Hortons. "Let's go to Echo Dale," she said. "I need to see the sky."

SHE'D ALWAYS KNOWN that Mark was a doggedly persistent man. That was one of the reasons she'd always liked him. When he'd heard about the identical genes, his first reaction had been to turn and walk away and keep on walking until it must have dawned on him that he couldn't simply abandon her—that he'd driven her here and would have to drive her home—but then, once he'd come back, he'd given her a chance to talk. She appreciated that—how stubbornly he was trying to understand her. He was trying to find a story he could believe, one powerful enough to account for how crazy she was. "You mean you weren't talking to anybody?"

"No. Ordering a sandwich. That was about it."

461

All she had to do was reinforce the story he already believed and that shouldn't be too hard because it was close to the truth. She had terrible insomnia, she told him, hadn't been able to sleep at night. She left her radio playing all the time. She went online and played Tetris. All-night restaurants wouldn't do because some asshole always tried to hit on her. Sometimes she walked on beaches but that was scary because she was alone. In the daytime she rode the SkyTrain lines from one end to the other. She walked from Kits Point to Jericho and back. "And not talking to *anybody?*" he asked her.

"No. Not anybody."

"And how long were you doing that?"

"I don't know. End of April. May, June. Most of July."

"Jesus, Ricki."

They were standing on the hill above Echo Dale Park in the same spot where they'd been last winter. It was summer now and she didn't care that sand flies were biting her ankles. She loved the big sky.

She could be just as stubborn as he was. "I'm not asking anything from you. You could marry Heather and have kids. You'd be a great family man."

The day was so beautiful that it was practically cheesy—an experience designed by the Medicine Hat Chamber of Commerce—fat sun, huge piles of cumulus clouds, a terrific heat radiating down but not too much for her. She missed this kind of heat. "It would be a gift," she said. "A gift to me. From you and Annalise. You'd never have to worry about me or the baby. I'd love it and take care of it. I'd give it the best start in life I could."

The little manmade lake below her was giving the local kids the illusion that they had a beach. The busses running out here even said "beach." It was funny, actually, but Erica had felt the power of the ocean and knew what a real beach was.

"The only answer to death is life," she said. Did she believe that? Of course not. But it had a good ring to it—was every bit as good as "life goes on."

"We're MZ twins," she said. "Our genes are identical." She had to keep repeating that. It shouldn't be a hard one for him to get—he was the science teacher. He just didn't understand the full implications of it.

He wasn't saying anything. She handed him the keycard. "What's this?" he said.

"A room in the Travelodge. I'm going to be—"

"Ricki, you're out of your fucking mind!"

"No, no I'm not. Listen." She wanted to say it as clearly as possible. "Most couples . . . When they've lost a baby, and then when one of them dies, most couples don't have the chance to have another baby but you and Annalise do. We would be— The world needs a person that's half you and half Annalise."

He could give her back the keycard. If she refused to take it, he could throw it on the ground. He could say, "Get in the car. I'm taking you home." He didn't do any of those things so she knew it was still possible. He was studying her like she was a coded message he had to decipher. "Jesus, Ricki, you're sure making me think outside the box."

"Yeah, I am."

"Would it give you something?"

"*Something?*— After Lise died, my period was—" That was wrong. He didn't give a shit about her period and he shouldn't have to. It was as regular as a clock now and that was all that mattered. "Thursday," she said. "Thursday afternoon. I'll be ovulating."

THE ROOM IN THE Travelodge overlooked the pool. Erica could smell the chlorine but she didn't mind it. She and Mark were naked in bed together. She was lying on her back. He was sitting next to her. They weren't looking at each other. "It doesn't help that I look like her, does it?"

"No."

She heard all of his anger and frustration boiled down to that one choked syllable. She also knew that it was pretty much all he *could* say. A woman would cry but he wasn't allowed to do that.

It didn't matter whether she felt anything but if *he* didn't feel anything, it wasn't going to work. How stupid of her. She'd thought that he would do whatever he used to do with Annalise. She'd thought that they could get in bed and fool around for a while and then it would be over— but no, he'd get an erection and lose it, get an erection and lose it. She'd had plenty of experience with boys who needed help—given the kind of boys she was attracted to, that wasn't surprising—but by the time she went to bed with them, she always knew them well enough to be able to guess what kind of help they needed. With Mark she didn't have a clue. It was probably weird—maybe even appalling—to try to make love to somebody who looks almost exactly like your dead wife. They probably should have done it artificially but somehow that had never crossed her mind.

"I must be just as crazy as you are," he'd said when he'd first walked in.

She'd thought it would help him that she was Lise's twin, would make things seem familiar, easy, but she could see now how wrong she'd been. If her goal was to get pregnant, she had to convince him that she was a distinct and separate person called "Ricki."

"Come here," she said. "No, you don't have to do anything. Just touch me." She guided his hand over her right shoulder and down her arm. "Can you feel it? Softball?"

"Yeah."

"And here. Pecs. I did bench presses. Lots of them. She never did. Can you feel it?"

"Yeah." He was actually smiling like she'd just let him in on some amazing secret.

"Okay, and feel my quads. Not like hers at all, eh? Not as developed. She had to jump over and over again. Can you feel the difference?"

"Oh, yeah."

"We built different bodies. It took us years, but we did it."

He was studying her. She sensed that he was actually seeing her now as he hadn't before—and she was actually seeing him, his broad jaw, high forehead, thick nose. Even in the dim flat light of the room his small brown eyes looked bright and warm. Nobody's idea of a handsome man, he was as solid and reliable as an old stone.

"Come on, Mark, just lie down, okay? Fuck the expectations. We don't have to do anything. If it works, it works. If it doesn't, that's okay."

He nodded—it was like saying thanks—lay back and stretched out next to her. He took her right hand and ran his fingers over it. "You've got rough hands," he said. "She had smooth hands . . . soft hands. She always put cream on them before she went to bed."

Now he was simply holding her hand. She couldn't begin to guess

464

what he might be thinking. "I hate that friggin' air conditioner," he said. "It's too cold in here. I hate the sound of it."

"Turn it off."

He got up and turned it off. She was afraid that he would get dressed and leave but he didn't. He got back in bed with her and pulled the sheet over them. "You know, Ricki, I always liked you."

"I always liked you too."

"But you never— I was never attracted to you."

"I was never attracted to you either."

He shot her a quick glance and then his body shook. He was trying not to laugh. It *was* funny. She heard herself giggle—and that got him laughing so hard the bed shook. "What the fuck are we doing here!" he yelled at the ceiling.

They kept trading the laugh back and forth—she would think she was finished with it, would catch her breath, but then he'd start again and that would set her off. She was laughing so hard that tears were streaming down her face and her chest ached. Finally they both lay there gasping for breath. She felt weak from it. "Jesus, Ricki," he said, "I just don't fuckin' know."

With the air conditioner off she could hear sounds from all over the hotel. Someone somewhere was running a vacuum cleaner. People were walking by outside in the hallway. She could hear kids splashing and playing in the pool. "You're genetically identical?" he said.

"We're MZ twins. Of course we're genetically identical. You should know that. You're the science teacher— Here, hand me that." She pointed at the tube of KY jelly on the bed table. She'd slathered herself with it. She hadn't been thinking about him at all.

She squirted a good-sized blob of it into the palm of her hand and then rubbed her hands together, warming it. She touched him. "Do you mind?"

"I don't mind."

She felt him come to life in her hands. "You'd think there'd be a lot of studies on the best way to get pregnant," she said, "but there aren't. So I'm just going on folk wisdom here. The deepest penetration is either missionary or rear entry."

"I'm not big on rear entry."

"Me neither, actually."

There was no reason to be in any hurry. He was getting hard now and she knew that this time he was going to stay that way. He slipped one arm under her, drew her closer and kissed her on the forehead.

She didn't want him to have to think, so when she felt that he was ready she arched up and guided him in. Missionary was not her favourite position but she wasn't doing this for pleasure—although in an odd way it *was* pleasurable. It wasn't exciting, wouldn't ever bring her to orgasm, but it did feel good—"satisfying" might be the word.

She was surprised that he didn't want to kiss her but that was okay too. He was staring off into the distance like he was looking for something that was miles away. She hoped that he wouldn't go on forever because that would hurt—but he didn't go on forever. He exhaled explosively and his hips jerked forward several times. It was like the last few blows hammering down a nail. Good work, she thought.

He was a big man and she felt squashed, claustrophobic, but she didn't want him to leave her yet. She could feel his heartbeat. "No, no. Stay in."

"Jesus, Ricki, I'm sweating all over you."

"It's okay."

He wiped sweat off her forehead. She didn't know whether it was his or hers. "You think we did it?" he said.

"We sure gave it a good shot."

She wanted to say her sister's name out loud but didn't want to hurt him. She didn't know if it would hurt him. He must have been thinking about her too. Annalise.

"Okay now?" he said.

"Okay."

He slowly drew himself out. If she'd been him, she would have wanted to take a shower but he began to get dressed. Then, in shirt and boxers, he glanced over at her, walked to the bed and covered her with the sheet. It must have felt wrong to him—inappropriate—that she was lying there naked while he was getting dressed. What a gracious gesture, she thought.

"Send me an email, eh?" he said. "It can just be a one-liner. Just say 'it worked' or 'it didn't work.' Okay?"

He had all of his clothes on but didn't look ready to leave yet. He pulled up a chair next to the bed. "I want you to promise me something. If it works, I'm Dad, okay? If you've got a man in your life, the kid can call him Bill or George or whatever, but *I'm Dad*. You understand what I'm saying?"

"I understand."

"I'll come visit whenever I can. If you ever need any help, I'm there."

"As long as I'm a university professor, I won't need any help. But it's good—"

"I didn't just mean money."

"Oh, sorry. That isn't what I meant. I didn't say it right. Fuck the money. Yeah, I want the kid to know that you're Dad."

"Okay, you promise?"

"Pinkie swear," she said, offering her hand.

That made him smile. He wrapped his pinkie around hers, stood looking at her. "You mind if I go now?"

"No. Go on. I just want to lie here for a while. They're great swimmers but I still want to give them their best shot."

She could see that he wanted to say something more but couldn't find the words. "Thanks, Mark," she said. "You're a good man."

"Okay, Ricki. You take care."

She was glad he'd turned off the air conditioner. She liked the late summer heat. She lay there so long that she drifted off, was nearly asleep, but even when her brainwaves changed, she never lost track of where she was. Eventually she got up, got dressed, and left the keycard on the bed table. She took the elevator down and walked across the lobby. She hadn't expected to see anyone she knew and she didn't. It was late afternoon and the light across the parking lot was long, hot and slanting. This is my hometown, she thought. It's good as it is.

30.

KAREN WAS TOO ANTSY to sit still. She checked the arrival times on the monitor again, saw that Jamie's plane had landed, walked back to the barrier that separated her from the hallway where the passengers would come out once they'd cleared Customs. Playing long-distance chess with Rob Clark was the last thing in the world she wanted to be doing, but that seemed to be what she was doing. How could she have been so stunned and stupid? She shouldn't have paid any attention to anything the twins had told her. As soon as she'd got Paige shipped off to camp, she should have flown to California, but now it was too late. She had no idea what Rob's latest move might mean. This flight had originally been booked for both twins, but Jamie was the only one who was on it.

Rob had called her from LAX. His timing had been perfect, worked out practically to the minute. He and the twins had been on their way to the airport when he'd got the call from Anderson Hill. The elusive headmaster had been away on vacation, but he'd just come back, and he would be absolutely peachy-keen delighted to meet with Devon and show him around the school. "Sorry, Karo, I know it's kind of abrupt, but not to worry, it's just another couple of days . . . unless Devon changes his mind, ha ha." Of course Dev was okay with that. Here, do you want to talk to him?

Again that strange stiff voice, that not-quite-right voice—"Don't worry, Mom, it's all good, ha ha."

Karen had been listening for deep subtext, and Devon's laugh had been badly wrong. It had sounded exactly like Rob's jolly-as-all-hell I'm-the-CEO fuck-you laugh. What was he doing, imitating his father?

Disaster—but what kind of disaster? Was Dev actually thinking of going to that appalling boarding school? What? Did he have Stockholm Syndrome? And what about Jamie? If the twins were separated, that was supposed to be the end of the world, the one-way ticket down the black hole. At the last possible minute Jamie had been dumped onto the plane all by herself so she'd probably melted down in flight. Whatever, Karen was going to have to deal with her. She was looking forward to dealing with her, actually. At least she'd finally find out what was going on.

Here were the first of the LA passengers. Family groups, moms and dads with their stunned kids. People looked vulnerable in airports, not just tired but incomplete, as though their shells had come off in flight. Now a cluster of Asian teenagers—on a school trip?—and some rumpled businessmen and more run-of-the-mill families, and then the slowest ones, the white-haired set returning from their vacations—but still no Jamie. Rob had assured her that Jamie was on the plane. She couldn't have simply vanished like somebody from the *X-Files*— Oh, but here she was, one of the very last, waving—"Hi, Mom!" My god, what had she done to herself?

Jamie was running up the end of the walkway to meet her. Surprised at herself, Karen ran too. Jamie's scruffy manga hairstyle was gone, replaced with a cute little bob—very dramatic—and could she actually be wearing a dress? It was kind of shocking, actually. But no, it was skirt-shorts in a one-piece. They caught each other in a fierce hug—another surprise—and Karen smelled sun and sweat, a nice smell, actually, straight from California, a summer smell—and something else with it. "You're not wearing *perfume*, are you?"

"Yeah. Just a little bit— Hey, Mom?"

"It's great to see you, sweetie. You look—" Something was seriously not right. Karen couldn't formulate it, but she could feel it like a sudden influx of the butterflies. There was a brand-new piece of luggage on the cart, a big one, baby blue. "What's with that?"

"Chris bought me a whole bunch of stuff, and I couldn't— I'm sorry it took so long. Customs wanted to check my bags." To Karen's questioning eyes, "No, just random. They didn't give a shit. Opened them up and went swish swish and like zipped them up again. Where's Paige?"

"Theatre camp."

"I knew that. Hey, Mom?" They were walking quickly. They were outside the terminal, smacked by the sun.

Karen had taken over the cart and was pushing it just as though Jamie was six. Jamie should be pushing her own bloody cart. Karen had been visualizing a virtual daughter, but here was the real one, utterly transformed and smelling like California, and it was too fast, or too immediate, or too— Karen felt dizzy and slightly sick, the first hint of that oops-I-might-faint feeling. It couldn't be the sun, could it? No, she was still worrying about Devon. "What on earth have you done to your-self, sweetie? You look so—" The word Karen had been about to use was "cute," but she censored it. "I love your romper."

"Thanks."

What a shock. Did Jamie actually have good taste in clothes? Could she have picked that perfect colour, that deep sea-blue? No, Chris had probably picked it. The mary-jane runners were cute. "Nice shoes."

"They're Sketchers. Mom?"

"They look comfortable."

"They are. *Mom!*"

Karen stopped just before the crosswalk and so did Jamie. Annoyed people were walking around them. "I don't believe you," Jamie said.

Out in the sun Karen could see in Jamie's irises flecks of her own amber reflected back at her. Then the fat summer day turned itself inside out like a T-shirt, and she couldn't believe herself either—that Devon could have fooled her for even half a second. He made a cute girl—just as she might have guessed if she'd ever had any reason to think about it.

"Chill, Mom."

"I am chilled, for fuck's sake. You didn't— Tell me you didn't enter the country on Jamie's passport."

He gave her his charming smile.

"Oh. God. Devon. And your sister—?"

"He's with Dad. They're going to call you."

Okay, Karen told herself, just keep moving—it's automatic pilot time. Like back in the day when Paige was a baby. Even with a nanny, four kids is four kids, and it's always one thing after another, and whether it's changing a diaper or coming up with a juice box or buckling somebody into a car seat, you have no choice—you can't *not* do it—but if you complete each task as it comes, just one bloody step at a time, everything will pass and eventually you'll be allowed to go to sleep. She hoisted in one suitcase and Devon the other. "Oh my god, Dev, you've got a Hello Kitty flight bag!"

"Stop staring at me. It's like awkward."

Karen slammed the trunk, walked around to the driver's side and got in. This strange girl—who was familiar but wasn't familiar at all, this complete stranger—got in on the passenger's side. Drive, Karen told herself. "Awkward?" she said. "That's a good one."

She should have paid for parking while she was in the lot; now she couldn't use the express lane—but what did that matter? Was she in a hurry? To get where? She'd been planning to take Jamie for sushi, and now she couldn't do that— Well, yes, she could, just not in West Van where somebody might know them. She should be furious with him, but she couldn't manage it. Devon—this eternal optimist whose central message was "it's all good"—this complete stranger who'd been living in her house for a year and a half, her charming son who was— Oh my god, of course he was gay, but what if it was more than gay? What if he was a transsexual?

"We, um . . . like switched."

"Of course you did. When?"

"Right after you dropped us off. Like you said goodbye and we went through airport security? We were way early, and we just . . . like switched."

"What? You traded clothes?"

"Yeah. We weren't like— We weren't that different. I had board shorts, and she had cut-offs and kind of a girl's top, and we switched, and—"

She waited for him to finish, but he didn't. She looked over at him. He was staring straight ahead through the windshield. It was the hair that really nailed it. His usual manga style had been androgynous enough for a boy, but this sleek cut with long sides and blunt bangs couldn't be anything other than a girl's—and she'd better change lanes or she'd miss Granville. "Where'd you get your hair done?"

"Some place in the airport."

"You're kidding me."

"No, Mom, why would I be kidding you? You got us there *three freakin' hours* before flight time, and we went through customs like . . . We had all the . . . like the letters and the tags, like UNACCOMPANIED MINOR, and we just shot right through."

"So what—? Seriously, did your dad and—" Karen seemed to be losing her voice. "I mean did Chris—?"

"Yeah. They thought I was Jamie and Jamie was me. Like the whole time. We were like what the fuck? They picked us up at the airport, and

471

Jamie's a lot taller than me now. So we didn't even have to— LAX is a freakin' zoo, and we're waiting for our luggage, and it's awkward, and Dad's like, 'Good grief, Devon, you're really growing up. I hardly know you,' and *that's Jamie*, and Chris is like, 'Rob, why didn't you tell me you had such a beautiful daughter? She's utterly *gorgeous!*' and that's me, and I am *not* gorgeous."

Karen had to laugh at that.

"And we kept worrying that they were going to get it, but they never did, and—"

Again, she waited for him, but he didn't seem able to finish this sentence either. She was in Marpole now, following Granville north on automatic pilot. "And so?" she said.

"Meh"—that odd teenage exclamation that could mean anything. "I'm *here*, okay? Across the border. Back in Canada. I'm *safe*, okay? There's nothing Dad can do to me. So you don't have to get into a big fight with him, or pay the Rottweiler a million bucks, or any of that shit. I want to live with you . . . if that's all right. Mom? I'll tell that to any judge who asks me."

NOW THEY WERE in Jamie's room, caught in a curious deadlock, standing there with the two suitcases, staring at each other. He'd shed his Sketchers inside the front door, revealing pink polish on his toenails, and that was the one little touch that was just too fucking much. They were in Jamie's room because, as Devon had just told her again, *he was Jamie*. "It's like weird," he said. "I've got all these clothes . . . But the way I'm Jamie isn't *like Jamie* . . . She's different. *I'm* different. So all these . . . Jamie won't want them. After we switch back. Some of the . . . Like the shoes won't even fit her, but . . . I guess they're mine. I should put them away or something. Should I be in my . . . in Devon's room? Right now I'm the girl. I guess this is my room now, huh?"

Was it? Karen had wanted to paint it a warm rose like her bedroom— the windows faced north, and the light could use all the help it could get—but Jamie had picked the old-lady lavender, so that's what it was. Jamie had been nine at the time, still a kid who enjoyed doing things with her mum, and they'd gone shopping together. Jamie had picked the furniture, and the drapes, and the duvet cover with its tender floral pattern that always felt sad to Karen, like a memory from a lost time. She could never understand how Jamie, the fierce little soccer star who refused to wear dresses, could have created such a melancholy old-school space for herself. No, Devon shouldn't be in Jamie's room.

Okay, but first things first. "Tomorrow we're going to have to get you into Dakila . . . well, maybe not Dakila, but somewhere . . . and get you turned back into a boy."

"No, not yet. I can't switch back till Jamie switches back."

"Come on, Dev, of course you can."

"No, seriously. We've got to do it together."

That was just crazy—but then the whole thing was crazy. "What? You're going to be a girl until she comes back?"

He didn't answer for a moment. "And besides," he said, "I'm perfect for Van An. Like for the cosplay."

"Van An?"

"Come on, Mom, you know. The Vancouver Anime Convention. Why do you think I came back early?"

Oh, right, the twins had been talking about it for months—the most important event of the year, more important than the Olympics, maybe even more important than Christmas. "Yeah, I'm going to be Makoto when he's the Nameless Princess." He'd glanced over at the framed poster when he'd said it.

It had been on the wall so long that it had receded in Karen's mind into mere decoration, but that was a mistake. A million times Karen had wished them gone, but there they were, still alive in all of their cheesy archetypal beauty. Girlish Makoto in his floral pajamas, all in white. Inappropriately sexy Kagami in her leather catsuit, all in black. His bare feet were *grounded* on the shiny floor. She was *suspended* in mid-air, hanging by her cat burglar's rope. Their identical eyes in their identical faces were staring at each other through the symbolic pane of glass, their identical expressions saying, *Oh my god, we're twins!*

"Like when Makoto escapes from the Meritopolis," he was saying, "they send out secret agents to assassinate him because he's . . . Like he's got a Net Weaver so he could fuck with their system. So anyhow, he's got to disguise himself, like—"

473

"Hey. Stop. Tell me the story some other time. So he disguises himself as a girl?"

"Yeah. Yeah, he does. A princess. He requests asylum in the Progressive Territories. He tells them he's a Meritoplian princess of honourable lineage but he can't reveal his name because then they'd—"

"Dev."

"Okay, okay, but they call him the Nameless Princess. Some of the characters even call him Nameless-chan. It's like . . . you know . . . cute . . ."

He had plunked himself down on Jamie's bed. "Book Five just came out. We got it in LA. It's crazy cool." He seemed to have run out of steam, was looking at her with troubled eyes.

"I'm going to have to tell your dad, you know."

He looked puzzled. "Why would you do that? You'd just make him feel like an idiot."

"I told him I'd call him when you got here. I can't very well call him back and *not* tell him—"

"Sure you can. And anyhow I texted Devon . . . Jamie. He told Dad I'm home safe, so you don't need to call."

She had to think about this one. She wasn't going to let herself get railroaded into anything.

"We just got our BlackBerries back," he said, "finally. Jeez, can Chris ever be a bitch!" His thumbs were going, sending a message. He'd had a manicure too, a French finish. That was just as bad as the pink toenails. Attention to small details like that— but wait a minute. They weren't *his* details. His nails looked exactly like Christine's. "Gels?" she said, pointing at them.

"Yeah."

"What? So you and Chris—?"

"Yeah, we did a lot of girl-bonding."

The sea-blue one-piece, the cute shoes, the manicure and pedicure, the boy-fuzz gone from his legs, the Hello Kitty flight bag, the brand new big blue suitcase full of stuff. Oh, Christine, she thought, you fucking idiot! She'd done to Devon exactly what she'd done to Paige.

He was still texting. "Everything's okay," he said. "Devon says—" and he looked up from his phone. "Weird, now I'm back here and you're

474

calling me Devon, I don't know what to call Jamie. All the time we've been gone, he's been Devon . . . Anyhow he's like, 'Dad's not even thinking about Mom.' They're having lunch with *Brandon* and his parents. Brandon's like . . . He goes to this freakin' boarding school where Devon's supposed to go."

"Does Jamie get along with this Brandon?"

"Oh, yeah, *Devon* gets along with Brandon just fine."

"She's been hanging out with him a lot, has she?"

"Yeah. *He's* been hanging out with him. Seriously, Mom, Jamie's not a *she* right now, okay? Yeah, he's been hanging out with Brandon and some of the other guys."

"That's just wonderful. And everything was— Is *he* just planning to go off to boarding school? This isn't a manga, you know. He may not be a she right now, but he wouldn't last a night in a boys' boarding school."

"We know that, Mom."

"Okay. Great. So tell me how you're going to get out of this one."

"What? You haven't— Look, Mom, there's nothing to get out of. Dad's always said he'd let Devon come back if he wanted. Like he's never said anything else. Like he says that over and over—" and he did a wonderfully accurate imitation of Rob's voice—"*I have never said anything else.* So, okay, if he does what he said he'd do, he'll just send Devon back. If he doesn't . . . if he decides to keep him . . . or, you know, pulls some kind of weird shit . . . well then Dad's gonna get exactly what he deserves, isn't he?"

THE VIEW FROM the deck was Vancouver-as-paradise, puffed-out sails dotting the water as the summer sun, that eternal jokester, grinned maniacally down on them. Dev's story was coming out in bits and pieces in no particular order. When he said "Devon," he meant *Jamie*—and so Devon was going off every day with Dad. Met all his business friends, even got to ride in a helicopter—"and playing *golf.* Dad's like, 'You should have seen him off the tee! It's straight, it's *sizzling*, it's damned near to the green. My god, he's *a natural!*' Jeez, that's what everybody always says about her. She's a natural soccer player, a natural surfer, a natural golfer, she's a natural *everything* . . . but anyhow, they've got to keep changing her handicap . . . *his* handicap, because he's beating them!"

Meanwhile he was stuck hanging out with Chris. "She ran out of things to do with me. Like how many times can you get your nails done? Seriously?" They played with Avery. She'd grown up a lot since he'd been there. She could walk, she could talk, her favourite word was NO! "Avery, how about a nice bowl of cereal? NO! We're gonna have a nice bath now, okay? NO!— I'm not a fan." But mainly Valentina took care of Avery, so they went riding—"Kind of scared me, but I pretended it didn't. Like I'm sitting on this big freakin' animal, what if she doesn't want me sitting on her?" And they went to the ballet. "It's a dressy audience, so I've gotta have a little black dress. Like every girl needs a little black dress, right, Mom?"

"Oh, absolutely."

"Not anything too, you know," and he drew a series of looping curlicues in the air to indicate overly frilly, "but *just a little black dress.*"

Karen couldn't stop laughing.

"So what's with you, Mom? You never got me a little black dress. Come on, get with the program."

He was laughing, too, and she saw something change in him. He was pleased that he could make her laugh— No, it was more than that. He was *relieved*. Well, of course. He'd turned himself into a girl, and she was *his mother.* He must have been worried sick about how she'd take it.

He'd been pacing from one end of the deck to the other, snapping up a piece of sushi each time he passed the platter. Now he plunked himself down onto one of the deck chairs. "Swan Lake and Coppelia and like that, things from the old white ballets. You should of seen it, just so . . . We had like these great seats, like so close you could like hear the pointe shoes squeak."

He seemed more relaxed now, and nothing about him felt like a boy in drag. Christine might have overproduced him—made him into something like a girl from an Aritzia catalogue—but there was no doubt that he *was* a girl. He was so convincing because he wasn't trying to be convincing.

Of course they had to go to church, all except for Dad. He always seemed to have something else he had to do. "Baptist, I think. I don't know. Like . . . oh my god, Mom, I can't even tell you. A gazillion people. They

476

project the hymns up on this screen, and there's like this little bouncing ball that tells you when to sing. Everybody's so *glad* to see you. Whoa!"

The most fun they had was with Brittany. "She's really nice. We told her we were switched. "She's like 'shut up! No way!' She's like hysterical."

"Was that a good idea?"

"Why not? Who's she going to tell? She hates Dad, and she thinks Christine's a total whack-job. We invited her to visit us in Vancouver, is that okay? Hey, is there any ice cream?"

"Yeah, I think so. Look in the freezer."

He filled a bowl for himself, brought it back to the deck. "You make a cute girl, Dev."

His brilliant smile—"Oh, thanks, Mom."

"But tomorrow we really are going to have to turn you back into a boy."

"No, Mum, *I told you.* I can't switch back till Jamie switches back. We're like entangled."

"You're what?"

"*Entangled.* Like in quantum mechanics. I know it sounds crazy, but— When they first found it— I think it was Schrödinger who found it. You know, the guy with the cat. Anyhow, the physicists were all like what the fuck! It's faster than the speed of light! That's like impossible. Even Einstein didn't believe it. He called it 'spooky action at a distance,' so anyhow, when you get two strongly related systems like me and Jamie—"

"Devon!"

"What?"

"*Stop that!* You guys are not sub-atomic particles. Let's start over. Why can't you—"

"Mom, *I told you, I told you, I told you!* I can't switch back till Jamie switches back. Like we've got to do it together."

"Come on, Dev, get real. Who are you supposed to be? If anybody sees you. Nobody's going to think you're Jamie. If you go anywhere—"

"I guess I'm not going anywhere . . . except to Van An. You gotta admit it's perfect. *I'm* perfect. Morgan and Avi are like— Hey, can they come over? Can they stay here? Things are like weird at their mom's place. I need to use the credit card, okay?"

477

"The credit card?"

"You told me to never buy anything online unless I ask you first, so I need to use the credit card, and I need— Oh, sorry about the salon in the airport. We couldn't really ask you, but we *had* to do that— Morgan and Avi already have their costumes, but I'm like— These stores in San Francisco, like they've got all this stuff from Japan, Baby SSB and Angelic Pretty, and they can send things FedEx so you get them the next day. Van An's next week, so—"

"Wait a minute. You're going ADD on me. Just shut up for a minute. We'll get to the anime convention later. And we'll get to your costume later. And Morgan and Avi and the credit card . . . we'll get to all that *later*. First you're going to tell me exactly what happened."

"What? Like I *have* been telling you."

"No, I mean— Okay, *why did you do it?*"

THAT WAS LIKE COMPLICATED. They're through customs. They walk all the way to their gate, and nobody's there. They've got exactly two hours and thirty-four minutes before flight time, and Jamie's like, "This sucks balls." They're sitting on the bench all alone, and she's like, "We've given up, haven't we?"

They knew what was going to happen. Everybody did. Their dad was going to pull some weird shit, and they were going to get separated, and they were just letting it happen. Why were they doing this?

Jamie's like, "You gave up first."

"No, I didn't. You agreed to it."

"Yes, you did. I never would of agreed to it except you agreed to it."

"You're playing soccer again. You've got all these new friends, and you just blow me off, what am I supposed to do?"

"I do not blow you off. Go take dance classes with Paige."

So they're going back and forth about who gave up first, and it's depressing. It doesn't matter who gave up first, they can't just give up and get separated. When they were together, they could deal with anything.

"Are we still identical?"

"Yeah we are. Totally."

"Okay then, we've got to stick together."

"Right. We can't get separated."

Jamie's like, "Erica told us to do the impossible, and we're not doing the impossible."

Erica! Okay, here she was—the thorny little knot in the narrative. Karen was finally going to hear about it. "*The impossible?* What does that mean? What were you supposed to do?"

"She never really— She didn't tell us what to do. Like climb a mountain or turn green, or some, you know, some weird shit. She's like, 'You guys are nuts. You can't learn to be identical, you gotta be born that way, so what you're trying to do is *impossible*.' She's like, 'Everybody's wishes things were different, but that's impossible. Everybody's rooting for you because they *want* you to do the impossible. So do the impossible.'"

What was that all about? Had Erica been doing some sneaky jujitsu on their minds? Was that supposed to keep them safe, give them some mysterious task that would . . . what? Distract them? Keep them from going down the black hole? "And Erica sounded depressed? That's what Bryan said you said. You thought she might hurt herself?"

"Oh, yeah. She was like seriously fucked."

"But why did you think Morgan and Avalon could do anything about it?"

"Because they're bodhisattvas and that's what bodhisattvas are supposed to do."

Really? "So they what? Pulled this intervention?"

"I guess so. Come on, Mom, we don't know what happened. We've been under like freakin' house arrest! I can ask Morgan and Avi when I see them. All they said is Erica's okay. She's in Medicine Hat."

Karen was so relieved she felt her eyes sting. "Tell me the rest of it," she said. "You're sitting in the airport. And then what?"

He couldn't remember who said it first—"Hey, let's switch."—but once it was said, they didn't have to talk about it. They just walked into the ladies and locked themselves into a stall. They were wearing identical Cons so they didn't have to switch them, but they switched everything else. "Remember that freakin' bra you made Jamie wear? She's like, 'I hate this fucking thing. Let's see how you like it.'"

Devon fluffs his hair up and pushes his bangs down over his eyes, and Jamie wets hers and slicks it back out of her face, and they sneak out of the ladies, like nervous somebody's going to see them, but there's still nobody around. Now they've got two hours and twelve minutes to flight time. So they're walking around the airport, looking at all the shops, and Dev's like, "Come on, Jamie, do you really think you can be me?"

"Yeah, I can. I know you really well."

"Maybe. But I don't know if *I can be you*. You're too freakin' weird and complicated."

"Don't try to imitate me. You don't have to do that. They don't know me. Make up your own Jamie."

She's like, "In order to ride the wave, your *mind's* got to ride it." When they were in Tassie and she rode the big wave, there was no way she could fall off her board. That's when Bryan told her it was all *in the mind*—and she was like, "whoa!" So she's like, "People fuck up because they're doing things they don't really want to do or because they don't believe they can do them."

Devon's thinking, yeah, right, I can make up my own Jamie. Then all of a sudden here's this salon or spa or whatever, and they look at each other. If they really want to do the impossible, then hair is the most important thing there is.

Devon's like, "Perfect. Let's do it," but Jamie's like, "I don't know. Awkward." They go inside, and Devon has to do all the talking.

"The girls in the salon are like, 'How much time have you got?' and they keep looking at our UNACCOMPANIED MINOR tags and shaking their heads. 'We can colour your hair in half an hour, no problem, but lightening your brother's . . . Well, at least he doesn't want to go platinum, ha ha. Maybe an hour and a half? How were you planning to pay for this? Any chance you could pay in advance?' So we stick the card in the machine, and just like you told us, Mom, we add twenty percent for the tip, and it goes right through, ZAP, and all of a sudden everybody's happy.

"Okay, what kind of haircuts? We've got to choose fast, and I'm like Japanese princess style, like *hime*, but the girl's not Asian so she's not in the loop. She shows me pictures, and I pick one, and she's like, 'Oh, that'll look cute on you,' and Devon— That's Jamie, right? So Devon picks like an ordinary boy's haircut, old school, and I'm done first, and the girl's like, 'We've got this great line of cosmetics,' so I buy some lip-gloss and stuff, and that's the second charge on the card, sorry, Mom. So anyhow we go back to the gate, and they're just calling for boarding. Okay, so now we're past the point of no return—oooh, scary. We've got our tags, so we board first, and I've got Jamie's passport, and she's got mine, but there's no problem. We find our seats, and I'm like, 'Okay, we've got three hours, and I'm gonna tell you every freakin' little detail about Dad and Chris and me and our house and like that, and you're gonna *remember* every freakin' little detail.'

IT WAS THE TIME OF DAY in late summer that Karen liked best—when the sun sank low enough to cast long honey-golden rays that transformed every object from ho-hum pedestrian into exquisite once-in-a-lifetime celestial. When she'd been married to Ian, she'd coped with things by not coping—she'd simply gone to sleep. He used to call her the crash-out queen. Too bad she couldn't do that now. Of course she had allowed the bodhisattvas to come over. They'd eaten up all the leftovers in the fridge—the non-meat items anyway—and now were upstairs in Jamie's room checking out all the new clothes packed into Dev's two big suitcases. They hadn't seemed the least bit surprised to see that he'd turned into a girl. They'd probably known all about it. He'd probably been texting them.

Karen had been working out all the possible variations in the twins' chess game, and if there was a flaw in their play, she couldn't find it. As incredible as it might seem, this pair of thirteen-year-olds had beaten the grandmaster, Robert Clark. Dev's take on things was absolutely right. If Rob turned out to be an honourable man—a man of his word—he would never have to know what they'd done, but if he turned out to be an asshole, then the endgame was going to be fairly brutal. Karen was sure that Jamie was just the right person to make it fairly brutal. No matter how hard she tried, Karen couldn't find a single reason why she should tell Rob a thing.

Upstairs, pulsing, that monotonous electronic music favoured by Bryan's twins—so they'd moved from Jamie's room to Twin Central. So what was it with Rob and Chris anyway? You'd think they'd never lived through puberty. If you've got fraternal twins and they're thirteen and slow developers, which one do you suppose would be the bigger, taller, stronger one—the boy or the girl? Oh, the idiots! And Jamie fooling her own father! Well, a man sees what he wants to see—wasn't that a line from a song?—but what if the whole thing blew sky high? Forget about maintaining an amiable relationship with Rob—he would be screaming on the phone, Jamie sobbing on the phone, and they'd have to send Jamie back, of course, and Devon? Well, she would keep him, and Rob could go screw himself.

And here was Dev on the deck with her, fully materialized. He'd shed his Aritzia catalogue look, was now in standard teenage girl summer uniform, cut-offs and a T-shirt—a baby-blue T-shirt with baby-pink roses exploding down the front of it. He was wearing one of those intensely red lipsticks that Bryan's girls favoured. Today's colour could easily be called "Screaming Marilyn."

"Mom? Can I use the card? It's for Van An. When Makoto's disguised—"

"I know that. You told me that." God, she hated that red lipstick on him. It actually made her kind of sick. Should she say so? No, probably not. "What is it you *want*?"

"A dress and a pair of shoes?"

"Okay, okay, okay. Buy yourself a dress and a pair of shoes."

That must not have been all that he wanted. He was still there. "Can Morgan and Avi stay here until like Bryan comes back from Tassie?"

"I thought they were staying at their mum's."

Well, yeah, they were supposed to, but like everything else, that appeared to be complicated. They didn't go back to their mom's house very much, hardly at all. They hated going there. They'd been sleeping at Bryan's house. No, Bryan didn't know about it, are you kidding? They hid a futon in a closet and unrolled it like whenever, but it was creepy being alone there at night. Okay, but why on earth didn't they go back to their mum's? Because the house was full of yabbos.

"Yabbos?"

Yeah, like the guys in Jason's band. Jason was their mom's boyfriend. He played the guitar, and they were supposed to be working on their songs, like for a CD, but they never worked on anything, it was party-on twenty-four-seven. And the yabbos were inappropriate. "Like, 'You girls are sooo hot. I bet you've got lots of boyfriends.' Like, 'Wow, imagine it with twins. Two on one, awesome!'"

Karen was furious. "Have they ever *done anything to them?*"

"No, but Morgan and Avi are afraid they might try, and then there'd be, you know, like major drama. Morgan and Avi don't take any shit from anybody, and they don't want any drama."

"They've got to tell their father."

"No, they don't. They really don't want to do that. They're afraid Bryan would go over there and clean up the house." Devon smiled. "That would be like major *major* drama."

Yes, he was certainly right about that.

"The yabbos ate their goldfish."

She didn't get it. "You know, Mom, like Morgan and Avi had a goldfish in a bowl, and one night the yabbos fried it and ate it. Morgan and Avi got up in the morning, and there was its little bones on a plate."

That was just too pathetic for words. "Of course they can stay here."

Devon went running off to tell the twins the good news, and Karen was left to contemplate the sun's last pomegranate smear. Thanks a lot, Bryan. Now she had six kids to worry about instead of four—and she was afraid of Bryan's twins. They were even more incomprehensible than he was, lived inside that closed-off space Erica called "the twin bubble," and god knows what reality they might have created in there. Bodhisattvas? Oh, really? Were they going to fill up her house with stolen road signs? Did they have sketchy boyfriends who would be hanging around? If she imposed a curfew on them, would they pay any attention to it? Would they pay any attention to *anything* she said? And Devon-as-a-girl was already modelling on them. It probably wouldn't stop with the red lipstick.

Now here they were, staring at her with their blank eyes. She was the grownup, so she should speak first. "Dev told me a little bit about what's been going on. You're welcome to stay here—"

"Yay," they said in unison.

"He told me—"

"Mom! You can't *do that.*" Devon looked utterly horrified. What on earth was he talking about?

"You can't say 'he.' Seriously. If you call me 'he,' you'll fuck everything up."

"Okay, okay."

"You can't screw it up, Mom. *Seriously*. Don't worry. When Jamie comes back, we'll switch back, but right now, *I'm the girl*, okay?"

"Okay. I got it."

Bryan's twins were still looking at her. They hadn't changed expression.

"All right, girls. *She* told me you were having some issues at your mum's. So it's okay with me if you stay here, but it's got to be okay with your mum too. I've got to call her."

"That is not a wonderful idea, Mrs. Oxley."

"She's pissed as a newt."

"They're like doing shooters and lines."

"Look, Morgan—"

"She's Avalon," Morgan said.

"Sorry. Look, girls, you know I've got to call her."

Dev picked up the phone from the patio table, handed it to Morgan. She punched in the number and handed it to Karen. It rang so long that Karen was about to hang up. Then somebody—maybe it was a woman—said, "Yeah?"

"Hello," Karen said, "is this Tracy?"

A woman's voice responded like a dim echo: "Is this Tracy?"

"Hello? This is Karen Oxley . . . ?"

"Hello," the voice said, "this is Karen Oxley."

Oh, my god, now what? As Karen waited, she could hear the sounds of a full-on party in the background—screaming, laughing, heavy metal. These people didn't sound old enough to be anybody's parents. They sounded like kids Cam's age—a bunch of drunken hosers. "I'm sorry to bother you. I'm Devon and Jamie's mother."

"Oh! It's *Dev*-on and *Jam*-ie's *moth*-er. It's Devonan *Jamie's* mother. It's Devon and Jamie's *mother*," and then Karen heard a loud wet hissing explosion—the sound of someone choking on their own laughter.

"Tracy?" Karen said.

"Tracy?" the voice said.

"Morgan and Avalon are at my house. Is that okay with you?"

"Morgan and Avalon are at my house. Is that okay with you?"

While Karen was trying to think of how to break through the echo, the woman hung up.

Karen had been wrong about Bryan's twins. She'd always had trouble seeing much beyond the too-long bangs and the sleazy makeup. The twins' eyes weren't "spacey" or "blank"—they were *watchful*. "You're living with us now, girls," she said, "but I just want to make sure we're clear on a few things. We've got house rules."

"We're cool with house rules."

"Our dad has house rules."

"All right, here's the first rule. You absolutely cannot go on calling me Mrs. Oxley. I don't care how polite that is in your family, it's not polite in mine. My name's Karen."

They were just standing there looking at her. Then Morgan said, "Karen?"

"Yes."

Avalon completed the question. "Can we get our cat?"

BRYAN'S HOUSE HAD a realtor's sign in front of it. Too bad he had to sell it quickly; if he could sit on it a while, he could make a killing, but that wasn't her problem, was it? Well, yes, in a way it was—she'd bought him his *next* house if he wanted it. Difficult man, she didn't think she'd ever understand him. He'd always said that his ex was barking mad, so how could he have pissed off to Australia and left his girls with her in a house full of drugged-out hosers? It felt like borderline child abuse. He could have left the girls with me, she thought. So why didn't he? Doesn't he trust me? The irresponsible asshole shouldn't flip the McKee house; he should *live in it*, give his daughters a stable home for a change. Didn't they deserve that?

Karen got out of the BMW, ostensibly to help look for the cat but actually to wander around in the night, brooding. She hadn't realized that she was mad at Bryan, and it was about Erica, of course. Not that she thought they'd *done anything*, but Karen felt— What? Left out? Well, if she'd been left out, it had been her own fault.

With no streetlights in this obscure part of West Van, the moon was the only light she had, and it was so woodsy that they might as well be on Bowen. The girls had vanished into three different directions, calling out, "Evinrude! Evinrude! Come here, kitty." What a hopeless mission. It could be anywhere. Cats aren't dogs. They don't come when you call them.

Teenagers saw adults as powerful beings qualitatively different from themselves—anyhow, that's how Karen remembered it—but the secret that teenagers didn't know was that a lot of the time adults were just kids playing grown-up. She was feeling a mysterious ache, a nostalgia or something much like it. Maybe it was a response to the moonlit night and the sadness of the children's voices calling out for their lost cat. She walked around the house toward the back. It was so dark in the shadows that she paused halfway, waiting for her night vision to kick in—then, when it did, continued on into a moon-drenched enchanted forest. How unreal—she was out in a fairytale landscape searching for a magical cat. And oh my god, there it was. Avalon was petting it. "Evinrude, you good cat, you waited for us!"

Karen had been imagining it as a fat tabby, but it was a thin grey thing, perfectly coloured to be invisible in the night if it wanted to be. She didn't like cats, but she was glad the twins had found theirs.

"Good kitty," Avalon was saying, "I bet you're hungry, aren't you? Oh, do we ever have a treat for you!"

Morgan had run back to the SUV, was opening the can of tuna—that and a blanket were the only things they'd brought to transport the cat. "You know, girls," she said, "cats don't like riding in cars."

"It's going to be fine," Devon said.

Reluctantly, Karen got into the driver's seat. "If that cat goes berserk—"

"No probs," Avalon said, and Morgan, the take-charge twin—"If she freaks, we'll throw the blanket over her."

"Drive slow," Devon said.

"Oh, you bet." Karen oozed the SUV onto the road.

At thirty clicks, it was taking forever to get home. Painfully attuned to the possibility of claws, Karen's skin was prickling. "Is she *still* all right?"

"She's cool."

Karen pulled into the garage. Morgan opened the door to the BMW, and the cat shot out of it like she had a rocket up her ass. She ran through the open door that led to the first floor and disappeared into the house. Karen had thought that cats were supposed to pad silently, but this one, running, had made a madly galumphing sound like a tiny pony.

IT WAS ALL TOO FUCKING MUCH, actually—the cat had hidden itself somewhere in her house and refused to come out. "Don't worry, Karen," Avalon said, "she's just scared because she doesn't know where she is."

"She'll come out when she feels at home," Morgan said.

"Doesn't she need a litter box or something?"

"Oh, no. She goes outside."

"She's a feral cat."

"She'll tell us when she wants to go out."

Karen wasn't so sure of that. That's all she needed—cat piss everywhere—but there didn't seem to be much she could do about it.

"Dev," she said, "seeing as you're the girl at the moment, you sleep in Jamie's room. Morgan and Avi can sleep in Twin Central." That was her indirect way of saying, *Don't even think about sleeping in the same room with the twins.*

Avalon was the warmer, more talkative, more accessible twin, so Karen decided to start with her. "Avalon? When you . . . ? Whatever you did with Erica . . . What was it? An intervention?"

"She really didn't want to come," Avalon said, smiling. "We had to like abduct her."

"Yeah, we had to like kidnap her," Morgan said.

"And we took her up the Grouse Grind."

"You're kidding."

"No, we're not kidding."

"She was cool with that . . ."

"once we got going."

"Like Dad wanted to show her the beneficence of the mind-body unity."

Karen didn't even know what to say. Now both unnerving twins were looking at her, waiting. "Oh?"

"And she sat with us a little bit," Avalon said.

"*Sat* with you?"

"Yeah. Like zazen."

Oh my god, Karen thought, this Buddhism stuff must be real for them. "Is she all right?"

"She said she was all right."

"She like texted us."

"She knew we'd be worried about her."

KAREN WALKED OUTSIDE onto the deck, leaned on the railing, and gazed at the jewelry of the night, at the moon's reflection riding in the water. She shouldn't have studied English literature in university. She should have studied advanced chaos theory.

Devon had followed her. In the dark, he made a slim silhouette, the sweep of his hair emphasizing the gentle curve of his cheek. It wouldn't be hard to think of him as a girl. If he was transsexual, well then she'd deal with it somehow. She would Google it and make herself a reading list—that was always a good start. She didn't know why, but she felt there was a way forward, something positive. The air was as soft as rustled silk. Then, with no warning, her mind executed a strange aerobatic maneuver—gave her a floaty sensation of ghosting through an enormously empty space that might have been left hanging loose, nearly forgotten. Was it that old nostalgia trick again, a memory? It felt like a flashback to the eternal summer she'd loved as a kid. Maybe it had been triggered by the girls and the smoky grey cat. "You ever feel how mysterious the night is?" she asked—a ridiculously cheesy line, but she was guessing that he must be feeling it, too.

"Oh, yeah! It *is* mysterious. It is. It's really *really* mysterious."

Bryan suddenly added himself to her mind, and she felt a pang of missing him as sharp as the lime scent he sometimes wore. You annoying asshole, she thought—but everything that had been pissing her off seemed to have dissolved into the empty space of the silken night. When you need to talk to somebody, you should do it, and the only time you've got is now. She could call his cell, but he rarely answered it. She didn't even know if his cell worked in Australia.

She found Bryan's girls in Twin Central, lying on the bed, watching something on Devon's laptop. "Do you girls have a phone number for your dad? At your grandparents? The landline?"

She shut herself into her bedroom. She didn't have a clue what time it was in Australia—hoped it wasn't four in the morning. She punched in the long string of numbers, and it started to ring just like a normal phone call. A man answered, she asked for Bryan, and there he was, as clear as if he was in North Van. "Hey, mate," she said, "how you going, owright?" Oh my god, how easy that was. She'd badly missed his huge laugh.

His mum was still hanging on, he told her. His brother John was with her now. They were all going back to the hospital later. The arseholes were a little too handy with the fucken morphine, if you asked him—the old girl was out of it most of the time—but they'd had some good talks right after he'd got there. Yeah, he was glad he'd got there in time—when she still knew who she was and remembered everything. "Arrogant bastards, they think they know what's best. I don't know about Mum, but if it was me, I'd rather have a bit of pain and still be able to think straight. But she's a fighter. Still hanging on. How's everything back there?"

"I've got your girls. They were . . . having some problems staying with their mum."

"Yeah? Thanks, Kay, that's big of you. I really appreciate that. You tell them if they get out of line, I'll kick their arses."

She didn't want to tell him about the drunken yabbos. He probably knew all about them anyway. "Bryan? I bought the McKee house."

That one stopped him. After a too-long silence, he said, "Yeah? Did you now?"

Okay, she thought, it's story time, and it better be amusing. She told him about Bob McKee sitting on her deck, the pathetic way he'd dropped his price every time he opened his mouth, getting advice from her brother, and finally arrived at the heart of the matter— "I bought it for you, if you want it. Instead of flipping it, why don't you just *live in it?* Find some other place to flip? Give Morgan and Avalon a stable home . . . at least until they're out of high school?"

"What? You're offering to *rent it* to me?"

"Oh, for Christ's sake, no. I wouldn't do that. We could be joint owners. It'd be an investment for you. I put a big whacking down payment on it. Could you pay the mortgage?"

"Oh, yeah. Yeah, I could pay the mortgage. No probs with the mortgage."

What the fuck am I doing? Karen thought. She hadn't realized it until she'd said it, but what she was offering could sound dangerously close to a marriage proposal.

"I don't know, Kay," he said. "It could be a— Big things like this have got to settle in my mind. There's a lot to be said for it, but— Let me think about it, okay? So? What did you end up paying for it?"

She'd held off on telling him that. She was afraid he'd think she was a bit of a fool. "One one. Exactly what you'd agreed to."

Yes, he *was* laughing at her. She felt her face flush. "It was a fair market price," she said, defending herself. "I checked it. Jesus, Bryan, why should I screw the poor bastard just because I could?"

He was still laughing. "Sweet bleedin' Jesus. You want to give me some of your merit, I'll take it. I could use a bit."

What was he talking about? "Merit?"

"Yeah, merit. You got a shit-ton of it, Kay. Everybody else in the world would have screwed him. Even I would have screwed him. But you didn't. If you were looking for right action, there it was."

31.

IT WAS *interesting*, she supposed—wasn't that the catch-all word you used for experiences that were nasty but educational like this one? Erica had never seen her office from this particular angle—lying flat on her back on the floor. The whole world seemed overheated—steamy, moist and fragile. She was sweating out of every pore.

"Leave your car here," Stacey was telling her. "I'll take you back to my place and you can just lie there and watch television. Then we can keep trying things until something stays down."

"That's really nice of you. Yeah, that'd be fun. Maybe later. But I want to see the kids." The Lynas twins and Devon were at the Vancouver Anime Convention over at SUB. They were supposed to meet Erica in her office.

"What if they don't show? Then we'd just be waiting around—"

"No, they're coming. They texted me. They got delayed . . . some contest or something."

Erica absolutely had not been ready for this. Why was it called *morning* sickness? That made it sound so benign and temporary. A fruit smoothie last night had been the last thing that had stayed down. This morning she'd thrown up the first half of a breakfast sandwich from the organic deli, then, an hour later, the second half. This afternoon she'd thrown up another smoothie, a cup of yogurt and just now, a banana.

"It's supposed to be adaptive, for Christ's sake," she said. "They've actually done studies on this. Apparently it's to protect the fetus from toxins in early pregnancy . . . when the organs are getting formed. But if you can't keep anything down, how's the fetus supposed to get any nutrients?"

"It's getting plenty of nutrients. It's sucking them out of *you*."

"Thanks, Stace. That cheers me right up."

"Try some water." Stacey offered her a hand. Erica took it, allowed herself to be pulled to her feet and then settled into one of the chairs where twins sat when she was interviewing them. She took the cup Stacey was offering her. "Don't gulp it, sip it."

"Absolutely." She hadn't expected Stacey to turn into such a mother hen but that was okay—she could use some mothering. She hadn't told Stacey that she was carrying Annalise's baby. She'd told her what she'd decided to tell everybody—that it had been a pleasant one-off with some guy she'd known in high school. He was a nice guy—this nameless fellow—but she wanted to raise her kid on her own.

She took a sip of the water—and then another. So far there was not a sign of that telltale lurch that would send her running for the bathroom. She heard kids' voices out in the hallway, said, "Here they are," stood up and felt the world tilt.

"Erica!" Morgan and Avalon—more than merely hugging her, they'd collided with her like two enormous puppies. How was she supposed to deal with all this animal energy? Dizzy and queasy, she hugged them back. "Hey, you got the school uniforms you always wanted."

"Yeah, we did."

"Sailor fuku."

They were manga schoolgirls perfect in every detail. "You look absolutely authentic."

"We *are* absolutely authentic—"

"They're *from Japan!*"

"Akime's aunt got them for us—"

"they're *real*—"

"like from a *real school*—"

"like their summer uniform."

A third kid had come trailing in behind them—a girl in a fantastic pink outfit. Stacey sent Erica an amazed look that said something like, *Oh my god, really?* It had to be Devon but Erica wasn't sure. If she'd seen him at Van An surrounded by other kids in costume, she would have walked right on by him. "Dev?"

"Yeah, it's me." He sounded tentative, almost apologetic. "I'm Makoto when he's the Nameless Princess." Now they all seemed to be caught in a let's-stare-at-Devon moment. "Akime did my makeup for the competition."

"It's like kabuki," Morgan said.

"Not full on," Avalon said.

"Kabuki light."

"Akime copied it from the manga," he said, "like from the colour pages." If the idea was to transform Devon's face into a mask, then Akime had succeeded. He wasn't dead white but close to it—a pale ivory—had sharp-edged black lines inked around his eyes, thinly arched eyebrows, a soft pink haze blended into his cheekbones, and a small brilliantly red mouth painted on, as shiny as if it had been shellacked. "Weird, huh?" he said. "When she showed me in the mirror, I'm like *what the—!* Boys play girls in kabuki. Did you know that?"

"No, I didn't know that."

He gave them a half-hearted curtsey, showing off his dress. "It's like . . . It's *real*. Like from Japan . . . California. I mean, you know, like from a store where they import things from Japan."

His pale pink costume was astonishing, actually—everything about it madly excessive. There was an enormous bow on his chest and two more just like it on either side of his mammoth poofy skirt. Rings of white lace descended from his waist and more white lace was slathered everywhere, even on the tops of his over-the-knee socks. The headdress had a fat pink rose in the centre of it, was decorated with more bows, tied with a broad ribbon under his chin to create yet another bow. There were even bows on the toes of his pink patent mary janes and bows at the tops of their high tapered heels.

"Oh my god, Devon," Stacey said, "you look exactly the way I wanted to when I was five." It was funny but not *that* funny—they must all have needed to laugh.

"And guess what?" Devon made one of his open-handed shrugging gestures. "I'm . . . just freakin' *stunned*. I mean like literally. We *won*. Like, you know, we won best intermediate cosplay."

"You're kidding. You won? Really? All of you?"

"No, no, not us—"

and ZAP, they were all talking at once—

"like a million girls in sailor fuku—"

"No, Dev and Jacqueline won—"

"She's like—"

"Don't tell them," Devon said, "I want her to be a surprise."

"Come on, come back with us—"

"like met Jacqueline, like on the first day—"

"you've gotta see her—"

"Oh. Hey. I forgot, this is Dr. Chou—"

"Yeah, Princess, get with the program—"

"I'm *Stacey*, okay? I've heard a lot about—"

"We *won*. I'm still like, what the fuck—"

"All this stuff, a prize pack—"

"The other skits were funny and we were so *not* funny—" and this surge of zingy collective energy seemed to be propelling them out the door. "You okay with this?" Stacey said.

493

Erica was absolutely okay with this. Her office had grown claustrophobic in the August heat—prison-like, stifling—but out in the world the sun was great, and the air and sky. The nausea had left her for the moment and she felt nothing worse than hungry—somewhat starved, actually, but that was okay too.

Ah, the cosplay kids—the closer to SUB they were getting, the more of them there were, brilliant in their costumes in the blazing afternoon light—a splendid rainbow, transforming the campus into real-life anime. The twins were right, a million Japanese schoolgirls—that seemed to be the favourite costume—and girls in elaborate dresses like Devon's, though none as elegant as his. The most interesting costumes were one-offs—specific characters from specific stories—like this pink rabbit and some sort of robot in a boxlike costume. "Who *are* these people?"

"There's Danboard. Don't know about the rabbit."

"Nobody could possibly know everybody—"

"Like some of them you've gotta ask—"

Where did the kids get these costumes? This wasn't like Halloween when you just slapped something together—this was serious. "Whoa!" from Dev. "Black Rock Shooter." A girl in high black boots and a cape, a sword in her hand, not much under the cape except what looked like a black string bikini. "Oh my god, is she ever hot!— Excuse me," raising his phone to show the girl what he wanted. "Okay?"

As Dev and the twins aimed their phones at her, the girl immediately took a dramatic pose, her sword raised, her expression mean and threatening.

"Thanks," the kids said and now it seemed to be Devon's turn—two boys in long black coats were calling out to him, "Princess, Princess—Nameless-Chan—" One of them was waving a camera.

"The boys just *love* Devon," Morgan told Erica.

"Shut up," he said but walked to where the boys were directing him—to the shade under a tree. He turned partially sideways and posed—one foot slightly behind the other, knees close together, toes turned inward. "Akime showed him how to stand like that," Morgan told Erica. "It's from kabuki."

494

Unsmiling, Devon stared down the camera. The shutter was click-ing and it finally occurred to Erica that she had a camera too. She pulled her phone out and took a picture of the people taking pictures of Devon.

One of the boys was inviting Morgan and Avi into the frame—"Come on, twins." Maybe this was the point of Van An—everybody taking pic-tures of everybody.

"How was your lunch with Celia?" Stacey was asking. Erica was so engrossed in the photography ritual that it took her a moment to connect—Dr. Celia Gergess from Gender and Women's studies. "Well, *she* enjoyed the lunch. Went back to her office and I threw up. Lovely, eh? She was very nice about it. I lay on her couch and she talked at me non-stop for two straight hours. Gave me a huge amount of stuff to read. Some of it's, um . . . kind of hard sledding. That theoretical stuff."

"Oh, I know! . . . So? What do you think?"

They were both looking at Devon. He was still standing in that strangely artificial kabuki pose. In his hyper-feminine pink dress, with that pretty mask for a face, he didn't look like someone in a costume as much as a life-sized doll—beautiful and creepy. "I don't know, Stace. He's the only one who knows."

"I see you've got the correct line."

Erica laughed. "I'm trying. The Dutch studies . . . That's what really interested me. They've been using puberty blockers for years. That's more than merely theoretical," and that was all she could say because the kids were coming back.

"Those freakin' boys can take my picture all they want," Dev told the twins, "but they're not getting my number."

"Make one up," Avalon said. "That's what we do."

There had to be at least a dozen Sailor Moon cosplayers around SUB— they were the only characters that Erica knew—and here, descending the steps, was an image truly out of a dream, a pale blonde princess in a formal white gown with a train so long that a tiny pink Sailor Scout had to carry it. "Oh my god, it's Princess Serenity!" Ooohs and aaahs from all sides. "And Chibi Moon—"

"Lovely," Devon said, "I *told* Mom to come out early to see the kids but she didn't want to."

Erica froze with her phone in her hand. "Your *mum's* coming out here?"

"Not until we call her and tell her to come . . . Like we should probably do that?"

With all that kabuki makeup on him it was hard to read his expression. "We thought you guys had talked to each other," he said. "Haven't you guys talked to each other?"

I AM A TRULY SHITTY PERSON, Erica thought—the words that automatically appeared in her mind whenever she remembered the unanswered email—but she wasn't the same person now. Some studies had shown that pregnancy made women moody but others hadn't found that at all. She didn't care about the studies. Yes, she was labile—could cry at the drop of a hat—and now under the hot August sun felt extraordinarily empty—hollowed out—and at the same time sensed a presence in her, a small warm spark of Annalise. It was too early in the pregnancy to be a real physical feeling so it must be a wisp of something she'd constructed out of her desires. Oh god, she was hungry. The anime kids were filling her mind with over-the-top images and she imagined eating a whole barbecued hog along with a bucket of roast potatoes— fairly grotesque when even water made her queasy. No, she thought, I am not the same person.

She had walked away from everyone and now was standing in the patch of shade under the tree where Devon had been posing like a boy playing a girl in kabuki. She could still see him—and Stace and the twins—small distant figures, part of the colourful crowd. "Who's to say what's real?" one of the twins had asked when she'd been living in the Temple of Intermittent Reality and it was a good question. The game these costumed kids were playing wasn't *make* believe, it was *dis*believe. The world that adults wanted to give them was ridiculous. Why should they believe in any of it?

The phone in Karen's house was ringing. Karen often allowed the answering machine to take it but she must have been expecting Devon because she answered on the fourth ring.

"Hi? Karen? It's Erica."

Karen's voice sounded shrill, strange—"Erica!"

Erica knew that if she didn't get it all out in a rush, she wouldn't be able to say anything at all. "Yeah, it's me, your lost penny. I'm at Van An with Dev and the Lynas twins and— Karen, I'm so sorry. I got your email. I read it a million times. It was important to me. I was . . . really touched. But I just couldn't answer. I'm *so* sorry. Can you forgive me?"

Maybe this was a bad idea. Maybe she shouldn't have been so straightforward and direct. Karen wasn't saying anything. Even under the shade of this tree the heat of the afternoon was huge, was unavoidable—like summer in the Hat, she thought. It made her feel like that, like a kid, connecting back to that, she and Lise riding their bikes in the sun. She saw now how she could shed everything and become one of these kids in this heat again—oh, and *pregnant*. Odd word. It continued beyond definition—and no sounds were coming back to her. Maybe Karen had hung up. It would be sad if she'd hung up. "Karen? Are you still there?"

"Oh, yeah. I'm here. Yeah, I'm still here. The email. It's okay. It really is. How *are* you?"

"I'm fine. I'm okay. I miss you too. That's what I wanted to say. That's what I would have said if I could have answered. How are *you*?"

"Ah— Erica? I'm sorry. This is kind of a shock. I'm having trouble talking. I'm sorry, I really— I don't— I'm *so* glad you called me."

But calling wasn't enough. If she was going to do it, she should do it right. "Look, why don't I— I'm here with the kids. Why don't I bring them home? Then you wouldn't have to drive all the way out— If you want to see me? I don't know if you want to see me. Or if you're busy?"

"Yes, please. It's— That's so sweet of you. Yes, of course I want to see you."

OKAY, ERICA THOUGHT, I've done it, now what? Stunned—empty, indistinctly sick, but no defined thoughts, nothing articulate—she had to balance on an edge that was already in motion. Searching for words like a grad student, she thought that she was, however, the one who had set it in motion and all that was required of her now, really, was to walk in the enormous heat of this nearby star, this blazing ball of burning gasses, toward the brilliant distant figures. *She* was the motion and she didn't even know what that meant. Devon, the Nameless Princess, was coming to meet her. "I talked to your mum," she told him. "I'm going to take you home."

Here were half a dozen kids from the Palmerston Anime Club and two girls she didn't know—in strange little hats and elaborately flounced dresses with poofy skirts like Devon's but dark, one in black, the other in an inky purple. "Alexis and Madison," Dev introduced them.

"Are you princesses?"

"No. We're loligoths."

"Gothic Lolita," Dev translated. "It's like a fashion . . . like from Harajuku."

Being surrounded by cosplay kids made Stacey look like she was in costume too—in plain white top, shorts and Nikes, she could be playing a cute high-school girl—and then Erica finally picked up on the vibe she was getting from everyone. They were all grinning madly at her—even Stacey—and it was exactly the kind of moony grin you get from people when they're leading you into a surprise party.

They were already stepping aside to create a walkway for her—and, as she was meant to, she was already walking down it. As the last of the kids stepped out of her way, there was revealed, waiting for her, not a girl playing Kagami from *Two from One Fire* but Kagami herself.

This was what "uncanny" must mean—the hairs on Erica's neck and arms were actually standing up. The girl was giving her a cold hard stare. Then she deliberately drew a knife from the sheath on her hip and aimed it at Erica's throat. "I am Kagami the Cat," she said, her voice low-pitched and forceful. "I steal from the living and the dead."

"The dead are easier," Erica said and the girl lost her cool, cracked up.

"Oh wow, you've read it!" Dev said.

The girl was offering her hand but then thought better of it. Her hands were absolutely filthy, grimy knuckles, dirt under the nails—just like Kagami's. "It's grease paint," she said, "don't want to get it on you . . . Hi, I'm Jacqueline Ma."

Everybody was laughing. "Hi, Jacqueline. I'm Erica. You got me good. For a few seconds there I thought you really were Kagami."

"Oh, but I am!"

"How on earth did you—? You've got everything exactly right."—Kagami's black leather catsuit—decorated with studs, crisscrossed with zippers and straps, hung with tiny pockets. She'd even found broad, flat round-toed climbing boots like Kagami's and had done something to make them look scuffed and battered.

"My friends helped me," indicating Alexis and Madison. "It took us *forever*," the girls chimed in, telling her how they'd done it. It wasn't real leather, it was pleather—an absolute bitch to sew. They'd torn apart an entire Book One and pinned up drawings that showed the catsuit from every angle so they could reproduce every detail.

"How do you even get it *on*?" Stacey asked.

Faint smile and wry delivery—"With considerable difficulty."

"She's been on a diet for months," one of the girls said.

"Your hair—" It was perfect too—the unruly mop that Devon and Jamie had reproduced in real life. "Oh, it's a wig."

"Yeah, I have long hair. It's pinned up." Jacqueline offered her knife to Erica. "See. Plastic. Couldn't cut butter. We're not allowed to have real weapons."

"Yeah, no real weapons," Dev told her, "and we're not allowed to lead anybody around on a leash."

"Even if they want to be," Morgan said.

Stacey laughed. "That's a shame."

They must have been waiting for Erica to arrive because now the entire pack was in motion, following Dev and Jacqueline. "Try the courtyard," somebody was saying, "like over by the fountain." They were going to do their skit again, Morgan told Erica. Alexis was going to videotape it.

The pack arrived in the courtyard behind the old library. Gesturing, Jacqueline blocked off the space where they would do it—in front of the fountain, not in the direct sun but in the flat bright light in the long shadow of the building. The kids were lining up, defining the space. When they'd done it on the stage, Dev told her, they'd had a time limit so they'd gone whipping right through it super fast but this time Jacqueline wanted to do it right. "She's in Theatre at Lord Byng."

499

"This is from Book Five," Avalon said. "Okay, so it's complicated. While they've been gone, like in the Temple of Intermittent Reality, all this shit happened—"

"Yeah, it's *really* complicated," Morgan said, "but anyhow Kagami gets promoted, or elected, or whatever, so now she's the Commander of the Fourth Army,"

"and they've won this big battle in the Disputed Territories and Kagami's taken all these prisoners and they're just kids—"

"like child soldiers—"

"Right, and Kagami's going to execute them all. She's got like this big mass grave dug"

"and Makoto's trying to stop her."

"Totally. And that's where the skit starts."

Jacqueline gestured for the kids to calm down. Alexis had her camera ready and gave the go-ahead. Jacqueline leaned close to Devon, whispering. Then she shook out her arms and hands, took a deep breath and went striding onto the implied stage. She was walking like an angry teenager storming off after a nasty argument.

Devon followed, taking short hurried steps, his heels clicking, skirt swinging. "Kagami," he called.

Radiating fury, she spun around to confront him.

His voice was stagey and a bit stiff. "They're just kids."

"Kids?" She spat the word out. "I was in the field when I was ten. Picking over corpses. I didn't hear anybody saying, 'She's just a kid.'"

Devon was visibly nervous, trembling, but it went with the scene, made it seem more realistic. "You kill too easily," he said.

Jacqueline was good. Taking her time, looking genuinely puzzled, she turned toward the audience, then back to Devon. "Is there a better way to do it?"

Not acting, just using one of his real-life gestures—spread hands and shrug—Devon walked away from her. His kabuki makeup was doing a lot of the acting for him.

"They're running out of soldiers," Jacqueline yelled after him. He stopped. "They have to use children now. Our strategy is working. We're winning."

With a swoosh of his skirts he spun around to look at her. Erica could see a change in him. He was letting go of himself. His voice wasn't stagey at all now. "What are we winning?"

She glared at him a moment, then exploded—"Who would want to fuse with you, you wuss!"

He was just as angry as she was—"I don't want to fuse with you either, you murderess!"

That was too much for her. She went storming off stage.

"You don't kill because you have to," he yelled after her. "You kill because you like it."

She froze. "That's not true!"

This was a big moment for Jacqueline and she was not about to hurry it. All of the force had drained out of her body. Her shoulders slumping, not looking outward at anything at all, she walked partway back—her feet lagging, almost stumbling. Devon never took his eyes off her.

Somebody had placed a manga on the ground as a prop. She bent, picked it up and offered it him. "Makoto? Read to me what it says in the Raintree Teachings. The verse about the tears of the slain."

Surprised, he took the book from her.

"I can't—" She was good—everybody could see how ashamed she was. "I never learned— War has been my school."

He stared at her a moment, then began flipping through the book. "The tears of the slain," he read, "sink into our soul-links and saturate our nights with sorrow."

Jacqueline made a dangerous move for an actor—turned away from the audience—but her drooping shoulders were eloquent. Turning back, she said, "I feel their fear. I feel their sorrow."

He extended a hand to her. "Then let them live."

She took his hand. "If we fused, would it stop this pain?"

"Kagami." He flung his arms around her.

She stood stiffly a moment, her arms extended—then hugged him back—then hugged him hard—and oh my god, she seemed to have blown her line, nothing audible but a muffled mumble.

But he stepped away from her, taking her hands in his, and asked, "What did you say?"

She spoke deliberately, going for clarity. "I said I would extinguish myself in you."

"You don't have to. We're two halves of one person."

They stood a moment, staring into each other's faces, then, suddenly, turned and walked toward the audience, their movements as synchronized as if they were dancing.

No one must have told Devon that actors should stare off at some distant point in the air. He looked directly at the watching kids on his left, spoke directly to them. "We have searched within ourselves and found the way. Your suffering is our suffering. You may return to your homes and families."

Jacqueline called out to the kids on her right, transforming them into her soldiers. "Bathe them and tend to their wounds and treat them with respect and kindness."

"You are free!" he shouted.

"Who are you?" Jacqueline's friend Madison shouted back.

Morgan echoed her. "Who has freed us?"

Jacqueline drew her knife from its sheath and held it aloft. "I am Kagami the Cat."

Devon made a deep ballet-style révérence. "And I am the Nameless Princess."

IT WAS AUGUST so the sun was still high and hot, but Van An was *so* over—the vendors disassembling their booths and packing up, the cosplay kids drifting away, only a few left, the stragglers who weren't ready to say goodbye. Jacqueline's friends, the two loligoths, had gone home a long time ago but Erica and her little posse were stuck in the cafeteria because Devon and the perpetually hungry Lynas twins absolutely had to have veggie burgers. Jacqueline was still with them. When Dev had asked if they could drive her home, Erica had said yes automatically but now she was hoping to god that Jacqueline didn't live in Surrey.

Erica was propping up the wall a few metres back from the table so she wouldn't get the full blast of the burgers and fries, but she had to get outside soon, away from the smell of grease. Her half a can of ginger ale was staying down—so far anyway—but she still didn't trust it. Stacey had joined her on the wall. "Quite a subculture these kids have built for themselves. Amazing the number of *Chinese* kids into *Japanese* culture. Wonder what their parents think . . . or their grandparents. I guess if you're fourteen, the war must be ancient history . . . Are you okay?"

"If we get out of here fairly soon, I'm okay. Smart girl, eh?" Jacqueline seemed to be the centre of focus now. Devon and the twins obviously adored her.

"Oh, yeah. Professor's kid. I know her dad. He's in Economics. Are you sure you want to drive to West Van? I can take them."

"I'm fine, Stace, really." That was a lie. "I won't go on the highway. If I feel queasy, I'll pull over." She was dreading the drive, actually—nervous about seeing Karen and seriously worried about the morning sickness. If you can't eat anything—if even keeping a few sips of ginger ale down is a problem—at what point do you end up in Emergency? Maybe after she dropped the kids at Karen's she should keep on going to Lions Gate and get them to hydrate her. "Come on, kids," she called to them, "get your act together."

In their short skirts and sailor blouses, Morgan and Avalon were dressed appropriately for the hot day but Jacqueline and Devon were suffering and had begun to deconstruct themselves. She had unzipped the top of her catsuit, revealing her collarbones shiny with sweat—had washed the fake dirt and grime off her face and hands, removed her wig and let down a torrent of glossy black hair. He'd shed his headdress, wiped off most of the kabuki makeup. "I so hate it when it's over," Jacqueline was saying, "when we have to go back and live with Muggles again." The kids were laughing at that, and finally they were up and moving.

As soon as Erica stepped outside, she began to feel better. The clear air was good and there was even a breeze. Maybe the drive to West Van wouldn't be so bad after all. "Where are you parked?" Stacey asked.

"It's Sunday so I got into the lot by the Psych building."

"I'm in the parkade."

They hugged each other goodbye just the way they used to do back in the day. Stacey still smelled like limes. "Should I be worried about you?"

"No, I'm okay. It comes and goes. Right now I'm okay." It was almost true. "Stace. Thanks for everything."

"It's okay." Stacey's smile communicated a complex bundle of emotions, but Erica didn't have the energy to decode them. She's a real friend, she thought.

Stacey waved to the kids—"Loved your skit!—and they called back to her, "Goodbye, goodbye."

Erica was the only one who knew the way so she walked on ahead, heard bits of an ongoing conversation drifting behind her. ". . . a mess in grade seven," Jacqueline was saying. "I was failing life . . ."

That was interesting. Erica stopped so they would catch up to her but, glancing back, saw that they'd stopped too. Okay, kids, if you want a private conversation, you've got one—and she walked on ahead again.

After a moment Morgan caught up to her. "Jacqueline wears Lolita *to school!*"

Now they were all catching up. Maybe they'd decided to include her in the conversation. "Just casual or otome kei," Jacqueline said, "I wouldn't do full-on classic or amaloli or anything like . . . The kids have got used to me now. 'Oh, her? She does *theatre.*' Nothing more needs to be said."

"She's got the haircut I wanted," Dev told Erica. "Exactly. The girl in the salon didn't have a clue about a princess cut—"

"Hime katto," Jacqueline said, "for sure. I've had mine since I was twelve. She didn't do too badly on you, Devon. Curved your bangs down when they should go straight across but you can fix that. She left enough on the sides to start the side-locks."

They'd arrived at Erica's Volvo. The twins got into the backseat but Dev and Jacqueline were still standing by the side of the car, looking at each other. "I'll cut it for you sometime if you want," she said.

He was looking directly into her eyes but didn't say anything. His silly pink heels gave him an extra few inches but she was still slightly taller than he was. "Your bangs should just touch your eyebrows, and your side-locks should probably be around here." She drew a imaginary line on his cheek. "Yeah, at an angle. That'd look pretty on you."

He still didn't say anything. He got into the back seat with the twins and Jacqueline got into the front with Erica. "I'm just up Dunbar," she told Erica. "You know where that is, right? Just drive up Dunbar and I'll tell you when to stop."

She turned around in her seat to talk to Devon. "Once it's grown in, it's kind of high maintenance. You have to cut your bangs and side-locks every two weeks, but that's not a big deal . . . and a real Heian princess would never cut the back, never, not once in her entire life."

"I don't know," he said. "It's exactly what I wanted but— I don't know."

Things were starting to feel a bit awkward but the twins jumped into the silence and began rattling on about *their* hair—"Can't do real hime katto— way too curly— did the bangs though—"

"*Love* your hair. Ginger's so special. I've got a ginger wig—" and on and on about wigs and costumes. Her dad was like, "Your hobby's kind of expensive, Jacqueline. We think you ought to pay for it yourself," so she had a job after school. Yeah, in a deli on Fourth. It *was* expensive, actually. Wigs, oh my goodness. She had a blonde one that was all ringlets—

Erica turned onto Dunbar. "Don't let me drive past," she said.

"Oh, no, I won't."

Devon said, "I don't know . . . like if I can keep it long. What would I do when I'm a boy?"

"Oh, you just brush it all back and put it in a ponytail. Or pin it up and wear a toque or a cap or something. When the back's still short like that, just put a little gel in it and part it— Slow down. I'm in the next block."

Erica pulled over in front of the designated house. It was an old-school Vancouver stucco with a small tidy lawn and some lovely eastern trees in front of it. "Great to meet you, Kagami," Erica said.

She wouldn't have thought that Jacqueline was a giggler but she was giggling. "Great to meet you too, Erica. Thank you so much."

Devon got out of the car and walked up the steps with her. They stopped in front of her front door—and stayed stopped. Whatever they were saying to each other seemed to be absolutely absorbing.

Eventually Morgan said under her breath, "Don't mind us. We're just delighted to sit here for like an hour or two."

Then Dev and Jacqueline were hugging—no, it was more than hugging, they were kissing. Not a little goodbye peck on the cheek, they were seriously kissing. "Come on, guys," Morgan whispered, "everybody can *see you.*"

It was awkward—it was extremely awkward. Erica felt herself blushing on the kids' behalf. "Oh, my goodness," Avalon said, "can't you just see all the little pink valentine hearts floating around them?"

Erica thought that she should probably look away but she didn't. Puppy love, first love—whatever—it might be hilarious ten years later but at the time it was excruciating. She and Lise had kissed boys for the first time, seriously kissed them, within a week of each other—hadn't planned it, just the way things happened with MZ twins. They'd been the same age as Devon—thirteen. Whew, she could still feel the intensity of it—like you might actually die of love. Jeff Havelka. They'd never really dated. The last she'd heard, he was married with a couple of kids and working in the oil patch.

Dev and Jacqueline finally managed to let go of each other. He walked partway down the steps, turned back. She gave him a *call me* gesture but didn't go into the house yet. He sighed, walked down to the car and got into the front where Jacqueline had been sitting. Neither twin said anything and neither did he. It was a late Sunday afternoon and Dunbar was empty so Erica made an illegal U-turn and headed back the way she had come.

She couldn't imagine three kids more talkative than Devon and the Lynas twins but they weren't saying a word. Erica drove down to Cornwall, followed it along by the beach to the Burrard Bridge, crossed the bridge and made the back-tracking turn that Karen had taught her, onto Pacific. She was the grownup so she should probably break the silence but she couldn't think of a thing to say.

While she was stopped by a light on Denman, Devon said quietly, "I wish Jamie was here. I really miss Jamie."

ERICA DROVE UP the steep incline of the driveway, arrived at the top, and Karen's spaceship-black BMW shouldn't have looked so alien—she had actually driven it. The kids were talking again and their voices should have provided a safety net but didn't. Karen must have been watching for them, was already running down the steps, and Dev was already out of the car yelling, "Hey, Mom, we won!"

Erica told herself to act normal but she wasn't sure she remembered what normal meant. She and Karen were hugging and Karen smelled like herself and Erica's eyes flooded. Oh, I am *so* pregnant, she thought. She could see that Karen wanted to say something but couldn't, her eyes filling with empathy—eyes that really were as amber as a wolf's.

Devon seemed oblivious to this adult drama, but the twins weren't, grabbed him and aimed him toward the house, leaving Erica and Karen a moment of privacy. It wasn't sadness exactly—Erica supposed it was what people called nostalgia—returning here where she had been almost happy, where she actually *had* been happy—however much she'd been suffering, however much she'd been crazy. The soaring glass and concrete, the towering hemlocks and cedars—"You look different," Karen said.

"So do you."

"I, um . . . I'm letting my natural colour grow in and— You're wearing makeup."

"Yes. Yes, I am," and Annalise's clothes.

"I don't know what to say. It's just wonderful to see you. I'll make tea."

She followed Karen up the steps and into the front hall where people shed their shoes. The twins had already taken off their loafers. Leaning against the wall for balance, Devon was unfastening the buckles on his patents. "So, um . . . what do you think of our nameless princess?" Karen asked her.

She's embarrassed about him, Erica thought. She doesn't need to be. "Their skit was magnificent."

"Yeah, Mom. You can see it later. Like Alexis is going to put it on YouTube."

The shiny colour of Dev's shoes reminded Erica of bubble gum and that was exactly how she felt—stretched as thin as a pink blown bubble. She shouldn't have driven to West Van. The drive had been too much. The whole day had been too much, actually. She steadied herself on the wall and kicked off Annalise's runners. Then they were walking past the steel-and-pine dining room and into the steel-and-granite kitchen and she was sitting down on one of the kitchen chairs. All that huge expanse of glass—windows—all that light— "I'm so sorry I didn't answer your email." She'd already said that. Did she have to keep on saying that?

"That's okay," Karen said. "I understand." She filled the teakettle and set it on the stove.

Erica knew that there was some polite verbal dance that she should be doing but she didn't have the energy to try to figure out what it was. "If I'd known that you and Bryan were a couple," she said, "I never would have stayed there. I saw him *as a man*, but a man like my dad or my brother. I haven't had any sexual feelings since Annalise died, and it just felt . . . There wasn't a trace of it."

Karen gave her a startled look. Maybe that had been too direct. Most normal people probably wouldn't be that direct. But Erica couldn't say anything more because Devon and the twins were coming back. They'd changed into shorts and T-shirts. "Mom! Sorry."

"What?" Karen snapped at them.

"Can Morgan and Avi like wash these in the wash machine?"—the sailor uniforms.

"What are they? Cotton?"

"Yeah, I guess. The label's in Japanese. They're *real* uniforms—"

"Cold water, gentle cycle. Use a little bit of Woolite. The white one."

The kids were gone again. Karen jerked the cupboard open, dumped half a dozen oatmeal-raisin cookies onto a plate, slammed it on the table and sat down directly across from Erica, looking at her. "Your email," Erica said, "I actually did answer it . . . in my mind. I just never wrote it down. You said that you missed me. Well, I missed you too."

Erica felt the sizzling sting of contact—wordless. "You didn't have to—" Maybe she shouldn't be talking but what else could she do? "You didn't have to apologize because you couldn't look at death. Nobody can look at death. If Annalise hadn't died, I never would have looked at it either. There's a . . . It's like a conspiracy in our culture not to look at it, not to talk about it . . . Death is the new sex— Hey, that's actually funny." She emitted a small stuttering laugh. Stop it, she thought. That's not normal.

But Karen was smiling. "It's okay." She isn't reacting to my words, Erica thought. She's reacting to *me*. "You can stay for a while, can't you?" Karen said. "How have you been?"

"I don't know how I've been. Karen, I— I really wanted to answer you—"

She had to make Karen pay attention to the words. She'd gone over and over them in her mind. "Listen. Karen. Seriously listen. Your idea that I might have reproduced Lise's car so I could kill myself in it . . . I didn't— Okay, I was totally phobic about cars, couldn't even ride in one without getting a panic attack, and I had to try and get over— So I was doing this flooding technique, and reproducing Lise's car was like— If you've ever been thrown off a horse, everybody tells you to get right back up on it again. If I could drive her Golf, the car she'd been killed in, then I would be—"

The kids were back *yet again*. They were truly annoying. Dev was carrying his pink dress on a hanger. "Sorry, Mom. Texted Jacqueline and she's like the dress goes to the dry cleaner, totally—"

"Hang it in the front hall closet. I'll take it—"

"But she's like wash the petticoat gently by hand and then hang it—

"Jesus, Dev, do you have to do this *now*?"

"Mom, it's been so hot, like disgustingly hot— Okay, so she's like hang it upside down. So it doesn't lose its poof. But what do we wash it *in*? What do we hang it *on*?" The kettle began to whistle.

"Oh, for fuck's sake. Wait a minute. Just go— Yeah, just go in my bathroom. I'll show you. I'll be there in a minute."

Karen jumped up, poured the water in the teapot, picked up the plate of cookies and gestured to Erica with her head—*follow me*. Now they were out on the deck in the open air and the fat ball of the sun was riding just above the ocean, throwing a long golden pathway to the east. Babying herself like a porcelain figurine, Erica arranged her body carefully onto a deck chair in the hot light. Maybe this wasn't the right time. Maybe she didn't have to say anything at all. "I don't fucking believe them sometimes," Karen said under her breath. "Be right back."

Erica's misery was beyond anything as simple as mere hunger. It had been well over twenty-four hours since anything had stayed down. She didn't have any choice whether or not to eat the oatmeal-raisin cookie—she'd already eaten it. The taste had been close to a transformative experience.

Erica felt sweat breaking out on her forehead. Was it the sun? Or the cookie? Her mouth was as dry as a bone. Maybe she should have some tea.

She poured herself a cup. She would have liked milk but Karen hadn't brought any. She took a sip and her stomach lurched. No, not a good idea. Here was Karen again, asking, "Did they actually win something?"

"Yes. Yes, they did." Oh dear, there was *no time.* That was the crucial thing that Karen didn't understand.

"We're like sleepwalkers," Erica said, "or like people walking around under the influence of a post-hypnotic suggestion . . . that's what you wrote in your email, right? Well, that really stuck in my head. I'm not sure what I think about subconscious motivations but I'm— Freud's a load of shit, by the way. Those guys had a hundred years to prove that stuff and they haven't proved any of it."

She felt depersonalized—listening to herself talk. "It's not like intelligent people haven't been thinking about this . . . a lot of papers and studies on it, and the first thing you have to do is define what you mean by 'subconscious mind' because a lot of what our brain is doing we're not consciously aware of, but that's not exactly what we mean by it, is it?"

Oh my god, it was like an inner floodgate had burst and all these words were torrenting out of her. "This is a roundabout way of saying that when you asked what I was doing in your driveway, I don't have a clear answer to that. So when I was up on the highway in the rain— This is me afterward, trying to reconstruct it, but I was aware of pushing the edge. I guess I wanted to see how close I could get. To dying. I think that's what I was doing— I even knew it. And then after the wreck, I was really terrified. Got the car off the highway and then— I don't know why I picked your driveway, but it does seem like a positive thing, I mean I could have just pulled off the road anywhere and . . . just sat there and died. But I didn't. You can call it 'the subconscious' if you want . . . and I ended up in your driveway."

Now what? She was still teetering on this challenging mental edge and it kept moving and there was nothing she could do except try to stay on it. "Yes, of course, I wanted to protect your kids but I wasn't thinking about that when I ended up in your driveway but from the very first moment I got an email from them— The very first thing they said on the very first page of their email was a suicide threat— So yes, of course I wanted to protect your kids.

"When you're thinking about suicide, it's very persuasive and it's hard to explain to anybody who hasn't been there, but I'd been there and— It's a feeling, large and just— It's hard to put it into words. Even when you're sure that death is absolute nothingness, you can still be attracted to it. Something in you wants to embrace the nothingness and— After Annalise died, I was sure I understood something about the world that I didn't know before . . . and single individual people mattered a whole lot . . . like these two particular kids in West Vancouver mattered a whole lot, and I had this crazy arrogance that told me that I could do something about it, that maybe I could make a difference because I'd been there too and I understood what they were feeling.

"So yes, I was attracted to your kids first because of that, because I wanted to save them, or help them, and you were right to guess that. And no, I am not going to hurt myself now. Sorry you had to worry about me so much—"

What a mistake that cookie was. She was going to throw up at any minute. Toss her cookie—that was a good one. She really should shut up.

Karen was looking at her sympathetically, curiously, somewhat amazed, actually.

"How am I? How the fuck should I know? I've always— But I mean— With a sample size of one you can't prove anything so what we're talking about here is subjective experience and all I can do is tell you— I've been where I—" *Shut up, Erica!*

"Where I lost my ability, totally, to test reality. That's very frightening. We all of us depend on this . . . want the world to be the same ten minutes from now or tomorrow or next week, don't want to suddenly see an entirely different world. But in the meantime, as to living my life— It's fairly problematical and about all I've been able to do is decide that if something feels right, I'll go that way, and if it— There's only one of me now so I've got to be both the tomboy twin and the girly twin and I wanted to change my brain chemistry and I *have* changed it— Oh, shit, Karen, I'm *so* sick. *I'm pregnant.*"

Karen actually changed colour—her face went totally white. "Who's the father?"

"Mark. Annalise's husband. It's Annalise's baby. She and I have the same genes so I wanted to— You want to hear irrational? Here it is. I wanted to give Mark and Annalise's baby back to the world. Oh god, Karen, I have the worst fucking morning sickness—" and that did it. She was crying. Not just a few tears, she was bawling. "I'm afraid, I'm afraid, I'm so afraid! *I've been throwing up water!*"

She felt Karen's hands on her, stroking her forehead and the back of her neck. "You poor miserable thing. You're all cold and clammy."

Erica couldn't do anything but cry.

"Listen," Karen said, "it's not so— I had it pretty bad with Cam. And then not so bad with the twins. But Paige, oh my god, I thought I was going to die. The first trimester, Jesus holy fuck. You just stay here, okay? You don't move, okay? Just try and calm down. I'm going to catch Safeway before they close—"

"Safeway?" It didn't make any sense.

"Yeah, there's a lot of things we can try. We're going to start with ginger."

32.

HERE IN THE SUMMER the view attracted everything to it like iron filings to a magnet—sweep of azure sky, dime-sized sparkles on the water, a good brisk breeze with a dozen sailboats racing in it—eternal August when every lovely day is much like every other, but this morning was different. Erica was different. When she'd got out of bed, she'd put on makeup, the faintest touch of it, and she was wearing her dead sister's clothes—just a summer top and shorts and runners, but they were cute in a way that Erica's clothes had never been—and she was pregnant, insisting that it was Annalise's baby—how weird was that? But the biggest difference— the most amazing, earth-shattering difference—was that Erica was *not depressed.*

For all those months while she'd been gone, Karen had remembered Erica as something like a pastel phantom, but here she was, fully inhabiting a human body, sitting on a deck chair in the direct light of the sun, a living breathing surprise, the same but not the same. The nausea seemed to have backed off for the moment, and she was actually smiling. "Are they racing?" she asked, pointing out at the sailboats. "Isn't that what you used to do?"

"Yeah, they are. I absolutely loved it. Do you know anything about sailing?"

"Oh, yeah," Erica answered, deadpan. "We do a lot of sailing in Alberta. Can't keep us off the water."

"Okay, look, they're beating, trying to see how close they can get to the wind. See, there's one poor guy who went too close, and he's in irons . . . going nowhere, his sails all loose and flappy, bluh. But look at the leader. He's got the angle just right."

Close-hauled—as she was remembering—when she'd been gradually transformed from a girlfriend into a sailor, bare feet hooked under hiking straps, her whole body hanging out over the water, feeling the spray of it—"God, it's so exciting when you're actually doing it! . . . Are you okay?"

"Pretty much." Erica patted her stomach where the nausea lived. "Just a touch of it."

Karen was happy. She'd begun by feeding Erica pickled ginger—"Hey, that tastes wonderful!"—and then ginger tea. It had all stayed down, so she'd tried her old standby, fruit flan—sugar, protein, and calcium, who could ask for anything better?—and that had stayed down, too. Delighted with each other, they had talked until cold blue light had lit the windows. They'd begun again where they'd left off, and they still weren't finished—no, not by a long shot. Just as before, they needed to tell each other *everything*.

"Do you want to try to eat?" Karen asked her.

"Yeah, definitely."

Drawn by teenage telepathy, the kids appeared just as Karen was opening the fridge. "Can we have a piece?"

"They're for Erica. I told you. She has *morning sickness*."

"Mom," Devon said, "you bought *three of them*."

513

Karen set the flan down on the glass-topped table on the deck. "It's like a mandala," Morgan said. What an odd thought—but she was right. Sunlight was reflected on the glass—too bright to look at directly—and gleaming on the ring of glazed peach slices, on the haze of sugar. It was almost too beautiful to eat, but Devon was already cutting it. So much for art. At least he had the good manners to offer Erica the first piece.

"Mom," he was asking, "do you have any more of those Laura Ashley dresses?"

"I think there's three or four of them. Why?"

"Can Morgan and Avi wear them?"

Jacqueline was having a party tomorrow night, he told her, and they were going to do otome kei—whatever that was. It was a big deal. They were going to meet Jacqueline's parents. A crucial bit of information was still not clear to Karen. "Jacqueline does know you're a boy, doesn't she?"

He smiled slightly. "That I was assigned male at birth? Yeah, she knows that. So do Madison and Alexis. But her parents don't. So I'm gonna be like this nice girl she met at Van An."

Assigned male at birth—where did he get that one? From the magical Jacqueline, of course. He'd found another older girl to model on—one who could play Kagami to his Makoto, one who was up on all the latest jargon, one who was going to introduce him to her parents *as a girl*. Karen's intuitive antennae were fluttering. It didn't feel right. She gave Erica a questioning look.

"Dev," Erica said, "can your mum read your emails? You know, the ones that you and Jamie sent me from Australia?"

Karen would have thought that he'd simply say yes, but he hesitated, frowning, and turned away toward the sun. "Okay. You want me to print them out for you?"

"How about Jamie?" Erica said. "We need her permission, too."

"Um, yeah. *Devon*. Right. I'll text him." His thumbs were already going on his phone. "He's like . . . He's pissed off at me. Sometimes now he doesn't answer my texts."

"Oh?" Karen said. "What's the problem?"

"He didn't get to go to Van An. He's like—" He shrugged. "He's not texting me back. I don't know if— Maybe he will later."

After the kids had wandered away, Karen said, "Pissed off? She's got every reason to be pissed off. She was looking forward to Van An just as much as Devon was, but she shouldn't be taking it out on him. What kind of game is Rob playing? Of course he must think that Jamie is Devon . . . Do you see any reason to tell him?"

Erica shook her head. It was true what everybody said about pregnancy—how it made women glow. Erica didn't need her sister's makeup. She was illuminated from the inside, her face radiant with colour, her eyes enormous and shining— And something else was going on in Karen's mind, some train of thought the kids had interrupted. She couldn't remember what it was but could still feel the ambience of it—something she wanted to tell Erica.

Out on the water the lead sailboat had rounded the buoy and blossomed with a big fat jolly balloon spinnaker. "Look," Karen said, "they've started on their last leg." Oh, *now* she remembered! "I liked being a sailor better than being a girlfriend. I can't even remember his name— Yes, I can. It was Ken Peterson. I used to date interchangeable boys. They were always the same type."

She could barely remember anything about them, but one of them was always required for the perfect summer—sun, sky, ocean, *boy*. Not that any boy would do—he had to be laid-back, laughing, sun-gilded, self-assured. Karen had to look good with him. How pathetic.

"Not pathetic," Erica said. "Just girl stuff."

Karen was about to say, "That's too easy," but then she thought, no, maybe it wasn't. It was fairly horrific what girls had to do to be girls. "I had to go through so much shit in high school," she said, "you know, to get into the club, with the cool kids, the popular kids, and it made me kind of . . . *hard*. That's not exactly the right word, but— Well, maybe it is the right word. God, I hated my first boyfriend."

"James Wellman?"

"Yeah. James. I went out with him until he went to UVic, but then . . . A boyfriend who wasn't around wasn't any use to me. I really did see boys like accessories right up until I married one of them."

She looked out over the water. "They're all on the last leg now," she told Erica, "running before the wind."

"That really means something? Running before the wind? I thought it was a metaphor."

"No, it's not a metaphor."

THE SUN AND the size of Bryan's girls—their physical presence—their blazing red hair, their freckles, and the Laura Ashleys fit them beautifully. "You girls look fabulous!" Nearly a year older than her twins, Morgan and Avalon were halfway through fourteen. What an age—Karen remembered the sheer mad adventure of waking up in the morning. Fourteen had been her last good year as a teenager—what a gloomy thought that was. "You can have those dresses," she said.

"Really? You're kidding!"

"Not kidding." She'd worn those dresses to look good with Ian when they'd been the perfect couple. He'd been the up-and-coming young hot-shit lawyer, and she'd been his candy-confection wife—anyhow that's the way they were supposed to look in public. "All that stuff from the '90s," she said, "take *all of it*."

"Oh, Karen, you're so lovely."

"Mom," Dev was asking her, "do you have any, um . . . little white gloves?"

That made her smile. "How old do you think I am? That's not my generation, that's your nana's generation."

"Do you have any kind of gloves, like, you know—"

"I *do* know. I know exactly what you want, and I can't help you. I'm not a gloves person. You really do have to make friends with your grand-mother."

"How about your shoes? They're too small for Morgan and Avi, but some of them like, um . . . sort of fit me."

This must be a hot button for him—he was actually blushing. "Okay," she said, "but not too high. Restrain yourself." Fat chance of that.

"You must think I'm crazy," she said to Erica after the kids were gone again.

"No," laughing. "I do *not* think you're crazy. I guess I have to keep saying that."

"What if I'm enabling some bizarre—"

"No, you're not. Let Dev enjoy himself. And it was really nice of you to give those dresses to the twins."

"It wasn't *that* nice. Isn't it about time I graduated from high school? Poor girls. They don't really have a mum, do they? And Bryan's a great dad, but he's a *terrible* mum."

They were both giggling just as though they were the same age as the kids. It was wonderful not to have to explain to each other what they meant. "I wish you didn't have to go," Karen said.

"I wish I didn't either, but— I'll call you later."

Erica was saying again all the things she'd said already. She'd made plans with her friend, Stacey, needed to go home and have a shower, needed to check on things at the university. Maybe she and Karen could get together later in the week. Dinner? If she could ever eat anything again—oh, and thanks so much for the ginger tea and the fruit flans— Karen had saved her life.

Karen knew exactly what Erica was doing: defining things, setting boundaries. She didn't want what had happened before to happen again— for them to drift into some strange undefined twinlike relationship. Okay, so she and Erica must be *good friends* now—wasn't that the proper category? You have nice visits with your good friends, and then they go away.

THE TEA HAD GONE COLD. It was still a beautiful day, but Karen didn't care—all the sparkle had left with Erica. When the kids exploded onto the deck, she was actually glad to see them. "Hey, Mom, we're going out, okay?"

Bryan's twins were dressed as usual—shorts, T-shirts, and flip-flops— but Devon was in Cons and shapeless baggy jeans, his hair tucked up under a reversed ball cap. He'd scrubbed off all traces of makeup and looked more like a boy than a girl. "Mostly emo boys," he was saying to the twins, "you know, like black polish—"

"You can always put your hands in your pockets," one of the twins said.

"Wait a minute," Karen said. "Going out? Where?"

Devon was waving his fingernails in front of her face, displaying the shiny French finish. "Gels! Like *baked on.* Oh. Mom. Jamie texted me back. You know, about the emails. She's like— oops— *He's* like, no way, absolutely, fuck you, no way. Sorry, Mom, that's a direct quote—"

"The little bitch," she said before she could stop herself.

"Chill, Mom, happy ending time. Like ten minutes later he's texting me back again. Changed his mind, ha ha, Mom can read them. Phew, right? Whatever. You can get like a kit to take it off, or you can do it yourself with acetone, but— Boys can wear nail polish, right?"

She finally got it—he was about to go out in public, and his nail polish was the only thing he was worried about. "*Devon!* What about Jamie?"

"What about *what?* It's all cool, Mom. If he changes his mind again, I'm just not gonna answer him. I printed them out for you, like right by the printer."

"Okay, okay, stop. Just where is it you're going?"

"Jacqueline's."

"I thought you were seeing her tomorrow."

"Yeah, but that's the otome kei party. We're just gonna hang out."

"Like a park by her house," Morgan told her. "Chaldecott Park. We Googled it."

Propelled by the collective mind, they were aimed for the front door. Karen was trailing along behind them. "If we miss the freakin' bus, it's like an hour before the next one," Avalon said, and then, in what felt like a private communication, almost a Shakespearean aside, Devon was saying, "The kids are used to seeing me in neutral mode, but if just one of them sees me in girl mode, my life's over."

"Karen?" Morgan was asking her. "Do we have a curfew?"

Curfew? She hadn't even thought of that. She'd better make one up. "Ten," she said firmly, but wasn't that too early? She'd said it, so she'd better stick with it. "And if you're out after seven, you've got to call me and tell me where you are."

She watched them jog down the driveway and vanish. When she went back inside, the house was ringingly empty. The emails were exactly where Dev had said they would be. It seemed like a lot of paper, more than she'd expected.

The first one began with: "Dear Erica, Are u ok? We havent heard from u for awhile & hope ur ok." Oh for Christ's sake, kids. Chat-room shorthand drove her nuts, especially "u" for "you." Why did they have to do that to Erica, a university professor?

Were all these from the twins? She flipped over to the next one. "Hey, Dev and Jamie, it's great to hear from you. I miss you too. It must be lots of fun to be in Sydney." That had to be from Erica. Devon must have printed out the whole exchange, both sides of it. Was she supposed to read Erica's side, too?

KAREN PUT LIQUID TEARS in her eyes and then patted her face with a cold facecloth. She'd been crying and didn't want it to show, but of course it did—her eyes were red-rimmed and puffy. She'd better wear sunglasses. Okay, so now for her next move—she didn't care where Erica was or what she was doing, she had to talk to her.

Erica answered on the second ring. "Where are you?" Karen asked her. "God, I sound like one of the kids."

"At John Lawson."

"You're kidding."

"Not kidding."

"You're still in West Van? I can't believe it. Where exactly?"

She was sitting on a bench aimed at the pier. It was high tide, and she seemed to be fascinated by the waves rolling in. Karen dropped onto the bench beside her. Erica must not have heard her coming—spun around, startled. "Oh. Hi. What's this?"

"The rest of the ginger tea." Karen had poured it into a Starbucks mug.

"Oh, thank you. That's so thoughtful."

Karen had also cut a slice of the kiwi flan that Erica had forgotten to take with her. She set the Tupperware container down on the bench between them. "You're an angel," Erica said. Why was she still in West Van?

Seagulls were wheeling over the water, enjoying the day just as much as the people ambling along the seawall. Erica was eating the flan too fast. "Do I ever need this! Walked all the way to Dundarave pier thinking I was actually going to eat a cheeseburger. How I got that idea, I don't even . . ."

"I read the emails," Karen said.

"Oh, good. What did you think?"

Karen was tempted to pretend that she hadn't read both sides of the exchange but then thought, no, this is no time for secrets. "I had to get over being hurt. I felt so left out."

"Of course you did— I'm sorry—"

"Don't be sorry. It's just that . . . Oh god. Jamie doesn't trust me."

"It isn't that she doesn't trust you, it's that—

"Oh, I know. Mum's just boring old Mum, right? But you're the outsider, the fair witness . . . and you've been an absolutely great role model for Jamie. You said all the right things to her. Oh, so you're James now? No problem. Let me tell you about the time when some girl took me for a boy . . . And it was such a natural conversation. That's how Jamie got to the point she could talk about what the kids did to her at Inglewood. God, those little bitches, I'd like to kill them."

If Erica had been great with the twins, they'd been great with her. "We were so happy when u & mom were GFs," they had written to Erica, "it was perfect for us. We were hoping that u would become part of our family." That's what I was hoping, too, Karen thought.

"You know what really got to me?" Karen said, "*one* of the things. A dozen things really got to me, and— Oh, Jamie, break my heart, why don't you? Maybe it's just me. I'm her mother so I'm prepared to love everything she does, but . . . She can't *spell*, but she can *write*. My god, it was a poem! *Bouncing off the bottom of the sea*, and *Morgan's like, don't fight me, Jamie, we're in the rip*. And then when she and Bryan go out again, she's *just watching it*. And Bryan! So cheesy, but it was the perfect thing to say to her. *There's nothing they can do to you. You've surfed the waves in Tasmania*. It was the happiest day of her life. I just bawled.

"I don't know whether to give Bryan a mentorship medal or strangle him. It was so fucking dangerous. I was imagining— 'Oh, yeah, we had a great time. Of course, Jamie drowned in the Tasman Sea, but other than that—'"

"I wish I'd read it right after she wrote it," Erica said, "but— Well, I didn't. And the crucial paragraph? The one where they say exactly what they want? Did you read it?"

"I don't know. Which paragraph? The one where they're talking about estrogen and testosterone? I couldn't make any sense of it. It just didn't— It seems like a perfect example of the Peter Pan syndrome. They don't want to grow up. They want to stay twelve forever."

"No, that's not what it says. It *is* confusing. I had to read it a dozen times. They *do* want to grow up. Dev wants to take something that will make him catch up to Jamie. Neither of them wants to turn into a woman, so their puberty shouldn't be driven by estrogen, but they don't like the idea of testosterone either. He wants to know if there's a mix of hormones they could take. Don't you see what they want? It isn't that they want to stay *twelve* forever. It's that they want to stay *the same* forever. And they were right. Medical science *isn't* ready for them. Well, except for the short term. The Dutch have done wonderful things with puberty blockers—"

"Eew! Come on, Erica, don't go there. It makes me sick just thinking about it."

"You know what else is sickening? The suicide rate among transgender children."

Their eyes met. Oh my god, did the new undepressed Erica have a dead steady gaze! "Okay, I'll think about it," she said, "just not right now, okay?"

She really couldn't think about it. Something at the centre of her felt tender and aching—as soft as a bruised plum. They'd been talking in a rush, but suddenly they seemed to have run out of words. If Karen had still been a smoker, this would have been the perfect time for a smoke. They were both watching the ocean—the ancient surf rolling in. "Erica? Why are you still in West Van?"

A short nervous laugh—"I just didn't— It was such a nice day, and I wanted to sit by the water for a while."

She's lying to me, Karen thought. Just a white lie, but still— "We used to come here when I was living with you," Erica said. "I like looking at the pier where you had your epiphany. That's the pier, isn't it?"

Karen felt her skin prickle. "Yeah, that's it."

"I looked for your apartment, too. I used to go to Kits Point and look for it. What is it you called it? Your quirky little apartment?"

Karen hadn't heard that before—anything about Kits Point. "I'll show you sometime. It'd be fun to see if you guessed it right."

What is she trying to tell me? Karen thought. She couldn't answer my email or call me, so that was the best she could do? Or is there something more?

The whole tone of the conversation had changed. No more easy flow. They weren't looking at each other. They were choosing their words carefully. "Erica? What are you going to do after the baby's born? Being a single mum is not lots of fun, you know."

"I'm not— I don't know for sure. My friend Stacey keeps telling me there's going to be an opening in her building." Whenever Erica mentioned Stacey, Karen felt a pang of jealousy. It made her feel mean and unworthy.

"It's a nice building," Erica said. "In the West End. All the apartments have little balconies. I know I've got to get out of . . . I hate the place where I'm living. So anyhow, if I moved into Stacey's building—"

"Stay with me."

Erica glanced quickly at Karen and then away. "Oh, Karen, you're so sweet."

"I'm not the least bit sweet. But I *am* serious."

"I know you are, but—"

Karen wanted to go on talking, explaining all the excellent practical reasons why Erica should stay with her, but something told her to keep her mouth shut.

"What?" Erica said. "You want me aiming my severed twin bond at you again? It's not entirely under my conscious control, you know. Look where it got us the last time."

"It was my fault the last time. I deserted you in Medicine Hat."

"No, you didn't. I was horrible. I burned you out. I burned everybody out. I knew I was doing it. I couldn't stop myself."

Everything that Erica was saying now Karen had heard before— how hard it was for an MZ twin to live in the world of singletons where everyone was supposed to be alone and isolated. She made it sound as though she'd been sentenced to life in solitary.

"Sorry," Karen said, "I don't think there's a different consciousness, something that us benighted singletons have and you guys don't. You think we're really different . . . mysterious and strange . . . not like you at all, but we're not."

Erica smiled. "Nothing human is strange to me."

"Oh, I remember that. *I am human, and nothing human is strange to me.*"

"You know that quote, eh? Neat. It was one of Annalise's favourites. I never got it straight who said it. It's like I don't want to know."

"I won't tell you, then."

"No, tell me."

Karen laughed. "I can't tell you exactly. It was one of the old Romans, but I can't remember which one. It was in Latin— Erica? Please stay with me. I love babies. It's just children that I can't stand."

"Oh, Karen. You know I can't."

This was just as scary as Karen had thought it was going to be. "The pier at John Lawson," she said. "It's not accidental that's where we are. You chose to be here. This is where I knew exactly what to do . . . but then, of course, I didn't do it."

Erica didn't meet her eyes.

"I love you," Karen said. "It makes me happy just being with you."

Erica was staring hard at the waves rolling in and breaking on the driftwood. Oh. Dear. What is she thinking?

"I love you too," Erica said.

"Stay with me?"

"Okay."

33.

"WHAT IS HE *doing?*" They were in Paige's bedroom with the door shut, having a mother and daughter conference, very much at Paige's request— well, demand was more like it. Paige had come back from camp to discover that the entire universe had become disordered. The most pressing matter appeared to be Devon. "He's wearing nail polish and lipstick. He's got a girl's haircut, and he's got his *legs waxed*. Morgan and Avi are even calling him 'she.' I don't care if he wants to pretend to be a girl now . . . he's always been kind of like a girl anyway . . . but what are my friends going to say?"

Oh dear god, Karen thought, why did she have to inherit the worst of me? The safest thing was to give her the twins' official line. "He and Jamie are going to switch back as soon as she gets home." Whether that was true or not was entirely another matter.

"Is he gay?"

"Oh, sweetie, if he is— Don't ever say that to anybody, okay? Promise? This is really important. I'm not saying that he is, but *if* he is, he has to come out to us."

"Oh, Mum, you know I wouldn't tell anybody, but— I think it's just mean what he and Jamie did to Dad and Chris. How could you let them do that? Just *mean*. If Chris ever finds out . . . Like she bought Devon all these dresses and things because she thought he was Jamie. How do you think she'd feel? She'd be totally like, you know . . . hurt. And Dad . . . I just don't understand how you could let them do it!"

"Paige. They just went ahead and—"

"Nobody ever asks me what I think! If anything happens, I'm always the last to know. None of you guys care about what I think—"

"Oh, sweetie, of course—"

"Morgan and Avi have just moved in with us and nobody asked me."

"I thought you liked Morgan and Avalon."

"I do like Morgan and Avi. That's not the point. Nobody *asked me*."

"How could I ask you? You were at camp. They don't even let you keep your phones at camp—"

"And what's Erica doing here?"

Wait a minute—that was a bit much. "What do you mean? I thought you liked Erica?"

"I do like Erica, but what about Bryan?"

"What are you talking about?"

"I don't care if you want to have a girlfriend, but I thought you were with Bryan."

"Now wait a minute. Erica is not my girlfriend—"

"Mum, you're sleeping with her."

Inhale deeply and stare out the window. You're the adult here. No, you do not yell at her, "You sleep with Lauren. That doesn't mean you're having sex with her." No, you do not say anything even remotely like that.

Paige must have read Karen's silence as assent. "What's Bryan going to think when he comes back?"

That was it—Karen snapped. "Paige! It's none of your bloody business who I sleep with."

Paige blinked rapidly at least a dozen times. That was a new one. Karen had never seen her do that before.

So much for being the only adult in the room. "Hey, sweetie, I'm sorry—"

"Take me to Lauren's."

KAREN AND BOB MCKEE had negotiated a short close—good for both of them—and he'd got the house stripped in less than a week. Karen had opened the kitchen cupboards, was running her fingers over the bare surfaces. "Clean as a whistle," she said to Erica. "He must have hired a cleaning crew. He's exactly the sort of guy who would do that."

"The kitchen's kind of ghetto," Morgan said.

"Dad's gonna want to do a shit-ton of stuff," Avalon said.

Karen hadn't told them that they might be here forever. Bryan had never responded to her offer, so he must still be thinking about it—and of course he had more important things to think about at the moment. His mum had finally died—"dropped her body" as Morgan and Avi put it. The funeral was two days ago, and he was coming home—on standby, the twins had told her. He could be here as early as tonight, definitely by tomorrow.

Karen led the kids upstairs. She'd dumped Paige at Lauren's and had been glad to get rid of her. The worst thing was that Paige had a point—she usually did—and what *was* Bryan going to think when he came home? "Nice old house," Erica said. "Feels homey. Lived in. I like it."

"Yeah, me too," Devon said. "It's friendly."

"But the bathroom!" Morgan was running her fingers over the old cracked snot-green tile. "Gross."

525

The twins were Bryan's kids, after all, and knew quite a bit about house renos. "Like we're definitely gonna be here for a year," Avalon said, "maybe two."

Karen clicked open the sliding French door and led Erica out onto the balcony. "Fabulous," Erica said. "It's almost the same view as your place, but somehow it feels totally different."

"We're higher, and slightly at a different angle. I'll bet Bryan will want to put a big deck here. The view's kind of wasted with this pissy little balcony."

Erica leaned on the railing and looked out over the water, the wind blowing back her hair. She had taken Karen seriously, and that was exactly how Karen had wanted to be taken. They'd driven over to Erica's munchkin-sized apartment and filled up the SUV with not all of her stuff but with a lot of it. Devon and Bryan's twins had helped, so it hadn't taken them long at all. If the kids thought there was anything out of the ordinary about Erica moving into Karen's, they hadn't said so, and Erica was fitting in just as seamlessly as she had the last time. But what if the twins had texted their dad about it? She couldn't very well ask them, could she? Damnable Paige— Well, it wasn't her fault. She'd just been pointing out the obvious. Oh dear, Karen thought, what am I going to do?

The kids had finished exploring the second floor, so Karen led them down into the basement rec room with its tacky teal carpet. "*Uber* ghetto," Avalon said.

"Dad's gonna gut this."

"Totally."

She popped open the creaky wooden door. Just as Bob McKee had done when he'd been showing the house, she'd saved the best for last. "Oh my god," the twins said simultaneously.

"Roses!" Devon said, almost whispering it. Every colour you could imagine—the signature red, of course—and sky yellow, baby pink, luminous white—late season.

"I love it when a garden's starting to grow wild," Karen told Erica. "When the roses get big and blowsy." Even the fallen petals were beautiful.

This time around Karen was seeing everything in more detail than when she'd first been here—the huge primitive ferns, the moss in the cracks between the stones in the walkway. She was glad that nobody had swept up the pine cones. "This is *so* BC," Erica said.

"Bob McKee's dad did this. You can see his mind at work. You can even get some sense of him," that old guy who'd been dead for years—not merely roses but splashes of perennials, flourishing in the sun. Karen knew some of them, the stunning lobelia—too blue to be true—and black-eyed susans, purple asters, and some other wildly blue flower. "Do you know what that is?"

"No, I'm not much of a flower person," and there was a bed of something else—bright red petals with honey-gold edges, warm brown circles at the centre.

"We could have such a great meet-up here," Devon was saying. "Orange-flavoured tea. Those tiny little cups—"

"Demi-tasse—"

"Yeah, and amaloli, full on."

"Totally."

Bryan had said that he'd plant vegetables out in the sun-drenched lawn beyond the garden—if it was his house. Karen could imagine the neat rows, the green crinkle of the lettuce, the fuzzy carrot tops. In the herb garden she broke off a sprig of lavender, smelled it, offered it to Morgan. "Scent your bedroom with this. Old lady smell. It'll help you sleep."

"Wow, yeah."

"You girls know your herbs? Thyme. Put some of this in your chili. And mint."

Karen was running her fingers over the battered old table. "Some people would want to get rid of this thing, but I wouldn't." It must have been there for years, weathering season after season, until the wood had cracked and turned powdery grey—like an image from a lost time—and she saw melancholy maidens in some sappy romantic painting sitting around it. Was that something like what the kids were seeing? Then in one of her intuitive flashes she understood how clever modern net-savvy teenage girls might want to wear utterly absurd dresses and sip tea in an old garden.

THE LIGHT ON THE answering machine in the kitchen was blinking. Of course somebody had called in the few minutes they'd been gone. Karen punched the button, heard her mother's maddening chipper voice. "Hi, it's just me. Your dad and I thought we'd . . . You know, on Saturday night? Devon coming home? You know how much he loves DQ cakes? We thought we'd get one and . . ."

Karen hit erase. No, Mum, she thought, *you're* the one who likes DQ cakes—and Saturday night? I don't think so.

The second call was from Cameron. He was stoked. He'd bought himself a Camry, pretty much thrashed but not too bad. He was going to bring the Lexus back on Saturday. Zach was coming in his truck. They'd stay over, and then he'd go back with Zach the next day—if that was all right?

Oh, for Christ's sake, Cam, not you, too. Mum and Dad, and Cameron, and even Zach who'd never been here before—all of them appearing on Jamie's first night back. Most definitely not a good idea. At some point Karen would have to call them back—not right now, some time later—and she couldn't even finish her thought because that damn grey cat had just jumped onto the kitchen counter. Karen was already in motion, rushing over to grab it, but the big reproachful eyes of both twins stopped her. "She just wants a drink."

"Then she'll get down."

"She's very clever."

"She knows where the water comes from."

Avalon had already filled the bowl from the tap and was setting it down in front of the cat. "She's very clean."

Karen looked to Erica for support, but she was grinning.

"But you're *pregnant*—"

"Not a problem. It's not cats you've got to worry about, it's *cat shit*. Evinrude goes outside, so there's no problem."

No problem? On the counter? Where the food goes? Thanks a lot, Erica. The cat was going lap lap lap lap lap and then pausing to look around suspiciously.

"I'm a professor at a world-class research university," Erica was telling her, "so of course I'm getting all my information from the mommy blogs. Cats are very clean."

Erica had just taken the twins' side in this micro-conflict, and Morgan and Avalon weren't even Karen's kids—they were *house guests*. She felt a little bit betrayed—but maybe she was overreacting.

"You guys can sit down," Avalon said. "It's almost ready." The girls—and that very much included Devon—were in charge of dinner tonight. They'd made a huge pot of every-vegetable-in-the-fridge chili. It had been simmering for a while. And they were making Japanese buckwheat noodles—soba. Over the last few days Erica had discovered that she could eat soba with salt and pepper. If she tried to add anything else, even butter or a bit of grated cheese, it sent her straight to the bathroom.

The girls had set the table with Grandmother McConnell's china. It was too bad that Jamie wasn't here to see it. In the kitchen Devon was pouring the soba into a colander in the sink. With her eyes, Karen directed Erica to look at him.

She'd been hoping that after his brief return to the world as a boy, he'd stay that way, but no. It was clear now that he wasn't merely putting up with being a girl until his sister came home—he was *delighted* with being a girl all the way down to his pink toenails. He was good with makeup, better than Bryan's twins. He understood that less is more. It was disturbing, actually, how good he was at it. "So is he?" she asked. When she'd said "transsexual" before, Erica had corrected her, so now she used what she'd gathered was the correct word. "Transgender?"

"It doesn't matter what I think," Erica said. "Or what you think or what anybody thinks. Gender identity is the most personal thing there is, and she's the only one who knows."

"Oh my god, you're doing it too! *She—*"

"Dev's definitely a she at the moment. We've got to respect that."

"I'm careful what I say, but I can't *think* she."

"Well, neither can I, actually." They both laughed.

"Come on, Erica, don't play games with me. I *know* he's the one who's got to decide, but you must have an informed opinion."

"Okay. Yeah, of course I do. You've read what they said in their email. It doesn't sound like Devon fits into the born-in-the-wrong-body narrative, does it?"

"Well. No. I guess not. But then what?"

"Just wait," Erica said, smiling. "She'll tell us."

Transsexual, transgender, whatever you were supposed to call it—what Karen knew about it was absolutely nothing. Ah, Devon, she thought, if anyone knows how much fun it can be, I do, but are you sure you want to walk down this road? She could tell him lots of things about it—that it wasn't always a whole lot of fun—but she guessed that he wouldn't pay any more attention than Jamie did. And what could she say? You know what, Dev? Sometimes boys can't tell the difference between a girlfriend and a dog.

Dinner was ready. "Say the sutra," Devon told the twins.

"Oh, no," Morgan said, "we don't need to do that."

"Yeah, but why don't you?"

"Come on, Dev, this is like awkward."

"Seriously, girls," Karen said, "there's nothing wrong with practicing your religion." Where on earth had that line come from? Some ancient policy manual?

The twins led them into the living room, bowed to a small statue of the Buddha—Sakyamuni himself, looking enigmatic and elsewhere, his eyes at half-mast but somehow also staring straight into yours. Morgan began the sutra, chanting it in a loud clear voice, "We wish, in joy and safety, that all beings may be happy at heart—"

"Whatever beings there are,"

"whether weak or strong,"

"whether large, middle-sized, or small,"

"whether we can see them or not,"

"those living close to us and those far away,"

"those already born and those seeking birth,"

"leaving none of them out,"

"may all beings be happy at heart."

"Amen," Karen said. Surprised, the twins stared at her. "Sorry," she said apologetically. "Buddhists don't say *amen*, I guess."

THE CHILI WAS PRETTY GOOD—although a few pounds of stew beef and some Italian sausages would have improved it. The kids had actually used every vegetable in the fridge, so she'd have to go shopping soon.

God, Bryan's girls ate like barracudas. "How's the noodles?" she asked Erica. "Staying down?"

"Okay so far."

"More ginger tea?"

"Sure."

"We can make it," Morgan said.

"You want some other kind of tea, Mom?" Devon asked her.

"Sure. Whatever."

"We drink green tea," Avalon said, "genmaicha."

"That's fine," Karen said, although she wasn't sure she liked genmaicha—the toasted whatever that was in it.

"Does Dr. Chou speak Mandarin?" Devon asked Erica, apropos of absolutely nothing.

"That's Stacey," Erica told Karen, and to Dev, "No. Her family's from Hong Kong. They speak Cantonese."

"Jacqueline's family's from Taiwan," he told them. "They speak Mandarin. She's like a true bilingual. Mandarin and English are *both* her first languages. Cool, huh?"

"Oh, yeah," Erica said, "it's great to have two languages."

"And they're originally from northern China. That's why they're so tall."

"So Jacqueline's tall?" Karen asked.

"Way taller than Devon," Morgan said.

He was offended. "No, not *way* taller. Just like a little bit taller."

"Totally," Avalon said, "like no more than ten centimetres."

"Shut up, Avi. And they're like Buddhists, too, and vegetarians. Not real strict with it. Her mom made us sweet and sour pork because she's like, 'All Western girls love sweet and sour pork.' And oh my god, the costumes Jacqueline owns. She paid for them herself. Did I tell you about the—?"

"Yes, I think you did," Karen said.

Poor Dev. He was utterly smitten. He didn't seem to remember that he'd told them much of this already—how nice Jacqueline was, and how smart she was, how cute she'd looked in otome kei. Karen had heard every detail of Jacqueline's perfect costume from the huge bow in her hair down to her patent oxfords.

531

"She does cosplay to explore various parts of herself," he was saying. "So she's been Momiji Sohma from *Fruitsbasket* and Gilbert from *Kaze to Ki no Uta* and—"

"You know, Dev," Karen said, "if you haven't read the manga—"

"Did I tell you about her name? In Chinese, her name's Ma Mei Jia. Mei means beautiful, and Jia means home . . . and it's also like the first syllable of Jacqueline, right? Jacqueline's sister and some of her cousins are all beautiful somethings. Her sister's Mei Xin, Beautiful Heart. Her cousins are Mei Lan, Beautiful Orchid, and Mei Lin, Beautiful Forest."

What was she supposed to say? "The Chinese are very poetic." She glanced over at Erica who seemed to be amused by all of this.

Karen was not feeling particularly charitable toward Jacqueline. If Dev was going to be a girl, he could surely find a more appropriate model, couldn't he? Jacqueline was already interfering in his life, and Karen didn't appreciate it. She'd sent him home with *a princess cut*. That, apparently, was the way a real Asian princess would have worn her hair back in the day. Jacqueline was good with a pair of scissors, and it was a cute cut—if you were a girl—but now Devon was determined to keep it. The back was supposed to grow forever, but at the moment it wasn't even down to his collar. He'd showed her what he could do with it when he switched back into a boy—wet it, brush it straight back, and part it. Then it just looked like a really bad haircut. "How old is Jacqueline exactly?"

"Um . . . Not much older than Morgan and Avi . . . just enough so she's a grade ahead of us. She's going into grade ten."

Karen did the math. "When's she going to be fifteen?"

"Um . . . I'm not sure."

"Of course you are. You know everything else about her."

"She's *already* fifteen. What freakin' difference does it make?"

"None. I was just wondering."

THIS WAS THE BEST TIME of day—when it was quiet, when Karen could actually take a moment to reflect. She liked watching the sunset on the deck with Erica. She liked the long twilight that was coming.

Erica had been checking things on her laptop. "How's the world?" Karen asked her.

"Looks like the US government agencies have been covering up how bad the BP oil spill was."

"Oh, right. Sorry I asked. Of course we're still destroying the world. I'll worry about it later."

The sun was just above the water. The number of times that she would sit quietly and watch the sunset were not infinite— Oh, stop it, Karen. Don't go all high-school-existential when there were too many practical things to worry about. "You met the fabulous Jacqueline, right? What did you think of her?"

"She's a nice girl. I liked her a lot. Everything Dev says about her is true. She's smart, she's talented, she's funny. Did you watch the YouTube?"

"Not yet."

"You should."

"Yeah, I guess—" Karen heard something in the kitchen—or she thought she did—and turned to look. "God, one of those idiot kids left the fridge door open. Wait a minute—"

She jumped up, ran inside, pushed on the fridge door, but it wouldn't budge. That didn't make any sense. But then she heard the big laugh from the other side of the door, jumped back and saw the speckled grin. He'd just popped open a bottle of lager. "Hey, Kay, how you going? Owright?" and from behind her the twins screaming, "Dad!"

34.

WELL, THIS WAS AWKWARD. It wasn't like Karen and Bryan had deliberately abandoned everybody. His kids had been so glad to see him—and
so had Erica, actually. It had been quite a jolly little reunion as they'd sat
around on the deck and Bryan had a few beer and Karen a glass of wine.
He'd talked about his trip, told them about his mum and her passing, and
then he'd said that he wouldn't mind a quick shower. "Use my bathroom,"
Karen had told him. After he'd been gone for about twenty minutes, she'd
said, "My goodness, I don't think there's any clean towels in there," and
off she'd gone. That was the last that anybody had seen of them.

Erica had cleared the table, loaded the dishwasher, wiped down
the counters and put the leftover food away. She'd washed the windows
behind the sink, taken the grates off the stove and scoured it with an SOS
pad, swept the floor and washed it. The dishwasher had run through its
cycle by then so she'd put the dishes away—and Karen and Bryan were
still closed away in Karen's bedroom. Also closed away inside Karen's
bedroom were Erica's clothes, her phone, her laptop, her bag full of university stuff and several books she might have enjoyed reading.

It was getting late. Every night Karen performed a ritual she called
"shutting down the house." Erica had gathered that was what you were supposed to do when you had children. With Karen out of the picture, was
that Erica's job now? Was she Karen's best friend, an honoured guest, a
member of the family, or what? How long had the invitation been meant
to last? Until Annalise's baby was born? Longer than that? She hadn't
been thinking clearly when she'd moved in here. Soaked with hormones,
she'd been feeling a soppy unfocused universal love. Stacey had warned
her but she hadn't paid any attention.

She turned off the lights in the kitchen and immediately all of the
night lights on the first floor came on. Their cool watery blue-green glow
made everything look sub-aqueous like the bottom of an aquarium—just
enough illumination so you wouldn't walk into the furniture. Creepy.
Was this extraterrestrial house really where she wanted to hole up for
her pregnancy? Was she hard-wired for what the baby blogs called "the

nesting instinct"? If there were any reputable studies on it, she hadn't been able to find them.

When somebody says, "I love you," you'd better be prepared to say it back or take the responsibility for hurting them. Erica couldn't say it unless she meant it so she'd been forced to think about it. She knew that grief had made her selfish. She hadn't been able to love anyone—not really—but now her ability to love was returning. She loved her family again, and she loved both sets of twins, and yes, she did love Karen and she'd told her that. But a boyfriend supersedes a girlfriend every time—well, unless you're an MZ twin and nothing can supersede that— but Karen was not her twin. Singletons create couples, and Karen and Bryan were a couple. She and Karen would go on being friends, but Erica shouldn't try to graft herself onto someone else's family. She needed to find a safe place for Annalise's baby. First thing in the morning she would call Staccy about that apartment.

So now what? Do the next ordinary thing, that's what. She walked upstairs, passed the closed door where Bryan and Karen were shut away, and continued on down to Jamie's room. Dev and the Lynas twins were lying on Jamie's bed, staring into radiance of Devon's laptop. "Bedtime, girls," she said and they just looked at her. Was that enough? Had she done her duty? Was the house shut down now? "That means you, Dev," she said.

She didn't care what Devon did, actually. More important was what *she* was supposed to do—go down to the guest room and sleep there, obviously. She was at the top of the stairs when she heard Dev's voice behind her—"Erica? Can I talk to you a minute?"

"Sure." She turned back and followed him into Twin Central. He pointed to Jamie's spot in the double monitor set-up. She sat down there and immediately her screen filled up with images—Devon as Makoto, Jacqueline as Kagami. What did he want? "Beautiful pictures, Dev. You guys look great."

"Don't we? We're all over the net."

They were looking at each other through the gap between the monitors. She could see from his eyes that he was upset. "Don't you want to be all over the net?"

"Jamie's seen like everything. She's watched the YouTube. She's so mad at me she won't even answer my texts."

Okay, Erica thought, some kind of crisis. She was the live-in psychologist so it looked like she was going to hear all about it. "She's mad at you?"

"Yeah. She's like, '*I'm* supposed to be Kagami, not some weird Asian girl you just met, and you switched back without me. Fuck you.' And I don't know, it's . . . I tried to tell her I didn't switch back without her but I guess I did. When I was Makoto disguised as the Nameless Princess, I did, and then when we met Jacqueline in the park— Jamie's coming back on Saturday, and it's gonna be—" His eloquent shrug told her how hopeless it was.

"Major drama? A big fight?" she said.

He watched her through the gap and didn't say anything. "What are you afraid of?" He still didn't say anything. "Is there anything I can do to help?"

"Yeah. Can you talk to her?"

"Of course I can talk to her. I'd be glad to talk to her."

"Cool. Let me show you something." He clicked out of the site. "All you have to do is Google Sailor Moon cosplay." That's what he must have done because images of girls dressed as Sailor Moon appeared on her screen. "Then you just scroll down and like eventually—" He found the image he wanted and clicked it to full-size.

Everybody knows what Sailor Moon looks like—the red, white and blue uniform with its super-short skirt, the sailor flap on the back and the big bow in the front, the impossibly long blonde pigtails. In this picture the kid playing Sailor Moon was Devon. "You're really cute." That was probably not an appropriate thing to say but what the hell. "You're perfect. You've even got the red boots."

"Yeah. Thanks. It was Taylor's old costume. She's heavy into cosplay, like super heavy. It didn't fit her anymore so she gave it to me. That's at Anime Expo. Me and Josh . . . like Taylor's mom took us. Taylor's mom's very liberal. She's like, 'Be who you want to be, Dev. All this boy-girl stuff is just so much crap anyway.'"

"Cool. How old were you?"

"Ten."

"Did you have fun?"

"Fuck, yeah. I was stoked."

He was staring at her through the gap between the monitors but as soon as he caught her looking at him, he looked away. "So you want to know what happened? It was my own freakin' fault. I was looking at the pictures and I left them up on the screen. Real bright, huh?"

Here was the story he must have wanted to tell her. Christine saw the pictures and that's what set her off. She foamed out all over Dad and Dev's life was over—he was totally cut. Everybody in his new school hated him but he wasn't allowed to see any of his old friends. Then it was summer and he was like stone grounded. He couldn't get his ass out of bed. He'd sleep most of the day and then he couldn't sleep at night. He was losing his freakin' mind.

"You were depressed."

"Yeah, I guess I was."

"I'm not just throwing the word around lightly. I'm telling you—you were honest-to-god clinically depressed."

"Yeah, I was. Fuck, do I ever know a lot about hanging yourself. The kinds of rope and the knots and like—"

"Yeah, me too." She hadn't planned to say that.

"When your sister died?"

"That's right."

"Why didn't you?"

She had to think about it. "I could give you a lot of bullshit, Devon. You know, all the sunshine crap about how great it is to be alive, but to tell you the truth, I don't know why I didn't."

"Yeah, me neither. I'm a chickenshit, I guess. A lot of kids hang themselves."

Then they were sitting there after midnight alone in Twin Central gleefully discussing suicide. How it should not hurt, or not hurt much, how it should be quick and idiot-proof but there really wasn't any method like that. Hanging meant strangling to death unless you wanted to do the long drop, and nobody in their right mind wanted to do that. They talked about manila versus nylon, about chairs and stools and step-ladders and where to tie the rope. There were other methods too. If Erica had decided to do it while she'd been back in the Hat, she would have driven out of town and gone to sleep in the snow. Devon had stockpiled his Dad's sleeping pills. Whenever there was a new prescription, he'd sneak out a few of them. Eventually he had twenty. He was pretty sure that was enough. But then Avery was born and Dad and Chris couldn't stand the sight of him any longer so they shipped him up to Vancouver and that changed everything.

"Me and Jamie, like what the fuck!" It wasn't just that they looked identical—they *thought* identical. They'd been going through the same shit and they'd even Googled the same shit.

"You know what's weird? Jamie figured it out first. I was gonna do it . . . when I got back home and school started. No doubt in my mind. And Jamie's like, 'Well, that'll be the end of me too because if one of us dies, then the other one will die too.'

"I'm like, 'Who are you? What are you talking about?'

"And she's like, 'We're *identical*. That's because we were split. So we're like two halves. If one half dies, then the other half will die too.'

"And then I finally got it. Oh! Right! We're *a whole system* so we're *entangled*."

Hearing this was positively eerie—it made Erica's skin light up with goosebumps. "So you've got to do it together or you can't do it? Okay, I get that. And how will you know when you're going down the black hole?"

"That's easy. It's when Dad's like, okay, Devon, here's the way it is from now on. You are *here* and your sister is *there* and blah blah blah and I don't want to hear any argument, that's just the way it is. Then it'll be like totally automatic. Then I'll know . . . and I'll know that Jamie knows it too and we're on our way. We don't have to call each other or talk to each other or like say goodbye or anything like that, we'll just do it."

The double computer setup was disconcerting, actually—peering through the gap between the monitors. If you didn't want to be seen, all you had to do was move over slightly. That's what he'd just done. All that was left of him was his voice. "Erica? Jacqueline sees a therapist. It wasn't— The first two were assholes but she finally found a good one. She's helped Jacqueline a lot, and I— I just don't know what to do any more. I'm like tired. Do you think that Mom would let me and Jamie see Jacqueline's therapist?"

THERE WAS PLENTY to read in the guest room—if you were a fiction reader but Erica wasn't. Even in August it was chilly down here, and she paced back and forth trying to think of what to do next. She wasn't sleepy—too much to think about. She had wanted to know how the black hole worked and now she knew. It didn't help.

There was no way she was going to leave yet. There was still too much in play. Jacqueline's therapist might be exactly what the twins needed. Karen seemed to think that the twins had outwitted their father but Erica wasn't so sure of that. It didn't matter what anybody told her, she *was* responsible for the twins and it cut both ways. They saw her as a friend and they had been responsible *for her*. She felt entangled—Devon's word—and not only with Karen's twins but with all of these people. She owed Morgan and Avalon big time. They'd saved her life twice—and that was no metaphor either. Then she heard someone padding carefully down the stairs. She was sure it was Karen and she was right. "I thought you must be down here."

"Yeah, here I am."

"Erica, I'm so sorry. We just— Bryan's just exhausted. From the long flight and the stress and everything."

Karen's golden eyes looked moist and a bit desperate. Erica could feel Karen's embarrassment radiating out in waves. She'd just had a good time in bed with her boyfriend and what was wrong with that? Nothing. "Don't be sorry," Erica said. "It's okay."

"Once he's asleep, he's out like a stone."

"Yeah, I figured that's what happened. He's really beat, eh?"

"Utterly thrashed— Are you okay? Any nausea? Do you need anything?"

"I'm okay. The nausea has kind of backed off for the moment."

Erica offered her hand and Karen took it. "Karen," she said, "it's *okay*."

ERICA DIDN'T WANT to wake up. But it looked like she had to. Annalise was shaking her gently the way she always did when something important was happening. Erica opened her eyes and saw that she and Lise were in their apartment in Edmonton. Okay, now all she had to do was remember what had been going on in her life when she'd gone to sleep and then she could fit right back into it.

Lise was dressed in a cute outfit—a white blouse, a pleated kilt, knee socks and flats. It wasn't like anything she ever wore. It was like the private school uniform that Jamie and the Lynas twins wore. Why was on earth would Lise be wearing something like that? It didn't make any sense. "Ricki," she said, "you've got to get up. We're going to be late."

Erica sat up in bed, saw that Lise had laid out clothes for her. They were exactly like what Annalise was wearing. That was very odd. They never dressed identically. But Annalise said, "Come on, Ricki, we've got dates." Annalise always picked the clothes for their dates so that explained it. Erica got up and got dressed.

Annalise was in the bathroom. She'd left the door open so Erica could talk to her. It would have been easy for Erica to ask her something, but she couldn't remember what she'd wanted to ask—although she could feel how important it was. Lise was putting on makeup. She was saying something about Mum and Dad. Erica couldn't quite hear her.

Erica walked into the bathroom and Lise turned to look at her. Erica saw in the mirror that she and her sister were absolutely identical. Someone else looking at them would not be able to tell them apart. Oh, she thought, Lise hadn't meant dates with boys. She'd meant expiry dates. That explains everything.

Erica began to wake up a second time and thought, no, that explains nothing at all. "But Annalise," she said, "I'm carrying your baby."

Erica sat up in bed. The dream could have been devastating, but it wasn't. It was the first time she'd dreamed of Annalise when it hadn't been one of those horrible PTSD dreams—driving madly to the hospital to save her, finding her body, seeing her broken body, freezing, not being able to move or even scream—but this dream had felt so plain and ordinary. Her memories might have become wispy and vague, but some module in her brain still had the ability to recreate Annalise so realistically that it had felt like she was actually there. It had left Erica with a sad complicated feeling. She had to get outside.

She slipped out of bed, pulled on her runners, and darted up the stairs. As she was crossing the interstellar twilight of the first floors, she saw that there was someone in the kitchen. She jerked to a stop, panicked, but then she knew who it was—a large dark form that could have been a lumpish piece of furniture except that it was moving, glinting with a sliver of light. "Can't sleep, eh?" he said.

"No." It was okay. She walked into the kitchen.

"Trying out the girls' chili." Now she could see the outline of the bowl in his hands. That's where the reflected light was coming from. "Not half bad," he said. "Could use a little sriracha, though. How you going, Erica, owright?"

"All right." She was trying not to talk too loudly and her voice sounded thin and fragile.

"Glad to see you," he said. "Yeah. So much for my Buddhist detachment . . . I'm not detached at all. I'm glad you're here and you're safe."

"I'm glad to see you too."

He opened the fridge. The light from inside was too bright, almost an intrusion. He pawed around, came up with a can of tuna, forked some out onto a saucer and set it on the floor. The strange grey cat was there instantly.

"Displaced you from your bed, didn't I?" At first she'd thought he'd meant the cat but no, he'd meant her. "Didn't mean to do that. Sorry. I won't do it again."

She told him the same thing she'd told Karen. "It's okay."

"Thanks for finishing up the painting. I owe you."

"No, you don't. It was the least I could do."

"Sold the bugger. Did I tell you that? While I was gone. The market was hot after all. Got better than asking. So now I'm back in the game. How about you?"

"I don't know, Bryan— I just dreamed about my sister. It was a good dream, actually."

"Yeah?"

Now he *was* addressing the cat. "You don't give a shit, do you, you old thug? No worries, mate, you're resting in your cat nature. Nothing to attain . . . A *good* dream?"

"It was so real."

"Yeah? Any realization you have in a dream is still a realization. Dōgen said that."

Bryan was following the cat and Erica was following Bryan. He opened the front door. "Out you go," to the cat, "go kill something," and to Erica, "People think cats are nocturnal but they're not. They like twilight best."

His voice had an unusually subdued quality—not focused, not insistent, almost like he was talking to himself. "I love this time of night. Love how quiet it is."

"I don't. Hate it, actually. It was the worst time for me . . . when I was depressed. I used to play Tetris." What an odd conversation to be having.

"This is the time when we used to get up in the monastery," he told her, "so I got to like it. You can get a lot done if you get up at four. Can always catch a few zeds later in the day. Works for me, anyway . . . Like the sutra says, 'With nothing to attain, bodhisattvas live without the walls of the mind.' But I still feel a wall or two. How about you?"

"Are you seriously asking me that?"

"Yeah, I am."

"Of course I feel walls around my mind. Doesn't everybody?"

"Sit with me?"

"Sure." She followed him into the far end of the living room where his girls had left their cushions. Oh, he must mean meditation.

"I saw the girls showing you. What did they tell you?"

"To sit cross-legged. Like this?"

"Hey, you've got a good half lotus."

"I didn't do anything to get it. I was just born that way."

"No worries. You use what you've got, right? Here, let me show you. Posture's really important. Scoot forward on the cushion a bit." He pressed his hand into the small of her back, guiding her into a more upright position. Then he pressed down on her knees. "Solid. You've got to get good and solid and grounded. Rock back and forth until you feel really good and solid.

"Yeah, your thumbs just touching, the right hand inside the left . . . you've got that right. And soft eyes. You don't want to close your eyes but you don't want to be looking at anything either. You want to be alert. You hear about how meditation is supposed to be relaxing? Bullshit. If you want to relax, take a hot bath. This is the hardest work you'll ever do. You've got to stay wide awake and alert. So what did the girls tell you to do next?"

"Count my breaths from one to ten."

"Good on them. Right. You count one on the inhale and it lasts all the way through the exhale and then you count two on the next inhale, you got that? You want to focus your attention on your breathing. Don't slow down your breathing, just let it be natural.

"Owright, now things are going to arise in your mind. When they do, you just watch them go by. If there's something pleasant, don't hang onto it. If there's something sad or horrible, don't push it away. If your mind goes wandering, pull it back to your breath. If you lose count, go back to one. And you just watch what arises and whatever it is, you just watch it go by. You watch it arise out of emptiness, and manifest itself, and vanish back into emptiness. And you watch the next thing arise and manifest and vanish. Just like the ten thousand things arise and manifest and vanish."

She didn't necessarily want to be doing this but Bryan was settling himself onto a cushion on her left. The first of the daylight was filtering through the windows—she should be asleep—but no, here she was sitting on a mediation cushion. Maybe she should give it a try.

EIGHT—breath slowing down, maybe it shouldn't be that slow, he said it was supposed to be natural, was it still natural? seemed to be flowing in a fairly natural way, now exhaling, imagine it moving inside like kind of mist—ah, here we go, starting over, INHALE—

NINE—how long was she supposed to do this shit, seemed like forever, forever, forever, suicide, an idea, except when it's not, EXHALE, shouldn't have talked to Dev, strap tightening, panic, kicking, screaming, clawing at her throat, no, don't want to see it, it's sick—sick, sick, sick—no, don't try to push it away, see what happens, oh my fucking legs—

TEN! with Annalise at the wave pool, just little kids, could hear the other kids giggling, how sweet was that? where *had* that come from? haven't thought of that for, oh Erica, quit chasing it, but years of things in the mind, forgotten? all right, we're at the EXHALE now, was it supposed to change anything? oh, that dream had been so real, and reality *was* intermittent, what a thought, and for one moment she'd felt like she was actually sensing something important, but what?—just watch the breath go out, breathe? strangling, god how horrible, we're back to that and we're starting over, let it go—

ONE! can't remember if forgotten, how long? seemed like *forever*, getting sleepy, maybe drop off, sleep like a big thick blanket, wool wool blanket blanket sheep, shut up! the opportunity? it was funny, actually, exhale and what was she hearing? Out in the world, it was the sound of Bryan's truck driving away.

35.

KAREN COULD LEARN to hate this place, this slab-grey nowhere—YVR. The minute you stepped into it, you were trapped in a nulled-out time zone where all you could do was wait. Too many people fit into the SUV, so there they all were, staring down the long inscrutable hallway leading from Canada Customs.

"I reckon the kitchen," Bryan was saying to Erica. "No way around it. Got to start there."

"Right," Erica said, "and that's major." She and Bryan seemed to have bonded over house renos—they were thick as thieves, actually—and Karen wasn't sure what she thought about that. She was glad they liked each other, but the universe was not unfolding as it should. After making her wait interminably, Bryan, that annoying man, had finally announced that, yes, he would go in with Karen on the McKee house. His twins had been ecstatic, had grabbed all of their stuff and gone shooting over there at the speed of light, and so had Bryan, leaving Karen and Erica alone together. Then something that had once been easy and natural had suddenly become awkward and embarrassing. Since the night of Bryan's return, Erica had been sleeping in the guest room, and Karen couldn't very well say, "Come back upstairs and sleep with me," could she?

Erica had been having long phone chats with Stacey, her overly helpful girlfriend, and Karen's intuition had kicked in and told her that Erica was leaving. That, of course, solved the problem, but Karen couldn't help a twingy stab of pain whenever she thought about it— Oh god, and she should stop going over it and over it and pay attention to the people around her. ". . . get our stuff from Mum's?" one of Bryan's twins was asking.

"Might be a bit of a gong show," he said.

"Yeah, but if we go at like seven in the morning,"

"they'll all be like passed out cold as mackerels."

"You're right on that one," Bryan said with a laugh.

Crackling with irritation, Paige had just come back from checking the monitor for the second time. "Her plane landed *like ten minutes ago!*" Paige was being a real little bitch. The transparent daughter whose feelings always showed was glaring at Devon, disapproving of him, and disapproving of everybody and everything, while Dev, oblivious to her, was bouncing up and down on the balls of his feet, wailing, "That's *all* I'd need, to *run into somebody—*"

"Chill," from one twin.

"Like nobody would even recognize you," from the other.

Devon had wanted Jamie to see at a glance that he absolutely had *not* switched back without her so he'd come to the airport as *full-on girl*. He'd consulted with the twins on exactly how to construct a full-on girl, and they'd provided him with the lacy white T, the too-short too-pink jean shorts, the polka-dot ballet flats, and the utterly revolting neon fuchsia lipstick. Driving out, he'd hidden on the floor in the back of the BMW—"If anybody sees me, my life's over!"—and now he was radiating anxiety like a rotating antenna—"Just my freakin' luck, somebody *from school—*"

"The girls are right," Erica told him. "We see what we expect to see. There's been lots of studies on this. Nobody expects to see you as a girl, so nobody will."

"Yeah," Bryan said, "seeing what's right in front of your nose, that's a hard one."

Ah, Bryan. Karen wished that what had happened had *not* happened, but there wasn't anything she could do about it. She'd walked into her

545

bedroom in all innocence, planning to do nothing but give Bryan a big fat fluffy white towel straight from the dryer, but just as she'd arrived, he'd stepped out of the shower—steaming clean, moist and warm—and the moment he'd seen her, he'd communicated his appreciation in the wordless way men must have done back in the day when people didn't wear clothes, and Karen's ability to think about much of anything had instantly vanished.

Come on, she told herself, *get out of your head*—and two utterly different conversations seemed to be running on either side of her. "... wear the lovely dresses that Karen gave us," Avalon was saying.

"and Jamie can do bishonen—"

"Totally. And you and Jacqueline can do amaloli—"

On Karen's other side Bryan seemed to be telling Erica one of his incomprehensible Zen stories. "Don't worry about what Bodhidharma had on his mind, you fuckwit. Go look at an oak tree."

Oh, and here were the first passengers finally, and they weren't going to have to wait any longer for Jamie—there she was, right there in the lead. *My god, Jamie, your hair!*—that was the first thing Karen saw—not a total buzz cut, but close to it. Jamie was pushing a cart with suitcases on it. In baggy khaki pants and a camouflage T, there was nothing she could possibly be but *full-on boy.*

"Jamie!" Karen called to her—an involuntary yelp—but Jamie was scowling, shaking her head NO NO NO. With an angry jerk of her shoulder she indicated the hall behind her, and fucking hell, *there was Rob.* Karen felt the shock of seeing him pass through her body like a low-grade earthquake. He was already waving and hallooing—"Karo. Hey! *Karo!*"

"Fuck," Karen said to Bryan under her breath, "that's Jamie's dad, *the twins' dad,*" and then amended herself again, "*my fucking ex.*"

"Bugger."

"Mu-*um!*" from Paige.

"Cool it, puss."

Erica was whispering. "What do you want us to do?"

"God. Fuck. I don't know. Pretend everything's normal."

Normal? Things couldn't be anywhere near as bad as they seemed, could they? Karen had defaulted to zombie mode and was ambulating toward the end of the barrier that separated the passengers from the real world. Hugging her daughter—brief and wretched—got two flat syllables—"Hi. Mum."—and then asshole Rob was squeezing her, and she was drowning in his brassy high-end aftershave. "Got to the airport, and I thought, my god, haven't been to Vancouver in years. Why not—?" and blah, blah, blah. She had no desire to follow his pathetic made-up story.

Bryan had leapt ahead to give Jamie a manly handshake. "Hey, mate!"—leading Karen to, um, introduction time. "Rob, this is . . . my friend Bryan, and—"

"Let me guess—" Rob's big fat jolly Americano laugh—"you couldn't possibly be twins, could you?"

"You think?"

"No way."

"Yeah, they're *my* twins," and Bryan sang out his own name and stuck out his hand.

"Rob Clark. Devon's dad—" and more blah, blah, blah as Bryan, grinning, appeared to be hanging onto Rob's every word and gazing into his eyes in rapt fascination. The inside of Karen's head was blurred out and buzzing, but she was somehow managing to produce a series of transmissions from her old-school etiquette manual— "Such a nice surprise— The guest room—"

"No, no . . . got a room at the Bayshore. Just a couple of nights— Dr. Bauer, I presume. Ha, ha." Most men would have made at least a minimal effort to hide their distaste, but Rob didn't.

With her tousled bedhead hair, flick of makeup, and her sister's pink runners, Erica looked like she was barely out of high school. "Erica," she said, but her eyes were saying, *I don't like you either.*

"Dev was—" Karen started. Wait a minute. She absolutely could not fuck this up. Devon was Jamie, and Jamie was Devon. She quickly overwrote herself—"Dev, you must be—" Jamie's passionate eyes were crackling at her— *So? Must be what?* Tired from the flight? Glad to be home? So pissed off at your father that you'd like to strangle him?

Here was the real Devon stepping into the mix finally—except that he was Jamie. "Hi, Dad."

"Hi, honey, it's so good to see you." Hug.

More useless words—a whole blathery torrent of them—and now, impelled by the grotesque improbability of this chubby grinning little goofball of a man, they had all agglutinated around Rob and were drifting toward somewhere he had in mind and they didn't. Karen was obviously the queen of her posse—all of them looking her way, waiting for the next cue—eyes, eyes, eyes, staring at her. *Oh my god,* she thought, *I'm in charge of the whole bloody lot of them!* Needing a stable reference point, she dropped her hand onto Paige's shoulder.

Rob was nattering about a nice family dinner. "Le Coq de l'Ouest? I'll make reservations. How about seven? Uh . . . and it really is *family,*" his eyes raking over Bryan and Erica to make sure they got the point. "I'm hardly ever in Vancouver."

Jesus, Rob, how unbelievably rude can you get! And Le Coq de l'Ouest? That was where Drew had taken her on their last date. Oh. Just. Lovely.

The rental car, that's where Rob was going. He'd already reserved some top-of-the-line sedan. "Go check in at the Bayshore and then come straight over to your place. Why don't my girls come along and keep me company?"

For a snaggle of take-up time they were all stuck decoding what "my girls" might mean. Devon had been stopped as absolutely as if someone had yanked his power cord. Paige's eyes were screaming *help,* but the only help that Karen could give her was an open-handed shrug meant to read as, *beats the hell out of me, kid.*

Paige stared at her a moment longer, horrified and not bothering to hide it. Then she deliberately plastered on one of her beauty-pageant smiles, turned to Devon and—and what?—took his hand. Holding hands like sisters, they followed their father.

"FUCK, FUCK, FUCK!" Jamie was yelling. Bryan had asked Karen if she wanted him to drive, but she'd said no because she wasn't the kind of woman who allows her boyfriend to drive her car for her. What that had got for her was maddening stop-and-go traffic on Granville Street. "So fucking pissed off," Jamie yelled from behind her—SLAM, BANG, THUMP. What was she doing? Punching out the seat? "Just decided? Fuck, really?"

Jamie must have been storing up her anger the whole flight—she was using up all the oxygen in the car. "First class? What's he think, I'm some kind of retard?"

"Your dad can't take Dev back, can he?" one of Bryan's twins was asking her.

"No way. We're back in Canada. We'll just sic the Rottweiler on him, right, Mum?"

"Right— Jamie?" But Jamie was in full transmission mode and not about to be interrupted. Every bloody window in the SUV was open, and with the traffic and the wind, Karen couldn't hear a lot of what Jamie was saying— something about Dad and Chris— what a fucking nut-bar Chris was— and if Dad ever found out they were switched, Dev would have gone straight to Jesus camp. "What camp?" Erica wanted to know.

Like *Jesus* camp. That's where Chris wanted to send him the last time—to work on his freakin' masculinity issues—"You mean some kind of reparative—?" But Erica didn't get to finish her question because Jamie had already jumped topics. "Total whack-job. Seriously! Brittany's mum's like, *Christine?* Whoa, you better watch out for her. She wants to get her sticky fingers into everything—"

"Jamie!" Karen tried again, but now Jamie was yelling about how pissed off she was that she'd missed Van An —yeah, saw the pictures on Facebook, loved the sailor fuku, *so freakin' jealous!* And Dev, oh my god, that doll dress from Japan? Sick. And like the YouTube—who was that weird Asian girl anyway?

"She's really nice. You'll like her."

"Fuck her!" Jamie had told her dad that she absolutely had to come back for Van An, but no, that wasn't gonna happen, he's like that freakin' boys' school—"Sure thing, Dad, I'm stoked!" and then she had to hang with Brandon. And the boys. "Oh my god, boys are fucking slime! Well, fuck them, they think Canada is igloos and mooses—"

Karen yelled it this time—"*Jamie!*"

"What?"

"Should we tell your dad what's happening?"

"No, no, no! *Devon.* He'd kill me. Like seriously kill me. He really wants Dad to think I'm him."

549

Wrong, Karen thought, but she wasn't about to try to talk Jamie out of it.

"What do you want *us* to do?" Bryan asked. "Should we piss off?"

"Yeah, probably," Karen said. "That'd make things simpler."

"No worries. We'll just go to our house."

"We can have a picnic!"—one of Bryan's twins.

"Yeah, in our garden!"

"Go to the deli,"

"get some veggie burgers"

"and potato salad and stuff"

"and Johnny's gelato!"

"There you go," Bryan said. "Takes care of us. How about you, Erica? You want to join us?"

"No, thanks." Erica sounded positively grim. "I'm not going anywhere."

THE VIEW FROM the deck was just as spectacular as it always was, but here they were trapped in the living room because this was where Rob wanted them to be—"Never been the sun lover you are, Karo."

But it was stifling, and Karen was sweating like a pig. At some point she was going to have to change her top. "Can you believe that, Karo? It's been *six years*. And I thought, why not? Life's too short, and . . . Well, and I wanted to keep you in the loop. Dev and I have been discussing a few things. Right, Dev?"

Jamie as Devon nodded. She looked exhausted. She'd been silenced.

It was getting to be the time of day when Rob most definitely needed a drink so Karen hadn't even bothered to ask. "Lots of peatiness," he said, savouring it. "Laphroaig? Sure tastes like it." She didn't know what the fuck it was. She'd found the bottle at the back of a cupboard, something left over from when he'd lived here. She smiled enigmatically.

There was so much tension in the room that Karen felt like she was inside a vacuum cleaner bag with the motor running. Erica was the one who'd thought of appies, had arranged them nicely on one of Grandmother McConnell's platters. That bit of hostess-work and the fact that she hadn't gone anywhere would have convinced Rob that Erica was, just as he'd suspected, *the girlfriend*. Rob sliced himself a slab of gorgonzola, deposited it on a cracker, and then began musing about what a great little house this was—telling Erica how lucky he'd been to pick it up when he did. "Blip in the market. Flat for high-end properties."

He ate the cracker, washed it down with another gulp of single-malt. "Won't say it was a steal, but . . . well, the price *I paid for it* . . ." He shook his head as though astonished at his own cleverness. "It's appreciated quite a bit since then. What's the assessed value now, Karo?"

You prick, she thought. "Oh, Rob, I don't remember."

"Maybe you girls would like to dress for dinner?" Rob was saying to Paige and Devon. Before now, Karen couldn't have imagined any situation that would have utterly silenced Paige—no, not miss sociability—but here she was, just as mute as everybody else.

"Oh, and Jamie," Rob said, "you're wearing a little too much makeup for a girl your age."

Dev shot Karen a quick look to show her how distraught he was. "Okay," he said. "Sorry."

Paige was the unknown factor in this bizarre equation. She didn't meet Karen's eyes, simply followed Dev out of the room and up the stairs.

"I did want to discuss family matters—" Rob to Erica.

Erica had settled into a chair well back from the action. She didn't respond in any way. She was giving Rob her hyper-intelligent house-cat look. Exasperated, he turned to Karen. Anything she said would be used against her, so she didn't respond either. Seated at the centre of the open floor plan designed for easy living—now hotter than hell and not a whisper of air passing through it—she heard Paige and Devon's voices upstairs—"the girls." It was too far away to make out what they were saying, but the emotional tone was coming through full tilt—urgent high-pitched words, distress, distress. It doesn't have to be like this, Karen thought. I could stop it right now. But she didn't.

Rob gave Karen a deeply disappointed look. He sighed, sipped. "All right," he said in the voice of the CEO finally getting around to the agenda, "Dev and I had a number of serious discussions. He's convinced me that an all-boys school is not for him. In spite of all the— You see, Karo, I do listen. I'm always prepared to be flexible."

Devon's best interests, he was talking about—yes, that had to be the number one priority here. Choosing exactly the right school was not a trivial matter. Excellence. Reputation. A proven track record. So in the meantime Dev seemed to be happy enough in West Van. But he really does want to come home. Soon. "Right, Dev?"

Jamie nodded again. Poor kid. Rob must have battered her down to nothing, got her to the point where she was ready to say anything just so he'd shut the fuck up—and oh my god, *now Rob was talking about Jamie.* "We were expecting a very difficult girl to get off the plane, a very disturbed young lady, and I have to tell you that we were pleasantly surprised. Is she on medication?"

"No," Karen said. Jamie's face was turning red. It wasn't just a little flush—it looked like someone was pouring red dye into the top of her head.

"Oh? Well, I must admit that we were quite worried about her. After that letter— Dev, you don't know this, but there's no point in keeping secrets now, is there? The last letter your sister sent you, we, ah . . . intercepted it. I'm glad we did, that you didn't have to see— Of course it took some time to decipher it . . . given your sister's learning disabilities. How is she doing, by the way? Is she making any improvements?"

"She's making *huge* improvements." Karen was staring at Jamie, trying to catch her eye, but Jamie wasn't looking her way.

"I'm delighted to hear that." Yes, Jamie was such a sweet girl, he was telling them. "A bit withdrawn. A bit shy. But very sweet. No trouble at all. Absolutely. Chris really connected with her— I'm sure we have Devon to thank for how well his sister is doing now, don't we? But he can't always be there for her. He has his own life to live, and it's—?" Rob gave Karen an ingratiating smile. He was searching for precisely the right words to explain this delicate matter.

Jamie was staring past her father. The red had drained out of her face as suddenly as it had come. Now she was turning white—sweaty, blood-stripped, scary, dead-man white. Karen looked to see what Jamie was seeing. Paige and Devon, in the little black dresses Chris had bought for them, were standing in the hallway frozen into immobility like a pair of pretty mannequins. When Chris had been creating these images of girlhood, she'd been deep in nostalgia-land, so she'd bought classic little-girl patents for Paige, and for Dev—oh, for god's sake—kitten heels. Dev had dutifully stripped off the teen-nasty makeup and done one of his less-is-more numbers. Paige had brushed her hair back Alice-style and held it with a hairband. They looked like they'd just escaped from an old Kodachrome slide.

"You see, we did decipher the letter," Rob was saying, "and— Whew! Well, let's just say that there were some very disturbing things in that letter. Some very dark fantasies. The kind of thing that you really do need a professional— I don't want to overstep my bounds here, but it's really not in Jamie's best interests for her to be so dependent on her brother, wouldn't you agree? Shouldn't we be making some arrangements for them to continue on with their separate—"

"Fuck!" Jamie leapt to her feet.

"No!" Devon screamed at her.

"*I'm* the fucking girl," Jamie yelled at her father. "Me, me, me!"

ZING, faster than Karen could add it up—strobe-fragments—Dev had kicked off his shoes, his bare legs and black skirt flying—"*No!*" Sped-up and racing, he couldn't possibly—but he was—already across the room. Hammering Jamie with his fists. "I hate you!"

Stunned, Jamie didn't even defend herself—but then she did, jerked her arms up to ward off the blows. "Ow! Stop it. Fuck!"

Jamie must have had enough. Came back at him—her whole body back at him—slamming him full force—grabbed him with both arms, and they went hurtling straight to the floor—BLAM CRASH—an end table and its lamp, exploding bulb, shattering glass. In some other part of the room a siren had gone off. Oh, that was Paige.

Erica! Now *she* was in motion, trying to get a grip on any part of the two writhing bodies. Kicking out, Jamie's leg smacked the bottom of the coffee table, sent it flying—cheese and crackers and platter and glasses—airborne— "Karen!" Erica yelled at her. Oh. Right. Do something.

This kind of physical shit had never been Karen's strong suit, but now she was up and out of her trance—trying to get her hands on Jamie. Erica had pried Devon loose from his sister. He was thrashing around in Erica's arms, kicking and screaming. Karen caught Jamie by one arm, hauled her to her feet, tried to hug her, but Jamie broke free—easily—and, crouching, turned on her, eyes as blindly furious as an animal's.

Karen had just felt the full force of her daughter's strength. Oh my god, she thought, she could kill me. Her only hope was that she was still Mum. "Jamie," she said firmly, "stop it."

Jamie straightened up, stepped back, panting. "He fucking hit me. You saw him."

"Yes, he did. We'll sort it out. Come on."

"Don't touch me!"

"Wouldn't dream of it. Come *on*," pointing Jamie upstairs. "Paige! Shut up." At the sound of her name Paige jumped at Karen, collided with her, was hanging on like a four-year-old. "Paige. Seriously. Nobody's hurting you."

Where was Erica? She still had a death grip on Devon. His face was muddy with snot and tears, but he'd subsided into a series of small yelps. "Rooms," Karen said, hoping Erica would know what she meant.

Then the whole bloody circus-crew lot of them were managing to ascend the stairs. "Asshole!" Jamie yelled at her brother. "You hurt me!"

"You hurt *me!*"

"You fucking hit me."

"I hate you."

"Fuck you."

"Enough!" Karen yelled at then. "I mean it." She pointed through the open door to Jamie's room. "Get in there. You're timed out."

"Sweet, Mum. How old are we?"

Jamie was through the door so Karen jerked it shut. "You," she said to Devon, "same thing." Erica got the message and pushed him into Twin Central.

Karen hustled Paige down the hall to her room. "Mum! It's not fair. I didn't *do anything*."

"I know you didn't."

She thrust Paige through the door and shut it. Breathe, she told herself. Isn't that what everybody always tells you to do? Both she and Erica were leaning against the wall. "Sorry," Erica said, "I think I'm going to be sick."

KAREN STOOD AT THE TOP of the stairs regarding the hallway of closed doors. Erica had vanished into Karen's bedroom, was presumably in Karen's bathroom throwing up. What would happen, Karen thought, if I walked out of here, got into the BMW, and drove away?

Her phone was in her pocket. Bryan hardly ever answered his phone, but he always checked his texts. The kids had agile thumbs, but she had to use her clumsy index finger. "Come back," she wrote.

She walked downstairs, straight into the kitchen, picked up the bottle, and carried it into the living room. Rob's face had reverted to CEO blank. She topped up his glass.

He was looking at the bottle. "It *is* Laphroaig."

"Yeah, I guess it must be."

"Do you want to tell me just what *the hell* is going on?"

"They switched," and then to make it absolutely clear, "Jamie is Devon, and Devon is Jamie."

"No. That's impossible. That's just impossible."

He seemed unnaturally calm. He drank. Looked away through the windows. Looked back at her, his face stiff and masklike. No, he wasn't calm at all. She'd seen him do this before—it was steely self-control. "Is this some kind of joke? If it is, I don't think it's—"

There was nothing more she could say to him.

"If I could just talk to Dev for a minute—"

"Do you mean Jamie?"

She saw the full impact of it finally register on him. "Oh, Jesus. Why?"

"It was their way of protecting themselves. They were afraid you were going to separate them. They're twins, Rob. You don't separate twins."

He walked away from her. When he began talking, he was addressing the view and not her. He *knew* something was wrong, he said. It was very subtle. He didn't mention it to Christine. He was afraid she'd think he was losing his mind. It had been a year and a half since he'd seen Devon, and kids can change remarkably at that age, but still— At first he'd thought that Dev might be on medication. He'd lost his— He didn't know how to put it. His sparkle? His exuberance? Then one night— It was his eyes. Rob looked into his eyes and thought, *that's not Devon*. But that was ridiculous. Who else could it possibly be? He felt like he'd entered the Twilight Zone—

"Rob," she said, "you can stay here and think about it all you want, but I've got three distressed kids upstairs."

"Yes. Right. Of course you do. I should go back to my hotel. I've got— I should talk to Christine? Shouldn't I?— I suppose I should cancel our reservation at Le Coq de l'Ouest?"

"Yes, I think so."

He looked like he was going to cry. "I was looking forward to it."

All she wanted to do was get him out of the house, and all she was doing was walking him politely to the door, but then, with no warning at all, he jagged to a stop, turned back to her, staring wild-eyed at her, and then in a madly convulsive gesture flung both arms outward, yelling—"Jesus, Karo, how could you do this to me?"

"What? What did I do?"

"Colluded," he yelled, shoving a finger in her face. "You *colluded* with them."

"What? You think I knew what—"

"Chris warned me about you. I should have paid attention, but— Good Christ, Karo, we lived together all those years. I thought we had— I thought *you* had some basic human decency. But you *colluded*— How could you *do this to me?*" He pounded his chest directly above his heart. Indicating what? That's where she'd shot him? "*This* is what I get for trying to be a decent human being?"

The image of him quivering—yes, that's what he was doing, *quivering with rage*—was so bizarre that she couldn't make any sense of it. No man in his right mind could act this way seriously, could he? It had to be a performance.

Now he was walking—no, *striding* like a commanding general—and he was headed the wrong way, not out the front door but back into the living room. "You've got it pretty sweet, don't you, my dear?" he boomed at her in a huge operatic voice. "Well, who gave you all this? Do you want to tell me that? And this is the thanks I get?"

It had taken her a beat too long, but she was catching up to him. No, it wasn't a performance. The great Robert Clark—the cool calm collected CEO—the man who got paid millions to sit on fancy-ass boards—the sagacious consultant on corporate governance and the banker's best friend—yes, right there in front of her eyes the great Robert Clark was losing his shit.

Now he was sputtering or stuttering—whatever—gasping for breath and then grabbing the next blast of words. "The truth of the matter, Karo— people are born male or female. XY or XX. Everybody knows that— obvious— self-evident— reproduce the species— but *you feminists*, oh my god, no! Healthy boys and girls— confused— latch onto them, get your fucking hooks into them— push your insane— Jesus, I just can't— Exploit their confusion— Poor kids get caught in the loop and can't get out— Mutilate their healthy young bodies to impersonate the other sex— But that's fine with you, right? You don't give a fuck, right?"

He was not a man like Ian, a man who might actually hit her—at least she didn't think he was—but instinctively she was staying well away from him. "Rob, Rob, Rob, just wait a minute, okay? Maybe we should have this conversation some other—"

"I can— Listen to me! I can— *How could you do this to me?* I was trying my best for Devon, but you— Chris and I were trying— Taking our responsibility seriously, but you—"

"Rob?"

"How could you *encourage* this sick confused behaviour? You've gone too far this time. I swear to god, I am not going to take this lying down. I can assemble a team of lawyers like you wouldn't believe. You're absolutely—"

"Rob?"

"You're absolutely *not* going to get away with it, you and your so-called doctor girlfriend— Doctor of what? Feminist quackery? I've had more than enough of this. What you're doing is child abuse!"

"*Rob!*"

"*What?*"

"Get out of my house."

JAMIE HAD BEEN standing at the top of the stairs listening to everything. Karen grabbed her, shoved her back into her room, and shut the door, and then Jamie was having one of her classic meltdowns—screaming and crying and bouncing around like a kicked soccer ball. "Fuck him! *Child abuse!* He's the one who did the fucking child abuse. Him and that fucking nut-job Christine. Fuck him, fuck him, fuck him—"

"Jamie—"

"*Learning disabilities?* Yeah, I'm the retard that can't spell. *Disturbing fantasies?* How could he just read my letter like that? He had no right. No right, no right, no right. *Everybody hates me.*"

"Nobody hates you."

"I fucked it. Dev hates me. He'll never forgive me. Oh my god, I want to die."

"No, you don't. Look, it doesn't—"

"I had to write it. Dev was like cut. How could they—? What they did to him was fucking— So I had to— I *hate* writing. I went on Google, like copied things out of Google, like I was *so fucking careful*. Nobody fucking believed me. Dev believed me. I was gonna hang myself when I got my period. Everybody hates me, I'm nothing, I'm not a girl, I'm not a boy, boys are fucking slime. *Slime.* Oh my god, the way they talk about girls, they hate girls, girls are fucking hos, they're cunts, 'Hey, Dev, you've gotta watch this—' Oh my god, it's a girl all tied up. Gag in her mouth. Getting fucked up the ass. 'How you like that, Dev? Pretty fucking hot, huh?'"

"Wait a minute, Jamie. Slow down. What did you say? You were going to—"

"*I hate fucking boys!* And I'm supposed to be a boy? I'm like, 'Oh yeah, it's hot. For sure.' I thought I was fucking gonna barf. Oh my god, I want to die, I'm nothing, I'm a freak—"

"Jamie, Jamie, Jamie. Wait a minute. Shut up. What did you say? You were going to hang yourself? When you got your period? *You were going to hang yourself when you got your period?*"

"Yeah, I was, but like— But afterward I couldn't. Like Dev— If I did, then Dev— We were entangled— So I couldn't."

Was this real or only more drama? Karen had to know. *"Where?"*

"What the fuck do you mean *where?*"

"Where were you going to do it?"

"In the garage. There's like this big pipe that runs along the ceiling, right? And then we've got like this little step ladder in the furnace room. I got the— The rope's still there." She pointed at her closet. "It's at the bottom of the box with my skates."

WHEN KAREN JERKED the door open, she was expecting to find yet another howling disaster, but Paige was a small silent package of evil-eyed fury. "Why *her?*" Jamie said. "It's none of her fucking business."

"Because she's your sister, that's why."

Devon hadn't waited in Twin Central—the jerk. He was in Karen's bedroom. Erica was lying on the bed, flat on her back, motionless, while Devon was sprawled out on the floor, leaning against the bedframe. Paige had changed out of her little black dress, but he hadn't, and he looked like a miserable little girl who has dressed for dinner and then been told that she has to stay home. "Thanks a whole fuck of a lot, Jamie," he said.

"Fuck you. You switched back without me. You got a girlfriend."

"*You* got a girlfriend."

"Rachel's not my girlfriend."

"You wish."

"Stop it," Karen said firmly, but they weren't about to stop it.

"Some weird-ass Asian girl you just met!"

Devon sprang to his feet. "Shut up, Jamie. That's fucking *racist*. I love her. We're going out."

"Going *out?*" Karen said.

She never would have imagined easygoing Devon blazing with so much anger. Now he was aiming it directly at her. "She's *not* too old for me, Mom. Lots of boys in grade ten go out with girls in grade nine."

"No," Paige said, "that's not it. Mum thought you were gay."

For a moment he was so stunned that his mouth was actually hanging open. Then he found one of his famous smiles. "Oh, my god. You did. You *did!* I can see it on your face. Come on, Mom, I would have *told you* if I was gay."

Not gay? Then what was he doing in that little black dress? Things were unspooling too fast. All three kids were yelling now—

559

"So what are you? A boy lesbian?"

"Shut up, Paige. Shut the fuck up." Jamie was making a leap for her little sister. Was she actually going to hit her? Karen sprang forward to interpose her body between them.

"I don't *care*. I just want to *know*."

"Bitch. You just shut up."

"No, Jamie, I will not shut up. Why don't you just tell everybody?"

"Tell everybody *what?* Come on, Paige, just *what* am I supposed to tell everybody?"

Okay, Karen could yell louder than any of them. *"Paige. Stop it."*

Paige actually flinched.

"There's nothing wrong with your sister, *absolutely nothing.*" Oh my god, the stress was insane—every muscle in Karen's body was vibrating.

Paige was staring at her with big hurt eyes. "I didn't say there was anything *wrong* with her."

If Karen had wanted silence, she certainly had it now. Jamie stepped back, putting distance between herself and all of them.

Erica got off the bed, walked over to Jamie, and put her arm around her shoulders. Jamie's lower lip began to quiver; then her eyes began to spill over with tears.

Paige was crying, too. "Nobody cares," she said. "Seriously, Jamie. Alana Bishop and Stephanie Ellis are going out and nobody fucking *cares*. Everybody likes them. They've got lots of friends."

"I'm sorry I hit you," Devon said. He wrapped his arms around his sister. "I'm really really sorry. Like seriously."

Jamie stood stiffly a moment, her arms extended uselessly outward as though she didn't know what to do with them. Then she hugged him back. She was crying hard now, wracked with it. "I'm sorry, too. I fucked everything— Fuck, fuck, fuck—"

This was as cathartic as could be, and Karen could let it run out to its watery conclusion without saying another word. Nobody would know she'd done that, but *she* would know, and she wouldn't be able to live with herself. "Okay, okay, okay. You guys can all have a good cry later. *Seriously.* Stop it— Erica? Can you tell the twins about puberty blockers."

"Yeah, I can do that."

Everybody turned to look at Erica.

"The Dutch studies— Oh, god, you guys don't give a fuck about the Dutch studies, do you?"

She switched to her professor's voice. "Puberty blockers won't reverse any changes that have already happened, but they'd stop you right where you are. They'd give you another couple of years to think about things, but eventually you'd have to go through *some* puberty or your bodies wouldn't mature properly."

Maybe Karen was going to faint. She had all the symptoms. She did what she always did—breathed deeply and tried to think about something else. "You could go off the blockers," Erica was saying, "and go through the puberty that matches your birth sex, or you could do hormone replacement therapy."

"We understand all that," Devon said quietly.

"If you want to do it, you're going to have to see a psychologist or psychiatrist. I can fast track you through ITS so you're not stuck on somebody's waiting list for a million years. You'd have to meet the diagnostic criteria in DSM-IV, and neither of you do, but I could coach you on what to say. Once you're approved, you could see Dr. Nitzberg."

"What would happen," Dev said, "if like— Okay, what if we let our bodies do their own thing and I added like a little bit of estrogen and Jamie a little bit of testosterone?"

"I haven't got a clue. You can ask Dr. Nitzberg, but I don't think he'd do that for you. I know what you want, but most doctors have a horror of non-binary genders. You were right. Medical science isn't ready for you guys."

"But can we get blocked?" Jamie was whispering. "Mum? Would you let us?"

Karen nodded miserably. "Yes. Jamie? If it's what you really want—"

Jamie looked like she was collapsing in slow motion, unfolding joint by joint. She sank to her knees, her legs splayed out on the floor. "Yes, please. As soon as possible, please." She tilted foreword, her face touching the floor. "Oh my god, thank you, Mum. Thank you, thank you, thank you."

"Dev?" Erica said.

He shrugged. "I don't know. I'm, um— I guess I'm cool with male puberty."

Jamie jerked upright. "You don't want to get blocked?"

"No, I don't think so."

"We're not—" Jamie had a hard time getting the words out. "We're not identical any more!"

Now Dev was crying. "We are! We are! We *are* identical!"

There were too many crying children here. Karen grabbed Paige's hand, nodded to Erica—*come on.* "You're the twins," she said to them. "You work it out."

Karen shut the door behind them. Even Paige was crying. "What on earth are you crying about?"

"I don't know."

NOW IT WAS Karen's turn. "Aw, Kay, you'll be right. You will."

"No, I won't. I'm never going to be right. I just agreed to let some fucking doctor stop Jamie's sexual development dead in its tracks!"

She was supposed to be mature Mum, but here she was hanging onto Bryan, weeping like one of her kids. "I want my daughter back!" The moment she'd said it, she knew how ridiculous it was. The daughter she wanted back was nine years old—and who the bloody hell was walking through the front door? Oh my god, it was Cameron. "Hey, Mum. Hey, Bryan. What's up?"

Fuck, she'd forgotten to call him back, and of course he'd brought Zach with him. The boys were carrying cases of beer. Karen had to stop the drama, look like she was in control. She should be able to do that, shouldn't she? She'd had years of practice. "Nice to see you, Zach," she said. "This is my friend, Bryan Lynas."

Bryan offered his hand, and Zach took it. "What's that?" Bryan said, "some of that fine Granville Island lager? Wouldn't mind one myself."

"Nice modest little place you've got here," Zach was saying to Cameron and then, after a beat, added, "but you've fixed it up real nice."

The boys cracked up, and, yes, it was funny, but Karen couldn't deal with it. She sent an imploring look to Bryan. He read her mind. "No worries, Kay."

She absolutely had to get away, escape to the deck. She threw herself down onto a deck chair. She'd thought that Erica was out here, but she wasn't. She should probably go looking for her, but she was stunned into immobility. Late August, and the days were getting shorter, twilight already settling in over the water, and that was nice with the lights, the reflections of lights. She just needed a few minutes in the twilight to try to recover, to try to rearrange her mind, and then maybe she could manage, but no, here was Paige shoving a phone at her. "It's Dad."

Her first impulse was to tell him to go fuck himself, but then she decided that she'd rather know what he was thinking than not know. "Yeah, Rob, what?"

"I, um . . . owe you an apology. Sorry I blew up like that. It was all . . . kind of a shock."

"Yeah, I know. It must have been."

"It was one of those unfortunate— I'm sure that both of us said things that we didn't mean."

Where had the "we" come from? Karen hadn't said anything. "Okay."

"You know, Karo, I just can't— There's no way I can figure out how to tell Chris. She's going to be absolutely devastated."

What was she supposed to say? Was she supposed to give a shit?

"I guess I'm going to wait and tell her in person. If I can frame it as a joke, a prank, something like that—? But it's— You know, Karo, I don't want to leave it like this. I've got three kids in Vancouver, and I don't see them all that much, so why am I—? Would you mind if I came back?"

"Oh, Rob, I don't think that's a good idea."

"I wouldn't be, ah . . . confrontational. I'd just want to, you know, *talk*."

Talk? What was there to talk about? Rob was, just as he claimed to be, flexible, but she didn't believe in this particular twist, this sudden reversal. He'd slipped and told her what he really thought, and he surely couldn't have changed his mind on any of it, could he? No, she didn't trust him for a minute. This had to be a new strategy, just more moves on the chessboard. What did he hope to accomplish? He surely couldn't imagine that Dev would ever go back to California. "Maybe tomorrow," she said. "Let me talk to the kids about it."

"It's just, ah . . . I don't want things to end up the way they did with Brittany."

Right. Brittany hated his guts. And this whole crazy reversal thing must have scared him badly. She could hear it in his voice. Or maybe he was only pretending to be scared as part of the new strategy. She was so tired of playing chess with him, but she seemed to be stuck with it. Okay, she could play it out to the crack of doom if she had to—no way Rob and bat-shit crazy Chris were ever getting their claws into Devon again. "Maybe I should pick up some pizza?" he was saying.

Pizza! She absolutely could not believe him. "If you're going to do that, Rob, get lots. I mean *lots*. At least half of it vegetarian."

KAREN FELT UTTERLY BATTERED, but she had to check on the twins and warn them that their father was coming back. They hadn't left her bedroom, but while she'd been gone, their mood had done a complete flip. No more weeping children—Bryan's twins had joined her twins, and the lot of them were positively manic. Oh, so that's where Erica had gone. She'd joined the kids.

"—didn't really," Dev was saying, "but I can see why you—"

"Totally you did!" Jamie said. She seemed to be the centre of attention at the moment—they were all talking to her.

"Makoto's a girl," one of Bryan's twins was saying, "when he's like—"

"No, he's not. No way."

"Yeah, he is. Like the Nameless Princess—"

"We didn't know what to call Devon," Morgan said.

"Couldn't call her 'Jamie,'" Avalon said. "It's like—"

"Yeah, I wasn't like you," Devon said to Jamie, "so they couldn't— They called me 'Princess.' Seriously— Hi, Mom. Are you okay?"

Nice of him to ask. "Reasonably okay. Did you guys make up?"

"Nothing to make up," Dev said. "Just networking issues. Like latency."

Jamie gave her brother a hard push, sending him stumbling backwards. "Asshole. We're not computers."

"Come on, twin," he said, "forgive me."

"Okay, I forgive you— We *are* identical," she said to Erica, and back to Devon, "but I still think you ought to get blocked."

"No," he said, "doesn't feel right for me. But I sure don't want to be a big hairy dude. You can get your hair removed . . . like permanently. Mom? Can't you?"

"Yeah, but it takes forever and it hurts."

"Meh," he said, dismissing time and pain.

"I wouldn't want to grow hair on my face," Jamie said. "Yuck."

"Are you going to wear a kilt to school on your girl days?" Avalon asked him.

"I don't know—"

"Yeah, you should," Morgan said.

"Totally," Avalon said.

"I don't know if I'm ready to be a martyr for the cause— Maybe."

"Erica?" Jamie said. "Can I call myself a lesbian if I'm not a girl?"

"I don't know the rules on that one."

"We'll ask Jacqueline," Devon said. "She'll know."

Karen was not following much of this. "Wait a minute," she said, "if you're— Jamie. Slow down. You're *not a girl?* Are you a boy?"

"No, no, no, Mum. I'm non-binary. That's *better* than a boy. God, I'd hate to be a boy. Boys are fucking slime."

"We *told you*, Mom," Devon said. "We're *identical*. We're *both* non binary. We *both* like girls."

"Dev was like texting me," Jamie said, "and I didn't get it. I thought it was like just more of his quantum crap. I didn't know if it was even a thing."

"We're the T in LGBT," Devon said.

"And Dad's the B," Morgan said.

"And we're *allies*," Avalon said.

"But wait a minute. If you're the T— Transgender?"

"No, no, Mom, it doesn't just mean *binary* trans. That's what everybody thinks, but it's . . . No. Anybody who doesn't identify with their birth-assigned gender is trans if they want to be. So we're trans. But we're *non-binary* trans."

"The binary is like male-female," Jamie said, "you know, like boy-girl. But we're non-binary, so we're off the grid."

"Jacqueline goes to an LGBT youth group," Devon said. "Can we go?"

565

"Yeah, I guess so. Where is it?"

"Kits."

Kits? Oh god, another reason to have to cross the bloody bridge.

"Jacqueline's best friends are a couple," Jamie told her. "How cool is that?"

"Yeah," Devon said, "Alexis and Madison. Alexis is out to her family, but Maddy isn't. It's kind of like, you know, harsh for her. Her parents are like super straight. And Jacqueline's non-binary like us. She isn't sure what kind yet. Sometimes it takes a long time to figure it out."

"And she thinks we might be genderfluid . . . 'cuz our gender keeps shifting around."

"Right," he said, "it's not stable. We're identical, so in our whole state we're every gender, and all you guys ever see are like collapsed outcomes."

Karen looked at Erica—is all this stuff *real?*

"I'll tell you about it later," Erica said.

"Okay, but—" There was the reason why Karen had come in here in the first place. "Okay, kids. Just stop for a minute. I've got to tell you something. Your dad's coming back."

That certainly did stop them. "What the actual fuck?" Jamie said. "What does he want?"

"Just to talk. That's what he says anyway."

"Shit," Devon said, "is he gonna take me back?"

"Absolutely not."

"Talk?" Jamie said. "Shit. Okay, we'll talk. Like we've listened to him plenty. This time he's gonna listen to us."

KAREN WAS FINALLY getting her moment in the twilight, but it was too late to do her much good. All she wanted was to sleep for a hundred years, but she seemed to have washed up on the deck like a piece of mute and useless driftwood. Bryan and his twins were talking about house renos. "Roof's top priority," he was telling them, "and I want to do solar panels, but then— Hell, if I'm gonna add a room over the garage, I've gotta do that *before* the roof, and I can't do *that* before I do the kitchen reno."

"We thought you'd do the kitchen first," Morgan said.

"Yeah," Avalon said, "that pokey little kitchen. No way."

566

Here were Jamie and Devon joining them. They'd changed into identical grey T-shirts with the Palmerston logo on them—old ratty gym wear—and cut-offs. Dev had parted his princess cut and brushed it back, getting the bangs off his forehead; Jamie had put the titanium studs back in her earlobes to match his. He'd cleaned most of his makeup off, and she'd put on a touch of pink lip-gloss. Dev saw Karen looking at him. "We're in neutral mode," he told her. "Hyper-genders are exhausting."

"Totally," Jamie said.

Karen could feel the nervous crackle coming off them—they were getting ready to confront their father. She looked across the deck to meet Erica's eyes, knew that Erica must be thinking the same thing. Bryan, oblivious to the teen drama, was still going on about his house—"Telling me it needs some walls knocked out, but I reckon I can't be adding any rooms till I've got the kitchen done—"

"Hey," Morgan said to Jamie and Devon, "do you guys want to see it?"

"Yeah," Avalon said. "Come on. You've got to see it."

Bryan's twins jumped up, and without another word all four kids were gone. "So much for whatever the old man might have been thinking," Bryan said, "dumb old fuck that he is." Grinning, he shook his head. "You know what?" he said to Erica. "You're a major player in this crazy family our kids have been slapping together. Why don't you come in with me on that house?"

Karen felt the fatigue leave her as suddenly as if somebody had whipped away a blanket. "What?" Erica said. "What are you talking about?"

"They must pay you pretty good out there at the university, right? So you come in with me, help pay the mortgage, and you've got some equity. Right?"

Oh. My. God. Erica must be just as shocked as Karen was. She was staring at Bryan, her eyes huge. "When your baby gets born," he said, "it'd have all these brothers and sisters waiting for it."

"Bryan, that's—" Erica shook her head. "That's crazy, isn't it?"

"Not any crazier than going around telling people you're pregnant with your dead sister's baby."

What a brutal thing to say. "Oh my god, Bryan," Karen said, "that's so—" and to Erica, "his Australian manners—"

Erica laughed. "No. It's okay. You don't have to apologize for him. I know him. I felt his hands on me when I was bouncing off the bottom of the sea."

Bryan laughed, too—one of his big belly laughs—and Karen felt something like a flare behind her eyes—but really it wasn't like that at all—and she spoke without thinking. "Don't fight us, Ricki. We're in the rip."

She saw an answering flare in Erica's eyes. "Okay," Erica said, "but you can't fight me either. I'm hard-wired for this stuff, but for you guys it's got to be learned behaviour."

"Is it now?" Bryan said. He was still laughing. "So give us our first lesson."

"Okay, I will. For starters, if we're going to do it, it can't be— Okay, there's not *Karen's* house and *Bryan's* house. They're *our houses*. You don't need to do a kitchen reno over there. The kitchen here is all we need. We could feed thirty people from this kitchen."

"Yeah," Bryan said, "you got it. The dining room here becomes the dining hall for the whole lot of us—"

"Right. And the kitchen over there— It's to process all the vegetables we're going to be growing—"

They were ahead of Karen but not by much. It *was* crazy—utter and total lunacy—but she could see it. "Move Cam over there," she said. "He's not here that much. Then Erica could have an office right next to mine. When the baby's born, it'll stay in the room with us—"

Paige had been so quiet that Karen had almost forgotten that she was still here. "Wait!" she yelled at them. "I don't get it. What are you guys talking about? What did you just *say*? We're going to mash everything together?"

"Yeah," Bryan said, "reckon our houses just got married."

"Sick!" and Paige, the perpetual messenger, leapt up and sprinted away.

THEY WERE ALL coming back now, Morgan and Avalon the first of them, flushed from running—"Dad, is it true?"

"We're all gonna be together? Even Erica?"

Bryan's twins had slid to a stop. They were so still they were like mirror images. "Oh my god," Morgan said, and Avalon finished the thought—"Our whole family's back together again after all these lifetimes. How cool is that?"

"Mum! Mum! Mum!"— the rest of them.

"The little room that looks over the garden," Jamie was saying. "*I want it!*"

"If Jamie goes over there," Morgan said, "can we stay in Jamie's room?"

"We'd even paint it"

"like daffodil yellow."

Good god, Karen thought, the bodhisattvas right next to me?

Cameron and Zach had emerged from the pit. "See," Cam said, "I told you they were all nuts. Mum? So where you gonna put me?"

Bryan was laughing at them. "We've gotta have a meeting. We'll sit down and work it out."

Oh for Christ's sake, the doorbell was ringing. Well, somebody would get it.

"In the basement over there," Paige was saying, "can we make like a little ballet studio with a bar and mirrors?"

"Easy," Bryan said, "but I'd have to lay down wood flooring. You can't be dancing on concrete."

"The living room in the new house can be the meditation room," Morgan said. "We could put the Buddhas in there—"

"paint it Tibetan colours—"

Who should have materialized in the front hall? This was just impossible—Karen's *mother*. Carrying a DQ cake. Karen's dad was right behind her.

Karen jumped up and hurried inside. "Hi, Mum. Hi, Dad."

Her mum's I'm-not-sure-I-approve voice—"My goodness, dear, looks like you're having quite the little party." Karen took the ice cream cake and discovered that her inner etiquette manual must have deserted her. She couldn't find a single polite word.

Erica had followed right behind her. Mum's eyes were saying, *Oh, the girlfriend's back, is she?* They'd never met Bryan. How was she supposed to introduce Bryan?

"A DQ cake, how nice," Erica said, taking it from Karen.

Devon was there, too. "Hi, Nana, hi, Papa—" What would her parents make of his waxed legs and pink toenails? Maybe they'd just think it was some crazy new teenage fad. "Mom. Mom! Can Jacqueline come over?"

"Mum!" Jamie was hugging her grandparents but she was looking at Karen. "If Dev's going out with her," she said to Karen, "don't you think I better meet her?"

"Mum!" It was Paige this time. "It's not fair. If Dev can have Jacqueline over, then I can have Lauren."

"Wait a minute, kids," Karen said. "Just give me a minute, okay?"

Now Erica was leading Karen's parents into the house and was putting the ice cream cake in the fridge, and Karen was still standing there pointlessly with nothing left to hold. Through the open door she saw that a shiny new-model black car had parked behind the others. The entire back seat was stacked with pizza boxes. *Karen,* she told herself, *you are not in charge of all this.* "Okay, eternal twins," she called to them, "get your asses out here and help your dad with the pizza."

End Note

Twin Studies, like all of my novels, is nailed firmly down in the time in which it is set. It opens on August 26, 2009, with the twins' first email and ends a year later in August of 2010. Since then, things have changed remarkably for kids like Devon and Jamie. For one thing, DSM-IV (that is, the fourth edition of the *Diagnostic and Statistical Manual of Mental Disorders*) has been replaced by DSM-V, thus changing the guidelines governing physicians. Near the beginning of the novel Jamie complains that she and Devon had to look all over Google, but they still couldn't find the right information. That's no longer true. Today the twins could find out what they needed to know in a matter of minutes.

Keith Maillard
Vancouver
May 6, 2018

KEITH MAILLARD is the author of fourteen novels, including *Two Strand River, Gloria, The Clarinet Polka,* and *Difficulty at the Beginning,* and most recently *Twin Studies.* He has won the Ethel Wilson Fiction Prize and was shortlisted for the Commonwealth Literary Prize and the Governor General's Literary Awards. Keith was born and raised in West Virginia and has lived in Vancouver for most of his adult life. He has been a musician, a contributor to CBC Radio, a freelance photographer, and a journalist. He teaches in the Creative Writing Program at the University of British Columbia.